THE COMPLETE MAGGIE KILLIAN TRILOGY

A WHAT DOESN'T KILL YOU TEXAS-TO-WYOMING ROMANTIC MYSTERY SET

PAMELA FAGAN HUTCHINS

SKIPJACK PUBLISHING

CONTENTS

SICK PUPPY (MAGGIE KILLIAN NOVEL #2)

DEAD PILE (MAGGIE KILLIAN NOVEL #3)

FREE PFH EBOOKS

LIVE WIRE (MAGGIE KILLIAN NOVEL #1)

A WHAT DOESN'T KILL YOU TEXAS-TO-WYOMING ROMANTIC MYSTERY

ONE

"Don't tread on me." Maggie mouths the words from the Gadsden flag flying proudly from the heavy-duty four-by-four in front of her at the traffic light. The curled rattlesnake sticks its tongue out at the world. She likes it, and she likes the banging desert-camo paint job on the truck, too.

She snares her hair with a red silk scarf, then pulls flyaway strands out of her lipstick. The air is changing, losing its summer-baked feel, and the afternoon sun sheds an early fall glow on the streets of Sheridan. Windows rolled down, she tips her face out and into the golden rays. She smells spruce, fir, and pine, and something else. Smoke. She breathes in the dry air through her mouth, and she tastes the smoke, too. Everyone in town has been talking about the wildfires to the northwest.

The light turns green and she rolls slow and easy down South Main, admiring the street art. In Wyoming, that means sculpture, not graffiti. She eases off the gas to stare at a bronze of a native woman dancing in the wind, head thrown back, buckskin and hair flying. It speaks to her, in her core, like most things about this throwback town. She accelerates again. She's drawing plenty of goggle-eyed stares in Bess, her vintage magenta Ford pickup, toting a *Beverly Hillbillies*–worthy mountain of estate- and garage-sale pickings in her utility trailer and the small truck bed. After three days in Wyoming, she's figured out that the looky-loos are not just eyeing the junk and the truck, either. The population here is skewed male. The Marlboro male, bearded variety, largely appearing womanless. If she was looking for a man, she could have her pick by sundown, never mind the gray streaks in her hair, the narrow gap between her teeth, or laugh lines around her eyes.

But she's not looking for one.

Well, technically, she is looking for *one*, but only one in *particular*. She brakes too hard at another red light and jerks to a stop. Something in the bed shifts, and her eyes cut to her rearview at the sound. *Please, Lord, no yard sale here.* The load settles. When she feels sure all is well, it only takes her a hot second to whip her phone out and open her Facebook app. Normally she's not much on lipstick or social media. But desperate times call for desperate measures. Crappy connectivity and data notwithstanding, she attempts to refresh Hank Sibley's profile, something she's done once every five minutes for the last week, ever since she typed "garage and estate sales, Sheridan, Wyoming" in her search engine and hit the road to go picking in his stomping grounds.

So far, he's been eerily silent. She's stalked him online for six months, ever since he showed up at her best friend Michele's house, a surprise addition to a dinner party that included Michele's brother, Gene. Gene and Hank were in Texas scouting for broodmares to diversify bloodlines for their Double S Bucking Stock business. The shock of seeing Hank had initially paralyzed her. He was a blast from her past—literally the most explosive relationship of her life. She hadn't been receptive to getting reacquainted at first, but pheromones and his dimples won out. Hank whisked her away for a week that nearly blew her world apart.

So she'd sent him packing, natch. Because once she regained her sanity and control of her libido, she couldn't forget that for fifteen years—after what he'd told her was the best night of his life, one where they risked death-by-mobster to be together—he'd never called. Never come to Nashville like she'd asked him to. Never contacted her a single time. He broke her freakin' heart. So much so that he spawned Grammy-winning songwriting—a good thing. And precipitated an ugly downward spiral that tanked her career and earned her back-to-back stints in rehab for a cocaine addiction that slid into heroin—a bad thing. Technically, she might have shared some of the blame, as did the unexpected death of her dad before she'd had time to go back and work childhood shit out with him. But Hank definitely ranked as a leading cause.

So sue her, he waltzes in and has this effect on her? It scared the crap out of her. *He* scared the crap out of her. She had no choice but to throw gasoline on that bridge and burn the fucker down.

But that was then and this is now. There's empty screen where his Facebook profile should be. She growls and checks the light. Still red. She pulls the page down to refresh it.

While she's in data limbo, her mind drifts back to the spring in Texas. The angry look in his eyes when he left had barely covered up his sadness and confusion. It had tested her resolve, but she'd held firm. Only, after he was gone, she'd realized it was too late for her to protect herself anyway. He was back in her head, back in her heart, back in her aching late-night dreams. She kept willing him to defy her edict to never contact her again. She longed for her phone to ring with his teasing voice in her ear. Of course he hadn't. It hadn't.

She'd finally decided she had to do something. So here she is in Wyoming, trying to casually run into him fourteen hundred miles out of the way from her normal life. Ridiculous. Yes, she knows it, yes, she should have just called and groveled, but she tamps down the thought. She's here now. And this is going to work, because she's going to make sure it does.

Anyway, Hank normally posts on Facebook once or twice a week. About the rodeos where Double S will be and how the horses and bulls are performing. The progress of the crop of foals, how the three-year-olds are coming along, and all of the achievements, accolades, and awards Double S is racking up in the world of stock contracting. She's been trolling their website and knows they don't have a rodeo right now—which is why she chose the weekend after Labor Day for her picking trip here.

The screen refresh is taking forever. God, how she wishes she hadn't gone cheap with T-Mobile, which doesn't seem to exist north of Denver. A car behind her honks. The light is green.

She salutes with her favorite finger. "Keep your pants on, buddy."

Hank's profile finally comes up just as she presses the accelerator. She has time to give the phone a good upward swipe, and she watches it like she's hoping for all cherries on a quarter slot.

There's a new post.

She makes a gentle left onto Coffeen Avenue, then props the phone on top of the steering wheel. Traffic is lightish, so she raises her knees to wedge against the steering wheel. Her right foot slips off the accelerator. The truck lurches out of its lane. The phone drops to the floorboard.

"Shit, shit, shit." She grabs the wheel and corrects course gradually so as not to flip the bumper-pull trailer. The truck has been pulling hard to the left for weeks now. Time to get the front end aligned and rotate the tires, as soon as she's home.

A tall delivery truck pulls in front of her. It's squeezing against both sides of the lane, and she can't search ahead for a place to pull over.

"Come *on*." She pounds her hand on the steering wheel.

Finally, she spies a parking lot she can get in and out of without clipping something with the trailer. She veers into it quickly. The building on the other side of the pavement looks straight out of *Gunsmoke*, with darkly stained wooden siding and forest-green paint on the door and window frames. TAXIDERMY is painted across the upper half of the store front in an Old West–styled script. A more modern banner flaps from rope attached to hooks in the wall: ASK ABOUT CHEMICAL-FREE BRAIN-TANNED SKINS, THE INDIAN WAY.

As she reads the words, Maggie feels a flicker—recognition?—but pushes it away. She doesn't give a single shit about the buckskins, dead heads, and trophies on the other side of the door. All she wants is to read Hank's post. She picks up the phone, which froze up in its scuffle with the floorboard. While the phone is rebooting, she turns up her sound system, the only modernization she's made to her World War II–era truck. Moors & McCumber's "Bend or Be Broken" comes on. She'd caught one of the Americana duo's shows on her way north through Colorado, where she'd picked up the *Live from Blue Rock* CD. She air-guitars along, her fingers still nimble ten years after she quit playing professionally, but she doesn't take her eyes off the phone screen. When her background appears—her pet goats, Omaha and Nebraska, named after the town she was in when she first heard one of her songs on the radio—she drops her imaginary instrument.

She types in her passcode. The phone rings. As she fumbles with the device, she accidentally answers the call. It's her mom. She doesn't say hello, prepares to hang up. If her mom calls back, she can let it go to voicemail.

"Maggie? Honey, are you all right?" Charlotte Killian's voice is loving, sweet, and worried. Perpetually worried.

Maggie closes her eyes and puts the phone to her ear.

"Margaret Elizabeth?"

"Mom. Hi. Yes, I'm good. What's up?"

"Oh, thank God. When you weren't answering my calls, I went by your place. There was a strange car out front, and no one answered the door when I rang the bell. I tried my key, but it didn't work in the lock—"

"Mom, I'm fine. And I'm traveling. I have a short-term renter. I'll oil the lock when I get back, but I'm glad you didn't barge in on her."

"Why didn't you tell me about your trip?" Her voice changes. Hurt creeps in, with an undertone of irritation. She'd gone to a lot of trouble. She always does.

Maggie takes a deep breath. Her mother has been distracted lately. After years as a widow with no social life, suddenly she'd begun dating men like a fickle sorority girl. But she'd settled on one. Edward Lopez. Michele's father, a veterinarian and a widower. Maggie had thought she could sneak off without her giddy, love drunk mother noticing her absence, but she should have known better.

What to tell her, though? Charlotte knew nothing about Hank. Not back then, not now. "I'm sorry. It was on a whim."

"You rented your house on a whim?"

"Sure. It's a thing, Mom. Everybody does it. Surely you've heard of Airbnb?" Which Maggie hadn't used, although she'd been inspired by it. She wasn't paying anyone a commission for something she could do herself through Craigslist.

The phone goes silent. Maggie considers coaxing her phone into double duty with the call and Facebook, but she's afraid it doesn't have the bandwidth.

Her mother says, "So, where are you?"

"Wyoming."

Her mother's reply is screechy. "Wyoming? What in the world?"

"I had a lead on some big sales. I've found great items for the shop." Her store, Flown the Coop, is a regional favorite, and she knows her Wyoming pickings will sell well at the Warrenton–Round Top fall antique show.

"Who's minding it for you?"

"I have a Blinn College student opening it on the weekends."

"The goats?"

"Michele is taking care of them."

Again there's a silence. Then, "And church?"

Maggie bites her lip. She watches a flatbed truck drive by pulling a gooseneck trailer. A border collie balances behind the driver's side, the wind in its fur. Wyoming is so fifty-years-ago, a throwback state, and the dogs love the freedom. Maggie loves hers, too. She doesn't want to get into this discussion with her ultrareligious mother. She'd abandoned her upbringing twenty years ago when she ran off to chase musical stardom. Her parents were both Wendish—descendants of refugees from ethnic and religious persecution in Germany who migrated to Texas in the 1850s—and had raised her in the restrictive community of their Lutheran church.

Maggie hadn't rejoined the church when she came home ten years later, but she attended services once a month to appease her mother.

Two years ago, Maggie learned she was adopted. Her birth mother had fled the same Wendish community to chase dreams of becoming an artist. Like mother, like daughter. Nature over nurture. It helped Maggie understand better her adoptive mother Charlotte's fears for her soul, but it didn't lead her back to religion.

"I'll only be gone a few days."

"When will you be back?"

"As soon as I'm done up here. I'll let you know."

"I have . . . I want . . . well, just call me when you know."

Maggie almost questions her mom about the hesitant words, but she lets it go. "I will, Mom. I love you. Tell Edward hello for me."

"I love you, too."

Maggie hangs up. As the home screen reappears on her phone, there's a voice outside her open window before she can pull up her Facebook app.

"Need any help, miss?" Male. Of course.

She nearly screams in her frustration. She peers over her shoulder at him, unwilling to turn fully away from the screen she's worked so hard to reach. The man is younger than her. Ten years, maybe, although exposure to the outdoors makes it hard to read. His eyes are gray, his sandy hair curly, but it's his lipstick-red lips that draw her eyes.

"Um, no, I'm fine."

"I saw you pull over. Texas plates. I figured with you so far from home, you could use a friend. I'm Chet."

He may be cute, but she doesn't give him her name. Or eye contact. "Yes. Well, I'm good. Thank you."

He doesn't leave.

She ignores him and pulls up Facebook and Hank's profile. *Thursday Night Jam tonight. Looking forward to some real bluegrass.* She smiles. Now she knows what she's doing tonight, as soon as she figures out where the heck this jam will be.

Chet is still hanging around by her window.

She beams at him. "Say, Chet, you wouldn't happen to know anything about a Thursday night jam around here, would you? Bluegrass?"

"At the Occidental?"

"Right. That's exactly where it is."

"Need a ride to Buffalo?"

She snorts. "Got my own wheels, son."

"Son? Hardly. But you can't turn a guy down because of his age."

Actually, she can and does. Often. She toodle-oo waves to him. "Nice to have met you."

She accelerates too hard, lurches, and drives off the curb with her trailer bouncing in her enthusiasm about this Occidental place. She needs to find it, map to it, hightail it there. First, though, she's stopping at her room in the Mill Inn—a Western kitsch, bargain option to the chain motels, built in an old flour mill, with a genuine 1940s model Ford pickup that is a close cousin to Bess. She has to drop off her trailer and get gussied up for this bluegrass-jam shindig. She laughs aloud as she thinks the words. But they fit her mood and her plan.

Tonight she's going to shock the pants off Hank Sibley, and he's going to like it.

TWO

An hour later, Maggie closes her Maps app, tired of letting that robotic wench Siri boss her around. She parallel parks Bess in one try on the quaint main street in Buffalo, in front of a creek-side establishment called the Busy Bee. The smell of smoke is stronger here, and the sky is hazy with it. It's odd, because the town is south of Sheridan, farther from the source. It must be making its way through Montana and down the east side of the Bighorn Mountains. She plants one boot on the ground. Gravel crunches underneath the ball of her foot. Shivers run up her arms. She's one step closer to reclaiming her destiny with Hank.

She slings her hobo bag over her shoulder and slams the door. Her tiered and ruffled prairie skirt circles her knees as she walks around the truck's front grill, and she adjusts the belt and enormous buckle at her waist. She stops to peek over the railing at Clear Creek. There's a pay dispenser of fish food. Tossing pellets in the stream—maybe the Wyoming equivalent of tossing a coin in a fountain for luck with Hank? She tosses a handful into the water. Foot-long trout shoot out of the shadows like food-guided torpedoes and disappear again in a blink.

She smiles and turns in a slow circle to look around. The town is smaller than Sheridan, with its well-preserved Western charm compacted into two blocks. Catty-corner across the street is a pocket-size park with a gazebo in one corner and a historical mural painted along the side of a brick building. There are a few liquor stores, of course, which she has learned always have bar seating inside as well. She has a strong urge to walk the sidewalks and peer into darkened windows and notes a Tex-Mex cantina, an Italian eatery, and a gift shop close by for future reference.

But she's not here to sightsee tonight.

She walks toward the Occidental, passing back by the little Busy Bee Café's weathered wooden front. In the cafe window is a flyer: LONG-MIRE DAYS, JULY 7, 8, 9, DURANT, WYOMING. Longmire. She's heard of it. A Netflix TV show, she thinks. But what does that have to do with an event two months out of date in Wyoming, and where is Durant? They need to update their signage.

Her phone buzzes. She digs it out of her bag and glances at it. Gary Fuller. The biggest country music star in Texas, one of the top performers in the country, and her ex.

I'll be home next month. I miss you. I miss your body. I miss us. I love you, Maggie.

Maggie exhales heavily. She and Gary have been on-again, off-again for years after meeting in rehab, theirs the best-kept hook-up secret in the industry. Last year he'd tried to convince her he was done with all the groupies and starlets and random sex. Was ready to settle down. With her. To have kids before it was too late for both of them. The only problem? That wasn't what she wanted. He was unwilling to let things continue as they were, so she ended it.

It wasn't until Hank reentered her life that she fully grasped why she hadn't wanted forever with Gary. She'd thought it was because she still wanted her own freedom. It wasn't, isn't. What she wants is Hank Sibley.

But Gary hasn't given up. She decides to put off answering him.

She resumes her short walk to the Occidental Hotel, which abuts the café. It's housed in a two-story red-brick edifice with striped awnings that extend over the sidewalk. The building stretches down the rest of the block. Potted mums in long narrow planters under the windows are as vibrant as her mood. Empty wooden rocking chairs flank the entrance.

Maggie pulls open the door and walks into the lobby. She gasps. The room is shockingly, opulently restored Old West. Gilded molding crowns the ceilings. Every piece of furniture is a period antique. Rich drapes hang over wood-framed windows. A fireplace dominates the corner of the room. Faded black-and-white photographs from the turn of the century or earlier depict cowboys, Indians, and the town of Buffalo in its early years. A gigantic mounted elk keeps a wary eye over the space. The lobby even smells authentic. Musty with a hint of leather. Every touch is perfection, and she knows how hard it is to get a restoration just right. She puts a hand on her breastbone.

"May I help you, miss?" The voice belongs to a woman with large square shoulders. She's sitting behind the reception desk, a marvel of beautifully preserved wood with a beehive of cubbies and roll-up closures.

Maggie tiptoes over to her. She whispers like she's in church. "The Thursday Night Jam?"

The woman smiles. Her lips and face are colored only by sun and wind. "It's next door in the saloon."

"Oh, sorry." Maggie turns to leave.

"You can cut through this hall." The receptionist points, turning her head and revealing a profile of the cinnamon roll–size bun on the back of it.

"Thanks."

"Have fun."

As soon as Maggie exits the lobby into the connecting space, she can feel the vibration of saloon noise. She passes a sparsely filled boutique and some bathrooms on one side of the hall. On the other is a bragging wall, with framed newspaper and magazine articles about the establishments and town of Buffalo. On the door to the saloon is a sign: WELCOME TO WYOMING. CONSIDER EVERYONE ARMED. *Except for me, unless pepper spray counts.* She pats her bag. When she puts her hand on the door to the saloon, it sends shocks from her fingertips to her scalp. Even her skin buzzes with anticipation. This is it. She's been waiting six months for this reunion.

She steps into the saloon with its blaring jukebox playing Chris LeDoux's "Copenhagen," and she laughs aloud. The place is just as perfect as the hotel. At six o'clock, it's packed wall to wall with people holding drinks, mingling, chatting. She'd been told all the tourists disappear after Labor Day, and she can see that it's true. This place is filled with locals. Fresh-scrubbed faces. Low-maintenance hairstyles. Faded blue jeans. Shirts ranging from ranch-work to Western dressy. Boots. Hats. Belts and buckles. And everyone has a jacket even though it's seventy degrees outside, prepared for anything and everything when it comes to the weather.

On the walls are heads of every beast native to Wyoming. A standing bear, midroar. A crouching mountain lion. Wolves, a coyote. Bobcats. Lynx. And that isn't even counting the hooved animals. Elk. Moose. Bighorn sheep. Mountain goats. Pronghorn antelope. Several types of deer. It's not her thing, but she also knows that Wyoming is an eat-what-you-kill state, with hunting a proud local tradition of survival and skill, unlike the wealthy, trophy-hungry big-game hunters that seem to proliferate from some other parts of the country.

She crosses a green-and-ivory checkerboard linoleum floor and bellies up to the bar. It's wooden, stained so dark it's almost black. She sees her reflection in a massive framed mirror behind crowded shelves of booze. Her fringed vest is too fancy. Her tank top too formfitting. Her teased hair too big. Her makeup too much. The only thing just right is her belt buckle. She looks down at it and nods at herself. So she stands out. It's always been her blessing and her curse. She has a sudden itch to jump back on Facebook and see if she can home in on Hank's whereabouts.

"What can I get you?" A bartender with the patchy facial hair of a teenager slaps a napkin down in front of her. He resumes pouring whiskey into a row of glasses, not looking at her.

"Wi-Fi password?"

He recites it, and she types it in. She pulls up the Facebook app. No new posts or comments from Hank.

Before she can order her drink, a man says, "Nice belt buckle."

Electricity jolts her, through and through. She licks her lips and pats the buckle. "This old thing?"

Hank Sibley laughs, deep, vibrato, rattling her chest. "I hear they're a dime a dozen. What'd you do, steal it off a dead cowboy?"

But they're not. She's wearing his authentic sterling silver 106th Annual Cheyenne Frontier Days belt buckle, the one he was awarded as bull riding champion that year.

"Something like that."

Although, technically, she didn't steal it from him. She took it off his bedside table in the Buffalo Lodge, the finest lodging establishment in Chugwater, Wyoming, which wasn't saying much. He'd been out getting them breakfast. She left him a note with her phone number on it and told him to come get his buckle from her in Nashville.

She turns to him, her foot propped on a toe, her back leaning against the bar. The current between them crackles—she's sure it's both of them, not just her—and she drinks in the sight of him. Still trim and muscular even though, since she's thirty-seven, he's got to be pushing forty. His hair is thick, although salt-and-pepper now, like hers. And best of all, he's still got those dimples. She feels a strain in her cheeks and realizes she's over-grinning at him. She dials it back, but it's too late. She knows her feelings are written all over her face.

His dimples deepen. His blue eyes sparkle. "Well, I'm sure it looks better on you than him."

She wants to rip his snap-front shirt off with her teeth. *Down girl.* She swallows down a big lump in her throat. "What are you doing at the Occidental?" Her voice comes out throaty.

"I live here, remember?"

"I knew you lived somewhere north of Denver and south of Canada."

"The better question is what are *you* doing here?"

"Hauling half the old junk out of northern Wyoming. You're welcome."

He dimples again. The air snaps and hums. "If you'd called me, I'd have taken you to dinner or something."

It's the "or something" she's here for. "Oh, you have a phone now? Because I seem to remember you didn't carry one before. Or use the old fashioned kind, for that matter."

"Still on that old saw, are you? That was fifteen years ago."

"Yeah, but since you never called me *again* since last spring in Texas, I just assumed it was a thing with you." She keeps her voice light.

He looks perplexed. "You told me not to call."

"Couldn't you tell I didn't mean it?"

He rolls his eyes heavenward. "You've got to be kidding me."

Maggie's holding bad cards, and she folds. "Anyway, I've had a change of heart."

"About?"

"Sending you away. Holding a grudge."

Hank's brow furrows.

Maggie's scared, but she's not stopping now. She smiles at him to cover her nerves. "Not letting go of the past. Missing a second chance for us."

"You told me you don't believe in second chances."

"I say the stupidest things sometimes. Don't listen to me."

"Hank, aren't you going to introduce me?" The woman that interrupts them is fresh-faced and unlined. She has a shiny pink Lip Smacker–type gloss to her lips. Her blonde—of course—hair springs in wisps around her face from a single fat French braid. In her boots, she is eye level with Hank, and her blue jean–clad legs seem to go on forever.

Maggie sees the blinds close over Hank's eyes. His dimples disappear. The electric current between them cuts out, leaving Maggie cold and in the dark.

He clears his throat. "Uh, Sheila, this is an old friend of mine, from back in my bull-riding days. Maggie Killian. Maggie, this is Sheila."

"Aren't you forgetting something?" Sheila Eskimo-kisses him. *Eskimo-kisses him. What the hell?*

"My, uh, girlfriend."

Maggie's stomach flips and churns. *Girlfriend? He can't have a girlfriend.*

Sheila raises her brow over wide eyes. "Maggie Killian? *The* Maggie Killian?"

"Ever since my parents named me." Maggie's voice is sour.

"Oh Em Gee. My mom *loves* your music. She plays it, like, *all* the time. You are totally her favorite singer ever. Well, you and Kaylee Storm."

Country-pop princess Kaylee Storm. Just her name brings up bile in Maggie's mouth. "That's . . . great."

"I literally just saw you online tonight, on my phone." Sheila puts her hand on Hank's arm, her fingers curling around his bicep. His eyes are wild, like a caged bear looking for an exit. "When we were at dinner, remember, sweetie?"

Maggie frowns at Sheila's hand. "I don't understand. Online?"

"Yeah. A big 'Where are they now?' type of thing. I texted it to my mom. She was totally excited, because she thought you were dead. The article talked about some big van crash that killed half your band."

"I wasn't with them by then." She hates it when reporters recycle old information about the accident and her past. Her nightmares about it will come back. It could have been her. Probably should have been. Not Brent, Davo, Celinda, Chris, and the groupie that had tagged along from Cheyenne. One of Hank's exes. Bambi. No, Fawn. But Maggie was spared, because she'd run off with Hank and quit the tour.

"And it said you're in some big movie coming out."

"Not in it. It's about me. Partly."

She socks Hank's arm. "Jeez, Hank, you never told me you were friends with someone who used to be a star."

Ouch.

At the far end of the bar, Maggie sees musicians tuning instruments. Over the sound system, a contemporary song starts up. One she heard over and over on the drive from Texas. It's catchy, even if a little too Caribbean pop for her normal taste. "Pretty is as pretty does. Throwing punches, just because."

Sheila squeals. "Ava Butler is the bomb. Don't you just love her? I mean, as a musician. And this song. Totes awesome."

Ava Butler. The name brings back a memory to Maggie. She'd known an Ava Butler during a period of her life she'd rather forget, although that didn't narrow it down much. Pre-rehab, but not by long. After her agent, Larry, quit her and she lost her recording contract. In Waco. A low-rent musical theater. The murder of a young actress. Ava stepping in to fill the lead part in the musical that should have been Maggie's. She'd been talented, Maggie recalls, but a slutty bitch who'd slept with Maggie's man-of-the-moment. And now, all these years later, she has a hit single, while Maggie is schlepping junk and being humiliated by a woman who is with the one man she has ever loved.

Maggie can't find words, so she just makes a noncommittal "Mm-hmm" sound.

"Hank bought me her new CD, dincha, baby? It's even better than her first one."

Maggie stares at the hollow of Sheila's neck, wanting to punch her, right there, just hard enough to stop her talking. She can't believe Hank has a child-girlfriend who loves Ava's *second* album and whose mother thought Maggie was dead.

If it counts for anything, dead sounds better to her right now than another minute in Wyoming.

THREE

Maggie turns back to the bar. Her cheeks burn as she keeps her eyes trained on the mirror. She hopes it looks like she's deep in thought, deciding on a drink, when what she's really doing is watching Hank and Sheila walk away. *That was just a little awkward.* Hank has his fingertips on the small of his date's back, guiding her with pressure just above the teeny waist of her sparkly-assed Miss Me jeans. *Awkward and devastating.* They take a seat at a table with another couple. From the back, it appears the man might be Gene—compact, muscular, dark-haired. *Great.* Someone she knows to witness her utter humiliation. He'll probably tell Michele, which means Maggie will get a call and have to talk about it. Something awesome to look forward to. She knows she should go say hello to him. It's the mature, *adult* thing to do.

But she just can't adult right now. Just. Can't. Adult.

A waitress twirls to a stop beside Hank. He holds up two fingers and says something to her. *Is his girlfriend even old enough to drink?* The woman with Gene has her light head tight with Sheila's even lighter one. Sheila points Maggie's way.

The bartender is pouring whiskey again.

Maggie is glad for a distraction from the two women talking about her. "Got any Balcones?" In the last few years, the Waco-distilled whiskey is her drink of choice. Alcohol's not great for her, but she's never lost herself in it like she did in the juice.

"Never heard of it. That a whiskey?"

"Yes. What do you recommend?"

He brandishes the bottle. "Koltiska. It's a traditional Western liqueur. Fifth generation family's secret recipes, distilled in Sheridan. You can try it with tea. They call that a TKO."

She gathers that the generation count matters a lot here. "I'm more of a whiskey drinker."

He pours a slug in a shot glass. "Try it."

She tips it back. It goes down hot, smooth, and tasty. "Pour me one. Just over ice."

As she waits, Maggie considers trying to find the article Sheila mentioned, the retrospective piece. They pop up occasionally, generate some interest in her and make money for the record company that traded her Flown the Coop, the land it stood on, and Bess for her albums, songs, and back royalties. Then the interest dies down. She decides her life is complete without reading the stilted prose of another hack rehashing her downward slide from the top of the music industry to drugs, mindless sex, rehab, and oblivion. The truth is far simpler, and far more complex than any of the journalists ever grasp.

The bartender adds another glass to a row on the counter and pours without pause. He slides it to her. "Run a tab?"

"I've got it."

Maggie turns toward the bass voice. "No, that's okay." *Pushy much? What is it with the men in Wyoming?*

The big voice belongs to a guy who's even steven with her five-foot-six-plus-boot-heels. He plunks a twenty on the counter. "Maggie, right?"

Had he overheard Hank introduce her to his teenybopper? "Um, yes."

He waits, holding eye contact. Maggie takes in his red flannel shirt and overalls. He's nearly as wide as he is tall, but not fat. Stocky. Muscular. Boulder-like.

She sips the Koltiska. It's good. Different from Balcones, but she's suddenly ready for things in her life to change. She imagines this is what it would taste like to drink out of a cold, clear mountain stream. "Thank you," she says to the drink buyer.

"I'd know you anywhere." His eyes grow squinty. "You don't remember me, do you?"

Maggie shakes her head. "I'm sorry—should I?"

"I met you in Minot. At the North Dakota State Fair. Back in 2002. My name is Rudy Simon."

"Hello, Rudy. Wow, a long time ago."

"You said you'd play a song for me. 'Troublemaker.' Then you didn't."

His words don't stir any recollections, but she doesn't doubt him. She played a lot of shows in 2002. She also drank a lot of Jack and Coke. "I'm sorry."

A man in his sixties—or it could be his eighties, hard to say in dim lights and with his Santa Claus facial hair—is speaking into the mic. She can't make out his words. When he finishes speaking, the musicians kick off a song. Maggie finds herself nodding to the upbeat tempo of old country. Really old—maybe the 1950s? She savors a sip of her drink, trying to place the tune, but she can't.

"You still owe me that song." Her benefactor's voice is hard and flat.

Maggie pretends she doesn't hear him. The musicians finish their number. Rudy doesn't take his eyes off her. Before she can think of a reply for him, a large man bumps into Hank's table. In the silence, four beer bottles clank, roll, and hit the floor. Everything in the bar seems to grind to a halt. Hank is on his feet so fast Maggie doesn't see him move. One second he's sitting. The same second he's standing. He's a head shorter and a feed sack lighter than the giant, but he's up in the guy's face, showing no fear, as if the guy is just another bull he knows he can beat.

All eyes are on the man and Hank. The men lean in, and it's clear harsh words are exchanged. Hank pokes him in the chest three times. Gene and the two women are up, too, and everyone is talking at once. The larger man shakes his head, laughs, and exits the saloon. The silence ends, instrument strings are plucked and strummed. Eyes swivel away from the spectacle and conversations resume.

"A little excitement," Maggie says, mostly to herself.

"That's nothing." The bartender points at the ceiling. "Original bullet holes, turn of the century. That was a little excitement."

Maggie glances up. Sure enough. Bullet holes.

"About that song." Rudy's voice is close to her ear. Too close.

Maggie rises, her drink in her hand. It's nearly empty. She drains it and puts the glass on the counter. The bartender raises a brow, and she nods. Her fingers are still around the glass as he refills it. She pulls a five from her jeans pocket and hands it to the bartender before Rudy can pay again.

"Sorry about the song. It was a hectic time."

"That's okay. You can sing it tonight."

Maggie steps away. "I don't perform anymore."

Rudy glowers at her. The musicians strike up another tune. Individually, they're fairly competent. Together, they're a riot of joy. As much fun as it looks, it doesn't tempt Maggie to join them, not one single bit. Writing and performing her music was her life. An obsession. Losing a career she loved so much, and along with it respect, cut deep. Like losing Hank had.

Maggie's not wired for losing. Her relationship with her guitar and her music is a private one now, one she controls. She puts nothing on the line anymore that she can't afford to lose. And tonight is the perfect example of why. She'd put herself out there for Hank again tonight, and now she's watching him with a woman young enough to be his daughter, if he'd started procreating in middle school. Gross, but possible. Just like the relationship. Maggie tosses back her Koltiska.

Something makes her glance toward the doorway, past Hank's cozy party of four. A male figure is silhouetted against the setting sun. He's muscular, slim-hipped, taller and heavier than Hank. He takes off a Stetson, uncovering curly hair the color of sand. Sheila and her friend are eyeing him, too, again with the pointing. *So rude.* A flicker of anger courses through Maggie. Doesn't that young twat know how lucky she is to be with Hank? As if Sheila reads her thoughts, she turns back to Hank. He shakes his head at her, then Sheila and her friend bust out laughing. Hank's eyes flick to the doorway, then back to his date. He's facing the guy, and he's cataloguing his every move.

As he steps farther into the bar, Maggie realizes she's seen him before. From the parking lot of the taxidermy shop. Ah, those red lips and unusual eyes. Chet. He's close to Sheila's age, from what Maggie remembers. Right now, that makes him perfect for her.

Maggie is buzzed. It's time to decide. Take it slow, or slam the hammer down. Sober, she's formidable, sexual. Across the line, she's supercharged. Doesn't care what she does—man, woman, inanimate object, her hand—as long as she gets there. All night long. She glances back at Hank and his child date. Back at Chet.

She nods at the bartender. "Make it a double."

She has his full attention now and holds the glass toward him. He hits her again.

Taking the drink, she says, "Nice to see you again, Ruben."

"Rudy."

She doesn't look at him. "Rudy, yes."

She starts toward the entrance to the saloon. The swivel of her hips is a primal drumbeat. She watches Chet as the rhythm catches his attention.

His broad smile is immediate, and Maggie knows he came here, alone, looking for her.

She stops in front of him and licks a few drops from the rim of her liqueur glass.

His eyes gleam. "I see you found the place."

"I see you found me."

"You're hard to miss."

The skin on her neck tingles from watching eyes. The liqueur courses through her. She reaches for his arm, runs her hand up it, squeezes. "So are you."

"Oh, sugar, you don't even know."

"But I'd like to."

"Drink up, and we can make sure you do."

She drinks. Shivers. Hands him her glass. She glances at Hank. He's turned his back, almost like he's done it so he won't have to see Chet and her. *Yeah, that's how I feel, too, mister.* She cozies up with Chet at the bar. He smells good, like someone she'd like to be naked with, and he's funny. They order a round from the bartender.

When he brings the drinks, Chet says, "Keep 'em coming, Frank."

She clinks her glass to his. "To new friends."

"God, your voice."

"What?"

"It's killing me. Feminine, but road rough. Like sex against a brick wall."

"Why, Chet, that's the nicest compliment I've gotten all night."

He moves in close so their breath mingles. "And I know who you are."

"I'd be worried if you didn't. We've met twice now."

"No, I mean I figured out that you're Maggie Killian. The singer."

Maggie taps his breastbone with her forefinger. "Aren't you the rocket scientist."

Rudy's nursing a drink a few feet away. He's been scooting down the bar, closer, closer, until he's elbow to elbow with Maggie.

Chet turns on him. "Give us some space, partner."

"It's a free country."

"Which means I'm free to kick your ass if you get any closer to my girl."

"She's not yours."

His shoulders bunch and an arm goes up. "That's it, buddy—"

Maggie puts a hand on his raised and flexed forearm. *Nice guns.* "He's an old friend. S'okay."

Chet drops his arm.

Rudy nods at her, but he doesn't speak to her again.

Two drinks later, Chet whispers to her. "I've had enough of hanging with my ex here. Wanna go somewhere private?"

She puts her bag over her shoulder. "Lead the way."

He takes her by the hand and pulls her toward the door. She hooks the fingers of her other hand through his belt loops. She turns to get one more glimpse of Hank, hoping he'll see what he's missing. But he and his group are nowhere to be seen.

Icy needles prick her heart. Chet hauls her to him by her ass on the sidewalk by his truck. The burly figure of her old fan from the bar lumbers in the opposite direction. Chet rubs his whiskers up her neck. The best way to forget that Hank has left with Sheila is to drown herself in some young, sexy cowboy before she gets the hell out of Wyoming, so she dives on in, lips first.

FOUR

Chet struts back from the Bison Inn lobby toward his pickup, grinning at Maggie. His red lips are delectable. She can't wait to taste them again. He waves a keycard back toward the tan stucco building. Two rough looking men and a woman whose cheeks and body scream meth appear from between some parked cars and fall in behind him. She's in black. A skin-tight black shirt under a puffy black vest. Or are those sleeve tattoos on her arms?

Maggie points at them, but Chet misunderstands and blows her a kiss.

The woman—with spiky blonde hair, a skeletal frame, and square shoulders—grabs him by the arm, spinning him. Maggie gasps. *What is going on?*

Chet's fists come up in a flash. He cocks an arm back, prepared to let it fly. As suddenly as he is poised to fight, he drops his arm. He wags his head side to side, no, no. Maggie watches, gaping, as the two men each take him by an arm, and he just lets them.

An oddly dressed woman steps into Maggie's line of vision, maybe drawn by the possibility of a fight. Is that a tan leather skirt? And a fringed shirt? Not that she has room to talk herself, in her fringed vest and tank. She's wearing her hair in two long black braids. Maggie rocked that look one summer on the road. The woman is behaving strangely, too, standing in a wide stance with her arms out slightly, like she's ready to fight. But whatever she's here for, she's in Maggie's way. She slides across the seat so she can see what's going on.

The blonde slaps Chet hard across the face, so hard that Maggie hears it in the cab of the truck, even with the windows up. The blonde shakes her hand, bent over at the waist, holding her gut and stumbling around. *She's laughing.*

The men release Chet and one slaps the woman a high five. She lets loose a combo of air punches and a high kick, then skips over to a group nearer the street huddled around a lifted Chevy one-ton with a home paint job in army green.

The fashion-impaired woman slips away, too.

Chet watches them for a moment. When he turns to Maggie, his head is down. By the time he's in the truck, though, he's grinning again, despite the bright red handprint on his face.

He swoops in to pin her against the passenger side window by the lips. Maggie gives back as good as she gets. The kiss is rough, but it ends after a few seconds.

Maggie nips his neck. "What was that about—offering yourself up for an ass-whupping?"

"When I'm wrong, I man up. I didn't do right by her, once upon a time. I get it. Worse for everybody if I fight back. Plus, I have a tire iron in my truck bed. I could put a stop to things real quick with her brothers if I needed to."

Maggie wonders if this is the ex-girlfriend they'd ditched in the Occidental. "So, you're too young for me *and* you're a man whore?" She slides her hand down his chest to the button on his jeans.

He laughs. "Neither." He grabs her wrist. "Let's save some of that for upstairs."

"Party pooper." Her hand retreats slowly.

He slides back to the driver's side, shifting to make his jeans more comfortable now that he's filling them out and then some. He starts the truck. "We're parking in back."

"Away from the woman you done wrong?"

"Away from everyone, beautiful. Where I can be alone with you."

FIVE

Maggie wakes to a spinning bed. Predawn light is peeping through a window with wide-open drapes. Above her, a warrior on a pinto pony has a bow and arrow trained on a US Calvary soldier. Beside her, a hulking form with the comforter over his head is snoring like a wood chipper. He rolls, taking the covers with him. Maggie grabs for them, but she's too late. She's naked and exposed.

The window-unit air conditioner on her side of the bed is working double time. Without the sheet, she's freezing. She wants clothes and the Excedrin in her bag. And a whole lot of water. Before she gets up, though, Maggie lifts the sheet. Last night is fuzzy, but she's ninety-nine point nine percent sure she left the Occidental with the young cowboy she met in the parking lot of the taxidermy store. It never hurts to be sure. And if there's even a chance it's Hank, that changes everything.

It's not. Hank, that is. The curly dishwater hair and muscular young body definitely belong to Chet. The fingernail scratches down his back belong to her. She trails her finger down one. That had to hurt. He groans and flips, quick as a cat, displaying a giant morning woody. The details of their hookup come back to her. Sexually, they were a hell of a match. Several times. She aches in the right places, but it feels all wrong.

At this moment, Hank is probably spooning his sweet young thing, while Maggie's freezing her ass off, God knows where, with her head splitting open from too much booze and her size extra-large mistake. A seriously delectable mistake, but with sobriety and thoughts of Hank, not one she has an appetite to repeat. Revenge sex only makes her feel better until it's over. And it's way, way over. Besides, if Hank doesn't know—and he probably wouldn't care—that she's with Chet, then it isn't even revenge. It's just a one-night stand. The rule for those is no lingering, sexy mornings. They lead to misunderstandings and man-babies with hurt feelings.

Hurt feelings . . . like hers. Damn Hank. Damn his girlfriend.

She has to get out of here. This room. This place. This town. This *state*. Away from the pain of thinking about what will never be with Hank. Maybe it's time to return some of Gary's calls. He's not a bad guy. He's the right age, unlike the pretty boy beside her. Gary cares. He can help her get over Hank.

Her phone rings. She slithers off the bed. Chet snorts and turns back over in a violent flop onto his belly. She winces. If he's not careful, he's going to break his impressive pecker clean off. Her phone rings again, and she scrambles around naked on all fours, searching for it. She finds it under her panties.

Nice. Starting the day with dignity.

It's Michele. She hits accept, grabs her bag, and slips into the bathroom. She shuts the door—no lock, or she would use it—and turns on the shower to cover her voice, but sets it to cold. She's going to want the hot water for the vigorous scrubbing she plans to give herself. He'd admitted to being a man whore. She remembers insisting on condoms, but she couldn't slip his whole body into one. So, yeah. Big-time shower.

Finally, she wipes the phone on a hand towel and whispers into it. "Hello."

"What took you so long?" Michele's voice is way too damn perky. "I thought you'd been abducted by a serial killer or something."

"It's really early." She holds the phone out, noticing her arm is almost not long enough for her to read the time. Screw this getting-old shit. "Six a.m."

"Seven here."

"Still an indecent hour. But I'm not alone."

"Anyone I know?" Michele's voice is hopeful. This bright Michele is a recent phenomenon to Maggie. Ever since she's known her, Michele has teetered between dangerous depression and mere deep sadness. Her husband was murdered, and getting over it has been hard. But she's finally succumbed to the persistent attentions of Rashidi, now her boyfriend. But given her own dismal situation with Hank, Maggie is missing the old Michele this morning.

"No." Maggie fills a plastic cup with water. She fishes the nearly empty bottle of Excedrin from her bag and takes three, finishing off the water. "But I saw *him*. Last night."

Michele's the only best girlfriend Maggie has ever had. Other women generally aren't Maggie's biggest fans, and vice versa. Michele is also the only person Maggie has ever told about Hank. Ever. That's including the therapists in the many mandatory counseling sessions during rehabs one and two. Michele is definitely Team Hank. When Maggie showed Hank the door, she and Michele had the only serious disagreement of their entire relationship. Pretty amazing given that Michele is a writer, a best-selling and semi-famous one. She wrote the tell-all book that Sheila had mentioned the night before, the one about Maggie's birth parents—her deceased artist mother, Gidget, and the very much alive former US senator Boyd Herrington, whose sister killed Gidget and tried to kill Maggie, Michele, and Michele's daughter, Annabelle. As much as Maggie hates the spotlight, it's a testament to her love for Michele.

"And?"

"He has a girlfriend Belle's age." She refills her water and downs it. Does it again. And again.

"No!"

"Yes." Maggie presses her back against the door and slides down until her rump is on the cold linoleum floor and she is sitting cross-legged.

"That, that worthless *pendejo*. Then who are you with?"

"You don't want to know. Even I don't."

Michele groans. "Oh, *chica, chica*. Are you okay?"

"Hungover. Humiliated. Homesick." Maggie picks at her cuticles. Her sunshine-yellow nail polish is chipping off. Apropos to her outlook.

"I worry about you."

"With good reason."

"And I hate to be the bearer of bad news at a time like this."

Maggie sticks her legs out straight and flexes her feet upward, stretching her thigh muscles. More bad news. "Hit me."

"Omaha and Nebraska. They're out again. They're like freaking Houdini and . . . another famous illusionist."

"There are no other famous illusionists."

"Any ideas on how to keep their asses penned up?"

"Shut the gate?"

"Ha ha. I am. But I'm wondering if your rental guest isn't. Or if someone else isn't. Because otherwise the goats are opening it."

"Seriously, the gate was open?"

"Yes. Multiple times."

"I'll text my guest."

"Maybe I could take them to Gidget's? Loopy could help me keep an eye on them."

Lumpy—or Loopy as Michele liked to call him—is a former Texas Ranger who had been Gidget's next door neighbor. Then Michele's when she rented the place for a year after Maggie inherited it. Michele had built a house on her own property, though, and moved out the previous spring. Now the old farmhouse was rented, and its gallery of paintings by Gidget and other famous artists Maggie had pulled for herself or loaned to museums and galleries. She was holding on to the place for sentimental reasons, at least until she could make up her mind whether to sell or remodel and move there herself.

"Sounds good. And I'll be home in a few days." Maggie gets up. With the cold shower going, the mirror hasn't fogged. She wishes it had. Her eyeliner and mascara make her look like a close cousin to a raccoon.

"Have you seen Gene?"

Does from a distance count? "No. Don't think I'm gonna this trip."

"Okay, well, be safe. I love you."

"Love you, too."

They hang up. Maggie sets the phone on the counter. There's a knock on the bathroom door.

Chet's deep voice says, "You in there, firecracker?"

Maggie closes her eyes. She can't hide forever. "My name is Maggie."

The knob turns. The door opens, and he pokes his head in. "Whatever your name is, you're a live wire, girl."

"And I'm not a girl."

"Looks like you need company." He steps in, still naked and his personal parts broken in the "on" position. His eyes roam over her body, and his eyes glisten.

Maggie pulls a towel off a shelf. It covers the most critical areas, save her meager cleavage and, she's sure, the bottom few inches of her ass. "Time to hit the trail, cowboy."

His eager face droops. Sad puppy meets American Gigolo. "But, I thought we had a good time last night."

"We did. Past tense."

"What did I do wrong?"

"You're too young."

He stands straighter. "I'm older than I look."

"So am I. Goodbye, Chet."

He reaches toward her face. "Hey, now. I rented the room."

She ducks away and points at the door. "And I thank you for it."

"Can I get your number?"

"No."

"Buy you breakfast?"

"Chet."

"Ask you to marry me? You'd make a real nice mama to my little girl. And I promise my mother isn't as crazy as people say."

She sighs. "Seriously."

"What, is an oil-production worker not good enough for you?"

"It's not that."

"Because I own my own ranch and house."

"Good for you."

"What if I told you I was about to come into big money—would I look better to you then?"

"Not really. Goodbye, Chet."

"Okay, okay. I'm going. But you can't ruin it for me. Last night was the best night of my life. And not just because you're famous."

If Maggie only had a dime for every time she'd been told *that*.

When she hears the door to the room shut, she goes to it, throws the deadbolt, and puts on the safety chain. Chet might have kept a keycard. Plus, she remembers a rough crowd in the hotel parking lot and the woman who'd slapped Chet. No use taking any chances in case her grudge extends to Chet's hookups, too.

Maggie returns to the bathroom and turns the shower water as hot as it will go. She works herself over with latherless soap and a sandpapery washcloth until her whole body is an angry scarlet. *Self-flagellation. Seems appropriate right now.* She keeps scrubbing.

SIX

After she's dressed in her clothes from the night before, she finger-brushes her teeth with water. She's still exhausted—in no shape for a desolate, lengthy drive toward Texas. Safety first. She sets her phone alarm for ten.

When she wakes, she feels less like death. She texts the guest at her house while she waits on the in-room coffee maker.

Leslie: Hi. Hope things are good. Pls keep gates closed & latched. Goats getting out. Thanks! Maggie

She notices a message from her birth father, Boyd. *I hear you're in northern WY. Big family secret: My mother is half Crow. Makes you an eighth. Reservation in southern MT. Huge powwow every August. Maybe we can go sometime.*

She knew she got her dark coloring from Boyd, but the source is a shock. The Herrington family is Houston high society and very political. She can't imagine that Native American heritage fifty years ago fit their mold. It pleases the rebel in her. And the connection to the people and history of the area stirs her. Is it crazy to think she feels it, has been feeling it ever since she got here? Which is sad, since she'll never be back. No way will she risk another encounter with Hank.

The coffee isn't quite ready, so she sends a quick reply to Boyd: *Scandalous. Compared to that, my existence is practically tame.*

Maggie splits her coffee between two cups and makes it as light and sweet as she can with the few packets of creamer and sugar available. She drinks the first coffee in the room. The other she carries with her. She takes an elevator down to the lobby, where she's reminded of the name of the place. The Bison Inn. The place couldn't be less charming if it were made of Styrofoam. Which it looks like it could be. And it's too much like the name of the Buffalo Lodge, where she'd once stayed with Hank. This experience taints the former somehow.

Meanwhile, her cute room at the very original, if cheap, Mill Inn is paid for and sitting empty half an hour north. She'd left her checkout open-ended, hoping she'd stay there in bed with Hank, naked and happily bruised, until she had to rush back for fall show. Her shower-roughened skin aches at the thought. She wants to head straight south now, but she can't. It's going to add an hour to her already long drive, but she has to return to Sheridan to pick up her stuff. She just prays her junk trailer is intact. Otherwise, the trip will be a *total* loss.

First, though, she has to find Bess. Chet drove here last night. But she has no idea where "here" is in relation to downtown Buffalo, where she parked her truck. She needs an Uber. Or a taxi.

She pulls up her Uber app. No dice. They don't operate within three hundred miles of here. Through the lobby window, downtown Buffalo is visible in the near distance. Her boots are comfortable. The sun is out. Walking will be good for her.

As she passes a nondescript reception desk tucked back from a claustrophobic lobby, the clerk calls out to her. "Management wants all our guests to know that your next night here is free."

The words are unexpected. Maggie stops. "What?"

He pushes back the sleeves of his hoodie, revealing burn scars. "You know, because of the murder."

Now Maggie sees scarring on his neck and ear that his longish hair almost hides. "What murder?"

"The dead guy? Out in the parking lot?"

"I have no idea what you're talking about."

"Oh, well, somebody bashed a dude's head in. Blood and brains everywhere, man. The police are still out there."

Jesus. Maggie shudders. Small towns aren't immune to bad people, that she learned back in Texas. She wonders how close she and Chet came last night to the same fate.

"This is the first time anything like this has ever happened in Buffalo. At least since I've been here. It's freaky, man."

"Very." She heads for the door, eager to get the hell out of there, but afraid of what she'll see in the parking lot.

"Wait. Don't you want to get the voucher for your free stay?"

She waves without turning. "Keep it." Through the front doors she can see an ambulance, a morgue vehicle, and flashing lights.

"The police want to interview everyone. Are you checking out?"

She pauses. If she could help, she would, but she isn't a witness. And her experience with police questioning is that it doesn't go quickly or easily. "Um, no. Just grabbing something to eat. Which reminds me, I forgot my wallet." She reverses course.

"What's your room number? I'll let them know."

Pretending not to hear him, she turns down the hall and studies the parking lot from a side exit. Yellow crime scene tape is stretched across the back of the parking lot. Four police cars block her view. The exit at the far side of the building is a better bet. Walking fast, she ducks out and makes tracks for the nearby Maverik gas station. There are no shouts for her to come back.

She stops at the station for a large sweet tea. Dehydration from too much alcohol. She doesn't shake hangovers like she used to. Sipping through a straw, she darts across the road and then under the interstate to a sidewalk. The sound of the tumbling water of a creek over rocks to her left competes with the rush of moving vehicles on her right. A truck struggles by with a load of cattle, spewing diesel and manure fumes in her direction. She covers her mouth and nose.

The fifteen-minute walk helps her regain her equilibrium from the bad night and weird morning. When she gets to her truck, she has the shakes from too much caffeine on an empty stomach. Food can't be delayed any longer.

Munching potato chips, a pickle spear, and a Reuben sandwich at the Busy Bee, she watches a young boy fish. He's persistent, casting over and over, until he catches a trout from the stream. He bashes its head with a rock and stuffs it in his backpack. Russian dressing gushes out of her sandwich onto her hands. The mix of sweet, sour, and salty in her mouth goes from pleasing to nausea-inducing in a second. The boy, the fish, the rock, the oozing sandwich guts—it's too reminiscent of the clerk telling her "Somebody bashed a dude's head in. Blood and brains everywhere, man." She puts her sandwich down and asks for her check.

She drives toward Sheridan, still feeling rocky. The wide-open plains and wildlife give her a boost. The herds of pronghorn are enormous. Fifty or sixty head apiece, bigger, she thinks, than a few days ago when she drove up. They munch the irrigated fields as if the crops were planted just for them. Birds of prey ride the thermals overhead. Hawks. A bald eagle. She's going to miss this. She's glad she's seen it.

Even as she's longing for escape, she sees the exit for Piney Creek, just north of Lake Desmet. Stalker that she's been, she knows that Double S is only a few miles away off Wagon Box Road. Her brain screams *no*, but her weak heart guides her hands to steer the truck down the exit ramp. Just one peek, she tells herself. See it with her own eyes, then beat it. She doesn't need Siri to direct her. She memorized this route, just in case.

A turn approaches on her right. A sign points the way to the FETTERMAN MASSACRE. It's the opposite direction from Double S, so she keeps going. The next road is on the left, and the signage there directs her to FORT PHIL KEARNEY and WAGON BOX FIGHT. There's no street sign, but it sounds promising. She takes it, and half a mile later comes to Wagon Box Road. *Small victories,* she congratulates herself.

Wagon Box, it turns out, is a dirt road. The truck's shocks are shit, so she slows, taking the opportunity to lower her windows. The smells of Russian olive trees and fresh mountain water from Little Piney Creek flood the cab. When she admired the silvery trees aloud a few days ago, she'd received a scolding. "They're invasive. Pests. Non-native. On their way out, one shovelful at a time." She doesn't care. They smell marvelous. She breathes deeply, letting it fill her senses. If clean had a smell, it would be the air in this valley. For the first time that day, she feels like there's hope for her. White-tailed deer graze in every direction. Flocks of turkey hens and their ugly broods saunter in front of her, herded by spectacular toms. The aspen trees along the creek rustle and shimmer, their leaves just starting to yellow. Although bumps and potholes jar her shoulders, she doesn't mind. She knows so little about the area, but suddenly she can imagine the ancestors she'd never known she had. Did they live and hunt here?

She sees movement in the thick aspens by the creek. She strains her eyes trying to find an animal. Nothing. Whatever it was, it's gone. Just as she returns her attention to the road, Bess hits a pothole. A big one. There's a loud *thunk*, then the truck stops moving forward. Something clatters, loud, but the engine is still running.

"Shit!" Maggie presses the gas. The engine revs, but the truck doesn't move.

After several more tries, she turns off the ignition. She'll just give Bess time to change her mind. When Maggie starts the engine, she gets the same horrible noise. She shifts to first and gooses the gas pedal. Bess stays put. Maggie tries reverse. Nothing doing.

"This isn't happening." She walks around Bess, patting her. "Come on, girl. It's rally time."

She crouches on the ground. Something big is hanging off the undercarriage, all the way to the ground. All the stress and disappointment bubbles up in her, and leaks out her mouth in a surge of curse words. "Fucking fucker."

She kicks a tire. Once. Twice. Three times. All she gets is a sore foot. But she knows it's not Bess's fault. Maggie was the one gazing off into the trees, distracted and goofy over wild animals and thoughts of her heritage. She'll have to call for help. But of course when she checks her phone, she gets a No Service message.

Why does Wyoming hate her?

In the distance, she hears the rumble of a truck. Heavy-duty, from the sound of it. Well, she'll hitch a ride, then. She hitchhiked plenty back in the day. But that was when she was younger and didn't feel the knife's edge of mortality at her throat. Wyoming people had been nothing but kind so far, but the men . . . they act awfully, awfully lonely. A life of sexual captivity in a dilapidated cabin doesn't appeal to her. She retrieves her bag from the truck, hangs it over her shoulder, and clutches the pepper spray inside it with one hand.

A flatbed Dodge dualie rounds the corner uphill from Maggie. The driver is male. Alone. She hitches her thumb as she squeezes the pepper canister so hard it digs into the palm of her other hand.

The truck rumbles to a stop, nose to nose with Bess. The engine's *bwah-bwah-bwah-bwah-bwah* quiets. Maggie stays by the door to her truck. A linebacker-size man slams the truck door. He's carrying an oilcloth jacket over one arm. Behind him, dark storm clouds are rolling in over the mountains. The sun fades away. A wind whips up, and the temperature drops, suddenly and noticeably. The man dons the jacket. Maggie wishes she wasn't in a tank top.

The man touches the brim of his cowboy hat. "Looks like you're having a bad day."

Maggie grinds her teeth. *Mister, you don't know the half of it.* "Appears so."

The big man halts five feet short of her. "Out of gas?"

"I wish." Maggie points at the ground under Bess. "I seem to have dropped some essential parts."

He walks all the way around the truck. When he comes back, he bends over for a look. He whistles. "Damn straight. Need a ride? A tow?"

Maggie's anger is giving way to a feeling of inevitability. She is doomed to a hellish and humiliating visit to Wyoming. "I may need both, if you could call me a tow truck."

He looks amused, his eyes crinkling in a weather-beaten face. "You won't find better than what I got here, as long as you're not needing a tow all the way to Texas." He jerks a thumb toward the back end of the truck, where her Texas license plate gives her away. At her blank expression, he adds, "I carry tow gear in my toolbox. I don't know about Texas, but out here, we're ready for anything, anytime."

Maggie stews on his words. He doesn't sound like he means that in a creepy way. She checks his finger. He's wearing a wedding ring. That decides it for her. She releases her pepper spray and sticks out her hand. This has to be fate, breaking down by Hank's ranch. Why not give in to it? Let it play out the way it is going to, without fighting it. The universe might still have a plan. "Maggie Killian. Thank you. If you could just drop me up the road at my friend's ranch, he can help me from there."

They shake.

"Patrick Rhodes. You've killed your truck in front of my place. Who's your friend?"

"Hank Sibley."

Something dark crosses Patrick's face, then he grunts. "No problem. At least you're pointed in the right direction."

Maggie ducks behind Bess to get away from an especially strong gust of wind. *It's colder than a witch's tit out here.* She wraps her arms around herself. The jacket she'd brought from Texas is in her suitcase at the Mill Inn, where it does her no good. Even though it's too light for the weather blowing in, it would be better than nothing. *I wasn't prepared for this place. Not for anything about it.* "Thank you."

"I can't tow you with your driveshaft dragging." He walks back to his truck bed, leans over it, digs around, then comes out with two wrenches and a hammer. "Give me a second."

He lies on his back, wriggling his shoulders and pushing with his feet, spurs catching on the dirt road, until he disappears under Bess.

Behind her, she hears another vehicle. It slows to a stop. She glances over. It's a monstrosity of a van, painted entirely in green-and-tan camouflage.

"Need help?"

She recognizes the driver immediately. The annoying fan at the Occidental. *What, are there only ten people in Wyoming?* "No, I'm good. Thanks."

He smiles and tugs down on his baseball cap. "If you say so, Maggie." He sprays gravel as he drives away.

She hears clanging and banging under Bess. It seems to her that it takes forever, but eventually a big metal part slides out, followed by Patrick.

After he puts his tools away and throws her driveshaft in his truck bed, he dusts off his jacket and jeans. "Sorry I left you out in the cold. Come get warm in the cab of my truck while I hook yours up."

She follows him, then diverts to the passenger side, which has a magnet on the door that reads RHODES ROUGH STOCK. He'd left the vehicle running with the heater on. Praise the Lord and pass the biscuits warm. She rubs her arms briskly to help it along.

Patrick turns his truck around, maneuvers it into place, and then gets out to connect a chain towline. While he's gone, Maggie cranks the heater up to full blast. Even better. She closes her eyes and lets the heat wave roll over her. Patrick's returning tools to the truck bed two minutes later. Maggie flips the heater back to low as he approaches. She's still cold, but hell if she'll admit what a flatlander she is.

He shuts the door behind him. "Double S is just a few miles up the road. Five minutes or so."

Five minutes until she springs herself on Hank, again. "Thanks."

"You live round here? We get lots of Texas transplants."

"No. Just visiting. Doing a work thing."

He nods. "How do you know Hank?"

An image of Hank's young, strong body, gleaming with sweat, in the Buffalo Lodge in Chugwater washes over her. She swallows. "Old friends. From way back."

He frowns and is silent for a moment. "Well, my truck will do the heavy lifting, but I need you to put her in neutral and steer and brake."

"Gotcha." Maggie returns to Bess, freezing. She should have left the truck on with the heater running. But that's not all that she's thinking about. Patrick's giving off bad vibes about Hank. *What's up with that?* She turns on the truck and puts it in neutral as instructed. She gives a thumbs-up.

Patrick returns one, then eases forward, taking the slack out of the chain. Bess rolls after him. He keeps his speed low. Maggie steers and brakes around the curves. Soon they reach the entrance to the Piney Bottoms Ranch, a cattle guard under a wooden structure with a weathered sign, the letters carved out and painted black. Underneath, another sign hangs on rings and blows in the wind: DOUBLE S BUCKING STOCK.

Maggie gets a sick feeling, like a bullied kid on the first day of school. Scared. Hoping things will be different. Excited despite herself.

With a tug from Patrick, Bess coasts over the cattle guard. It rattles Maggie's teeth, but that doesn't distract her hungry eyes from taking in this place she's imagined for so long. Hank's home. The skies are just clear enough for a good view of the spread. Corrals, red barns, and two arenas—one covered, one outdoor. Horses everywhere. The square bodies and short necks of cattle in the distance. On a slight rise above the livestock structures are the human-type abodes. A two-story house, a smattering of cabins. Farther in the distance and a few hundred vertical feet up the side of a mountain, a tall cabin perches under a green metal roof. It's set back into ponderosa pines, a regal overlord to the working class below.

Shoot me dead and call me Edna. It's even more beautiful than she'd imagined.

Patrick pulls to a stop in front of the central house. He walks back to her truck, extricating himself from his coat. Maggie rolls down the window.

"You need this more than me."

She takes it. "Don't mind if I do. I'll get it back to you."

"It came to me on the way over here. I've seen you before. Last night at the Occidental."

"Oh?" She doesn't remember meeting him. She wasn't that drunk, was she?

"We didn't meet. I saw you talking to Hank. Anyway, welcome to Wyoming."

"Thanks. I was leaving today. Looks like I've been delayed."

"Rotten luck for you. Maybe not so bad for me, if you'd let me take you to dinner."

"Oh, that's nice of you. But . . ." Her voice peters out.

"You got someone?" He frowns. "I thought Sibley was with that Morris girl?"

Young Sheila must be a Morris. "No, I mean, yes, he has a girlfriend."

"Just a sec." He makes a trip back to his truck. When he returns, he hands her a card. "Here's my number. Just in case. Now let's get you unhooked."

Maggie gets out to watch. As Patrick unlatches the hook and chain, the low-hanging clouds close in again, shrinking her world down to a radius of a few hundred foggy yards. The temperature drops. Even with the jacket on, she's still chilly and hugs herself. A man walking toward them from the barn complex materializes out of the fog. Her heart recognizes the shape and gait. Hank. Stiff-legged and consternated.

"Rhodes," Hank shouts. "What the hell do you think you're doing?"

Patrick ignores him as he puts up his towing gear.

Hank keeps advancing on Patrick with a menacing look on his face. "I said what the hell . . ." Hank sees Maggie, and his angry words peter out. "Maggie?"

If she had any doubts before from Patrick, now she's sure there's no love lost between these two. But she's perplexed about Hank's reaction. Had the old Hank had a temper like this? She lifts a hand in greeting. "Surprise."

Hank's gaze roves back and forth between her and Patrick. "I don't understand."

"I was out sightseeing. Bess broke down in front of Patrick's place. He brought us here." Her words leave out a lot, and she hopes Hank will let it slide.

His eyes narrow, asking. She looks away, answering.

Patrick interrupts their silent conversation. "You need anything else, Maggie?"

"Nope. I've busted up enough of your day. Thanks."

He moves a few inches closer. Loud enough for Hank to hear, he says, "Use that number and I'll come back for my coat, and whatever else you have to offer."

What about his wedding ring? She takes a step back, unwilling to be a prop in their stage routine. "You take care."

Patrick drives away. Raindrops begin to fall to the ground, but they're quickly replaced by ice pellets.

"You probably have questions." Maggie uses her hand to shield her face from the sleet.

"In there," Hank says, pointing to the barn. He puts his coat and arm out. She ducks under the shelter he offers, and together they run down the slope to the outbuildings.

SEVEN

Hay is stacked floor to ceiling on one wall of the barn, up to the loft groaning with more of the same. A fine dust of hay powder floats in the air and covers the floor. Maggie sneezes and fights the urge to scrub grit from her eyes.

Maggie weaves her almost-true story about sightseeing, truck trouble, and giving Patrick the name of the only person she knows in Wyoming, who luckily happens to live on the next ranch over. She omits everything to do with shacking up for the night with Chet in Buffalo. No sense volunteering irrelevant information. Or so she tells herself. This close proximity to Hank already feels high-risk. Like standing on a wet floor using a blow-dryer. No sense in jumping into the bathtub with it.

"That's screwed up," Hank says. If he thinks there's more to her story, he keeps it to himself.

"Story of my life." She wriggles her nose to prevent another sneeze. "I've got to get Bess to Sheridan to a mechanic."

A black-and-white dog slinks into the barn. Maggie has an impression of long hair and short legs before it disappears behind a bale of hay.

Hank shakes his head. "Everything in town will have closed at noon. Not that Mother Nature cooperated, but most folks knock off early to head up to the mountains. It's usually the last snow-free weekend of the year up there. Let us take a look at the truck and see if we can fix it."

"Us?"

"Me. Gene. Our hand, Paco. He used to work at an auto repair shop. One of us will figure it out."

"That sounds promising." She sighs and pushes damp hair off her forehead. "I have a trailer full of antiques and a room full of my stuff in Sheridan, too."

"We'll get you on the road before you can say spit."

But now that she's here, she's wondering why exactly she's in such a hurry to leave. She hitches the belt buckle and smiles.

EIGHT

Maggie is about as useful as teats on a boar hog for the next hour. Hank and a hand he introduces as Andy tow Bess to a cavernous shop at the edge of the livestock complex. Maggie tries not to stare at Andy. His work shirt looks home sewn and blousy, his trousers a soft denim with a dress-pants overlapping waistband. The coat he hangs neatly on a peg doesn't appear store-bought either.

"What do you think of our shop?" Hank asks. He's beaming like a proud papa.

From the outside, the "shop" is just like any other metal warehouse. Inside, it's like a high-end garage and smells of petroleum products and rubber. Walls of shelving, pegs, and racks hold tools and vehicle parts. Stacks of tires in a wide range of sizes tower along the walls. There's even welding torches, industrial jacks, and a grease pit with guides for wheels on either side.

She puts her hands on her hips, trying not to look like she's posing when she is, wishing she had showered and changed clothes. "Impressive."

"Lots of heavy equipment here. Tractors. Off-road vehicles. Trucks. Gotta keep 'em running."

Patrick had said people have to be ready for anything, anytime in Wyoming. At Double S, they are, she thinks. The two men position her truck over the pit, with a lot of pushing and, on Hank's part, cursing.

"Are you trying to break my heart today?"

His words are a jolt. Hers was the heart broken on this trip. "What?"
Hank points at her jacket.

She looks down. RHODES ROUGH STOCK is emblazoned over her left breast, along with the silhouette of a bucking bull.

"You're representing for the enemy."

His words trigger a memory of harsh words and an altercation at the Occidental. Hank and a big guy. That had been Patrick, she realizes. Patrick and Hank are enemies. Or competitors, at least. She glances at the emblem again. "Sorry."

"Andy, throw her one of our jackets. And burn that one."

Andy straightens a round-brimmed hat over his boyish face. He's young. Too young even for Sheila. Maybe in his late teens? He rummages in a cabinet and unfolds a khaki all-weather jacket with the Double S logo on it. He brings it to Maggie then holds his hand out for her Rhodes jacket.

"I need to return it."

Hank guffaws.

Andy nods, backing away, eyes on the toes of high-heeled cowboy boots.

Maggie takes off the Rhodes jacket and stashes it on the bench seat in the truck. Several strands of fringe come off with it. She dons the Double S jacket and twirls. "How do I look, boys?"

Hank breaks out his dimples. "Like we need to feature you in our advertising."

Maggie unleashes the sultry in her voice. "My picture in this jacket and 'Ride 'em, cowboy' below it?"

He shakes his hand like it's hot. "Let 'er buck."

Andy flushes crimson.

Hank and Andy climb down into the pit with a toolbox and Bess's driveshaft. For ten minutes, there's a steady series of clanks, thuds, and man sounds. Every so often, one of them says something to the other.

When it grows quiet, Maggie drops to a cross-legged seat near the truck. Cold metal under the tush. It's uncomfortable, but she has a view of Hank's profile, so she toughs it out.

In a casual voice, she asks, "So, Hank, how long have you been dating Sheila?"

Hank speaks, but it's to Andy. "Why don't you run get Paco? I think this one's beyond us."

"Sure thing, boss." Andy appears and nods to Maggie as he trots out of the shop, putting on his jacket midstride.

Hank climbs out, wiping grease from his hands with a dingy rag.

"Everything okay?"

"With your truck? Not really."

"Did you hear my question a minute ago?"

"About me and Sheila." He still doesn't answer her, tosses the rag onto a workbench.

"Yes."

He leans his still-fine Wrangler-clad butt against the workbench. "Three months, I guess."

Maggie stands and starts walking around near Hank, examining tools with her hands. She picks up a socket wrench. "She seems like a nice girl."

"She is. Very nice."

She works the grips on a pair of needle-nose pliers. "What does she do?"

"She's a teacher. Third grade during the week. Elementary-age Sunday schoolers at the Methodist church on the weekends."

"Oh. That's great." Maggie squirts compressed air from the nozzle of a long hose. The explosive noise and kick make her jump. "Oops." She puts it back in its holster.

The door opens and slams against the interior wall. Andy and a swarthy, attractive man with a mischievous air and thin mustache follow it. Andy wrestles it closed behind them.

"Can't fix it, Sib?" The new man—a fireplug—rubs his hands together and hustles to the truck. "Howdy, ma'am. I'm Paco." His accent reminds Maggie of Edward, her mom's beau and Michele and Gene's father. First generation out of Mexico.

"Maggie. Thanks for your help."

He walks around Bess and whistles. "That's a sweet ride, *mamacita*."

Hank's eyebrows shoot toward his hairline.

Paco doesn't seem to notice. "And your driveshaft just fell off? Without any warning?"

"Right into the road. One end of it, anyway. I was driving, hit a pothole, heard a *thunk*, and my Bess was out of business."

"Hmm. Well I ain't never seen no bolts on a driveshaft loosen themselves. You had any work done on your truck recently?"

"No. It's been a while."

"Let me take a look." He disappears under the truck.

Hank moves to the edge of the pit, watching him. Maggie gives in to the magnetic pull and joins Hank. He sneaks a glance at her.

Before she can bedazzle him with a sultry smile, the door opens and closes again. Maggie looks to see who has joined the party, and the familiar face of Gene Soboleski grins at her. A flicker of irritation pulses through her. Interrupted, when things with Hank were moving in the right direction. *Argh.*

"Maggie May. In Wyoming. At Double S. Wow." He's a fast mover, and he hustles over and gathers her in a hug, crushing a Cheetos bag against her back. The two of them had really hit it off the previous spring in Texas. "How's that sister of mine? And my father?"

"Michele is writing like a mad thing on her new book and preparing for the premiere of her Maggie movie."

"I read my sister's book." He grins, wads up his Cheetos bag, and shoots it like a free throw into a tall black trash can. "I thought it was about the fall of the Herrington political dynasty."

"Hell-o. The title is *The Love Child and Murder That Toppled the Herrington Dynasty.* Me." She taps her chest. "The love child."

He laughs. "And are her father and your mother still two lovebirds sitting in a tree, K-I-S-S-I-N-G?"

"Waay too much."

Again, he laughs. "We're going to be stepsiblings, aren't we?"

Maggie smiles back at him. "Magic Eight Ball says signs point to yes."

"Speaking of which, Hank pointed you out to me at the Ox last night. Sorry I didn't get a chance to say hello. You looked . . . occupied . . . and we had to go. School nights for our dates."

Occupied. So that's what the kids are calling it these days. Maggie doesn't blush or look away. He'd hit the nail on the head about school nights, though. Two grown-ass men dating virtual *children.* "What's your girlfriend's name?"

"June. But she won't be my girlfriend. I'm not hankering for the job of instant dad to somebody else's kid with a girl half my age."

She knew she liked Gene for a reason. "Probably smart."

Gene grins. "Andy says you're stranded with us."

"For now."

He pats her shoulder. "Hey, I'm sorry about that big online article about you."

"What?"

"The 'How the Mighty Maggie Killian Has Fallen' piece. Sheila showed it to us last night."

Maggie's stomach drops. That doesn't sound like the "Where are they now?" retrospective Sheila had described. "Did you read it?"

"Um, yes?" He makes a teeth-bared wincing face.

"That bad, huh? And that's really the title?"

"Yep. But anyone that knows you knows different."

Paco's voice from below Bess interrupts them. "No can do, Sib."

Hank, who's been pretending not to listen to Gene and Maggie, groans. "I thought you could fix anything?"

"It didn't just come loose, man. Take a look."

Hank takes the driveshaft that Paco is holding up from the pit.

"See the end of it? It looks like it melted."

Hank frowns as he turns the heavy metal in his hands. "I thought something looked strange." He sets it in the truck bed. "That's why I sent for you."

Maggie feels a flicker of panic.

"Right?" Paco says.

Maggie paces the floor near the truck. "Use super glue. Duct tape. Whatever you have to."

Paco peers out from under her truck. "You're kidding, right?" He looks at Hank. "She's kidding?"

Maggie pushes her hair back, still pacing. "Sort of."

Paco hoists himself out of the pit. "No can do. You need a new one."

"Can we get it in town?"

Paco frowns, wiping his hands on a rag from the workbench. "Maybe. But these old trucks, lotta times you gotta hunt one down. Like from a used parts dealer."

Hank takes Maggie's elbow. "Stop pacing. You're wearing the floor out."

"Would you rather I punch something?"

"As long as it's not me." He lets go of her. "How about we tow it to the Ford dealership. Maybe you'll get lucky."

She looks at her phone. It's four thirty. "Shit. They're about to close."

"We'll call on the way. Then they can start on it first thing in the morning."

She sighs. "Okay. I guess that's my only option. And you can drop me by my hotel."

"Nonsense. You don't have a vehicle. We'll bring you and your trailer back here. You'll stay in the guest cabin."

Gene's forehead wrinkles. He opens his mouth, then shuts it.

Maggie's heart feels like someone has lit a nice fire inside of it. Hank wants to drive her to town. And he wants her to stay here. She's done more with less. "If you're sure I'm no bother."

Their eyes lock. The fire inside her crackles.

"I'm sure. Andy, can you take her to the guest cabin? I'll pick you up in fifteen minutes, Maggie."

Andy salutes.

"Thank you." Maggie follows Andy to the door, putting some sass in her back view.

Just before the door closes behind her, she hears Gene say in a low voice, "What are you thinking, having her stay here? You're playing with fire, Hank. And if Maggie doesn't burn you again, Sheila will."

NINE

Hours later, Hank and Maggie roll back onto Piney Bottoms. The storm had broken while they were in Sheridan. The temperature yo-yoed back into the high seventies, and the sun is bright, like Maggie's mood. She's with Hank. In Wyoming. He's been chatty, even flirty. And Sheila isn't around. Life. Is. Awesome.

The only negative is that the dealership's service department was, as expected, closed, and they hadn't picked up when she called. Hank parked Bess in their lot. Maggie dropped her key in a night drop and left a detailed voicemail about the truck, the broken part, and the need for speed. Now all she can do is pray, and blow up their phone as soon as they open in the morning.

Hank brakes in front of the one-bedroom cabin Andy had taken her to earlier. "Dinner is in fifteen minutes at the main house. We have a communal dining room and a cook, although Trudy is so good she's more like a chef." He grins. "Be late and you'll incur the wrath of my mother."

Maggie's heart goes into orbit. He's asking her to dinner. With his mother. She feels hope. She loves it here. She never wants to leave.

"See you then."

Hank clears his throat. "Um, no. I've gotta go. I'm late for a thing."

She freezes, hand on door handle. She sees several strands of fringe on the seat between them. "A thing?"

Hank looks out the window.

"A date?"

"Sheila has a dinner with some of her fellow teachers."

Maggie stares at him, trying to mask the pain stabbing her through the heart.

"From the, ah, church."

She lets out a bark of laughter. "A group dinner date with Sunday school teachers?"

"What's wrong with that?"

"Are you shitting me? Hank Sibley's big Friday night is partying with church ladies?"

His brows furrow, but he dimples. "Listen, wiseass."

Maggie, for once, is immune to the dimples. Her voice turns edgy. "Better to be a wiseass than a dumbass."

"Now I'm a dumbass? Why?"

"For giving up your fun. And dating a *child*, no less." Maggie gets out with her guitar, bag, and suitcase. She slams the door, then walks around the truck toward the little cabin.

Hank rolls down his window. "What the hell, Maggie?"

She ignores him, keeps walking.

His volume increases. "You left me. *Twice.* Fifteen years ago in Cheyenne. Six months ago in Texas."

Maggie wheels. "Left you? That's rich. You never *called.*"

Hank shakes his head. "Everything's always someone else's fault, isn't it, Maggie? I told you why I didn't call. You didn't show up on my doorstep, either. And after Texas, you told me never to call you again."

Maggie drops her bags and stalks back to his window. "Just—"

He barrels on. "I never got married, I have no children, and life was going to pass me by if I kept waiting on you. So I didn't. Finally. And I'm seeing a good woman who happens to love working with kids. Forgive me if she's not as much *fun* as you. She's also not as dangerous. Because she cares about me and not just herself." He snorts. "You're the most self-centered person I've ever met."

Hank sprays mud in a hasty departure from Maggie.

Some of it splatters on Maggie. She jumps back then slaps at it with more ire than intention. "Self-centered?" His words sting.

Once, long ago, a friend had said to her, "It must get lonely, never thinking about anyone but yourself." But she's not selfish, is she? She's always had that drive, that focus. It was key to her success as a musician, while it lasted. And after the music, she needed it to survive her addictions, to claw her way back from the humiliation of losing everything. No one helped her. She had to look out for number one. What did Hank know? It's not like he stayed in touch, worried about her, knew anything about her.

But as she grabs her bags and walks to the cabin, all the air rushes out of her in a whoosh. She doesn't want to think about his reasons for not calling all those years ago. Because when she does, she has to face some ugly truths, like the ones he'd told her in Texas. About his career-ending head injury. His dad coming down with Lou Gehrig's disease, then dying. His obligations to his family. Even about the crushing disappointment he felt returning to an empty hotel room and her note. The depression—her word, not his—he'd endured.

And then there was *her*. Her pride keeping *her* from calling *him*. Her very public death spiral. Drugs, alcohol, sex, betrayal of the people around her.

By the time he had it together, she was falling apart—and disappearing.

She opens the electric tape gate around the grassy cabin yard gingerly. Andy had explained to her yesterday that it's to keep loose livestock from eating the grass. He'd claimed it's not turned on now, though. He'd grabbed it and slid tape back and forth through a slot in a fence post to prove it to her. She wants to believe him, but she doesn't want it to zap her.

Zap. A funny word to cross her mind. Zapped is exactly how she feels with her quick fall from emotional high to low. She just wants to crawl into bed and stay there until her truck is fixed and she can tuck tail and run back to Texas.

When she gets to the front door of the cabin, she's met by the black-and-white dog she saw earlier in the barn. It looks like half the herding dogs she's seen in Wyoming, only with its legs sawed off at the knees. A border collie mix, but mixed with what?

The dog stares at Maggie with naked hope in its eyes.

"What are you looking at, fucker?"

The dog wags its tail and licks its lips. The tail does double duty as a broom on the porch floor and a bass drum mallet to the cabin wall.

Maggie pushes past the dog and into the unlocked cabin, then returns to the porch for her suitcase and guitar. In the few words he'd spoken earlier, Andy had explained that she could lock the cabin from the inside, but that the ranch doesn't issue keys for locking up from the outside.

"We don't need them," he'd said.

Now, with the descent of the sun, the cabin is dark inside. Maggie flips on a light switch. Nothing happens. She keeps trying until she finds a working lamp in the kitchenette and one on the bedside table.

She's starving. She checks the mini-fridge. It contains nothing but water and a miniature tray of ice in a compartment that's in desperate need of a defrost. The cabinets aren't much better, although there are packets of instant coffee. Piss in a mug. She'll pass on that.

Dammit, she can't let Hank Sibley drive her into an emotional free fall. She's stronger than this. Dinner at the house is her only chance at some chow, and she's going to get something to eat. A shower and outfit change will have to wait. In the low illumination, she opens the miniscule closet and drops her bag on the floor, then closes the accordion door to keep it from falling out. She props her guitar case sideways against the outside of the closet. Then she barges out of the cabin and toward sustenance.

The dog looks up from digging a hole in the little grass yard.

"You really are a fucker, aren't you?"

All she gets as an answer is more tail-wagging.

No one answers her knock at the house.

Maggie lets herself in. "Hello?"

Silence is the only response.

She's early, so she takes a moment to look around the large front room. It's filled with brown and black leather easy chairs and couches arranged around a gargantuan rock fireplace. A big-screen TV is mounted above the mantel. Old photographs of horses, cattle, and landscapes cover all the wall space not taken up by animal heads. Each mount has a plaque below it. The type of animal, gender, site of the kill, date, name of the hunter, and how it was killed. She notices several are Hank's and is surprised to see "bow" as the weapon on a buck deer and an antelope.

Three doorways and a staircase lead out of the room. A peek through them shows her two doors lead down hallways. When she opens the third, she's met with the sound of voices and the smell of food. Inside is a long plank table for ten in a room paneled in whitewashed shiplap. Rusted relics hang on the walls, a testament to the ranch's history. A PB branding iron. A wooden-handled scythe. Barbed wire. A big rectangular casement opens on an industrial-size kitchen with all modern appliances, except for a wood stove the size of a Chevy sedan. The shiplap carries over into the kitchen space, contrasting with dark green painted cabinets and thick wooden countertops.

Conversation halts as Maggie enters. Men occupy the seats at the dining room table, save for a gray-haired woman, who has to be Mrs. Sibley.

A slim, pale man with thinning hair sits beside her. He nods at Maggie. Gene is at the far head of the table. Paco and Andy sit across from each other.

The silence is like a pair of hands around Maggie's neck. She makes her way to an open seat beside Gene and looks back toward the door.

Mrs. Sibley is tiny in her wheelchair. A full plate of food and a bowl of cobbler are in front of her, along with a tall glass of what looks like milk. She stares down a long nose at her with flinty dark eyes. Maggie curtsies, then regrets it, feeling like a suck-up.

When Mrs. Sibley finally speaks, her voice is shrill, her eyes locked on Maggie. "No dogs in the house."

Maggie looks around and sees the black-and-white dog beside her feet. It must have snuck in when she opened the front door. "Fucker," she mutters loud enough for only Gene to hear.

He makes a strangled noise, and his eyes sparkle.

"Sorry," she says. "I didn't see her. I'll take her out."

At the front door, the dog hunkers down and makes itself limp and heavy like a fifty-pound bag of flour, but Maggie muscles it out. She's back to the dining table in less than a minute.

"You're late." Mrs. Sibley sniffs.

Food is already circulating. The men heap their plates. If Maggie wants to eat, she'll have to claim her share fast, but she's last in the food chain. She eyes the serving bowls and platters stalled at other plates.

Gene leans toward her. "Her name is Louise."

"Hank's mother?"

"No. The dog. She's a stray. Trudy—our cook—started feeding her. Now we can't get rid of her."

"Great. But what is Hank's mother's name?" The basket of rolls finally gets to her. She takes two and stuffs the first in her mouth, without butter. She looks down. More fringe in her lap. She has to change clothes before the outfit she is in disintegrates completely.

"Mrs. Sibley. Well, Evangeline. Vangie. But I don't recommend you call her anything but Mrs. Sibley."

Mrs. Sibley shouts, "I can hear you."

Gene raises his voice, too. "Mrs. Sibley, this is Hank's friend, Maggie Killian. Maggie, this is Mrs. Sibley. She's the matriarch of this place."

"The Piney Bottoms Ranch has been in my husband's family for three generations, I'll thank you to know."

Gene whispers. "Aka Double S, since all we run here now is the stock contracting business. But technically, it's Piney Bottoms. And we don't use all of it. A shame."

For a deliciously inappropriate moment, Maggie wonders whose bottoms in the family are piney. She decides prickly pants Mrs. Sibley is the most likely inspiration for the ranch's name.

"What?" Mrs. Sibley shouts.

"I said it's a lovely ranch, and Little Piney Creek is where it gets its name," Gene says.

Or it could be named after the creek bottoms.

A panicked look crosses the old woman's face. "Where's Mr. Sibley? He works so hard. He deserves his supper."

The man next to her pats her back. For the first time, Maggie notices he's wearing blue medical scrubs. "Mrs. S, he'll be fine. We'll save a plate for him."

Again Gene whispers, this time softer. "Alzheimer's. She thinks her husband's alive. He's been dead fourteen years now."

Which reminds Maggie about all the loss Hank endured, while she was writing "fuck Hank" music and angry that he didn't come chasing after her. Well, if he'd called, she could have helped him. She could have been his rock through all of it. *If you'd been willing to give up the music that took you away from him in the first place.* She shushes her conscience. It's bad enough when Hank says the kinds of things he did earlier without her own brain getting in on the abuse.

"Pass the potatoes?" Andy says.

"Hi, Andy." She hands him the bowl, which has finally made its way to her, after adding a dollop to her plate. They're nearly yellow with butter, just how she likes them.

"Hello, Ms. Killian." He adds two scoops to his plate. Seconds.

"Maggie."

"Um, Maggie."

"Thanks for your help today."

"Of course." He takes a bite, chews, swallows. "Is that a real Frontier Days buckle?"

Maggie had forgotten she had it on and again wishes she wasn't still in last night's clothes. "2002 bull riding champ. Yes."

Paco makes a clucking sound. "But that was . . ."

"Hank. Your boss. Yes."

Gene jumps into the conversation. "He wouldn't have won it, if not for Maggie."

Paco grins. "You and the boss man were, um . . ."

Maggie smiles. "A thing." She scrapes the last of the meatloaf onto her plate then adds a huge portion of salad, since it's barely been touched.

Gene laughs. "That's one way of putting it."

Emboldened, Andy blurts out, "Is it true you're a musician?" His cheeks suffuse with color, and he ducks his face.

"I was."

He lifts his eyes. "You don't play anymore?"

She smiles. "I play. It's just not how I earn my daily bread."

"But isn't a musician someone who plays and sings?"

His words poke Maggie in her soft underbelly. She puts a hand to her middle. "I'm no longer a *professional* musician."

"What instruments do you play?"

"Anything with strings, including the piano. I can eke out a tune on a saxophone, and my percussion skills are passable."

His eyes widen. "You play everything with strings?"

"Well, not a harp. And I prefer guitar, fiddle, mandolin, and ukulele. But I also play bass—upright and electric—cello, and lap steel."

He shakes his head. "I would love to hear you play. Where I come from, we don't have instruments, but we sing. Music is my favorite thing, besides horses."

"I brought a guitar. I guess I could play a little if you'd like."

"Do you know 'Amazing Grace'?"

Maggie smiles, despite her day and her own damn self. Most nineteen-year-old boys don't ask formerly famous musicians to play "Amazing Grace." They ask for her big hits. "Buckle Bunny." "I Hate Cowboys." "Never Mind, Don't Call."

Or Miranda frickin' Lambert.

But "Amazing Grace"? That's what's different about him, she realizes. Religion. Only it's not a religion she recognizes, and it must account for his odd getup.

"I'm finished," Mrs. Sibley announces.

Her caregiver is up quickly and backing her wheelchair away from the table. His plate is half-full. Mrs. Sibley's plate and cobbler bowl are empty.

Everyone stands.

"Good night, Mrs. Sibley," they chorus. "Good night, Tom."

So that's the caregiver's name. Tom. Maggie is slow getting up, but she joins in.

As Tom wheels Mrs. Sibley out, everyone retakes their seat. It's quiet enough to hear the flap of a hummingbird's wings, much less the voice of a querulous woman.

"What's that woman doing in there with my sons? She's rude. And where are Laura and Mr. Sibley?"

A doorway opens, then closes, cutting off the sound of Mrs. Sibley's voice. Then there's a giant exhale, and the men all start talking at once. Spoons clank serving bowls. A woman with red hair in a low bun brings out a giant cobbler, minus a square in one corner, and gallon of ice cream.

She sets them in the middle of the table and smiles at Maggie. "I'm Trudy. Did you get enough to eat?"

"Nice to meet you. I'm Maggie, and it was delicious. Thank you. With that cobbler, I'll be fat and happy."

Trudy wipes her hands on a white chef's apron, leaving the flour on her nose and forehead. "I don't see you ever fat, but baking is my specialty. If you're here long enough, I could pad your bones a little."

Maggie raises her hand. "Sign me up."

Trudy passes out warmed bowls, then disappears back into the kitchen.

Gene takes a double helping of cobbler. "Trudy is trying to get into the Culinary Institute of America. I can't decide if I wish her well or would do anything to keep her. You just don't find cooks like her out here." He scoops ice cream onto the cobbler, and it starts to melt and pool beside the cobbler. "You do know where you are, right?"

"Between Buffalo and Sheridan."

"No, I mean the significance. We're right along the old Bozeman Trail. You can still see the ruts of the Trail near here. Over by the site of the Fetterman Massacre."

Maggie serves her own dessert, less than half the amount of Gene's. "I saw signs to that earlier. Which side did the massacring?"

"The Indians. They lured a hundred soldiers from Fort Phil Kearney"—he points with his spoon, roughly in the direction Maggie had come from earlier that day—"into an ambush and killed every one of them."

"This is a dumb question."

"Only dumb if you don't ask."

"Why did we even need the trail?"

"It led to the Montana gold rush up near Bozeman. And it was in violation of a treaty that promised all this land to the Indians. Then the US decided it needed to build forts—a further treaty violation—to protect the people using the trail."

"So all those men died in the massacre because of gold?" Maggie feels overly full suddenly and puts down her spoon.

"That's one way of looking at it. Anyway, the fort didn't last long. A year after the massacre, the gold rushers abandoned the Trail for the Union Pacific Railroad. Then the soldiers left, and the Cheyenne burned Fort Phil Kearney down."

"Poetic justice."

"Maybe so. But the Indians still lost in the end."

Maggie isn't sure how to feel about that.

Andy and Paco push their bowls back and leave together, calling their good-nights. Maggie takes her last bite, savoring it. Trudy wasn't lying. Her baking is to die for.

Gene stays with Maggie. "Days here start early. Most everyone's headed for bed. You need anything?"

He leads her into the community room. Paco is at a desktop tucked into a built-in cabinet and shelving unit. Andy flips through channels, stopping on *The Real Housewives of Orange County*. He turns it off when he sees her.

Maggie ticks a mental checklist. Sheila to meet someone her own age. Hank to surprise Maggie in bed tonight. The Ford dealership to return her truck tomorrow. Nothing Gene can help with. "Nope. I'm good."

"All right. You have Wi-Fi in your cabin, but nothing else. You're welcome to hang out here in the community room if you'd like. There are books, games, puzzles, a desktop and printer, and a TV. If you use the TV after eight, keep the volume low so Mrs. Sibley can sleep. Breakfast is at six a.m. after the first round of chores is over."

Six a.m. is after the first round of chores? Not musicians' hours, or junkers'. Maggie is glad she doesn't work on a ranch. "I think I'll turn in early, too. It's been a tough day."

They part ways outside, where Louise is waiting for her. The dog jumps and wiggles, tripping Maggie at the step off the porch.

"You're not making yourself very welcome."

Louise falls into step beside her. It's just dusky enough that Maggie is glad for her company. In a day of wild weather fluctuations, the temperature now is mild and the breeze from the northwest is light, pushing the scent of the livestock in the corrals away from the house and cabins. The setting sun throws a silver sheen across the wild country to the north and west, while the mountains cast a shadow on the ranch. Horses nicker to each other. A bull snorts to her immediate right and she jumps, surprised at his presence, and glad to see he's on the other side of a barbed-wire fence.

By the time she reaches the covered deck of her cabin, it's a dim twilight out. Like a human thermometer, she gauges the falling temperature. Sixty-ish. She pauses for one more look around. The moon is rising, enormous and yellow. Gray clouds slide across it, blocking most of it from view. From this vantage point, she sees the huge pine trees that dot the complex like the shadows of giants. They appear on the verge of walking about, a la *Lord of the Rings*. A big, dark bird wings past, screeching.

Everything about Wyoming is mercurial. *Don't blink.* Something canine howls. Louise joins in, and Maggie shivers. A dog friend is sounding better all the time, even an annoying stray.

"Want to come inside with me, Fucker?" She ruffles the dog's ears.

Louise licks Maggie's wrist with fast tongue darts.

"You can come in, but no licking. Gross."

The two go inside together. Maggie turns the lamps on. For the first time, she really studies the place. Dark corners consume big triangles of the interior. The furniture is heavy, hand-hewn pine with wine-colored cushions that look blood red in the low light. The artwork runs toward violence and death. A Native American on a sprinting pony, shooting an arrow into a buffalo already riddled with them. US soldiers and Native Americans squaring off in battle. Two hounds battling a mountain lion on a snowy mountain precipice. It's creepy.

Just then, tiny feet scurry across the floor somewhere near her.

Maggie squeaks and hops toward the bed. She puts her hand to her chest. "Just a mouse. Get a grip."

Louise wags her tail against Maggie's guitar case.

"Don't tell."

Maggie digs the bottle of Balcones she brought up from Texas out of her suitcase. She tosses the belt and buckle in the case and stuffs it deep under her clothes. Then she dons her pj's and knee socks, washes her face, and walks to the little kitchen for a glass, on tiptoe to minimize what her socks touch. She empties a few ice cubes into the glass. The tap snorts then spits out winter-cold water. She dilutes the whiskey, just barely, and settles back in bed with her phone. She draws some Balcones into her mouth and holds it there, hoping to dilute the intensity of her feelings. She's in limbo, not wanting to feel them, but not wanting to numb them. When she took the numbing route before, it led to treatment, and rehab isn't her favorite place. But she's an older, wiser, steadier person now, without the temptations and pressures of life as a music star. At least she hopes she is. She swallows. Liquid fire. But the Balcones doesn't taste right after her drink last night. What was it called? Koltiska? When she gets her truck in Sheridan, she'll have to pick up a case of it to take home with her.

The cabin feels isolated, like she's the last person in the world stuck in the last place on earth. Mindless entertainment is in order, the company of imaginary friends. She opens the app on her phone, but T-Mobile has no signal here, surprise, surprise. She selects the Double S Wi-Fi, but it asks for a password.

"Really?" She shakes the phone at the sky and whoever is up there delighting in her misery.

She needs a distraction from the loneliness and the places her mind wants to take her, like Hank-and-Sheila-ville. Her regrets about her one-night stand. The weirdness of the dead body at the motel that morning. Her broken-down truck and imprisonment here. She surveys the options. Her guitar? One of the dusty paperbacks on the old bookshelf by the front door? Neither appeal to her. She pads to the kitchen. She'll let the Balcones bottle keep her company in bed. Her iPhone doesn't need Wi-Fi to play music. She sets it to her favorite playlist: All Things Lucinda. Sipping whiskey to "Can't Let Go," she pulls her covers up to her chin and gives in to the thoughts she doesn't want to think.

TEN

"Grrrrrrr."

Maggie hears growling. She hears the snarls of a mountain lion and the yelping of a mangled dog. Maggie's panting and her heart is racing. She feels the ground under her feet. She's running, slipping, sliding down a snowy mountainside. It's so damn *real*, as is the woman leading her to safety. *Come, daughter,* she says, even though with her long black braids and buckskin clothes she doesn't look like Charlotte or Gidget.

But she sees a flashing number on the bedside table. It reads 12:01. That can't be right. She saw the clock before she fell asleep, and it said 12:53. Power outage, maybe? That could make it flash. Of course. That's it. And the mountain lion and the woman—that was just a dream. She's under a quilt in a cabin, not out in the snow. As she calms, the dream slips away and her surroundings take shape. It's not much lighter in the cabin than the night before, but it's definitely almost dawn.

Then she hears the growling again. She has a fleeting memory of a dream about a hurt dog, but the rest of the details are gone. Poof. Like her relationship with Hank.

"Louise? What is it, girl?"

The growling intensifies. Maggie props herself on her elbow and rolls to face the door. Louise has her nose to the jamb. On the other side of the door, Maggie hears scuffling. Footsteps? Probably. Animal or human?

"Who's there?" Her voice cracks. She tries again, shouting. Did she throw the lock before she got in bed with the Balcones? God, she hopes so. "I said *who is out there?*"

The scuffling quiets. Louise whines. Maggie slides out of bed. It's colder than she expected. Her toe stubs something hard. It rolls away from her. The Balcones bottle. She ignores it, rifles through her bag for her pepper spray. Louise joins her at the window, where Maggie slides the curtain aside a few centimeters. Maggie flips the switch for the outside fixture, but the light doesn't come on. It figures. First thing today, she's asking for a package of lightbulbs. And the Wi-Fi password.

The dog's tail thumps Maggie's leg. Louise seems relaxed now. Maggie lets out the air she'd been saving up in her lungs. There's nothing on the porch. But on the horizon is something spectacular.

The sun is rising. Red. Orange. Yellow. Pink. Sedimentary layers of flame glow above the dirt and rock, like a Technicolor stage set. Against the backdrop, Maggie watches a small herd of white-tailed deer make an entrance. They leap a fence at center stage, one after another. She's entranced. And a little irritated. She wants to hate it here. She almost does, and then something like this moment happens, over and over, and it turns her upside down again. Hank and Wyoming. Wyoming and Hank. Why is it that she can't quit either of them?

Since she's up and not under attack, Maggie finds a kettle and fills it with water, then showers and dons clean clothes—her warmest—while it heats. No red scarves. No tank tops. No fringe. It's not just the cooler temperatures either. She feels as dead-out as the lights in the cabin. Not a live wire. Not even the burned-down nub of a match.

She wraps herself in the quilt and takes a mug of the instant coffee to the porch. It isn't as vile as she'd feared. The air is crisp and smells loamy. A musical chirping pulls her attention toward a fence post where a bird with a brilliant yellow breast preens. Hoofbeats, snorts, and stomps add percussion to the melody. Steam rises from the corrals. Something inside Maggie stretches and cracks.

If this is her last day in Wyoming, she wouldn't have wanted to miss this.

The sound of human voices startles her. She thought she was the only one up. But it's Paco and Andy, entering the house.

Gene holds the door for them. "Breakfast is almost on, boys."

She can't believe how sound carries here. Or that early chores are over, and she's about to miss breakfast. She throws the quilt back onto the bed and ditches her mug. Louise jogs beside her to the house. This time,

Maggie tells the dog to sit at the door. Louise stares at her without comprehension.

"Fine. Have it your way. Stand. Sit. Whatever. Just don't come in."

Louise still tries to squeeze past Maggie through the open door. Maggie pushes her back outside with her boot. When she enters the dining room, she's met by the strong smell of manure and man sweat on Gene, Paco, and Andy. She's not in a position to complain, seeing as it's their hard work that's putting food on the table for her, free of charge. The clock reads five minutes until six.

"Good morning." She rounds the table toward the chair she used the night before.

Mrs. Sibley stares at her from her wheelchair across an assortment of beverages. A coffee carafe. A tall bottle of milk. Clear plastic pitchers of juice, in colors suggesting apple, orange, and grape. "Who's that woman?"

Tom takes her speckled hand. "Maggie Killian. She's a guest."

"She's not my guest."

Maggie tries a smile on her. "I'm a friend of Hank's. And Tom, nice to meet you. I guess we were never officially introduced last night."

He smiles. She sees exhaustion in the lines around his eyes. "Nice to meet you, too."

The old woman's voice is cross. "Hank isn't allowed to have friends spend the night. He didn't do his chores."

Gene enters on the tail of the exchange. "I'm sure he'll finish them today, Mrs. Sibley. And Maggie won't be any trouble."

"She looks like trouble."

Maggie can't argue that. She sits by Andy.

"Morning, ma'am."

"I'm not your mother. How about you call me Maggie?"

"Where I come from, ma'am is respectful."

"Where I come from, it means you're old."

He smiles like he's afraid someone will catch him at it.

Trudy sets a plate of biscuits next to a matching platter of scrambled eggs. The woman's hands are red and dry, much older than her face. Trudy wipes her hands on her apron. She mops her strawberry-blonde brow with the cuff of a long-sleeved Western shirt. The outfit screams rodeo, from Maggie's perspective, including the glittery embroidery she sees on the back pockets of Trudy's jeans as she goes back into the kitchen.

The eggs are striated with cream cheese. Maggie's mouth waters. After all that Balcones last night, she needs those eggs bad. "So, where do you come from, Andy?"

His voice is soft. "Ashland."

"Where's that?"

"Montana."

"So how'd you end up working in Wyoming?"

Andy shoots a glance at Gene. Maggie catches Gene's smile as he encourages the younger man to speak.

"It's, um, ah, I'm on Rumspringa, ma'am. I mean Maggie."

"Rumspringa?"

Andy stuffs a biscuit into his mouth.

Gene answers for him. "Rumspringa is a period when the Amish youth can leave their communities and experiment with life outside. A time for them to make adult decisions on the path their lives will take, before they're baptized into the church."

"Oooh." Maggie gets it now. Andy's dress. His manners. His reticence. He's Amish. She's never actually met an Amish person before Andy, and she knows very little about them.

Paco toasts Andy with a cup of coffee. "I'm teaching him the ways of the world. The English world. I keep trying to tempt him with beer and dancing, but I guess I haven't introduced him to the right girl—yet."

Andy's face goes tomato red. He serves himself eggs and fills his mouth.

"Not yet, young man," Mrs. Sibley barks.

Maggie is stuck on one of the things Paco said. "The English?"

Gene answers again. "All of the rest of us. The Amish speak Pennsylvania Dutch in their communities. We speak English. Thus, we're the English."

Trudy emerges from the kitchen with more dishes. She's strong and steady with her armloads of food. Three dishes this time, and they look heavy. Bacon and sausage on one, an assortment of butter, jams, hot sauces, and ketchup in a basket, and hash browns in a shallow round dish. Everyone leans toward the food.

Maggie wonders why they don't dig in.

"Mr. Sibley will lead us in the prayer," Mrs. Sibley announces.

Gene clears his throat. "He's not in, so I'll bless the food, if that's all right, Mrs. Sibley."

Maggie realizes that Mrs. Sibley is referring to her dead husband, and that Hank isn't coming to breakfast. Gene says grace, but Maggie is oblivious. She's preoccupied with Hank's absence. She knew he was going out with Sheila, so it shouldn't be a surprise to her that he's not here. Still, she hopes he's just sleeping in, not sleeping with Sheila. God frowns on premarital sex with a Sunday school teacher, she feels certain, and she knows she sure as hell does.

"Amen."

As soon as Gene utters the word, the men descend on the food. A pre-served plate is in front of Mrs. Sibley again. But she's not eating. Her lips are pinched and her nostrils flare. She glares at Maggie every few seconds.

Maggie whispers to Gene. "She really doesn't like me."

Gene grins. "You have that effect on women."

Maggie rolls her eyes at him. The first of the breakfast dishes reaches her, and she scoops out a sizable portion of scrambled eggs. After last night's meal, she knows she won't get a second chance.

She passes the platter to Andy, who adds to the mound of eggs on his plate. "So you're Amish, huh?"

"Yes, ma—Maggie."

The hash browns and bacon arrive back-to-back, requiring Maggie's attention for a second. "I'm Lutheran, but Wendish."

He looks at her blankly, then serves himself hash browns and shovels in a bite with a piece of bacon.

"The Wends, my people, live in a community away from town. Very religious. Very different from the other people in the area."

He slathers a biscuit with butter and jam. He nods, still chewing.

"I've never been to an Amish community, but I imagine they're similar to the Wends in some ways."

Andy swallows. His biscuit hovers near his mouth. "Are you Anabaptists?" His teeth sink into the biscuit and jam oozes out.

"Ana what?"

He talks through his food. "Anabaptists." He chews, swallows, then restarts. "We believe baptism is an adult choice, and, if you're baptized as a child, you must be rebaptized as an adult."

"Oh. Then no, we're not Anabaptists. I was baptized twice. Once as a baby and again when I was five. It didn't do much good. Maybe they should have kept trying." Maggie samples the eggs. Cream cheese and chives. Perfect texture and seasoning. And not what she would have expected on a ranch table in Wyoming. The hands don't seem to mind the hoity-toity eggs, judging by the empty platter.

"Do you drive cars and use electricity?"

At the end of the table, Tom says, "You need to eat those delicious eggs before they get cold, Mrs. S."

Maggie glances at the old woman. Yep, still glaring at Maggie. What had Andy asked? Did the Wends drive cars and use electricity? "Yes."

"We don't."

"Everything here must be very different to you, then."

"I'm used to it. My father and brothers and I have worked for the English since I was a boy. But now I can choose to do whatever I want. Because of Rumspringa."

Mrs. Sibley bangs her spoon on her glass. "Quiet! Quiet, children. I can't digest my food with this racket." Then she turns to Tom. "I have somewhere I need to be."

Her food is still untouched.

He jumps to his feet. "Yes, Mrs. Sibley."

As the others had the night before, they call their goodbyes to her. She ignores them all. Trudy brings a dish cover for Mrs. Sibley's plate. Maggie wonders how Hank deals with his mother's illness. It must be incredibly hard.

Paco says, "Did you hear Chet Moore was murdered yesterday?"

Chet? Maggie drops a biscuit and chokes on the bite she'd just taken. She reaches for her orange juice and gulps quickly. Her eyes water. She tries to remember Chet's last name, the Chet she hooked up with, but she can't. Moore doesn't sound familiar. Maybe it's a different Chet. She hopes it is. Coughing some more, she feels conspicuous, but no one glances her way. They're all focused on Paco.

"What happened?" Gene asks.

"Dunno much, except they found him in the parking lot of the Bison Inn with his head bashed in."

His words are thunder in Maggie's ears. "Oh God!"

All heads swivel in her direction. She balls a fist and presses it to her mouth.

The coincidence was too much. Chet. Murdered. Only hours after he left her, only hours after they'd been intimate. Just outside the hotel where she slept. Oh God. Oh God. He was so vital, so strong.

"Maggie?" Gene is in front of her, hands on her forearms. He gives her a shake. "Maggie May?"

Her mouth hangs open. She feels shocked and sad for a moment, but then a horrible thought occurs to her. She was probably the last person to see him alive. Other than the murderer, of course. The police would be reconstructing Chet's last hours. They'd know he stayed at the Bison Inn. But no one knew they'd spent the night together. The room was in his name. When Chet checked them in, she'd stayed in his truck. The next morning, he'd left alone, and she'd made the walk of shame back to Bess hours later. And she hadn't given the desk clerk her room number, thank God. Relief courses through her, along with a sickening guilt. No one would know she was with him there. She doesn't want everyone and his dog knowing her business. She especially doesn't want Hank to know about her hooking up with Chet after finding out about him and Sheila.

She looks away from Gene, down at the biscuit she'd dropped. Everyone is looking at her. They're wondering why she's lost her shit. She has to calm down. Figure out how to act. Concerned first, because she met a guy who may be dead now. But not devastated or terrified. Those would be inappropriate. But upset would hit the right note. So, upset. That will be easy enough, because she's very, very upset.

She takes a deep, shuddering breath. "I, um, met a guy at the Occidental. His name was Chet. I hope it's not him? He bought me a drink. Too young for me, so I sent him packing, but so nice and really cute." She's babbling and her voice sounds like a strangled cat, but she holds her face steady in a concerned expression.

Gene nods, looking at her with a confused expression. "Um, yeah, Chet was at the Occidental."

Maggie shifts gears to sadly upset, which comes out more authentically, amongst the other bigger, scarier feelings she's hiding. "Oh my God. This is . . . horrible. Do they know who did it?"

Paco says, "He was a hound dog. And that *chica* he used to date, she's stone-cold crazy, and her brothers are dangerous. They're all into meth now. If it wasn't the crazy *chica*, my bet is a pissed-off husband or boyfriend."

Gene releases Maggie and turns back to Paco. She keeps one ear on the conversation and the other turned inward. The woman who slapped Chet. The men who held him still for her. Was that not enough for them? Did they come back and kill him?

Beside her, Andy's voice is sonorous. "God take his soul, and may he rest in peace."

Maggie's mind races. It doesn't matter that no one saw her with Chet at the Bison. Because half the town can place them together at the Occidental. Chet had bought her drinks. They'd walked out together. Gene had probably even seen them.

Paco pours himself more coffee. "I heard he checked into the Bison the night before. Only reason for that is a hookup."

Maggie's throat closes. People are already talking about Chet spending the night with a woman. It won't take them long to come looking for her.

Gene whistles. "Must have been someone he wanted to impress to shell out for a room."

Paco grins. "What's it to him? He makes good money. Or made, anyway. Worked for a drilling company."

Andy chimes in. "Isn't that wasteful, when he has a perfectly good ranch with a house?"

"Sounds smart to me. A woman's got a lot of time to change her mind on a forty-five-minute drive."

Maggie remembers the urgency on her part, the need to have sex with Chet immediately. To feel like she'd shown Hank. But shown him what? She feels sick. She hadn't shown him anything. And now Chet was dead.

Gene puts both hands on the table. "Well, I'm sure the police will figure it out. We sure won't sitting around here gossiping. Time to get to work."

Chairs push back, and the men leave quickly, not dawdling in the community room like the night before. Louise dashes in the door as the hands exit.

Maggie stays frozen in her chair. Maybe she should call the cops. But what did she have to tell them? She doesn't know anything about Chet. Certainly nothing about how he died. The police would delay her departure. Her personal business would become public information. She needs to get on her way as fast as she can get Bess fixed. Forget this whole horrible trip ever happened.

But if she's still here and they haven't caught the killer by then, she can always call the police Monday.

"For now, I've just got to chill." She speaks her thought aloud.

Louise whines and nudges her hand.

Maggie pats the dog's head. "I know. Easier said than done, girl."

ELEVEN

Maggie paces in the direction of the paddocks, not eager to return to the cabin. It's not even seven a.m. The Ford dealership won't be open yet. She forgot to get lightbulbs and the Wi-Fi password. She's stranded with nothing to do, so she might as well make the best of it. Take a walk with Louise. Get some exercise. Burn off some of her stress. Clear her mind.

She marches on toward the gate, Louise her shadow. Andy canters out of the stable yard in front of her on a big buckskin gelding. He points his horse toward higher elevation, roughly in the direction of the big house on the mountain. Paco drives off on a four-wheeler. A blacksmith is shoeing a horse beside a farrier truck, his hammer clanging like a bell as it strikes nail and shoe.

Her phone vibrates with a text. She checks it—shocked she has service here—still walking.

Michele: *Did you get ahold of your renter? Are you on your way home? Goats are at Gidget's.*

Maggie stops. Twenty-four hours later, the world is a much different place than when she'd talked to Michele.

No, I'll try again. Bess broke down. Delayed. Thanks on the goats.

She almost updates Michele that she has definitely talked to Gene since she's staying at Hank's and oh yeah, by the way, her hookup was murdered, but she doesn't have the oomph right now. She hits send.

Then texts her guest again. *Leslie, hey, I didn't hear back from you. Just want to make sure you're OK.*

Michele: *OMG so sorry. Keep me posted!*

Michele would be double sorry if she knew the whole story. Maggie pockets her phone and resumes her walk. As she nears a pen in the warren of livestock enclosures, she notices a glossy black horse. The massive animal whirls and stares at her. Maggie climbs on the bottom metal rail and holds her hand out, palm down, over the top. The horse looks away.

"Come here, sassy. I don't bite."

"You're a stranger and a meat eater. She's a mare conditioned to be on the lookout for threats to the herd. Of course you bite, and she knows it." Gene runs up the rails with hands and feet, and swings over to sit atop the fence.

"I'm not a horse lover, but I could make an exception."

"She knows that, too." Gene opens his hand. In his palm is a horse cookie. "Lily, Lily girl. Cookie. Come get a cookie, Lily."

The horse walks over in slow motion, her ears pricked forward. She reaches her neck out to its full length, then stretches her lips to take the cookie from Gene while remaining as far from him as possible.

He laughs. "Same old Lily girl." He digs in his pockets and hands Maggie some cookies. "You can give her a try, but don't touch her face. It's a blind spot for a horse. She considers it pushy. Rude on a first date."

"Got it."

Louise stands on her hind legs, pawing the air with her front paws.

"And don't feed the circus animal. That dog is a beggar. She eats at the barn with all the other clawed critters every morning."

Maggie slips Louise a cookie after Gene turns away.

"I hear her chewing."

She climbs the fence and sits next to him. "Here, Lily. Here, my pretty. Come get a cookie." She holds out her hand, palm up.

Lily swings her head to look Maggie over, then swings it back to eyeball Gene.

"She's okay, Lily girl."

Lily repeats her slow-motion walk, but she comes all the way up to Maggie, presenting the side of her neck. She whisks the cookie daintily from Maggie's palm with velvet lips.

"She likes me."

Gene shakes his head. "She's Hank's, so I guess it figures."

"I can't help it if she has good taste."

"Give her a rub under her mane, like you're giving a person a neck massage. Kind of up on the crest. You'll feel the muscles there."

Maggie slips her fingers under the long, coarse hair and strokes the horse's neck. "Wow. Thick."

"She's mostly Percheron. Their necks are very strong."

"I don't want to hurt your feelings, girl, but you've got a giant ass, too." Probing the arch of the muscle, Maggie kneads it gently. Lily bobs her head in time with Maggie's massage. "Aren't Percherons draft horses?"

"They are."

"I thought you raised buckers?"

"We do. A bucking horse has to be sturdy. Lily adds size and strength to the bloodline."

Maggie whispers in Lily's ear. "All that and a pretty face."

"The most successful and famous bucker in Wyoming history was half Percheron. Steamboat. The horse on the license plate."

"No pressure, girl." Maggie gives Lily an extra good rub where her muscles converge behind her ear. "Is she always this big? Her gut is huge."

"No, she's pregnant. This will be her third foal. The first one is just starting out. She's a peach."

"Does she buck?"

"With great enthusiasm and a lot of strength, when we ask her to. But it was never her career. She's a nice ride, actually. Just antisocial. Well, not as much with you. Are you usually this good with horses?"

"I don't know. We didn't have horses when I was growing up. I've ridden some, but really, I don't have much experience."

"You're a natural. Maybe you're part Indian."

Maggie smiles. "I am. One eighth Crow."

"That may explain it. They were incredible horse people. Many still are. And you almost qualify for enrollment."

"What?"

"You can enroll as a tribe member if you're one-quarter Crow."

Does my father know? "Closeness only counts in horseshoes, I guess."

"It doesn't change the fact that you have Crow ancestry. It may have something to do with what Lily senses in you."

"That sounds like superstitious stereotypical BS." She smiles at him as she says it.

Gene laughs. "Superstitions and stereotypes have a source, sometimes. I'm just saying it could matter. Don't be all closed-minded about it."

Lily tosses her mane and Maggie catches a glimpse of the arched muscular neck she's been petting. It makes her look regal. Maggie reaches for Lily's nose, wanting just one more feel of its cushy softness, but Lily backs away.

"I told you she doesn't like to have her face touched."

"You can't blame me for trying."

"Oh, but I can, Maggie." He turns his torso to face her. "Or should I call you Lily?"

"Why would you call me Lily?"

"Because you back away whenever anyone tries to get close."

Ouch. His words catch her off guard, but she doesn't let him see he's wounded her. "Can't a girl be hard to get without a guy being mean about it? Don't listen to him, Lily."

He hops down. "If you say so, Maggie."

TWELVE

Back in the cabin half an hour later, Maggie can't call the mechanic because she has no cell signal. And no Wi-Fi. She hoofs it with her canine new-best-friend up to the barn area, hoping to find someone who can help. The place is a ghost town, except for livestock, and none of them offer up the Wi-Fi password. Maggie is about to go in search of Trudy or Tom—although she doesn't relish an encounter with Mrs. Sibley—when a familiar truck pulls up.

Hank.

She flags him down, struggling not to think about him being fresh off a sleepover at Sheila's.

He parks a few yards away and gets out. "Good morning."

"Morning." She brandishes her phone. "T-Mobile doesn't exist in Wyoming. I need to call the dealership."

He tosses her his phone. "Their number should be in my Recents from yesterday."

She nods, keeping her eyes averted. "Want me to bring it to you at the house when I'm done?"

"I can wait." He crosses his arms, exposing his triceps and causing his shoulders to bunch up nicely.

Maggie has a moment of temptation. She could pretend to fumble finger around and read his most recent texts with Sheila first. But she doesn't want to subject herself to their mushy talk. Or worse, sexts.

She pulls up his call log and finds the dealership number based on the time the call went out. Five minutes after five the afternoon before. She presses it. When she reaches the service department, she introduces herself and refers to her message and her truck.

"Yessirree, we got your message and that colorful little pickup of yours. That's an oldie. Nice truck." The voice is young and Southern. Alabama. Mississippi. Louisiana at the farthest west.

"Thank you. Do you have the part to fix it?"

"Can't say. Can I call you back when we've had a chance to look? Busy morning here."

She gives them Hank's number.

"That's not the one you left on voicemail, is it?"

"No, but it's the only one that will work."

"Alrighty then."

"Thank you."

She ends the call and hands Hank his phone.

"Any luck?"

"Zero progress. They'll call back on your phone."

He pulls on his lips, the ones that have been kissing the wrong woman. "Well, you've got some time to kill."

"Tell me something I don't know."

"Can't do that unless I take you on a tour of the place. How 'bout it?"

"If you're sure it's okay with your girlfriend."

"Why wouldn't it be?"

Maggie is slightly offended. She scoffs. "Please. Women hate me."

His dimples light a fire in her core. "Oh, that. Well, don't worry. I haven't told her about us."

"Ashamed of me?" She tosses her hair behind her shoulder.

"Do you tell your dates about me?"

"Point taken."

"Come on. Let's grab a four-wheeler. There's things to see that my truck can't take us to."

"Can we tour on horseback?"

"You ride?"

Barely. "I grew up in Texas, didn't I?" She points. "Can I take Lily?"

"How'd you meet my ornery old girl?"

"We buddied up this morning. Gene introduced us."

He starts walking into the stable. She follows. "She's nobody's buddy."

He grabs some rope halters.

"She's mine."

"Prove it. Bring her back here to me."

Maggie throws some swagger into her walk. "You don't think I can."

"I don't."

"And if I do?"

"I won't charge you rent on the guest cabin."

She laughs and jogs to Lily's pen. She should have asked Hank for cookies. But when she checks her pocket, she finds one left over from earlier. She enters the corral, holds it out. "Cookie, Lily girl. Cookie."

The mare lowers her head and walks slowly to her. She lips the cookie from Maggie's palm.

"Look at that. You make me feel better without even trying." Maggie loops the lead line around the horse's neck. The halter end looks like the complicated rope puzzle she carried on tour with her one summer, one she never solved. "Nope. Not even trying."

She applies gentle pressure on the loop, still facing the big animal. Lily doesn't budge.

"Don't make me look worse in front of Hank."

Lily swishes her tail.

Maggie turns toward the barn, sighs, and leans against the rope, applying steady pressure. To her surprise, it goes slack so fast she nearly falls. She walks forward and hoofbeats clomp behind her. Lily keeps coming, even through a gate, until they reach grass, where she buries her nose and refuses to budge.

"Give her a minute. She's been cooped up staring at that all night." Hank's voice is close. Ten yards away, inside another paddock, he has haltered a gray horse. "And close the gate. Rules of the range. Always leave it like you find it."

Maggie salutes him as she closes the gate. When Lily's mouth is stuffed with grass, she pulls. Lily pulls back, slightly, and keeps eating.

"When you want her to stop eating, use rhythmic tugs. Fast. Or even just shake the lead rope. Like this." He mimes shaking the lead.

Maggie tries it.

"Don't be a pansy. Harder."

"Who are you calling a pansy, bucko?" She shakes more vigorously. Lily lifts her head.

"Good. Turn away from her. Now you can pull steady, until she comes, then give her slack. Yeah, like that. Get her in line beside you, moving with you. And walk faster. That way she can't eat."

When Hank's suggestions work, Maggie beams. It's like she's learned a secret language.

"The halter would make everything easier."

"Now why didn't I think of that?"

"You don't know how."

"Nope. I could do it if it had a buckle."

Hank and his horse fall in beside her. He hands the lead line to Maggie. "You take Wolf. I'll tie her halter."

"Hi, Wolf." Maggie stops with both horses. "No. Teach me."

Standing close with the horses and Hank creates a cocoon of warmth and intimacy. Maggie feels tingly. She watches Hank, listens, and emulates his motions when it's her turn. She's soaking him in until she catches a womanly scent. Yuck. He smells like perfume. Like Sheila. She takes a step back. It feels like a violation of her intimacy with Hank, which she knows is absurd. She has no claim to him. But she feels what she feels.

"What's the matter?"

Maggie adjusts Lily's halter to take up slack like Hank had shown her, then ties it off. "Nothing. I just needed room to work."

Her short-lived rebound from her funk over, Maggie is silent as they groom, saddle, and tack up the horses.

Hank leads Lily to a mounting block. "You'll want to use this."

Maggie nods, then climbs up the steps and into the saddle on the tall mare.

Beside them, Hank mounts Wolf. He's a foot shorter on his quarter horse than Maggie is on Lily. "How's the weather up there?"

Despite her mood, she's awed by the difference in her perspective from Lily's back, especially when Lily ambles out, rocking Maggie along with her. "Holy shit, it's like I'm riding a freakin' elephant. How tall is she?"

"Eighteen hands."

"Which is what, in people terms?"

"Four inches per hand. Seventy-two inches. That means she's six feet tall at her shoulder."

"And your horse?"

"Fifteen hands. Sixty inches or five feet."

"She seems so much bigger than him. More than just taller."

"That's because she's thicker, stronger. Wolf is a cow pony. He has a big ole quarter-horse butt, but he's fairly slight elsewhere. She weighs two thousand pounds to his thousand fifty."

"Girl power."

"Mare power. Her foals are big, strong, and athletic. We breed her with a stallion that's much more high-strung, so they're not as laid back as she is. Lots of fire in 'em."

As they ride through pastures of tall grass, she watches Louise sprint through them in a crazy zigzag pattern. Sometimes only the tip of her erect tail is visible. Maggie realizes that the grass isn't all dead and brown like it appears from a distance. The stalks are green. Only the tops are brown, where everything has gone to seed. It's not all grass, either. There's a fair amount of some blue-green plant. Maybe it's what gives the hillsides the silvery sheen she'd noticed the day before.

She points up into the foothills, to the tall cabin she'd noticed when she first arrived with Patrick. "Whose cabin is that?"

Hank smiles. "Ours. We call it the summer cabin. It was my dad's favorite place in the world. We'd have lived up there year-round if Mom would have agreed."

"Why didn't she want to?"

His voice is wry and affectionate. "Winter. It's hard work getting up there. Worse getting down."

"You love it?"

"I do. Just another way I'm like Dad, I guess. I get up there as often as I can. We had a fire up near there a few years back, too. Lightning in the middle of a rainstorm. It's so dry here this time of year that it doesn't take much. I guess I feel protective."

Hank hops down several times to open wire gates for them. Louise keeps them within sight, but constantly works the far edge of that range.

To Maggie, it feels like they've ridden miles and miles. "Are we still on your ranch?"

"My mom's ranch. Double S leases space. But yes, it's five thousand acres, so we won't leave it today." He points to the north. "A ways past our northern boundary is the site of the Wagon Box Fight. It's an interesting nugget of history."

Her voice is teasing. "Ah, my tour has started."

"Girl, you're more lucky than you'll ever know. A bona fide Cheyenne Frontier Days champion and local landowner is taking you on a personal tour of his ranch. And giving you a history lesson. I'm not even charging extra."

"I thought you said it was your mom's ranch."

"I'm about to revoke your tour pass, woman."

"Just a stickler for facts."

He wags a finger at her. "As I was saying about the Wagon Box Fight before I was so rudely interrupted, about thirty soldiers and contractors from Fort Phil Kearney held off the Lakota Sioux by tipping the wagons on their sides in a circle for protection. They called the heavy back ends wagon boxes, hence the name of the fight. Of course, they also had breech-loading Springfield rifles, and the Sioux didn't."

"Was that a good thing?"

"Not for the Sioux. They fought hard for this land—so did the Cheyenne and Arapaho—when the US built forts along the Bozeman Trail."

She pats herself on the back for asking Gene about the Trail last night, so that she doesn't have to ask Hank now. "What about the Crow?"

"They aligned themselves with the US. Some say it was because the other tribes were their enemies, but others say it was more that they recognized the inevitability of defeat by the US troops."

Maggie had just learned more about the Crow in thirty seconds than she'd learned her entire life. It was weird to think her ancestors had fought with the US troops against other Indian nations. She suddenly had an itch to get her hands on books about the Crow. What was even stranger was she wanted to read them.

They ride in silence for a while, except for intermittent riding tips from Hank. Maggie watches Lily's ears swivel every time she hears a sound, whether it is Maggie's voice, a bark from Louise, the wind, a bird, or the clank of Wolf's shoe on stone.

"See over there?" Hank now indicates something to the east.

Maggie catches sight of movement. A bouncing motion. Horns, fast-moving white rumps. Louise chasing them. "Antelope. They're beautiful."

"And if we were looking for them, we'd see white-tailed deer, pheasant, turkey, sage grouse, and a little farther into the mountains, elk, mule deer, and other game animals. Moose. Bighorn sheep. The Native Americans really prized this area for hunting and winter camps."

"So they fought for it. Along the Bozeman Trail."

"They did." He smiles at her like a prize pupil, something she's never, ever been. "And they had some great victories, too. But when the dust settled ten years later, they'd all been pushed onto reservations far, far inferior to this." He sweeps his hand around them. "The Crow made out better than the others, but they still lost their way of life."

"That's horrible."

"To the victors go the spoils. And now my family owns this ranch. I can't pretend I don't love the place and want to keep it. But I get a twinge every now and then, and I see their spirits."

"Whose spirits?"

"The warriors, I believe. And I'm not the only crusty old cowboy around here who'll tell you the same. Especially around the battle sites. Once I was out hunting with Gene and another buddy, and we came into a mountain meadow. Up there."

Maggie pictures the cabin on the mountainside overlooking the ranch. "By the big cabin?"

Again, he gives her a look that shows he is pleased with her answer and the attention to the area it shows. "That direction, but miles farther up. My horse spooked. I was looking around for what startled him, and on the other side of the meadow, I saw two warriors on ponies, everyone dressed and painted for battle, including the horses. Gene saw them, too. I raised my hand, and they raised theirs. I turned to show our other friend, and when I looked back, they were gone."

"I didn't take you for a woo-woo type of person."

But as he told the story, Maggie got a woo-woo type of feeling. She can't put her finger on why. Recognition, maybe? It's almost like she's seen a spirit herself, except she can't remember it happening. Ever since Boyd told her about her Crow ancestors, she's felt a closeness to the area that's bizarre, really. Like she's romanticizing it. And she's not a romantic person. If a spirit sighting happened at all, it was probably back in her drug days. Hallucinogenics had never been her friend.

"You didn't take me at all, as I recall." He raises a hand. "Sorry, I shouldn't have gone there."

"You shouldn't have. But maybe that's what made Fucker bark last night."

"Who?"

She points to the black-and-white dog chasing a jackrabbit one hundred feet away. "Fucker. I guess her real name is Louise. She's adopted me."

"Nice name." He reins Wolf closer to Lily. The mare pins her ears back. Wolf dips a shoulder to move away, but Hank holds him close to Maggie and her horse. "It could have been a spirit. Or it could have been an animal. The rodents are attracted to our trash. And where there are prey animals, there are predators. We not only have the antelope and deer, we have cattle and horses. Lots to interest the meat eaters."

"That's comforting."

He laughs. "Most likely it was just the wind. Which we have more of than anything."

It hadn't sounded like the wind. More like scuffling. But maybe that was just something blowing across the porch? "If there are predators, then how come there are so many antelope and deer?"

"The predator ranges are shrinking due to people but we still have this unbelievably nutritious grass. Thick, tall, and high protein. So we get a lot of grazers with too few predators for natural balance, then the grazers don't leave enough forage in the winter for our livestock. Hunting has always been critical in this area, for survival, but it's also an important part of our ranch management."

That explains the head mounts of the animals back in the ranch house, she thinks. "When is hunting season?"

"Depends on the animal and the weapon. Right now is mostly bow hunting. And bear. I can't wait to get out there." He stops Wolf and looks around him appreciatively. "A hundred years ago this region was free-range—no fences. Can you imagine that?"

Maggie scans the countryside around them all the way to the horizon. She sees fences, roads, houses. What would this place have been like before them? "I can't."

"Hundreds of thousands of horses and cattle roamed here. Compare that to these little bands of ten to twenty horses per pasture you're seeing now. The horse industry was huge."

"What happened to it?"

"Automobiles. Trains. Airplanes. Tanks. Humvees. Back then, herds of horses ran wild, and the ranchers would round them up when it was time to break them or sell them. Mostly for war and transportation, but also some for racing, polo, showing, cowboying. Even for meat."

"What?"

"Meat. Sadly, that was often the source for the US to fill the food commitments to the reservations."

"Sometimes I hate us."

"Me, too. And horses like Lily, or rather, draft horse stallions—Clydesdales, Shires, Percherons, Belgians—were turned loose in the herds to increase their size. Like we're doing here. Except instead of breeding horses to be hardier for a job they love, the purpose was to put more pounds of meat on the hoof."

Maggie gasps and reaches down to pat Lily's neck. "Oh my God. Don't listen to him, Lily."

Three white-tailed deer explode from a stand of tall, thick buckbrush. Wolf whinnies and rears slightly as he whirls. Lily reverses direction with a snort, then does a funny four-footed dance in place.

"Whoa, girl." Maggie is terrified she will fall off. Her hand shoots down to grip the saddle horn. But the centrifugal force of Lily's roll-back surprises Maggie. She stays mostly centered in the saddle. "Just deer. We're okay."

The bigger horse calms and gets back on course while Hank is still dealing with Wolf's excitement.

"And that's the difference between a hot-blooded cow pony and a cold-blooded draft horse," Hank says, when he catches up with them. "Hey, see that cabin across the creek there?" He says creek as if it is spelled c-r-i-c-k. Crick.

The creek in question looks almost as big as a river to Maggie. It's tumbling at a good clip down a rocky bed. The water is mesmerizing. Once she'd seen it, her eyes hadn't strayed beyond it. Now she lifts her gaze and sees a ramshackle building. From this distance, she would have called it a shack instead of a cabin and wonders what the difference is.

"Yeah. Is it yours?"

"No. Our property ends just on the other side of the creek. See the fence?"

She squints. "I do now."

"The cabin belongs to our crazy neighbor. Electrician by day and fence destroyer by night."

"What?"

"He has a bad habit of taking the fence down so his cattle can get to our water. Water is life up here. Water rights are wealth. And, there's a section down. Again." Hank lifts a hand in greeting. "That's him, watching us."

Maggie sees a short, wide man near a camo panel van with SIMON ELECTRIC painted in neon yellow block letters on the side with a phone number below it. What is it with camo vehicles in Wyoming? Wasn't there one in the Bison Inn parking lot, when she was there with Chet? She sees it in her mind's eye. No, it was an army-green truck. Close cousin to camo. It had belonged to the awful woman who slapped Chet.

Chet. Ugh. She doesn't want to keep remembering Chet. But how can she forget him? She was naked with him less than two days ago, and now he's dead. Hank hasn't brought up the murder, and she's not about to, but she wonders if he knows about it. And, if he does, whether he remembers Maggie with him at the Occidental. God, she hopes not.

Lily huffs and shifts, responsive to Maggie's slightest signals, intentional or otherwise.

The crazy neighbor either doesn't see them or is ignoring Hank.

"Whatever." Hank lowers his hand. "This is our turnaround point. If we had time, I'd take you on the dime tour." He points up into the rugged foothills. "Gene got his antelope up there last year."

"Thanks for the nickel tour anyway."

"No problem."

As they turn around, Maggie says, "Hopefully when we get back, I'll have good news from the dealership."

"Sorry to tell you this, but I have signal out here. They haven't called."

"It's suddenly not so urgent that I get back." She gazes into the foothills. They tug at her, call to her. She's never been a mountain person, and Hank's told her about the predators that roam up there. But the longing is stronger than her fear of them and the unknown.

"I need to get back. Gotta get some work done before I have to knock off early." Hank urges Wolf in front of Lily.

Maggie has a bad feeling she knows why. "Oh? Something fun?" Her voice is brittle.

"Um, dinner with Sheila."

"The Sunday school teachers again?"

"No."

"My next guess is Mommy and Daddy, because I'll bet she still lives at home."

He gives her the side-eye. "Half-right. Dinner with the parents and Sheila's baby sister."

Half-right is twice as bad. If Sheila doesn't live with her parents, that means Hank can shack up with her all he wants. Maggie can't compete with a young, pretty woman who is sexually available. She's just been fooling herself. Going riding with Hank isn't stolen time. It's just opening up the wound so there's more surface area for the salt to sting when it's poured on.

"Yah, Lily." Maggie squeezes the horse's sides with her legs and presses gently with her heels. The mare is sluggish to respond, so Maggie repeats her command with firm intention. She needs to get away from this pain, and the quickest path back to Texas is on the back of the big black horse. Louise, excited, yips and snaps at Lily's heels.

"Hey, wait up," Hank calls.

Maggie whispers to Lily. "There are more cookies for you if you lose him." She knows Wolf can catch them, but right now, she needs a Hank-free moment.

The pregnant mare somehow finds a higher gear, and the wind in Maggie's face gives her the sensation that it's driving all her troubles into the distance behind her.

But then Hank and Wolf surge ahead, and it just feels like blowback in her face.

THIRTEEN

When Maggie trots Lily into the stable yard ahead of Hank and Wolf an hour later, Gene, Andy, and Paco are emerging from the main house. Her stomach growls. They'd missed lunch.

The *clop-clop* of the two horses' hooves is loud on the road. Gene turns toward it, sees them, and waves.

"Look at you and Lily."

Maggie asks Lily to stop. She does, but manages a few cheater steps toward her paddock. "Yee-haw."

"Missed you this morning," he says to Hank. "Minivacation?"

"Yeah, right. I took Maggie on a tour." Hank sounds defensive.

Lily makes eager throaty noises that vibrate Maggie's legs.

Maggie holds her back. "My truck's not ready."

"There's fence damage again, out near Simon's place. I need to check on Mom, but I can make repairs after."

Gene shakes his head. "A buyer called. He's coming in to look at the three-year-olds."

Paco says, "Andy and I can mend the fence."

"Thanks," Gene and Hank say in unison.

A truck pulls up, a Rhodes Rough Stock magnet on the door.

"What's he doing here?" Gene asks, to no one in particular.

Patrick Rhodes unfolds his large body out the driver's-side door. He reaches back in the truck and first grabs his hat and jams it on, then retrieves a tissue-wrapped bouquet. Sunflowers with giant nodding heads. He nods at the men and walks up, spurs jangling, to Maggie and Lily. Paco and Andy exchange a knowing glance and hotfoot it for the barn.

Patrick touches his hat brim. "Maggie."

"Hello, Patrick." Maggie glances at a glaring Hank.

"I saw these in town. They reminded me of you."

Maggie points at his left hand. "What does your wife think of you buying flowers for other women?"

"I'm a widower."

"And a motherfucker," Hank mutters.

Maggie relishes the awkward tension. Serves Hank right. "Thank you. My favorite."

"Can I hold your horse? Or break your descent?" He reaches toward Lily's face.

She backs up with a snort.

"Shh, girl." Maggie pats her neck.

Hank growls. "Lily stands for dismount on her own."

Maggie screws up her lip. Just what she wants—an audience as she tries to figure out how to get off. She swings her right leg over as she stands in the left stirrup. Then childhood memory takes over. She levers her upper body and stomach against the saddle for balance and kicks her left leg backward out of the stirrup. Free of the saddle, she hops to the ground.

Which is much farther down than she expects, and she keeps going, right onto her fanny in the dirt.

No one laughs.

Maggie winces. "For my encore, I'll dive off headfirst."

Patrick offers his left hand, the flowers clutched in his right. "Happens to the best of us."

"Liar." She takes his hand.

He lifts her to her feet and then some. She ends up closer to him than she likes and he keeps hold of her hand. She feels the eyes of Hank and Gene, and wonders how much of Patrick's help is to irritate them, and how much is to woo her.

She takes the flowers and her hand, then steps back. "Your jacket is in my cabin. I can run get it for you."

Patrick bows slightly at the waist. "Let me take you to dinner at the Wagon Box Inn tonight. You can give it to me then."

Maggie doesn't remember Patrick as this courtly from yesterday. She stares into the bouquet. Hank has a date. She has no particular interest in Patrick, but why shouldn't she go? It's a free meal. She missed lunch. In affirmation, her stomach growls. And it seems like a good way to piss Hank off. "A girl's gotta eat. What time?"

"Six?"

Lily bumps Maggie with her nose.

"Whoops. I need to take care of my horse. See you then."

Patrick goes to his truck and drives away, leaving a heavy silence behind.

Maggie tilts her chin up. She leads Lily to the hitching post by the tack room.

"Just be sure to wear your new jacket tonight," Hank calls after her.

She wants to make a dramatic exit, but she remembers Bess and turns. "Crap. I have to call the dealership."

Hank rides over and hands Maggie his phone. To Gene, he says, "I'll meet you at the outdoor arena in half an hour."

"Fine." Gene shoots Hank a meaningful look that Maggie doesn't understand. Then he walks to his four-wheeler and drives off.

Maggie pretends she isn't mulling over the look. She hits the number for the Ford dealership in Hank's Recents. Hank and Wolf join Lily at the hitching post.

When Maggie connects with the service department, the Southern mechanic says, "It sure 'nough looks like someone took a blowtorch to your driveshaft. It must have been holding on by a thread. Who'd you piss off?"

"The list of people I haven't pissed off is shorter. Are you sure it was sabotaged?"

"Well, I wasn't there when it happened, obviously, but that's my guess."

"Do you have a replacement?"

"No, ma'am. We don't stock parts on those old-model pickups. You have to hunt down stuff like that."

"I don't care where from, or what it costs. I just need it as fast as possible."

"We're closed for the rest of the weekend, but I can get on it first thing Monday."

All the ma'ams are starting to grate on Maggie. He doesn't sound *that* much younger than her. But between him and Andy, she's starting to take the hint. Next thing she knows, someone will call her Grandma. "Can I pay extra for someone to stay late and do it? So it can be shipped today?"

"Sorry, ma'am, it's just me left in here. We actually closed fifteen minutes ago, and I gotta go."

"First thing Monday, then?"

"Yes, ma'am."

After she thanks him, she hangs up and stomps in place double time for a few beats, shaking her fists. "They don't have it. They won't even start looking for one until Monday."

Wolf is already unsaddled and brushed out. Hank unbuckles Lily's throat latch and removes her bridle. "Did I hear you say sabotage?"

"That's what the mechanic thinks. I don't know."

"Shit. Do you know anyone who'd do that to you?"

"Not in Wyoming." Then she remembers the crazy chick who'd slapped Chet. Chet had said he'd seen his ex at the saloon. So she could have seen them together. Not appreciated it. Taken it out on Maggie's truck. But with a blowtorch? It seems like a stretch. "At least, I don't think so. Maybe a few in Texas."

"Wouldn't necessarily have been here. Maybe someone wanted you to break down on the way here."

Gary? One of his exes? There was a Jenny last year. She'd shown up a few times at Gary's when Maggie was with him. "Not out of the question."

Hank squeezes below his bottom lip. "I don't like it."

The sabotage would bother her more if Maggie wasn't *most* concerned about getting out of Wyoming. She paces in a tight figure eight, trying to come up with a solution that gets her on the road south today. Tomorrow at the latest. She doesn't have one, and suddenly her eyes are hot. She's screwed. Trapped in a front row seat to Hank's relationship with Sheila.

"I'll check back into the hotel."

His voice is firm. "I want you here. It's safer." He disappears into the tack room.

When he returns, Maggie says, "It's not like it was a bomb. It's just a part that fell out in the road. Even if it was sabotage, it wasn't done to hurt me. I'll be fine."

Hank's voice is incredulous. "Someone took a blowtorch to your drive-shaft. That's not friendly, Maggie. Out here, you could break down where someone wouldn't find you for days. Which I think could end real badly."

Hank has a point. Besides the sabotage, though—if that's even a real thing—it's going to cost an arm and a leg to get the part here. She's not exactly cash rich. Which is ironic, since she inherited a ranch, a vintage

Jaguar, a Warhol painting, and an extensive art collection from Gidget. But none of those jingle in her pocket. The money she'll save on a hotel bill will go a long way toward fixing Bess.

"If I have to stay here, then thank you."

"Think of it as a dude ranch vacation." He grins at her with his damn dimples. She wants to poke them with a sharp stick. "Some people pay big bucks for a week at a place like this."

A week? She'll flay herself alive if she has to spend that long suffering through the Hank-and-Sheila show. And that would just be more time for people to figure out she was the woman in Chet's hotel room the night before his murder. Neither are things she wants any part of. Surely it won't be that long. She can't let it be. She needs to spend some time coming up with a Plan B, ASAP. Maybe look at plane tickets for her and shipping costs for Bess. To do that, she needs connectivity.

She rubs Lily between her eyes. "I don't mean to be a fussy dude guest, but can I get the Wi-Fi password and some lightbulbs?"

Hank uncinches Lily's saddle and hefts it off her back. Holding it in one hand, he removes her blanket with the other. "Wi-Fi password is Buffalo2002. Capital B."

Buffalo . . . which could be the town, the animal, or the Buffalo Inn where they'd spent their one night. In 2002. Which makes it pretty clear which it is. "You're kidding."

"It's an old password. Don't make it into a big thing." He won't meet her eyes and rushes on to say, "I'll bring you some lightbulbs after I check on my mom."

Dammit, she doesn't want to feel this flicker of hope again. A smile threatens to break out. Ridiculous. She's being ridiculous. "I'll put Wolf and Lily up."

"Brush the sweat off her first. Check their water, too."

"Yes, sir, Sergeant, sir." She salutes. It's strangely satisfying to be asked to help. "I'd feel better about staying if you put me to work, actually."

"Aren't you the eager beaver?"

He has no idea. Maggie smiles. "I'm serious."

"What? Doing laundry? Chopping vegetables? Mucking stalls? We don't have much call for a picker, of guitar strings or old junk."

"Any of those. Or I could refresh the cabins with stuff I find around here. Even pull a few items from my haul this week." Maggie is surprised at herself. *Where did that idea come from?*

He purses his lips. "Might be wasted on us guys. I'd say you could tackle the main house, but my mother's been known to pepper unwanted visitors with buckshot. Or worse."

"I prefer my ass without holes. But think about it. I've got time on my hands."

FOURTEEN

At the cabin, Maggie stops with her hand on the screen-door pull, Louise beside her. The front door is slightly ajar. She knows she closed it, because she's paranoid in the land of single men and predators. Especially after her nightmares and Louise's growling episode.

"Inside, Louise."

The dog stares at Maggie but doesn't move.

"You're no help."

Maggie pushes the door open further with her toe. Her neck prickles, and she rubs it with her hand. The sensation of eyes on her skin makes her feel exposed, naked. She turns slowly, her eyes darting and scanning for movement. Nothing. She feels foolish. Maybe the latch on the door is sticky. Or maybe someone brought her supplies and didn't shut the door well.

But as she steps into the cabin, her skin feels itchy all over. Like someone or something is watching. She leaves the big door open, and Louise darts in just before the screen door slams behind her. Maggie examines every item and surface, opening drawers, cabinets, and closet. Nothing appears disturbed.

Then she kneels at her suitcase and rifles through it. Her hands feel hot and her chest cold. She knows instantly someone has been in her things.

And her belt and buckle are missing.

"No, no, no." She paws through the suitcase again, searching for the hard metal that should be impossible to miss.

It's been her most prized possession all these years. She's never misplaced it. The thought of it being gone is like losing Hank all over again. Louise whines and flops down against her leg. Maggie drops her head in her hands. She didn't cry in Texas when she sent Hank packing. She didn't cry when she learned about Sheila the other night. But now the tears come, ever so slowly, but they come. Once they start, they build and build until she's sobbing, her back rising and falling, her breaths choking gasps.

When the worst of it subsides, Louise licks her leg with darting tongue movements.

"Stop it. No. Gross."

Louise withdraws a few inches. Maggie wipes her cheeks and stares into her messy suitcase. The tears dry up, but she's in a trance of sorts, mulling over how much like this suitcase her life has become in such a short period of time. She had her shit together. She really did. Until six months ago. Now? She's just as messy as it is.

After what seems like an eternity, there's a tap on the wooden frame of the screen door behind her.

She swivels toward the sound and falls on her rump, vulnerable. Again. Then embarrassed.

Hank sees her and pulls the door open a few inches. "I don't remember that as a favorite position of yours."

"Whatever." She rolls to her knees, then stands. Can he see her ravaged face in the dim light of the cabin? She's glad for all the burned-out bulbs.

"I brought you some stuff." Under his arm is a package of lightbulbs and another box. In his left hand is a long gun.

"There's no need to shoot me."

Hank extends the rifle to her. "More like don't shoot me. I thought maybe having this would make you feel safer. At night. With the critters and sabotage and all."

And the theft of the buckle. His buckle. She almost blurts it out. But if she tells him, he'll see how it has gutted her. She's not open to more humiliation a la Hank right now. So all she says is "Thanks," and she takes the rifle.

"This is a .300 Win Mag. A good all-around rifle for around here. Do you know how to shoot it?"

Maggie's father had the same gun when she was a girl, for deer hunting in the mountains, something he made a pilgrimage to do every year he could afford the trip. "Well enough."

He sets a box of ammunition on a low coffee table then holds up the lightbulbs. "I'll just put these in your fixtures and be on my way."

Maggie sets the rifle in the corner near the head of the bed, butt to the ground. "I've got it."

"If you're sure."

She reaches for the lightbulbs.

He pulls them back. "Are you okay? Really."

She hesitates. Again, she almost tells him about the missing buckle, the open door, and the sensation of being watched. But she doesn't want it to seem like she's using drama to keep him around, and she can't prove anyone was here, that she didn't leave the door open, or that she hadn't just misplaced the buckle. Hank has another life. One that doesn't involve taking care of her. He's had every opportunity since she arrived to express an interest in rekindling their relationship, and he hasn't. She needs to get the hell out of Dodge with what's left of her pride, not cry to him that she's scared and ask him to fix it. Besides, since when has she admitted to being afraid of anything? Never, that's when.

"Really. I'm fine."

He points at her eyes, his hand brushing the skin of her cheek ever so softly. "You're kinda, um—"

His touch is like fire.

A gasp erupts from her. All her resolve, all her rationality is at risk in an instant. She chokes out an answer. "Allergies. It's nothing."

The air between them grows thicker, and her vision turns hazy. *Can he feel it, too?* Electricity builds. She moves an involuntary step closer to him. He licks his lips. *Yes, he feels it.* She leans in until her lips graze his.

He crushes his mouth against hers. She comes at him like a hungry lioness.

Then his phone buzzes. He trips over his own feet jumping back from her, then swallows and pulls the phone from his pocket. Glances at it. His face falls.

She grasps the lightbulbs and wrests them from him.

He lifts the phone. "I shouldn't have done that, music girl." He uses the nickname he'd given her fifteen years ago. "I'm sorry. I have to go."

They stare at each other for a few seconds, then like smoke in the wind, he's gone.

MAGGIE'S BRAIN is scrambled from the kiss. Did it mean anything? Does Hank regret it? She hates having to go out with Patrick in this state, but she's hungry enough to eat her arm. If she just had some Miracle Whip to slather on it she probably would. What she should have done earlier is go in search of snacks at the main house, but she'd fallen asleep in the cabin dreaming of Hank with her laptop open, before she'd even tried out the Wi-Fi password, much less followed up on her plans to research travel options.

So thank God she'd said yes to dinner.

She sees Patrick's truck roll past her window at one minute past six. She hadn't told him which cabin is hers. She downs a shot of her dwindling Balcones before grabbing her bag and his coat. The sun is descending behind the mountains and the temperature has fallen twenty degrees since her ride with Hank earlier. She's glad for the Double S jacket over her jeans and thin Johnny Was top. She touches her waistband. It feels barren without her signature buckle. Hank's buckle. She touches her fingertips to her lips.

Maggie exits the tape gate to the cabin's yard. She waves at Patrick. He doesn't see her. In the opposite direction, Hank's truck appears, heading toward the main gate. He passes Patrick without either man raising a hand.

When Hank draws even with Maggie, he stops and rolls down his window. "You have my number in case of trouble?"

She snorts. "What—you're going to leave your girlfriend and prospective in-laws to come to my rescue?"

He clenches his jaw. "You're a single woman, stranded in Wyoming. And you're good-looking. You're a hot commodity."

"I have pepper spray, and I'm not afraid to use it."

"I should have brought you a handgun instead of a rifle."

"Relax, Hank. You're not responsible for me."

"I know. But this is my fault."

"That Bess broke down?"

"That you're in Wyoming."

Maggie looks away quickly. "You and a killer estate sale." She points at Patrick. "My date's waiting. So is yours."

"Maggie, I'm sorry."

She can read the tea leaves. "About what? Earlier? Don't worry about it. It was nothing."

"It wasn't nothing. But it can't be anything."

"Drop it." She summons false bravado and winks. "Don't do anything I wouldn't."

"Just take care of yourself." He rolls his window up and drives on.

All the charge drains from her like an old battery. Maggie has an uncharacteristic longing to run after him, beg him to bag Sheila and whisk her away. But she'd never. A girl has her pride—or what's left of it after she's stranded in Wyoming.

So, instead, she trudges toward the main house. Patrick's truck backs up, then turns around. He pulls up next to her.

She opens the passenger door. "Hey."

His eyes light up. "Damn, you get better looking every time I see you."

"It's the great Wyoming lighting. You clean up good, too." Which is true. He does. He can't help it that he's not Hank.

He eases the truck out the gate and turns toward the town of Story. "So, Maggie Killian, what brought you to Wyoming?"

"I buy old stuff, restore it, and sell it."

"Don't they have old stuff in Texas?"

"Sure. I was looking for different old stuff than what everybody there has." It's not *un*true.

"I'm trying to picture this business."

"It's like that show *Junk Gypsies*."

"Haven't seen it."

"Have you seen *Fixer Upper*?"

"Is that the show with the goofy husband?"

"Um, maybe." Probably. Although Chip Gaines is ratings gold. "And my business is sort of like that. But without the goofy husband and television crew."

"Okay." His face says now he thinks I'm the goofy one. "When are you headed back?"

"Yesterday. Until my truck broke down. Now, whenever it's ready."

"It's a nice time of year to visit."

"If you like all four seasons in one day."

"More for your money around here, for sure."

He's right, though. It's a gorgeous time of year to visit. Maggie's eyes drink in the scenery. On her left, two sandhill cranes pose like giant feathered praying mantes. The mountains are a dark silhouette against the edge of a brilliant sunset over their peaks. The truck descends around a curve to the creek bottom in the little town of Story. Lodgepole pines close in around them. They cross Little Piney Creek, which is mostly a bed of rocks, on a narrow bridge. White-tailed deer forage near the stream.

Patrick points at a brick building, one story, with a fenced playground.

"That's the elementary school." They rumble over a one-lane bridge. "There's the fire station. They're busy this time of year. The humidity is so low, the fire risk is way up."

"There was lots of smoke last week. And I noticed the creek is dry."

"Yeah. At least we got a little rain. Down there's the library. The post office. The Story Store."

"Someone didn't overthink that name." Maggie holds up a hand. "Wait. Could we make an emergency supply stop? The larder is bare in my cabin."

Patrick throws the truck into a U-turn. "Sure. We're a little early for the reservation."

Inside, a grizzled cashier greets Patrick. "Tonight's shot is Tequila Sunset."

Maggie is half listening, half musing over a counter crowded with lottery tickets, fishing flies, and local crafts.

"Tequila Sunrise, you mean?"

"Nope." He grins. "It's my special concoction."

Patrick pulls out his wallet. "Want one, Maggie?"

"Why not?"

The cashier hands them two plastic shot glasses. Patrick holds his up, and Maggie touches hers to it. It's like cough syrup, thick, sweet, and mediciney. Maggie controls her gag reflex, just barely.

She sets the cup back on the checkout counter. "Be right back."

The interior of the store is jam-packed. While a good part of the store is groceries and household goods, the largest share of the floor and cooler space is for beer, wine, and liquor. Maggie grabs pricey bananas, coffee, bread, squeeze Miracle Whip, Swiss cheese, turkey, tortilla chips and salsa, and a bottle of Koltiska Original Liqueur. Now she can avoid the torture of meals at the main house.

Back in the truck, Patrick turns onto a road that looks enchanted and a little spooky.

"I'll throw bread crumbs unless you promise me you aren't taking me to visit an old witch who eats little children."

"Huh?"

Hank would have gotten her sense of humor. Gary, too, for that matter. "Never mind. I was just being silly."

Maggie doesn't volunteer any other witticisms. They pass cabins on one side and a dated drive-up motel on the other with larger-than-life painted wooden forest animals. Three does bound across the road in front of them and disappear into the sky-high pines. Maggie tilts her head back, staring up into their tops, which blend into the fading light.

The truck turns, reclaiming her attention from the sky. An authentic wagon box is mounted on a tall pole at the entrance to the parking lot. A sign reads WAGON BOX INN. The inn itself is a rambling affair built of huge logs and set against another idyllic stream. Majestic pines and a deep lawn surround a wooden deck.

Patrick escorts Maggie into a vestibule, up a broad carpeted staircase, and through another set of doors. "The restaurant here is pretty good. The bar is even better."

"My kind of place."

An orange-haired woman in a pink paisley top is needlepointing what looks like a bear with a fish in its mouth. She doesn't put her project down. "Hi, Patrick. Your table's ready."

"Donna." He touches his hat.

She stays inside the reception booth, making no bones about giving Maggie the once-over.

Patrick leads Maggie to a table for two. Maggie looks back and sees a woman with a gray beehive whispering with Donna, their eyes on Maggie. She gives them a broad smile, which appears to startle them, and they break apart.

Maggie orders Koltiska over ice.

"Original or KO ninety?" The waitress makes eye contact, but with only one eye. The other's off doing its own thing.

"Hmm. Ninety proof?"

"Yes."

"Make it ninety. Over ice." Just one, she thinks. Because there's no way I'm ending up Patrick's angel of the morning.

"And your usual, Pat?"

He nods at her. She scurries away.

"Excuse me for a moment."

"Of course."

Instead of going to the bathroom as she expects, Patrick makes a lap of the packed room. His hat and spurs are perfectly in tune with his environment. He takes his time, shaking hands and holding court, sans Maggie. That's okay. The last thing Maggie wants is for people to know her name, especially as Patrick's date. She connects to Wi-Fi and fiddles with her phone. There's another message from Gary, but hours earlier.

I'm in town. Coming by to see if you're decent. Hope you're not.

She has to write back to him soon, but by now he's figured out she's not in town.

When Patrick returns, their drinks have arrived—something amber in a whiskey glass for him. She puts her phone away. They order their dinners, and Maggie takes a big swig of KO 90. She savors the heat. Instant recharge of her tired battery.

A crusty old-timer with two percent body fat and wrinkles like the Grand Canyon moseys in, making straight for their table. He and Patrick greet each other with gusto. Patrick doesn't introduce Maggie. Within seconds, the newcomer brings up Chet, his barely audible voice whistling through a missing front tooth.

"I hear he took up with a woman Thursday night. Not from around here." He wiggles bushy white eyebrows.

Maggie pushes her hair behind her ear. This is news she needs to hear, even if it's bad.

"Where from?"

"No one knows. She's a mystery."

Patrick looks amused. "Are you suggesting a mysterious black widow brained Chet?"

The old-timer wheezes and coughs. "It could happen. 'Cept you're thinking about when a woman marries a feller then kills him for his money. Chet was working at Crazy Woman Exploration. Not exactly rich."

"He had the ranch, too."

"But no wife to kill him for it."

"There's always his mother."

The old-timer swells up. "I dated Beth Ann's big sister in high school, I'll thank you to know, and I won't stand for those types of insinuations about her."

Patrick laughs. "Sorry, pardner. I didn't mean anything by it. So, who do the police think did it, if it wasn't this black widow?"

"If they know, they ain't saying."

Patrick sneers. "Well, if we're waiting on local police to crack the case, we may never find out whodunnit."

Their ribeye steaks arrive, still sizzling on the plates, melted butter running down their sides, with layered potato casserole on the side. The old-timer leaves. Maggie eats like one of the Double S hands. Patrick doesn't speak during dinner, and she's glad. Her mind is preoccupied with the news that Chet's hookup has been labeled as an out-of-towner. That's a step in the wrong direction as far as her anonymity is concerned.

A familiar figure passes their table. A thirty-something man with a patchy beard that makes him seem a decade younger than his skin and smile wrinkles. When he passes back by, he nods to her. She nods back. His identity hits her. The Occidental bartender. She watches him return to the receptionist, who hands him a takeout bag. He shoots her one more glance, this time giving her a two-fingered salute at forehead level. And a smile. Then he walks out of the vestibule.

Small towns. You can't go anywhere without seeing everyone you know.

When they finish their meals, Maggie turns down another drink, dessert, and coffee. "So, what's the story with you and Hank?"

Patrick slips a credit card into the check holder. "What do you mean?"

"The bad blood. The dirty looks and snide comments."

The waitress shows up quicker for the card than she has with any of their drinks and food all night. "I'll be right back, Pat."

"We're competitors."

"Oh, come on."

"Maybe he just doesn't like me."

"But you seem like a popular guy, if tonight's any indication."

"Maybe I just don't like him."

"All right. You don't have to answer."

He smiles, but it isn't a happy face. "We go back. Way back. And if you want any more of the story, you'll have to charm it out of me on a second date."

Maggie is confused. He's barely interacted with her, now he wants a second date? Maybe he's unusual, or maybe this is how men date in Wyoming. Either way, she doesn't do pressure. She spent too many years yielding to it in the early days of her music career, with bruises on her knees indelibly burned in her memory, tainting record contracts and Nashville gigs.

There'll be no charm for him.

The waitress presses the folder into his hand. "Thanks for coming in, Pat. See you soon."

Patrick signs the check. Conversation over. In fact, conversation doesn't resume until Patrick walks her to the door of her cabin. Maggie scurries ahead of him, trying to avoid what's coming, because it's not going to be him.

He catches her arm. "You're not in a hurry, are you?"

Louise comes out of the shadows to Maggie's side, almost invisible with her black fur against the night sky. She's growling, and the ruff on her neck is high.

Patrick jumps back. "Goddamn dog scared the shit out of me."

The bag of groceries bangs against her leg as Maggie escapes behind the screen door with Louise. She drops the safety latch as surreptitiously as she can and pats the dog's head. Another protector. Maybe Hank put her up to it. "Rough day. I need some shut-eye."

"Rain check?"

"I'll call." She won't. "Thanks again."

Still, Patrick doesn't leave. "Say, didn't I see you with Chet that night at the Ox?"

His words knock the wind out of Maggie. She rushes her answer into the space left by her uncomfortable pause. "The man who was murdered? That Chet?"

"The only one from around here. Speaking of which, you're not."

Maggie scrambles for mental footing. *Sadly upset, that's how I play it. Just like before.* "He bought me a drink. Such a nice man. So sad."

"I bought you a drink tonight. Guess I'll have to watch my back." Patrick puts two fingers to his hat and disappears into the dark.

Maggie closes the door and leans back against it, waiting until she hears his engine noise receding. Had he been accusing her of something? Threatening her? Her head swims and she sees spots in her side vision. Monday. She had planned to call the Buffalo police if she wasn't out of here by Monday. Now, Monday is impossible for Bess. Maggie's going to have to reveal herself to the police soon, or someone else is going to beat her to it.

But first she has to figure out a way to tell Hank, one where she doesn't seem like a total slut.

FIFTEEN

Maggie pours herself a Koltiska over ice and sips. She has a reprieve on her confession tonight—Hank is with young Sheila and her family. She'll tell him first chance tomorrow. The thought makes her sag like her grandmother's pantyhose. It was already a lost cause for her with Hank. So why is she so terrified to tell him about Chet? It's not like it will change things.

A cold, wet nose presses into her palm.

"Hey, Fucker. Help me secure the perimeter?"

Louise rewards her with the disgusting, stabby licks.

"Not okay." Maggie jerks her hand away.

The dog is certainly a mixed bag. Sweet but disgusting, protective but annoying, cute but disobedient. And she certainly seems to have adopted Maggie.

Maggie locks the front door and searches for signs of intruders. In the cabin, the reconnaissance operation takes less than two minutes. Maggie doesn't see any signs of disturbance. More important, Louise is calm. Maggie loads the rifle anyway—safety on. As she's doing it, she sees HANK SIBLEY engraved on a plate screwed to the stock. She rubs her thumb across the plate, then slides the rifle on the ground under the bed, within easy reach. Then she unpacks her groceries and puts them away.

"What now, girl?"

Louise sits by Maggie's guitar case and wags her tail.

"You like music?"

The tail wags faster, whether because Maggie is sweet-talking her or because Louise is a guitar aficionado, Maggie doesn't know.

Maggie looks at her phone. It's only eight thirty. *Why not?* Some old habits die hard, like some old loves, and she's neglected this habit far too much lately. She sets her drink down and kneels, her knees cracking. She opens the case. After her belt buckle, she loves this Martin more than any other material thing in the world, and she takes good care of it. On the road, other musicians had made fun of her for obsessing over it, but she'd always believed her music would only be as good as her instruments. No bashing guitars onstage for her. She became known for her natural virtuosity, her ability to play better than any of the musicians hired to back her.

But that was a long time ago.

As always, the first thing she does is check the ambient temperature and humidity on a portable monitor. The weather is far drier and colder here than Texas. She's been careful not to leave her baby near any heaters, and she hasn't opened the case in Wyoming, so conditions have remained fairly constant for the guitar inside. Fifty percent humidity and seventy-five degrees is ideal for it. Too much humidity is especially bad, which is a challenge in her old Texas house in the summer.

Conditions in the cabin are actually quite good. The humidity is right at fifty percent, the temperature at sixty-eight. It will be cooler on the porch, but with the heat from her body, it will be perfect. She wipes the instrument with a warm, damp cloth. Then, without taking off her jacket, she puts the strap over her neck. It's like a hug. She holds the Martin close, hugging it back. She runs her hand across the embroidered peace signs on the strap, a homemade gift from her mom when she was in middle school, pre-Martin. She'd played a cheap Kmart instrument back in the day.

She greases her fingering hand with Vaseline, grabs her pick, and walks out to the porch with Louise and her drink. She settles on the porch swing and puts her drink on a patio end table beside it. Silvery moonlight spills over the strings on the instrument in her lap. It's like a celestial blessing. Her stress eases. This was the right decision.

"Thank you, mother moon." She strums the guitar and tunes it. Louise cocks her head from side to side and whines. "Are you singing or complaining?"

The dog doesn't answer.

When Maggie has the guitar ready, she pauses, waiting for inspiration. In the silence, she hears an odd cry, like a rattling bugle. Her fingers begin moving on the strings. She exhales and closes her eyes. A song takes shape, and she smiles. A confidence-building opener—her muse knows what she needs. It's the introduction to the first song off her multiplatinum *Buckle Bunny* album. "I Hate Cowboys" was also her first country number one, and it hit the top spot on several other charts as well. The album and song should have been the beginning of a long, award- and reward-filled career. Instead, they were the beginning of her end as a professional musician.

But that doesn't mean she doesn't love every song she wrote for the album. She's proud of them. They came from her heart, out of the broken place left after Hank, and the hopeful place that hadn't been crushed. Yet.

She sings the words, pouring her heart into it. People think the song is funny. She doesn't. It's an anthem to her heartbreak. Her voice cracks. There's a new poignancy to it for her after seeing Hank again. Kissing him. And losing him again. Louise vocalizes along with her. Maggie pauses. She knows she plays tight. No off-key sounds to elicit the funny moans and whines coming from the dog's throat.

"You are singing, Louise. Very nice." Then she starts up again.

I hate cowboys—especially bull riders—I hate cowboys.
   Their buckles look funny,
   And they call their girls bunnies.
   I hate cowboys. Damn bull-riding cowboys.

The song's joke has always been on her. She finishes it and plays through the entire album. As she prepares to strum the opening chords of the final song, the eponymous "Buckle Bunny," she hears a noise just beyond her field of vision. A sneeze? At the same time, Louise barks crazily and charges toward the sound.

"Who's there?" she calls. Her voice is shrill. She stands, ready to run for the rifle. Why hadn't she brought it out here with her?

A figure materializes, both hands up. "It's me, Ms. Maggie. Andy. I was in the stables checking on a sick horse. I heard you playing and had to come listen. Your music is beautiful."

Maggie exhales and sits down with a thump, sending the swing back into the wall. She's light-headed. "Oh, Andy. You scared me."

He looks everywhere but in her eyes. "Is it all right if I listen some more?"

"Sure, come have a seat."

Louise slumps at Maggie's feet again, silent now that her work is done.

Andy steps onto the porch. He's still in boots, a cowboy hat, his denim pants, and one of his odd long-sleeved work shirts, but gone are the chaps the hands wear by day. "If you're sure you don't mind."

Maggie points to the swing. "So you said you don't play?"

"No, ma'am."

She gives him a dirty look.

"I mean, no. But I want to learn. But I don't have an instrument, and there's no one to teach me."

"Well, you're in the right place." She hands him the guitar.

"Oh no, I can't—"

"Hush that. You can. Do you know how to hold it?"

Even in the dark, she can see his blushing smile. He puts the strap over his neck like Maggie had earlier and holds the guitar awkwardly in front of him.

"Good. Now, we'll start with something fun and easy."

"Could you teach me 'Amazing Grace'?"

Maggie grins. "Sure. You just need to learn a few chords." Maybe she could convince him to learn "Stairway to Heaven" or "Smoke on the Water" later. Or maybe not.

Louise puts her head on her paws, and Maggie could swear the dog is smiling, too.

SIXTEEN

The next morning, Maggie sleeps in. She'd crashed well after midnight, her sleep interrupted repeatedly by the eerie night sounds. She's exhausted and has no desire to rub her own nose in Hank's absence or endure Mrs. Sibley's ire. Plus, if by some miracle Hank was at breakfast, she has delayed the difficult conversation she plans for later today. Maybe that's the most important reason for hiding out in bed an extra hour or two.

She pads over to the kitchen once she's dressed, hair in a messy bun, teeth brushed, and water splashed on her face. She brews a big pot of coffee to go with her turkey melt, then enjoys them on the front porch. Sitting out in the crisp morning air, she feels peaceful, despite everything. Partly because of the sounds of cattle and horses, but also because of the music the night before.

She'd worked with Andy on "Amazing Grace" for nearly an hour before he'd begged off to get some sleep. Sundays aren't exempt from pre-breakfast chores. In that short time, he'd mastered the chords he needed, and they'd sung the hymn together. He has a rich bass voice with nice range.

When he left, Maggie had poured herself another drink and done something she hadn't done in ten years: written music. The song that came to her is far from complete, but she's calling the work-in-progress "Stranded."

Unfortunately, after that she'd pulled up the "How the Mighty Maggie Killian Has Fallen" piece. It was horrifying. The author rehashed Maggie's admittedly sordid past, exploiting the high profile of Michele's *Love Child* book and upcoming movie. What the author had not done was make an effort to chronicle Maggie's life since her meltdown, other than give stalkery types the name of her store and the town she lives in. *Hip hip hooray for lazy journalism.*

Maggie shakes her head, remembering the aftermath of Cheyenne, the crash that killed her touring band, and all the highs and lows since then. Then she banishes it from her mind. She's already got ten pounds of shit to stuff into a five-pound bag today without forcing the past in, too.

She stretches and yawns. Louise had run off when she let her outside at dawn, Maggie assumes to go for her own breakfast at the barn. She's still nowhere to be seen. The fog that had rolled in the night before is slowly lifting, fashioning a white skirt around the waist of the mountains with the dark rock and forests of the higher elevations sticking out like a women's top above it. A white cap sits on the tallest peaks. With a start, she realizes that white is new snow. The changing of seasons is early and abrupt. Maybe winter's initiative is a sign to get her ass in gear, too. She doesn't have to be in Texas to work. There's a whole trailer-load of junk here with her, waiting for her attention, and she's sure any tool she needs she can find on this ranch.

In minutes, she's at the trailer with a pen and notebook. She's unfastening the tarp when Louise appears. "Where've you been?"

The dog grins, wiggles, and wags.

"I don't suppose you can help me with this?"

The dog flops into the dirt in a shaft of sunlight streaking through the clouds.

"I'll take that as a no."

Maggie folds the tarp and secures it with the tie-down straps. It's high time to identify, inventory, price, photograph, label, and post the pieces that are salable, and to make a list of items that need an intervention or reinvention. She sets to it, moving like a dervish between the trailer, the piles she assembles by category, the notebook, a Sharpie and masking tape for labeling, her phone for pictures, and her laptop for pricing research and inspiration.

She tackles the bulky items first. A Singer pedal sewing machine cabinet. A coffee table with legs made of horseshoes. A sideboard that has a future as a TV stand. Within half an hour, she sheds her jacket. The piles grow. The dog sleeps. She fills pages in her notebook. Hours pass. She stands back and surveys her half-empty trailer. She's kicking ass. If she keeps after it, she can be done by lunch, reload the trailer except for items she wants to work on here, then spend the afternoon updating her website. She decides she's earned a short break.

With a banana and more coffee, she settles on the porch with her laptop. Hank hasn't driven past since she's been working, and from here she can confirm his truck is not home. Good. That means she can put off the yucky conversation even longer. She turns her attention for the next half hour to a project she thinks of as Operation Escape from Hell—researching travel options.

It sucks the life out of her. She can't find any combination of flights and junk shipment that costs less than a thousand bucks. She can shave off five hundred by hopping a bus. But all of that is before repair and transport of Bess.

And what does this expenditure buy her? Not much. The earliest she can leave is Monday. If she's lucky, Bess will be fixed by Tuesday or Wednesday. Is a day or two worth it? And, if it is, can she even afford it without selling off a kidney or one of her inheritance treasures? She pulls up her bank account and compares it to her budget for show season.

It's a gut punch. She'll be lucky to fix the truck, limp home, and survive the show. She can admit to herself, too, that she'd secretly hoped to find an option that got her out of here before confession time.

Louise noses her hand. The dog is like an emotional barometer.

Maggie strokes her floppy ears. "I should have never left Texas. Everything's broke. My piggy bank, my heart, and my truck." She sighs. "I'll put a few paintings up for sale, but without a miracle, I'll have to tough it out. Do what I can from where I am." *Face the music with Hank.*

Her phone rings from somewhere. The in and out cell reception is enough to drive her bonkers. She puts the laptop down, and follows the sound. She runs to the trailer and finds the phone on the ground under the tailgate.

"Hello," she says, out of breath, without taking the time to look at the caller ID.

"Hey, it's Michele. Are you exercising?"

"Do you know me even a little? Running for the phone at fifty-two-hundred-feet elevation nearly killed me."

Michele laughs. "That's my girl."

Maggie walks back to the shaded porch and her laptop. "What's up?"

"I thought you'd be on the road home, but it doesn't sound like it."

"No, I've run into a snag with Bess. I'm waiting on a part and a fix."

"Well then, you're not going to like this call. More bad news."

Maggie slumps against the wall of the cabin. "I'm a human punching bag—hit me."

"First off, the goats are fine. Lumpy is watching over them like Papa Bear."

"Bears eat goats."

"You know what I mean."

"Go on."

"Jerry called me," Michele says, referring to the kid Maggie has working Flown the Coop on the weekends. "He said he tried getting ahold of you first."

Maggie scrolls to Recents. She has a missed call from the kid. And a voicemail. "Crap. I missed it. Signal up here is the shits."

"Okay, well, I'm with him now. And with Lee County's finest. Your store was broken into last night and ransacked."

Maggie moves to a rocker and sits heavily. "No."

"I'm sorry. There's more."

"I don't think I want to hear it."

"Jerry said Gary came by yesterday, right before closing time."

"My Gary?"

"Well, your former Gary, unless there's a new development you haven't told me about."

"What was he doing there?"

"Throwing a temper tantrum that you weren't there, especially after Jerry told him you were in Wyoming."

She should have answered his messages. "Not good."

"Jerry's telling the deputies about it now."

"Gary wouldn't."

"Probably not, but I wanted you to know. Sounds like he was pretty pissed."

"If he wasn't before, he will be after he gets dragged into the investigation."

"The deputies said they'll call you later. I gave Tank and Junior your number."

"Thanks."

"I'm hanging around until they're done. Rashidi is with me. He's going to board up the windows and door."

"It's that bad?"

A Buffalo Police Department cruiser pulls through the gate and slowly makes its way up the drive. Hank's truck is following it. Maggie's stomach threatens to eject coffee, turkey melt, and banana.

"Honey, it's really bad. A lot of damage. Maybe some theft. Jerry's trying to help the deputies figure it out."

"Well, thank you. You, Rashidi, and Jerry."

"One more thing. I went to your house to let your guest know."

"Leslie."

"Yeah. There's a car there, but no one is answering. There's vehicles from the sheriff's department all over the yard now because of the break-in at the store, and still no one has come out."

Maggie kicks herself for not pushing harder with Leslie. She has to get ahold of the woman. "And she hasn't answered me either. I'll see when she's supposed to check out." Should she ask Michele to let herself in to check on Leslie? Before she can decide, the police car and truck stop in front of her cabin. "Listen, I have to go. I'll call you later. Thanks again."

"Sorry. Love you."

Maggie ends the call. Hank gets out and meets the officers beside the vehicle. They talk like the old school chums they probably are, then head toward the porch, and Maggie.

SEVENTEEN

The first officer to speak only has an inch or two on Maggie, if that. She suspects he's wearing lifts in his shoes. His hair is white-blond and his blue eyes milky. "Maggie Killian?"

Shit. I'm too late. She avoids looking at Hank. "That's me." She stands and smooths the legs of her jeans. Her heart is racing so fast it hurts.

"I'm Detective Lacey. This is my partner, Detective Johnson." He thumbs toward his colleague, a woman taller than him. Her head is mostly covered by incongruous Shirley Temple–like curls.

"Nice to meet you." Which it isn't, but she can't say what she really wants to: *Go away and leave me alone.*

Lacey continues. "We're here to talk to you about Chet Moore. Did you know him?"

Out of her peripheral vision, she sees Hank. His mouth is open, his arms crossed. "I met a guy last Thursday named Chet. I don't know his last name."

"Can you describe him for us?"

"Early thirties. Taller than him. Thicker." She points at Hank. "Curly hair. Light brown, dark blond. Unusual eyes. Gray."

The detectives look at each other. Lacey nods.

"That's him." Lacey leans against the porch railing. "Where did you meet him?"

"In Sheridan. Outside a taxidermy shop."

"Tell us about it."

"I was pulled over to make a phone call. He stopped to see if I needed help. I told him I didn't."

"That was it?"

She walks to the other end of the porch, putting space between herself and the detectives. "No. I was at the Occidental Saloon later. He showed up there. Bought me a drink."

"Go on."

She hesitates.

"Ms. Killian, we have a witness that saw you at the bar with him."

"Is that all? I just told you I was there. So now you have two. Who was the other?"

"That's not relevant."

"Chet is dead."

"So you know that?"

She scoffs. "Everyone in the area knows that. Now you're here talking to me. That makes it relevant. Whoever sent you to me did it for a reason."

"And what is that?"

"I don't know. You'd have to ask them. But anyone in the Occidental could have told you I was talking to Chet." She ticks on her fingers. "Hank here. His girlfriend, Sheila. Gene Soboleski and his date—sorry, I don't know her name. The bartender. Do you want me to go on?"

A slideshow of faces fast-forwards in her brain. The musicians. Rudy from North Dakota. Patrick. And every other patron in the place. She doesn't kid herself. With that shitty new article out about her, Sheila could have had the whole bar gossiping about her. Add to that she's memorable looking. Every single one of them *might* have recognized her.

"Not necessary. The same witness saw you get in Mr. Moore's truck."

That information chills her. She didn't see anyone when she and Chet left. After processing this for a moment, she nods at Hank. "Is he here officially? Because I'm not comfortable discussing my personal life in front of him. Especially not if he was your witness."

Hank's face is stony. "I can wait by the truck." He stalks away, fists balled.

When he's gone, Maggie says. "Awkward. Hank and I used to date." She takes a deep breath. "Yes, I left with Chet."

"Then what?"

Maggie looks around for Hank. He's leaning against his truck, arms crossed. Sound carries out here. She lowers her voice. "We spent the night at the Bison Inn."

Lacey doesn't follow her lead. His voice sounds like a bellow. "And?"

"He got up the next morning and left. I slept in. I had lunch at the Busy Bee, then came here."

"And you're aware that he was killed that morning outside the hotel?"

She shakes her head. "I wasn't at the time. I heard about it yesterday."

"Why didn't you come to us then?"

"Why would I? Because I'd heard maybe someone I knew had died?"

"Because you'd spent the night with him."

She sits on the rail, one leg on the ground. "I'm sure I'm not the only woman who can claim that honor."

"You were the last person to see him alive."

"How would I have known that? Even *now* I don't. In fact, my money is on the person who killed him seeing him last. And that *sure* wasn't me."

"But don't you think you might have information that will be helpful to our investigation?"

"No, I don't. When he left, he was alive. I never saw him again. I'm sorry to hear what happened to him. Very."

Lacey chews on his lip and nods. "Just a moment."

He motions to Johnson and they step away from her, heads together, voices low. Maggie takes the opportunity to watch Hank under lowered lashes. He's frozen in place, arms still crossed, and looks steaming mad. When their tête-à-tête is over, Lacey and Johnson box her in on her side of the porch.

Lacey continues to lead. "So let's go through this again. When you were still at the hotel, did you know he'd been murdered?"

"Wait—don't you need to read me my Miranda rights?"

"You're not under arrest."

"Does that mean I don't have to talk to you?"

The cops share a glance.

"It would help us out a lot if you do. And, if you don't, we can't promise we won't pick you up and read you your Miranda rights then."

Maggie weighs the bad options, then throws up her hands. "Fine."

"So we were asking if you knew Mr. Moore had been murdered. When you left the hotel."

"No. I knew there was a crime scene in the parking lot, but it had nothing to do with me, and I left."

"We don't have a statement from you."

"Because no one took one."

Lacey glowers. "No one asked you to give a statement?"

"No."

"Not when you checked out?"

"I didn't check out. Chet booked the room."

Johnson nods at Lacey.

"Did you see anyone suspicious or who might have indicated they intended to harm Mr. Moore?"

"I was wasted, Detective Lacey. I saw Chet, naked, and the inside of the hotel room."

Johnson smirks.

Lacey narrows his eyes at his partner. "What about in the parking lot?"

"That night?"

"Yes."

"I saw him talking to some meth-head-looking people on his way in, but I stayed in the truck. It didn't go well. In fact, a woman slapped him."

"Can you describe them?"

"A group of white people with tattoos. Two men and a blonde woman. That's it—it was dark, I was fifty feet away. And did I mention wasted?"

"Did you hear their conversation?"

"No. When Chet got back in the truck, he told me she was a woman he hadn't treated well, and that he had it coming."

"Anyone else you can think of?"

"No."

"At the bar?"

"He got a lot of female attention at first. Hank's girlfriend, Sheila, seemed to find him especially attractive. But he came straight to me."

"Did anyone seem upset about that?"

"Not that I saw."

"Hank?"

"Unfortunately, not in the slightest." She feels Hanks eyes burning into the side of her face and hopes he can't hear her.

"Did Mr. Moore talk about anyone being after him or upset with him?"

"Detective Lacey, we weren't exactly *talking*."

"Is that a no?"

"It's a no."

"Did he ever tell you where he was headed or whether he intended to meet anyone on the day he was killed?"

"Not that I remember that night. Our first real conversation was in the morning. He asked me to take a shower with him. I said no. He asked me to marry him and be the mother of his little girl. I said no. He pouted. I said goodbye. He left."

Detective Lacey looks at his feet. She sees him grinning. Then his head pops up. "Moore doesn't have any kids."

"I suppose he doesn't have a crazy mother either? Because he told me he had both."

Johnson holds up a hand toward Lacey, stopping the line of conversation. "Anything else?"

Maggie sighs dramatically. "What are you looking for—sexual positions? Um, missionary, doggie, and me on top. Number of orgasms? Him, three, I think, me, five. Is oral sex legal in Wyoming? Because we did that, too."

Johnson's mouth opens, then snaps shut quick as a mouse trap.

Lacey says, "No wonder he asked you to marry him."

"Is that all, detectives?"

"Just one more thing. Did you have anything to do with the death of Chet Moore?"

Maggie tosses her hair, dander up. "Zero. I did not kill him. I did not see him killed. I do not know who killed him. I don't know anything about him, really, except that he seemed to have a hard-on that never quit."

Lacey's pale skin colors. "We don't need quite that much information, but thanks. Also, we'll need you to come in and make a statement."

"I thought I just gave one."

"We need it typed up and signed."

"You'd make some poor administrative employee listen to this?"

Lacey's voice is dry. "Well, you could tone it down some."

"Do you need me to go in now?"

"Tomorrow. Make it two thirty."

"Fine."

"And we need you to stay nearby until this is settled."

Maggie jumps to her feet, and the two detectives back up a few steps. "Whoa, whoa, whoa. I live and work in Texas. You want me to stay until you crack this case? What if that never happens?"

"We can talk about it more after you give your statement, but, for now, at least through Friday."

Friday. Six more days of suspended animation. "You can't force me to put my life on hold."

"Don't make us, Ms. Killian."

Maggie groans. "Do you even have any suspects?"

"We aren't at liberty to say at this time."

"Is that a no?"

"It's exactly what I said."

Which doesn't inspire confidence in Maggie about them wrapping the case by Friday, or turning their attention away from her, for that matter. The detectives return to their car and make their goodbyes with Hank. Maggie walks to the porch steps.

As soon as they're gone, Hank is in her face, a soft drink can sloshing and dangling from his hand. "What the hell is going on, Maggie?"

EIGHTEEN

Maggie puts her hand on a support beam and stares out at the mountains. "It seems I was possibly the last innocent person to see Chet Moore alive."

"Meaning?"

"It means I spent the night with him, before he was killed in the parking lot of the hotel as he left."

"Innocent." His eyes drill into hers. "Not the word I would have used."

"I didn't kill the guy." Hank's judgy attitude and disappointment is what she's been afraid of, and it sparks her wick. She purrs. "Although I guess you could say I nearly did, but he wasn't complaining."

"Nice, Maggie."

"What? You object to how I spent the night?"

Hank crushes the can against the porch beam, sending caramel liquid squirting out. "A one-night stand? Yeah, I object."

Maggie steps away from him. "You didn't seem to object the times I spent the night with you."

"We were different."

Maggie can't argue with that. "And we're different now. Because you have a girlfriend, and what I do is none of your goddamn business."

His blue eyes darken. He looks away to the mountains. "I guess not. But the trouble you bring to this ranch is."

"Trouble? I didn't bring Chet here, and I didn't do anything to him."

Hank's smile is a death mask. "I wondered if you'd admit it."

Maggie's head spins. "Admit what?"

"That you spent the night with him."

"You knew?"

"Of course I knew. You were all over him at the Ox. You left with him. We drove out of town right behind his truck, and you pawed each other at every red light."

Maggie feels like she's going to puke. How well does she even know this man? They had one night together fifteen years ago, and almost a week in the sack earlier this year. She obviously missed out on cues to some important traits. Like his temper. And that he can be a huge asshole. "You told the police about me."

"Nope. I didn't tell anyone. I was too humiliated that someone I used to be with would hook up with a douchebag like Chet Moore. If you'd do that, what wouldn't you do? And now the police are here. You know the old saying. Where there's smoke, there's fire."

"You think I *killed* him?"

"Maybe not that. But I don't know what I think about *you* anymore, Maggie."

NINETEEN

Monday morning, Maggie is updating her website from the cabin porch, skipping breakfast at the main house, again. Work is a good way to keep from thinking about the harsh words between her and Hank, not to mention the edict from the Buffalo detectives that she stay in town through Friday. She can't do anything about the latter, and she doesn't want to face up to the former. She uploads a photo of the Singer sewing machine and types in a price and description, then posts it to her website. It will sell fast and for a good price, she's certain.

Her phone rings. Caller ID announces LEE COUNTY. As in Texas. She'd forgotten about the break-in at Flown the Coop. A week ago it would have been a huge problem. Now it doesn't even make the cut into the top two worst.

"Maggie Killian," she says into the phone.

The voice is officious. "Junior Jones, Lee County deputy sheriff."

"Am I being punked? Like I don't know who you are." Maggie pictures the Ichabod Crane look-alike deputy with the Dudley Do-Right demeanor. He's mooned over her for years. "And you realize it's an indecent hour where I am?" With the time difference, it makes sense Junior is at work in Texas.

He relaxes, but not much. "Sorry. I'm following up about the break-in at your store."

"I hear it was a break-in, vandalism, and theft."

She hears a car honking in the background on Junior's end. "True. I hate it for you, Maggie. We'll try to find who did this."

"It's crap. And I'll never get my junk back. You know it."

"You got any enemies?"

"Oh, come on. How long have we known each other?"

"Long enough. Consider it a rhetorical question. List them please."

"Honestly, Junior, I don't know anyone who would do something like this. Even the people I've pissed off. But while you're investigating it, look into who would sabotage my truck, because I'm broken down here in Wyoming and can't leave." Of course, she doesn't know what kind of douchebag would steal the belt buckle either. A text message flashes across her screen.

Michele: *Did Tank or Junior call you?*

While the answer is obvious, Maggie can't send it now.

Junior says, "What do you mean?"

"Just what I said. My truck was sabotaged. I'm stranded."

"It wasn't somebody up there who did it?"

"I don't know. But I barely know anyone here. And someone in Texas vandalized my shop. Stands to reason they could have been the one to take a blowtorch to the end of my driveshaft, too."

"Like Gary Fuller?"

"Definitely not Gary. He's too careful of his public image. He's never even admitted our relationship in public."

"He was yesterday, loud and proud."

"Jim Beam probably factored into it."

"No doubt." In the distance, she watches Andy and Paco rope a bull that had gotten out of its pasture and refused to be herded back. One over the horns, one catches a back heel. "Maybe one of Gary's ex-girlfriends. One in particular. Jenny. She's a nutjob. And some dumbass reporter just released a bunch of personal information about me, including the name of my store and the location. You could get her number from Gary."

His words come out slowly, and she imagines him licking a pencil and writing it down. "Oh. Kay."

"Are you at my place now?"

"No."

"Next time you go by, can you check on my tenant? She's not answering me."

"Do you have reason to think we should enter forcibly?"

"No, but I wouldn't mind if you peeked in the windows."

"When will you be back?"

Leaving out the reason why, Maggie says, "A week or less. You can coordinate with Michele about access until then."

"I'll need a statement from you when you get back."

"Fine." *Get in line.* "Oh! And can I get started on an insurance claim, send an adjuster out?"

"Sure. Have them give me a heads-up, though. Criminals revisit crime scenes. We don't want him getting hurt, by the bad guys or the good guys."

"Thanks, Junior. Keep me posted."

"Of course. Drive safe, Maggie."

She smiles at the last bit. That's more like the Junior she knows. She hangs up. She responds to Michele's text: *Just hung up the phone with Junior. Calling insurance now.*

After she initiates a claim, she holds her coffee mug to her face to warm it. The morning air is chilling her nose. She sets the cup down. Movement along the road catches her eye. Someone heading her way. Hank lifts his hand, and the pressure in Maggie's chest is immediate. She doesn't wave back. She'd spent the night tossing and turning, regretting that she'd napped instead of booking tickets Saturday afternoon. That she'd played music instead of doing it after dinner. She could have been out of here first thing Sunday morning, before the police showed up. Before the ugly scene. Staying at Piney Bottoms before was hard. It's become cruel and unusual punishment, and counterproductive. Now she's stuck in Wyoming.

But she doesn't have to be stuck *here.* She can ask Patrick for a ride to Sheridan. Check back into her hotel. Rent a car. Drive down to Buffalo. Push things along with the Buffalo police and their investigation. Keep working on Flown the Coop business from afar until Friday, when she will run like the wind and never come back. She quickly types a search in a new tab: Rental cars Sheridan, Wyoming. In another, she pulls up the Mill Inn site. As soon as Hank leaves, she'll make it happen.

Hank's voice is cautious. "Good morning. Missed you at breakfast."

She looks up. As he draws nearer, she sees he's wearing something odd across his shoulder.

"I missed you there the last two mornings."

He stops short of the porch. Now Maggie recognizes his shoulder ornament as a compound bow and quiver of arrows. They stare at each other. Hank's eyes look tortured. Maggie's are flinty.

"It's bow season. I thought I'd get in a little practice this morning. Want to come?"

His angst is like fingers of flame reaching out for Maggie. She glances down at her laptop. The time in the upper right corner is seven thirty. She opens her mouth to say no, then closes it.

"Please. I need to talk to you."

Like kindling, her yes ignites. "Okay."

"I'm headed there now."

She nods and follows him through a gate and into a pasture behind her cabin, to a grassy section against a stand of pines. There are three targets backed by round bales of hay six feet high. Louise bounds to and fro around the two of them.

Her voice is still flat. "I didn't know there was a shooting range out here."

"Only for bows. We have some heavy-duty backstops for guns, farther from the buildings."

Hank's phone rings. Maggie tenses and looks away. An intrusion from his girlfriend is even worse after his judgment about her tryst with Chet. Never mind that she judges herself and expected him to. It still sucks.

"It's the dealership."

Maggie's insides unclench.

Hank presses the screen. "Hello. Hank Sibley here." He pauses. "She's right here." He hands Maggie his phone.

"This is Maggie Killian."

The Southern mechanic's voice is instantly recognizable. "Good news, Mrs. Killian."

Maggie wants badly to correct the Mrs., but she holds her tongue. "I like good news."

Hank sets down his quiver and nocks an arrow into his bow.

"We found you a part."

Mixed emotions flood her, Hank's nearness causing a short in her circuitry. The Clash's "Should I Stay or Should I Go" was one of her favorite songs as a young teen. The Clash. Appropriate. Running through her head now, it amps up her giddiness and confusion. Lust. That's it. Any time she's within three feet of Hank, she's lust crazy. She needs to go home. Period. "That's great. How soon can you have it installed?"

"Welp, first we gotta get it here. It's in Florida."

"Florida."

"Yes, ma'am. They can overnight it."

"So, tomorrow."

"Actually, no. Wednesday. Overnight in Wyoming takes two days, if they get it out for shipment today, and if the weather holds."

"Weather holds? You mean like snow. It's only September."

"Right. It should be fine. But sometimes it isn't. You just never know."

She squeezes her eyes shut. She hears a thud and opens her eyes again. There's an arrow just left of the bull's-eye in the center target. Louise whines. Maggie strokes her ears.

"So do you want us to order it?"

"Yes. Please." She recites her credit card information.

"We'll get you up and running as soon as it comes in. Don't you worry."

"Thank you." She hands the phone to Hank.

"What did they say?"

"Wednesday. Or Thursday."

"I'm sorry."

"Yeah." Then, despite herself, she smiles. She's becoming as mercurial as Wyoming. It wouldn't have made a difference if the part could come earlier. The police have grounded her until Friday. The part will be installed before she can hit the road. Her voice is almost cheerful as she says, "Fuck my life."

"About that." He lays the bow on the ground. "Um, I was wrong. Yesterday. I'm sorry."

"No argument here. You've got no right to be jealous."

"I don't know what came over me. Seeing you with Chet, well, there's more to it than you know."

Maggie snorts. "To it, or to you?"

"Both."

In her strange new mood, another song from her distant past comes to her. She hums a few bars, then sings a line about a live wire.

"What's that?"

"'Psycho Killer.' By the Talking Heads. I thought it was appropriate."

He pinches his lower lip. "I know you're no murderer."

"Just a slut."

"No." He takes her hand. "You're you, which is exactly who I think you should be."

"You could have fooled me." Her words are light, but her voice is husky. She summons her pheromones. Channels the lust that's tormenting her.

"We've had our rough patches."

"You think?" Maggie laughs and leans closer. *Kiss me, Hank. Kiss me again.*

"But I think we're hitting our stride. And I'm sorry about that kiss. I shouldn't have done that to Sheila or confused things between us. We're friends now. For the first time. And I'm here for you, whatever you need."

His words are like mule kicks, with twice the punch in half the package. Maggie straightens and pulls her hand away.

"Did I say something wrong?"

"No. Thank you." For cover, she points at the bow. "Can I give it a try?"

He stares at her, looking like she's a puzzle piece he can't quite fit in. "Sure." He launches into an explanation of how to hold the bow, sight, and shoot.

Maggie nocks an arrow. "Carbon fiber?"

"The arrows? Yes."

She lifts the bow and extends it in front of her with her left arm, then draws the bowstring with her right. She aims through the magnifying front sight. When she lets the arrow fly, it hits the target within inches of Hank's shot. Louise makes an anguished cry that sounds like a human baby.

"Nice!"

Without acknowledging his comment, Maggie fires three more arrows, each one closer in, until on the fourth, she hits dead center. The focus and effort are a godsend. The heat inside her has cooled. Her pheromones are at bay. Louise is not as good. She cowers at Maggie's feet, moaning. Maggie is perplexed. She's heard of dogs scared of loud gunshots, but never arrows.

Hank has watched silently until then. "Okay, so you're a hotshot. Where'd you learn?"

She shakes off the last of her funk. "Camp champion. Must be like riding a bicycle. But I've never hunted or shot a moving target."

Hank holds out his hand for a turn. "You're one sexy badass, woman."

Just not sexy enough. Maggie relinquishes the bow.

Hank shoots, but his arrow pierces the target farther from the bull's-eye than any of Maggie's shots. He shakes his head. "I'm usually better at this."

Her voice is dry. "I'll bet that's what you tell all the girls. It's nothing to be ashamed of."

"Seriously, besides worrying about you and feeling like an asshole, I got some bad news last night. I think it's messing with my aim." With the bow still in one hand, Hank bends and swipes a tall blade of brown grass. "You may have noticed there's no love lost between us and Patrick Rhodes?" He chews on the stem.

Maggie nods. "Slightly."

"Pretty bad coincidence our biggest competitor on the rough stock circuit has the ranch next door."

"Keep your friends close and your enemies closer."

Hank picks up the quiver and bow and walks toward the targets, Maggie alongside. "Yes. And we found out that he underbid us on the contract for the National Finals Rodeo."

"Which means what?"

Hank pulls an arrow out and returns it to the quiver. "Which means that for the first time in eight years, we won't be the stock contractor for the National Finals Rodeo. Patrick will. It's a really big deal, and he's going to rub our noses in it."

Maggie adds arrows to the quiver from each hand. "That sucks."

"It does suck. And our horses are far better. He has some great bulls. I could have understood if they'd split the contract—I still think our bulls are better, overall, but I could have lived with him getting the bulls contract. But he lumped in his horses on his deal, and the NFR didn't even give us a chance to match his bid."

"Would you have matched?"

He sighs. Arrows loaded, he walks back toward Maggie's cabin. "We couldn't have. It's too low. Sets a bad precedent that leads to unprofitability."

Louise runs ahead of them, tail up, her relief at the cessation of the shooting session obvious.

"So he'll put himself out of business."

"One can only hope. If he keeps this up, someone is going to put him out of business for good, six feet under. I'd be happy with that honor myself."

"Hank, can I ask you something?"

"You can ask. Whether I answer depends on what it is."

"Patrick said your feud goes way, way back. He made it sound like something other than rough stock. And he said if I wanted to know what it was, I should ask you." She almost adds the part about Patrick's suggestion that she could charm it out of him, but she doesn't want Hank focusing on the wrong issue.

"He did, did he?"

"Yes."

"There's your answer, then."

"But you *didn't* answer me."

"You asked if you could ask me a question. I said you could, but whether I'd answer it depended on the question."

Hank's answer is the beginning of a headache for Maggie. "Oh."

Hank stops by the gate to the tape fence around Maggie's yard. "Well, I'm getting back to work. Are we good?"

Maggie thinks of her plans earlier to move to Sheridan, rent a hotel room and car. Hank's apology makes it seem like a whole lot of trouble for nothing. "We are. Except for one thing."

A look of something almost like fear flashes across Hank's face. "What is it?"

"Can I borrow a vehicle to drive into Buffalo? I have to give a statement at the police station. And I may have a few other things to do over the next few days."

Hank relaxes. *What had he thought I was going to say?* "I'll commandeer you something to drive. We've got Mom's old Tahoe. I should have thought of it earlier. You can drive it until you get yours back. If you'll come to lunch, I'll give you the keys."

"That old battle-ax hates me."

"Who, my mother?"

"I'm sorry. I didn't mean that."

"Sure you did. And it's okay. But she doesn't hate you. She acts like that to everyone now. I wish you'd met her before Alzheimer's. She's a different person inside."

His words stir something in her. Memories of her own dad. She pushes them away but not before a thought jolts her. Her dad's health precipitated her retirement from music. Hank's dad's health did the same to him, minus the rehab stints. And now his mother has Alzheimer's. It must be so hard for him. "If you say so."

"Anyway, I'll have a surprise at lunch."

"What?"

"Hence the use of the word surprise."

Maggie has had far too many surprises this week, none of them good. But still, when she opens her mouth, what comes out is "See you there."

TWENTY

Maggie returns to the cabin, cursing under her breath. A lunch surprise. And she fell for it. She has to immunize herself from Hank. Before, her solution was cocaine. Lately, her alcohol consumption is way up, and it had already been over the recommended daily allowance. Mindless sex hadn't worked too well for her either. Exhibit number one: Chet Moore. And she's not the yoga, meditation, or random-acts-of-kindness type. She opens the cabin door, lost in thought.

The back door slams shut.

"Hey," Maggie yells.

She freezes, but only for a split second. Then she runs for the rifle, grabs it, and sprints to the back door. It's closed, but unlocked. She searches her memory. Had she left it locked? Surely she had, as paranoid as she's been after the belt buckle went missing. She looks around the cabin. At first, nothing appears out of place. Then she sees her guitar case. It's unlatched. She opens it.

Her precious Martin is there, and she cries out in relief. *See? I just left the door unlocked. The wind opened it. Then when I opened the front door, the change in pressure slammed the back door.* She lifts her guitar to hold it close, and that's when she notices the peace sign strap is missing.

"Son of a bitch!"

Someone has touched her baby. They've taken her belt buckle and her peace strap, and stolen her inner peace along with them. She hears a bark from the front porch. Louise had gotten trapped outside. She lets the dog in and consents to a flurry of face kisses.

"Come on, girl."

Together they walk out the back door. *I'm an idiot.* Why hadn't she done this in the first place? She might have caught a glimpse of whoever made off with her strap. She scans the landscape. The pasture where she and Hank had been shooting. The forest beyond. Pastures on either side. Horses in one. Cattle in another.

But no humans.

She searches the ground for footprints. There's no trace, except an unlocked back door, unlatched guitar case, and missing strap. She lifts her gaze, concentrating on the near view. The yard is bare of bushes, but her eyes arrest on the tape fence protecting the grass from loose livestock and other hooved creatures. The tape is sagging. She follows it to the right, then to the left. One of the white plastic fence posts is misplaced. It's not stuck in the ground, and it's side by side with the next post, hanging slanted from the tape itself.

Odd. Had the post been like that before? She hadn't done a fence check. Besides, what would a pulled-up post have to do with anything?

And then she gets it.

If someone ran out through the backyard, they had to go under the fence to escape. Which meant lifting it, in a rush. The tape is strung through notches in the posts. She remembers Andy showing her how the posts can move freely along the tape. Now she can visualize a man with an arm over his head, tape in his hand. The post is jerked out of the ground and sliding down the raised tape, coming to rest when it hits the next post in line.

Shit, shit, shit. Someone had run out the door, right as she was coming in the house, and he'd left under the tape, right here, while she was checking her guitar.

She examines the grass. There are no footprints, but could there be depressions from footsteps? She's no tracker. She glides her hand over the grass. It seems crushed to her.

"What are you doing?"

She startles, whirls. Gene is standing inside the back door.

"Why are you in my cabin?"

He holds his hands up. "I knocked. No one answered. I hollered in— you weren't here, but the back door was open. I came to see if you wanted me to saddle Lily for you. It's a pretty day for a ride."

Maggie drops her shoulders, which had risen up her neck. "Sorry. Someone just ran out the back door of the cabin. I'm missing a few things. I'm jumpy."

"What do you mean?" Gene is by her side in a few quick strides.

She tells him about the belt, the guitar strap, and the slamming door, and shows him the fence post.

"Did you tell Hank?"

"No."

"Maggie May, you should have told one of us."

"I was hoping I was wrong, when it was just the buckle. That I'd misplaced it. But I wasn't. Someone is coming in and stealing my things."

He clomps around, but wide of the path she suspects the intruder used to flee, his eyes trained on the grass. He ducks under the tape and keeps walking. She tents her eyes and watches him.

"There's definitely been someone here. Boot prints." He points at the ground. Native grasses, rock, and sagebrush grow beyond the yard, with visible patches of dirt occasionally.

"That could have been any of you guys. Everyone in this country wears boots."

"Not like these. Come here, but be careful. Don't mess up the trail."

She joins him, staring at a print in the dirt. Gene takes a close-up picture with his phone.

"That's a tactical-boot print."

"What's a tactical boot?"

"See the tread at the forefoot? And no square heel print?"

"Yeah."

"Everyone here wears cowboy boots, because we ride all the time. Our prints would have smooth forefoots, and you'd see a differential heel. These are more like hiking boots. Or work boots."

Maggie nods. "I see it."

"Whoever it is wears a wide boot. Maybe a ten or so. We need to call the cops."

"I have an appointment this afternoon to give a statement. I can report it then." She wants further involvement with them like she wants a hole in her head, but this shit is getting scary.

"I heard. Sorry."

She cuts her eyes away. Of course he has. Everyone knows about her rendezvous with Chet now. And those that don't know her are speculating, like the old-timer at the Wagon Box Inn. Did she do it? Hell, even the people that know her are probably wondering. It's exactly what she hadn't wanted to happen.

Gene's voice is gentle, sympathetic even. "But the Buffalo cops don't cover us. We're under the jurisdiction of the Sheridan County Sheriff's Department out here. In Sheridan."

"Great."

"They're not bad."

She rubs her temple. She officially has a whopper headache. "It's a belt buckle. And a guitar strap. They'll laugh at me."

"It's a break-in."

"The door wasn't locked."

"It doesn't matter. Besides, aren't you forgetting something?"

"What?"

"The break-in and theft at your store in Texas."

Maggie scowls. And the sabotage, but she doesn't bring it up. "How'd you know about that?"

"Michele. Do you think they could be related?"

Michele. Best friends don't rely on fresh-out-of-the-box stepbrothers to update best friends on their significant life events, like murdered hookups, cop visits, truck sabotage, and break-ins. Not if they want to stay best friends, which Maggie does. Michele's the only best girlfriend she's ever had. Hell, only best friend of either—any?—gender. She's got to call her. And Junior, dammit, because if there's even the slimmest of chances these events fourteen hundred miles apart are linked, he needs to know. "If they are, I don't see how."

Gene shakes his head, lips in a line. "You've got a big red target on your forehead, Maggie. I'd call the sheriff if I were you."

"You're not me."

"Suit yourself. But if you don't, I have to. And I have to tell Hank."

"Fine. I'll call."

"When?"

"On my way to Buffalo."

"Good. I'll tell Hank at dinner."

"You're pushy."

He grins. "I care about your safety."

She holds up the rifle she's been carrying around with her. "I have this, and Louise. But it would be nice to have a key so I could lock up."

"I can get you that. And I'll talk to Hank. We could move you up to the house with him and his mom."

She bobs her head. "Or not."

Gene doesn't laugh. "About that."

"About what?"

"You and Hank."

Maggie tenses, doesn't look at him. Stares at the cabin, thinks about bolting.

As if reading her mind, Gene walks to the back door. "Me and Hank have been together longer than most married couples. I knew him before and I knew him after you left him with nothing but a scrap of paper in Cheyenne. When he hurt his head at the next rodeo. When his father took sick and died. When we struggled to get this business off the ground. When his mother slipped away and became a different person. When he saw you had destroyed yourself and it nearly killed him. Honestly, for a long time I thought he was going to follow you off the deep end."

Maggie can't help it. She meets his gaze, her eyes searching for any exaggeration in his words.

"He tried to contact you, you know."

She closes the ground between them and grabs Gene's elbow, all pretense dropped. "What? Why didn't he tell me?"

"Pride, I guess. He got escorted out of one of your shows in Denver by bouncers when he tried to go backstage. Cussed out by your agent. And turned away from your rehab clinic because he wasn't family."

"He would have told me."

Gene enters the cabin and checks the doorknob. Now he's the one avoiding eye contact. "Ask him."

A tear slips down Maggie's cheek. "I didn't know."

Gene walks to the front door and examines that knob, too. "He said he sent letters to the only address he could find back then."

She mulls that one over until the answer comes to her. "My publicist. But I didn't get them."

Gene walks from window to window, making sure they're locked. "Now, how was he supposed to know that? He just finally gave up. It was a bad time for him, and he had to get it together."

"Oh God." Maggie scrubs the tears away. Hank could walk up at any moment. She doesn't want him to see her like this.

"And when he found you again in Texas? That's probably the happiest I've ever seen him, by the way. Happier than when he met you, even though you were meaner than a snake." He smiles at her. "But then Hank's always liked a little mean, in bulls and in women."

"I—"

He holds up a hand. "And the worst day? When you sent him back to Wyoming without you last spring. Because he knew then exactly what he'd lost."

Maggie's voice escalates. "But he hasn't lost it. I was scared. I'm here now. Ready for a second chance."

He holds up one finger, then two, then a third. "Higher mathematics tells me this would be a third chance."

She groans. "If he just hadn't hooked up with the Sunday school teacher, we'd be together now. She's a child, Gene. He's dating a child."

"What'd you expect—he'd sit around pining for you? Waste the rest of his life turning down women who weren't you, again? You hurt him. Twice."

"He hurt me!" Maggie drops her face.

Gene shakes his head. "Well now, holding on to that must make it all better."

She knows she hasn't given Hank enough credit, hasn't believed in him enough, and the realization rocks her. She doesn't deserve a third chance.

Maggie doesn't watch Gene walk out, just lies down on the bed and cries softly, until a cold, wet nose pushes against her face.

There's a rapping sound on the screen doorframe.

She yelps.

"The offer still stands on saddling Lily, although I don't imagine you feel up to it now."

"I sure don't want to hang out here." She wipes her tears and stands. Riding Lily sounds Zen. Or as close as she can get to it, with her life like a swarm of mosquitos in a bug zapper.

TWENTY-ONE

Gene makes a step out of his hands and flexes his legs. Standing beside the tall mare with the big belly, Maggie stares at him from under a cowboy hat. He's pretending none of the emotional conversation earlier happened, and she appreciates it.

"Put your foot in my hand. I'm giving you a leg up."

"Ah. Last time I used a mounting block. That worked pretty well." She manages a half smile. The Excedrin she took before she left her cabin is starting to work on her headache.

"We're expanding your capabilities."

Even with his help she struggles to capture the saddle horn and mount gracefully. "Getting on this creature, I'm like a bear on a balance beam."

"Bears are pretty graceful. I was thinking more like a fish flopping around in the bottom of a boat."

She gives him a middle finger salute.

"There's the Maggie I know and love."

"Aww. You love me."

He rolls his eyes. "Stay within sight and shouting distance, in case you have trouble."

"I'll be fine, Grandma."

He pats Lily's rump. "Take Louise with you."

Maggie rides out. She plans to follow the route Hank used for her tour, but that is soon foiled by closed gates. There's no way she's getting on and off Lily without someone around to help. Plus, closed gates could mean bull encounters on the other side. *No, thank you.* Even without bulls, she's nervous as a long-tailed cat in a room full of rocking chairs. Lily seems jumpy, too.

Maggie follows fence line until Louise leads them to an open gate half a mile away to the south of ranch headquarters. The land there is rugged, with deep gulches filled with trees and rimmed with rocky ledges. Louise flushes five white-tailed deer from a draw. Lily snorts and hops, then plants her feet.

Maggie grabs the saddle horn. "Easy, girl." She strokes the glossy black neck.

Lily huffs, then sighs and continues on. The land slopes uphill toward the mountains. As they draw closer to them, the pitch upward dramatically increases.

"Let's just go to the top of this ridge, then we can turn around."

Lily's shoulders roll as she climbs. She stops for a breath and snatches a bite of grass.

"Come on." Maggie nudges the horse with her heels and gets no response. "Yah, Lily."

The mare ignores her. She's stopped in the midst of tall shrubs with sagging branches of deep red berries. Lily shoves them aside to get to the grass underneath.

"Carrying a big foal in there must be hungry business." Maggie gives in and puts the reins over the saddle horn. She snaps a selfie with her body turned so Lily's head is in the shot, then takes a few pictures of the scenery. She shoves the phone back in her pocket. Lily is chewing with determination, her mouth stuffed with grass.

Maggie gathers the reins. "Enough. Let's go." She squeezes with her legs, nudges with her heels, and gets nowhere. She kicks the horse's flanks. Lily keeps eating. Finally, she gathers her courage and smacks Lily's shoulder with her palm. Maggie's hand burns. Lily doesn't flinch, but she slow-walks forward up the ridge.

"Phew. I thought we were spending the night there."

When they crest the ridge, Maggie sees that she's come upon the neighbor's shack across the creek that marks the boundary of Piney Bottoms Ranch, by coming in a big circle in the opposite direction from her ride with Hank. Hank's crazy neighbor's place. She's peering into the distance, looking to see if he's there, when Louise gives a shrill yip. Maggie glances toward the sound. It's followed by a deep roar, then the sound of something large crashing through bushes and onto the trail behind them. Her heart lodges in her throat. It's a black bear—at least she hopes it's a black bear and not a grizzly and wishes she'd asked Hank or Gene about them—that becomes a blur as Lily spins and bolts with far more agility and speed than Maggie would have expected from a very pregnant draft horse.

Her long-ago camp riding lessons didn't cover fleeing the scene of a bear. She clings to the saddle horn and tightens her legs. For a split second, she considers reining Lily in, but she wants away from the bear as bad as the horse does. While the horse is moving fast, it's not smooth. Maggie is coming up onto the saddle horn with every lunge. She pushes down through her feet, fighting for stability. Her legs start to move with Lily's rhythm, and finally Maggie starts to feel more secure and risks a head turn. The horse trips on a rock and nearly sends Maggie over her head before she gets a look behind them. When Maggie regains her balance, she's appalled at the rough terrain. How is Lily even upright?

"Easy, girl." She pulls on the reins and shifts her body position back in the saddle. "Easy now. Whoa, Lily." Maggie is careful to keep the weight of her heels off the mare's flanks, not wanting to accidentally encourage any more pell-mell flight over uneven, rocky ground.

The horse begins to slow. She's blowing so hard Maggie can't hear if there's a bear behind them or not. But Lily would still be running if the bear had followed them. Maggie pants, too. She pats Lily. "Good girl. It's okay."

Lily clatters to a walk. Maggie lets herself go limp for a moment as the adrenaline spike ends.

Just then, a man steps out of the bushes. He's carrying a white five-gallon bucket and what looks like a dustpan with teeth.

Lily shies sidewise before Maggie can react. She lists in the saddle and grabs for the saddle horn. She manages to stay on, but only because Lily stops and turns to face the man.

Lily stretches her neck out toward him.

"Maggie?" he says. "Maggie Killian?"

Maggie pushes the hat that's fallen over her eyes back on her forehead. The man in front of her is wearing faded blue-jean overalls with a long-john top underneath. He's stocky and short. The man who bought her a drink and asked her to sing a song for him at the Occidental. She'd refused. Performing was her old life. She doesn't owe anyone an on-demand show like a trained circus monkey. Still, she squirms a little in her saddle. Chet had been pretty rough on him.

"Rudy."

"You remembered my name this time." He continues advancing toward them until he is right in front of Lily. He sets his bucket and weird contraption down and reaches up to Lily's face.

"Um, she doesn't like you to touch her face." Maggie expects the horse to pull back from him.

Lily holds her ground. Rudy rubs Lily's forehead. The mare's posture is so chill, it's like she's napping.

"What about her face?"

"Never mind." Maggie shrugs. "You scared us. We were running from a bear."

"I was out picking berries and heard galloping. I expected a horse, but not a rider."

Louise appears and runs into the little group. She circles Rudy, sniffing his ankles. Then she growls and bares her teeth.

"Louise, stop it."

The dog's hackles rise. She chokes off her growling and whines.

Rudy backs up a step. "She's protective. That's good."

"She's a disaster. She's the one that chased the bear out after us."

Louise takes up position between Maggie and Rudy, at Lily's shoulder.

Rudy clucks to Lily and feeds her something from his pocket. He takes hold of the cheek strap of her bridle with one hand.

Maggie's heartbeat speeds up again, like it did with the bear. Something about Rudy handling Lily with Maggie on her back feels like a violation. And why is Rudy out here on Piney Bottoms land picking berries anyway? Suddenly, she wants to be back at the ranch with people. Her people.

"Well, nice to see you. I have to go."

Rudy doesn't look up at her. She hears the crunching of Lily's teeth again.

"What are you feeding her?"

"Horse treats. I always carry them out here."

"By out here, you mean on Hank's place?"

Now he looks up. "I live just across the fence. On the other side of the creek there." He points. "And the Piney Bottoms Ranch belongs to Vangie. Mrs. Sibley."

Rudy is the crazy neighbor, Maggie realizes. "You know what I mean."

He steps toward Maggie's knee, still holding Lily by the bridle.

Louise growls again.

"Where are you off to in your big hurry?"

"I have an appointment in town."

Rudy nods. His face is impassive, but his eyes twinkle. "Does it have anything to do with that douchebag?"

"What?"

"He's not good enough for you anyway."

"That's none of your business."

"You and Sheila have the same taste in men."

Maggie's blood boils. She'd thought Rudy was talking about Chet all this time, but obviously he means Hank. Is she that transparent? "And that's none of your business either. So, if you could let go of Lily's bridle, please?"

He holds his hands up. "Sorry. I thought I was helping. You don't look like an experienced rider. In fact, I'm surprised they let you out here by yourself on a valuable broodmare like her."

"I'm fine. She's fine." She neck-reins Lily away from Rudy and gives her a little bit of pressure with her heels. The mare responds slowly, reluctantly, her attention still on Rudy and his cookies.

"You know your way back?"

"Um . . ." Maggie realizes that Lily's flight has left her a little disoriented on the direction back to the stable yard. She hates admitting it to Rudy, though.

"Follow that fence line." Rudy points to a few strands of barbed wire off to Maggie's right. It's a fairly steep descent to it. "You can stay on this ridge until it meets up with it. The trail's more gentle up here, which will be good for your horse. It also goes by a pond, so you can get her a drink of water."

"Thank you." Maggie's voice is stiff as she walks Lily off on the ridge. "Louise, come."

Louise obeys, but she lurks behind them.

Maggie feels Rudy's eyes on her back. She turns.

"You should let someone know she bolted, so they can make sure she didn't strain anything," he says.

"Okay." Maggie rocks in the saddle, urging Lily to walk faster. The mare picks up the pace by the smallest possible increment of effort.

When they're almost out of earshot Rudy shouts, "And good luck on your interview with the police."

TWENTY-TWO

Back at the barn, Paco examines Lily—who keeps her face turned away from him—and proclaims her no worse for her bear flight. He pats her large posterior. "You're bigger than he is, Lily. I bet that ole bear ran away from you faster than you did from him." To Maggie, he says, "Where'd you see it?"

"Out near the crazy neighbor's—Rudy's—place. Eating berries."

"Yeah, that area near Simon's acreage is a great place for pre-winter forage."

"Could it have been a grizzly?"

"Not around here. We ain't got nothing but black bears. Now, the western half of the state, they got grizzlies. A whole lot of grizzlies. They've been known to come all the way into town in Cody. But not here."

"Thank God."

"Did you keep your seat?"

"Yes. I'm fine."

"Let me cool her down for you, since she got a workout. I'll put her up, too."

"If you're sure, that would be great. I'm kind of wrung out."

"I'm sure. The ornery old girl prefers you to me, but she doesn't always get what she wants. None of us do."

"Doesn't she like you?"

"Not really." He laughs. "I make her work. And no cookies."

Lily turns her head and Maggie could swear the horse rolls her eyes at Paco.

"See you at lunch, then. Thanks."

"No *problema*, senorita."

Maggie and Louise walk to the cabin. There's an old tan Tahoe with a note under the windshield wiper parked out front. *Here are some wheels for the rest of your stay. But you'll have to come to lunch if you want the keys. Hank.*

Oh, Hank. After everything Gene told her, she has a sudden urge to talk to Hank. Not tell him she's sorry per se, but to—oh hell, fine, whatever, to apologize. It's like an itch between her shoulder blades, the kind infuriatingly just out of reach. One she needs him to scratch when he forgives her.

Inside the cabin, Maggie checks her phone. It's eleven forty-five. She has a list as long as her arm of calls to make, but there's no time before lunch, which is at noon sharp. She promised Hank she'd be there for his surprise. So, she'll make the calls on the drive to Buffalo. With her headphones, because she's safety-conscious like that. Now it's time to step it up.

She washes her hands, glances in the bathroom mirror, wipes a dirt smudge from her nose, and adds neutral lipstick. Her hair is big, windblown, like she's been riding a horse. She fluffs it some more. When on a ranch, do as the cowboys do. She arrives at the main house with five minutes to spare.

"No," she tells Louise, when the dog tries to squeeze past her into the house.

Louise flops to the ground and gives her sad eyes.

"Those things won't work on me. I know you'll be fine."

The smell inside is tantalizing. From the doorway to the dining room she sees why, as Trudy sets a platter of fried chicken next to mashed potatoes with a pool of butter on top. There's also dishes of green beans, creamed corn, and, of course, Trudy's biscuits. Her stomach growls.

"Excuse me," a male voice says.

Maggie turns and sees Tom trying to wheel Mrs. Sibley in.

Maggie is blocking the door. "Of course. Sorry."

Mrs. Sibley grouses, but to no one in particular. "Who's she? Family only."

Behind Mrs. Sibley, a familiar face appears. Dark eyes crackling with energy under pixie hair of the same color. Exquisitely feminine elfin

LIVE WIRE (MAGGIE KILLIAN NOVEL #1) 137

features and pink bow mouth. Whipcord thin body muscled and strong enough to control a racehorse, Maggie knows, because it's Hank's sister, Laura, and she's a jockey. Or was a jockey, until she retired not too long ago.

Laura says, "Mom, it's not family only. We eat with the hands."

"They're the same as family. She's not."

Tom pushes Mrs. Sibley into the room. With Laura near her, Maggie is shocked at the resemblance between mother and daughter. She shouldn't be. They're family. And she knew very well what Laura looked like, since she'd met her in Texas, at Michele's. But Maggie hadn't noticed the resemblance the first few times she was around Mrs. Sibley. Now it's unmistakable.

Laura spots Maggie. She smiles, but it's a waste of facial muscles, because the expression in her eyes makes it clear she doesn't mean it. "Maggie. Hank said you were visiting."

"Hello, Laura. I wouldn't say visiting. Stranded. My truck broke down when I was up here on a work trip."

"Oh. Work trip. Gotcha."

Stung, words fly from Maggie's mouth like a flock of larks startled from a tree. "How are things in New Mexico? With the ranch and camp? Mickey and Farrah?"

If Laura is impressed that Maggie remembers she runs an equine therapy camp on a New Mexico ranch with her husband, Mickey, and teenage daughter, Farrah, she doesn't show it. "Fine. Thank you."

Heat rushes to Maggie's face. She's confused and a little hurt. She and Laura had gotten along fine in Texas. What had happened to make her treat Maggie like a fungus? She moves to the far end of the table, to the seat she'd chosen at her other meals, away from the Sibleys, next to Gene.

He pats her hand. Is that sympathy she sees in his eyes? Andy nods hello on her other side. She smiles at him. Then Hank enters the dining room and relief floods through Maggie.

"Hey, sis. Hi, Mom." He kisses the two women and waves to Maggie.

Maggie tosses her hair, ready for Hank to make everything better for her with his mother and sister. She feels warm and tingly with anticipation.

Hank turns back and gestures for someone to follow him in. "Sheila, let me introduce you to my mother, Evangeline Sibley, and my sister, Laura."

Maggie's tingles turn to a thousand stabbing needle pricks.

The young blonde enters with a starlet wave.

Hank had invited Maggie to the grand introduction of his girlfriend to the family. *Is this his damn surprise?* If so, it's fitting in a week of bad ones. Obviously, things between Hank and her aren't quite as wonderful as Maggie thought.

Sheila's voice leaves a pink bubble gum aftertaste in Maggie's mouth. "Hello, Mrs. Sibley. Laura. So wonderful to meet you both."

Laura stands, and the two women hug. Sheila leans down to Mrs. Sibley and kisses her cheek. Mrs. Sibley grimaces and pulls away. Maggie smiles.

"Time for my lunch," Mrs. Sibley says, giving Sheila the cold shoulder. "We can't wait on your father any longer. Bless the food, Hank."

Over their mother's head, Laura and Hank share a pained look.

Sheila says, "Laura, how nice you can visit."

Laura sits back down. "It's good to come back home for a few days. Summer camps are finally over. Mickey is at a conference on the newest innovations in inseminating horses. My daughter Farrah is off to the University of New Mexico. The timing is right."

"That's great." Then Sheila sees Maggie. Anger flashes over her features and is just as quickly gone. "Oh, Maggie. Hi. I heard you're squatting in the guest cabin."

Maggie opens her mouth in an O, then snaps it shut. If you can't think of anything nice to say, better not to say anything at all, her mother always says. She'll follow her advice this once.

Mrs. Sibley's voice is a bark. "Grace, Hank."

Hank launches into a prayer as if it's an emergency and he's driving the fire truck. Maggie seethes at him from her end of the table. Some surprise. He's either clueless or mean. She doesn't know which to hope for.

After grace and filling of plates, Sheila beams at Hank, then turns toward his mother. "Your son was so sweet last night, Mrs. Sibley. He took my parents and little sister out to dinner with us."

Mrs. Sibley doesn't look up.

"What does your little sister do?" Laura asks in the uncomfortable silence.

Sheila giggles. "Oh, she doesn't do anything but go to school. She's only nine."

Under her breath, Maggie mutters, "They're practically twins."

Gene nearly chokes on a bite of fried chicken and hits her knee with his.

Laura's voice is polite and friendly. "Oh wow. Are you the oldest?"

"No. I have a big brother. Like you do."

Sheila's perky voice and expressions are making Maggie nauseous. She plans her getaway in case she heaves. She'll go right behind Sheila, and if she happens to blow on that pretty blonde hair, well, it won't be Maggie's fault.

"How old is your brother?" Laura asks.

"Thirty-five."

Laura's lips move like she's talking to herself. Then she says, "So if he's thirty-five, and your little sister isn't even ten yet, that's twenty-five years between them. And your mother is . . ."

Sheila shoots a look at Hank, who's studying his mashed potatoes. "A saint." She puts a hand on his arm. "Hanky Panky, don't forget we've got Chet's funeral this afternoon. We need to get going as soon as we finish lunch."

The idiotic nickname almost does it for Maggie. She tenses, ready to flee.

Hank's voice is taut like a barbed-wire fence. "We're fine."

Maggie relaxes. She may be pissed at Hank, but that doesn't stop her from doing a little internal fist pump that he's unhappy with Sheila. The woman is easy to root against.

Sheila fakes a pouty face. "Somebody isn't happy he has to skip a hunting day with his buddies."

Laura swallows a miniscule bite of corn from the child-size portion on her plate. No wonder she's so lean. Maggie glances at her plate. Three pieces of chicken and a generous scoop of all the sides. A biscuit, plus one she's already downed. She's always had an overactive metabolism, but she feels like a glutton.

Laura puts her fork down. "Hunting season. God. It's like all the men in Wyoming go into rut when the animals do."

Sheila leans toward her. "Tell me about it. Hank got all cranky and ran off and left me after our date last Thursday so he could spend the night in the mountains and be ready to go after an elk at dawn."

"What'd you get?" Laura asks him.

Hank mumbles around one of Trudy's biscuits. "Skunked."

Maggie frowns. Hank told her he hadn't been hunting yet. His eyes lift slowly and find hers. They stare at each other for a long moment. He shakes his head at her, just barely. A chill ripples through Maggie. Hank hadn't spent last Thursday night with Sheila, and, unless she's drastically misreading things, he'd lied to Sheila about hunting. All of this after he'd seen Maggie with Chet. The chill sneaks up and over her scalp.

Where had he been?

No. She can't get sucked into caring. Not her problem.

She pushes her plate back, her fried chicken nearly untouched. She's had enough of this drama. She's got to get away from here. She'll convince the police to let her go back to Texas. Hell, she'll find the killer herself and gift wrap it for them if she has to. *But what if it's Hank? Nonsense. Hank's no killer.* So she'll have to find the killer who isn't Hank. Meanwhile, she can put Bess up for sale online. If the truck sells before it's fixed, she'll use the money for a plane ticket and to ship her junk back to Texas.

As if reading her mind, Laura says, "Maggie, when are you going back to Texas?"

Maggie glances at Hank. He's no longer looking at her. *Good.* He's the only one who knows she's been ordered to stay until Friday, and why. "As soon as I can, but I'm waiting on a part. Until then, I'm staying out of the way, and preparing all the great junk I bought here for a fall antique show."

Gene wipes orange Cheetos dust from his hands onto a napkin. His was the only plate Trudy had added them to. "And keeping Lily exercised. I hear she got her speed work today, Maggie."

Hank's head snaps up. "What?"

"Maggie took Lily out, and they ran into a bear. At least that's what Paco told me."

"Is that true?" Hank asks her. His eyes are navy blue, dark and dangerous.

Paco brandishes a biscuit. "Truth."

Saved from answering, Maggie reaches out to her plate. She fills her mouth with potatoes, hoping to end the conversation.

"Were you hurt?"

Maggie motions to her full mouth. Hank folds his arms over his chest. She shoots him two thumbs-up.

Sheila's eyes are darting back and forth between the two of them. It's been five whole minutes since she was the center of attention. A crease between her brows deepens.

Gene isn't done ratting Maggie out. "Maggie's had a big day. Someone's been stealing her things out of her cabin, and today she spooked him in the act."

Maggie mutters, "Traitor. You said I had until dinner."

Hank comes off his chair. "How come I'm just now hearing about this?"

Maggie picks up a chicken leg and stabs it in his direction. "This is the first time I've seen you since it happened."

"Gene?"

"Ditto." Gene doesn't even look at his partner, but the corner of his mouth is twitching. "Oh, Maggie, I almost forgot." He digs in his pocket, comes up with a key on a ring with a leather strap, and hands it to her. "Cabin key. So you can lock up."

Gene is using me to get Hank riled up. Sheila's face contorts, turning her features unlovely, and suddenly Maggie understands. Gene doesn't like Hank's girlfriend. But after their earlier conversation, she doesn't think Gene's Team Maggie either.

Hank forces words through gritted teeth. "Did you call the sheriff?"

Gene says, "Maggie promised she'll call them this afternoon."

"And I'm going to." She locks eyes with Hank, the contact giving off sparks like two light sabers in battle. "They didn't take much."

"It happened here on the ranch. The Sibley ranch. You and I need to talk about this."

Maggie leans toward him, her tone and clipped words the equivalent of squaring off and bumping chests. "After I get back."

"Where are you going?" Laura's face scrunches.

"Oh my God, Hank told me about your police interview!" Sheila's voice is exultant and her eyes reptilian. "That you were the last person to see Chet alive before he was murdered. That's so sad. And he is—was—totally hot. You naughty, naughty girl, spending the night with him."

"I, um . . ." Hank says, then trails off.

Laura's eyebrows are in her hairline. "You're a suspect in a murder investigation?"

Maggie glares at Hank, then Sheila. "Just giving a statement."

Sheila smiles, then bats her eyes. "Then how come they're not letting you leave town until Friday? Isn't that almost like being arrested? House arrest or something?"

Maggie wants to kill Hank for flapping his big mouth. This must be why Gene doesn't like Sheila. The woman is a passive-aggressive beast. Maggie wants to kick her ass all the way back to the elementary wing of the Sunday school where she teaches kids to ask themselves "What would Jesus do?" *Not act like you, mean girl.*

"Pie, anyone?" Trudy is balancing two on each forearm. "Chokecherries are in season. I have homemade whipped cream and vanilla ice cream coming up, too."

Maggie wants to kiss the cook for the timing of her interruption. "Make mine a double."

"It's pie, not whiskey, Maggie," Laura says.

Maggie's voice is badlands dry. "Who said I was talking about pie?"

TWENTY-THREE

After taking time to write a quick Craigslist ad for Bess, Maggie feels marginally less homicidal, although the ad gouges a chunk out of her soul. She and Bess have been together for a lot of years, bad, better, and pretty good. Emotional survival, however, comes first. She closes her eyes and clicks to post, then takes a second to breathe.

When she's recovered, she puts Louise out and hustles to the Tahoe. It's way too early to leave for Buffalo to give her statement, but she doesn't want Hank to corner her about the intruder in her cabin. Or for any other reason. She's still seething about him arm-twisting her to come to lunch with his mother, sister, and girlfriend. Some surprise. He had to have known how bad it would suck for her. Or he should have. Either way, she's pissed. Not to mention rattled about his lies. The only question is whether he's lying to Sheila, to her, or to both of them. Killer dimples and eyes like the deep end of the ocean don't make up for all that.

No, she definitely doesn't want to be alone with that jackweed Pinocchio.

She jams earbuds in her ears before she's even exited Piney Bottoms Ranch. She has so many people to call she can't keep them straight. Sheridan County to report the break-in. Junior with Lee County in Texas. Gary. Michele. And, while she's at it, her mom and Boyd deserve to hear from her, too. The "who first" decision is made for her when her phone rings.

She braces herself and answers. "Hey, Gary."

"Maggie, what is this bullshit—" is all she gets before static breaks up the call.

"Gary? Hello, Gary?"

The line spits, crackles, and squeaks.

"If you can hear me, I'm so sorry. I should have gotten back to you sooner. And I hate that you've gotten dragged into this business with my shop. I'm coming home soon. I'll call you. I promise." She smiles. Dodged a bullet on that one. *Thank you, Wyoming and T-Mobile.*

Washboard road bumps jostle her phone out of her hand. It lands near her feet. She leans over, trying to keep one eye on the road, but she can't quite reach it. She slides it toward her hand with her left foot. Still no dice. Steering straight and slow down the middle of the road, she dives down for it. Her fingers knock it further away, toward the door. She stretches, wiggling her fingers.

A horn blares. Maggie shoots upward and jams her brakes at the same time. Her head cracks into the underside of the dash and then the steering wheel. The Tahoe jerks to a stop. She jukes around the wheel and her mouth drops. She's on the left hand side of the road, nose to nose with a huge white truck. The first black person Maggie has seen in the state of Wyoming is barreling toward her window. She deserves an ass-chewing. She rolls down the window, ready to woman up.

"Listen, I'm—" she starts to say.

"Lady, are you okay?" The man's pupils are dilated and nostrils flaring, but his voice is nothing but concerned.

"Yeah, I'm fine. I'm so sorry."

"I nearly hit you."

"More like I nearly hit you. Really, I can't apologize enough."

His expression changes, and his head tilts slightly. "Hey, I know you."

"I don't think we've met."

"You look so familiar. My names Brendan Tucker. Does that ring a bell?"

"Nope. Again, my apologies. But I'm late for an appointment."

"Yeah, I gotta get to a funeral." Maggie wonders if it's Chet's he's going to, like Sheila and Hank, but she doesn't ask. "But you be careful. If you run off the road here, it won't go well for you."

For the first time, Maggie notices the steep embankment to her left, the one she'd been careening toward before Brendan honked. Beyond the twenty-foot drop-off is fast-moving Little Piney Creek. "Thank you. I will."

Shaking, she rolls her window up and accidentally gooses the accelerator, spraying gravel. The man is going to think she's crazy. Or on drugs. She's been both before, but right now she's only dazed. Completely sober, and she nearly kills herself, after all the years she survived drunk and strung out. It's funny, but she doesn't laugh.

She gives herself until she reaches paved road to pull herself together before she makes her next call. Deputy Junior. She presses his number in her Recents. As his number is ringing, she passes a series of houses with small acreages on the creek. The houses are well kept, if modular and bland, with four times their value in motorized vehicles out front. RVs, ATVs, snowmobiles, tractors, and trucks, with at least one at each place that looks like it hasn't run in her lifetime. In the last front yard before the turn onto the highway, five trucks are arranged in order of their apparent death. Over-the-hill, vintage, antique, ancient, and decomposing.

Her call to Junior ends up in voicemail. "I had a break-in up here in Wyoming. Some of my things were stolen. I thought you should know. Call me."

Maggie defies death merging onto the seventy-five-mile-per-hour inter-state in between a truck hauling a trailer full of black cattle and an eighteen-wheeler weaving in the wind. She white-knuckles the steering wheel through a gust of wind. Four calls to go. Boyd, Mom, Sheridan County, and Michele. She sets the Tahoe's cruise control to one mile per hour over the speed limit. A ticket outside Casper on the trip north taught her not to target nine miles over in Wyoming like she does in Texas.

When the controller catches, she rolls her shoulders and neck. "Ah."

Cruise control is a luxury Bess doesn't offer, one in a long list. Seat heaters. Defrost. Airbags. A back seat. Maybe trading up to a newer vehicle wouldn't be all bad. She looks around the front seat and dash of the Tahoe. Compared to Bess, it's completely devoid of personality. Bess has style. Atti-tude. A one-of-a-kind paint job. When Maggie crawled out of her second rehab stint with only the decrepit shop to her name, she found Bess under a mountain of trash in the barn. It was love at first sight. The first bright spot in a long dark spell. She nursed the truck back to health while she healed. Bess and the new Maggie are synonymous. Vibrant, unapologetic throw-backs, two star-shaped pegs in a world of round holes. Contemplating parting with her—well, it shows how close Maggie is to the end of her rope.

Maggie's eyes burn. The feeling is more than guilt, loss, or sadness. She's scared of the person she was before Bess and Flown the Coop. Back when she'd lost Hank and was circling the drain. Now here she is again, and one of her safety nets is up for sale and the other violated and vandalized. But let the chips fall where they may, she has to get back to Texas and save herself, with or without Bess.

She'd just prefer they make the trip together.

Heaving a sigh, she returns her mind to her list and tackles it in order of difficulty, Mom first.

Her mother answers on the first ring. "Maggie, honey."

"Hey, Mom."

"Are you home?"

"No, just calling to give you an update."

"And?"

"I'll be home by Sunday or Monday."

"You're going to just miss the Lindenhauers' big estate sale." Her mother delights in monitoring local papers for deaths and property liquidations in the area. Maggie has a news clipping service that does the same thing online, but some of her best junk has come from Charlotte's finds.

"Do you want to shop it for me?" Maggie developed her eye at Charlotte's knee.

"Oh, honey, I wish I could." Charlotte doesn't elaborate.

Maggie puzzles this over. The mom she knows would jump at the chance. But she's not up for twenty questions. "Listen, I don't want to alarm you, but I have some bad news."

Charlotte's voice goes up an octave. "Are you hurt?"

"No, nothing like that. There was a break-in and some damage at Flown the Coop. Probably some drunk teenagers. I just wanted you to hear about it from me."

"Oh, honey, I'm so sorry. And right before the fall antique show."

"No worries. A minor speed bump."

"Does this have anything to do with that new antique store that's opening near you? The owner is bragging about how he's going to put you out of business. I try to ignore that kind of gossip, but he burns me up."

"I don't know what you're talking about."

"Hmm. He's been telling people he tried to buy your place but you turned him down."

Maggie remembers an offer from months before. She hadn't taken it seriously. A man with far too high an opinion of himself had walked in and demanded to know how much she wanted for the Coop. His visit was like an earthquake, his vibe and mannerisms so at odds with the store that she'd had a vision of it falling down around their ears. She'd sent him packing. She dredges up his name. "Rickey Sayles?"

"That might be him."

"So he bought a place. Good luck to him, then." He'll need it, because she's going to make him eat his words about putting her under.

The low-gas indicator lights up on the dash. *Damn Hank.* She'd been rushing to avoid him. They stock bulk fuel for the equipment at the ranch, and she could have filled up there.

"Have you talked to Michele?"

"Not today. Why?"

"No reason. Can we plan on dinner Monday night? Remember, I need to talk to you."

"Monday night."

"Yes."

Maggie almost argues in favor of a phone call. She stops herself. *Don't be a shitheel.* "Monday it is. Bye, Mom." She ends the call.

A sign announces Buffalo. She veers onto the first exit and stops at the Maverik. While gas is pumping, she takes the easy way out with Boyd. A text.

Sending up smoke signals from WY. Having a run of bad luck. Haven't seen any Crow. Home in a week.

Maggie feels moderately virtuous and completely drained. Both living parents dealt with. She assumes the nonliving ones are keeping an eye on her whenever the fancy strikes, but she whispers a hello to them both anyway.

"Maggie, isn't it?" a male voice—it's always a male voice here—asks.

She puts her hand on the gas nozzle and pretends not to hear the guy.

"Excuse me, miss?"

He didn't call her ma'am. She can reward that. "Yes?" She turns to him. It's the Occidental bartender. Patchy face.

"Were you at the Ox last week?"

"You introduced me to Koltiska."

"I thought it was you. We keep running into each other. The Wagon Box, here."

"I keep running into everyone I've met." The gas nozzle clicks off. She replaces it on the pump.

"You're not at the service."

Maggie screws on the gas cap and shuts the cover. "Excuse me?"

"Chet Moore's funeral. I thought, well, you know."

"I barely knew him." She punches no to decline a receipt.

He cocks his head, like he's listening to something far away. "I heard you two were getting married."

Maggie busts out laughing, then reins it in. "That's preposterous. Where do people come up with this crap?"

"Sorry."

"Not your fault."

"Well, if you're not getting married, I guess that's good news for the rest of us."

"Not for long." She lets herself back in the Tahoe.

"Wait."

She leaves the door open a crack.

"Let's trade numbers."

She smiles. One thing she won't miss about Wyoming is the edge of desperation in the men, like she's the only source of warmth for a long cold winter. "Let's not. You take care now." She closes the door and pushes the electric lock button.

TWENTY-FOUR

The Buffalo Police Department is across the street from a church for the Jehovah's Witnesses and next door to a bowling alley. Up the street is the looming hulk of the Bighorn Mountains. *A town that has it all.* She still has fifteen minutes before her scheduled statement, so she heads into downtown. She can tackle the next call on her list. Sheridan County Sheriff's Department. Only she forgot to Google the number before her drive. She remembers using the Wi-Fi at the Occidental and parks out front. When she has signal, she makes the call. After several transfers, she's connected to a deputy. Bad cell reception eats his name, but she doesn't let that slow her down.

"I'd like to report a break-in and theft."

The reception improves. His voice is deep with an underlying sense of fun threading through it. "A burglary."

"Same difference."

"Address?"

"I'm not sure. Piney Bottoms Ranch."

The bartender strolls into the Occidental, seeming not to notice her.

"Who am I speaking to?"

"Maggie Killian. I'm staying in the guest cabin there."

"Ah. Okay. We can send someone out to the Sibley place to take a statement later this afternoon."

"I'm . . . out today."

"Okay. I'll have someone call you to schedule it, then. I'm off the rest of the week. Any items we should be on the lookout for in the meantime?"

"A 2002 Cheyenne Frontier Days belt buckle."

There's a long silence. "That's the year Hank won. I don't think I've ever seen him wear the buckle."

"He hasn't. I've had it."

She can hear a smile in his voice. "Anything else of value?"

"A guitar strap embroidered with peace signs."

"Seriously?"

She scrunches her eyes shut. Exactly the reaction she'd feared. "It has great sentimental value. But there's nothing else."

"Gotcha. Maggie Killian. Burglary. Guest house. Piney Bottoms."

"You know where Piney Bottoms is?"

The deputy laughs. "Part of our job to know the county. Piney Bottoms takes up a nice chunk of it. I'll have someone call."

"Okay, then. Thank you."

Maggie drives back to the police station. She trudges into the station like she's heading for a saltwater enema. To her surprise, the process is anti-climactic. A city employee hands her a piece of paper and a pen, and directs her to a small room with a table and chairs one small step up from the folding variety to write her story.

When she's almost done, Lacey appears and mashes a chair across from her. Seated, he looks taller than when he stands. "You get it all down?"

Maggie pushes the paper toward him. "Want to double-check my work?"

He reads it, nodding, then hands it back. "This will do."

"Have you gotten any good leads?"

"I'm not at liberty to talk about the details of the case at this stage of the investigation."

"I'll take that as a no."

Lacey shrugs. "Honestly, our best lead is you."

Her face feels like boots a size too small on a shoe stretcher. "You're cracked."

"You're the one with means and opportunity."

"Means?"

"His tire iron."

"He was killed with his own tire iron?" She remembers Chet telling her he kept it in his truck bed. Handy for him, but unfortunately handy for someone else this time. She shudders. Poor Chet. He might not have been the one for her, but he wasn't a bad guy, and no one deserved what he got.

"Yep."

"Well, I was at the hotel. So was his truck. But I had no motive to kill him. And anyone could have gotten hold of his tire iron." A face flashes into her mind. Dimples. Navy blue eyes. She rejects it. Hank may be a liar, but he's no killer.

"What if I told you we had a witness that overheard the two of you arguing, and him refusing to see you again?"

"I'd say someone is very confused or a big fat liar-liar-pants-on-fire."

"I'd say it's motive."

"If that had happened, it's motive to tell him to fuck off, not to kill him. But it didn't happen."

Lacey stares at her with his strangely milky eyes.

Maggie leans forward on her palms. "Come on, detective. Doesn't Chet have a string of unhappy exes, one-night stands, and cheated-on husbands and boyfriends? He could have work rivals. Creditors. Maybe he was black-mailing someone. Dig deeper. I'm not your killer."

Lacey keeps staring at her.

"Did you talk to the slap-happy meth head and her brothers? The ones who were pissed at Chet?"

"We haven't been able to track them down."

"I'm sure you'll find them soon. It's a small town. But it's not *my* town. I wish you Godspeed, because my livelihood depends on me leaving Friday."

"I wouldn't get in too big of a rush, Ms. Killian."

"Can't I sign some sort of agreement that I'll come back if you need me to? It's not like I'm going to Costa Rica. Just Texas. Wyoming's ideological sister state. Maybe it would help if you thought of it as 'South Wyoming.'"

Lacey stands, a short man once again. "I'll be in touch."

Maggie makes a strangled sound in her throat. "I'll never get to go home unless I solve this for you. You're not even trying."

"I don't recommend it. This is a police matter."

"Maybe. But it's also a Maggie matter when you're holding me hostage in Wyoming and taking your sweet time."

His voice grows hostile. "You'll think *hostage* when I arrest you for interfering with a police investigation. I'm not afraid to throw your famous butt in jail." He sucks in a breath, and when he exhales, the hostility drains from him. "Good day, Ms. Killian."

Fuming and mumbling suggestions for what inanimate objects Lacey should have sex with, Maggie finishes up her statement. She stops to have it notarized with a department admin. As she waits, her mind is in turmoil. She has no experience catching murderers, but she'd spouted off a list of potential suspects for Lacey without even trying. What's wrong with him? Is he lazy? Stupid? Or is she just expedient because she's from out of town?

"Sign here," the admin says. She presses her finger so hard the tip turns red, indicating a line in her notary book.

Maggie scrawls her signature. "Am I done?"

"All done," the woman chirps. Her eyes are beady and birdlike, too, but her hair is the curly steel wool of a black sheep.

Maggie reminds herself it's not this woman's fault. She chokes out a "Thank you."

"You're welcome, Ms. Killian."

Maggie rounds the corner to the lobby. Patrick Rhodes is coming down another hall, their paths set to intersect.

"Hey, Patrick," she says.

The big man ambles up to her. "Hey, pretty lady."

"What are you doing here?"

"Giving a statement on the Chet Moore case."

"Me, too."

He nods. "They asked me about you."

"Surprise, surprise. What did they ask?"

"Just what I knew about your actions and whereabouts, since you spent his last night with him and all."

"They told you that? Assholes."

"No. I heard that over breakfast at the Busy Bee. I felt half-famous by association."

"That's great."

"Sorry. No offense. Let me make it up to you. Buy you a drink."

She remembers his solo lap of the Wagon Box and the way he'd given her the creeps at the end of their date. "Why, so you can show the mystery harlot off to your cronies?"

He grins, his laugh lines crinkling. "Actually, there's a few things you may want to know about Chet Moore."

She feels her eyebrows shoot up. Creeps or no, this is an opportunity she can't pass up. "Lead on."

Maggie drives the Tahoe downtown and parks behind Patrick, just short of the creek.

She joins him on the sidewalk, and he points to a neon sign for a bar called the Century Club. "They're just about always open."

A cloud of cigarette smoke greets them, flashing Maggie back to playing for coins in a tip jar and shots of cheap whiskey. The interior is tight, poorly lit, and dominated by a wooden bar on the left and a pool table on the right, where a lanky cowboy is breaking as a redhead leans on her cue, waiting. The decor is mainly courtesy of big beer. A Miller High Life clock. A neon Coors wall hanging. A Pabst Blue Ribbon light fixture over the pool table. Flyers announcing beer specials cover nearly every inch of the mirror behind the bar. Maggie sees—barely—two men and a woman seated on stools lift a hand in greeting, not at her. Patrick lifts his in return.

The bartender tosses his long brown ponytail over his shoulder. He plonks two napkins on the counter and nods at Patrick.

"Budweiser." Patrick points at Maggie.

Maggie pulls a credit card out of her wallet. She scans the bottles. This isn't a craft-beer-and-specialty-liquor type of place, but she tries anyway. "Koltiska and tea."

The bartender grunts and swings his head toward a bright yellow poster-board sign. CASH ONLY is written in block print. "Jack all right?"

"Fine."

Patrick puts a twenty down.

Maggie says, "Thanks."

A text comes in for Maggie from Hank: *I called the sheriff. Theft on our property is my business.*

Maggie types fast and hits send: *Beat you to it.*

"There's your boy." Patrick raises his beer toward a 2002 Cheyenne Frontier Days signed photograph of Hank.

Maggie is drinkless. The bartender is refilling whiskeys for the patrons along the bar. "Not my boy."

"Didn't you play there that year?"

"Yep. How did you know?"

"I saw your show. You were amazing."

"Still am."

He swallows half his beer in one chug. "And I heard about you and Sibley."

Maggie gyrates her upper body over the bar, trying to catch the bartender's eye. "Ancient history. I thought we were here to talk about Chet."

"Keep your panties on, if you can. Although I hear you have trouble with that."

"Fuck you."

He chuckles. "If you want, it can be arranged."

"Don't hold your breath." Maggie's starting to regret coming with him. Especially sober.

The bartender wipes down an infinitesimal square of counter space that's already clean.

Maggie clears her throat. "Excuse me. Jack and Coke when you get a chance?"

The bartender nods and keeps wiping.

"What does a woman have to do to get a drink around here?" She snaps at Patrick, angry with him and the slow service.

"This is a local hangout."

"And I'm not local."

Patrick purses his lips.

"Can you help me out?"

Patrick taps the bar with a knuckle. "Darrell, can you get my guest a Jack and Coke, please, seeing as you already have my money?"

Darrell the bartender shoots Maggie a glance. He pours her drink, then hands it to her. "I don't believe we've been introduced."

"Darrell, this is the world-famous Maggie Killian." Patrick's emphasis on *world-famous* borders on sarcastic.

Maggie imagines Patrick's head filling with helium until it explodes. It helps.

The woman a few stools down from Maggie leans out around her companions. She takes her time checking Maggie out. Maggie returns the favor. Tattoos cover the woman's arms and shoulders under her tank top. The short spiky blonde hair, sullen expression, and skeletal frame look familiar to Maggie.

Darrell puts up the Jack. "Maggie Killian? Never heard of her."

"Maggie, this is Darrell, the proprietor of one of the finest bars in the west. Since 1900."

"Never heard of him."

Darrell throws back his head and laughs, his lips retreating donkey-style over tobacco-stained teeth. His merriment ends in wet, phlegmy coughs. Without another word, he walks to the jukebox.

"Friendly." Maggie slams her mostly-Coke onto the bar. She should have ordered a double.

"He grows on you."

"Like a wart, or more like athlete's foot?"

"Speaking of things you want to get rid of, how come you haven't ditched Wyoming?"

"The part for my truck won't get here for a few more days."

"I've got one just like it, you know."

"One what?"

"Old Ford pickup. What year do you drive?"

"1942."

He drains his beer and sets it down loudly on the bar.

Darrell hollers, "Refill?"

Patrick matches his volume. "Do bears shit in the woods? One for Maggie, too." He lowers his voice. "Mine's a forty-four. Doesn't run. We could probably scavenge you a part off it."

Maggie knows better than to hope, but her heart leaps. "I need a driveshaft."

"Yeah, I think mine might work."

"That would save my life." Never mind that she's under town arrest by the police. She isn't counting on the mail-order part until she sees the whites of its eyes. The Mill Inn has an ancient Ford truck out front, she remembers. If Patrick's truck doesn't yield a driveshaft, maybe that one will, for the right price? "I just listed my truck on Craigslist. I figure if there's a collector in the area who wants to buy it quick, that could solve my problem, too."

Patrick raises his eyebrows. "Craigslist? No one around here uses that."

"What do they use?"

"There's a kind of swap-meet AM radio show you can submit on."

Maggie rolls her eyes. "I need a bigger audience."

"A lot of people use UpCycle on Facebook."

"UpCycle." Maggie sends herself a note to post Bess there. "Got it."

The jukebox suddenly blares Darrell's choice, too loud for the time of day and nonexistent crowd. Patrick drums the beat on the bar top. Maggie's voice singing "I Hate Cowboys" rings out. "The ones from Wyoming try taking girls home, and they don't think the word no applies." She hadn't realized how true that line was when she wrote the song. It feels like a dang prophecy now.

"What's so funny?" Patrick asks.

She shakes her head. No reason to explain the joke, but she suddenly likes Darrell. "The life, times, and tragic death of Chet Moore. Time to spill."

Darrell sidesteps behind his bar. He draws another Budweiser for Patrick and brings Maggie her refill with a wink.

In the silence after the song ends, Patrick wipes foam from his lips and says, "Mr. Chet Moore."

The conversation amongst the people next to them stops.

Maggie feels a coolness descend over the bar. "Did you know him?"

"Of course. He's from Sheridan, but everyone around here knows him, even back when he was just a boy. Played football at Sheridan High. Linebacker. At the University of Wyoming, too. Until he blew out his knees, people thought he'd go pro. He dropped out of college after that and came home. Kept himself busy with the ladies and nightlife when he was around, although he worked two weeks at a stretch in the oil fields, if I'm not mistaken."

"Does he have any enemies?" Maggie hears a snort from a few stools down.

"Plenty. He's always been too pretty for his own good. Makes it easy for him to move from woman to woman. But I guess I don't have to tell you that."

Maggie's been cast as the female lead a time or two in the story Patrick's telling, including this time. Chet had chased *her*. But she keeps her lip zipped and finishes her second drink.

Patrick continues. "So there's more than a few women unhappy with him, plus from time to time he doesn't check first whether they've got a fella."

"Got any names?"

A barstool scrapes back. With no warning, the spiky blonde inserts herself between Patrick and Maggie. Up close, her dark eyebrows clash with her hair. She's a dead ringer for Xena the Warrior Princess after a bad flu, albeit with an edgier hairdo. Her shoulders flex. When she speaks, her voice is tight with rage. "You the bitch with Chet the other night? The one the police think killed him?"

"Whoa now, missy. Calm down." Patrick tries to block her access to Maggie, but he's too slow.

Xena shoves Maggie in the center of her chest with two stiff fingers. The two men, even bigger than Xena, although just as undernourished, move in close behind Xena on either side.

Maggie's had her share of bar fights, or so she's been told, since she doesn't remember a single one of them. She doesn't budge. "What the hell is wrong with you?"

"You fucked my boyfriend, and you fucked up my life, that's what's wrong." Xena's nostrils flare, drawing Maggie's eyes to a delicate gold nose ring.

"Who are you?"

The woman spins on a boot heel. "Come on, guys."

They follow the angry, malnourished Amazon toward the exit, each of her steps rattling glass on the shelves. A wallet chain swings from her hip, hitting her thigh well below the exposed pocket and frayed edge of her blue-jean shorts. The men are WWF rejects. Tattooed arms wasting away jut out of their wifebeater Ts, untucked over jeans. The three are wearing identical biker boots, like they're part of a gang, or at least a dress-up club.

Of course. Maggie shouts, "Hey, you were at the Bison Inn. I saw you slap Chet."

The blonde shoots Maggie the bird as she and the men push through the exit.

Patrick deadpans, "You're not real popular in here."

"Tell me something I don't know."

The door shuts behind the three people the Buffalo police can't seem to find, one of whom just might have bashed in Chet's head with a tire iron only a few days ago.

TWENTY-FIVE

Patrick and Maggie are the only patrons left in the Century Club.

Darrell sweeps the used cups left by his departed customers off the bar. "You owe me another round for driving off all the customers."

Patrick laughs. "Whoops, sorry."

Maggie says, "Switch me to Diet Coke, and I'll keep drinking."

"And Jack?" Darrell asks.

"Nah. Got a long drive." And no desire to bump uglies with Patrick.

"Bud," Patrick says.

Maggie fans her shirt. She hadn't realized she was sweating. "Who was that?"

Darrell's soda dispenser spits and coughs, then emits a stream of Diet Coke. "Lisa Whitefeather."

"Who is she to Chet Moore?"

"Girlfriend, on and off. Since high school. One of several."

Maggie does the math, or at least guesstimates. "Ten years?"

Darrell sticks a straw in the Diet Coke and pushes it to Maggie. "Plus a few."

"And the toughs with her are her brothers?"

"Yep."

Ten plus years is more than long enough to get sick of Chet sleeping around, or cheating on a sister. Maggie feels a frisson of excitement. Maybe she really *can* crack this case and break herself out of limbo—she's already further along than the police just by finding Lisa and her brothers. But she can't be reckless. About the Whitefeathers or Lacey's threat to toss Maggie in jail. "Should I be watching my back?"

"I think they just like to talk tough."

Patrick hands Darrell another twenty. "Glad I hadn't told you about her yet, Maggie. Who knows what she would have done if she'd heard me talking about her. I know her name, but I didn't know her face."

Darrell spirits the twenty away in a cash drawer.

Maggie nods. "An angry woman."

"At you, anyway."

"Chet and Lisa seem . . ."

"Like an odd couple?"

"At the very least."

"Chet and Lisa were mostly off. She gets around."

"Shocking."

"Couple of kids by a couple of guys. But she and Chet always seem to end up together again. Like Sodom and Gomorrah." Darrell holds up two bags of Lays. "I think you need to spend a little more money to make things up to me. Chips?"

Patrick puts his wallet on the counter. "You've about cleaned me out."

Maggie pops open a bag and munches a potato chip, thinking. Lisa. Kids. Could one of them be Chet's daughter? It might explain her anger. And if he wasn't doing right by the two of them, it could be a powerful motive to do him harm, especially when mixed with drugs. "Who could tell me more about them?"

Darrell leans between them. "His mama."

"If she's heard the rumors about Chet and me, she'd probably make me about as welcome as Lisa did."

Patrick shakes his head. "She hates Lisa. I've courted Beth Ann a time or two, and you should hear her complain about that girl."

"His mother? Isn't she . . . older?"

Darrell makes an mm-mm-mm sound. "She's a looker."

Patrick says, "Had Chet real young. Maybe I could vouch for you. She works just down the block at Reride."

Maggie polishes off her Lays and licks her fingers. *Or I could lie about my name.* She doesn't want Patrick along for the ride.

Darrell eyes her empty bag. He tosses a Snickers bar her way. She catches it. "On the house."

"Thanks." Maggie tears into the Snickers like she's been on a week-long fast. She wishes she had a do-over with Trudy's lunch chicken.

"Welcome. If I were you, I'd talk to his crewmates over at Crazy Woman Exploration. They live together on shift. Know each other's business."

"Good idea. And maybe a landlord? Or a roommate?"

"He doesn't have either of those. Inherited the family ranch when his pa kicked it a few years back."

"Why didn't it go to his mother?"

"Jeb Moore owned it before they married. And long after they divorced."

"So who gets it now that Chet is gone?" Maggie's no lawyer, but having just been through the distribution of Gidget's estate, she's pretty sure the ranch would pass to the child, unless Chet willed it to someone else.

"I'll bet Beth Ann can tell you." Patrick stands. "Come on, I'll give you a ride."

Maggie stares into her Diet Coke. A heavy silence falls. Patrick doesn't seem to notice. Maggie looks up at Darrell.

He nods. "Gotta get something from the storeroom." He disappears through a door toward the back of the establishment.

Patrick cocks his head. "What storeroom?"

Maggie puts a hand on his arm. "I need to talk to Beth Ann alone."

"You're gonna get buffaloed again. You need me to make sure your drinks are served and people talk to you."

"I'll be fine."

"If you're trying to tell me you're not interested, I hear you. But I didn't get where I am by taking no for an answer."

Maggie almost sings the line of her cowboy song. "I'd expect no less. Thanks for the drinks. And the information." She slings her bag over her shoulder and makes for the door.

Patrick's spurs jangle as he walks behind her. "Good luck, Maggie."

During the short walk to Reride, Maggie remembers the driveshaft Patrick promised her. *Shit.* Well, even if he gave it to her today, she couldn't get it up to Sheridan to the dealership before they close. She'll text him later and arrange to pick it up tomorrow. A sign in a window announces she's reached Reride. It's only four fifty-five, so Maggie pushes the door. It doesn't open. That's when she notices an index card taped inside the glass door: CLOSED FOR FUNERAL. NORMAL HOURS TOMORROW.

TWENTY-SIX

Well, shit on a stick. Nothing more Maggie can accomplish in Buffalo today, then. She retrieves the Tahoe and sets off for Piney Bottoms. She hasn't driven north for five minutes before her phone rings.

"Hello?"

Michele's voice is far too clear, so Maggie can't miss the irritation in her tone. "You're in so much trouble, missy."

"Super. Let me put my headphones in so I can enjoy every second." Maggie steers with her knees while she gets set up. "Okay. What did I do now?"

"You talked to the police without having counsel present."

It's terribly inconvenient for Maggie that Gene and Michele have discovered they are siblings. Both had been lonely onlys before and are now practically joined at the hip. So, duh, Maggie doesn't need to fill Michele in on Chet's death. Or the cop's visit. Or probably even the last time she visited the loo. "I'm sorry?"

Michele sounds more like the Mexican side of her family when she's upset. "*Mierda.* The cops are not your friends. You should have called me the second they showed up. I could have found you an attorney. Or stayed with you on speakerphone." In addition to being a best-selling author, Michele is also an attorney. And an annoying overachiever, from Maggie's point of view.

"Michele, I didn't kill the guy. I didn't even see who did. Honestly, I don't know anything about it."

"It's a *murder* investigation. It doesn't matter if you did it. They need a suspect. They have all the power. You could go to jail. For life. Or worse."

Maggie almost asks Michele how long is worse than life in jail. "Calm down. You're going to blow the speaker on my phone."

"This isn't funny."

"I know. I'm sorry. You're right. I should have called. My brain froze when they showed up."

"You should have called when you found out he was murdered. Much less when they showed up."

"When you're done boxing my ears, can you tell me what I should do now?"

Michele growls. "Where did you leave things?"

"I went in and did a written statement today."

"Let me guess—still without a lawyer."

"You're my lawyer. So that's a good guess."

On Maggie's right, Lake Desmet looms, like a miniature ocean in a moon crater. She'd read about it in a pamphlet in Sheridan. It's a natural lake, the undrained basin between two creeks, formed from a collapse over an underground coal seam fire. Around the shores, the red hills are rugged and barren, without a tree in sight other than the anemic ones planted at a few houses on widely spaced tracts. The wind has died down. The late afternoon sun throws sparkles on the rippling surface of the water. It's calm. Peaceful. A stark contrast to Maggie's life.

"Being your lawyer is giving me a headache." Michele's sigh is withering. "Do they have any suspects?"

"Just me, apparently."

"They told you that?"

"A Detective Lacey said I'm the closest thing they've got."

"This is serious."

Maggie signals too late as she takes the steep, winding exit ramp off the interstate. "I know. But they're ignoring the obvious. I came up with a list longer than his johnson, which I don't think is saying much, without half trying. Starting with the guy's nutso ex. And did I mention the victim is that young cowboy I spent a night with?"

"Your hookup is the victim?"

"Yes. His name's Chet. It feels disrespectful to call him my hookup now that he's dead."

"Did they read you your rights or anything else weird or scary?"

"No, unless you count being on town arrest through Friday, at a minimum. And them threatening to throw me in the pokey if I interfere with their investigation." Maggie slows the Tahoe by Fort Phil Kearney, then stops altogether for two Angus cows crossing the road in front of her. They leisurely chew their cud and deposit cow patties halfway. She honks. They lift their tails and waddle off.

"I count those."

"I thought you might."

"Okay, give me a name. I'll call them."

Maggie almost argues with her, then changes her mind. Michele on fire is a force of nature. She wants the inferno on her team. She gives her Lacey's name. "And, Michele, thank you."

"You're welcome. I hear you talked to Junior, too."

"I did. And left him another message. I'd already told him about my truck being sabotaged, but I needed him to know about the break-ins."

"Yes, I heard about those, too."

Gene is nothing if not thorough. A fly fisherman whips his line back and forth over his head, then lets it settle on the waters of Little Piney Creek. He waves at Maggie as she drives past him kicking up a cloud of dust.

"Hopefully the adjuster has contacted you about going out to the shop."

"Already taken care of. And your goats are alive and calling Lumpy 'Daddy.'"

"What would I do without you?"

"You'd be an even bigger menace to society. Did you talk to your mom?"

"Yes, why?"

"Hey, Rashidi's on the other line. I'll call you after I've talked to Lacey. Try not to draw any more attention to yourself in the meantime, okay?"

"Who, me? Never."

TWENTY-SEVEN

Louise is so excited to see Maggie that she chases her tail in a circle until she falls in a heap.

"You're not the smartest dog I've ever met." Glancing up the slope to the main house, Maggie sees Hank's truck. She hustles into the cabin to minimize the chance of interaction with him or other humans, but shuts only the screen door. Earlier, she'd told him she'd talk to him later about the break-ins. Now it seems like a crappy idea. The weather is a perfect seventy degrees. She might as well enjoy it, because it will be hotter than Satan's house cat when she gets back to Texas.

She's jacked up and motivated to regain control of her life, so she sets up her laptop and jots down a to-do list, drumming her short fingernails between items as she thinks.

1. UpCycle Bess
2. Text Patrick about driveshaft
3. Mill Inn about their truck
4. Crazy Woman Exploration?
5. Beth Ann Moore
6. Avoid Hank

She's made it through number one—posting Bess to UpCycle—when there's a knock on the doorframe of the cabin. Louise wags her tail and goes to greet the visitor. Maggie closes her eyes and prays for a natural disaster, just in case it's Hank.

"Maggie?" It's Andy's voice.

She cancels the prayer. "Hey, Andy. Come on in."

"Um, maybe you could meet me out here?"

Maggie's instantly suspicious of another bad surprise. But his request makes sense. He's religious. The cabin is small. There are no chaperones for their mixed-gender interaction. "On my way."

She opens the door, relieved to see he's alone. "What's up?"

Andy scuffs his feet. "I was wondering . . . could you give me another guitar lesson?"

"Of course. Is now okay?"

"If it's not a bother."

"No bother. I'll just send Louise out to keep you company while I get the guitar."

Louise is enthusiastic about the plan. Maggie stops to watch them through the screen door. Andy throws sticks for Louise, patiently coaxing her to bring them back instead of running off with them. The game continues far past when Maggie would have grown tired of it. A warm glow spreads in the center of her chest. Boy and dog. It's a winning combination.

She returns to the porch with her Martin case. Andy joins her, cheeks pink from running around with Louise. She hands the case to him, unopened. He unfastens the latches as carefully as an altar boy walks down a church aisle with a lighted candle.

He licks his lips then caresses the guitar. "It's beautiful."

"Thanks. I've had it since I was about your age, I'd guess."

He lifts it from its velvet cradle.

"The first thing we have to do is make sure we take care of her. That conditions are right." She explains the ideal temperature and humidity and shows him the monitor. "Wyoming in September is heaven for guitars."

His wide-mouthed smile reveals crooked teeth. He closes his lips quickly, but the corners keep tilting up.

"We'll wipe it down when we're finished, but for now, all we need to do is tune it." Maggie does it by ear. "Sounds good tonight, don't you think?"

"Very."

She wipes Vaseline on her left fingers and offers the jar to him.

He mimics her actions. "You play so nice. Could you, um, play something? Before me?"

"What would you like to hear?"

"Any hymn. I like them all."

Maggie grins. How had she come to this place where her adoring fan was requesting covers of religious tunes? In the last year of her solo performances, she'd played all originals for crowds in the thousands. But whatever this nice young man asked for, he would get. They'd covered "Amazing Grace" last time. The only other hymn she remembers in its entirety is "How Great Thou Art."

"I lost the strap, so watch how I hold it. It will feel a little different when you try it than it did last time."

He watches her intently without answering.

She strums a few chords then starts singing. Andy's eyes are wide and shining. By the time she reaches the first chorus, he's swaying and singing along with her. He keeps singing for the rest of the song.

When the last note dies out, she hands him the guitar. "Show me what you remember from last time."

Andy takes the guitar, holding it like a lover. Within a few minutes, he's figured out how to balance the instrument without its strap and re-mastered the chords for "Amazing Grace." They move on to "How Great Thou Art."

Watching him fumble his way through the song, Maggie's soul feels lighter. Sitting outside with this scenery and this gentle soul—this is how religion should be. She'd be a front row regular at any church that could make her feel like this.

After half an hour, Maggie says, "It's dinner time. I was going to make myself a turkey melt. I've got chips and salsa, too. Care to have a porch picnic?"

"Um, that would be nice."

"Do we need to let Trudy know we're not coming?"

"No, it's leftovers night."

"Okay. You keep practicing. I'll be right back."

She hurries inside and assembles turkey melts in a hot skillet. While they're cooking, she pours waters and takes them outside, then returns to flip the melts. She tucks the half-eaten bag of chips under an arm, balances a bowl of salsa on a plate, and delivers them as well. Andy sounds stronger and more confident. She gives him a thumbs-up. Finally, she piles the turkey melts onto a second plate. She sets them on the porch table and sits. Andy is putting away the guitar and latching up the case.

Maggie tears a bite off a turkey melt from the pile. "Is it a full house up there tonight?" She jerks her head toward the main house.

"Hank's not back from Sheridan." Andy takes a melt off the pile.

Chet's funeral. With Sheila. But his truck is parked at the house—they must have taken her car. "Ah. Did anyone else go?"

"No." He stuffs half a turkey melt in his mouth.

Maggie looks away. Manners apparently aren't enforced at Andy's family table. She flips a tiny piece of cheesy tortilla to Louise. It's a terrible throw, but Louise snatches it out of the air quick as gunpowder. "So, Andy, are you a hunter?"

He nods. A string of cheese hangs from his lip. "Yes, ma'am. I mean yes, Maggie."

"Have you gone yet this year?"

"I went Friday morning, real early. Paco covered for me." He frowns.

"What's wrong?"

"It's . . . nothing. Just a thought."

"Go on and tell me. It looks painful in there."

"It's bow season."

"So I gather."

"I don't have my own."

"Yes?"

"Hank let me borrow his."

"How nice of him." Maggie is not inclined to think favorably of Hank yet, so her voice is dusty dry.

"You don't understand."

"Obviously. Why don't you tell me?"

His face radiates agony. "Today at lunch, Hank's girlfriend said he told her he was up on the mountain hunting. But he couldn't have been, because I had his bow."

For a moment, Maggie exults. *Suck it, Sheila. He lied to you, not me.* But then all his unaccounted for hours crash down on her. Where had Hank spent the night if he wasn't hunting, after he'd seen Maggie with Chet?

"Did you see Hank that morning?"

"Not until I got back from my hunt near on lunchtime. I got an antelope." He smiles, but it's watery.

"Congratulations. Here at the ranch?"

"Yes, ma'a—aggie." He stumbles over his mishmash of words.

She keeps her voice light. "And everything seemed okay with Hank?"

Andy stirs the salsa with a chip. "Not really."

"What do you mean?"

He looks up at her suddenly, the tension ebbing from his face. "Come to think of it, he must have borrowed Gene's bow."

"Why's that?"

"Because he had blood all over him. You know, on his arms and clothes." He returns his attention to eating, satisfied he'd solved the mystery, crunching through all the chips within minutes.

Maggie throws the rest of her melt to Louise. She's too nauseous to eat now. Hank had told them at lunch he'd been skunked on his hunt. So why did Andy see him covered in blood?

There has to be an innocent explanation. Just damned if she knows what it is.

TWENTY-EIGHT

After dinner, Andy leaves. His revelation about a bloody Hank has Maggie wound up. She crawls in bed with her guitar and songwriting notebook. Sipping Koltiska on ice, she hums a melody to match her mood, then picks it on the guitar in G minor with augmented chords, which Louise sings along with.

> *When you tell your truth*
> > *It comes in twos*
> > *That way you*
> > *Don't have to choose*
> > *Now your double*
> > *Is my trouble*
> > *Make it go, make it go away*

She jots down the words then writes *"Double" by Maggie Killian* at the top of the page. By the time she finishes roughing out the song, she's deliciously, gloriously, totally drunk. The empty Koltiska bottle sits on the bed beside her. Even in her inebriated state, though, she knows when she's on to something, and this song is *something*. It's moodier than most of what she used to write. Hell, she's moodier than she used to be. She's a closing-in-on-middle-age woman with a life that's gone off the rails. She's earned her moody creds. Fuck happy. Fuck ironic. Fuck everything.

"Fuck yeah." She plays the song again, singing in full voice.

Louise growls.

"Don't be so sensitive." Her voice slurs a little. She rests her head against the wall. "Whoa."

A knock at the door seizes her breath. *Not Hank. I can't face Hank.* She pretends she isn't there.

Louise keeps up a low, snarly growl.

After a minute, the knock sounds again. What if it's the person who stole her buckle and strap? The rifle is in the corner. She stands. The room wobbles like she's trying to surf. She weaves over to the gun and rests a hand on the barrel. Maybe this isn't the best idea. Her bedside lamp is on. She was singing at the top of her lungs and playing the guitar. The Tahoe is out front. Whoever it is knows someone is here.

She calls out, voice cracking. "Who's there?" She clears her throat, irritated that she's being a wimp. Louder, she repeats, "Who is it?"

The squeaky female who answers is a surprise. "Sheila."

Maggie picks up the guitar, plays a *wah-WAH*, then puts it on the open case, without falling over after it. Sheila's possibly the only person she wants to see less than Hank. She tries hard to sound sober and indignant. "I'm in bed."

"This will only take a minute."

Fine. You want some of this, you got it. Maggie pads to the door in bare feet and a worn white T-shirt that shows off her long, lean legs. She's never been scared of skin, and she's not putting on clothes for Sheila's sake. The young bimbo is not her favorite person, especially after forcing her out of bed.

Maggie throws the door open with the lamp backlighting her form. Louise presses against her ankle. In a husky voice, she says, "Someone better have died."

Sheila is in a black knit dress and black boots, her hair clipped in a messy fall. Her eyeliner feathers below her eyes like she's been crying. "He did. His funeral was today. But then you know all about that, don't you?" Sheila's eyes pop. "Don't you have a robe or something?"

Advantage, Maggie. She loves the role of aggressor. The cool night air rushes in. Her nipples harden and she arches her back. "How nice of you to think of me, but no, sadly, I don't." Even though it's chillier than she'd like, Maggie turns on the porch light and steps outside. Louise follows. "You, back in the house."

Louise slowly walks back in, head down.

Maggie lets the screen door shut behind the dog. She turns back to Sheila, moving into her personal space. "Now, what'd you drag me out of bed for?"

Sheila steps back, stumbling when her boot heel catches in the planking. Maggie catches her by an elbow, then grabs the other. She pulls Sheila close, most of her nearly naked body touching Sheila somewhere.

"You smell like a distillery."

"You don't like it?" Maggie knows well the impact of her sexuality. It doesn't discriminate on the basis of gender. She disturbs everyone, whether in a good way or a bad way, and right now, she's enjoying Sheila's discomfort.

"Let go of me. What's wrong with you?"

Maggie makes a purring sound in her throat. She disengages slowly. "You seem to be having a strong reaction to me. Don't worry, honey, that's natural. You should see what being this close to me does to a red-blooded man."

"Like Chet?"

"Hmm. You seem about his age. Did you go to school with him?"

"I did, as a matter of fact. He was . . . nice."

"You're the only one who thinks so. You must have been friends. So do you know anything about him having a daughter?"

Sheila's face blanches. "No. Who's saying that?"

"He did. When he asked me to marry him."

"You're full of it."

Maggie leans toward Sheila again. "Hey, did Hank tell you about us?"

Sheila twists away. "He did. He said it's all in the past."

Maggie straightens and runs the bottom of one foot up the inside of her calf, stopping at her knee in a half tree pose. It's suddenly very breezy between her legs. "That's cute."

"You need to stay away from him."

"Why? Are you afraid you can't hold on to him?" Maggie licks her lips. "Maybe I could share. The three of us might have a good time together."

"Are you some kind of *lesbian?*"

With the alcohol coursing through her veins, Maggie can be anything. "I'm an equal-opportunity fuck, Sheila darlin'. It's one of my many charms."

"You're a sick . . . witch, and I want you gone from here."

"Sheila, do you think Hank always tells you the truth?"

"I mean it. Tomorrow. You leave. Or I'm going to tell the cops you confessed to me that you killed Chet."

"You do you. I'll do me." Maggie laughs. "Maybe I'll do someone else, too."

"You've already *done* enough."

"We'll see." She twirls on tiptoe.

"Oh my God, cover your ass. And put on some underwear."

"You're the one who dragged me out of bed." Maggie winks over her shoulder. "Something to remember me by." In the distance, a tall woman with long dark hair, dressed entirely in white appears. "Wait." Maggie reaches out toward her.

Sheila's expression mirrors Maggie's. Surprised. A little frightened. "What is it?" Sheila turns, following Maggie's gaze.

Maggie peers harder into the darkness, then blinks to focus. The woman disappears. Maggie's unsettled, but she covers it with a grin. "Wouldn't you like to know?"

TWENTY-NINE

Maggie wakes to a crushing headache and a bad, bad feeling. She pats the bed around her. Her hand strikes glass. Cylindrical glass. The Koltiska bottle. She must have drank it all. She keeps patting. Next, her hand finds her notebook and pen. She pushes herself up. Songwriting. The bad feeling returns. If she was writing, she had to have been playing her guitar, too. Her guitar. Where is it? Had she crushed it in her sleep?

Squinting, she looks around her. The guitar isn't on the bed. She gets up on her hands and knees. Her head pounds and the bed spins. On one of its rotations, she catches sight of the guitar lying across its case. Safe. On another rotation, she sees Louise lying at the door with her head on her paws.

Relieved, she lowers herself onto her elbows and presses her cheek into the quilt. Her mouth is dry. The water glass on her bedside table looks upside down from this angle, but she can tell it's empty. She drags herself off the bed and stumbles to the kitchen to refill it. The bad feeling returns.

She lets Louise out, then, as she's climbing back in bed, she has a flash of memory. Herself, on the porch. Feeling angry and vicious. Sheila there, shell-shocked.

Oh God. Sheila. She'd toyed with the girl, taunted her, punished her. Not that Sheila didn't deserve it for dragging her out of bed to order her off Piney Bottoms. But Maggie isn't proud of indulging herself. If this was a test of her emergency response system, then she's uncovered a weakness in her coping mechanisms. Maybe she isn't as wise, strong, and steady as she thought. What if she'd been out somewhere? If someone had come along with a dime bag and she'd had a pocketful of change? *Dear God, protect me from myself.*

The last thing she remembers from the night is imagining Hank alone in his bed a few hundred yards away. She had an idea. She could crawl in with him and remind him of her best qualities. Fuck him so hard he wouldn't even be able to whimper the name of his wrinkle-and-gray-free girlfriend.

She hadn't. The younger Maggie would have.

Maybe she is strong and steady enough. But man oh man. Hank is going to kill her when he finds out the things she said. If he doesn't already know.

Maggie peeks out her blinds. Lily is pacing in her paddock. Maggie feels a longing to saddle the horse and ride far, far away, if only she wouldn't barf the second she walked out her door. She closes her blinds. Sheila threatened to lie to the cops about Maggie if she wasn't gone today. Maggie puts a cool hand to her forehead. Screw Sheila. Maggie feels like dog crap, and she's not going anywhere.

She chokes down a banana and coffee with Excedrin, then forces herself into Coop business to keep her mind off last night. Once she gets to work—processing orders, emailing with the adjuster about her claim and her college-age helper about packages to mail, and uploading new items to the website—time speeds up. Her stomach doesn't reject the food. After three glasses of water, she starts to feel somewhat better. Good enough to look at Facebook. She's surprised to see fifteen notifications, roughly fifteen times her normal haul. They're inquiries about Bess.

I saw that truck last week. It's fine. So are you. Can I get a test ride?

Delete.

Hey gurl, nice wheels. Do you take cheks? I'll pay full price for delivery.

She Googled the address in the middle of nowhere in northeastern Wyoming.

Delete.

More of the same. Delete. Delete. Delete.

Ms. Killian, We resell classic vehicles. I'm very interested. Please call. Rod w/ HotRod Motors

So she calls, and Rod is legit. Scary legit. Wants-to-come-see-Bess-today-and-take-her-away-forever legit. Makes-her-stomach-hurt-so-bad-she-knows-she-doesn't-want-to-sell-Bess legit. She stalls him until Wednesday afternoon. By then she'll know for sure whether she'll be able to get a driveshaft before the cops let her leave, from Patrick, the custom-parts shop, or Mill Inn. Which reminds her of her list from the night before. She picks up where she left off: number two.

She shoots Patrick a text: *Do you have the driveshaft? Maybe I can pick it up this afternoon, if so?*

Mill Inn: she pulls up the Contact Us form on the Mill Inn site since she's not in the mood for a phone call.

I was a guest last week. Random question. Your old Ford pickup out front— what year is it, and would you sell the driveshaft if it will fit my truck? I could have a replacement sent to you ASAP, but I'm broken down and need to get my truck fixed and be on my way back to Texas.

Crazy Woman Exploration: she jots down the number and address.

Beth Ann Moore: she hunts for the woman's contact information online, but with no luck. This isn't unprecedented, in Maggie's experience. She does her fair share of online people-searching, since she tracks obituaries in hopes of getting first looks prior to estate sales. Numbers are getting harder to find with the widespread use of cellphones, and if people don't own or lease homes in their own names, their addresses aren't instantly available either.

Maggie opts not to spend money on a people-finding website. She'll try Reride, see if they'll give up Beth Ann's info. And if the past is any indicator, she's much more likely to be successful in person than on the phone. She fries the last of her tortillas, turkey, and cheese in a skillet and eats them while driving into Buffalo.

As she pushes the front door of Reride open, a bell jingles. She smells something with a sweet just-out-of-the-oven scent as she enters a huge unpartitioned space with flickering fluorescent lights. Sales merchandise crowds the floor. Women's clothes. Men's. Saddles and tack. A section for cowboy hats. Tall shelves of footwear. Books. Jewelry. Knives. Trinkets, kitsch, and whatnot. Above an opening on the far wall, a sign reads THE COLD DISH FROZEN YOGURT.

And she'd thought her own Flown the Coop was an overload to the senses.

A curvy, fit woman with a chic gray haircut that matches Chet-gray eyes pops up from behind a circular rack of blouses. "Welcome to Reride. Let me know if I can help you with anything. All T-shirts are half price, on account of tourist season is over." She picks a hanger off the rack and waggles a pink shirt at Maggie. The words CRAZY WOMAN are emblazoned across the chest. "Crazy Woman. It looks like it fits you."

It takes Maggie a second to realize the woman means the shirt, and not the words on it. "Thank you. I'm actually looking for Beth Ann Moore." Maggie steps closer. A large box of blouses is sitting on the floor in front of the woman.

Her smile sparkles, and she juts a hip in her tight jeans. "You're looking at her."

Maggie had expected to come, hat in hand, begging for Beth Ann's phone number, address, or work schedule. Chet's funeral was yesterday. Wouldn't a grieving mother be in the fetal position under layers of blankets in a cave-like room this soon after losing her son? What is his mother doing at work? And she's not just *here,* she's perky. Her attitude, her breasts, and her butt.

Maggie masks her thoughts with a smile. "Oh, good. I hope it's okay I came here. My name is Maggie Killian. I'm so sorry about Chet."

"Maggie Killian? I just read an article about you on the internet. You look great. Obviously my son thought so, too, if the rumors are true about you two."

"Um . . ."

"I can't believe it. My son sleeping with someone famous like you. That's so cool."

Maggie takes a few steps and presses a hand against a pillar. The woman is giving her vertigo. "Well, yes, um, thanks, I guess. That's not actually why I came by. Or not really."

Beth Ann eyes her up and down. "You don't look as old as I thought you would, either. Maybe this fitted shirt would work for you?" She puts the pink one back and holds up a baby blue shirt the size of a postage stamp.

"No, thank you. I don't do bare midriff. But I'm only thirty-seven."

"Oh, well, that's not so bad. Chet was about to turn thirty."

"A very mature thirty."

Beth Ann puts a hand beside her mouth like she's telling a secret, but she doesn't lower her voice. "Half the women my age would have jumped in the sack with him, too, or so they tell me. Don't be embarrassed. He was a beautiful boy. A good-looking man. His dad, Jeb, was like that, too. *Exactly* like him. Both of them complete horndogs until the end."

"I'm . . . sorry?"

"Me, too. If Jeb could have kept it in his pants, we might have stayed married." She snatches a yellow blouse with fancy white embroidery from a different display and thrusts it at Maggie. "Try this one."

Maggie takes it, holds it up to herself. At least the size is right, even if nothing else about it is.

"But I'm getting what's mine in the end, anyway."

"Excuse me?"

"When me and my ex divorced, I got squat. He'd inherited his family ranch young. Before we were married. And when he died, he left it to Chet."

"I see."

"But with Chet dead, I figure it's mine now. I've already moved my stuff back to the house. Honey, I don't think yellow's your color. Why don't you try this orange one?" Beth Ann snatches back the yellow, replacing it with an identical blouse in orange.

"That's . . ."

"Great, thank you, I know. I've just got to figure out what to do about the big fat mortgage Chet put on the place. And a stack of bills on the kitchen table, unpaid. I sure can't afford the payments. Naughty boy. It's not like he needed money. Had a ranch of his own that was free and clear until he stuck that thing on it. Mind you, he couldn't afford to ranch it and had to lease it out for grazing to cover the taxes, but he had himself a good job. His salary better not just have been paying for that fancy new truck of his. Although I guess that's mine now, too. I hope so, because I drove it to work today. And his bank statement right there on the table doesn't offer me much comfort. His account is drier than the Powder River in August. I'm about to pull him out of the grave and snatch him bald-headed."

Mortgage? That was new information. Along with everything else Beth Ann was vomiting up. Maggie had worried the woman wouldn't talk to her at all. Now she worries she'll have to shove a sock in her mouth to stop her. "Which bank is it? Maybe they'll refinance."

"Help me? I don't think so. It's Rocky Mountain National. They closed my account there after I bounced a few checks. Assholes."

"I understand."

"Well, I'm going to miss the boy. Really. But I always figured he'd outlived his time by about a dozen angry husbands already. Or at least one breakup too many with that Indian skank."

"Lisa Whitefeather?"

"The one and only."

"She doesn't look Indian."

"She's not. Not really. Her dad is one quarter Cheyenne. If that. He hangs on to that family name like a drowning rat to a piece of driftwood. And the way he dresses native. I'm probably more Indian than him."

Maggie nods, thinking she and Lisa Whitefeather are both watered down too much for membership in their respective tribes. "People are saying that I killed him. I just want you to know that's not true. Besides that one night we spent together, I didn't even know him. And I'm very sorry he's dead."

"I figured. What kind of woman bashes a man's head in, anyway? That's some pretty angry stuff. Messy, too. Hey, we have some new scarves that would look great with the white streaks in your hair. They're sparkly."

"It was all just awful." Maggie follows Beth Ann to a rack of scarves, considering her comment. It's true. Very messy. She still hasn't washed the outfit she wore to and from the Bison Inn that night. She ought to gift wrap it and drop it off at the police station with a note saying *NOT COVERED IN CHET MOORE'S BLOOD. LOVE, MAGGIE.*

In a cheerful voice, Beth Ann says, "Course, if you did do it, God will send you Satan's way, and they don't need my help. So I figure one way or another, you'll get what's coming to you. If you did it. I think purple's your color." She throws a scarf over Maggie's head, then tosses a tassled end over her shoulder.

"Which I didn't."

"Great. And that's definitely the look for you. You're going to buy it, aren't you?"

"Um . . ."

"I'm paid on commission."

"Just one last question. Does Chet have a daughter?"

Beth Ann's good humor slips for the first time. She scowls, revealing her age in a spider web of creases on her face. "Are you saying I look like a grandmother?"

Maggie isn't in a position to alienate Beth Ann. She touches the purple scarf around her neck. "I'll take one in red, too."

THIRTY

Maggie exits Reride oddly exhilarated, two scarves richer and forty bucks poorer. On the street, she pauses, her mind swamped with information. She'd hoped to learn something about Chet and Lisa, so she could paint Lisa as a viable suspect to Lacey. Her first salvo in a the-other-guy-did-it defense. But she'd gotten more than that, at the same time as nothing damning about Lisa. Beth Ann, a ranch-grubber with a heart of stone. Chet's empty bank account and new mortgage.

Where had his mortgage proceeds gone, besides to the shiny new truck Beth Ann is driving already? She ticks possibilities. Drugs. Gambling. An investment. Chet's claim that he was about to come into big money, unless he was just blowing smoke up her skirt. Child support for a daughter Beth Ann didn't believe he had. Of course, with Chet's bed-hopping, he could have ten kids with ten women. Money for Lisa—maybe he was helping her out, maybe she was blackmailing him. Or maybe someone else was.

The rabbit trails lead in a myriad of directions and bring her no closer to a trip back to Texas. Or to satisfying her apprehensions about Hank. She banishes him from her mind. This isn't about Hank. It's about getting home, not a hurtful, untruthful man who is unaccounted for at exactly the wrong time and shouldn't have had blood on him Friday morning.

She washes two Excedrin down with the last of the water in a bottle stashed in her shoulder bag as she ponders her next move. She could head back to Piney Bottoms. Maybe the driveshaft is in. She checks her phone. No messages from the dealership, Patrick, or Mill Inn.

Scratch that idea.

Call Lacey with the information Beth Ann gave her? He'd just minimize it, and he might even make good on his threat to charge her with interference.

Definite scratch.

She could move to the Mill Inn. Avoid another conflict with Sheila or any interaction with Hank. But that would mean no more Lily, Louise, Andy, or Gene. Okay, or Hank, dammit. She needs an explanation from him. She deserves one.

So . . . scratch the moving idea, too.

Down the street, past the Tahoe, she sees the Rocky Mountain National Bank, like fate. It's here. She's here. She can drop in, ask a few questions, and maybe figure out where Chet's money went, possibly uncovering a few more suspects for Lacey in the process. Or maybe she'll learn nothing. Either way, she's on a scent, her juices flowing, with nothing better to do.

And she knows what she'll get if she doesn't try.

She starts walking toward the bank, mulling over an approach. She is and always will be a performer. All those nights in her early days, playing for bar crowds uninterested in her or her music. She'd had a few short sets to find a way to draw them to her. Sometimes she hadn't given a shit, not wanting to feel like a sellout. Other times she'd relished the game, mostly when she was hungry and broke. Mother, sister, lover, friend, artist, wild child, daughter. When it suited her, she could play a role—and fill a tip jar.

It had suited her with Beth Ann, and she'd nailed it.

She feels a growing sense of purpose and optimism as she walks toward the bank. At the entrance, she wrestles one side of a double door open to the usual afternoon gale. When she stumbles into the lobby, she blinks. The inside walls are entirely lined with rock. Real rock. Big black and gray rocks with thick mortar holding them together. When her eyes adjust to the dark interior, she gawks. It's like the inside of a volcano. Or a cave deep in a granite cliff. There's a rock-covered counter in front of a tall, wispy teller. A rock fireplace and a brown leather couch bookending a smiling woman seated at a desk. A rock-surrounded window in an office, a suited-up man looking through it at her, his door closed.

The decorator stalled out on inspiration after the word "rocky," and the result was a train wreck.

A chipper voice bounces like a rubber ball toward Maggie from the woman behind the desk. "Welcome to Rocky Mountain Bank. May I help you?"

Maggie approaches her, downplaying her Texas accent. "I hope so. Maybe. But it's a very private financial matter." She makes a point of looking around the lobby at the other two humans in view.

"Rocky is the man you need." The cheerful woman points at the office. "Soundproofing and a door that shuts. Can't get more private than that."

Rocky waves, looking like he heard every word.

Maggie doesn't bother debating with her. "Thank you."

Rocky meets her at the door to his office with his hand thrust out. Maggie gets a whiff of something chemical-y. Mothballs? They shake, then he shuts the door, takes her arm, and escorts her to the chair in front of his desk.

He sinks into his high-backed chair. Dark brown suit in a Western cut melds into dark brown leather with brass studs. "I'm Rocky Mountain."

Maggie stares at him, not sure how to respond.

"Just kidding. My name is Rocky Hancock."

She laughs, late, hearty, and fake. This guy is going to make her feel like a sell-out, apparently. "Maggie Killian."

"Oh yes, I recognize you. I'm a big fan." He reaches out his hands, raising and lowering them with his head slightly bowed.

"I didn't know I had any big fans. At least not anymore. Thank you."

"How can I help? You said it was"—he makes big air quotes with his fingers—"a very private matter?"

She lowers her voice to a husky whisper. "Yes. I'm, uh . . . well, I don't suppose you've heard about me and Chet Moore?"

"I heard. You two. An item. Maggie Killian and a fellow Sheridan High Bronc." He waggles his eyebrows. "Lucky bastard." Like her sleeping with a local is a credit to all men in the area.

"For a short period of time." She starts to minimize their relationship, but his expression changes her mind. "Not long enough. He asked me to marry him."

"You were getting married? Congratulations. I mean, I'm so sorry he's gone."

She wipes at her eyes, sidestepping his question. "I was just talking with Beth Ann, and—"

"Oh, that woman." His eyes roll, but then he assumes a solemn expression. "She's . . . a former customer."

Maggie looks up under her lashes, glad for the second coat of mascara she applied to cover her rough night. "He knew she had her problems, but he loved her. I feel responsible for her now that he's gone."

"You'd be taking on a big project, I tell you."

She nods sadly. "Beth Ann said Chet mortgaged his place, was behind on payments, and has an empty bank account. I'm worried he unintentionally left her in a bad position."

He looks down his nose like he smells a fart. "How did she claim to know that?"

"A stack of mail on Chet's dining room table. She can't figure out what he needed all that money for, and I didn't know what to tell her. Do you know?"

He shakes a finger at her like she was a naughty child. "If I knew, I couldn't tell you."

"You can't?"

He winks. "I don't know."

"What?"

"No, I don't know what he needed it for. Get it?" He laughs.

Maggie can't muster a smile. He's making no sense. And isn't funny. "I hoped talking to you would help me understand what happened to him." She sniffs, tries to look like she's holding back tears. "If there was something to celebrate, I could be proud of him. Or some problem he had, I could help. Especially with his mother left holding the bag."

Rocky chews the inside of his bottom lip, like he's working a wad of chewing tobacco. "Well, there's one thing I can tell you, because I didn't learn it from him. But you'd need to keep it between us."

"Oh?"

"My wife works the front desk at the law firm here in town. She said he came in and left a big fat retainer check with them a few weeks ago. Right after he got the mortgage money from us."

"Really? For what?"

Rocky looks around like the walls have ears. "I'm not disclosing attorney-client privileged information here, because Jaycee isn't a lawyer. Plus, it was written right on the face of the check her boss sent her here to deposit. When she told me, it finally made sense why he was driving down from Sheridan to do business here."

"Why?"

"To keep other people out of his business."

"Oh." The irony is so rich it nearly gags her. When Rocky doesn't continue, she adds, "Well, what did it say?"

"For custody of my daughter."

Maggie leans forward, gripping the edge of his desk. "That's wonderful news. We had such a whirlwind courtship that he didn't tell me the name of his daughter. What is it?"

"That's a good question."

"Her mother, then?"

"An even better one."

THIRTY-ONE

Maggie's phone vibrates. She pulls it from her bag. The words LEE COUNTY flash onscreen. Rocky gave her what she came here for, and Junior's call is as good a way as any to end this interview. She holds her phone up. "I have to take this. Thank you for your help, Mr. Hancock."

"Rocky. And of course. My condolences again for your loss."

Maggie shakes his hand again then presses accept call as she exits the office. "Hello?"

Rocky rushes ahead of her toward the entrance.

The male voice in her ear says, "Maggie Killian, please."

"Speaking, Junior." She waves goodbye to the woman who helped her earlier.

"Hi, Maggie." She can almost picture Junior's blush. "I got your message. I'm sorry to be bothering you on vacation again."

Rocky opens the heavy exterior door. She smiles sweetly and nods to thank him. "I'm not on vacation." She walks toward the Tahoe, glad for the big sky after half an hour in the dark cavern of the bank.

"Oh—uh, okay. I, um, I'm calling you with an update on the break-in at Flown the Coop."

Maggie feels like her life is a treadmill set faster than she can run. The break-in at her shop. Not to be confused with the break-ins at her cabin here. "Thank you. Tell me something good."

"Wish I could. We met with Gary Fuller. He wasn't too happy about it."

"I can only imagine."

"He's got an alibi. And there's no physical evidence to tie him to the damage."

"Good." She stops, bracing her hands on the bridge railing for a moment to look up Clear Creek. No little boy fishing today. She walks on.

"But there's nothing we can tie to anyone else either. Tons of fingerprints, of course."

"Touching the merchandise is encouraged."

He sighs. "I wish you had security cameras. And an alarm system."

"I'll install them when I get back. Did you hear I have a new competitor down the road that's bragging about putting me out of business?"

"Yeah?"

"Rickey Sayles. He tried to buy the place from me. I said no."

"You have reason to think he'd do this?"

Reaching the Tahoe, she leans against the warm metal. "Hell, I don't know. Doesn't sound too friendly, though."

"Got it. I'll follow up." She'll enjoy Junior hassling him. Serves him right for bad-mouthing her. "Michele's been out to the store with the insurance adjuster."

"Good."

"Also, your employee said he doesn't think things were stolen."

The vandals were obviously assholes of very little taste. "Thanks, Junior."

"One more thing."

"Yes?"

"We need a statement from your rental guest. Leslie. She didn't answer the door. I, uh, peeked in the windows and didn't see her. Michele went in. Her stuff was there, but she wasn't. If you'll send me her information, I can follow up with her."

"As soon as I'm back to my laptop."

When she ends the call, Maggie pauses with her hand on the door handle of the Tahoe. She looks at the signage on the building directly in front of her. It reads LAW OFFICE in gold gilt letters flaking at the edges. *Why not?*

She enters onto a narrow wooden stairway. At the top, she passes black-and-white photographs depicting Buffalo at the turn of the previous century. Horses hitched in front of a new-looking Occidental. Cattle plodding down a muddy main street. Cowboys sporting waxed mustaches with twisted ends. Beyond the pictures, she finds a door with a glass window warped with age. Maggie puts her nose as close as she can get to the glass without touching it. Through the ripples, she makes out a very short, very pregnant woman squeezing sideways to get behind a reception desk.

Maggie opens the door.

The woman tucks bobbed red hair behind mouse-like ears. The hair swings back to her chin. "Good afternoon. Do you have a meeting with John?"

"I'm hoping to."

"Grab yourself a coffee or tea. I'll see if he's available. Your name?"

"Maggie Killian." Maggie sets up a cup and a hazelnut cream pod, and starts the Keurig. She's starting to drag. Too much Koltiska last night. *The beginning of a song.*

"Oh," the redhead says in an all-caps tone.

Maggie keeps her hand on the coffee cup but cuts her eyes to the woman. "Are you Rocky's wife?" She thinks hard. Her thinker works better on more sleep and less liquor. "Um, Jaycee?"

"Ye-es," she says in two syllables.

Maggie smiles like that's the best news she's heard all day. "He talks about you. So nice to meet you."

"You're . . ."

Maggie waits her out. *The one that slept with Chet? The last one to see him before the murder? The whore of Babylon? Take your pick.*

The woman opens her mouth wide like she's trying to gobble a tennis ball, then snaps it shut. Whatever she was going to say, she thinks better of it. "I'll check with John." She waddles out of sight.

Maggie adds three creamers and as many sugars, stirs, and drinks the coffee in a few quick gulps.

Jaycee reappears. "He can see you for a few minutes. But one of his daughters has a volleyball game. If this will take longer than that, I'll need to schedule you for a better time."

Maggie throws her coffee cup in the trash. "Perfect."

"This way, then."

She follows Jaycee down the short hall. The shorter woman backs past the doorway, but her pregnant belly still extends into the entrance to the attorney's office. Maggie sidles through, bumping into it.

"So sorry."

"No problem. It seems to always get in the way."

The man in the office speaks. "That'll get worse for eighteen years before it gets better."

She giggles. "John Fortney, Maggie Killian. Let me know if I can get either of you anything."

The man who stands to greet her is even shorter than his pregnant receptionist and half her weight. "Ms. Killian. Please. Have a seat."

Jaycee retreats.

Maggie steps into an office tricked out like a railroad museum. A heavy black metal signal light hangs from the ceiling, its red, yellow, and green lenses dark. Sepia photos chronicle progress across the plains, interspersed with crossing placards and Union Pacific memorabilia. An antique surveyor's transit is displayed on his desk.

She gestures around her. "I'm in the business of old stuff. Yours is amazing."

"Thanks. My great-great-grandfather came out here to work on the railroad west. Never left. You're not from around here, though. Am I right?"

"Texas."

"And local gossip links you to a deceased client of mine. Is that why you're here?"

"Does a girl have no secrets?"

"Not in Buffalo, Wyoming. I'm not sure what I can tell you, but I'll help if I can."

Maggie reads her audience. Wedding ring. Family man. Like her late father had been. "As you know, Chet was determined to win custody of his daughter."

The lawyer tents his hands and flutters his fingers on the underside of his chin. "Go on."

"He was concerned about her. I want to see if there's anything else I can do for her. It's what Chet would have wanted."

His eyes drill into hers, searching for the hidden truth.

Maggie holds hers steady.

"Awful fast."

"What?"

"Your relationship."

She looks askance at him. "Haven't you ever been in love?"

"No offense, Ms. Killian. You're a looker. But that doesn't jive with the Chet I know."

"What doesn't?"

"Talking about his daughter, for one."

"I can't speak to the old Chet. But the one I knew proposed the day after we met." It feels good to tell the truth. She smiles. "And he loved his daughter."

"If he's even the father. We'll know in a few days."

Maggie admires his photos some more while she deliberates. "If he's the father, would that make the girl his heir?"

"It would."

"Because he didn't have a will."

"Look, if you're trying to lay claim to his ranch, you're out of luck. His mother's alive, even if this girl doesn't turn out to be his."

"I don't want his things. I just want to see Chet's wishes carried out. Frankly, his mother has already moved into the ranch house and is driving his truck. She has *no* idea she may be losing a ranch and gaining a grand-daughter."

He spins in his chair and carefully extracts a file folder like a Pick-Up Stick from a credenza stacked eight inches deep with crisscrossing files and papers. He opens it, flips pages, snaps it shut, drops it on his desk, wiggles another out.

After checking it, he tosses it across the desk to her. "Chet wasn't going to win any custody case. I told him as much. Lisa had called the cops one too many times on him, with the black eyes and broken ribs to get everyone's attention. Chet claims she was blaming him for things another man did, some bartender, but he couldn't prove it."

"Chet would never." Would he? He sure hadn't hit back when Lisa slapped him in the parking lot of the Bison Inn.

"He's won his share of bar fights."

"But hit a woman?"

"Can't say. This is all I know." He taps the papers in front of her.

She takes her time examining them. It's a stack of photos of Lisa in hospital gowns. Her hairstyles change over the years, but the damage to her face is much the same over time. Black-and-blue bruising around her eyes. Blood below her nose. Busted lips. Whoever did this to her should pay.

She shudders. "Thank you for showing them to me, John. You're right. Lisa's wouldn't have let him have custody of their daughter without a fight."

The attorney pulls the folder away from her. "Who said anything about Lisa being the mother?"

THIRTY-TWO

Maggie is jacked, like finding-a-missing-Andy-Warhol-painting-in-a-falling-down-shed jacked. Like a-sold-out-concert-with-two-standing-ovations jacked. She runs down the stairs, her bag bouncing against her hip. She's just blown open Chet's life and unearthed multiple viable suspects without breaking a sweat. Beth Ann, to get the ranch. Lisa, because of the abuse. God knows who, about the money. And the mystery mama, over custody. While John-the-attorney refused to tell Maggie her identity, the police could subpoena his records. Maggie shouldn't have to do all the work.

She needs to call Lacey.

But as she passes the Century Club she remembers Darrell's advice: talk to Chet's crewmates. She'd Googled them earlier. Their headquarters are two hours south in Casper, but she entered the number in her phone. She mulls it over. She's on a roll. Without more, Lacey might write off her tips. It's four o'clock, and the Crazy Woman Exploration office may close at five.

In the bright afternoon sunlight, she turns toward the creek. She presses the number and holds the phone to her ear.

A gravelly male voice says, "Crazy Woman."

Maggie flinches. Crazy Woman is ubiquitous in the area because of Crazy Woman Canyon, the natural wonder and local lore immortalized in *Jeremiah Johnson*. No one knows for sure who the crazy woman was or how the canyon got its name, but every time she hears the words, Maggie takes it as an accusation.

"I'm trying to locate someone who worked with Chet Moore." Maggie starts walking up the street along the creek, in the direction of the mountains.

"Chet?"

"Yes. He—"

"Died. Yeah, we know. A shame. Good worker. We hated to lose him."

"Yes, me, too."

"No, I mean, we hated losing him when he quit. A couple of months ago."

A path from the street juts toward the cottonwood-tree-lined creek. Maggie veers onto the trail, her heart thrumming. Chet had quit his job months ago. No one she'd met mentioned it. Maybe none of them know. Somehow it feels important. The morning before she'd jettisoned him at the Bison Inn, he'd said he was coming into big money. She'd chalked it up to braggadocio. But what if it was true? She tried to remember his exact words. He hadn't said he had *already* come into money, which he could have truthfully claimed since he'd cashed in on the mortgage proceeds. He said he was *about to* come into it.

"Oh yes, that. Such a shame."

"So what do you want with his crew?"

"I, um, was seeing Chet."

"Like a girlfriend."

"Like that."

"Must have been new."

Maggie crosses a bridge and rejoins the path on the opposite side, then follows its curves. "Yes. Everything happened . . . so fast. And now I need closure. He loved the guys he worked with. I thought if I talked to a few of them it would . . . help."

"Why not—he and Brendan were good buddies." He rattles off a number. "Got it?"

Maggie stops in deep shade. The cottonwoods along the creek are as tall as the old lodgepole pines near the Wagon Box Inn in Story. "Hold on." She types the number in a text to herself then hits send. "Got it. Thank you."

"He's off shift now. If he's sober, you'll probably be able to reach him." He hangs up.

Maggie smacks her phone in her palm, one, two, three times. The plot is thickening, better than an old episode of *The Rockford Files*. And she should know, since she rode sofa-shotgun with her dad for every episode. Even if Maggie wasn't a suspect, even if she wasn't worried about whether Hank was involved, this shit was impossible to resist.

She presses the number.

When Brendan answers, she hears clanking glasses and bottles, and someone shouting, "Another round for me and my friends," then, "Hello?"

Maggie heads back toward downtown, walking and talking again, going through the same spiel. Introducing herself, claiming she was Chet's fiancée. Getting a read on Brendan.

Halfway through, he interrupts her. "Wait, I know you."

"I don't think so."

"Chet texted me a picture of you." Ice clinks against glass. "That dickhead hadn't returned my calls for six weeks but he texted me a naked picture of the woman he wants to marry. You gotta love him."

"Did you say *naked?*"

"And then you almost ran off the road and killed yourself yesterday."

"Oh. You do know me."

"May I say Chet has—had—damn good taste."

"Do me a favor. Delete it."

"Um, yeah, sure."

Maggie sighs. She knows he's saving it.

"Dammit. Why'd he have to go and die? There was nobody as much fun as Chet." Brendan's voice cracks.

"I know. And he missed hanging out with you. He told me he was planning on calling."

"We had elk permits for bow season. We were gonna get our bulls together."

"That's what he said. I just wish I understood why he would have quit such a good job. Especially when he loved working with you."

Brendan clears his throat. "'Scuse me? He hated this job. Only did it so he could get a mortgage on his place and pay child support—you do know about Phoebe? Shit. I hope I didn't spill the beans."

Phoebe. Yes! She pumps her fist in the air like she's marking the beat for a backing band. "Oh yes. All about Phoebe."

Maggie hears sounds behind her. Footsteps, maybe? She scans in a three-sixty but sees nothing. The sun sinks early and thoroughly here on the east side of the mountains, and she realizes it's not nearly as light out as it was when she started her walk. She speeds up.

"It was a big secret, but I kept it. He was crazy about that kid." Brendan's voice thickens. "Of course, finding out so long after the fact, I told him he couldn't be so sure she was his, but he just dove right in anyway."

"He adored her." Maggie crosses her fingers as she launches into a whopper. "I always figured that's why he was hoping to come into big money. So he would have something for her." Again, there's a noise behind her. She stops to get a better fix on it. The noise stops, too. She grabs the pepper spray from her purse and walks even faster.

"Exactly. I offered to go in on it with him, but he said he couldn't drag me into something so risky. Plus he wanted it all for Phoebe."

"He said it was a big surprise. Wouldn't tell me what it was until it was a sure thing."

"That's Chet for you. Cagey SOB. Heart of fuckin' gold."

"Now that he's gone, I wish I knew. So I could be proud of him for it."

"It'll be public knowledge soon enough, with Phoebe the better for it. Just got the news the day after he died."

"And what was it?"

"He drilled on his ranch."

"Drilled. For oil."

"Oil. Gas. Whatever he could find."

"And?" The sound behind her now seems like a buffalo stampede to her ears. She doesn't bother to look back. She just takes off running, phone to her ear, pepper spray in hand, and bag whapping her hip.

Brendan chuckles. "Little Phoebe won't be rich, but it will keep the ranch in the family for a long, long time."

THIRTY-THREE

After the call, Maggie stops in the parking lot by the baseball field. She has a stitch in her side after her sprint, so she walks in circles with her hands behind her neck, elbows up. When the cramp subsides, she shoves her phone in her bag, then picks up the pepper spray she'd dropped in the street. Moving in a slow circle, she makes sure that whatever was following her stayed down by the creek. Satisfied, she puts the spray away.

She has signal—a miracle—and asks Siri for the number for the Buffalo Police Department. It's a few minutes until five. She has a brief moment where she wonders if Michele will be mad at her for calling. This is an exception. She's calling about other people, not herself.

"Buffalo PD." The man sounds annoyed.

"Detective Lacey, please."

Without another word, he transfers her to Lacey's voicemail.

"Detective Lacey, this is Maggie Killian. I ran into Lisa Whitefeather and her brothers at the Century Club. And Chet's mother at Reride. Between the two of them and a few friends, I learned that Lisa has filed multiple battery charges against Chet. Seems like motive for her and her brothers, if you ask me. I also heard Chet quit his job a while back and put a mortgage on his ranch. Turns out he recently found out he has a daughter named Phoebe and was trying to get custody from the baby mama, who can't be too happy. This isn't going to be good news to his mother, either, who thinks she's getting his ranch. But she won't, because he died without a will, and it will go to his daughter. I could go on. Anyway, my point is that this town is full of suspects who had a motive to kill Chet. I hope you're investigating them, because I sure as hell had nothing to do with it."

She ends the call, feeling like a badass.

Her adrenaline surge ebbing, her mind returns to Hank. She wants desperately for Lacey to crack the case, to name a killer. Then she'll ask Hank where he was Thursday night and about the blood on his clothes Friday. He'll be appalled she was worried about it and tell her some story fitting for a former bull rider who spent years living in truck beds and trailers in rodeo arena parking lots. She'll laugh at him and her fears.

And then she'll be off to Texas and wash her hands of her temporary imprisonment in the wilds of Wyoming, Hank Sibley, and his ridiculous girlfriend.

She takes off toward the Tahoe, which is just around the corner on Main. Suddenly she hears footsteps behind her, again, heavy ones. Shooting a glance over her shoulder, she breaks into a run. A large, dark figure is approaching fast.

"Wait up, Maggie." She recognizes the voice. Patrick Rhodes.

She slows to a trot, then a walk, then stops. "You scared me."

"A woman on her own needs to be cautious."

"Was that you back there?" Maggie points to the trail by the creek.

"Back where? I just saw you as I was leaving out the back of the Sports Lure."

"All right." She has no reason not to believe him, but her uneasiness has returned full force. She resumes fast-walking back to where she parked the Tahoe.

He matches her pace easily with his long strides eating up twice as much ground as each of her steps. "I'm grubbing at Winchesters on the way home. Join me? You have to eat at Winchesters if you're spending a week hereabouts. It's an institution."

Not a "place known for its fabulous food," but an "institution." And getting into a habit of hanging out with the big man isn't overly appealing. Having people associate them together is even less. "I should get back."

"You think they're going to wait dinner on you at Piney Bottoms?"

And, on the other hand, he's right. They wouldn't. And her cupboard is freshly bare. "Okay. But I'm paying my own way."

"Of course you are. And I have that driveshaft for you."

She stops at her borrowed vehicle. "You could have mentioned that earlier."

"You're welcome."

She rolls her eyes, her head turned so he doesn't catch her at it. "See you there."

In the Tahoe, Maggie asks Siri for directions to Winchesters, then sets off with a strange and unwelcome sense of security. She hadn't realized until her data challenges how much she relies on technology. She's not the same woman who drove herself to gigs from coast to coast, never having enough money for a pay phone and relying only on the atlas she'd stolen at her first gas stop out of Giddings, that's for sure.

Halfway to the restaurant, her phone rings. The display identifies the call as coming from the Sheridan County Sheriff's Department. She picks up.

A male voice barks at her before she can say hello. "You Maggie Killian?"

"I am."

"You're not one for returning phone calls, I take it."

"What?" She pulls up at a red light.

"I left you three voicemails between yesterday and today."

She flips her phone to voicemails. Nothing. "I'm sorry. I didn't get them. My phone hates Wyoming."

"What?"

"Never mind."

"I'm Deputy Travis. I took the complaint when Hank Sibley called about the burglaries. I'm calling to set a time to come out to Piney Bottoms to take your statement."

"I called, too." Green light. Maggie accelerates toward the steakhouse.

"I didn't get that message."

"Guess we're even, then."

"How about I come now?"

Siri tells Maggie they've arrived at the destination. Maggie whips into a small parking lot in front of a tan building with a green metal roof and trusses. The sign confirms Siri's announcement that they've reached their destination, crossed Winchester rifles and all.

"I'm not actually there. How about tomorrow morning, say about ten or eleven?"

"Good." He hangs up.

She stares at the phone for a moment. Deputy Travis has all the finesse of a charging rhino.

She sees Patrick's truck. Somehow, he'd beaten her to Winchesters.

Inside, she finds him conversing with the hostess, full flirt on, which from a man of his size is a whole lot of flirt. Maggie hangs back, just in case the hostess is buying what he's selling.

"Right this way." She grabs two menus and leads the way. She's almost as tall as Patrick, and she moves ponderously, like she's wearing full-body armor instead of too-tight jeans and a light flannel shirt. She drops the menus on their table, pivots, and retreats. *Not buying.*

Patrick sits, and Maggie pulls out her own chair.

A waiter appears, his skin pink and corn-fed. "Drinks?"

"Dewar's, neat," Patrick says.

"Iced tea."

Patrick raises his eyebrows at Maggie.

"Coming right up," the waiter says.

She pops her menu open and starts reading. Almost immediately, Patrick begins entertaining walk-by guests at their table. She keeps her head down to avoid introductions. Patrick doesn't offer them anyway.

The waiter plunks down a basket of bread without breaking stride.

Patrick catches him by the arm. "We're ready to order."

Out comes a pocket-size flip pad and miniature pencil.

"Chicken potpie," Maggie says.

Again, she gets an uptick to Patrick's eyebrow. "Ribeye. Rare." He waggles an inch of liquid in his glass. "And another of these."

The waiter finishes a scribble. "Got it."

When he's gone, Maggie puts her bag on her shoulder. "I'm hitting the ladies room."

The hostess is back, and she stops at their table. "I'm on break."

Maybe Ms. Personality is buying after all.

Patrick smiles at the hostess and says out of the side of his mouth to Maggie, "Take your time."

Her iced tea isn't going to carry her through this dinner. Maggie detours to the bar. "Koltiska Original on ice. Double, tall."

Booze may make her hot to trot, but she's immune to Patrick. She puts a ten on the counter and takes her drink to the bathroom with her. There, she splashes water on her face. She looks like she feels—wrung out. Using paper towels, she blots her face then uses lipstick on her cheeks and lips. She fluffs her hair and pushes it away from her face, studying herself in the mirror.

"Hang in there, Margaret Elizabeth. You have suspects for the cops. You have a driveshaft for Bess. You'll clear the air with Hank, and then get the hell out of Dodge."

She leaves her empty glass beside the sink and returns to their table. "Fastest chow in the west" should be Winchesters motto—their food is already on the table.

"Sorry," she says.

Patrick waves his empty fork in the air. He's chewing an enormous hunk of beef, if the bulge in his cheek is any indication.

Maggie breaks the crust on her potpie with a big spoon. Steam rises out of the hole. She scoops up a bite and blows on it.

Patrick swallows without choking to death. "I guess you know Hank's pretty pissed at me right now."

Maggie remembers how upset Hank was when he told her about Patrick nosing Double S out of NFR. "You think?" She tastes the potpie, adds salt.

He grunts, a cross between a chuckle and a cough. "All's fair in love and war. Especially war."

"Business is war?"

"In a manner of speaking."

"By 'all's fair,' do you mean you did something *un*fair to Hank and Gene?"

Patrick grins, his mustache rising like it's on puppet strings. "You might have noticed I'm popular around here."

Maggie stifles a groan. "You're certainly social."

"Everybody loves me. Hank, well, as nice as Gene is, he can't make up for what a sour jackass his partner is."

Maggie just stares at him, unable to form words.

"It pays to make friends, Ms. Killian."

"No doubt," she chokes out.

"So I did someone a solid for a little bit of information about the Double S bid."

Maggie's hackles rise. "That's *not* fair."

He salutes her with his nearly empty second double Scotch. Or at least she thinks it's his second. "As we were discussing."

"I'm done discussing with you. Hank and Gene are my friends." She pulls a wad of cash from her wallet. "I've lost my appetite."

A woman's voice interrupts her. "Maggie."

Maggie drops the cash in the middle of the table and looks up into the pixie face of Hank's sister, Laura, then down to the haughty profile of Mrs. Sibley. "Laura. Mrs. Sibley. Good evening."

"Patrick." Laura's voice drips acid.

"Look at you, pip-squeak. You sure did grow up right. Pretty and successful. I know your father would be so proud."

"You have no idea what he would think."

Patrick puts his hands up. "Whoa, what did I say?"

To try to prevent a nuclear reaction, Maggie says, "Laura, Mrs. Sibley, I guess I'll see you back at the ranch."

Laura sneers and pushes her mother's wheelchair past them. "I'll be sure to watch for the Trojan horse at the gate, Maggie."

Her comment is surprisingly painful, like pulling on underwear that picked up a grass burr from being washed with work jeans. But now that Maggie knows what Patrick did to get the NFR business, she can't fault Laura much.

THIRTY-FOUR

Half an hour later, headlights on high beam glare into her eyes from her rearview mirror. She puts a hand up to block the assault, then steers the Tahoe through the entrance to Piney Bottoms. The cattle guard shakes her brain against the inside of her skull, and the potholes jar her so hard her neck cracks. Or maybe she's a little on edge after the disastrous end to dinner.

"Dimmer switch, asshole."

It's late. When she left for Reride hours before, she had no idea she'd be out the rest of the day. Change of season here is more dramatic than she's used to, fourteen hundred miles north of her normal. The shorter days seem shorter sooner. The duration of the dusk-time Frogger game the Wyoming deer play with the driving public, longer. Dark is truly dark, especially on cloudy nights like this one. She knows she's lucky she isn't on the side of the road with a deer-shaped imprint in Mrs. Sibley's Tahoe.

The driver with the brights on turns into the ranch, too. With all that's happened—truck sabotage, break-ins, thefts—is this some creeper following her home down the lonely back roads?

Maybe not. The vehicle might carry a guest for the main house. She'd even be glad for Sheila right now.

But no such luck. The potholes jerk the headlights around like they're having a seizure, but they keep moving inexorably toward her cabin. Damn, how she wishes she'd met with the Sheridan deputy today. She grips the wheel, tensed and considering doubling back to the main house for safety in numbers. But no. She doesn't want a scene with the Sibleys. She'll be fine. Louise will be on the porch, ready to rumble. Maggie will run inside, flip on the lights, and grab the rifle.

As she parks, the other driver flicks the brights on and off.

She puts her bag over her shoulder, keys in hand, and shoots out like an arrow from a bow. With Louise barking and jumping around her, she fumbles at the tape gate.

"Back, girl. Back."

Louise ignores her. Frustrated, Maggie rips the pole out of the ground and drops it, like her thief had. She runs over it to the porch. The other vehicle pulls up. She tries to jam the keys in the lock, fumbling blind in the pitch dark.

"Dammit!"

A man's voice five feet away asks, "Why are you in such a hurry?"

She screams and drops the keys, then scuttles backwards. "Who's there?"

The porch creaks under a rocker. Ice settles in a glass.

"Not who you're expecting, apparently." The clouds part, and a sliver of moonbeam illuminates Hank's sullen face.

Her hand flies to her throat. "Hank. What are you doing here?"

"I came to talk to you. But I see you've brought company."

"Thank God you're here. That truck's following me. I was terrified."

They stare at each other. Hank's face relaxes. He sits forward.

Then a second man's voice calls out to Maggie. "I got something you're going to like, Maggie."

She groans. Patrick. The asshole.

Hank stands, knocking the chair back into the cabin wall. "Whatever, Maggie."

She closes the distance between them, reaching out for his arm. "It's not what you think."

Patrick's voice grows closer. "Ready or not, here I come."

"Oh really?"

"I didn't know it was him."

"Well, now you do." Hank lurches, and his drink sloshes.

"You're drunk."

"You're a traitor."

"That's better than being a liar," she shoots back.

Suddenly the moon is completely uncovered. Hank doesn't react to her accusation. Maggie sees the set of his jaw and the fists of his hands as he barrels past her to get to Patrick.

Patrick is visible now, too. He's carrying something bulky. "Sibley. Does your little blonde know you're here?"

Hank doesn't break stride until his fist meets Patrick's jaw. The older, larger man staggers back. There's a dull thud as he drops whatever it is he's carrying. Louise darts back and forth between Maggie and the men, barking and lunging.

Patrick clutches his face. "What the hell?"

Hank rears back for another strike, but this time Patrick ducks under it. He's faster than Maggie would have given him credit for, fast like a bull, and Hank is drunk like a skunk. Not that Patrick is sober, but in the battle of relativity, Hank loses the round. Shoulder first, Patrick hits Hank like he's ramming a tackling sled, wrapping up Hank's torso, driving him all the way to the ground. Hank lands with an "oomph."

"Stop it! Stop!" But the night swallows Maggie's words.

Hank twists and wrenches himself free, then jumps back to his feet, still agile in the face of a charging bull after all these years, even drunk. The men stand and circle each other like overdressed sumos in a ring. Then the moon slips back behind the clouds. Maggie hears grunts, groans, curses, and the sounds of body parts slamming into each other and the ground. Louise's barks resound in a circle around the dark hump of wrestling men. To Maggie, the fight seems to go on forever. She's just about to fetch the rifle— shoot in the air to break them up—when their noises stop.

Maggie approaches cautiously. "Are you idiots done?"

Neither of them answers.

She moves closer and stubs her toe. "Shit." She leans down and gropes until she connects with something big. Hard. Metal. She slides her hands over the shape. A driveshaft. She'd rushed out of Winchesters so fast, she forgot all about the part. "He brought me a driveshaft, Hank."

The men still ignore her. Both are panting. One of them spits.

"Hank Sibley, did you hear me? I just about broke my toe on a drive-shaft Patrick brought for my truck."

When Hank speaks, it isn't to answer Maggie. "You stole our contract, Rhodes."

"This isn't about the contract and you know it."

"Cocksucker."

One of the men stands. There's a swish, swish, swish of hands brushing dirt and grass off jeans.

Patrick says, "Maggie, let me know if I can help you getting back to Texas. I'd want to get the hell away from this clown, too."

A day-bright light pierces the clouds as the moon comes into view again. Hank dives, going for Patrick's legs. Patrick kicks out, and Hank makes a gurgling sound. Louise stands guard over Hank, who's kneeling and slinging blood from his fingers.

She grimaces. "I meant what I said earlier, Patrick. But thank you for the part. Are you okay?"

Patrick's voice sounds whistly as he walks to his truck. "Other than the tooth somewhere in the yard and my broken nose?"

"I'm sorry."

"Not your fault." His truck door opens. "Good luck, Maggie." The door slams shut.

The truck roars off. Maggie lifts the driveshaft, putting her back and legs into it. It's too heavy for her to carry. She'll come back for it later. With a wheelbarrow. She drops it. Louise sniffs at the hunk of metal, then returns to Hank.

Maggie joins the dog. One of Hank's ears is dripping blood from a clear imprint of Patrick's teeth. His bottom lip is the size of a kielbasa. An eye is puffed shut.

Maggie crosses her arms. "You realize he was helping me?"

"Unethical. Stole from me. Cheats. Lies."

"Maybe so. But you treated me like it was my fault."

Hank rolls onto his side. He rests, wincing, then pushes up on an elbow. "You brought him here."

"I did not, and you know it. Why were you on my porch?"

"If you're with him, you need to stay with him."

"You're a bad listener."

"Fine." Hank crawls on all fours. A bloody string of saliva hangs from his mouth to the grass.

Louise noses at his face, then licks his eye. He growls at the dog, who backs away. Maggie sighs and kneels beside him, putting a hand on his back. He swipes it off.

"Still feisty? Suit yourself." She gets up and walks to the cabin, using the flashlight on her phone to find the keys. She unlocks the knob and stands with her hand on it. "I told Patrick to get lost tonight. After he bragged about what he did to get the NFR contract."

Hank sways to his feet. "What did he do?"

"He paid for information and a chance to bid last and lowest."

Hank bellows like a bull on his way to becoming a steer. "The fuck you say."

"You already suspected as much."

"But I didn't *know* it."

"Well, now you do." She throws open the door to the cabin.

Hank wheels. He points in the air. "Stay away from him. You hear me? Anyone else. Just not him, Maggie. Not him."

Not Patrick, but also not Chet. She thinks about his reaction to both men. His jealousy and anger. He has no right. Not when he's with somebody else.

"So, what if I were to go with, oh, I don't know. The bartender at the Occidental."

"He's bad news."

"Of course he is." She turns, letting the screen door shut, and points at him. "You don't tell me who I can be with, and I won't tell you. Speaking of the witch, do you need me to call Sheila to come kiss your boo-boos?"

"I'm serious. Not Patrick."

"You're pathetic. Go home."

"I am."

"Good." Maggie slams the cabin door and leans against it, shaking with something. Rage? Maybe. She wipes away a tear.

Or maybe not.

She hears an engine fire up. She'd expected him to be walking back to his house. Is he taking the Tahoe? She flips on the porch light and pulls the curtain back from the front window. Hank fishtails his truck around from the side of the cabin. Well, that accounts for why she didn't see it when she drove up. Instead of turning toward the main house, though, he careens into the darkness, toward pastures, high prairie, and big animals.

She watches his taillights recede, then drops the curtain. "Dumbass."

But with his absence, she feels completely alone. Scary alone. She'll sleep with the rifle beside her tonight. Or she would if she had it. But she won't. Can't. Because when she turns to get it, the rifle isn't there.

THIRTY-FIVE

The next morning, Maggie skips the group breakfast, instead taking Louise and the driveshaft to Sheridan. She second-guesses herself hard the whole way about the night before. She'd decided not to call the sheriff about the missing rifle, since Deputy Travis was already scheduled for the morning. In fact, she'll have to hustle to get back from town in time to meet him. But worrying about the rifle and who'd taken it from her cabin—her locked cabin—kept her up all night, without a bottle of Balcones or Koltiska to help her through.

She'd gotten so sleepy, she'd started hallucinating. Twice, she'd been sure she'd seen an Indian woman standing over her bed. Once, wafting a burning sage smudge stick over her bed. The other, chanting in a singsong voice, using a language she didn't understand. Both times, Maggie had closed her eyes to shut out the image. The first time, it worked. The second time, when she opened them, the woman was still there. She'd closed them again and screamed bloody murder, and the woman had disappeared.

Maybe if she'd called Travis, she wouldn't be questioning her sanity this morning. Or maybe it wouldn't have helped. Either way, she can't go back and change her decision now.

Her first stop in town is the dealership, where she sucks down burned coffee from their lounge while the service tech retrieves the hunk of metal from the Tahoe.

He's the same one she's been talking to on her calls. His red Roll Tide T-shirt stands out in a sea of Cowboy brown and gold. He returns carrying the driveshaft like it's a six-pack of beer. "Your dog gave me a good barking-to."

"She's awesome like that."

"Funny looking, too. What is she?"

"Half border collie."

"Like a dwarf collie?"

"Corgi mix, maybe. Or a terrible accident with a table saw."

He laughs. "I'll try to get you going today. Tomorrow at the latest."

His words are like a spark plug. Maybe things will go her way today, which would be great for when she talks to Hank. She's definitely talking to Hank.

She has time for a green smoothie from the Golden Rule. But when she sees their cinnamon rolls, she caves. Driving back to Piney Bottoms with the wind in her hair, she alternates sips from an extra-large dark coffee, light and sweet, with bites of warm cinnamon roll, stopping only for gas and a four-pack of KO 90. Because the gas station is also a liquor store. And a wine bar. Things to love about Wyoming.

Before leaving the pump, she holds up the last bite of cinnamon roll. "Don't tell anyone what a softie I am."

Louise gobbles it and wags her tail. Hair swirls in the cab from her tail storm. Her eyes beg for more.

"That's all I've got. Besides, you ate your dog food this morning anyway, little piggy."

Maggie makes it back to the ranch with half an hour to spare before she expects Deputy Travis. But a white Sheridan County truck pulls through the Piney Bottoms gate just ahead of her. Maggie waves to the deputy. A hand rises. When the truck reaches the split in the entrance road, it veers toward the main house instead of continuing to her cabin. Maggie follows. She assumes he's planning on checking in with the owner before talking to her.

Then she takes her foot off the accelerator. Louise cocks her head. The Tahoe slows to a crawl. Is she ready for the Sibleys yet? Poised with her foot over the pedal in indecision, she suddenly mashes it down. She hopes Hank's there, hungover and squirming with his shiner, busted lip, and chewed-on ear. *Time for him to face the music,* she thinks.

Two deputies are already walking to the door when she gets out behind their vehicle. One has a unique, skipping limp, the other a three-inch-long beard like half the other men in the state.

She calls after them. "Hello! I'm Maggie Killian."

They turn and stop.

The unique deputy frowns. "Yes?"

"Aren't you here to see me, about my intruder and the things that have been stolen?"

He puts his hand on his gun. "No, ma'am. Do you live here?"

Maggie stops, eying his gun hand. *What the hell?* "No. I'm in the guest cabin."

"I need you to head back there, then. This doesn't concern you."

"But I don't understand. We had an appointment."

"Ma'am, get back in your vehicle and leave, please."

Hank opens the front door and steps onto the porch. Even after an ass-whupping, he sets off electric butterflies in her belly. Framed in the doorway is his mother in her wheelchair, Laura behind her with a hand on each handle and a frown on her face.

"Can I help you?" Hank says.

"Are you Hank Sibley?" the limping deputy asks.

Hank's battered, swollen face folds like a squeeze box. "George, that's a stupid-ass question. You know I am."

The other deputy approaches Hank and halts a few feet away.

George holds up a hand. "Gotta do this by the book. Hank Sibley, you're under arrest for the murder of Patrick Rhodes."

Maggie gasps, earning her a glare from George. Patrick is dead? Hank is being arrested for his murder? Her heart drops to her knees, and the rest of her almost goes with it.

George shakes his head at her. "I told you to get along."

No way in hell is Maggie leaving. Hank searches her face through his one good eye. For what, she isn't sure. She reaches toward him, and his hand rises as if to touch hers, but ten feet separates them.

"Hank, Ernie's going to snap the cuffs on you now while I read you your Miranda rights."

"Is that really necessary in front of my mom?" Hank lowers his voice. "She has Alzheimer's. Can't I just agree to come along with you and sort this out in town?"

"I'm sorry. Procedure. Put your hands behind your back."

Hank holds his wrists in front of his waist. "Come on. At least do it where she can't see. And could you keep your voices down, please?"

The two deputies share a long look, Ernie questioning, George giving a grudging nod. Ernie snaps cuffs over Hank's wrists, then puts a hand on Hank's elbow as George recites the Miranda warning in a low monotone.

From the doorway, Mrs. Sibley's voice is screechy. "You boys. What do you think you're doing? Mr. Sibley has work to do. You go on, now, and let him be."

"It will be fine, Mom. Let's go inside." Laura pulls back on the wheelchair. To Hank, she says, "I'll be half an hour behind you."

Maggie suddenly loves Laura for the anguish in her voice.

Mrs. Sibley pushes her feet to the floor and drags them. "No. I'm not going." Her eagle talon fingers grip the armrests. The veins in her neck pop like a weightlifter on a world-record dead lift. The flesh around her eyes suddenly sinks and darkens. "Goddammit, I said no!"

The deputies walk Hank toward the white truck.

"Hank," Maggie calls. She's choking on something. She can barely get his name out. "Hank."

Mrs. Sibley has fought Laura to a standstill. She points at Maggie. "That woman. That woman is trouble. Take her. She's the one you want."

Maggie can't disagree. If she hadn't gone to Winchesters with Patrick, if she had remembered to get the driveshaft from his truck before she drove to the ranch, then Hank and Patrick wouldn't have fought. If she hadn't told Hank what Patrick had said, then Hank wouldn't have torn off into the wild blue last night, to do God knows what, God knows where.

She puts the mental brakes on. She has no idea why they're arresting Hank, but nothing she knows proves he killed Patrick. So he drove off. So he was mad. It proves nothing.

Nothing.

She follows the men to the Sheridan County truck.

"Stay back, ma'am. If I have to tell you again, you're coming in, too." George opens the back door.

Ernie assists Hank inside.

Hank stops half in, half out. "Maggie, have Gene send our lawyer."

"Of course."

He shakes his head. "This is all a big misunderstanding. You know that, right?"

"Yes." *Maybe.* "Do you need anything else?" *Sheila?*

"No. I'll be fine. Thank you."

"Come on, Hank. You can talk to your girlfriend later."

Maggie almost says, "I'm not his girlfriend." Instead, she blows Hank a kiss.

His lips form a kiss back, then he climbs the rest of the way in the vehicle, and George shuts the door behind him.

THIRTY-SIX

Maggie runs to the barn. No Gene. Andy and Paco are unloading bags of feed.

Out of breath, her words burst out between gasps for air. "Have. You. Seen. Gene?"

Paco tips his hat back. "He went out to doctor an injured horse. He should be back soon. Can I help?"

Maggie hears an ORV coming toward them. "No. I need Gene."

"Lily misses you. Do you want to take her some sweet feed while you wait?"

She can't think about Lily right now. Or anything but Hank. "Later."

Andy tosses a fifty-pound bag onto a stack as high as his head, making it look no heavier than a pillow. "Hey, Maggie, do you think I could maybe have another guitar lesson tonight?"

Gene steers the ORV into the barnyard. Maggie doesn't answer Andy. She charges out the door, meeting Gene before the engine stops running.

"Hank needs you."

Gene puts an empty Cheetos bag in the ashtray and grabs a big leather veterinarian bag from the seat beside him. He climbs out. "What's new?"

"I'm serious." She lowers her voice. "Patrick Rhodes is dead. Some Sheridan County deputies arrested Hank. He asked me to have you send the attorney."

The vet bag lands in the dirt. "Paco, you're in charge," Gene calls out.

"Thank you, Maggie." Then he jumps back in the ORV without another word and roars off.

The sound of a vehicle rattling over the cattle guard comes from the direction of the front gate.

Paco joins Maggie. "What's going on?"

Another white county truck approaches the barn. Adrenaline courses through her. Maggie pulls her jacket tighter. Now what? Are they here to arrest her, too?

A lone occupant idles the truck outside the barnyard. He rolls down his window. "Deputy Travis, Sheridan Sheriff's Department. I'm looking for Maggie Killian."

Maggie raises her hand like a student who has to tell the teacher she forgot her homework. "I'm Maggie."

"Where were these break-ins Hank called about?"

Fight or flight fades, leaving Maggie weak. The deputy isn't here about Patrick Rhodes. *Thank God.* "I called, too."

"You going to show me or not?"

Maggie points. "The last cabin. That way."

"Want a ride?"

A walk will give her time to pull herself together. "No. I'll meet you there."

"Suit yourself." Travis rolls up his window and drives ahead.

Maggie sees nothing but the toes of her boots on the walk to the cabin. She rubs her arms and chants aloud to herself, "Everything will be all right. Everything will be all right." When that doesn't work she switches to "Not about Hank. Not about Hank." Gene passes her, driving like a bat out of hell toward the gate. Toward Sheridan and the sheriff's department. They raise hands at each other, salutes rather than waves.

Maggie's almost to the torn-down tape gate when she remembers the missing rifle. She'd been planning to tell the deputy about it, but now she isn't sure. Hank could have taken it when he was waiting on her. It belongs to him, after all, and he has a key to her cabin. She needs to ask him about it. She can't bring it up to Travis. That or anything related to Hank and Patrick's altercation. Too risky.

She pastes on a smile—she goes for relaxed and welcoming—and steps over the tape on the ground. "Deputy Travis, thank you for coming."

On terra firma instead of in his truck, the deputy reminds her of a grizzly bear. Big, hunched, lumbering, with dark hair and a sizeable belly.

He's marking in a spiral notebook and looks up at her. But when he speaks, it isn't to her.

"Sheila. How are you?"

Maggie stiffens and glances in the direction of Travis's gaze. Her blonde nemesis is walking up, right behind her.

"Travis, hello." Sheila gives Maggie a wide berth.

To Maggie, Travis says, "Pardon me for a minute. Sheila and I grew up together from the time we were in kindergarten."

"Seems like yesterday." Sheila stands on tiptoe to hug him.

"How is little Phoebe? She still the spitting image of your mother?"

Sheila smiles up at him. "Yes, and my parents spoil her rotten. Got her another pony for her ninth birthday."

The two keep chatting, but Maggie tunes them out. She's staring at Sheila. Remembering her staring at Chet and whispering to Gene's date, June, the week before at the Occidental. Wondering how many little Phoebes there can possibly be in the Sheridan area. Realizing Sheila has to be Chet's baby mama, the one he was fighting for custody of their daughter.

The one with a compelling motive to see Chet dead.

Sheila's voice slices into her thoughts like a hot knife through Jell-O. "Maggie, did you hear me?"

"Sorry. What?"

"I said I came by to see Hank on my way back from a school thing in Sheridan. I can't find anyone. Do you know where he is?"

Maggie's blood boils with hatred for this woman who has sat by and let the police hound Maggie about Chet, when she has vital information for them that she's kept to herself.

Well, two can play hide-and-seek. "I haven't the foggiest." And she gives Sheila a sweet, wide-eyed smile.

THIRTY-SEVEN

Several hours later, Gene knocks on Maggie's door. His olive skin is pasty, his eyes hollow.

Maggie pulls Gene into the cabin. "How is he?"

"Subdued. Exhausted after his interview."

"What makes them think he did it?"

Gene shakes his head, sighing. "Hank went over to Patrick's last night. They had a noisy fight. Several of Patrick's hands were there. They're saying Hank was drunk and promised to kill Patrick. Multiple times."

"It's just an expression. Lots of people say it."

"But not right before the person they say it to is murdered."

Maggie drops her face into her hands. Beside her, Louise whines.

Gene takes Maggie's shoulders. "Look at me." She lifts her head partway and lowers her hands. "Hank swears he didn't do it."

"I know."

"Patrick was shot with a rifle. And everyone in Wyoming has a rifle."

Maggie turns from Gene, walks into the kitchen area, leans on the counter palms-first. "Last night, though . . ."

"What about last night?"

Maggie shakes her head.

Gene urges her again. "What is it, Maggie?"

She straightens and takes two glasses from the cabinet. "Want a drink?"

Gene scrubs his forehead with the back of his wrist. "Sure."

She puts ice cubes from a freezer tray into the glasses, then pours each of them roughly two shots of KO 90.

She hands Gene his drink. "Hank lent me one of his rifles. For my protection."

"Yes?"

"When I got home from Buffalo last night, it was gone."

Gene's face furrows. "And?"

"And Hank was here. On my porch."

"Hmm. Do you think he took it?"

"I have no idea. Right after you left this morning, Deputy Travis came, about the thefts and break-ins. I told him about the belt buckle and the guitar strap. About the person running out and under the fence. But I didn't tell him about the rifle. I don't know why. I was just . . . afraid to."

"Maggie—"

"Gene, what if it's the rifle that killed Patrick?"

Gene's expression is grim. "There are some things you need to know." He motions for Maggie to follow him, and they go out to the porch.

Louise flops inside the door. An afternoon storm has rolled in. Lightning flashes. A few seconds later, thunder shakes the roof over the porch. The air is greenish black and heavy. Maggie smells the sweet odor of ozone, like someone has dumped a bucket of chlorine into the clouds. Hail strikes the roof, small and high-pitched at first, then bigger chunks fall with deeper and deeper tonality. Rain joins in. Maggie remembers her piano lessons as a child. Adagio speeds up to allegro, until the sound is continuous, like a snare roll with a bass drum backbeat. Overspray mists the porch. Maggie wipes moisture from her cheek.

Water beads on Gene's forehead as he stands, hat in hand, at the railing. "Hank killed a man once."

Maggie sinks into the porch swing. She's surprised, but she's not shocked.

"It was self-defense. He was never charged with anything."

Maggie blinks away spots in her vision. She concentrates on her breath. "Tell me."

"Hank owed some people money once. Back in Cheyenne."

"Cheyenne."

"Yes. You remember?"

Of course she remembered. Hank had agreed to lose in return for increasing payments each round, so that Cristiano Valdez, the son of a Brazilian crime boss, could win at bull riding at Frontier Days. Then she and Hank met, and she'd told him she'd go out with him if he won. She'd only been flirting, hadn't realized the deadly serious price of her demand. A lovestruck Hank had double-crossed the Valdez family. He and Maggie spent a night on the run from them, before Maggie left for Nashville. Then Hank and Maggie hadn't spoken in fifteen years.

"I remember."

"They came after him. More than once. The first time was right after the head injury that retired him. After he was home. His dad was sick. His mom was overwhelmed, depressed. Two guys ambushed him coming out of the Mint Bar in Sheridan. Hank made it to his truck and held them off with a length of pipe. Took a chunk out of one of them."

"Don't mess with Hank."

"You have no idea." Gene smiles without mirth. "The second time was here on the ranch. Again, two guys. His mother was in her garden. One of the men grabbed her. The wind was blowing in the right direction, so Hank heard her scream. He had a rifle with a nice scope, and he sighted them in it from out there." Gene points into the pasture north of the main house. "He saw his mother clobber the guy holding her and break away. The guy pulled a gun on her, so Hank shot him."

"Oh my God."

"His mother got away. The other guy ran."

"And then what?"

"The guy he shot had fired his gun as he went down. Died with it in his hand. Hank had his mother to testify. The sheriff's department wrote it up as self-defense and the county attorney declined to prosecute. As far as I know, the Valdezes left Hank alone after that."

"Thank goodness."

"Yeah. But it sure isn't going to look good now. Especially because Patrick used to work for them."

"Them who?"

"He was the go-between for the Valdez family with Hank, back when this all started. When Hank reneged on his deal, he ended up on Patrick's bad side, too. And vice versa. Then Patrick got into stock contracting and moved his operation here. It's been an uneasy peace ever since."

Maggie's mind goes whirling and tumbling back in time, to the Hank she knew fifteen years before and the choices that led to this moment. To the Valdez family—the record deal they'd dangled in front of her if she chose Cristiano—and their long reach. "Oh God. There's history. And the rifle." Maggie's heart plummets. "It will look like his weapon of choice. And that he doesn't have a problem pulling the trigger."

"Maybe. That's what I'm afraid of. Even worse if it turns out that Patrick was shot with one of Hank's guns."

The hail suddenly stops. In its wake, Maggie's voice sounds unnaturally loud. "You don't think Hank would . . ."

"Kill someone unprovoked? In cold blood?"

"That."

Gene stares into the rain like he's searching for a truth that may wash away. "Maggie May, I've known him for more than twenty years. And, no, I don't think he'd kill unprovoked. Give him a good reason, though, a real good reason, and he'd do what he had to do."

Maggie weaves her hands together in her lap. Gene's words cut both ways, toward the good Hank and the bad. *But Hank swears he didn't kill Patrick, and that's what matters.* "I'm glad I didn't tell the deputies about the rifle.

"Me, too."

Gene's phone rings. He rips it from his pocket so violently it falls to the porch. He crouches to get it. "This is Soboleski." He listens, nods. "On my way."

"Hank?"

"The judge expedited bail. I'm heading back into town to get the money and pick him up."

Maggie squeezes her linked hands. Surely they wouldn't spring him this quickly if they really believed he'd murdered Patrick. Would they?

THIRTY-EIGHT

After another sleepless night—this time worrying about Hank and hearing nothing from anyone—Maggie feels like a human pincushion. She's dressed in boots, jeans, and her Double S jacket, pacing the porch, hobo bag over her shoulder. Considering a drive to Buffalo to talk to Lacey about Chet and the status on that investigation. Anything to kill time, or she'll come out of her skin. She sees Gene leaving the house, though, and all thoughts of Buffalo evaporate.

She runs to catch up to him, dodging a few muddy spots. The rain the day before was violent, but short. Somehow her boots still kick up dust, too. *Oh, Wyoming, make up your mind.* "Hey, Gene, wait up."

He walks back to meet her. "You weren't at breakfast. Or dinner last night."

"I have wheels, so I can eat where people don't hate me."

"I don't hate you. Hank doesn't. Paco and Andy don't. I don't think Tom or Trudy have anything against you, either."

"Mrs. Sibley, Laura, and Sheila do."

Gene grins. "True. But Sheila wasn't there."

"Fuck a bunch of Sheila. Why isn't she here for Hank?"

"Because he hasn't told her about his arrest."

"She'll find out."

"Exactly what I told him, but he said he wasn't up for dealing with her yet."

Maggie isn't up for dealing with her ever. They're closing in on the barn, but Gene detours for his truck.

Maggie's phone rings. It's the Ford dealership. She answers, midstride.

Her Alabama friend says, "Your truck's ready when you are, Ms. Killian."

She puts her hand over the phone. "Hey, my truck is ready. Any chance you can drop me in town to get it?"

Gene grabs keys from his pocket and twirls them on his fingers. "You're in luck. I was just heading in to pick up some vaccines at the vet."

Into the phone she says, "On my way. Thank you."

Maggie slings her bag onto the seat and climbs in after it.

"How is your truck ready so fast? I didn't think the part would be in until late today or tomorrow."

"Remember how I told you Hank was at my cabin when I got home night before last?"

"Yeah."

"There's more to the story than that." She fills him in on Patrick's old truck, the driveshaft delivery, and the men fighting in the yard.

Gene looks gut-punched. "Man, Hank better hope they don't call you in for questioning."

"It would help if I knew whether he told them about it, before that happens."

"I can't help you there. He refused to talk about it last night. Then he didn't come to breakfast today. I haven't even seen him."

Acid backs up Maggie's throat, burning her mouth. She'd misled Gene about using the Tahoe to go for food. She's had nothing but coffee since lunch yesterday. She's far too anxious for food. They bump along Wagon Box Road in silence while the radio plays new country. Nothing annoys Maggie like new country. She turns it off.

Gene shoots her a look. "Make yourself at home."

"Not for a second longer than I have to."

"Does that mean you're leaving us to go deal with your problems in Texas, now that you'll have your truck back?"

Maggie had forgotten about her Texas problems. She's officially at the end of her rope. They'll keep. For now. "I can't until I get an official farewell from the Buffalo PD."

"They haven't made any progress?"

"Not even with my help." She fills him in on the things she learned, minus the name of Chet's daughter, her mother's identity, and her unreturned voicemail to Lacey. She leaves out her concerns about Hank, too, just as she had with the detective.

"The baby-mama angle is promising." Gene turns onto a paved road.

Maggie doesn't answer.

"I said the baby-mama angle is promising."

"I heard you."

"You don't agree."

"I do. I also think Lisa and her family are worth a hard look."

"Then what is it?"

"What is what?"

Gene navigates the cloverleaf entrance to the interstate. "Your voice is funny. You're holding something back."

Maggie feels like she's eaten a bowl of sawdust. She opens the lid on a half-drank bottle of water and swigs it down.

"Help yourself."

"Thanks." She decides to probe Gene further. If she can trust anyone, it's this man. "Do you know anything about Sheila having a daughter?"

Gene's head bobs back, and his chin recedes into his neck. "I've never heard that. One she gave up for adoption?"

"I'm not sure."

"What are you not telling me?"

"Nothing certain. It's only a guess. And your answer tells me you can't confirm or refute it."

Gene's brow furrows, then he hits the steering wheel. "Are you suggesting Sheila is the mother of *Chet's* daughter?"

Maggie bites her lip.

"That's crazy."

"It could be her."

"Give me one reason why you think it is."

"Because Chet's daughter's name is Phoebe. And so is Sheila's little sister's."

Gene is so lost in thought he drives the truck onto the shoulder and has to correct it back onto the interstate. "Sorry."

"Well? Do you know any other little girls in the area named Phoebe?"

"Who says Chet's daughter even lives around here?"

Maggie watches out the window as they take the exit into town. An RV dealership, Heartland Kubota. After the turn, Taco John. The Mill Inn. "Nothing to say she doesn't."

The silence between them is long and awkward. Gene pulls into the service area of the Ford dealership. Maggie starts to get out, but he puts his hand on her arm. She pauses, looking back at him.

"Maggie, this sounds like an issue for Sheila and Hank. Not for you and me."

Maggie gets out, nodding in thought. "Thanks for the ride." She agrees. It's not an issue for her and Gene. *But it's time for it to be an issue for Hank and me.*

THIRTY-NINE

Hank is saddling Wolf by the barn when Maggie returns to Piney Bottoms, Louise lounging in the dirt beside them. She pulls Bess to a stop at the barn. Her hands are frozen on the steering wheel.

Maggie spent the whole drive home hashing out her approach with Hank. She has questions for him. Important ones. But Hank also needs her. Yes, he has a girlfriend, but she's a mere child, and Hank hasn't even told her about the trouble he's in. How much help can she be? And, sure, Laura is here, too, but that's not the kind of support Hank needs. Hank needs someone who understands what it means to be in trouble, whose life hasn't always been picture-perfect. He needs Maggie, whether he realizes it or not.

And she's here in Wyoming because she needs him.

She's never been a quitter. She's failed publicly and spectacularly in her life, but she's never quit. So she's not quitting now. She is going to get her answers. And she's going to figure out, once and for all, if there's a chance of a future for the two of them. If there is, she's going to fight for it. If there's not, she's going to be here for Hank, then leave knowing she gave it her all.

She's never been more scared in her life.

She pries her fingers from the wheel and gets out. Her hands are shaking and her face is hot. Louise sniffs her with the enthusiasm of a month's separation instead of two hours. Distracted, Maggie reaches down to stroke Louise's head and misses. The dog readjusts herself under Maggie's fingers. The scratch doesn't last long.

Maggie stuffs her keys in her purse and throws it back in the truck. She steels herself. Hank is in a dark place. She feels it on her own skin, like a cold sweat. "Hey, Hank."

Hank's face is stormy, a dangerous look she hasn't seen since she broke up with him in Texas. "Hey." He pulls the cinch strap so hard that Wolf snorts and bends his neck to give Hank a dirty look.

"What are you doing?"

Hank fastens Wolf's breast collar and back cinch. He hefts a saddlebag over Wolf's haunches and ties it down. Maggie approaches the side of the horse's head with her palm down. Wolf turns to it and sniffs, then chews and swallows. She scratches the T-spot on his forehead. He closes his eyes. His head droops a few inches.

Hank begins fastening his bow and quiver onto the side of Wolf's saddle. Maggie remembers what Andy told her, how Hank lent the boy his bow on the morning Hank told the others he was hunting, but was still covered in blood when Andy came back from his own hunt. She doesn't want to think about it yet. Soon, though. She'll get Hank to clear this all up and more, soon.

First, she has to keep him from pushing her away. "I asked what you're doing."

"Riding out to hunt."

"Where's Sheila?"

Hank grunts. A few seconds of silence later, he says, "She's already tagged her antelope with her dad."

Good. Sheila is still on the outside. "We need to talk, Hank. Let me go with you." She holds a breath, waiting for his answer.

"Don't you need to be on the road?"

"What?"

"Back to Texas in your purple truck." He tugs on straps that are already tight and doesn't look at her.

Does he want her gone? In her heart, she refuses to believe it. "Magenta. And I can't. Not until the police clear me to leave. Because of Chet."

He slips a bit into Wolf's mouth. "I'm grounded because of Patrick."

Maggie backs up to give him room to finish bridling the horse. "We may end up in adjoining cells."

Hank folds Wolf's left ear down for the headstall, then the right. He fastens the throat strap and jiggles the chin chain to straighten it. "Are you going to get Lily or not?" He digs in his pocket and comes out with some horse cookies that he drops in Maggie's hand. "But your dog can't come."

"She's not my dog." Maggie thinks of her regal golden retrievers, two years dead. Of her twin goats, Omaha and Nebraska, that took their place in her heart. She doesn't need a goofy pint-size border collie.

"Oh, she's yours, all right." In a derisive voice, he sings to the dog, "The stars at night, are big and bright."

Louise howls along with him.

"Great. Come on, girl." Maggie jogs off, stopping with Louise at the dog run by the barn first.

Louise stares at her balefully from behind the chain-link enclosure.

"Don't look at me like that. I'm sorry. Really."

She heads next to Lily, who watches Maggie approach, big black head over the fence.

Maggie scoops up the rope halter, opens the gate, and slips inside. "I've missed you, Lily girl."

Lily crunches a cookie while Maggie ties her halter.

"You look even more beautiful than usual today. Ready to help me with your dark and impossible owner?"

Lily noses Maggie, looking for more cookies.

Maggie clucks and tugs Lily into a slow trot. When the two reach the hitching post, Hank has all Lily's gear ready. He saddles her in the time it takes for Maggie to fasten her lead line and holds the bridle out to Maggie. Gene and Hank have tacked Lily up for her every other time Maggie's ridden her. Maggie takes the bridle, staring first at it, then at the very tall horse whose ears are higher than Maggie can reach. She peeks at Hank under her lashes. He's studying her, expressionless.

"Okay." She holds the bit up in front of Lily's mouth, thinking. The horse licks it. Maggie smiles. She puts a cookie in the hand by the bit, then lowers it. Lily follows the cookie. When the horse has her head low enough, Maggie stops her hand. Lily takes the bit and the cookie both at once. Maggie positions the chin strap and manhandles the headstall over Lily's ears. The mare chomps without protesting or lifting her head. Maggie finishes with the chin strap, then curtsies for Hank.

"Ready?"

"Ready." She stands at Lily's shoulder, waiting for a leg up.

Hank mounts Wolf, then pushes the brim of his hat back to scratch his forehead. "Are you coming?"

Maggie's not sure why he's testing her, but she's not about to fail. She searches for something to climb. There's nothing, and the ground is flat.

Hank nudges Wolf closer. "Grab her mane, close to the saddle. Put your toe in the stirrup and stay as close to her as you can. Use the mane to pull yourself up as you jump. Use your other hand on the cantle."

"What's the cantle?"

"The thing that keeps your ass from sliding off the back."

"Got it."

"Be careful not to lever your body out from her. Straight up." His voice is slightly less curt.

"Easy for you to say."

"Try."

"I don't want to hurt her."

"It doesn't hurt her. Trust me."

Trust me. She wants to tell him how hard that is to do right now, when she knows he's lied. That's one strike. Then he went after Patrick, drunk, when he should have left well enough alone. That's two strikes against trust. Hell, he's kissed her when he's dating another woman. That should be strike three. But no matter how many strikes he has, she also knows that if she wants him to trust her enough to tell her the truth, she has to show him some trust of her own.

Drawing in a deep breath, Maggie follows his instructions. Her first try ends several inches short of success. The saddle creaks, but at least it doesn't slip sideways. And Lily doesn't move a muscle.

Maggie flops back to the ground like a fish. "I can't."

"Try again. You were too tentative with her mane."

Maggie mutters. "Sadist."

Hank makes a sound that might be a laugh. Maggie's heart lights up like it's hooked to a generator. She would try fifty more times if it would make him happy. She takes another deep breath, hooks her heel in the stirrup. She feels ridiculous, like she's hanging by her heel from a trapeze, a low-rent circus act. *The things a woman does for love*, she thinks. This time she hops a few times on her straight leg before bending deep to access her thigh power. As she jumps, she channels her anger at Hank, magnified by the power of her love for him, into a massive jerk on Lily's mane. She uses all her upper-body strength and tightens her core to keep her progress vertical.

At the apex of her ascent, her body is high enough to swing her straight leg over the mare's broad back, where she bangs her knee to a stop on the cantle. She collapses across the saddle horn, her legs in a flying herkie, the jump she'd mastered her one year as a high school cheerleader. She had been the worst on the squad, both in terms of skill and attitude, before she'd run away for Nashville. She's feeling just about the same now as she did then. Sucky.

"Don't stop. Use that stirrup leg now."

Maggie doesn't have a hand to shoot him a bird since she's clinging to Lily's back like a baby spider monkey. She pushes off her stirrup leg and crawls the rest of the way into the saddle. Zero grace, but she makes it.

"Nicely done."

"Liar." Now that she's on Lily's back all by herself, her anger and bad attitude fades. That was kind of badass.

"You'll get better at it."

Her heart quickens, liking the sound of that. "If she'd moved a muscle . . ."

"You'd be eating dirt."

"With my butt."

He laughs for real, even giving up a quick flash of dimples. "Come on." He issues some invisible signal to Wolf, and the gray takes off at a slow lope.

"Thanks for waiting on us, butthead." She clucks as she squeezes with her legs. "Don't let him get away, Lily. We're making progress."

It's all the encouragement the mare needs. She gathers her bulk and catches Wolf, and Hank and Maggie ride out at a lope, side by side.

FORTY

When the horses slow for a breather, Hank says, "So, you said you wanted to talk to me. Talk."

There's a firestorm of questions burning its way through Maggie's head. It's so intense that she can't pick just one.

Despite his earlier dimples, Hank is still edgy. "Well?"

"Cool your jets. I'm trying."

"How about I go first, then. What possessed you with Sheila?"

Maggie is taken aback. She'd been so caught up in what she needed to talk to him about, she'd forgotten about her scene with Sheila. "Um, you're talking about . . ."

"You making her believe you and I are carrying on behind her back. And she said you made a pass at her?"

"Believe me, if I'd have made a pass at her, she wouldn't have told you what we ended up doing. I just . . . pushed on her a little."

"Jeez, Maggie."

"Well, you did kiss me."

"We kissed each other. And I said I was sorry."

"I heard you."

"Sheila chewed my ass."

"There appears to still be enough left to work with." One good thing has come from Hank turning the tables on her. She doesn't feel like sparing his feelings anymore, and her words burst forth like a fireball. "Speaking of which, why the asswipe move insisting I come to lunch the other day for a 'surprise' only to shove the big reveal of your girlfriend to your mom and sister down my throat?"

"What? That wasn't my surprise. I didn't even know Sheila was coming."

His words sprinkle drops of cool rain on her hot emotions. "Really?"

"I just thought you'd like seeing Laura. I was excited about her visit."

"She hates me."

"Maybe she knows you went to dinner at Winchesters with Patrick Rhodes."

Just like that, he fans her flames again. "Maybe it's something you told her about me."

He shoots her a withering look. "If you mean does she know I asked you to share my life and you said no, again, then yes, it's something I told her. We're loyal like that."

The horses amble on. Maggie is oblivious to their surroundings, to the weather, to the animal under her. The conversation isn't going well. At all. And she's barely started on the things she needs to talk to Hank about. She fights to contain her raging thoughts, to keep them from exploding all over him and making things even worse.

"You're killing me. If you're not going to say what you had to say, why'd you come?"

"Obviously not for the pleasure of your company."

"What'd you expect? I'm having a bad day. I was arrested for a murder I didn't commit."

His horrible attitude is wearing her down, and her voice is sharper than she intends. "Hank, are you forgetting I was there when you fought Patrick?"

Hank jerks Wolf to a stop. The horse tosses his head and chews at the bit. "Are you fucking kidding me? You think I killed him?"

"How should I know? You took off from my cabin after attacking him for no reason, and next thing I hear, you've chased him down and fought him again at his place, and then he's dead."

"No reason? You have no idea all the reason I have."

"No thanks to you. But don't worry, Gene filled me in on your *past*. Patrick working for the Valdez family. The Valdez thugs coming to town. You fighting them off with a tire iron. Defending your mom by shooting one of them with a rifle."

"Gene has a big mouth."

"Whatever. None of that is going to help you much with the deputies now, and I need to know what happened, and what you told the deputies, for when they question me, Hank."

Hank spurs Wolf, who takes off like a rocket. Maggie urges Lily to catch him, but the gelding leaves her like she's standing still. Maggie doubts Lily could have stayed with Wolf even if she wasn't pregnant and wanted to. And she doesn't want to. Maggie slows the mare to an easy trot. Ahead, Wolf is a gray streak across the waving brown prairie. When Maggie can barely see it anymore, the gray streak slows, then stops. Ten minutes later, they overtake Wolf. He's grazing with his reins over his saddle horn. Hank is lying on his back nearby, head cradled in his hands, shoulders propped on a boulder.

Maggie and Lily stop beside him. "I shouldn't have told you what Patrick said."

"I shouldn't have chased after him and picked another fight. Don't blame yourself. It wasn't just what you told me. It was a lot of things."

"Like what?"

Hank smiles. One side of his mouth, one dimple. It's enough to kickstart Maggie's pulse. "He shouldn't be making moves on you."

She hates that she loves hearing him say this. "You've got a girlfriend."

"I don't think I'll ever be okay with the thought of you with someone else. Especially not him. But he was alive and well when I left for the summer cabin."

She hadn't asked where he stayed yet, and she ticks this off her burning list of questions. "The summer cabin?"

"The one up on the mountain."

"I know where it is. You told me about it."

"It's where I go for solitude."

This makes sense. She believes him. But she can't stop now. "The police say Patrick was shot with a rifle."

"Yeah. And I defended my mom with a rifle. They're trying to make a thing of it. Ballistics will clear me."

"But how, if there's no weapon?"

"Because the bullet won't match any of mine. And none of mine had been fired."

Unless the shot was fired from his stolen rifle. She's scared to bring it up. But she has to. She will. She just needs a minute to figure out the right way, to get her courage up. When she does, she'll ask him about Sheila, Chet, and Phoebe, too. "I wish there was a way to clear me that easy in the Chet mess."

"I wish you'd never left the Occidental with Chet."

"Hank . . ."

"What? You don't like that I'm jealous? After the stunt you pulled with Sheila, you don't have much room to talk."

Touché. She changes course. "Were you at the summer cabin the night you told Sheila you were going hunting? After you saw me with Chet?"

He cocks his head at her. "Yes. Why?"

"Did you go fight with him, too, like Patrick?"

"I didn't like the douchebag, and I hated seeing you with him. But he's not worth my time."

"You lent Andy your bow."

He sits up, jumps to his feet. "What did you say?"

"You lent Andy your bow. But you told Sheila you went hunting."

"I lied to Sheila. And then it snowballed, and I had to lie to everyone at lunch. That wasn't a good moment."

"Hank, Andy saw you that morning. You were covered in blood."

"What are you saying?"

"I just need to understand what happened."

"You came out here alone with me to ask me if I killed Patrick, and now Chet? You either already know the answers, or you have a death wish yourself."

"You won't hurt me."

"Why's that?"

"Because you love me."

"Aren't *you* the smart one." His tone is dark. His face is darker.

He whistles for Wolf. The horse trots back to him, and Hank slips him a cookie. He clears his throat, and his expression relaxes to normal. Or semi-normal. As normal as he gets with a murder charge hanging over his head. "Real cowboys don't use horse treats. Now you know all my secrets." He remounts and takes off at a trot.

Maggie isn't letting him run off again. She and Lily stick with them from the get-go. The horses eat up ground in a slow trot, their riders silent again. Maggie wants to tell Hank she loves him, too. That she believes in him. She needs him to answer her questions, to clear the air, but she believes in him. In them.

"Hank . . ."

He rushes to cut off her emotional tone. "What's the holdup with the investigation into Chet's death? Don't the police have any suspects?"

"No, none. Unless you count me. Even though there's a list as long as my arm of people with motive, which I don't have a lick of."

Hank stares at her. Can he hear the tremor in her voice? "Like who?"

Is he testing her? Teasing her? Serious? She watches him, treading lightly and carefully. What if she blurts out "Sheila?" But she holds it in. Finally, she says, "I think that's a question for the police."

At the top of a broad ridge, Hank stops Wolf. Without permission, Lily joins him in the rest. Maggie looks around. She recognizes the view in one direction, although she's seeing it from a new angle. The creek, the fence at the property line, Rudy's ramshackle place.

"I've seen a big buck out this way recently. Let's hunker down and wait."

"Okay." Maggie urges Lily forward a few feet, wanting distance from Hank and the disturbing thoughts still swirling in her mind. The grass crunches under the horse's hooves. She sees movement in the distance on the far side of the ridge. "Is that an antelope herd?"

Hank whirls in his saddle. He grins. "Hell yeah. No time to hunker down. Do you want to take the shot? I'll let you have my tag."

"No, that's okay." Maggie's in no shape to operate a weapon with her mind in a muddle.

In a few swift moves, Hank liberates his bow from Wolf's side and throws the quiver over his back.

The herd is moving. Maggie's emotions are roiling and her mind aflame. She feels swept along by a force bigger than herself, like she's caught in the middle of the running hooves with no way out but to speak.

"Whoa, boy." Wolf stands like a statue. Hank nocks an arrow and takes aim.

Maggie's secret erupts out of her before he can shoot. "I know about Phoebe. That she's Sheila and Chet's daughter."

Hank cuts his eyes to her without dropping his bow and arrow. "So do I."

Oh God. Hank *knows*? That gives him almost as much motive as Sheila. More, in some ways. And now that her fears are pouring out, she can't stop the flow. "And your rifle. The .300 Win Mag you lent me. It was stolen from my cabin two days ago."

Hank's bow arm falters. "What the hell?"

A loud *pow* rips through the silence, the sound lingering for several seconds. Lily jumps, then hotfoots in place. Maggie gathers the reins in.

"Oomph."

The sound is from Hank, and Maggie turns toward him. His body slumps, then lists sideways. He topples from the saddle to the ground. Wolf prances and rears beside him.

Maggie screams. "Hank."

There's a second *pow*. Wolf spins and falls. The sounds he makes are purest animal agony. He writhes and kicks, his hooves dangerously close to Hank.

Lily panics. Her back end catapults upward, but with a funny twist. Maggie pushes down with her feet and tush. She reaches for the saddle horn, but Lily's next buck comes too fast. The force of her motion flings Maggie's arms upward. Lily leaps forward and to the side. Maggie feels air between her butt and the saddle, then, as her feet fly up and out of the stirrups, she thinks Gene was right—Lily bucks with enthusiasm and strength. Then she's floating, like a dying bird, several feet above Lily's head. But not for long. The ground comes, hard and fast. Maggie lands hard—rump first, shoulder and ribs second—in the space where Lily was a moment before.

Pain shoots up Maggie's rear and back. She groans, rolls onto her elbows, and drags herself, hips flat against the ground. Lily's hooves jackhammer the ground, then grow rhythmic and softer as she bolts away. Maggie twists, trying to find Hank. Wolf's thrashing body is in the way.

"Maggie," Hank calls, his voice a rasp. "Are you okay?"

"I'm not sure." She can't catch her breath, but she forces words out. "Are you?"

"I've been shot."

Of course. It's the only thing that makes sense. Hank and Wolf. She pants and keeps dragging her inert body toward Hank, around Wolf's sharp, flailing hooves. "Who would shoot at us?"

"Don't know. Maybe a poacher. Somewhere north of us. Can you walk?"

Maggie tries to stand. She doesn't make it, but her hips rise enough for her to crawl on her hands and knees. From this height she can see Hank, beside his bloody horse. She must be in a state of shock, because everything feels like it's moving in slow motion, including her emotions. She feels bad for the squalling horse, but she has to get to Hank, and it seems to be taking her forever.

Finally, she reaches him. He's bloodier than Wolf, and it takes all her will power to remain calm. Hank needs her.

Another *pow* sends Maggie flat on her belly. It's followed in rapid succession by two more, with the three protracted sounds overlapping for a brief moment.

"Shit," Maggie says.

"Maybe not a poacher."

After a few seconds of silence, she raises herself on her elbows again. His cheek looks uninjured, and she touches it. "Where did it hit you?"

He points slowly at his side with the hand and arm cradling it. The other arm hangs limp. "Hurts like a sumbitch."

She has to get help. Her panic rises again and she feels like the sky is expanding and pressing her down. Maggie pulls out her phone and checks it. "No signal." She yells at the heavy sky, "Fuck you, Wyoming." She returns it to her pocket. "Do you have yours?"

"Shirt pocket."

She pats it gingerly, but there's no phone. Scanning in concentric circles, she spots it ten feet away lying beside a rock. She crawls to it. It's broken nearly in half. She tries to turn it on anyway. Nothing happens. Horse hoof, she realizes.

She crawls back to Hank. "Broken. I could build a travois and drag you out. If there were any trees. But there aren't. Not any closer than there." She points to the edge of the woods up the side of the mountain, a half mile or more away.

"No tools. No lashing. Try again."

"I need to get you out of here."

Hank winces. "You need to go for help."

She looks around for her horse, hoping for a miracle, but doesn't see the mare, just a dark wall of clouds closing in. "Lily's gone." She rises to her knees, weight off her hands. Her tailbone sends pain shooting through her like fireworks. Still, it's progress.

"Go to Rudy's. Not too far. Call Gene. Tell him . . . tell him I'm where he got the buck mule deer last fall. And take my gun."

"Gotta get you outta the line of fire, first. And stop the bleeding."

"I'm fine."

Maggie ignores him. She becomes aware that Wolf's cries are softer and farther apart, but she can't worry about him. She has to help Hank. She grabs him under his arms. This time, she's able to stand, but when she pulls he doesn't budge. "Come on, dammit." The harder she pulls, the worse it hurts.

She bends her legs, tears streaming down her face. "Fuck off, pain."

Using all the strength she has, she drags Hank one foot, then falls on her injured butt. She screams.

"It's okay, Maggie. I'll be fine."

She ignores Hank and hooks her arms under his again. Sweat joins her tears. On her next try she gets him another foot before she crashes to the ground, weeping. Then eighteen inches, then two whole feet. Finally, she props him behind a rocky outcropping. She takes off her Double S jacket. She wads up a sleeve and forces it against his wound.

Hank's face whitens, and he cries out. "Argh."

"You've gotta press here."

He nods. He tries to get his hand in place, but he can't get the right leverage to apply pressure.

"I can put a rock on it. Or you can roll on your side."

"Rock won't work." He rolls over onto the jacket, grimacing.

Maggie shoves a rock under the coat and him, forcing the wad of fabric further and tighter against the wound.

Hank gasps, "You're enjoying this."

"Not one iota." She grasps his face. "Don't you die on me."

"Too ornery. But I could use help."

"What do you need?"

He dimples, and she's done for. He has a girlfriend. He's killed a man before. Maybe others. Probably not, but there's not time to be sure. Because fuck if she doesn't love the shit out of this man. She always has. She always will. And that's all that matters right now. She presses her lips against his. Hard at first, then soft, and her lips cling to his.

Lightning flashes around them and thunder cracks almost instantaneously. Maggie's body electrifies and it's almost as if it levitates. Their lips break apart. She squeals. The unmistakable scent of ozone fills the air.

"That helps, music girl. Wow. I think the earth even moved."

It helps her, too. "Yeah, it was okay."

She gets more dimples, then his eyes roll back. "Hank?" She shakes him. "Hank?"

His eyes flutter open. "Hurts a lot."

"I have to go. I have to get help for you. Can I do anything for Wolf?"

He groans. "Damn good horse. Can he stand?"

Wolf has quit struggling. His big barreled rib cage rises and falls with his breaths that are far too slow. "No. I'm sorry."

Hank makes a choking sound, then holds the rest of his feelings in. "Me, too."

Maggie stands, grabbing Hank's bow.

"Take the gun. Bows aren't for emergencies."

She has to leave his gun. For whoever shot at them, if it isn't a poacher. The thought rips her insides raw. The shooter could still be targeting them. Or on his way here. Hank has to be able to protect himself. Besides, he has a decision to make. About Wolf. One that he needs a gun and a bullet to carry out.

She puts as much sass in her voice as she can muster. "What, haven't you seen Daryl with his bow on *The Walking Dead?*"

He shakes his head and smiles. "You're something else, Maggie Killian." Then he coughs.

She sees blood on his lips, whether from splatter or from his insides, she doesn't know, but it's powerfully motivating. "I'll be back as soon as I can." She turns and jogs, limping painfully, in the direction she prays will take her to Rudy's house.

FORTY-ONE

"Damn you, Lily."

How is it that Maggie's spending most of her time going uphill, when it looked like Rudy's house was down below her, last time she saw it? She struggles her way through thick sagebrush, keeping her profile low, in case the shooter is still out there. The long-legged, four-footed Percheron would have breezed over the rough terrain Maggie is stumbling over. Rocks. Cactus. Buckbrush. Hummocks, gullies, and sinkholes. Maggie doesn't bother picking the thorns and stickers from her clothes anymore. Or the dirt and rocks ground painfully into her palms from breaking falls. Somewhere in the distance, she hears an engine, like an ORV. It's heading in the same direction she is. Eastward, down through the foothills.

A *crack* blasts behind her. She gasps and drops to a hunched-over crouch level with the flora around her. Dust tickles her nostrils, followed by the bitter, spicy smell of crushed sagebrush leaves. After a few seconds of silence, she rises, slow and cautious. It was definitely a gunshot, but it sounded different than the ones earlier, at least to her ear. Sharper, less drawn out. As her fear subsides, she realizes why. Wolf. Hank's handgun. He'd put the horse down. It's the humane thing to do, but another blow in a lengthy barrage. She doesn't have time for sadness now, though. She fights her way onward.

At the top of the rise, she looks back. Hank is no longer in view. But there's something else she does see. A curl of smoke rising from trees half a mile and at a higher elevation from where he'd gone down. Had he crawled to the woods and started a signal fire? As she stands watching, flames ignite in the upper reaches of the pines, exploding like a gas fire. Even from this distance, the boom, crackling, and hiss carries its way to her ears. That's no signal fire or campfire.

It's a forest fire.

The fear she felt before mushrooms into a panic that threatens to consume her. She's paralyzed for long moments—too long.

A strange delirium slips over her. She hears things she shouldn't hear and sees things she shouldn't see.

"Go." The voice that commands her is brusque but feminine. "Go fast." A woman appears out of the gulch on a small paint horse. She's riding bareback, her long legs dangling below its belly.

"Can I borrow your horse?" Maggie croaks. She waves her hand at Rudy's place. "It's so far." She turns to measure the distance with her eyes. When she returns her gaze to the woman, she says, "Or you can go . . ." Her words taper into nothingness. The woman is gone.

"Jesus, Maggie, get a grip." Maybe she's breathing in things she shouldn't. Or dehydrated. Whatever it is, she has to get going, pronto. Get to Rudy's before her mind is totally gone, and it's too late for Hank.

She whirls to take off at a run, but her leg slides into a wide burrow. She barely has time to worry what kind of animal lives in a den that big— Coyote? Badger? Fox? Rattlesnakes?—before the shrieking pain in her tush demands all her attention. She crawls on all fours up and out of the hole, dirt and rocks flying out from under her feet. When she's a safe distance away, she flops panting and contorted on top of the quiver and bow, but she doesn't care. It's her second fall, and her butt throbs with red-hot pain. She remembers how she felt in rehab. The withdrawals, her screams. It was bad, but she was strong enough to beat it.

She's strong enough to beat this. To get help for Hank. A waterproof jacket and rock aren't enough to staunch his blood flow forever, and now there's fire on the mountain, too.

The pain has broken her out of her delirium at least. No more hallucinations or hearing the voices of nonexistent Indians. She forces herself to her feet. After a few hopping steps favoring her injured side, she breaks into a trot, then a lopsided run. She runs, and runs, and runs, and keeps running, barely seeing where she's going until she reaches the creek. She charges in without slowing, her breath coming in dry sobs. She feels exposed here. Vulnerable to the shooter. But there's nothing she can do but move fast and low. The rocks wobble under her feet. Water splashes to her knees, shockingly cold.

Past the creek, she picks her way across the barbed-wire fence—down again—and up the grassy slope to Rudy's shack, shivering. Wet and jacketless, she's suddenly aware the temperature has fallen some fifteen degrees since she and Hank left the barn. Smoke curls upward from the chimney in Rudy's shack. It's a good sign. Rudy is home. Or was home recently. Running on a grassy yard now, she pulls out her phone to check for a signal as she sprints the last few yards to his door.

Nothing. Always and ever unreliable.

She turns back toward Hank. She puts it back in her pocket at the door, then knocks, sending needles through knuckles. "Rudy? Rudy! Help. Are you in there?"

She waits, listening, but there's no answer. She needs his phone. She tries the doorknob. It turns, and she pokes her head into his house. "Rudy, it's Maggie Killian. I'm coming in to borrow your phone. I have an emergency."

No answer.

It's dark inside, and it takes her eyes several seconds to adjust. At first, all she notices is clutter. The man is a packrat. Stacks of magazines teeter next to a fire crackling in the grate. Cardboard boxes line one wall. Above them, plastic and paper bags in the hundreds hang from hooks. Her eyes move to the kitchen on the opposite side of the room. Stacks of plastic containers cover most of the counter space, up to a sink with a large window over it. There's no curtain, and she sees Lily outside. Her Lily. With Rudy. The mare is nibbling something from Rudy's hand as he rubs her forehead, a rifle strapped to his back. A four-wheeler is parked just beyond the two of them.

Maggie starts to call out for Rudy again, but she sees a set of keys and a phone between the crowded stacks on the kitchen counter, ten feet away, behind a couch that's acting as a bookshelf. She lurches over to the phone like the Hunchback of Notre Dame, dragging her bad leg. It's a cordless landline phone. She presses the power button. No dial tone. Shit. She turns slowly, trying to see into, under, on, and around the mess, but there are no other phones in sight.

It's then that she becomes fully aware of her surroundings. The walls are covered like the floors and furniture, with not a bare spot to be found. There are posters. Flyers. Photographs. Album covers.

And they're all of her.

Her hand flies to her throat, and she steps up to the biggest one. It's a concert poster for the North Dakota State Fair, fifteen years ago. Maggie Killian and Crew. She's on an outdoor stage, somewhere, and her hair is elevated an inch higher at the crown than she wears it now, blowing in a stiff breeze. She's all leg in high-heeled boots and a frayed-hem blue-jean miniskirt that barely covers the essentials. The belt hanging around her hips is one she wore pre-Hank, a string of silver conchos. Someone had drawn a heart shape around her in red marker.

Why would Rudy have this? Then she remembers what he'd told her at the Occidental. It's the event where he met her, in Minot, North Dakota.

Magazine and newspaper articles are crammed into the mix on the walls for a chilling pictograph of her history. A *New York Times* article lauding her for standing up to shock jock Aaron Cryor when he harassed her on his radio show. Album and single charts. Grammy award nominations and her one win. Boozy photos on glossy magazine paper of her with a succession of forgotten men. A write-up about the musical theater in Waco she'd performed in after she lost her record deal. Gossip-rag pieces tattling on her rehab stints. Even the recent "How the Mighty Maggie Killian Has Fallen" entertainment blog piece is tacked to the wall.

The creepfest is most recent in the kitchen. Stuck to the refrigerator with a Wyoming Cowboys Football Schedule magnet, she finds a brand new photograph of her from last Thursday night, talking to Chet. His face is no longer recognizable, since it's blacked out in pen, the marks made with such force that they tore the photo paper. Another defaced photo hangs underneath it by a strip of Scotch tape, this one of her with Patrick, from the back, walking into the Wagon Box Inn. A third recent photo, also taped, is of her on Lily, riding beside Wolf and a man whose face has been removed from the picture, too. Hank.

Her Hank, who's lying shot and bleeding a hard mile away, with a fire bearing down on him.

And Rudy is outside stroking the face of the mare that doesn't like to be touched. Feeding her treats. Goose bumps pimple Maggie's flesh. On her arms, her chest, and her neck. There's something so off-kilter about it. About Lily, Hank, Patrick, Chet—and Rudy's crazy all-Maggie decor.

About Rudy. Is this what she thinks it is? The rifle. The four-wheeler. Yes. Yes, it is.

She hears a noise outside the front door. Boots stomping off dirt? There's nowhere to hide. No time to run. If it's Rudy, he'll know immediately she's seen all of this. That she knows what it means. He's an ox, and she won't stand a chance unless she strikes first.

She pulls the bow from her shoulder and nocks an arrow, firms her stance, and aims for the door.

It swings outward, creaking.

Rudy strolls into the living area, her guitar strap around his shoulder like a pageant sash. He smiles. "Maggie Killian. You've come to see me." His smiles droops when he sees her bow pointed at him.

She pulls back the string as he grabs for the rifle strapped to his back. She releases it as he slips his finger in the trigger and pulls, too late. Her arrow strikes him in the left shoulder. His shot reverberates in the small, crowded space. Maggie's ears feel like they're imploding, but the bullet goes high and wide and the rifle clatters to the floor.

Rudy bellows and grasps the shaft. Maggie grabs another arrow from the quiver. He sees her preparing to shoot and lumbers to the door, his hand sliding up to the fletching before he grabs the doorframe and propels himself outside.

Maggie runs for the keys on the kitchen counter by the dead phone. Maybe there's one to Rudy's van. She's got to find a phone or cell signal. Behind the keys is a belt and a big shiny Cheyenne Frontier Days buckle crammed between plastic towers.

The buckle, the strap on Rudy's shoulder, and the rifle on the floor? She glances back at the rifle on the floor. A .300 Win Mag. Even from this distance, she's sure of it. All of them, things taken from her guest cabin at the ranch. Her things. Now that she's made the connection, another mystery unravels: Lily letting Rudy feed her and pet her. Rudy's been sneaking around the ranch, breaking into her cabin, stealing things, and visiting *her Lily* while he's there.

She grabs the keys and the buckle and races out the door. Even with the dark clouds, the outside light blinds her for a moment. When she gets her bearings, the first thing she sees is Rudy, staggering toward the creek. He crumples on the bank.

Good. She hopes he never gets up again.

She rounds the cabin quickly, looking for Rudy's van, and finds it on the side of the shack. She jerks the door open. Inside, she jams key after key into the ignition. On the third try, she hits pay dirt. The engine turns. She floors the accelerator and fishtails down the long driveway, praying she's not too late.

Within minutes, it is clear that she's lost. Hopelessly lost with not a farmhouse or vehicle in sight. Which means no phones. The only thing she's seen on the rutted, one-lane road is cows, deer, and barbed wire. She sobs as she drives, praying aloud. "Come on, T-Mobile. Please, God, let Wyoming cut me just one break. I'll do anything. Just please help me save Hank."

She doesn't expect an answer from God. Not after the way she's treated him all these years. That's why she's so stunned she nearly drives Rudy's van into a fence when her phone rings.

She mashes the brakes to the floor. The van shimmies and bounces to a stop over the washboard, pulling even farther toward the fence. The phone clatters to the floorboard on the passenger side.

"No, no, no!"

Maggie throws the van in park. She dives after the phone, landing with her head against the glove box, her stomach on the passenger seat, and her palms in a three-bag-thick layer of old fast food and rancid ketchup. She holds herself up by her head and digs like a mole for her phone. She presses it and a soggy white bun to her face, her hand slimy with moldy tomato.

"Hello?" She pushes herself up with her other hand, leaving a yellow handprint on the seat.

"Maggie. This is Gene. Lily just galloped into the barnyard without you. Are you okay?"

Maggie babbles so incoherently even she doesn't understand herself. But Gene does. Somehow.

"Let me confirm before I call 911. Hank's shot, he's where I got the buck muley last year, and there's a forest fire?"

"Yes." There's so, so much more. But that is all that matters.

"I'll call you as soon as help is on the way."

Maggie isn't about to drive farther in the wrong direction, where she might lose signal again. While she waits on Gene to call back, Maggie wipes her hands and face with her dirty shirt. A sticker scratches her face. She's sure she's making muddy streaks on her cheeks, if her hands are any indication. Still, it's better than food waste smeared from ear to ear.

She pulls up her Maps app and follows the roads from her position back to Piney Bottoms. She takes back every curse she uttered about Lily. She's giving her a double ration of oats when she sees her next. And she gets out of the van, hits her knees in the dirt, and prays again. God deserves a huge thank-you, too, and a reminder that there's a long way to go before Hank's safe.

This time she picks up on the first ring when Gene calls.

He speaks before she can say hello. "There's ground and air rescue on the way, and fire fighters. I gave them GPS coordinates."

"It's really rugged out there."

"They'll get him with a helicopter. The ground crew is just in case. And they'll have ORVs."

"There's more. It wasn't important enough to slow you down." She tells him about Rudy. All of it. "He was still alive when I left. And the rifle was in the cabin. They need to know. He's dangerous."

"Jesus, Maggie May. Thank God you're alive."

"Let's just hope Hank is."

"He's tough. You've gotta believe that."

"I do." She sniffs back another sob. "I do."

He patches her through to the sheriff and stays on the line while she updates the dispatcher with everything to relay to the deputies en route. They drop the third line.

"Can you find your way back here?"

"I've got it mapped."

"I'll take Laura and head to the hospital."

"I'll meet you there."

Back at Piney Bottoms fifteen minutes later, Maggie races past the barn. Paco is outside washing Lily. He waves with one hand. Maggie waves back. She slams the camo van into park in front of the cabin before the vehicle even stops moving. She hates having it here. It's like Rudy is here somehow, again.

Inside, she doesn't take time even to wash her face. She wants out of here. Not just out of here to go to Hank. Out of here completely. This place where her privacy and peace were violated. She doesn't know where she'll go, but she knows she won't be coming back to this cabin.

She grabs all her things—including Louise—guns Bess north, coaxing the truck to its top speed of eighty miles per hour and holding her there, all the way into Sheridan.

FORTY-TWO

Maggie pulls her hair back in a handheld pony. It's snarled and matted. She releases it again and looks at her hand as she lowers it. Ground-in dirt, thick with a greasy sheen from Lily's coat. A wide stain of Hank's blood, flaking where it's thickest but also deep in her pores. She hadn't changed before coming to the hospital, other than to slide the belt through her belt loops and fasten the Cheyenne Frontier Days buckle. There's no patch of clean left on her T-shirt, the nastiest of it the fast-food detritus a la Rudy. Dirt, burs, dog hair, and blood cling to the new holes ripped in her jeans.

She rests her head against the wall and slumps, turning her attention to the mass-produced Western art on the walls of the waiting room. Tans bleeding into pinks and oranges and back again until the palette reaches greens. It's soothing. She lets her mind go, relaxes into the scene.

"Maggie?"

The Betty Boop voice breaks Maggie's trance. "Sheila."

"What's going on? Is Hank okay?" Tear tracks streak the foundation on Sheila's cheeks. She's in jeans, Keds, and a Buffalo Elementary T-shirt, hair in a high ponytail.

The handful of people in the room stare at Maggie and Sheila. Old men, bones razor sharp inside jeans held up by suspenders. Matching women, only slightly softer in body, but their faces steely and inscrutable. Waiting for whom? For what news? Maggie only knows they aren't here for Hank. She is.

Maggie gets to her feet but doesn't touch the other woman. "He's out of surgery. In recovery. That's all I know." *Because I'm not family, but then, neither are you.* "Laura and Gene are with the doctor now."

"Oh God. Is he going to die?" For a Wyoming woman, Sheila's near-hysteria is surprising. A woman has to be tough to live here.

"I don't think so." Underlying fear laps at Maggie's calm, but she keeps it out of her voice. Hank is alive only because Gene knew where to send the helicopter and rescue team. Hank had lost so much blood. But the doctors said the bullet hadn't done serious internal damage. It could have been much worse. The worst. But it wasn't.

"I'm nearly thirty. I've spent all this time on him. He can't die." Sheila throws herself onto a couch and starts to sob.

Maggie isn't up for coddling Sheila. "Yes, it would be such a tragedy for *you*. And Chet Moore's daughter, of course." Maggie considers the horrible irony of it all. So many people with motives to do Chet in. All that she uncovered about the mess that was his life. None of it in the end having a damn thing to do with why he died.

No, that was all on Maggie.

Sheila's waterworks shut down fast. She glares at Maggie. "What did you say?"

"Nothing." She wants to claw at the selfish younger woman, but makes a hasty exit instead.

Unsure of anything other than she needs to keep her distance from Sheila, Maggie paces the hallways of the hospital. Works the kinks out of her sore butt, and wonders if she should get an X-ray, but decides no—it's not like they can put a cast on her ass. Grabs a coffee and drinks it black when she discovers the caddies are empty of creamer and sugar. Checks on Louise out in the truck for the umpteenth time. Stops at the information desk to check Hank's status but learns nothing new.

On her tenth lap of the facilities, her phone rings. It's Boyd.

"Hey, Boyd."

He sounds concerned. Paternal. Kind. "Maggie, I ran into Michele. She told me what's going on. What can I do to help?"

"Thanks, Boyd. I'm going to be all right."

"At least let me run interference with things on your place here."

"I think Michele and Deputy Junior have that taken care of." Junior. Saying his name jars something loose in her mind. What has she forgotten about Junior? Then it comes to her. She forgot to send him the contact information for her renter, so he can get a statement from her.

She'll do it when she gets off the call. "I'll be home in a few days, anyway."

"Do you need a place to stay?"

No, thank you. Boyd's warmth can't make up for his wife's chilliness, although Maggie doesn't blame her for it. Maggie's existence was a shock to her, part and parcel of events that torpedoed her husband's plans to run for president of the United States. Not to mention all the baggage of the bad reputation Maggie drags around.

Besides, Maggie plans to sleep in her own bed. "I'm good."

"We'll grab dinner, then."

"Of course. Thank you."

After they hang up, Maggie searches her email and finds an old string with her renter, Leslie DeWitt. It has Leslie's home address and phone number. Maggie forwards it on to Junior with a message: *Better late than never?* While she's on her phone she checks the messages she's ignored for hours. Her mom. Gary. Nothing new from either of them.

Michele: *I talked to Lacey. Call me.*

She will. Later. Right now, she's too anxious. She makes three more laps of the hospital, then runs into Paco, Andy, and Gene on the ground floor.

"Cops are looking for you." Gene gestures toward the waiting room.

"Thanks. I think." She enters. Buffalo Detective Lacey and Sheridan County Deputy Travis. A cross-jurisdictional dream team. She raises a hand in a sort-of wave.

They walk across the room toward her. Sheila is nowhere to be seen.

Maggie tries to muster up the energy to deal with all of this, but her voice is dull. "I heard you were looking for me."

Lacey nods, his white-blond hair swinging forward, in need of a cut. "Let's take this out in the hall."

She leads them, then turns.

Lacey hikes a thumb at Travis. "Sheridan County brought Rudy in. He's in the hospital here."

She sags against the wall. "Thank you." Light-headed, she leans over with her hands on her knees.

"An arrow was still in him. If the shot were an inch further to his right, he'd be dead."

Maggie curses her bad aim, but she simply nods.

"Your arrow?"

"Yes. He shot Hank and he was coming at me with a rifle."

"Did he point it at you?"

"Yes. Did you find it?"

Travis moves closer, his big presence oddly comforting. "Yes. In the doorway, where you said it would be."

"Good."

"It had a name engraved on it. Hank Sibley."

Maggie sighs. "A .300 Winchester Magnum."

"How'd you know that?"

"It was stolen from my cabin."

Travis scowls at her. "You left that out of the list of items you gave me yesterday."

"I'm sorry." She makes a gesture at the world in general. "My brain was fried. Still is."

"Having all the information helps us solve crimes faster."

"At Rudy's, you saw the other stuff, right? The strap he stole from me at Piney Bottoms? The stuff about me posted everywhere?"

"We saw it all. It was compelling as to motive in a few recent events."

Maggie snorts. "Just a little. That rifle. Have you confirmed it was the one that shot Hank?"

"We have people looking into that right now."

"I think it will be the same one that shot Patrick Rhodes. And Wolf, too."

"Who's Wolf?"

"Hank's horse."

"Yeah, I'm sorry about that. Anyway, it's roughly the same caliber rifle that shot all three, as you seem to know."

"I only know what my gut's telling me."

Travis says, "We saw the pictures of you with Chet and Patrick, too. And Hank." He points at her waist. "I see you found your belt buckle."

"I'm sorry. It was at Rudy's. I didn't think, just grabbed it as I ran out. It means a lot to me."

The cop and deputy look at each other.

Travis says, "I wish you hadn't done that, but we can let it slide."

"I guess I'll need to come in and give a statement?"

"At some point. You've got other fish to fry today."

"Thank you."

"But first, we have something we need to talk to you about."

Maggie pushes off her legs and stands again. She presses the back of her hand against her forehead. "What now?"

"We found something else at Rudy's. Chet Moore's wallet."

"He didn't get it from my cabin. I never touched it."

Lacey puts a hand on her elbow. "There are fingerprints all over it."

"You're kidding me, right? You're coming back at me again, after everything you saw at Rudy's? I don't know how much more of this I can take."

Travis puts a hand up. In a voice so soft it seems impossible that it comes from a man of his size, he says, "You're misunderstanding us. Rudy's fingerprints were all over it. Yours weren't."

For a moment, she's confused. How did they check for her prints? But then she remembers. Her fingerprints are on file from old drug arrests. She never thought she'd be glad for her past, but she is now. Rock solid evidence tying Rudy to Chet. "That's better."

Lacey nods. "And we had the Whitefeathers in for questioning. They remembered seeing Rudy in the hotel parking lot after you and Chet went inside."

Travis smiles at her. "Between you and me and the fence post, there's no doubt you didn't kill Chet Moore, or that Rudy is the one who did. Or that he took your stuff and, yes, killed Patrick Rhodes."

"It's about time." She lets her head fall back against the wall with a crack.

"And if you ever want a job," Lacey adds, "you should apply with the Buffalo PD. You did a great job on the case this week. You really stirred up some shit with your voicemail."

"But I didn't figure it out until it was too late, and then only by nearly getting Hank killed." And she still doesn't have any idea how Rudy managed the break-ins in Texas at the same time as the break-ins in Wyoming. Or if he even had anything to do with them or the sabotage of her truck. But those are problems to solve another day. For now, the mess here is untangling from her and from Hank, and that's enough.

"You figured out more than we did. As your attorney stressed several times when she was reading me the riot act earlier."

Ah, yes. Michele did talk to Lacey. Maggie almost smiles. How she loves her Chihuahua-size friend with the chops of a pit bull.

"Maggie?" Gene's voice interrupts.

The officers step aside for Gene and Laura.

Maggie throws her arms around the short cowboy. "Do you have an update?"

"We do. He's going to be fine. You saved him, Maggie."

Maggie shakes her head. "More like I nearly got him killed." She buries her face in his shoulder. "It was my fault. Hank getting shot. Chet dying. Patrick. They were my fault, too. Everything is my fault."

"Not everything." He pats her.

She turns her face to him like he's the sun in December. "Nearly."

"What are you talking about?" Laura asks. "What did you do, Maggie?"

Gene's voice is firm and his face hard. He faces Laura. "She solved the murders and saved Hank's life."

"She said it was her fault."

"She's very much mistaken about that, as you'll hear confirmed from law enforcement if you don't believe me."

Laura glances at Lacey and Travis, who are still close enough to hear every word. Both men nod.

Laura lifts her hands. "I'm sorry. I'm on edge. Worried about my brother."

Gene shrugs. "It's okay. We all are."

Maggie grabs Gene's elbow, pulling him away from Laura and bumping into Lacey as she does. "Gene, I was wrong."

Gene pushes her back and holds her by the shoulders. "Wrong about?"

"Hank. Me and him. Us. I can't let Sheila have him. We belong together."

Gene smiles. "Don't tell me. Tell him."

"I sort of told him I loved him earlier. When I thought he was going to die."

Gene chuckles.

"But, Gene, I don't deserve him. Even that annoying twit Sheila deserves him more than me."

Behind her, Lacey laughs. Maggie turns and glares at him.

He wipes the mirth from his face. "We'll just be getting out of your way."

Travis says, "I'll call you about a statement. That's all for now. Good luck, Ms. Killian."

The two law enforcement officers retreat down the hall and out of sight.

Gene shakes his head at Maggie. "Love isn't about deserving."

Maggie sniffs and wipes her eyes. "I'm a dangerous person. I hurt everyone. Hank especially."

"But you really love him, don't you?"

"I do. So much."

"Then you should let him know. Not when he's bleeding to death on a mountain. Let him decide whether you're too dangerous for him. He's always been something of a risk taker." Gene winks.

Maggie laughs.

Pounding feet interrupt the moment. Sheila sprints down the hall toward them, ponytail bouncing.

"Where has she been?" Maggie asks.

Gene whispers. "They moved Hank to recovery."

Laura moves in to rejoin their conversation. "She forced her way in when I went out to talk to Gene."

Sheila practically skips up to Laura, Gene, and Maggie.

"What is it?" Laura asks. "Good news about Hank?"

She beams. "We're getting married. Hank and I are getting married! My Hanky Panky's going to be a daddy!"

Laura and Gene gawk at the girl.

Sheila is having a baby? Maggie takes a deep breath. Yes, Maggie is dangerous. She's not the best person in the world. But even a mess like her won't wreck this for Hank. Fatherhood. It's bigger than her. It's more important than her feelings. Hank's girlfriend is pregnant. Maggie loses.

She chokes the words out like a hairball, but she does say them. "Congratulations, Sheila."

"I have to go call my mother." Sheila runs out toward the lobby, her phone to her ear.

After she's gone, Gene says, "Well, son of a bitch."

Laura looks conflicted. "Hank's always wanted children. Maybe this is a good thing?"

Head buzzing, Maggie takes a deep breath. She pulls the belt and buckle from her waist and hands them to Gene.

He pushes them back to her. "Don't, Maggie."

"I'm not getting in the way of that." She looks straight into Laura's dark eyes. "No matter what anybody here thinks of me, I'm better than that."

Laura looks at Gene, then back at Maggie. Tears glisten in her eyes. "I've never—"

Maggie shakes her head. "Just stop, Laura. You're his sister. I get it."

She squares her shoulders, lifts her chin, and walks away. Past Sheila jabbering on the phone, past Paco and Andy hovering over coffee cups near the front door, all the way to the parking lot, all the way to Bess.

Maggie stalls, letting Louise out for a potty break and dumping her water bowl, then putting her back in the truck. What she's waiting for, she can't say. She knows she can't be waiting on Hank. He's in a recovery room bed. Engaged to Sheila. With a baby on the way. He's not coming after her. She and Hank are through. After fifteen years, she's truly lost him.

A tall woman with long black hair in a low ponytail and some kind of buckskin-colored suede pants and matching top eyes Maggie good as she walks toward the hospital. Maggie watches her go, feeling a magnet pull to follow her back inside. To beg Hank to change his mind, be a daddy to his child, but to love her. To make it okay for her to stay. Which is *insane*. When all she has wanted for the last week is to be gone from this godforsaken state of pain. Her heart is just playing tricks on her mind.

Well, she's too smart to fall for her own shit.

She's going to get her trailer of junk and go home. She'll make it there in time for the fall antique show. Fix up her shop. Browbeat Junior until he solves her case. Smooth things over with Gary. Shower Michele with appreciation. Hug her goats. Eat with the only father she'll have for the rest of her life. Let her mom tell her whatever secret it is she's dying to get out. Yes, that's what's going to happen. And she's not going to cry a single tear, because Hank is going to be happy, something she could probably never make him—not as mercurial and dangerous as she is, as they are—and she is not going to screw that up.

But she waits another five minutes anyway. The sunlight is incandescent on the mountain range with its jagged black teeth chomping at the sky. She breathes in the scent of the Russian olive trees wafting up from the creek one last time—the invaders on their way out, like her—and savors the fingers of wind in her unruly hair.

When no one and nothing stops her, she reaches in the half-open window and ruffles Louise's ears. "It's just you and me now, Fucker."

She hops in, eyes dry, and puts the truck in gear, pointing Bess toward the interstate, south and home to Texas.

SICK PUPPY (MAGGIE KILLIAN NOVEL #2)

A WHAT DOESN'T KILL YOU TEXAS-TO-WYOMING ROMANTIC MYSTERY

ONE

Maggie brakes for a tumbleweed the size of a small pickup. The giant weed rolls across Highway 87, bouncing off a DON'T MESS WITH TEXAS sign before resuming its course south. In the rearview mirror, the New Mexico sunset is a Technicolor backdrop to the zombie chorus line the dead bush and its brethren form on a barbed-wire fence. They're like the display of coyote carcasses Maggie'd seen a few miles back. *If the hanging coyotes are a warning to predators, what are the tumbleweeds warning?* By the brown, barren look of things, the fauna thinks the message is for them.

She rescues a whipping strand of hair from her ChapSticked lips. Lipstick and a headband had been out of the question when she left Colorado Springs without sleeping, in a hellfire hurry to get back to Giddings. Home. Her home.

She turns to the panting border collie–corgi mix in the passenger seat. The dog's black-and-white hair is levitating, but the wind is hot. "This is as good as it's gonna get, Louise."

Louise whines, circles, then sticks her nose out the window.

Maggie's phone plays a portentous series of chords on the seat beside her. She'd set new notification tones last night, as soon as she was out of Wyoming. Time for change, across the board. This sound is for a text, and it tells her two things. First, she's back in the land of cell service. Second, her phone survived being thrown at the door of the bathroom stall in Raton, after flaunting a text from Hank, the love of her life and breaker of her heart.

Hank's text had read: *Was it something I said?*

Something he said. *Funny.*

Defying death now, she presses the phone for his contact information. His picture pops up, and she enlarges it. He's in profile, smiling and showing off his delicious dimple. A Stetson covers his dark hair. His shirt is open at the neck, right where she used to like to kiss him.

Well, not anymore.

She puts the phone down, stretches her eyes wide, and rolls her neck. With another vat of coffee, she can make it to Wichita Falls for a few hours —she prays—of sleep, leaving her an easy five hours tomorrow. Driving outside the hot hours is appealing, due to her broken air conditioner. And pretty much any hours the sun is out are hot in Texas in mid-September.

Maggie switches feet on the accelerator to give her aching right foot a stretching break. No air conditioner *and* no cruise control. Worst of all, her tush doesn't appreciate the long hours driving. When a thirty-seven-year-old woman gets bucked off a muscle-bound draft horse six feet at the shoulder, it isn't pretty, and Maggie had bitten the dust only the day before, courtesy of Hank's Percheron Lily. A sad pang takes her by surprise. It's not only Hank she's going to miss. She'll miss Lily. The mountains. The wildlife. Everyone at Piney Bottoms Ranch.

A lone woman walking on the shoulder of the highway catches Maggie's attention. A long gray French braid hangs down her back. As Bess and the trailer pass her, she turns and makes eye contact with Maggie. A shiver runs up Maggie's arms. The woman's face is ghostly white. A blue scarf encircles her neck. Maggie takes her foot off the gas. Should she stop and offer her a ride? But the pale woman wasn't hitching.

Maggie powers on, regardless, restless dog beside her.

An hour and forty-five minutes later, the speed limit drops as she enters Amarillo. Maggie switches off Lucinda Williams, who's rasping about why she "Changed the Locks." She scans for radio stations on the new stereo in Bess, her vintage pickup. *Magenta* vintage pickup, a color never intended by the Ford Motor Company, Maggie is sure. But it suits Bess, and Bess suits Maggie. She loves every rusted spot on the underbelly and dent in the hide of the truck's close-to-seventy-five-year-old body.

Maggie catches the tail end of a commercial that doesn't sound like it belongs on Spanish-speaking, Christian, or talk radio, so she stops. The commercial ends, and a pop song with a hip-hop edge comes on. There's something else to it, too. Steel pans, maybe?

Maggie groans. Her finger hovers over the scan button.

Louise makes retching noises.

"I know. It's not my thing either."

Over the wind and highway noise, Maggie recognizes the song and the singer. A hit from last year: "Bombshell" by the It Girl of the moment, Ava Butler. Maggie was the It Girl once upon a time, too, before she pissed it away. Maggie *hates* Ava Butler, and not just because Ava's success makes Maggie feel like Jennifer Anniston reading an *Enquirer* article about Angelina Jolie's perfect Brad Pitt babies. No, Maggie hates her because the two women costarred in a cheesy musical in Waco, Texas, and Ava stole Maggie's part.

And Maggie holds grudges.

Louise retches again. Her sides begin to heave, and her legs quiver.

More than just good musical instincts? "Oh. Oh no. Louise, wait. Stop. No!"

Leaving the station as-is, Maggie puts her blinker on and veers across three lanes of traffic—setting off a barrage of horns—toward an abandoned building with a buckled blacktop lot. When she's pulled in far enough that her trailer isn't sticking out in the road, she grabs the leash and snaps it on Louise. She doesn't want Louise blowing chunks on the driver's side, so Maggie scoots across the bench seat, maneuvers over the stick shift and sick dog, and opens the passenger door.

"Ouch." Her sore tush complains about the sudden activity. She gives the leash an awkward tug. "Come on, Louise."

Louise doesn't budge. Before Maggie can make it past the line of fire, Louise deposits two cups of soggy dog food and cheeseburger across the seat, the floorboard, and Maggie's hobo bag, boots, and jeans.

In a voice more empathetic than angry, Maggie says, "Oh, Fucker."

Louise wags her tail. In their one week together, Louise has decided that Fucker means "I love you" in Maggie-speak.

"Quit smiling at me."

The dog flops down in the vomit, like she's just too weak to stand another second.

"Oh no, no, nooo." Maggie shakes her leg to dislodge vomit from her boot. She counts back the days since she's slept. Three, maybe? She can't take this. "So much for Wichita Falls."

A police cruiser pulls up behind her truck, lights wigwagging.

"Perfect."

The cop takes his time running her plates. Given her recent problems with the law in Wyoming, Maggie decides to sit tight and wait for him, half in and half out of the truck, instead of cleaning up like she wants to. A few minutes later, a stocky officer with red hair and a full but not bad-looking face saunters to the passenger side. Maggie doesn't have to roll down the window, at least, which is good, since she's managed to get dog barf on her hands.

"Good evening. I'm Officer John Burrows, Amarillo Police Department. Are you having a problem, ma'am?" The cop bends down to peer in the door, hand on his holstered gun. His voice is small-town West Texas. Give her five more minutes and she'll place the county, ten and she'll peg his town. Sound and Maggie are friends, and she's great with accents, especially Texas ones.

Maggie points at Louise. "My dog just barfed all over the place. And me."

He coughs and steps back. "Are you aware you made an unsafe lane change before you exited the roadway?"

Maggie sighs. "I used my blinker."

"You cut off traffic."

"Louise had just done her Linda Blair-in-the-*Exorcist* impression."

His expression is stony. Maybe he hadn't seen the movie. The vomit scene. Or maybe he has zero sense of humor. "License and insurance, please."

"Do you have a paper towel or something? My hands are covered in dog puke."

He lowers his Ray-Bans and squints friendly green eyes over them at Maggie, Louise, and the vomit. "Sorry, no."

"The longer I sit here, the worse it's going to smell. I have dirty laundry I could use for cleanup, but it's on my utility trailer. Can't you just write me a ticket while I get out and start scrubbing?"

"That's not protocol, ma'am. I need you to hand me your documentation and remain in the cab." He slides his aviators into his shirt pocket.

"Of course you do." She wipes her hands on her thighs and slips open her bag, trying not to transfer barf from the bag to her person while she does. The officer's attention is on a flip pad of ticket forms. She swipes her license through the vomit before she holds it out to him. "License."

He takes it without looking up. When he notices the vomit, he grimaces, pulling one finger at a time away from the license. Then he glares at her.

She pretends not to see him as she rummages in the tiny glove box for her insurance card. When she finds it, she manages to leave a perfect set of puke prints on the paper. Her lips twitch. "Here you go, sir."

He pinches it by one corner. "Wait here."

"Can I please clean up now? I know my license matches the registration you pulled on the truck, along with my clean driving record and up-to-date insurance. Please?"

Louise wags her tail, each sweep stirring up wet chunks and sending them flying.

"Fine."

Maggie retrieves dirty laundry and wipes down the interior, the dog, and herself—not that it does much good—while still maintaining the presence of mind to flip off two truckers and a carload of teenage boys who honk and shout at her as they pass. She rebags her dirty laundry and tucks it under the trailer tarp, then fastens the bungee cords.

The officer reappears by the truck bed as she's walking toward the cab. "I've written you a warning."

"Really?"

"Really. Sign here." He taps his ticket pad, handing it and a pen to her.

She verifies that everything on the ticket is correct, then signs her name. He tears off the ticket. "Please be more careful."

"Yes, sir." Maggie salutes as she takes it.

"Also, my sister and her husband own a hotel. The Sundowner. They take pets. You can clean yourself and the pooch off better." He offers her a business card. "Tell her I sent you."

"Thank you. I might do that."

"It's downtown. Right next to Pumpjack's. And tonight is karaoke night there. It's a big draw. Fun."

"I'm not feeling much into fun."

His jaw flexes, eyes sparkle. "I know who you are. Maggie Killian. You're famous for fun."

She raises her eyebrows. "Lies, all lies. I promise."

"Think about it. Seriously, it's the place to be on Thursday nights in Amarillo."

It hits her. "You're going, aren't you?"

Finally, he grins. "I am. And I would really love it if you'd sing 'Buckle Bunny.'"

Her music seems a lifetime ago to her. A really long, hard lifetime. "Maybe. And thank you. For only giving me a warning, and for the info about the hotel. I've had a really bad week."

He nods in sympathy. "I read the article online."

The "How the Mighty Maggie Killian Has Fallen" article posted on an entertainment blog last week had made her sound like a train wreck. Correction: an even bigger train wreck.

She doesn't bother telling Burrows that the article isn't a fraction of what made her week bad. That she spurned a Unabomber-type fan—Rudy —in Wyoming, where she'd gone to win Hank back, under the pretense of shopping for junk at estate sales. That the fan then used a tire iron to bash in the head of Chet, the cowboy she'd had a one-night oops with after Hank introduced her to his much younger, Sunday school–teaching girlfriend, Sheila. How Bess broke down, leaving her stranded at Hank's ranch, where the police zeroed in on her as the murder suspect and basically put her on house arrest in Wyoming. That meanwhile in Texas someone vandalized Flown the Coop, her antique shop, at the very same time the crazy fan invaded her Wyoming cabin and stole Hank's rifle and her two most trea- sured possessions—Hank's Frontier Days bull riding champion belt buckle and a guitar strap embroidered by her mother. That the same rifle was used to kill a neighboring rancher—Patrick, who had taken her out to dinner— and to shoot Hank while he was out riding with Maggie. How Maggie managed to run for the crazy fan's cabin, find the rifle, buckle, and guitar strap, shoot the crazy fan, leave him for the sheriff, and get help for Hank in time to save his life. Then, just when Maggie thought she and Hank might have a chance, Sheila announced a baby on board and her engagement to Hank.

Yeah, it was a sucky week.

Maggie parts ways with the officer and takes his advice on the Sundowner.

An hour later, Maggie strips out of her vomit clothes and puts them in a tub of hot water. She scrubs them with the thin bar of hotel soap. After she rinses the laundry and hangs it to dry, she drags Louise into the bathroom.

Maggie tries to lift her. The dog turns herself into something like a cruise ship anchor. "Come *on*, Louise."

The dog shrinks heavily into the floor.

Maggie jerks Louise up and into the tub. She washes the dog's long fur three times. After a thorough rinsing, Maggie pitches the soap into the trash and grabs the remaining towel. She's already used the other one—plus the hand towels and the tiny tube of shower gel—on the interior of the truck. The squatty dog leaps from the tub and shakes, flinging water from her body.

"Lew-*eeze*. Thanks a lot."

Maggie buffs her dry. When she's done, Louise poses at the door, throwing a look over her shoulder at Maggie like a short-legged model on a catwalk. Maggie shakes her head and opens the door for her. Louise beelines for Maggie's open suitcase and rolls in her clean clothes.

"I'm shipping you back to Wyoming."

Louise settles into the clothing, her chin on the edge of the suitcase, her tail wagging like a fan above her.

Maggie retreats into the bathroom. It smells like wet dog and barf, and she's out of hot water. Still, she has the shampoo and conditioner she's saved just for herself, and clean is clean. When she's done, she drips onto the bath mat and blow-dries her wettest areas.

She's utterly exhausted, physically, mentally, and emotionally.

After cranking up the air conditioner, she pulls back a thin coverlet and flops naked onto the sheets. She stares at the popcorn ceiling. Bed sounds so good, but so does a couple of drinks. Because she not only wants to sleep, she wants to be numb. She rolls over and does a visual search for a minibar. None. She elbow-crawls on her stomach to the phone and presses zero.

"Front desk." The woman's voice makes *desk* into a two-syllable word.

"Do y'all have a bar?"

"A what?"

"A bar. With liquor."

"Yes, ma'am. Our restaurant serves Miller Lite, Coors Light, and Budweiser. And a house white and house red. Wine, I mean. You can even get them with room service if you'd like." Her tone is one of pride, and Maggie wonders if she's speaking to Burrows's sister. She'd been in such a hurry at check-in that she hadn't mentioned him.

And she'd forgotten she's in the damn Bible Belt. Maggie rolls on her back and closes her eyes. They want to stay that way. "Thanks." She doesn't explain to the woman that wine and beer aren't liquor.

"Do you want me to transfer you to room service?"

"No, that's okay."

Louise hops onto the bed and licks Maggie's cheek with tiny tongue darts.

Maggie hangs up the phone, ducking her face away from the squatty dog. "You know I hate that."

Louise stares at her solemnly.

"And if you think I'm feeding you anything tonight, you've got another think coming."

Louise lowers her nose and gazes at Maggie with contrite eyes.

Maggie groans and levers herself off the bed. She's held out since Raton, but she finally reads her messages. Hank's texted twice since her phone-throwing meltdown, which brings the grand total since she left the hospital up to ten.

His latest: *Gene gave me the belt buckle. What's up with that?*

Gene Soboleski. Hank's best friend and business partner in the Double S, a bucking stock contracting business. Brother of Michele, Maggie's best friend.

Maggie doesn't answer.

She dresses in a rush, feeling naked without the buckle—she's had it the entire fifteen years since Hank won it bull riding in Cheyenne. She'd thrust it into Gene's hands the day before, then fled the state. Maybe Hank will give it to Sheila. Maggie doesn't care. She's done with Hank Sibley.

Another text comes in from Hank. *I'm worried. Please call.*

She doesn't answer him. Worried. Yeah. She's worried, too.

She's worried about where she's going to stay when she gets back to Giddings. She'd stuck her toe into the whole vacation-renting-by-owner craze and rented her house. Now she's returning earlier than planned, and she can't freaking remember when Leslie—the short-term renter—is due to leave.

She's worried that someone will steal the trailer of Wyoming junk out in the hotel parking lot.

She's worried about how she's ever going to whip all the new items and her shop into shape in time for the massive Warrenton–Round Top fall antique show her livelihood depends on. That she's worn out her welcome with the friends and family who've been covering for her while her life was falling apart in two places at once, fourteen hundred miles apart. *Shit. Note to self: check in with Michele for an update on the investigation and insurance claim.*

She's so worried, in fact, that she knows the Sundowner beer and wine selection aren't going to cut it, no matter how wrung out she is. In the bathroom, she paints her face and diffuses her long, curly dark hair. She pulls a tiered blue-jean skirt, red tank top, and long, laced vest from the suitcase. They're wrinkled and smell like Louise, so she doubles up on perfume. She adds gypsy hoop earrings and her favorite high-heeled cowboy boots.

In the bathroom, she sets a full water dish on the floor. "Here you go. I'll be back in an hour to take you out. No more barfing."

Louise doesn't lift her head from the pillow she's claimed on the double bed. A week ago, Louise was a stray sponging off the ranch dogs at Piney Bottoms, the site of Hank and Gene's business. Louise adopted Maggie, maybe drawn to her because Maggie was a lonely stray like her—or maybe Louise just sensed Maggie was an easy mark—and Hank had made it official. Before Louise, Maggie'd had two golden retrievers, Janis and Woody. She'd thought she'd never open her heart to another dog after their deaths, yet here she is, heart definitely cracked.

From the hotel, Maggie takes a right, toward bustle and bright lights. Immediately she comes upon a bar with an orange-and-blue neon sign that reads PUMPJACK'S. The entire front of the establishment is glass, giving the place the look of a repurposed Rexall Drug. She enters, and off-key singing and loud backing music assault her ears. On her left, a DJ is working from a karaoke station beside a small stage where a large man is slurring his way through "Strokin'." Scrawled in white marker on the glass of the window behind them is THURSDAY KARAOKE SEVEN TIL MIDNIGHT, which she reads backward from the inside. She looks at her watch. It's already ten o'clock.

For a second, Maggie considers bailing.

A man leans close enough to be heard over the bad singing. "Maggie Killian. You came."

In body if not in spirit. She barely recognizes redheaded Officer Burrows without the Ray-Bans and uniform. "Hey."

He guides her farther into the bar. The décor is primarily antique metal signs from oil and gas companies, stuff that would resell well in Maggie's Flown the Coop. Even away from the speakers, Burrows has to talk close to be heard. "Did you get a room at my sister's place?"

She nods.

He smiles. It makes wrinkles around his nice green eyes. "I already checked the song list. They have some of yours on it."

Maggie shakes her head vehemently. "Not happening."

"Want a drink? Maybe you'll change your mind."

She glances toward his hand. No wedding ring. Booze electrifies her sexuality, and she doesn't allow her switch to be flipped around an inappropriate partner, just in case. Not that she's choosy. Availability, safety, and ability, those are her criteria. She nods at Burrows. He beckons her to follow him to the bar where he orders a Corona for himself.

The bartender, who doesn't look old enough to drink or legally obtain the tattoos all over his body without his mommy signing for him, motions for her to order.

"Koltiska Liqueur on ice."

"Strike one." He holds up a finger.

"Balcones Whiskey on ice."

A second finger goes up. "Strike two. Will you swing for the fences or play it safe?"

"Jack."

He claps. "And she's on base. Sorry we don't carry the others."

"I'll believe you if you pour a double."

He shrugs as he pours, and keeps pouring. "Not my bar."

Maggie downs her double Jack like it's sweet tea.

"Thirsty?" Burrows asks, eyebrows up.

"Did I mention my week sucked?" She holds up a finger and nods to the bartender.

He slides one to her then throws his hands up when she catches it. "Through the uprights."

She rewards him with a smile, and he winks. To Burrows she shouts, "Ladies room."

Burrows gives her a thumbs-up. She returns to find a third drink waiting for her and hears her name blaring over the speakers.

"Next up is Maggie, with 'Buckle Bunny.'"

Maggie slits her eyes at Burrows. "Not cool." She remembers standing in the Occidental Saloon in Buffalo, Wyoming, a few days before, telling a psycho fan that she wouldn't perform in public when he demanded she sing a song she'd dissed him on years ago. She would have traded a yes then for Burrows's ambush now, in a heartbeat.

Burrows puts a palm on his chest. "I put you on the list before you came. Just in case. It fills up fast. Don't do it if you don't want to."

The DJ is watching the crowd, looking for his tardy performer. "Is that her, John?" The DJ points their way.

John nods.

"Hey y'all, it looks like Maggie has stage fright. Let's give her a little encouragement."

The crowd cheers. Maggie wonders if it counts as assault on an officer if she punches Burrows. She'd rather turn back to the bar and let the bartender show her his tattoos than sing here. But with everyone looking at her, Maggie is afraid she'll be recognized. One picture to TMZ and she's labeled a snotty bitch too good to party with the locals. Out they'll trot all her failures again, for her mother to obsess over with her church friends.

The drunken crowd chants at the DJ's urging, mob-like. MAG-GIE, MAG-GIE, MAG-GIE.

She holds up a finger to the DJ and downs her drink. Warmth flushes her face and her body buzzes. By the time she finishes the song, her drunk will have caught up with her and she'll be on her way to fast forgetting. She glares at Burrows one more time. His return smile sticks in her craw. She balls her fists, and stalks to the stage.

"Here she is, folks. Maggie, doing 'Buckle Bunny.'"

Conversation noise continues unabated in the bar. Inspiration strikes. She's performed the wrong songs for the wrong crowds too many times to risk her own beloved material here. She stops at his monitor. "How about 'Bombshell' instead? The Ava Butler song."

"No problem." He presses a few buttons. "Make that . . . Here's Maggie, doing 'Bombshell.'"

The crowd whoops. Apparently "Bombshell" is more popular than "Buckle Bunny." *Louise has better musical taste than these rubes.*

Maggie's never sung Ava's hit other than in the privacy of her own truck, and then with a healthy dose of sarcasm. But she knows she has more talent in her left pinky than Ava has in her whole body. She's going to give herself the gift of blowing Ava's version out of the water, even if the only witness will be the few Pumpjack's patrons sober enough to listen.

She launches herself into it. No warm-up. No run-throughs or blocking. Nothing like the old days. Just her instincts and what *Rolling Stone* once called the voice of a wayward angel on a three-day bender. By the time she reaches the end of the song, the crowd has gone from surprised to shocked to raucous. Burrows is doing a Magic Mike impression while people around him jump up and down and sing along to the chorus. When Maggie finishes, she lifts a fist and drops her head. The crowd raises the roof.

Okay, so sue me. I have a voice and I ain't afraid to use it.

TWO

"Holy shit, what-what-what?" the DJ shouts into his microphone. "I think we have a ringer. Okay, Pumpjackers. I'm willing to break the rules if y'all want to hear some more of that. What do you say—Maggie again?"

The crowd chants and claps, more mosh pit than mob now. "Maggie, Maggie, Maggie."

From the right, a tall blonde woman touches Maggie's hand. "Maggie? As in Michele's friend Maggie?"

Maggie whoops and jumps off the low stage to embrace the woman. "Emilyyyy. I forgot you live in Amarillo."

Maggie had met Emily the previous spring at Michele's, when Emily was visiting with Laura, her partner in an equine therapy camp business. Hank's *sister* Laura. Hank and Gene had been with them. Sparks had flown between Maggie and Hank—not the good kind. At least not then. The next week, they'd generated a lot of heat, first between the sheets, then during Hank's implosion when Maggie sent him back to Wyoming without her. Maggie pushes the memory away. Thinking about Hank hurts.

"What are you doing in the feedlot capital of the world?"

Maggie laughs. "Singing karaoke."

The DJ interrupts. "So do you want to do 'Buckle Bunny' now, Maggie?"

"Hell no. More Ava Butler. Your pick."

Burrows presses another drink into Maggie's hand. "You are freaking incredible." He and Emily hug.

Friends, obviously. Maggie drinks like a camel that's just crossed the Sahara.

The DJ nods. "More Ava Butler. Got it."

"Why are you singing Ava's songs?" Emily asks.

The way Emily says Ava's name is almost like she knows her. But Maggie doesn't have time to ask Emily about that or answer her question, because the music starts. Burrows and Emily step aside, heads together, deep in conversation, until Maggie begins crushing "Fire on the Mountain." Then they join the crowd in a fist-pumping sing-along with Maggie.

When it's over, the DJ holds his hand up. "Whoa there, Maggie." He rolls back from his monitor and stands. "Okay, y'all, I got the scoop. This here is not a humble karaoke amateur. This is Maggie Killian. Maggie *frickin'* Killian. I thought I heard an alt-rock vibe to her "Bombshell." She's retired from the biz, but she was a *huge* star. And apparently a big fan of Ava Butler."

Maggie doesn't correct him about Ava. People cheer and rubberneck around each other at her. Some snap selfies of their big faces in front of her on the stage. She imagines one hundred simultaneous Facebook posts going up. She'd figured she'd be identified, but it's time to step out of the limelight, even a dim one. She bows at the waist, waves, and joins Burrows and Emily, who have joined a larger group.

Burrows hands her another drink. Maggie is thirsty. She gulps it down.

Emily hooks her arm through Maggie's. "Oh my God. I just realized I've seen you perform before. When I met you at Michele's, I had no idea that you're famous."

"Famously infamous. Or I used to be."

"You're amazing."

"Thanks." Maggie is about to ask her about Ava, and about where Emily saw Maggie perform, but Emily's already speaking again.

"Jack, Wallace, Ethan, this is Maggie. She's Michele's best friend." Emily smiles at a tall, slim man with dark skin and hair and arresting amber eyes. "Maggie, this is my husband, Jack—"

"Hot husband." Maggie shakes his hand, then purrs. "Nice to meet you, hot husband Jack."

Jack turns red and mumbles something unintelligible.

Emily stands on tiptoe to kiss Jack's cheek. "Jack's not much of a talker."

She touches the elbow of another man. "This is Wallace. He triathloned with Michele back in Houston. He's one of my best friends."

The man who sticks out his hand has floppy hair with blond highlights and a body type Maggie recognizes from Michele's endurance events.

"So you're a psycho like Michele?" Maggie asks.

He raises his hand. "Guilty."

With one word, Maggie identifies him as Houston. West side. Maybe Katy.

Emily bumps Wallace with her hip then turns to the last man in the party. "And this is his husband, Ethan."

A thin, very well-dressed black man with eyelashes like a mascara ad kisses Maggie's hand. "My pleasure."

Dallas. Oak Lawn area. "Which makes it mine." Maggie nods at Emily. "I like this one."

"Excuse me." A group of middle-aged women are standing near them. Their spokesperson says, "Could we get your autograph, Maggie?"

"No problem." Maggie signs her name a handful of times. She poses for pictures and allows herself to be hugged. When the women leave, she says, "Damn. I'm drunk."

Wallace raises a glass to her. "Delightfully so."

And in that moment, everything in the last week, especially the last two days, crashes over Maggie in a wave. Like a balloon with a pinhole leak, Maggie deflates. Her legs are rubber. Her lids are heavy. She's tired like she's been pulling a sled of bricks all the way from Wyoming, and she can't make it another step. Not a single one.

"I should jet. It's been fun, but I'm bushed."

"Don't go," Ethan says. "You haven't seen Wallace do 'Rhinestone Cowboy' yet. I promise, it's life-changing."

Maggie feels it coming and tries to turn away, but she's not fast enough. She doesn't do tired well, and this is more than tired. It's tired, hurt, sad, and drunk. A tear leaks out and runs down her cheek. She swipes at it angrily, then laughs at herself. "I'm sorry. That sounds badass, Wallace. But I have to go."

Emily stops her with an embrace. In Maggie's ear, she whispers, "What's the matter?"

Never mind that they're not close, that Emily's friends can hear them, or that Maggie is by nature a closed diary with a padlock and key, Maggie spills her story on Emily's shoulder. All of her story. All the way back to meeting Hank in Cheyenne fifteen years before. It comes out in a boozy rush, and she doesn't stop even when Emily has released her and the group is clustered around Maggie, nodding her on.

"It all started when Hank, this bull rider, was taking money to lose, which I didn't know at the time. I told him I wouldn't go out with him unless he won. So he did. I broke up with my band so I could stay there with him. They were really, really pissed. Davo, Brent, Celinda, Chris. Oh my God. I can't believe I remember their names. They tried to kidnap me and make me stick to the tour with them. But I didn't. Which is a good thing because I'd be dead if I had—they crashed the van. Very sad. Anyway, these South American gangsters chased Hank and me all over Wyoming that night. The next morning, when Hank went to get us breakfast, my agent called, and instead of firing me, he bought me a plane ticket to Nashville to write an album with Patty Griffin. He did fire me, later, but I was already famous by then, and that's not part of this story. So I left Hank a note to call me and went to catch the flight."

Emily's eyes widen as she puts two and two together. "Are you talking about Laura's brother, Hank? The one you were fighting with at Michele's?"

"Laura didn't tell you?"

"No. She knew?"

Maggie's shoulders lift and fall. "Knew. Knows."

"She's in big trouble. But go on. You left for Nashville, and then what?"

"He never called. He broke my heart."

"You mean you hadn't talked to him in all that time until you saw him at Michele's?"

Maggie holds up two fingers in the sign of scout's honor. "Not once in fifteen years."

"Okay, wow. That's awful. But how does that get us to tonight?"

"I've just been to Wyoming to see Hank."

The group, hanging on her every word now, says "Ooooh" in unison.

"In Texas last spring, he wanted to get back together. I didn't hate him, but I was still mad. I said no. Then I changed my mind. When I got to Wyoming, he already had somebody else." Tears trace a path down her face, but she doesn't seem to notice.

"Oh, hon, I'm so sorry." Emily pats Maggie's back.

Maggie nods. "Me, too. But it doesn't make any difference. And now he's engaged to Sheila and they're going to teach Sunday school together and make babies. I might as well get back with Gary." She lifts her empty glass. "Fuck 'em, right?"

Emily, Wallace, and Ethan make eyes at each other. Burrows stares into his beer. Jack looks like he wants to be anywhere but there.

Wallace leans in. "Gary?"

"Yeah. Gary Fuller." Too late, Maggie remembers she doesn't ever tell anyone about Gary. He's been a secret since the beginning. What is wrong with her, blurting out stuff like that?

"The country music star, Gary Fuller? The one whose little sister Kelly has *the* number one single on the iTunes country charts and just kicked off a nationwide tour?"

Maggie snorts. "Gary's manager spoon-fed Kelly the song, and she doesn't have an album to back it up." The modern-day equivalent of Tiffany's mall tour circa 1987 for "I Think We're Alone Now." Kelly's big break was singing backup for Gary earlier that year. She wonders what he thinks of her solo efforts.

Wallace's eyebrows shoot skyward. "Ooh, and I hear he's the frontrunner to take the country coach slot on *The Singer* now that their ratings are slipping. You-know-who is going to be F-I-R-E-D."

"And you know all of this *how?*" Ethan asks.

Wallace shimmies his head. "What? Just because I'm gay I can't listen to country music? Maggie is a Texas legend."

Ethan smiles at the others. "More like he obsessively reads *People*. Since he was in training pants."

Wallace holds up a hand to his husband. "Don't listen to him, Maggie. You were saying, about Gary Fuller?"

Maggie sighs. "I broke up with him. He's very, very mad at me."

"Because of Hank?"

"No. But I haven't taken him back because of Hank."

Wallace grins. "Okay, not to be stalkerish, but I already knew all of this, except for the part about Gary. I read about it online today. I never dreamed I'd be meeting the real Maggie Killian tonight." He leans forward, hand cupping one side of his mouth like he's sharing a secret. "It's such a relief when I don't get suckered into fake news."

"See?" Ethan shakes his head. "You read too much garbage online, babe."

Maggie's tear-streaked eyes are red but alert. "I don't understand. Knew all of what?"

Wallace and Emily exchange another look. Emily slides a finger across her throat.

Wallace smiles at Maggie. "Hey, I have an idea. Did you eat? Why don't we get you some food?"

"I need to walk my dog."

Emily, Wallace, and Ethan laugh, but nervously, like Maggie's lost her marbles. Even Jack smiles.

Burrows says, "I think she's serious."

"I am. My dog, Fucker, threw up in my truck, which is how I met Officer Burrows. Otherwise I'd be in Wichita Falls about now. That's why I didn't have time to eat."

Wallace nods. "Makes perfect sense. Then let's get food and go walk Fucker. Unless—" He waves between Maggie and Burrows.

Maggie shakes her head quickly. "Not a thing."

Burrows looks crestfallen for a moment, but he rallies with a brave face. "I've got an early morning. Maggie, nice meeting you. See the rest of you soon."

Maggie waves. "Thanks for getting me onstage and wasted."

"Yeah, John." Emily rolls her eyes. "Always a great idea with someone who has famously done rehab. Multiple times."

Burrows winces. "Sorry. Didn't think of that."

Maggie wags a finger at Emily. "That was for coke. I'm much better with liquor."

After Burrows leaves, the group orders food from a bar menu. Maggie chugs waters while they chat and wait, suffering through karaoke performances that range from rutting goat to cat in heat. When the food comes, Wallace, Ethan, and Maggie bid farewell to Jack and Emily and walk back to the Sundowner, to-go bags in hand.

Maggie fetches Louise, who is elated when they rejoin the two men on a grassy area behind the hotel. They stand beside a picnic table, eating their burgers while Louise runs in circles.

Wallace finishes first. He wads up his burger paper and throws it in the trash can outside the hotel's back door. "It's been such a hoot meeting you, Maggie."

Ethan holds a thumb up and nods. His mouth is full and he's still got three-quarters of a burger to go.

Maggie swallows a too-big bite. "Come to my shop and buy some antiques. Hang out with Michele and me."

Wallace smiles. "Text me the details, and color us there."

The three swap phone numbers.

Maggie hugs her new friends. "Thanks for escorting me home. And making me eat. Good call."

Wallace studies her face. "Are you sure you're going to be okay tonight?"

Maggie flaps a hand at him. "I'm fine. That thing earlier—already over it. Never better."

"All right, then. Are you ready, Ethan?"

He holds up his half a burger, but he nods, hand in front of his mouth.

Maggie waves, then they walk away arm in arm. Louise is still cavorting along the line of bushes edging the building, sniffing out trash. Maggie fears more vomit is in their future. When the two men are out of sight, she pulls her phone from her jeans pocket. For a hot second, she thinks about texting Hank. She'd like to give him a piece of her mind, something like "You sorry no-good son of a bitch, why don't you love me like I love you?" But that would mean admitting to herself and him she *does* love him, not to mention caving in and calling him. Instead, she pulls her go-to move whenever she feels rejected: she calls Gary Fuller instead.

He answers on the first ring. "Maggie."

She still feels boozy, but boozy sexy instead of boozy sad. "Hey, baby, I miss you."

"Here Without You."

Her lips curl up slowly. He's talking to her in song titles. It's a good sign. She answers with the artist. "Three Doors Down."

She hears him muffle his phone. It doesn't keep her from hearing the woman's voice in the background. "I have to take this," Gary says. Then Maggie hears her say, "You're crawling out of my bed to take calls from her?" A door slams. Then another.

"Where were we, gorgeous?"

Maggie doesn't give a fig about the other woman, whoever she is. Gary's never pretended to be anything but a horndog, even when he and Maggie were together. It's probably Jenny. She's a nutjob and hates Maggie, but she makes herself available to Gary. Very available. "About to have phone sex because it's urgent, urgent."

He laughs. "Foreigner. We can do better than that. Where are you?"

"Switch me to FaceTime."

Gary might be shit as a boyfriend, always on the road, sleeping with whatever groupie catches his fancy in every town, but he's sexy as hell. She switches their connection to FaceTime and his video comes into view. He's shirtless. Because he stays in great shape for the cameras, his chest and abs are chiseled. His shoulders make a yummy inverted V, and his collarbone begs for her tongue. His sandy blond hair is mussed from whatever he took his shirt off for.

His green eyes, though, look at her like she's the only woman in the world. At least for now. "Better?"

"Much."

"Damn, you're beautiful."

She wants to ask if she's prettier than the woman in the other room. She figures she's older. In fact, she doesn't get it. Gary can have and does have any woman he wants, eighteen and up—or so he claims, anyway. Why thirty-seven-year-old her?

"Thank you. You're not bad yourself."

"So where are you?"

"Amarillo by Morning."

"George Strait. Amarillo? I won't ask why."

She bites the inside of her lip. Guilt is swelling inside her, demanding she deal with it. Now. "I'm sorry you got dragged into the thing about the vandalism at my shop."

He nods, slow and rhythmic, like he's bobbing his head to music she can't hear. "That sucked."

"And for ending things between us."

"That sucked worse."

"Are you still mad at me?"

"Not mad enough, apparently."

She hears the woman's voice again. "Are you coming back, Gary?"

His jaw bulges as he clenches his teeth. "Sorry. Just a second." He turns his face, leaving his movie-star handsome profile onscreen. "No." He throws a T-shirt over his shoulder, giving her a quick glimpse of the enormous gold ring he insists on wearing. He adds a diamond to it for each million records he sells. Pretty soon he's going to need to switch to something bigger. Like a bracelet. Or a belt. The background behind him blurs as he starts moving.

Maggie hears keys jangling. "Where are you going?"

"My truck."

"I didn't tell you to stop what you're doing."

"I lost my appetite."

Her forehead creases. She leans toward the screen. "I can't make any promises, Gary."

"I can be very persuasive." He winks at her. "But I'm not asking for any."

"You were. Before."

"Yeah, and then you left me. I've had six months to rethink things." He smiles, opens a door, shuts it behind him. Bugs buzz a globe light behind his head. "Just get your ass home. Tom Clarke is coming to town tomorrow, and he's about to discover I'm upgrading to a new manager, so he can focus all his attention on his hot new clients. We can celebrate my independence from that thieving jackwipe together. And my other good news, which I'll tell you after I've fucked you until neither of us can walk."

Maggie doesn't want to get into Gary's latest complaints about his manager. Gary should have shitcanned him a decade ago. A pang of loneliness echoes inside her. She wants it to be Hank on the screen, Hank telling her to come home. She wants to point Bess north and leave now. But that won't happen. God knows she still needs someone who will scratch her itch, and Gary knows all her itchy spots. That has been enough before. It can be enough again, can't it?

Louise noses her hand.

Maggie fondles the dog's ears reflexively, offscreen.

Onscreen, Gary's face holds the possibility of salvation. She closes her eyes to save his image for when she'll need it. When she opens them, she tilts her head. Her hair swings forward, silky against her cheek. Baritone vibrato and soaring soprano twin in her inimitable voice. "Keep the bed warm, music man."

THREE

Maggie's hangover remedies have kicked in by the time she nears Round Top the next afternoon. Alka-Seltzer, a gallon—literally—of water, and a Joe T. Garcia's Mexican food lunch in Fort Worth counterbalance the sweltering heat sans air conditioning. It was at Joe T.'s that she'd read her texts while she paid her bill.

The first was a surprising group text initiated by Wallace, with Ethan, Emily, and Michele: *Hey, new girlfriend. Have a safe drive.*

She'd smiled and replied: *Heading straight to see that friend you asked me about ;-) Gonna wash that Wyoming man right out of my hair.*

Wallace responded immediately with *OMG send pictures. Or video. Kidding. Sort of.*

Maggie laughed, pocketed her credit card, and read a text from Gary: *You're bailing, aren't you?* It made her squirm. He knows her well.

Maggie: *Eric Church. "Like a Wrecking Ball."*

She'd hit the road again singing songs from his *Outsiders* album.

No, this time she isn't bailing. Who would have ever thought Gary Fuller would be a safer place to land than Hank Sibley?

Hank. He'd still been blowing up her phone during the drive—she'd ignored his texts at Joe T.'s, out of self-preservation—but it had slowed from an incessant shelling to an occasional shot. She gets it. During her week on Piney Bottoms, things between them had become electric. He'd kissed her. She'd saved him. They'd come close to rekindling things, until Sheila's news. Because Maggie had run, Hank didn't get to tell her thank you or explain himself or say goodbye. It wasn't fair to him. He hadn't done anything wrong, but that didn't change the facts or how bad they hurt.

She'd kept her mind mostly off him by voice-dictating lists of things to do.

- Take Michele dinner and a gift.
- Prepare for antique week.
- Repair the Coop.
- Create "junque" from Wyoming haul.
- Meet with insurance adjuster.
- Get a report from the Lee County sheriff's department about the incident.
- Clean up after the renter.
- Pick up Omaha and Nebraska from Lumpy.
- Fix Bess's air conditioner.
- Call Mom and Boyd.

About that time, she'd sniffed, smelled a hint of dog puke, then added a last item.

- Get Bess professionally cleaned.

Other than that, she'd surfed radio stations, run a mental best-of-Maggie-and-Gary slideshow to get herself in the right headspace, and thanked the good Lord that Louise kept her breakfast down.

Now, on Highway 290, she notices a new antique venue. It's in a white metal building that's been standing vacant ever since she can remember, halfway between Burton and Carmine. Cars and trucks crowd the dirt lot out front. A big sign hangs over the door: CRUSTY CRAP. Underneath, a smaller sign reads RICKEY SAYLES, PROPRIETOR. A decrepit black fringed buggy leans on its traces near the front door.

Maggie groans. Rickey Sayles. He'd tried to buy the Coop from her a few months before. When she turned him down, he opened his own shop. She's been told he's bad-mouthing her to any who will listen, bragging that he's going to kill off the Coop. That makes him a viable suspect for the vandalism, in her opinion.

"Bless your heart, Rickey." She salutes Sayles's new venture with a bird, then exits south toward Round Top.

Fifteen minutes later, she parks at Royers Round Top Café. There's a very full low-sided rain-collection tub under a porch gutter. She lets Louise out for a drink. The dog jumps in and thrashes happily in the water.

"Not what I had in mind," Maggie informs her.

She puts the wet dog back in the truck and heads inside. At the counter, she orders their Steak Special OMG! for two, to go. With Texas Trash pie, Gary's favorite. A whole one. She may not be in love with him, but their sexual reunion, if nothing else, is cause for celebration, as is the good news he promised her. And what is better for celebration than a place like Royers, whether dine-in or to-go, especially with pie? She orders two more, Chocolate Chip for Michele for her help with the Coop, and Pecan for Lumpy, for hoteling her goats.

She admires the interior with eyes fresh from her time in the wild, wild west of Wyoming, where there is nothing like Royers, not even close. Posters, flyers, photos, and curios in a rainbow of colors are plastered over every square inch of ceiling and wall. It's like a big welcome-home hug.

While she's waiting on her food, Maggie texts Michele.

Maggie: *I'm back.*

Michele: *So I hear, through the Amarillo grapevine.*

Maggie: *The rumors of my behavior are grossly exaggerated.*

Michele: *I love you. Sorry you've had a tough time. Go easy on Gary.*

Maggie: *Not in my playbook. I love you, too.*

Michele: *See you soon?*

Maggie: *Tmrw.*

In an attack of daughterly guilt, Maggie quickly texts her mother next.

Maggie: I'm back, Mom.

Maggie stares at the phone, expecting an immediate answer, but none comes.

A waitress with multicolored pastel hair slinks up with Maggie's food, interrupting her texting. Heather has always been Maggie's favorite, and her hair clashes perfectly with the frenetic vibe of Royers. "Here you go, Magpie. How's Boyd?"

Boyd Herrington, former senator and presidential candidate, is Maggie's birth father and a Royers regular. He's not to be confused with her nonfamous—and no longer living—adoptive father, who was an ultrareligious member of the Wendish Lutheran community. Boyd is now a lobbyist, and about to be immortalized on the big screen, like Maggie, thanks to the true-crime book Michele has penned and the movie soon due for release: *The Love Child and Murder That Toppled the Herrington Dynasty.* Maggie, of course, is the love child. At the center of the book is the murder of Maggie's birth mother, Gidget, an artist and gallery owner and an escapee from the Wend culture, like her daughter. Maggie's adoptive mother, Charlotte, was none too pleased when Gidget bequeathed Michele the task of finding her long-lost daughter, or that Michele was successful and wrote about it. But Boyd? Boyd is pleased as punch about Maggie, the book, and the movie.

"Boyd is Boyd." Maggie smiles. "I've been out of town a few weeks, so I haven't seen him." She hands Heather her credit card.

Heather swipes it through the reader. "I hear ya, hon. How his wife puts up with his shenanigans, I'll never know."

Boyd is a man whore, like Gary. Maggie would have to give that parallelism some thought, some other time. Boyd had even hit on her once prior to learning she was his daughter. She shudders. Thank God she doesn't go for slick, rich older guys, especially not after she'd suffered through a few too many creeps in the early days of her music career. Heather hands Maggie a curly slip of paper, and Maggie adds a twenty percent tip and her signature.

"Thanks, Heather."

"Don't be a stranger."

Back in the truck, Maggie offers Louise a piece of roll. Louise gulps it down.

"What, no thank-you?"

Louise grins and wags her tail.

During the drive to Gary's, Maggie drums the steering wheel and works on her a cappella rendition of "Bombshell." She only hates herself a little for enjoying it. The sun is setting, and traffic is light. A little silver sedan crosses over into her lane headed into town when she's halfway to Gary's house. She smashes her palm into the horn, steers right, and tries to keep Bess off the shoulder. Ditching while pulling her trailer could be fatal. The sedan driver reacts and returns to the other side of the road.

"Crazy-ass!" Maggie shouts.

After that heart-thudding encounter, she has the road to herself.

When her pulse is more normal, she sings again. "Bombshell, baby." She thumps her chest like Ava does in her videos.

Maggie laughs, until she sees dark gray smoke in the distance. Her brow furrows. As the daughter of a volunteer firefighter, she grew up understanding the language of smoke.

She mutters aloud. "It's too dry for burning. Grass and wood smoke is grayish white. Oil and plastic burn black. Dark gray . . . dark gray is bad."

She presses the accelerator. Bess strains for more speed as they ascend a hill. Around the last corner before a long straightaway to Gary's, flames shoot skyward and disappear into gray smoke.

The source, when she sees it, breaks her into a cold sweat. It's Gary's old wooden house. His jacked-up red Chevy Silverado is outside, parked way too close to the burning house. Flames lick outward, threatening to devour it.

"Shit, shit, shit."

She fumbles for her phone as she floors the accelerator. Using her knees to stabilize the steering wheel, she presses 911, SEND, and the SPEAKER button. Holding the phone to her ear with one hand, she takes the turn to Gary's too fast. Bess careens off the pavement onto Gary's driveway. For a moment, Maggie loses control. The trailer fishtails.

"No!"

Maggie mashes the brakes and grabs the wheel with both hands, trying not to jackknife. The phone slides off the seat into the floorboard. Louise joins it.

A calm female voice says, "911. Please state your emergency."

"House fire." Maggie shouts toward the phone, first giving the address. "Gary Fuller's place. I've just pulled up. His truck is parked outside."

"Please hold while I dispatch emergency response."

"I can't hold. There could be someone inside. Like Gary."

"What's your name, ma'am?"

"Maggie Killian."

"Ms. Killian, please remain in your vehicle and wait for the firefighters."

"Not a chance."

Maggie gets as close to the house as she dares, then shuts the engine off and jumps out before the truck's completely stopped. The fire shoots sparks that reach her hood, but she doesn't care. She throws open her door and jumps out, falling to her knees. She scrambles up, Louise hot on her heels.

"Gary," she screams. "Gary, where are you?"

Louise is barking hysterically, but all Maggie hears is the answering roar of the fire. She needs to get in, to figure out if Gary is inside, but the door is inaccessible. The entire front side of the house is engulfed in flames. Her heart pounds faster than the hooves of a racehorse. House fires are her worst nightmare. Once, when she was only eight or nine, her dad was called to a house fire. He didn't have time to take her home before he responded.

"Stay in the car no matter what. Your mom will be here soon," he'd told her, his brown eyes stern, his voice an order. "Promise me."

"Yes, sir, Daddy," she'd said, but she'd barely been listening to him.

He'd left her in the car. Maggie had never seen a serious fire before. She was curious about what her gentle farmer father did on his mysterious hero callouts. The leaping flames were mesmerizing to her. She snuck out of the car to get closer. But her fascination turned to terror when a woman about her mom's age suddenly burst out an upstairs window along with the sound of shattering glass and earsplitting screams. The woman ran through the air, arms and legs churning, which was bad enough.

But what made it truly horrifying was that she was on fire. Her granny-style nightgown. Her long blonde hair. Her house shoes. When she hit the ground, her screaming stopped. A firefighter leaped onto her, wrapped her in a heavy blanket, and rolled her over and over. To Maggie, it looked like an alligator wrestling its prey, something she'd seen on TV.

Maggie had run for the car and slammed the door behind her. She buried her face in the tweed upholstery that never lost the smell of smoke after that night, no matter how many times her mom shampooed it. She'd jammed her fingers in her ears to block the sounds. When that didn't work, she'd sung to herself. She still can't hear "Ring of Fire" without thinking of that night, to this very day.

Since then, burning buildings—and the thought of people inside—haunt Maggie. But today she's more scared of finding out later that Gary was in the house and that she could have saved him if she'd tried than she is of the flames.

Maggie charges toward the back of the house. Gary spent an obscene amount of money to have a yard designer install native grasses and flowers that thrive year-round. It's a geographically correct flora obstacle course now with tall brown grass and late-blooming yellow flowers. She zigs, zags, and hurdles her way across it. Halfway through it, she catches her foot. The ground knocks the wind out of her and something hard and sharp digs into her knee. She kicks her feet in a panic and twists to see what has her. Her boot is caught in a hose snaked between clumps of prairie grass. As she extricates herself, she sees a long slit in the hose. It doesn't make sense to her, but she has bigger problems. She frees her foot. Her knee is throbbing, but she ignores it. She scrambles to a crawl, fights to get herself upright, and takes off again at a run.

Her voice cracks with strain. "Gary. Gary!"

The flames are even worse in the back than in the front. His bedroom is back here, looking out on rolling hills, pasture, and oak groves. Is he inside? She prays he's not. That he's in town having dinner with his manager. Or that he got out earlier, and he's on the other side of the house wielding a hose, unable to hear her.

But what if he *is* inside? He might be okay. He could have wrapped himself in a wet blanket. Or be hidden from the fire under his desk. Anything is possible. An image of the flying, burning woman with her churning arms and legs flashes through her mind again. Her breath catches. The only thing certain is that Gary's chances of surviving—if he is in there —are decreasing by the second.

And she's the only one here, the only one who can help him. She can't search the grounds first. She can't wait for the firefighters. She has to *do* something.

She studies the antique French doors to his bedroom. On the other side of the glass, the drapes are ablaze. She wraps her hand in the lightweight fabric of her top and tries the knob. The heat is searing. It won't budge. She jerks her hand away. The doors are flimsy and insubstantial by modern standards—she'd helped Gary pick them out at an estate sale in Brenham— but still too sturdy for her to break down. Even if she kicks out the glass, the panes are too small for her to crawl through.

She'll have to break down the doors. But if she does, then what? She doesn't even want to think about it.

There's a gardening shed on the edge of the backyard. She sprints over to it. It's unlocked. Finally, a door she can get through.

"Something heavy. Come on, Maggie. Something heavy."

Fueled by adrenaline, she hefts a pickax over her shoulder. It will do. She runs back to the house, slower with the weight of the pickax. She hesitates at the door. Maybe Gary will come running out if she breaks a hole for him, because the last thing she wants is to go in that house herself.

"Please, God," she whispers, "don't make me have to go in there."

Planting her feet, she swings the pickax with all her might like a giant bat at the doorframe. Wood splinters. Glass shatters. At the end of her swing, the weight of the pickax pulls it from her hands, slinging it into the room.

For half a second, she feels a strange sucking of the air around her into the house, like an inhale from something monstrous and alive, then flames exhale with a giant whoosh. Maggie falls backward, shielding her face, screeching with pain. Her four hundred dollars' worth of Johnny Was top ignites, just like the gown on the woman she'd watched jump through the second-story window nearly thirty years ago. She hugs herself and rolls, smothering the fire with the dirt and her body. When she's out of the range of the hungry, fiery monster reaching for her through the bashed-in door, she lies still as a corpse. She smells soot and tastes dirt, but she doesn't move. She feels relief that she's not in the house, then crushing guilt.

A wet tongue licks her cheek.

"Gary." Her voice is weak. She coughs. "Gary." She kneels, butt on her heels, hands bracing on her knees.

The tongue of fire no longer laps from the house. Louise whines, then darts through the broken door.

Hoarse and croaking, Maggie crawls after her dog. "No!"

A suited firefighter appears in her peripheral vision, grabs her shoulder, and yanks her back. "Ma'am, stop," he says in a bass voice.

For a moment, she thinks she's hearing her father. But that can't be. He's dead. Long dead. Her mind returns to the present. She struggles to break the man's grip. "No. Gary. Louise."

The firefighter peers at her burned clothing then speaks into a radio clipped to his chest. "I need an EMT."

"Help them, please."

Maggie tears her eyes away from Gary's room. A fire truck is parked on the side of the house, and an ambulance beside it. Lights are flashing. Sirens are wailing.

"Holy shit," the firefighter says.

Maggie's gaze jerks back to the maw of the fire. Her dwarfish black-and-white dog appears. She's carrying something in her mouth. The firefighter rushes to help Louise, and Maggie is on her feet, sprinting.

She's shouting their names. "Gary. Louise."

But when Louise clears the door and bounds toward her, Maggie's shouts fade. The unreality of what she sees robs her of thought and voice. Just as Louise reaches Maggie, the firefighter tackles the burning dog and smothers the flames. Maggie slumps to the ground, numb, the blackened finger of her former lover in the grass beside her where Louise dropped it, still wearing his ridiculous gold ring.

FOUR

Shivering in a shock blanket, Maggie croons to Louise and rocks the dog like a baby. Maggie had only submitted to treatment from the EMTs on the condition that they treat Louise first. Miraculously, while Louise has less of her long fur, her burns are relatively minor. The EMTs warn Maggie to monitor the dog's coughing and breathing but assure her that Louise appears she will heal just fine. Better than a human would, because dogs are resilient that way.

Maggie will heal, too. Her arms are red, with a few blisters. She lost a good bit of her eyelashes, eyebrows, and arm hair. But all of her physical injuries are cosmetic and temporary.

"I don't understand. How did Louise get out alive?" she asks a firefighter. A genderless, nameless, faceless, shapeless person as far as Maggie is concerned. A disembodied voice from a sooty face and a body in bunker gear.

"Because she's short, and she wasn't in there long. Two or three feet above the floor, you're fine. Up high burns first. That's why we coach people to stop, drop, roll, and *crawl*. Once the ceiling starts to rain burning materials onto the floor, the floor catches, and that doesn't work anymore. Your dog made it out just in time."

"But not Gary." Maggie's voice breaks.

Louise licks her face.

"No. Not Gary."

"How did this happen?"

"You'll need to talk to the fire marshal about that."

"Who?"

The firefighter points at an unmarked SUV with a light on top parked next to a phalanx of Fayette County Sheriff's Department vehicles. "If you're ready, we can go over there now."

Maggie stands.

Louise squirms out of her arms.

"Let me put her in my truck first."

The firefighter follows her to Bess. At the truck, Louise resists, almost clinging to Maggie. Maggie lifts her and shoves her in, slamming the door before she escapes. The dog starts barking madly and jumping like she's on a pogo stick. Maggie feels guilty turning away. When she does, she nearly plows into a perimeter barricade of plastic sawhorses and tape that had been erected while she was with the EMTs.

The firefighter grunts and removes a helmet. "Your dog is worried about you." Long, silky hair cascades down her shoulders.

"I've only had her for a week. It's crazy. I can't believe she went into the fire. She's never even met Gary."

"Some dogs are like that. Special."

Maggie wishes they'd arrived earlier, so Louise could have been special for Gary when he was still alive.

The firefighter leads her to the fire marshal. "Ma'am, are you ready to interview Maggie Killian? She called the fire in and was on scene when we got here."

The woman is writing on a paper attached to a clipboard. She turns to Maggie, not the firefighter. She's short and thick in a red bunker jacket open to show the suspenders on her coveralls. Shoulder-length steel-gray hair peeks out from her helmet. "Now is fine. Thank you."

"Yes, ma'am." The firefighter walks away without another word to Maggie.

The fire marshal stares at Maggie through horn-rimmed glasses, sizing her up. "Maggie Killian."

Maggie nods, wondering what someone who sounds so East Coast is doing in small-town Texas. "Yes."

"I'm Karen Rosenthal, fire marshal for Fayette County. Let's get a deputy from Fayette County to join us."

"Okay."

Karen waves over a bowling ball of a man in a sheriff's deputy uniform. "Deputy Troy Mason, this is Maggie Killian."

Maggie and the deputy shake.

"She called in the fire. Ms. Killian, start from the beginning."

Maggie pulls the shock blanket tighter around herself. "I was coming to see Gary. I picked up dinner at Royers and drove out here. I saw dark gray smoke from a distance, then I came around the last bend in the road and saw the house in flames. I called 911."

"Was there anyone here when you arrived?"

"I didn't see anyone outside, but I don't—didn't—know about inside. Gary's truck was here."

"No other vehicles, no signs of other people?"

"No."

"You didn't see anyone leaving?"

"No."

"An explosion?"

"No."

"Explosives, accelerants, matches, lighters, or anything else that might be used to start a fire?"

"Nothing."

"Smell anything odd?"

"Just smoke."

"Why were you here?"

"We were . . . we used to be together. I've been traveling. I called him, and he asked me to come over."

Troy cuts in. He's got a thick, slow Texas accent. "How long since you seen him, ma'am?"

"A few months, I guess."

"Talked to him?"

"I heard from him a lot. He didn't, um, he didn't take our breakup well."

The fire marshal's eyes are big and shrewd behind her lenses. "Were you familiar with his house?"

"Very. I helped him remodel and furnish it over the last few years."

"Any electrical issues, to your knowledge?"

"He had the whole house updated and rewired. It was old and crappy before that. But I don't know if he had any current problems."

"Did Mr. Fuller smoke?"

"No. He is—was—a singer. He believed it was bad for his vocal cords."

"Would you characterize him as suicidal?"

Maggie shakes her head. "Do you know who this man is?"

"Gary Fuller."

"Gary Fuller, international country music star, the biggest entertainer out of Texas since George Strait. He had a very healthy self-esteem, stoked by the admiration of an adoring public. I don't think he's been depressed since I've known him, which is over ten years. Certainly not suicidal."

"That doesn't mean he hasn't been. Or wasn't recently."

"If our breakup is any indication, he was sad, he got mad, he got over it."

"How do you know that?"

"He was with another woman last night. To me, that was the normal, confident Gary."

A firefighter—one of rank, Maggie assumes from the patches on the uniform—pulls Karen aside. The two have a brief, whispered conversation with Troy listening in. The firefighter nods, then ducks under the barricade and trots back to the house, talking into the radio the whole way.

Karen and Troy return to Maggie.

Maggie wipes her eyes.

Karen says, "Are you okay, Ms. Killian?"

"Rough night. The fire. Gary. And all the firefighters. My dad was a volunteer firefighter here in Fayette County when I was a little girl."

Karen's eyes drill into hers. "And?"

"And . . . nothing. I'm just emotional. Memories and present circumstances colliding."

Troy picks up the conversation where they'd left it before he and Karen stepped away. He drawls, "Who was the other woman with Mr. Fuller that night?"

"I didn't ask."

"Did it upset you?"

Maggie snorts. "Not in the slightest."

Troy and Karen look at each other. The fire marshal nods at the deputy. Troy says, "I'd like to talk to the people close to him, to get a feel for what was going on in his life and who was in it."

Maggie shivers. She just can't get warm. "It sounds like you think someone set this fire deliberately. Like they *killed* him."

The two answer at the same time.

Troy says, "We can't rule anything out."

"Premature," Karen says. Then she adds, "I'm not at liberty to give out additional information at this time."

Something about her tone raises hackles on Maggie's neck and suspicions in her mind. "Am I a suspect?"

"I wouldn't say *suspect*. I'm investigating the cause of the fire." Troy crosses his arms. "I'm investigating other potential crimes."

Maggie says, "What would you call me, then?"

Karen shrugs at Troy.

He says, "A person of interest with potentially key information."

Maggie closes her eyes. She's been down this road before. Last week, in fact, as public enemy number one after the death of her cowboy fling, Chet. It's ludicrous they're homing in on her for Gary's death now. She could come up with a list as long as her arm of people that would benefit from his demise, if Fayette County wants it. For now, she'll say as little as possible beyond the facts. "I called 911. I was injured trying to save him."

"Ah, the sheriff himself has arrived." Karen beckons a tall man in a ten-gallon straw cowboy hat. To Maggie, she says, "You'd be shocked how often a person sets a fire then has second thoughts. Even more stick around the scene to glory in the aftermath. Or to get treated for their injuries."

"It wasn't me."

"I certainly hope that's what we find. For now, just give us your contact information for a follow-up interview." Karen puts a new sheet of paper on top of the stack on her clipboard and holds it out to Maggie.

"And let me guess—don't leave town."

Troy's eyes have been on his boss, who is consulting with a man who appears to be the fire chief. He cuts them to Maggie for a moment. "Spoken like a woman who's heard it before, I'd say."

Maggie fumes, but complies, the blanket falling from her shoulders, the pen digging into the paper. Gary is gone. Gone *forever*. Another man close to her has succumbed to violence. First, Chet was bludgeoned to death. Then Patrick, a Wyoming rancher she went out with a time or two, was shot dead. Next, Hank, the love of her life, barely survived a rifle shot. And now Gary, her former boyfriend, is dead. Never mind that the fire marshal and a deputy are eyeing her like the easy answer to a hard question barely a week after she was a suspect in Chet's death. That pales in comparison to the more obvious truth.

She's a freaking black widow.

FIVE

After Maggie's written her list, the fire marshal and deputy release her.

Maggie drives by rote toward her house, her hands white-knuckled on the steering wheel. It's nearly ten p.m. The lapse of time between now and when she'd first seen the dark gray smoke is like a black hole in her life.

She groans. Louise lifts her head, checking on her. Maggie fondles the dog's ears. How is she going to come to grips with never seeing Gary again, after he'd been in her life, in one way or another, for a decade?

Her heart hurts. Gary's family will be devastated. They're a tight-knit clan, all nine of them—his mother and his seven siblings and their families living in houses Gary built for them on a family compound near Boerne, outside of San Antonio. Well, six siblings, since Kelly is of the Nashville world now. Who is going to tell them? And how will they react when they hear she was there when it happened?

There will be a service for Gary. Maggie will have to go. She groans again. From day one, Gary's mother, Merritt, hasn't been Maggie's biggest fan, citing ample and readily available evidence that Maggie was trouble. Merritt's gossip rag obsession makes Wallace's fascination seem like a passing fancy. She had to know that Maggie had dumped her golden boy. The recent smear story online about Maggie in the bad old days will just add more fuel to Merritt's fire. Maybe Maggie hadn't fulfilled Merritt's worst prophecies of tanking Gary's career, saddling him with unwanted children, dragging him into addiction, and sucking him dry financially. But

Mama Fuller still mourned that he never married a Miss America, a princess, or a Hollywood actress befitting her boy's stardom, and she laid that squarely on Maggie's shoulders. Maggie thought it probably had more to do with the fact that Gary was tied to his trailer park mama by her short apron strings, but no one asked her.

Her phone rings as she pulls up to her dark house. Without looking at caller ID, she answers. "Hello."

"Maggie." It's Hank's voice.

For a moment, Maggie loses her sense of direction. She's disoriented in the darkness, unsure of up, down, left, or right. She shakes her head to dispel the vertigo. "Uh, hey, Hank." Her voice sounds scratchy. She clears her throat.

"Why did you leave? Why are you ignoring my calls and texts? I mean, really, what the fuck is going on? I don't get it, Maggie." His voice sounds raw like hers. Fire raw.

"Not now, Hank."

"When, then?"

Good question. Never, maybe. "I don't play second fiddle." Especially not when first fiddle is carrying his child.

"What?"

"Lose my number."

"I—"

She ends the call and turns the phone over so she can't see the damn dimple-cheeked picture of him. She'd cry if she didn't feel so numb from the fire and Gary's death. It was such a mistake to go to Wyoming. She'd been right to rebuff Hank last spring. She should have just left him—them—in the past. *Note to self: change my phone number.*

She pulls up in front of the Coop and sees a moon-silver car in her headlights. *Shit. The renter.* Maggie had driven here on autopilot, but Leslie must have another night or two left in her visit. She'll look it up later. For now, she has to find another place to stay.

It's too late to show up unannounced at Michele's.

Maggie texts Michele: *Got room for me at Nowheresville?* She uses Michele's nickname for her property and new house.

Michele: *Just tonight or forever?*

Maggie: *Tonight. Need shower, whiskey, shoulder to cry on.*

Michele: *Mi casa es tu casa. What's wrong?*

Maggie: *I'll tell you when I get there.*

She reverses Bess and the trailer back onto the road and makes the short drive to Michele's new house. She and Louise alight and traipse to the door. The cicadas buzz in the trees, vibrating Maggie's very bones. The humidity feels oppressive after Wyoming, and the night air smells to her like decay.

Michele opens the door before Maggie can knock. "You smell like smoke and look like hell."

Maggie opens her mouth to explain and breaks into sobs instead.

"Oh, honey, come inside." Michele pulls Maggie through the door and into her arms. "Whiskey first?"

Maggie nods, unable to speak through choking noises that seem bigger and louder in the high-ceilinged entryway. She hears scrabbling claws and a territorial growl. She chokes down another sob and steps back. The only stranger-looking dog in the world than Louise is Michele's Gertrude, a Rastafarian-like mix of sheepdog and pug. Her locks tremble as she stares down Louise, the intruder to her peaceful domain.

Louise wags her tail and holds herself rock-still for inspection. Gertrude makes a lap around her and sniffs her hind end. Then something changes, and all of a sudden the two dogs are chasing each other around the living room, barking happy barks.

Michele raises her eyebrows. "Who's your friend?"

"Consolation prize from Wyoming."

They move to the kitchen. Maggie climbs onto a cowhide stool and leans on the tan granite countertop. Michele pours from a bottle of Balcones and adds a few ice cubes. She hands Maggie the drink and guides her to the couch with fingertips between her shoulder blades. "Start talking."

So Maggie takes a deep breath, and she does, until there's nothing left to tell.

SIX

The next morning, Maggie is officially cried out and even more sleep-deprived. Hank. Gary. The roar of the fire. The work in front of her to restore her shop. More Gary. More Hank. On repeat, all night long.

Throwing off the quilt, Maggie staggers to the en suite bathroom. Michele's Mayan art looks like it was created to hang on the earth-toned tile wall. A multicolored glass butterfly figurine takes flight from a sage green soapstone countertop. A glass-walled shower with a river-stone floor promises tranquility. She ignores the shower, opting only to splash water on her puffy eyes. She stares into the mirror, seeing herself in the light of day for the first time since the fire. Without eyebrows and lashes, she looks like a minor actress in a slasher flick, right before her short role ends. She peeks under the bandages on her arms. The EMT told her to put aloe vera on them—Neosporin if they start to look infected—and change bandages daily. So far, it doesn't look bad. Just ugly. She'll pick up supplies later.

She pulls on jeans and a snug T-shirt that says VINTAGE MODEL across her free-range breasts. Her Martin guitar in its hard case is propped against the wall. Good. She remembered to bring it in last night. Now that she's returned Hank's belt buckle, it's her most prized possession in the world. It and everything else in her truck bed and trailer could have been destroyed last night. Fire. Water. Whatever other shit the firefighters dumped on the blaze. Her material things are nothing compared to Gary, of course, but they still matter to her. She presses her temple. Coffee. She needs coffee.

She tiptoes barefoot to the kitchen. Gertrude and Louise are playing tug-of-war with a thick braided rope in the doorway to Michele's office. Maggie joins them at the door and pokes her head in.

Michele is sipping coffee from an oversized mug, sitting behind the compact antique desk Maggie found for her the year before. The moment Maggie saw it, she knew it was the perfect size and style for her friend.

"I've been reading about Gary."

Maggie asks, "Does my name come up?"

Michele winces. "It does."

"As a suspect?"

"No. Just as a former girlfriend, and the one that found him."

"Well, that's something, at least."

"They'll find out who did this. I'm so sorry, Maggie."

"Me, too." Maggie flops into a chair. It rolls backward, and she arrests it with her feet. "Thanks for the ear last night. And everything else. The shop. The investigation. The insurance claim. My goats."

"Thanks for the pie." Michele had insisted on helping Maggie unload Bess, which was a good thing. All the Royers bags and boxes had made it into her refrigerator.

"Not in the same league."

Michele blows a raspberry, making light of Maggie's serious tone. "You'd do the same for me."

"Still. I owe you."

"I'll claim it in decorating advice."

"Your place is looking great."

"Belle tells me it looks too new for a country home named Nowheresville."

"Your stepdaughter is a smart young lady, but rustic takes time. We'll find the right pieces, one by one. Speaking of your brood, how are Sam and the baby?"

"Good. Charlie is visiting Sam's father. It's a busy time of year for Sam with baseball, and Robert needed his baby fix."

Maggie smiles. It's sincere, if droopy. Michele's teenage son had a baby boy his senior year of high school. Halfway through his freshman year on a juco baseball scholarship, his young wife was murdered. To say the kid had been having a rough time was an understatement. As a result, Michele balances very hands-on grandmothering with her writing schedule, the pro bono legal work she insists on doing to help out in their rural county, endurance triathlon training, and a super-sexy boyfriend—Rashidi, a hydroponic farming expert from the Virgin Islands who works for the Texas A&M Extension Service. Hydroponic as in "plants grown in water, fed by fish poop from live fish in the same tanks." Maggie doesn't understand his field, but she likes him almost as much as she likes Michele's stepdaughter and son.

"So where's your man?"

"Refugio today. He's doing workshops and helping with installations. He'll be back tonight."

Maggie walks into the kitchen to Michele's Keurig. She prefers a good percolator, but Michele has tossed out even her old drip pot in favor of pods.

"Are you ready to talk about Flown the Coop?" Michele follows her and leans against the countertop, cradling her mug.

"Give me some good news. Please."

"I do have one good bit. It turns out your renter, Leslie, is super nice."

"My renter." Maggie pops in a pod and positions a thick, oversized plain white mug with a chip under the spigot, then closes the handle and presses START.

"Yes."

"How did you finally meet her?" At the time of the vandalism to the Coop, Michele had been unable to track Leslie down.

"She's been around the house and chatty the last few times I've been over to meet adjusters and deputies and contractors."

"Well, that's good, I guess."

"Yep. What's better is that you have Gidget's old Jaguar in storage and the Andy Warhol you inherited from her in a museum."

"Tell me about it. If they'd been damaged in the shop, I'll bet the adjuster would have gone ballistic."

"And all Gidget's paintings. Thank God they were in your house."

Maggie's stomach tightens at the thought. Besides being worth a fair amount of money, they are emotionally irreplaceable to her. "Oh, I talked to Junior again," Maggie says, referring to the Lee County deputy working the Coop vandalism case. "I gave him a few suspects to run with."

"I wonder how Gary's death will impact his investigation."

"Me, too. Did you talk to Gary after he found out he was under suspicion?" Maggie tests her coffee. Too hot. She blows on it, then sets it down.

"Yes, he came by the Coop to see the damage for himself."

"I thought he was supposed to stay away."

"You know he was never any good at doing what he was told."

Maggie smiles sadly. "One of the things I loved best about him."

"Anyway, he was none too happy. He gave me and Leslie an earful about the incompetence of Lee County. And he threw in a few choice words about you, too."

"She was there?"

"Yes."

Maggie purses her lips, thinking. Gary *had* been really angry at her. Humiliated by her. Jealous of her other men. But he sure got over it quickly when she called. Besides, his method of revenge was to screw younger women, not to trash her livelihood.

Michele points at the refrigerator. "Greek yogurt. Blueberries. Granola in the pantry."

Maggie gathers ingredients, a bowl, and a spoon. She moves her coffee to the island beside Michele and assembles her breakfast. An apple fritter fits her mood better, but she'd never find one here. Michele tends toward boringly healthy.

"So, how did you end up with a date planned with Gary last night, anyway?"

Maggie's compromised emotional bandwidth had led to limited details in her storytelling. She's not much better this morning, but coffee is helping. Yogurt will, too. "I drunk-dialed him from Amarillo." She takes a bite.

"You were getting back together?"

"No. Just planning to engage in adult activities."

Michele shakes her head.

"What?"

"I'm really sorry for what you've been through. I'm sorry Gary is dead. I know you have a lot of history, and you cared about him."

"I hear a *but* in there somewhere."

"But I know you, and there's no way you're getting over Hank without someone to, um, you know. Help you exorcise the demon."

Maggie takes a big bite and talks with her mouth full. "I have no idea what you mean."

Michele laughs and swats her. "Speaking of Hank, I've noticed you're not wearing your belt buckle."

"His belt buckle now. Like it always should have been."

"Are you okay?"

"Not really." She'd filled Michele in on his engagement and great expectations last night. "But I gave it my best shot."

"You did. I'm proud of you. And I'm jealous you got to see Gene. I want to go visit him."

"He's really awesome. If only he wasn't business partners with and living on the same ranch as Hank, I'd go with you."

"Listen, I have some conference calls, and my editor is expecting my input on her revisions to my work-in-progress later today."

"*Baby's Breath?*"

"Yep. Are you going to be all right if I bail on you?"

Maggie waves a spoon at her. "Lots to do."

"Don't forget to put calling your mother on that list. And Boyd."

"I texted Mom last night. No answer."

"Yeah, she's on a cellphone hiatus."

"So my timing is perfect."

"Not nice."

Maggie grins. "Seriously, what do you mean?"

"Charlotte is on a getaway without her phone. She has news, but I'm sworn to secrecy."

"About what?"

"I'm not supposed to tell you."

"No fair. How long has she been gone?"

"Just since yesterday. But that's all I'm going to say about it."

"Oh, goodie. If she's not here Sunday, she can't try to drag me to church."

Michele smirks and disappears back into her office.

Maggie finishes her yogurt parfait, then lets Louise and her new best friend Gertrude out. She returns to the bathroom and makes herself more hygienic and presentable, then flops onto the bed to brave her phone. She has a voicemail from Junior asking for a meet on her shop. Fine. She'll call him in a minute. Condolence messages on the Amarillo friends group text. Had Michele told them, or did Wallace get the news from People.com? She replies with a sad face and *Thank you.*

Then, a text from Hank, shortly after their call the night before: *I thought we were good. What have I done? And by the way, thanks for saving my life.*

Maggie deletes it. She can't let his gratitude soften her resolve. But she was pretty amazing, if she does say so herself. When Hank was shot while he and Maggie were out antelope hunting, she'd gone for help, first nailing the shooter with an arrow shot from Hank's compound bow, then arranging for a helicopter and rescue team. She'd do it again if she had to. But that doesn't mean she'll answer his texts.

The doorbell rings. She hears two barking dogs, then Michele greeting someone. A male voice answers.

Michele hollers. "Maggie? It's Boyd."

Maggie sets her phone down. *Well, that didn't take long.* She joins Boyd in the great room.

Michele's phone rings. She glances at it, then holds it up to show she has a call to take. "Sorry." She answers it as she's closing her office doors behind her.

Boyd beams at Maggie. "There's my beautiful daughter. I heard you were back." He holds up a palm. "No, actually, I heard you left town. Not from you. Then I heard you were back. Again, not from you. I'm starting to get a complex."

Maggie hugs him. "Hi, Boyd. It was a spur-of-the-moment thing, in both directions."

"I also heard some bad news. About Gary Fuller."

"Yeah."

"Are you okay?"

"Just sad." Maggie brushes hair back from her face, tucking it behind an ear.

"I'll bet. I'm really sorry. If there's anything I can do, let me know."

"I will."

"Hey, what's wrong with your arms? And your . . ." Boyd leans closer, staring at her face.

"The fire. It's not as bad as it seems."

"Tell that to your eyebrows, because they're not looking so good."

"They'll grow back."

"It's all over the news that you were there. Not just local. CNN, et cetera."

"Swell."

"The price of celebrity. Speaking of which, how would you feel about me running for office again?" He locks his eyes on her and leans in, his signature move. Voters love it. People think it shows his sincerity. Maggie thinks he knows he's still a handsome and charismatic man, even at nearly sixty.

"Ambivalent."

"That's a ringing endorsement."

"It's up to you. Not my business."

"It will impact you. Keep your name in the news. You'll have to deal with reporters and talking heads."

Michele rejoins them, watching the father-daughter exchange like a tennis match.

"You do you. I'll worry about me."

"It just seems like with Michele's movie about us and all, the timing is good. My name recognition will be high."

Only a politician would look at the disclosure of his secret love child and the murder of his baby mama by his sister and former campaign manager as good PR. Maggie shoots him a thumbs-up, out of words.

Michele grins. "You guys are coming to the premiere in Austin, right? I have tickets for everyone."

Maggie grumbles. "If my eyebrows grow back in a week."

"Two words: eyebrow pencil."

"Do you promise me I won't hate the performance of the actress playing me?"

"You're such a snob. She's great."

"She's all flash-bang-boobs. Big-budget movies. You know I wanted a real actor."

Boyd says, "My wife and I will be there. Thanks for the tickets. I'm sure that's what my churlish daughter meant to say."

Maggie shrugs. "Or not. Thanks for coming by, but now I have things I gotta do. Lunch later this week?" She kisses Boyd's cheek.

"Perfect. And I can introduce you to my campaign manager. Run through some ideas she has."

Maggie rolls her eyes. "Let's not and say we did."

SEVEN

Later in Giddings, Maggie drops by the feed store for dog food and goat treats, then the grocery store for bandages and ointment. She can't pick up her goats from Lumpy until she has her house back, but it makes her feel better to buy them something. Her sunglasses and the light jacket of Michele's she'd borrowed on her way out the door help cover evidence of the fire, for which she's grateful. At both stores, she fends off curious stares and condolences, gestures she knows are meant more to elicit information about Gary than to make her feel better. Barely anyone knew about the two of them until he died.

Leaving the parking lot of the grocery store, she sees a man who looks familiar. He's tall. Very, very tall. Handsome, too, from what she can see under a John Deere ball cap pulled low on his forehead. His hands are jammed in his pockets. He passes, walking the other direction, and she sees a Skoal-can-like faded outline in the back pocket of his city-boy jeans. Not from around here. Maybe she doesn't know him after all.

Before she goes anywhere else, she needs gas. She stops in town at the Valero c-store. As she's pumping, a man's voice calls her name. She looks around, hoping he's speaking to a different Maggie.

"Yes, you. You're Maggie Killian, aren't you?" The voice belongs to a grungy-looking guy with acne on both cheeks.

"Who are you?" The pump clicks off. Tank full.

"I'm a reporter. I was hoping for a comment about Gary Fuller's death."

Maggie jerks the nozzle out so fast she spills gas on the concrete. She jumps back to avoid getting splashed. It gets on her hands anyway. She replaces the nozzle, then screws the gas cap back on. "Buzz off, cub."

"Were the two of you back together? Did you catch him with another woman?"

She ignores him.

"Did he tell you he was going to be the newest coach on *The Singer* and whether it ended his friendship with Thorn Gibbons?"

She opens the door to Bess. Thorn Gibbons. The guy in the grocery store parking lot *had* looked like the TV and music superstar from Connecticut, the one who likes to pretend he's real country and is just as famous for beating a charge that he and his college lacrosse team had roofied a teenage girl and taken turns with her as he is for his music. He and Gary had never been friends. Just acquaintances in the biz. And Gary hadn't said a word about *The Singer*. Maybe that had been his good news. *Hmm, if he was Thorn, why would he come to Giddings?*

"Give up, already."

"Is it true he fired his sister Kelly from his band? And that you're a suspect in his murder?"

She slams the door, teeth gritted, and pushes down the lock. Damn reporters. Vultures. Or, in this guy's case, baby vulture. She should have expected they'd show up for the death of a star of Gary's wattage, but she doesn't have to like it. And now because of the little twerp, she and Bess smell like gas. But he got her attention with one tidbit. Had Gary really fired Kelly? She can't imagine what would be bad enough to make him do that. He doted on the kid. Young lady. She couldn't be more than seventeen. So, woman—barely.

Working through the to-do list she'd created on the drive yesterday, Maggie decides to call Junior for a report on the investigation. She paws through her bag, but she can't find her phone. She searches the cab. No dice.

The reporter knocks on the window. "Come on, Ms. Killian. I'd still like a word with you. Tell me about the fire, at least."

She pretends he isn't there.

She digs deep to remember where she last had her phone. Boyd rang the doorbell. She was reading a text from Hank. The bathroom at Michele's. That's where she left it, dammit. That nixes a call to T-Mobile for a new phone number, at least for now.

Without a backward glance at the baby reporter, she drives away. Since she can't call Junior, she drops in at the sheriff's department. It's noon, and he's eating from a brown bag at his desk.

"Maggie." His neck flushes. Junior has never quite realized he's ten years younger than her, or that she's not interested. He stands, like a pocketknife unfolding. He scratches his crew-cut hair. "Been hoping to talk to you."

"I got your message. Left my phone at home. Is this okay, me stopping in?"

He wipes his hands on his trousers, then wraps wax paper around his sandwich and seals it in the bag. "Works for me. Come on."

He leads the way into a small room with a Formica-topped metal table and a few low-budget rolling armchairs. The walls are bare. It's a step up from an interrogation room. A very small step.

Maggie sits in a chair. It sinks in on one side of her tush. "You guys figured out who vandalized my shop yet?"

"Not yet. Not much to go on. What's with the sunglasses?"

"The fire at Gary's last night. It got my eyebrows and eyelashes."

"I'm sorry. About that and about Mr. Fuller."

"Were you able to clear Gary before he died?"

"We can't much rule anyone out yet."

"Except for me, I hope. I was in Wyoming."

"I wasn't saying . . ." He stops.

Maggie prods him. "Do you need anything else from me?"

"Well, your statement. And I was hoping you've had more ideas about who might have done this."

"Honestly, my money's on drunk teenagers. But did you look at Rickey Sayles? Or one of Gary's latest bed bunnies? Jenny was the last one I knew by name."

"Your renter said she hasn't seen anyone come and go except Michele. And Gary."

Maggie can't resist bedeviling him, especially after he ducked her question. She puts a hand over her breastbone. "You think Michele did it?"

He blushes again. "Of course not."

"Any direct evidence it was Gary?"

"No."

"Well, I know you'll do your job to the best of your abilities."

Junior looks down. Maggie feels guilty, for half a second.

Then Junior says, "What were you doing out at his place last night anyway?"

She's surprised. He isn't usually this direct with her. Or nosy. "A little something called none of your beeswax."

He looks away from her and toward the ceiling. "The fire marshal called. She wants to work together. Thinks there could be crossover between the vandalism of your shop and the fire that killed Gary."

"I don't see how."

"You said Gary was angry at you."

"So he told me, and everyone else that would listen."

"But you were going to see him."

"We'd buried the hatchet."

Junior sucks in his upper lip and rakes it several times with his teeth. He twists in the seat of his chair like he can't get comfortable. "That's not what the emails between you say."

Maggie snaps up in her chair. "How are you reading our emails?"

"He left his phone in his car. No password."

"So read our texts."

"We did. There's nothing about you going to his place. Or a buried hatchet."

Maggie's brain races. What's happening here? This feels like it's a suspect interview in a possible arson-murder case. "That's bullshit, Junior. I can't remember the last time I sent Gary an email, anyway."

He recites an email address. "Is that you?"

"Yes."

"Appears you emailed him plenty. And they paint a very different picture."

"In what way?"

"That he dumped you."

Maggie can't help it. She laughs. Obviously her attempts to keep the fact that she's in love with a cowboy in Wyoming who's marrying another woman have been too successful. "What? He did not."

"That he slept with other women and you got mad."

Maggie stops laughing. "You're serious."

"Yes."

"He always slept with other women. I slept with other men." And a few women, but she doesn't volunteer that information. "We had an open relationship."

"The emails also said he wouldn't take you back, and you were coming over to make sure he understood you weren't taking no for an answer."

Maggie freezes. She never sent any such thing. None of them. Is Junior lying? Or is someone setting her up? But who? And how? One thing is for sure. She can't continue this conversation without knowing more, and not without her lawyer. She'd talked to the cops once before without Michele, in Wyoming. She'd learned her lesson and good.

Her chair rolls back and smashes into the wall as she gets up. "I came here to talk about vandalism at the Coop, in good faith. Not cool, Junior. We're done here."

"What's that smell?"

"What smell?"

"It's like gasoline or something."

"It is gasoline. Leftover from yesterday when I committed arson." She slits her eyes at him. "As if. I got gas in my truck on the way here, and I spilled some on myself, not that it's any of your business."

"Okay. What about your statement?"

"Kiss my ass. There's your statement." She rushes out, angry and dazed. She needs to call Michele. *No phone. Dammit!*

In her truck, she drums her fingers on the steering wheel. *What to do, what to do? Think, think, think.* Her brain spins like a pinwheel. She puts her hand out as if to stop it, but it speeds up. She imagines little plastic pinwheel fins hitting her fingers.

Fine. She can't fix everything at once. Or anything at all. After the last week and especially after Gary's death last night, she's a mess. She needs . . . What *does* she need? What will make her better? The answer is usually booze and sex at times like these. But the image in her mind is different, sudden, and strong. A little wooden farmhouse. Her own queen-size four-poster bed. Coffee percolating on her gas stove. *Front Porch Pickin'*, a simultaneously melancholy and joyful painting of a guitarist by her birth mother, Gidget, hanging over the fireplace mantel.

She needs home. She steers Bess toward her house. *After. I'll consult Michele after.*

When she pulls into the small parking lot, her American flag is waving in the breeze from its pole on the front porch. There's a sign over the door: FLOWN THE COOP. The outside of the house is a kaleidoscope pattern of painted boards, weathered so the palette is muted. Rustic impressionism. Her heart swells. The first time she saw this place, her hopes had been low. So much dirt, grime, and trash. She'd gone treasure hunting in the depths of the barn. Found the rainbow of reclaimed boards stacked against a back wall. In a brilliant flash, she'd seen what they could become. She set to work. Bringing the vision to life had given her hope and the strength for the long, hard excavation and restoration project that turned into a new life.

A woman appears, walking down the flagstone path around the side of the Coop. Even from fifteen yards away, Maggie can see she's wearing heavy makeup, large sunglasses, a voluminous sundress and a floppy hat. Very American-tourist-goes-to-the-beach. It seems like camouflage, but Maggie's not one to point fingers at the moment. The woman is smoking a cigarette, her eyes cast down. She doesn't look up, like she's unaware of Bess, unaware of Maggie. Maggie slams the truck door and hurries to meet her. That brings the woman's head up. She reverses course.

Maggie chases after her, passing a busy hummingbird feeder and a sign that reads PRIVATE RESIDENCE. "Wait."

The woman speeds up.

"Leslie?" she calls. She isn't even sure it's her renter. Leslie checked in after Maggie left for Wyoming, so they hadn't met.

The woman pauses with her hand on the doorknob of the *other* house. Maggie's home. The one unseen from the road, only accessible from behind the store. "What do you want?"

"Hi. I'm Maggie Killian. The owner. Are you Leslie?" She closes the gap between them.

She nods. "I know who you are." Her face and startlingly blue eyes have a flat expression that matches her voice. Under the pancake makeup, Maggie thinks she sees a scar on her lip and under her eye, but she's still beautiful, if icy.

"I'm sorry." She points at the cigarette. "No smoking at my place."

Leslie drops her cigarette and crushes it under her sandal.

"Great. Well, I just got back in town. I was checking to see when you're leaving. It's today, right?"

"I have two more nights."

Maggie frowns. She wishes she had the contract with her. She could have sworn that it ended today. But so much has happened in the last week, so many mind-stressing things. She doesn't trust her brain. "All right, then. I'll just drop my trailer out back and check on some things in my shop. Sorry for all the traffic in and out after it got vandalized."

"You should warn people if you're at a risk for crime." She talks like an old woman, but it doesn't look like she's any older than Maggie is.

"Well, I'm not. Or I haven't been, anyway. But again, I'm sorry about that. Is everything okay otherwise?"

"Yes."

"I'll be in and out some. Let me know if you need anything."

Leslie nods and goes in the house.

"Wait. Your cigarette butt."

Leslie shoots her a look. "I'll get it later." The door closes.

Maggie stares after her, then picks up the butt, pinching it in the middle, her face puckering with disgust. Something about Leslie that she can't pinpoint seems familiar—Voice? Eyes? Shape and gait?—and at the same time completely foreign. Leslie sure had a lot more personality on the phone and via email. Well, all the deputies and insurance people probably had her miffed.

Maggie pulls her trailer to the back of the property and unhitches it in front of the storage barn. Then she returns to her beloved store, steeling herself for what she'll find. When she flips on the lights, the devastation takes her breath away. Everything on the shelves and counters has been swept to the floor. Broken glass is everywhere. Items on the wall hang askew. Others lie smashed on the floor. Her favorite installation piece, a photo booth she made of salvaged doors, is splintered and collapsed. A butcher-block table rescued from an old industrial application is covered in red paint. She forces herself to walk all the way in and examine every item. Almost everything will require at least minor repair, and some things will never be the same.

A little more mess sure won't make it worse. She returns to the trailer and spends the next half hour unloading her Wyoming haul into the barn. She hears a car pull up in front of the Coop but ignores it until the sound of footsteps behind her demand her attention. When she turns to see who it is, she gets a nasty surprise. It's her customer-turned-competitor, a tiny slip of a man, with more hair in his mustache than on his head.

Before he can speak, she says, "You've got some nerve showing up here, Rickey Sayles."

"I heard you had some trouble."

"I'm sure you did."

"You're a sister in arms. I came to offer my help."

Maggie huffs. "I don't need any more help from you."

"I'd be happy to renew my offer to buy the Coop."

Maggie gets in his personal space, finger stabbing at his chest, but not touching. "Get off my property now. I've told law enforcement about the threats you're making around town. I've got my eye on you, Sayles."

Sayles doesn't flinch or back away. He doesn't even blink. "My offer isn't going up, Maggie."

"You can put that offer where the sun don't shine."

Looking like a librarian disappointed in a loud patron, he shakes his head. "You know where to find me, then."

"Oh yes. I most certainly do." Maggie points toward the parking area.

Sayles disappears the way he came.

Maggie finishes unloading the trailer, fuming and muttering. She brushes dust off her hands, then locks up both buildings and leaves.

She has no idea how she's going to be ready for antique week, but she *will* be ready, and she's not selling out, to Rickey Sayles or anyone else. Starting tomorrow, that has to be her sole focus, round the clock. Heartbreak over Hank and grief about Gary won't bring them back. Worry about wrong-minded law enforcement won't pay the bills.

And there's no way insurance will begin to cover all she's about to lose if she misses her biggest sales opportunity of the year.

EIGHT

Maggie drives too fast on her way back to Michele's. Without the trailer, Bess feels like a horse unhitched from a wagon. Maggie just wants to get away from the mess at the store, the smarmy Rickey Sayles, and the weird vibe from Leslie. The farther she gets from her house, the more convinced she is that Leslie was supposed to have checked out that morning. She would never have left her house rented this close to the antique show. She had always planned to come back from Wyoming and gear up for it.

Suddenly, she's sure Leslie is lying. Absolutely, positively sure. Maggie doesn't want to wait to confront her. She wants her house back. She wheels the truck around, barely hitting the brakes as she U-turns. She pushes Bess as fast as she can go through the gravel on the curves. Steering the truck in the center of the road, she makes the last turn before her house and nearly plows into another car head-on.

She slams on the brakes, steering to the right, grateful she left the trailer by the barn and doesn't have to worry about whether it will jackknife or flip. To her surprise, the sedan stops, too. The driver, a man about her mother's age, leaps out of the silver car and runs to the passenger door of her truck. Maggie shoves her hand into her bag. It comes out with her pepper spray, which she holds out of sight in her lap. At her door, the man leans over, panting.

Maggie cracks the window. "Are you okay? Sorry if I scared you."

"Maggie." He stands up, leveling startling watery green eyes on her. His thin white comb-over has flopped to the wrong side and hangs in a long, limp arc.

It's been a few years since she's seen him, but she knows him. Gary's manager. "Tom." Tom Clarke. Late of Nashville, but unable to completely hide the Georgia in his voice. "What are you doing out here?"

"Looking for you. Can we talk?"

Maggie feels nervous butterflies in her gut. Something is way off about him. She and Tom aren't exactly buddies. He's one of the few people in the world that knew about her and Gary, back when, other than their families and a very few friends. They've dined together and watched Gary perform together, but they've also argued over what Tom called her unhealthy influence on Gary. She'd backed Gary when he refused to move to Nashville and turned down songs better suited for Luke Bryan. That wasn't unhealthy. It was just less lucrative than what Tom had in mind for Gary.

But now his cash cow is dead. The man before her seems desperate. Then it hits her. Gary was going to kick Tom to the curb. He'd mentioned thievery and other clients. Had he gone through with it? She grips the pepper spray tighter. "What's going on, Tom?"

"Not here."

"If you want to talk to me, then talk. You're sounding like a crazy person."

"I don't know who else to talk to. Gary is dead. And I'm afraid people are going to think I killed him. Did he say anything to you about me before he died?"

Um, yeah. But she ignores his question. "Why would they think you killed him?"

He looks around, his eyes wild. "Because I was supposed to meet with him yesterday."

"About what?"

"That's not what's important. What matters is I didn't show up. I was late. By the time I got there, he was long gone."

"I'm not the one to tell. You need to go to the authorities."

"I can't."

"Why not?"

He shakes his head violently.

"Did you kill him, Tom?" Maggie holds on to her pepper spray for dear life.

"I'm a lot of things, Maggie, but I'm not a killer."

"Yes." She pokes the bear. "You're greedy, a climber, and a thief, and we both know Gary knew it."

He stares at her for a moment. "I shouldn't have believed you would understand." He runs back across the road toward his car.

"Wait! Where are you going?"

But he doesn't answer, just wrenches his door open and sprays a rooster tail of gravel as he guns his sedan in the direction of the highway.

NINE

At the Coop, Maggie parks Bess inches behind the bumper of the silver Taurus she assumes is Leslie's car. She pauses, hands trembling. What the hell had that been about with Tom? He'd scared her. She knows she has to tell the authorities—will any of them believe her? But she's here now to deal with Leslie. The Tom issue can wait a few more minutes. She takes three deep, calming breaths, then gets out of the truck.

At the door to her home, Maggie knocks so hard it rattles glass in the side window. No one comes to the door. Her knuckles are smarting, so she pounds the door with her palm. When that doesn't work, she stalks back to Bess and honks the horn, long and loud, over and over.

Maggie has just given up on the horn and is returning to the door when Leslie finally steps onto the porch.

"What do you want? I was sleeping." Leslie crosses her arms over a perky chest. Boob job, Maggie realizes.

"Our contract ended today. You were supposed to be out at eleven a.m."

"Sorry, but no. I emailed you about staying two more nights. You said yes. And I sent you the money for it."

Maggie scowls. That isn't the same answer as earlier. "Two more nights? That's news to me. And I didn't receive any payment."

"Check your PayPal."

Maggie had turned off PayPal notifications long ago. She hates all the services that insist on emailing her if someone so much as farts in their app.

She'll have to look at it later. But she's standing her ground now. "I need you to pack up and vacate my home."

"Are you calling me a liar?"

"Let's just call it a misunderstanding, as long as you leave."

"I'll do no such thing."

"You're a squatter."

"I'm a renter, and I'll call 911 if you continue to threaten me."

"I haven't threatened you."

"Are you calling me a liar again?"

"I'll be back. Don't make me bring a locksmith."

The woman shuts Maggie's own door in her face.

TEN

Maggie leaves the compound, her emotions in a jumble, Louise riding shot-gun. She has no destination in mind. The wind through the windows blows her hair up and around her head and face. She holds it back with one hand and steers with the other. Moors & McCumber's "Take Me Away" is just loud enough for her to hear it over the road noise. Her heart pounds along with the upright bass. The song is a perfect match for her confusion, tension, and grief.

She cruises east on Highway 290. When she realizes she's almost to Brenham, she decides to reverse her course. She doesn't have any interest in heading into town. As she swings around into westbound traffic, she notices a long line in front of a small tan brick building. A black sign reads TRUTH. She's heard of the place, a sort of mecca for worshipers at the altar of Texas barbecue.

Truth. She rolls the word around in her mind. Truth. The truth is Maggie's all kinds of screwed up. She accelerates, putting her mind on autopilot as Bess eats up the miles. She takes a left past Burton. The truck attacks the dips like a heavy car on a roller coaster. *Six Flags Over Texas. The Runaway Mine Train ride.* In middle school, she'd endured the heat and the lines to ride it seven times in a row on a class trip to the amusement park. She loved the sensation of jerking around corners, diving down descents, struggling up hills. Always taken by surprise by the unknown in front of her.

She doesn't love it so much now that it's her life. She needs a destination. Enough of this floating. It's killing her slowly.

The smell of something charred fills her nostrils. Suddenly, she knows exactly where she's headed, and she doesn't have to change her course to get there.

As she rounds a sharp curve, she comes upon parked vehicles lining the road on both sides, as far as her eyes can see. Brake lights flash, and she slows Bess. Her grief sharpens. All these people are here to rubberneck at the site of Gary's death. In the distance, there's a grayish mess where there used to be a house. A place where she spent countless hours with him. Working. Laughing. Talking. Not talking. Naked, clothed. Mostly happy. A refuge for them both. A place where they'd taken care of each other over the years, mostly in blessed seclusion. A friendship, she realizes.

Now it's gone. He's gone. They're gone.

She's close enough to see the crime scene tape, the county vehicles of the investigators, and the mass of bodies pushing up against the fence. Snapping pictures. Leaving balloons, stuffed animals, flowers, and other tributes hanging from the barbed wire at the edge of his property. As she passes, she sees grief-stricken, tear-streaked faces. Faces well-known to her in some cases. Neighbors. Customers. Friends. People who are part of the landscape of their community. Some trigger frissons of recognition she doesn't have time to pin down. Others, she can't place at all. Nonlocals. But Gary is a megastar. She wonders how far people have come to be here. Are they making a pilgrimage, creating a shrine to a fallen hero?

Then a voluptuous woman with long wavy red hair turns and catches her eye. There's no doubt Maggie knows *her*. Jenny. The hookup who'd taken her affair with Gary a little more seriously than he'd expected. The one who'd shown up at Maggie's house to roust Gary from bed. Only Gary hadn't cowed and begged Jenny's forgiveness. He'd told her to get lost. That between her and Maggie there was no choice and never had been.

Jenny had been humiliated. Now, she just looks enraged. It chills Maggie. The redhead flips Maggie off, and her lips stretch back over her teeth as she screams something at Maggie.

Too late, Maggie realizes Bess sticks out like a sore thumb. People are leaning toward one another and heads are turning. Eyes are staring, fingers are pointing, more mouths are shouting. Maggie Killian, they're saying. His lover, they're saying. His killer, they're speculating.

Her breathing grows shallow. It was a mistake coming here. How could she have thought she'd find sanctuary and a balm for her emotions? She wants to pass the cars in front of her, get the hell out of Dodge, but traffic is gridlocked in both directions. She's trapped. Watched.

Icy pins prick her hands. She's gripping the steering wheel too hard. She stretches them one at a time, keeping her gaze straight ahead on the bumper of the car in front of her, as she tries to wish herself home.

ELEVEN

Back at Michele's, Maggie emails her to-do list to her laptop and adds to it:

- Find out about Gary's service.
- Evict Leslie.
- Tell Michele about Tom.

She'd decided against calling law enforcement about Tom on the way home. Michele would want to be with her when she makes that call. Or make it for her. And Maggie will wait for Michele.

Now that she's back with her phone, it's time to change her phone number. She pauses with her finger on the number for T-Mobile. It feels so irrevocable. And Hank hasn't called in more than twelve hours. Maybe it's unnecessary? But if history teaches anything, she knows one of these days he will call, and she can't guarantee she'll have the strength to resist him when he does.

Asleep at Maggie's feet, Louise snores like a braying donkey.

"Thanks for the vote of confidence."

Maggie calls T-Mobile and orders the change. They try to talk her into driving to Austin for a new SIM card at a T-Mobile store, but she doesn't have the time or patience. They promise it will arrive within a few days. She'll just have to stay strong until then, if Hank even calls.

With a storm in her chest, she returns to working on her list, detailing steps to take in the restoration of the Coop. Her fingers pound the keys like hail on a tin roof.

"What's into you?" Michele walks into her kitchen.

"My life is in the shitter."

"Colorful, but not specific."

"We'll just go with the big-ticket items." Maggie ticks her forefinger. "Lee County is joining forces with Fayette County because of the common links between the vandalism at Flown the Coop and the fire at Gary's."

"What common links?"

"Me. And their earlier suspicions about Gary."

"I don't get it. Have they even ruled out an accident at his place?"

"I know, right?" Maggie pushes her laptop back. "They claim there's email—only I didn't write them and have never seen them—on Gary's phone, between us, that makes it look like he dumped me and I went to his house to threaten him."

"What?"

"It's nuts. And the texts between us confirming our plans? They're not there."

"Did they Mirandize you?"

"Negative. But Junior most definitely tried to surprise me into incriminating myself."

"I hope you told him you wouldn't talk to him without a lawyer."

"You would have been proud of me. As soon as the bullshit started, I did. But I'd probably talked too long before then anyway, because I thought it was just about the Coop."

"I'll call them. They're only to communicate with you through me. Promise me."

"You already have so much on your plate."

"Please. You're my best friend."

"You're mine. And the *best* best friend ever. When you do call them, we've got something to offer. Gary's manager, Tom Clarke, pulled me over about an hour ago. He was acting crazy, saying he went to see Gary last night but that he was *long gone*."

"What?"

"Yeah, Gary had called him in to fire him, but Tom says they never met."

"So Gary didn't fire him?"

"I'm not sure. I told Tom to call the cops. He said he was afraid they'd arrest him. For some reason he thought he should come to me. But when I wasn't sympathetic, he changed his mind and left in a big hurry."

"Where is he?"

"I have no idea. But I thought you'd want to tell law enforcement about it when you call."

"Thank you. Any more big-ticket items?"

"Lots, but I'll only bore you with one. My tenant is a Grade A bitch and a liar."

"Leslie? She's been nothing but nice every time I've met her."

"Then she hates me for some unknown reason."

"She loves your place and the town. She wants to move here."

"Well, she practically is. She's insisting she extended for two more nights and paid me for them."

"Did she not?"

"My memory is that she was supposed to have left this morning."

"By *memory* you mean . . ."

"The stuff you get from the thing between your ears."

"Right. Well, do you have a written contract?"

"Yes."

"Let's take a look."

Maggie scrolls through her email.

"Do you not have it saved to your hard drive?"

"I thought I did. I was looking for it before you came over here."

"What about your deleted items?"

Maggie grimaces. "I had a lot of time on my hands in Wyoming. I cleaned out my inboxes, filed stuff, deleted things, and, um, I emptied the trash."

"And you've searched?"

Maggie types *Leslie* in her search box and presses ENTER. Nothing comes up. She tries *rent* and gets random emails with *parent, torrent,* and even *Trent Reznor,* but no rental agreements. "Nothing. Not even the email where she asked for an extension and claims I told her she could stay."

"*Mierda.* You and your obsession for deleting."

"Now is not the time to cure me of my ills."

"Okay, so was she through Airbnb or HomeAway? Or what's that other one?"

"It doesn't matter what it is. I did it through Craigslist."

"You what?"

"I did a direct VRBO. I didn't want to pay the fees to those online shysters."

"Oh, Maggie."

Maggie holds up her hand. "Did I not already tell you now is not the time?"

Michele makes a zipping motion over her lips. "So you've got no contract other than your memory?"

"We had a contract."

"Which, if you didn't make her leave this morning, is extended and ratified."

"I have Leslie's verbal assurance now that she's moving out in two days."

"Verbal contracts are binding. If you accept it, you have a new contract. Otherwise, you're stuck trying to prove up your old one, and force her out now. Which is next to impossible, practically speaking."

"This blows."

Michele's eyes light up. "Change of subject. Let's search for email between you and Gary. We can prove Junior was wrong. Or lying."

"They can't lie to me, can they? That's like *entrapment*."

"Sounds like, but isn't." Michele snorts. "Perfectly legal."

"It shouldn't be."

"You're preaching to the choir."

Maggie types *Gary* as her search, and a slew of emails appear, dating back for weeks. "This doesn't make sense. We haven't emailed each other."

Michele and Maggie scan them together. Maggie's stomach turns over. They're the emails Junior told her about.

"I've never seen these before. And I deleted all my other email with him while I was in Wyoming. I would have deleted these, too. These are new. Even though some of them are before then. This doesn't make sense."

"Girl, who have you pissed off?"

This topic has come up more than once in the last week. "I seem to get that question a lot."

TWELVE

The doorbell chimes. Louise and Gertrude race toward the door, toenails sliding on the tile, barking crazily.

Maggie shuts her laptop, thankful for the interruption. "You're popular today. Me, Boyd, and now another guest."

"Introvert hell." Michele heads for the door. "It's probably Rashidi's friends. Well, his and Katie's. They're staying for a few days."

"Who's Katie?"

"My law school roommate. I've told you about her. And Emily used to work with her."

"Right. I remember."

In the entryway, Michele greets a woman with an island lilt to her voice like Rashidi's and a man with a Texas drawl.

Maggie ponders feeling guilty that her goats are still boarding at Lumpy's place. The former Texas Ranger lives next door to a property Michele inherited from Gidget and deeded over to Maggie. Lumpy's a soft touch, and Maggie knows her babies are in good hands. Still, they probably think she's deserted them. They deserve to be home, eating the treats she bought them.

Her thoughts are interrupted when a man enters the great room. He's blond and built. Shorter than Maggie normally goes for, but magnetic in a *Top Gun* sort of way. Michele follows him. Bringing up the rear is a black woman in spike-heeled sandals and a Lycra sundress appropriate for the heat but nothing else, trying not to fall over Louise and Gertrude. She's eye-popping.

And Maggie's eyes do pop. Because she knows her. Ava Butler, her old nemesis and the annoyingly omnipresent voice on her radio. The one whose singles Maggie belted out at karaoke in Amarillo.

"What the actual fuck?" Maggie hears someone say, then realizes it's her.

Ava's male companion stops short, assessing Maggie with a professional once-over, like he's deciding if she's about to physically assault someone. Okay, fine, yeah, she wants to. Ava-fucking-Butler, here in Michele's house?

Ava looks away from the dogs tripping her up. She spies Maggie and hesitates for a beat, then bursts out laughing. Cackling, really. She bends over with her hands on her thighs and literally howls.

Maggie pushes back from the kitchen table where she and Michele had been working. "It's been a long time."

Ava straightens and wipes her eyes. "A long hard time for you, I hear, and I believe it, the way you look."

"Fuck you." Maggie wants to put her sunglasses and jacket back on to hide the fire damage, but she's not giving Ava the pleasure.

"You wish."

Michele holds up both hands. "Whoa, whoa, whoa. What's going on here?"

The man crosses his arms and a smile spreads over his face. "Shh, Michele, it's just getting good. Let's see where it goes."

Michele tries again. "I take it you know Ava and Collin?"

Maggie heads for the liquor cabinet and her bottle of Balcones. "FYI, I'm off Balcones, Michele. I drink Koltiska now."

"Duly noted. And off topic. Answer my question, since you've insulted my houseguest."

"Cussed her, too," Collin adds.

"You not helping, baby." Ava slips into the island patois Maggie remembers well. It made her want to slap Ava back then in Waco. It makes her want to tackle her and put her in a choke hold now.

Maggie pours a generous double. She holds it up in a mock toast toward Ava. "Ava and I met while doing musical theater in Waco. Back when she was just a backstabbing nobody."

Ava curtsies. "And you a wash-up coke-snorting has-been."

"Fuck you again."

"Wait," Michele says. "I went to a musical theater in Waco, when I was there for my law school reunion. An actress was murdered and the show was called off after act one. And you guys"—she points at them—"you guys were in it! How did I not realize that until now? Maggie, I've known you for years and never placed you in that show."

"Is that supposed to be a bad thing?" Maggie drawls.

Michele frowns. "That poor actress who died. So sad. Anyway, you were both incredible!"

"So you were the one in attendance," Maggie says.

"Maggie too wasted to notice if the theater burn down, much less how many people in the audience," Ava says, and snaps her wrist.

Michele raises her hand with her palm facing the two women, like a teacher quieting kindergartners. "Enough of that. Maggie, if you're pouring, does anyone else want one?"

Collin lifts a finger. "Just like yours, Maggie. And I'm Collin, by the way. Ava's baby daddy."

North of Dallas, his voice tells her. South of Oklahoma. "You poor, poor man."

"Lucky man, more like it," Ava says.

"I remember the lucky man you had when I knew you. That hot *CSI* actor. Really hot."

Ava switches out of her accent and suddenly sounds boringly Middle American. "The man's a slut. He'd fuck a dog if that was all that was handy."

Collin whistles. "Maggie slept with Zach?"

Ava smoothes her dress over her flat stomach. "Not exactly. I'll take a double as well."

"Speaking of sluts, Ava did actually sleep with my boyfriend at the time." Maggie smiles angelically. "Michele, a drink for you?"

Collin cocks an eyebrow at his girlfriend.

Ava shrugs. "Zach and I had split up. I hated Maggie. It seemed like a good idea at the time."

Michele says, "I'll wait for Rashidi."

"The wait is over, my love." Rashidi appears behind her and kisses her neck.

Ava launches herself at him. He twirls her in a hug. Her accent returns. "I miss you ass. How much of that you hear?"

"Enough." Rashidi shakes Collin's hand, kisses Maggie's cheek, and returns to slip his arm around Michele. His accent comes out thick. "Welcome home, Maggie girl. Sorry about Gary."

"Thank you. Drink?"

"I take a Shiner."

Michele nods. "Shiner for me. I have a feeling some of us need to pace ourselves. And referee."

Maggie hands out the drinks. As Ava grasps hers, Maggie holds on to it. "Baby daddy. So no more Zach?"

"God, no."

"Good call. He's a little effeminate." Maggie releases the drink.

Ava freezes, then giggles. "True dat."

"How many babies with Tom Cruise here?" Maggie nudges her head in Collin's direction.

Ava turns off her island accent again without missing a beat. "One. I have a daughter, and we have a son."

"Handsome devil, like his dad," Collin says.

"They're staying with Collin's sister, Katie, while we're here. She sings with me sometimes, too."

Maggie nods. She remembers that Ava's newer music includes a soprano with a twangy voice, more than backup, less than shared top billing. Ava Butler with Katie-somebody-or-other. The relationships start to make sense to her. Katie, law school roommate of Michele. Singing partner of Ava. Sister of Collin. Old boss of Emily. Thinking of Emily reminds her of Amarillo, and of karaoke. "Just so you know, I sing your songs better than you."

"Oh, I know."

"Huh?"

"Emily sent me the video."

"Wait. Emily what?"

"Somebody put it up on YouTube. You're trending on social media. Thanks for making me money—it kicked my sales up."

"I haven't even gotten online since I did it. I had no idea."

Ava raises an eyebrow and sips the Balcones. "You like my songs, then?"

"They're all right." Maggie remembers singing them driving home the day before. Catchy for sure, dammit.

"I'll admit your versions were the best I've ever heard from anyone but me. Talent never held you back."

"No, I did that all by myself."

"Seriously, even though I'm not big on folk or whatever—"

"Alt-country. Texana."

Ava bobs her head. "Whatever. But even though it's not my thing, your stuff is good. Respect."

"Thank you. Yours, too."

"Not like the already-been-chewed bubblegum all over the place lately. Kelly-what's-her-name."

Maggie can't disagree about Gary's little sister.

"Do I sense a truce?" Rashidi says.

Ava and Maggie give each other the slant-eye.

Maggie nods. "For Michele's sake."

Ava smiles. "As long as she doesn't come near my man."

Maggie smiles back. "Good thing for Collin I don't have one for him to worry about you with."

Michele says, "Speaking of which, I can't vouch for Maggie's mouth or behavior. She's having the bad day to end all bad days, which includes three dead ex-boyfriends and getting dumped by the fourth."

"Damn, girl." Ava lifts her glass at her.

"Thanks for the share, Michele. You left out being a murder suspect and having a squatter living in my house, but I think you hit the major high points." Maggie stretches her arms over her head as she arches her back. She purrs, "But I can't catch nobody doesn't wanna be caught."

"Bottoms up to that," Collin says, raising his glass.

THIRTEEN

Too much Balcones later, Maggie falls asleep in her semipermanent room at Michele's. She bolts upright in the wee hours of the morning. Her room is pitch dark, but her heart is hammering. There's someone in the room with her. Or is it just an impression left from a bad dream?

After long moments with her breath held, listening, she punches her pillow and digs her head into it. There's no one in the room. She's being ridiculous. Half an hour passes. Maggie doesn't fall asleep. She tries to count sheep, but all she sees are disgustingly happy couples jumping the fence. Rashidi and Michele, Ava and Collin, Emily and Jack, Wallace and Ethan, Hank and Sheila. Hank and Sheila? That pisses her off and brings her fully from relaxed and groggy to wide awake.

She sits up, then gets the feeling again. Like someone is watching her, from close by. She slinks down and pulls the covers over her head. That gives her the bed-spins. She sits up.

And screams.

A woman with a fat gray braid tied with a scarf in a big bow at its end is rocking in the chair next to the window. Her legs are long, her hands clasped in her lap. Are those roses and skulls on her plaid shirt? Wisps of hair frame a moon-shaped, moon-colored face. Her eyes are so dark they're like cutouts against the night sky.

She turns her face toward Maggie and puts a finger over white lips.

"Who are you?" Maggie whispers.

The woman stops rocking. Sad tears flow down her cheeks in a silver river. Like Maggie has disappointed her somehow.

"What are you doing here?"

A knock sounds at the door. Maggie jumps. The woman in the rocker disappears.

"You okay in there?" It's Michele's voice.

"Bad dream."

"You drank too much."

"You didn't drink enough."

"Night, Maggie."

"Night."

Maggie looks back at the rocking chair. Moonlight streams into a seat empty except for a blue scarf with a field of white stars. No, she thinks, that can't be from the woman she'd seen. She wasn't real. It was a dream. The scarf has to be something Michele or someone left there earlier.

Michele is right. She drank too much.

FOURTEEN

Morning is a gut punch to Maggie. Had she slept at all? She groans, rolls to her stomach, and puts a pillow over her head. She hears Louise even through the pillow. Maybe that's what woke her. A dog needing to go out. *Shit.* She sits and hangs her feet over the edge of the bed. Her stomach lurches. A tongue laps at her toes.

"Louise, stop."

Floppy black-and-white ears rise above the mattress, followed by a black button nose and shining eyes.

"What time is it?"

The dog cocks her head.

Maggie leans down into her hands, elbows on her knees. The room tilts. Last night is a blur. Why did she drink so much? The string of awful events of the last two weeks wash back over her, ending with the appearance of Ava Butler in Michele's living room. As bad as all the rest is, Ava is the explanation for the hangover.

"As long as you don't like her, we're all right."

Louise gives the wood floors a good sweeping with her bushy tail.

The dog goes to the door and whines again. Maggie opens the door just enough for Louise to push her way out. Seconds later, she hears barking and human greetings for Louise and a "What did you do with Maggie?" which she ignores in favor of a shower and toothbrush.

Fifteen minutes later, the world is less like the rocking deck of a ship.

The morning after drinking never gets any easier, no matter how much she practices. She soft-foots into the kitchen. The clock on the stove says it's nine. Too damn early. Is it too much to hope that Ava and her hunky man have left for the day?

"Good morning, Maggie. You look like shit." Ava sets a pod into the Keurig. "I was making this for me, but you clearly need it more than I do."

Maggie shoots her a bird. "Good morning, everyone."

Rashidi is standing behind Michele, his hand on her shoulder, an empty plate in front of her. "We saved you some breakfast." He points to a plate with corn tortillas, scrambled eggs, refried black beans, salsa, and a sprinkling of shredded cheese.

"Thanks."

Michele sees Maggie scanning the room and guesses what she's looking for. "Dogs are outside."

"Ah, good."

The front door opens and Collin appears in running shorts and shoes, dripping sweat down his bare, bulky chest. "Damn, it's humid here." He walks straight to Ava. Before she can get away, he wraps her in a wet hug.

"Ick, Collin, no." But she turns in his arms and kisses him, long and hard.

Maggie snatches her plate, looking away. She doesn't bother warming her food, just plants herself at the bar and shovels it in. Her stomach rebels, but she's not about to let it win, especially not with all the mushy-gushy lovey-dovey going on around her—just like when she tried to count sheep. It's enough to toss breakfast over, if her hangover isn't.

Collin releases Ava. "Maggie, that funny-looking dog of yours is carrying a possum around in its mouth."

Maggie flinches. "Dead?"

"Well, I didn't stop and check its pulse, but that's my guess."

Louise, a bloodthirsty killer? Her golden retrievers had tried to catch squirrels and other small animals, but they were too floppy and goofy to ever succeed. Maggie pictures Gary's finger in Louise's mouth. Bile rises in her mouth. But Louise had been trying to save Gary. That was different. *Must think of something else.*

"That's disgusting," Ava announces.

"What's up with you today, Maggie?" Michele rises, gathering empty plates and taking them to the dishwasher.

Ava sets the fresh cup of coffee beside Maggie's plate. "Here you go.

Maybe some caffeine will take a few years off around your eyes." She points at them. "Dark circles."

Maggie flips Ava off again. Her finger is going to stay nice and limber with her nemesis visiting. She turns toward Michele. "Gonna try to bribe Leslie to check out early." *And escape this damn love nest as soon as humanly possible.*

"You should quit stressing about it. You're welcome here."

"I know. Thank you. But I need to get back to my life."

"Good luck, then."

"Need some muscle?" Collin asks. "Rashidi and I could crack some heads."

She offers a tepid smile and a wave of her fork. "I'll be fine."

"Suit yourself." He swats Ava on the tush. "I'm hitting the showers, with or without you, woman."

"Without? Bite your tongue." Ava takes his hand and they disappear down the hall.

"Jesus." Maggie slugs coffee, welcoming the tongue scald.

Rashidi laughs. But he takes Michele by the hand. Maggie hears him whisper to her. "Separate hot-water heater on the other side of the house."

"Get a room," Maggie mutters.

Rashidi and Michele disappear into the master suite. The silence in the kitchen turns deafening. Half the food is left on her plate, but Maggie scrapes it into the trash and puts her cutlery and plate in the dishwasher. The coffee is coming with her. She doesn't see her bag, but she knows just where she'll find it, no matter where she left it—the coat and purse rack Michele keeps by the door. Michele enforces order on her world and the people in it. Maggie grabs the bag, lets Gertrude in, and joins Louise outside, rubbing her bouncing head on the way out to her truck, until they pass a furry mound in the yard.

Collin is correct. The possum is dead.

"Oh, Fucker. What have you done?"

The spring in Louise's step grows springier. Maggie ushers the dog into the truck. Inside the cab, it feels like a swamp. Midmorning in mid-September, and no humidity or temperature break yet.

The leather seats are damp on her thighs. She pulls her homemade blue-jean miniskirt down—formerly her favorite pair of jeans, until they sprung too many holes—and levers her butt and legs up by pressing her back into the seat. She turns on the truck, rolls the windows down, and sets the vent to full blast to push out the heat. Louise's tongue lolls out as she pants, and Maggie tries not to think of the dead possum it's been touching. Or the other things she's seen in the dog's mouth. Nasty.

The familiar drive between Michele's Nowheresville and her own Flown the Coop isn't lovely this time of year. The summer sun has long since burned the grass to a crispy brown, the flowers died in June, and the heat shimmers off the asphalt like it's a desert instead of central Texas. It's truly hotter than she imagines hell to be. Hell. The thought of it brings Gary back into her mind. She hopes he made it up to the good place, even though he always claimed he wanted to spend eternity with the fun crowd down below. That makes her smile, which makes her eyes leak.

She lets the tears drip, lost in memories. The two of them had met in rehab. A recipe for disaster if there ever was one. But he'd been a bright spot. A brash young performer defusing bad press from a DWI and near-disastrous traffic incident under his manager's orders. Tom was protecting his future, but Gary met falling-star Maggie. After her release, she spent a week with him at the decrepit farmhouse he was renting near Round Top—the one she'd later helped him restore, and the same one that had burned to rubble two days before. At the end of the week, Gary hit the road and they kissed goodbye. Her record label went belly-up. Of all the crazy coincidences, the owner owned a compound of buildings nearby in Giddings and offered them to her in lieu of royalties on her last album, which he sold to another record company. Speculative future royalties on a tanking career or a few acres, buildings, and contents? She chose door number two.

Giddings. Close to her parents in La Grange, but not too close. She found Bess and other treasures in the ramshackle barn. She discovered a knack for repurposing. Not too many months later, she opened Flown the Coop, named for her escape from addiction and rehab. Gary came back from touring straight to her new doorstep nine months later. For the next decade, their relationship followed an easy pattern of on-when-he-was-home and off-when-he-toured.

She smiles and makes a turn from one gravel road onto another. Gary had shot to the top, like she had once upon a time. He'd never understood why she refused to go back to the life. Why she insisted he keep her a secret. Why she refused to go on tour with him, which he swore would have been the saving grace of their relationship. Maggie didn't want a saving grace. She got what she needed from him, and when she didn't, she got it from someone else. And he'd loved every minute of his stardom. She envied him that. Hers had chewed her up and spit her out in the wake of Hank.

Her smile disappears. Hank.

The sun glints off the hood of Leslie's car. She parks behind it. "Ready for this?"

Louise follows her out of the truck and around to the house. On a deep inhale, Maggie knocks. This time, Leslie answers the door quickly, almost as if she's expecting her. Her hat and glasses are gone, revealing thick sandy hair and tight facial skin with a scar beneath one eye.

She pins Maggie in place with her eyes. "Yes?"

Louise makes a break for the inside of the house.

Leslie blocks the dog with her knees. "Control your animal."

It's my damn house. Maggie grabs Louise's collar and hauls her back a few feet. "Louise, sit."

The dog's bottom hovers over the ground.

Close enough, Maggie thinks. "We need to talk."

Leslie's shoulders lift and fall with no change in her expression.

Maggie takes a step toward the door, but Leslie doesn't let her by. "All right, Leslie. How about a hundred and fifty dollars to vacate my place today?"

Leslie holds out a sheaf of papers to Maggie. "We have a contract and extension."

Maggie takes the papers. It's a set of printouts of the contract and some emails. *Well, damn.* "I'm offering new terms."

"A refund, then?"

"I guess."

"No."

Maggie grits her teeth. "On top of the refund?"

Leslie shakes her head.

Maggie hears a noise inside. A person or an animal? She tries to see in, but Leslie is blocking her view. "What would it take, then?"

Leslie shuts the door in Maggie's face. Louise yips, a loud, shrill bark that surprises Maggie.

She nods. "I know. Total bitch." Standing on the steps, Maggie flips through the papers, then texts Michele an update. *Leslie refuses to leave but gave me a copy of the contract and the missing email about an extension. Dammit. Dropping both on your desk later.*

Maggie and Louise walk to the truck, only to find themselves blocked by a Tahoe from the Lee County Sheriff's Department. Junior waves. Maggie meets him halfway, working up her ire along the way.

"Please tell me you're taking my renter to jail so I can get back in my house."

"Huh?" He lifts off a Lee County Sheriff's Department ball cap and scratches his scalp through his buzz-cut hair.

"Never mind. If you're here to harass me, you'll have to do it through Michele from now on."

"She made that quite clear when she called. But it's not about Gary or the Coop. I hate to do this, but I have to let you know I'm this close"—he holds his hands a few inches apart—"to citing you for animal neglect."

Maggie glances down at Louise. The dog looks fat and happy to her. "What are you talking about?"

"Your goats keep getting out. They're going to get run over, Maggie."

"That's impossible. Lumpy has them."

"He may have, but they're not with him now." He thumbs toward his vehicle. "They're filling the back end of my ride with pellets."

"Oh shit, Junior." *Literally.* "I'm sorry. I had no idea. Give me a hand, and we'll tie them in the back of my truck."

Louise high-steps beside them to the Tahoe. Junior puts his hand on the rear hatch.

"They're fast. How about we each catch one as they make a break for it?" Maggie moves to the right.

Junior nods. "One, two, three." He opens the door.

Two goats leap into the void. Maggie catches seventy-five pounds of black flying fur. "Oomph. Gotcha, Omaha."

Nebraska and Junior hit the ground. Nebraska scrambles with three legs, but Junior doesn't release his grip on the fourth. After he hauls the reddish-brown goat in, he squats, then hefts. Louise helps by barking her fool head off and nipping at the heels of the goats.

Maggie holds Omaha tight. The goat struggles, freezes, then struggles again. "Stop it, Louise." The dog continues barking. "I have halters and leads permanently tied into the front corners of the truck bed."

"I didn't go to police academy for this."

"You're *county* law enforcement. Livestock are in your jurisdiction."

Junior grumbles and uses one hand to drop the small gate on the truck bed. Maggie backs her butt onto the lowered gate, then swings her legs around until she can rise up on her knees, then her feet. She clamps Omaha between her legs while she wrestles him into a halter.

"So close, and yet so far, you little monster." She ties the halter and releases her leg grip.

He shakes his body from his shoulders through to a tail wiggle, then he butts her knee.

"If you can't have freedom, you'll take loving, huh?" She scratches behind his horns where he likes it best. "I missed your stinky butt. And your brother's." Over her shoulder, she watches Junior. He's clumsier than she is, but successful. "Thanks, Deputy." She uses her other hand to give Nebraska some scratches and loving, too.

Louise jumps into the truck bed with them, bringing the body count in the small space up to five. She snuffles along the floor, until Maggie realizes she's hoovering up goat poop.

"Stop it, Fucker."

Junior hops off the gate. "What did I do?"

Maggie considers laying into him about their last conversation at the sheriff's department. "Not you. The dog."

"Her name is Fucker?"

Louise wags her tail at him.

Maggie shrugs. "It seems to fit."

"No comment." Junior gives Maggie a hand down. He slams the gate. "Next time, I ticket you."

She salutes him. "I'll find a way to pen them up at Michele's, unless you want to evict my tenant."

"Bring me the right paperwork, and I will. Until then, you're on your own."

On her own. Alone. Yep, more than he can possibly know. "Until then, I guess I can count on you for illogical insinuations and animal cruelty charges."

"There's nothing illogical about following where the evidence leads."

"I hope you remember that when you actually get some."

FIFTEEN

Maggie sticks her head through the door of the Coop. She wants to make sure it's okay, but that's ludicrous. Clearly it's not okay. It's a wreck. Exactly the same as yesterday.

Why would someone do this to her things, to *her*? It feels so personal. For a brief, guilty second her mind goes to Gary. Personal. He's the only one that has—had—a personal stake in her around here. She's a junker, for God's sake. Unless someone is pissed off for paying too much for repurposed vintage farm and industrial junk, whose feathers does she ruffle? Well, not counting her liaisons. But that brings it full circle back to Gary, since she hasn't romped with anyone but him since before Hank's reentry into her life. Except in Wyoming, and the romper in question was already dead by the time the damage was done to the store.

But if Fayette and Lee County law enforcement personnel are right, it may be someone who also had a beef *with Gary*. And while she can't think of someone out to get her, she wonders if it's time for her to share her growing fire suspect list with law enforcement, to get them off her tail.

But that can't take precedence over getting her business in order. She shuts and locks the door. She has to jump-start her cleanup and repair. That and fulfilling web orders, of which there's a few days' backlog, since her part-time employee quit coming in after the vandalism and store closure. She's eager to get started. Good hard work is cleansing and a great distraction. She'll tackle the store as soon as she deals with Omaha and Nebraska.

From the Coop, she drives to Lumpy's little ranch. Well, actually, she drives past it and makes a U-turn in front of Gidget's old place first, just to eyeball things. *Thank the Lord for good renters*, she thinks, watching a thirty-ish man in a dirty ball cap, jeans, and long-sleeved plaid shirt mow in even rows across the pasture with the tractor. Two kids and a rangy tan dog are playing in the front yard of the little white house. Cows are grazing in a separate pasture on the other side of the drive.

She creeps up the lane back to Lumpy's and drives to his house, where she parks under a tree for the shade. If she'd known she would be coming, she could have brought him his pie. She stops, remembering the night before. Pie. They'd eaten all the Royers pies. And the Steak OMGs. *Dammit.* No pie left for Lumpy. She'll have to think of a new thank-you gift for him later.

Leaving her bag in the truck and goats in the bed, she heads for Lumpy's door. Louise makes a hasty reconnaissance while Maggie bangs on the door off and on for a full minute. No one answers. Lumpy lives alone. His truck is home, which is weird, since he's not coming to the door. But from time to time, a former–Texas Ranger buddy will pick him up for a fishing trip.

She gives up and returns to Bess, whistling for Louise. The dog races back, her body nothing but a black streak, straight for the goat-pen fence. Maggie expects her to jump it, but instead, the dog doesn't alter course. Maggie braces for a horrible collision.

None happens.

One moment Louise is on one side of the fence, the next she's on the other. She barrels into Maggie's knees for praise and a hug, but Maggie steps around her. She examines the spot the dog went through and finds the mesh cut cleanly at the corner of every square, from the bottom of the fence to the top two squares. The cuts create a triangular door into and out of the pasture.

Maggie steps back, arms crossed. "Some bastard cut the fence. At *Lumpy's*." Random vandals? To let Omaha and Nebraska out? Or targeted at Lumpy? It's impossible to say.

After a minute to think about it, her skin crawls. She feels watched. She scans the property, but sees no one. She can't fault Lumpy's absence. He provided solid fencing in a pasture with a pump-fed water tank and float and lots of good forage. The goats should have been fine. Someone had done this on purpose. Lumpy had made lots of enemies during his years as a Ranger, and he still monitors the police scanner 24/7. As a result, he keeps his stick in too many pots, stirring up trouble. Maybe this is someone getting back at him.

She fetches her phone from the truck and types him a message. *Where you at? Someone cut your fence. I took my goats.* Before she hits SEND, she thinks about the logical next step. Lumpy has calves in the pasture, too, and even though they're still a hundred yards away and not the sharpest animals on God's green earth, they could wind up on the road. There's a spare stack of goat panels leaning against the barn.

Before she gets to work, she can't resist reading new texts in the string with her Amarillo friends.

Wallace: *So, you and Ava, BFFs?*

Emily: *Not funny, Wallace.*

Maggie replies: *What she said. ;-)*

She stuffs her phone in her back pocket and gets to it. The panels are unwieldy, but she pries one away from its pals and lifts it from the middle. She walks it over to the ruined panel, first with one end digging up the grass, then with the other end dragging through it. She props it against the fence and returns to the barn for baling wire, cutters, and pliers. Once she has the right materials and tools, she makes fast work of removing the clipped panel and replacing it with the intact one. She secures the new panel on each end with twisted wire.

When she finishes, she gets her phone out and adds to her Lumpy message: *I fixed your pasture fence.* Then she hits SEND and wipes her brow with her forearm. The sweat leaves a muddy track on her arm. She suspects it has a match on her face, so she uses the inside of her tank top to clean her forehead. The dirty streak on her shirt confirms her hunch.

Her stomach growls. She decides it's lunchtime, but she's got a load of animals. It only takes her a minute to decide whether to go to Tractor Supply for goat panels or pay Lumpy back his materials later. She reverses the truck up to the panels. As she scoots each one into the truck bed, she coaxes Omaha and Nebraska to step into the open squares. She borrows the roll of wire and cutters, too.

She sends Lumpy one more text: *I owe you goat fence*

Back at Michele's, she pulls the truck into the shade on the side of the house. Since she doesn't have T-posts or a post-hole digger, she leans the corners of the panels upright against slender-trunked cedar trees. Rashidi had cleared all the lower branches off the trees near the house, God bless him. She wires the panels into place on the tree trunks, creating a rough circle. Really rough. More like an octagon with whiskers, given that a few panel ends stick past the tree they're joined to, but it works. She leaves the end of one panel unwired to make a gate. Finally, she gets the biggest tub she can find from Rashidi's gardening shed and links hoses together to reach all the way to the near edge of the jury-rigged pen. She fills the tub with water, adds two goats to the pen, and voila, Michele has a goat ranch.

Louise jumps into the tub for an impromptu bath.

"Out." Maggie remembers Louise outside Royers. Before the fire. The dog likes water.

Louise dunks her head, then jumps out and shakes the excess water off on Maggie's legs.

"Fucker."

Louise grins up at her. Maggie takes a picture of the new goat pen and its contents and texts it to Michele. *Sorry? I hope this is OK. Lumpy's fence got cut. He wasn't home.*

Maggie is feeding the goats their new treats when she hears crunching gravel from the front of the house. The sound of an engine, too.

A typing bubble appears immediately, and Michele's answer follows seconds later. *Why didn't I think of that? Totally fine. I just talked to Papa and Charlotte. Don't be surprised if they show up looking for you.*

The vehicle engine noise stops. A car door slams. Then another.

"Yoo-hoo. Maggie?" The voice is high and sweet.

Louise cocks her head and whines, asking Maggie about the new voice.

"It's Mom," Maggie informs the dog. "She's okay. Sort of."

Louise takes off like a bullet toward the front of the house.

Maggie straightens her dirty top and skirt, wipes muck off her knees, and lifts her shoulders and chin. "Coming, Mom."

She wobbles through the clumpy grass in Michele's side yard. At the corner of the house, she adopts a determined strut, marshaling courage and the right attitude to face her mother. When she reaches the front yard, she sees a low-slung Shelby Cobra in the drive. Michele's father, Edward Lopez, is squatting beside it, petting Louise. He's a handsome man, with olive skin and dark hair going to gray, wearing chinos and a golf-type shirt. He waves at Maggie.

Walking toward Maggie, arms extended, is her mother. Charlotte is radiant in a white scoop-neck T-shirt, boots, and patchwork-quilt-patterned prairie skirt. Curling strands of hair have escaped Charlotte's French twist to brush her face, ears, and neck. She's a more demure version of Maggie, although with the help of L'Oréal, not a much older-looking one.

Maggie moves straight into her mom's hug. "Hi, Mom. Edward."

"Finally, you've returned!" Charlotte says, backing out of the hug but hanging on to Maggie's arm like her daughter will run away if she lets go.

To Edward, Maggie says, "I was gone for seven years once. Now I can't leave for seven days."

He squeezes her shoulder. "Let's get out of this heat." He walks ahead of them and opens the door.

Courtly. Always. A very likeable man. Michele dotes on him.

"Wait," Charlotte says. "Maggie, your arms. What's with the bandages?"

"You heard about Gary?"

"Yes."

"So you know I was the one who found the fire and called for help. It . . . got me. A little. My arms." She takes off her sunglasses. "My eyebrows and eyelashes. I'll be fine."

"It's all so horrible. I'm sorry, honey."

"Thank you, Mom. It's very sad."

"I always worried your father would die in a fire. But he never got hurt in all those years as a volunteer. Not once."

At the door, Gertrude greets Louise. Maggie steps aside to let the dogs play in the front yard. Once inside, the air is too cool on Maggie's sweaty skin. She wraps her arms around herself and heads toward the kitchen, dropping her sunglasses on the counter.

"I'm making coffee. Anyone else?" She grabs a mug from the cabinet.

Her mother and Edward follow her. They shake their heads no, looking at each other like guilty teenagers.

Maggie closes the cabinet. *What's going on with them?* She inserts a Rainforest Blend pod into the Keurig and starts it. "You've been dying to talk for days, Mom. Whatever it is, spill it."

Charlotte claps a hand over her mouth. Behind it, her lips curve into a huge smile. The light catches something sparkly on her hand.

"Hold it right there." Maggie comes around the counter and takes her mother's wrist. She holds the left hand in front of her and examines the ring finger. The light catcher is a diamond. A big one on a slim gold band. "You got engaged?" She looks to Edward for confirmation.

He takes a deep breath, and his eyes shine like the diamond. "Tell her, Charlotte."

Charlotte places both hands on Maggie's cheeks. "We got married, honey."

Maggie's eyes widen. She's so surprised, she doesn't even smile. "You don't let any grass grow, do you?" The two have only been dating a few months.

Edward dips his head slowly, then raises it. "Not when I'm lucky enough to have a woman like your mother."

Maggie finally chuckles. "Congratulations."

Charlotte draws Maggie into another hug. "You're not mad we did it without you?"

"Of course not. It's your life, not mine. I just want you to be happy. When did you do it?"

Edward says, "Last weekend. We've been on a little honeymoon in Austin."

Charlotte pulls back, still hanging on to Maggie by the elbows. "I feel guilty we didn't have a church wedding."

"I think God will forgive you, Mom."

"So we're having a short ceremony and reception at St. Paul tonight. Just punch and cookies after, with our family and friends. Will you be there?"

Maggie contains the groan that threatens to escape. She wonders how many friends Catholic Edward really has in the Wend community and Lutheran congregation. But Michele's mother was a Methodist. He's probably used to being the odd man out. "Sure, Mom. Whatever you want."

"I'm so glad. And your nice Wendish renter will still be here, so she's coming, too."

"Leslie?"

"Yes. Leslie. What a sweetheart. She loves our church. She's been coming to the ladies home Bible study this week. Did you know the same reporter that's been bothering me about you interviewed her? Anyway, she even sang with the choir Sunday. She has a beautiful voice. Not as pretty as yours, but the best we have in that group. She used to sing professionally, you know."

Maggie's jaw drops. "Wow."

"She said you've accepted her offer on your house. She makes such a lovely addition to the community, and she's been yearning for a Wendish home for years."

"What?"

"A Wendish home. She grew up outside the community. But—"

"No. The part about me accepting her offer."

"Oh. She said she's buying your house."

"She most certainly is not."

Charlotte sits on a barstool, her body slumping a little. "But I don't understand. She said you're moving into Gidget's and—"

Maggie pushes her hair back with both hands. "I have long-term renters at Gidget's. Good renters. Leslie is a short-term vacation renter. My house is not for sale. Did you not think I would tell you about something as important as I'm moving?"

Charlotte sniffs. "Well, you hadn't told me you were traveling to Wyoming."

"That was for one week. To go to an estate sale." She omits the part about trying to reunite with Hank since it's beside the point now anyway. "Which is way different than moving."

"Maybe to you it is. But I'm your mother."

Maggie sighs, but it comes out more like a growl. "You must have misunderstood her."

"Maybe so."

"She's probably looking at buying someone else's house."

"I guess."

Edward steps between them. He smiles. "Can I get one of those coffees after all?"

Something moves in the backyard and Maggie glances out the bay window. She can't see the goat pen from inside the house so it's not them. Normally the only things out there are oak and pine trees and an occasional deer. This time is different. A white-as-a-corpse woman is standing on the patio, nose almost to the glass, a fat French braid holding the hair off her face. Maggie is pretty sure she's seen her before. Or maybe she just looks like the woman from her dream earlier?

She smiles at Edward. "After I find out what that woman in the backyard wants."

Edward and Charlotte both look out the window.

"What woman, honey?" Charlotte asks.

Maggie's eyes seek out the spot where the braided woman was a moment before. Now the backyard and woods beyond it are empty. "Huh. That's weird. She's gone now."

The front door bangs open. Maggie takes a few quick steps in that direction, worried it could be the strange woman she'd just seen, now barging into the house. First a male voice floats in, then a female one. The door closes. Ava and Collin appear, arms wrapped around each other, cheeks flushed. Not the woman from the backyard.

Collin straightens and releases Ava. "Well. Hello."

Maggie says, "Collin, Ava, may I introduce you to my mother and Michele's father. Charlotte and Edward Lopez. They're newlyweds. Collin and Ava are friends and houseguests of Michele's."

The two couples exchange greetings. Collin and Ava congratulate Edward and Charlotte.

Ava slips her arm back around Collin. "We're just, um, going to change clothes."

They giggle their way upstairs and shut their bedroom door.

Charlotte and Edward exchange a glance, then burst out laughing. Maggie shakes her head and groans.

SIXTEEN

With Omaha and Nebraska's plight resolved, Maggie and Louise make it back to Flown the Coop by noon, careful to avoid crossing paths with Leslie. Maggie's barely unlocked the door when her phone rings. Caller ID tells her it's someone with her insurance company. She stuffs her keys in her bag and sets down her laptop, a sandwich, and a thermos of ice water, then answers.

"Maggie Killian speaking."

A voice so deep it's almost inaudible comes on the line. "Maggie, this is Franklin Best. I'm the adjuster on your claim. I'm in your area, and I thought I'd see if you're available for me to come by and get your statement."

Barry White. Johnny Cash. Elvis. Maggie tries to picture him. "On a Sunday? Well, feel free. I'm at the shop this afternoon."

Louise chases a mouse out the front door.

"Perfect. Half an hour?"

"Half an hour."

They end the call. The heat is oppressive. Maggie doesn't want to turn on the air conditioner because of the broken windows, but she finds an intact fan and sets it up, leaving the front door open for circulation. She pulls her thick hair into a ponytail off her sweaty neck. She tries to secure it with a rubber band from the counter, but it breaks.

"Shit." She drops her hair.

Louise pads back into the store and flops down in front of the fan.

"Where have you been?"

Her tail thumps, but she doesn't answer.

Maggie shuffles the soundtrack from O *Brother, Where Art Thou?* on her phone, since the iPad that doubled as her cash register and stereo system didn't survive the attack on the store. When that's successful, she digs into the web orders. Running back and forth between the piles of damaged merchandise and the laptop at the counter, she checks availability and drafts emails apologizing for the delay, or in some cases, the impossibility of fulfillment. She's pleased to see that several of the Wyoming items she posted while stranded in the Cowboy State have already attracted buyers.

Hank's face flashes in her mind, and for a moment her heart free-falls. Why hasn't he called or texted? She'd thought she didn't want to hear from him anymore. Now that she's initiated the phone number change, she's not so sure. *Be careful what you wish for, right?*

With a mental shake, she refocuses on the web orders. She'll replace the sold items with new inventory tonight. She's selective about what she posts, since inventory can change so quickly. But to keep people interested at all price points, she likes to rotate a constantly changing variety of products. Frankly, she sells a lot of T-shirts, socks, and locally sourced merchandise. That's a blessing today. She stores most of them in the barn except for a few display items, and nothing in the barn was damaged.

When she's through the order backlog, she starts fulfillment, order by order, then adds the tracking information to each of the draft emails before sending them. She's only finished half the packages when a voice deep enough to rattle glass—if there was any left—resounds in the silence between the ending of "I Am a Man of Constant Sorrow" and "Down to the River to Pray."

"Maggie?"

The inside of her store is dark from the boarded-up windows, and because Maggie hadn't turned on the lights when she came in. A man in the doorway is backlit by the sun. It isn't Barry, Johnny, or Elvis. More Rick Astley, circa 1987, with a red pompadour that doesn't quite go with his indigo jeans and company golf-style shirt.

Louise rushes the door, growling, but a beat slower than her normal protective self.

"Louise, come."

The dog ignores her command. That much is normal, anyway.

"She's friendly. Sorry. I'm over here on your left." Maggie waves after she sees his eyes track her voice.

He moves, light as a dancer across a stage set, through the stacks and wreckage. "In the flesh. Wow. So nice to meet you." He holds his hand out the last ten feet as he approaches, grabs hers, and gives it a hyperactive shake.

"You'll forgive me if I'm not as enthusiastic, given the circumstances. Coming back to this mess was a real downer."

"I'll bet."

"Is it okay for me to start cleaning up and fixing things?"

"I've got what I need, picture-wise. Usually our insureds check with law enforcement too, but, if they're a go, you're a go."

Maggie doesn't give two shits what Junior and crowd want after they've insulted her with insinuation and suspicion. They hadn't told her not to, and that's good enough for her. "Great. I'll get the contractors in ASAP, then."

"Your friend Michele already got quotes for us."

Maggie pats a stack of papers she'd found on the checkout counter that doubles as the shop desk and storage cabinet. "Got 'em."

Franklin clears his throat. He picks up a chipped corbel and examines it, or pretends to. "I expected you to be more burned than you look."

"What?"

"I heard about the fire at Gary Fuller's. And how you tried to save him."

"My dog did more than me." Maggie nods at Louise.

"There was a picture with the article online, so I would have recognized you anywhere."

"Picture of me? What article?"

He stretches taller and puts down the corbel. "People.com. Lead story. The picture was of you singing in a bar in Amarillo."

"Oh. My." She hasn't led People.com in many years, and she doesn't want to now. Especially when no one had even contacted her before they ran the story. But she needs to read the article. Even if it hurts, she needs to know what law enforcement and the rest of the world are being fed about her.

"It even mentioned the break-in here, and a bunch of stuff about your trouble in Wyoming. The upcoming movie about you, too. Mostly it was about the fire at Gary Fuller's, though. And, um, history stuff. It was great." He bounces on his toes, then frowns. "Other than they called you a black widow. That seemed a little extreme."

Exactly what she'd thought of herself as, so Maggie can't fault them much. She remains silent.

Franklin's frown grows stricken as the silence stretches. Finally he blurts out, "On the way here I heard some of your songs on the radio."

"The oldies station?"

"No, it was a Houston country station. They played a whole set of yours and Gary Fuller's music. They talked about your ties to Houston. Like your birth parents, Boyd Herrington, and the gallery your mother owned there. And the movie, of course."

"How . . . nice." Maybe it *would* have been better to get her record rights instead of this shop. *Nah.* She's done with all of that. "Well, as you can see, I'm fine." She holds up her arms. "Just some minor burns." She drops the sunglasses she's wearing to hide her singed lashes and brows down her nose. "And my eyelashes and eyebrows sacrificed themselves like they were supposed to."

Franklin pulls out his phone and rotates it several times in one hand. He holds the phone up. "Could we, I mean, would you mind if we were in a picture together? One without your sunglasses?"

Thinking it better to replace speculation with truth, Maggie beckons him with her fingers. "One. And I'm fine with you posting it, but not selling it. Got me?"

"Absolutely." He snaps a picture, and then shows it to her. "Is this okay?"

"Sure."

"Is it true that after you quit your band they got in a crash and everyone died?" He rushes to add, "That's what it said online. It's so sad."

His words are a blow to the solar plexus. She knows she wasn't responsible for the wreck. Highway patrol blamed it on a deer who leaped in front of them on the Wyoming interstate. But if she hadn't run off, if the band hadn't chased after her and Hank, if Davo hadn't been so upset when he got behind the wheel, then maybe he would have reacted faster. Kept the van on the road. Not rolled it into a ravine.

She'd reached out to all their families. Sent flowers. Found out the record label had settled with all of them. Her brain knows it wasn't her fault. Her heart just never believed it. At least that's what her counselor had told her in rehab.

"One person survived." Celinda Simone. The only other woman in the band.

"Do you still keep in touch?"

Maggie had never spoken to Celinda again. She'd tried, after reading she'd had something like a dozen surgeries, but couldn't reach her. Maggie steps back, hugging herself. His questions are intrusive and painful. "Franklin, if you don't mind, I don't like talking about that part of my life."

"I'm so sorry."

"It's fine." Maggie sighs.

"I've been going on. I'll stop. It was just surreal. I was pinching myself that I was on my way here to meet you."

"It's okay. Let's just get my statement done."

Franklin appears contrite, and he works fast. The statement takes ten minutes, with no surprises.

Afterward, he clears his throat, looking reluctant to leave. "Obviously we can't pay out until law enforcement is done and we get a copy of their report. Just in case of the unlikely event of insured involvement."

Has Junior put a bug in his ear? Maggie rolls her eyes, but with her face turned away from him. "I understand."

"I mean, I'm not saying there is. Just, you know, doing my job."

"It's been a shit week, though, Franklin, and I'm running out of capacity to let anyone's job roll off my back."

"Yeah. I get it. Well, thanks again. For the statement. And the picture. I'll be in touch when things progress or if I need anything else." He turns to go, then spins back to her. "And I'm very sorry about your boyfriend. He was a great musician."

Maggie wouldn't classify him as a boyfriend or as great. Successful, yes. But that's not the same thing. "Thank you."

"You're better, though. The DJ was saying so, too. Iconic."

Dinosaurs are iconic. Or are they just extinct? Like me. She manages to say, "Thanks," then waves goodbye.

She locks the door behind him and turns on the air conditioner. Damn the electricity bill. Louise doesn't react other than to groan and roll over with all four paws in the air. Maggie finishes filling the online orders, washing the road dust off the Wyoming finds, and triaging those and the shop contents into four piles: ready, easy-fix, hard-fix, and trash. She photographs the trash from every angle, then loads it onto the trailer. Hard-fix she pushes, drags, and carries into the barn. Easy-fix she crowds into a staging and work area behind the counter, which allows her to keep creating while tending to customers.

Sweat soaks through her tank top and runs down her arms and legs. Her stomach growls. She wolfs down her sandwich and drains the last of her ice water from her thermos before dusting, sweeping, and mopping. She checks her phone when she's done. It's past three. But she wants a semblance of order. She needs it. So she spends an hour putting out the merchandise and arranging it artfully. She uses space to her advantage, along with additional inventory from her barn storage. The Coop ends up looking more customer-ready, save the broken windows. Now, if only the house was Maggie-ready, she'd feel a lot better.

Michele's voice interrupts her. "Knock, knock."

Louise lifts her head, wags her tail, and resettles her jaw between her paws on the concrete floor. Maggie studies her dog. She hadn't even gotten up when Michele walked in. What's wrong with her?

She smiles at Michele, though. "God, I hope you brought cold beer."

Michele holds up a can. "Will a Diet Coke do?"

"Like a life raft to a drowning man. Gimme." She scrunches her fingers to hurry Michele over.

Rashidi follows Michele into the shop, along with Collin and Ava. Michele hands Maggie the Diet Coke.

"Wow, you work hard. This place a war zone last I see it." Rashidi's island lilt and diction seems appropriate somehow.

"Yah mon." Maggie winks at him.

Ava raises her perfect, full brows and runs a finger across the spotless display nearest the door, a set of middle school lockers repurposed into a cabinet. "You must have been working hard. You're looking rough."

Maggie is too tired to rise to the bait. She drinks the entire can of Diet Coke without pausing.

"Great place," Collin says. "Impressive collection of road signs."

Maggie salutes him with her empty can before ziplocking it into her sandwich bag. "Tip of the iceberg. I have an entire warehouse out back."

"You open for business?" Ava waggles a T-shirt two sizes smaller than Maggie would have suggested for her.

"Not to the public, but I take money anywhere, anytime."

"I'm shopping, then. Collin." She hands him a hot-pink satin purse.

He pops a hip out. "How does this look with my nail polish?"

The others laugh as he follows Ava around the store.

Michele touches Maggie's dirty elbow. "I hear you got the news."

On a day in a week of a lifetime overfilled with news, good and bad, it takes Maggie a moment to remember. "We're sisters."

"You okay with it?"

"If they're happy, I'm happy. And I think they're happy. Are you?"

"I am. I . . ."

Ava looks up from examining the sock display. Her voice goes back to the islands. "Michele think they move a little fast. But everyone else think Michele move a little slow."

Michele snorts. "I wouldn't have put it that way."

"So when you gonna make an honest man of me?" Rashidi demands.

Michele shakes her finger at him. "No pushing."

"I gonna be pushing, pulling, and everything else to get you to the altar if I have to."

Michele actually smiles at his response, a far cry from a year ago when a declaration like that would have resulted in her locking herself in her room and Rashidi out of it.

"Get a room," Maggie advises them. "And it *was* fast, Michele, but your dad is safe with my mother. She had a gadabout spell, but she's a woman of GAWD and will make him a fine wife."

Michele turns to Rashidi. "I need a minute with Maggie."

He makes a face at her. "Well, fine, then." Then he winks at Maggie and chases down Collin and Ava. "Load up, Ava. You can afford it."

Michele puts her head so close to Maggie that their hair mingles, the short Hispanic sister and the taller part-Crow, part-Wendish one. No one would mistake them as blood relations, but their hair color is a perfect match, if you don't count Maggie's artful gray streaks. "I got a call from Junior today. Lee County and Fayette County—including the fire marshal —want to set up a joint interview with you."

"Lovely."

"They suggested now."

"Uh-uh. I've got to go get ready for the wedding thingy at Mom's church."

"Which is why I told them I'd check with you for Monday."

"If I have to, Monday isn't the worst day."

"Chin up. We'll get to the bottom of this."

"We've got to figure out the email clusterfuck."

"I have a technology expert who can take a look at that starting tomorrow. It's going to be okay, Maggie."

Maggie says, "Thanks, sis," and winks, but in her heart she thinks *It's never going to be okay again.*

SEVENTEEN

Maggie shortcuts to her bedroom through Michele's side door. She wants no more of the canoodling twosomes. She flops onto the bed with Louise, who is as lackluster as she is. They both groan. Next up, Maggie has her mom and Edward's ceremony and celebration. She stares at the orange-peel pattern in the ceiling. Balcones would help, if daytime drinking weren't so ill-advised before a church ceremony. She has two and a half hours to self-medicate somehow. What would Michele do in her position? Her friend and new sister is a paragon of self-control. She'd go for a run or a bike ride or a swim or something. Those are out of the question for Maggie.

But she can do Michele-light.

She pulls a free beginner yoga video up on her laptop and a yoga mat out from under the bed, where Michele keeps it for guests, as if everyone is as health conscious as she is. Maggie strips to her underclothes and follows the video. For the next ten minutes, she ducks from dog kisses on the mouth and realizes the full extent of how she's been betraying her own body. It's stiff, and her movements are anything but strong and fluid.

"We have to do better, Louise. Exercise. Eat right. Sleep more. Drink less."

Louise agrees, her tail wagging extra hard.

"We could do daily goat yoga. Offer it to the antique show guests as a draw to the Coop."

Louise barks and sits up with her paws raised.

"You're feeling better, I think. I'm sure they'll think you're cute, too."
Louise paws at Maggie with one leg.

"You think I'll feel better if I take you for a walk?" Maggie checks the
time on the laptop. "I've got fifteen minutes."

She turns off the yoga. One refrigerated water bottle to-go later, Maggie,
Gertrude, and Louise stop at the pen to put halters on the goats, then make
a circuit of Nowheresville with them, detouring through the greenhouse
buildings that hold Rashidi's home hydroponic farming equipment and
experiments. Louise stops every few hundred yards to retch or squat.

"That's what you get for killing possums." Should she take Louise to the
vet? But the dog is bouncier after every bout of sick. She's fine, Maggie
decides. Just ate something that doesn't agree with her.

A lukewarm shower feels cool on her skin post-walk. To save time, she
skips a hair-washing in favor of dry shampoo. She throws on light makeup
and draws on some nearly symmetrical eyebrows. A long-sleeved silk top
covers her burns and works with a blue-jean skirt in a pencil shape that she
can wear with a pair of Old Gringo boots.

When she emerges from the bedroom, the house is empty except for her
and the dogs. She still has an hour before she has to be at the church. For a
brief moment, she considers opening the Martin case. Getting out her
beloved guitar. She could work her way through the new songs she'd
written in Wyoming, the first in years. Maybe pick her way to a few new
melodies. But she's just not up for it. Playing is an extension of her
emotions, and she doesn't want to feel anything more than she already does.
Normally in an emotional muddle like this she'd be seeking out a hassle-free
sexual partner. If she lived in a metropolitan area, she might have been a
Tinder-hookup kind of girl. But she's not in the mood for sex as a salve
either, maybe for the first time in her adult life.

"Louise, Gertrude, guard the house."

The dogs hop up on the couch.

"Good, just like that."

Maggie gets behind the wheel of her truck. Like Bess has a mind of her
own that strangely thinks like Maggie's, the truck takes her to Los Patrones
in Giddings. Or so Maggie tells herself. She feels better after yoga and a
walk, but not that much better, and Los Patrones is the closest fully stocked
bar to the church.

She parks and pats the dash. "Thank you, Bess."

Inside, she perches on a stool at the bar. NFL football blares on a TV to
her left. She inhales the savory smell of sizzling fajitas being carted past her

to a six-top table crowded with ten people. Above her head, red metal letters spell out CANTINA BAR, and almost touching her forehead, margarita glasses hang upside down from racks. Not much around town is open on a Sunday night, so the place is hopping.

She settles for a double Balcones and pulls up People.com on her phone. Reading about herself may negate the soothing effect of the whiskey, but she's put it off long enough. The article about her is still the top story on the site. "Gary Fuller and the Black Widow," she reads. As Franklin had told her, there's a picture of her singing karaoke at Pumpjack's in Amarillo, although the main photo is one of her with Gary. One from her private stash. The only person she'd ever shared a copy with was Gary, via text. The two of them were in his kitchen. Their faces are smashed together for a selfie. Blueberry pancake batter is smeared across her cheeks like speckled war paint. She remembers that morning, maybe two or three years ago. The day after he'd returned from a tour. The morning after a welcome-home party between the sheets.

She reads quickly, and her mouth drops open. The recycled shit in the article is irritating, but some items are flat-out defamation. They list her rehab stints, including a third round that never happened. They cite lovers she's never met. And they name her as the cause of the deaths in her band-mates' crash, never mind that she wasn't with them or even there. Other stuff is naked, irresponsible speculation. That Gary's legions of redneck-crazy fans are saying she might have caught Gary with another woman, that she might have killed him and set the fire to hide it. As "evidence," the site includes a picture of fans holding a vigil outside his home. Hundreds of them. And quotes an unnamed source close to the investigation as saying they have "no other leads at this time." But the part that's most upsetting? People.com claims a witness in Amarillo outed her affair with Gary and their Friday meet-up before it happened, as reported on the TMZ enter-tainment blog.

Maggie scrolls through TMZ until she finds the post. Sure enough, they'd posted a scoop on Friday afternoon. "Secret Affair Between Gary Fuller and Fallen Star Maggie Killian Rekindled." *What the hell?* Her blood boils. TMZ credits an anonymous tip from someone in Amarillo, Texas, where they claim she'd last been seen belting Ava Butler karaoke songs. They link to the video on YouTube. The last assertion is the clincher: *Gary and Maggie are planning a sexy rendezvous at his ranch in Texas tonight. Don't do anything we wouldn't do, kids!*

"Son of a bitch!" She thought people only found out about them after Gary's death, because she was at the fire, and because of her admitting the relationship to law enforcement. But she was wrong. It doesn't take much to narrow down possible identities for the rat. The only people she'd told about Gary were in Amarillo. Emily, her husband Jack, Officer John, and her new buddies Wallace and Ethan. Of those, one is obsessed with online gossip. She seethes. And she'd offered up the information about her date with Gary on a text string with the group.

Maggie forwards the link to Michele in a text. *One of your Amarillo friends is not mine. And I need an attorney to sue the shit out of People.com for libel.* Then she forwards the TMZ link to the Amarillo friends group, with no comment.

"You were talking about my ex-husband?" the bartender asks. Her name escapes Maggie, but the woman talks like a sailor and looks like a grandmother. She's wearing a T-shirt that says BAKING FOR MY GRANDKIDS IS MY SUPERPOWER. She even smells like cinnamon. Or maybe that's the Fireball she's pouring for another patron.

"What?"

"I heard you yell *son of a bitch.* Got here as fast as I could."

Maggie laughs, although it's bitter. She takes a deep breath to pull herself together, then changes the subject. "Y'all need to carry Koltiska liqueur."

"What the fuck is Koltiska? Is it from Texas?"

"Nope. Our sister state to the north. Wyoming. Separated from Texas at birth."

"I won't order any out-of-state shit, Maggie. You know the rules."

"You can always get smarter."

The bartender slides a shot glass to her. "You're such a needy bitch. This is new. Try it."

Maggie passes her empty glass. She doesn't pause to check her drunk. She's only had one, albeit a double. This will be her stopping point. "What is it?"

"Don't be so goddamn pushy. Try it, then I'll tell you."

Maggie knocks it back. She shudders and wipes her mouth. "Well?"

"Rebecca Creek Whiskey."

"Tastes like Crown to me."

"Yeah. But way fucking cheaper. And I can't give it away. Here, let me fill you up again. On the house."

No way is she turning down a freebie. Maggie holds out her shot glass for the top-off, then throws a twenty on the bar. "Thanks for taking care of me."

Grandma bartender salutes her.

Maggie is about to drink her whiskey and leave when a man takes the barstool next to her. He's big, but lean. He turns to her, so she shoots him a glance and snorts. Light blue eyes, blondish-brown curls under a John Deere cap. Stonewashed jeans that are more about optics than country living. Perfectly scuffed boots. A T-shirt that shows off gym muscles and is too tight for ranch work.

"Maggie Killian?" he asks.

"And you're Thorn Gibbons, right?"

His eyes flit around, like he's making sure no one heard her. "I'd appreciate it if you'd keep that to yourself. Nice to see you again."

She almost laughs. His fake country accent can't decide if it's Tennessee, Oklahoma, or Texas. "We've met?"

"Well, sort of. I opened for Gary once in Houston. You were backstage. We were introduced, but it was a long time ago."

Maggie has zero memory of it, but he could be right. "Sure." She tosses back her shot.

"Had, he, uh, mentioned me lately?"

"Should he have?"

"Just wondering."

A seriously random thing to wonder about. But she's met a lot of performers obsessed with what other people say and think about them. She was just never one of them. "Well, we hadn't been in touch."

"But I thought, you, um, talked to him before he died. Weren't you on your way to his house when you found the fire? At least, that's what I read."

"Can't always believe what you read. I'd think you would know that."

He exhales. "Sure. Yeah."

"What brings you to town?"

"Um, I had a gig in Austin. I drove over to see Gary. I should have checked the news before I came."

"What do you mean?"

"Well, I didn't know until I got here. About him . . . the fire."

"Oh. Yeah."

"It rattled me, you know? He gave me my first break. He was like a big brother to me." Thorn's voice cracks melodically. He wipes dry eyes.

"I'm sure his death rattled a lot of people," she says, thinking of Tom Clarke. "So why are you still here?"

"What do you mean?"

"Didn't I see you yesterday morning? At the grocery store in town?"

Thorn studies his hands, which are wrapped around the body of a long-neck, covering the label. "No. I was sleeping one off in Austin."

An internal siren goes off in Maggie's head. "Huh. You've got a twin in Giddings, then."

"Does anyone know what happened to him yet?" He starts picking at a corner of the label.

"You mean other than he burned to a crisp?"

Thorn flinches.

"I don't think so."

He stands, setting his empty bottle on the bar, label away from her. But she recognizes a fancy city-boy beer bottle when she sees one. "Well, it was good to see you. I just wanted to say hello."

"You going to be in town long?"

"No. Headed back to Austin to catch a flight to Nashville."

"Take care."

"You, too."

She watches the flashy stitching on his jeans pockets as he walks to the exit. A slinky-bodied woman with a pouf of peroxide-blonde hair almost trips in her spike-heeled boots in her hurry to get to him. Maggie expects him to duck her, since he's trying to go unrecognized. Instead, he takes her hand, and together they push through the door and out of the restaurant. Maggie frowns. Another decidedly odd encounter. And probably an untruthful one.

Her phone rings. Fearing it's Michele—or worse, Charlotte—she flips it over. But it's neither of them. It's Gene Soboleski, Michele's half brother. Hank's best friend. *Come on, T-Mobile and USPS. I need that new SIM card.* She almost doesn't answer it, but then changes her mind. Gene is her friend, too.

She jumps up, finger in her other ear to block the clank of glasses and silverware. She presses accept with the thumb of the hand holding the phone. "Hello?"

"Maggie May, it's Gene."

"So I see and hear." Using her tush, she opens the door and steps outside, into the dusk of an early fall evening in Texas.

"It's kind of an emergency."

Her breath exits her lungs in a whoosh. Hank. She drops onto Bess's bumper, a poor excuse for a seat, but all she has between her and the ground as her legs go wobbly. "What's wrong?"

"Hank's been out of sorts since he got out of the hospital. About you."

Not the kind of emergency she'd feared. She draws in a deep breath and gets a snoot full of the pain of Hank's baby and engagement. "Not my problem."

"He disappeared yesterday afternoon. His truck's gone. Sheila's on my ass. I haven't heard from him."

She grabs hold of his words like a life preserver. He and Sheila are fighting. "Sounds like she's having trouble keeping him on the leash."

"Help me out here. Have you seen him? Talked to him? Heard from him?"

"Not in a few days. And, Gene, I'm in the process of changing my phone number so that I *won't* hear from him."

"I was hoping he came chasing after you."

You and me both. "Sorry to disappoint you and Sheila."

"Maggie—"

"I have to go. I'm headed to your father's wedding reception."

"What?"

"Yes, Edward married last week."

"Married *who*?"

"My mother. Which makes you my stepbrother now."

"Damn. Maybe that's why Michele called me so many times. Guess I should have answered. And now I have another new sister."

"Lucky you. So as much as I'd love to keep talking about Hank and his pregnant fiancée, I have to go."

She presses END CALL. Enough wallowing. So Hank has cold feet and is drunk somewhere, maybe riding a bull for old times' sake. That's Sheila's problem, not hers.

And thinking about it could just break her heart.

EIGHTEEN

Sober enough. That's how Maggie thinks of herself. She puts one foot in front of the other as she tightrope walks into the church, ever so carefully. She doesn't stretch too hard, but she gives herself a little pat on the back. She's not even late for the service. A small miracle, given the monumental setbacks she'd endured at Los Patrones. Learning she has a traitor amongst her new friends. Reading the lies being spread about her. Running into Thorn. And getting the call from Gene. Gene, about Hank.

Damn Hank Sibley and damn Gene for calling. She can pretend to Gene that she doesn't care where Hank is and call it Sheila's problem, but she can't lie to herself. She craves Hank, longs to see his name on her caller ID. His face at her door. He's like a sickness, sapping her strength, leaving her weak and vulnerable. But she's going to protect herself from him. She's changing her phone number, soon. And she won't even be in her home until tomorrow when Leslie leaves, and Maggie's homelessness ends. If he shows up—which he won't—she's safely tucked away at Michele's.

In the meantime, she can call Hank and hang up. Just to see if he'll answer for her. To reassure herself he's all right.

Or she could if she had no pride or spine left.

"Shit."

Heads turn inside the vestibule. She rolls her lips inward. *Must not curse aloud.* Talking to herself in general is a negative in church, even more so when she's drunk enough to swear, too. And—oh hell. All right. Yes, she's drunk. How else is she supposed to handle all this? People staring, asking about Gary and everything they've read online—and yes, she's upset about what's going on and sad about Gary, but he's gone, and he isn't who she loves.

She loves Hank. She fucking loves Hank. She doesn't want to, but she does, and it makes her want to scream and tear at her hair. Instead, she keeps advancing into the church to witness yet another union of happy lovers. Insult to injury, even if it is her own mother and she should just be happy for her.

"Maggie." She turns to a tall, distinguished man with thick salt-and-pepper hair. His suit is custom-made. His shoes are Italian leather, bought in Milan, or so he claims. This is the man she's come to know as her birth father in the last two years.

"Boyd."

He kisses her forehead and hugs her to his side. Then he chuckles. "Don't let anyone strike a match near your mouth, honey."

"What are you doing here?"

"It's your mother's wedding and reception. Of course I'm here."

"Were you invited?"

He busts out a laugh. "Your mother and I share a common interest. You."

"So you're saying you were invited?"

"Yes." He grins. "When I called and asked if I could come."

"I knew it."

Two church ladies appear on Maggie's near horizon. Tonight they'll lecture her about the impact of her week-long absence and recent notoriety on her mother, along with suggestions about how much good it would do Maggie to have more Jesus in her life. These are the women who have prayed for Maggie since her infancy, and it hasn't done any good so far. She has no misconceptions it will start working for her now.

But whether she likes it or not, she braves them and the "church of the Wends" once a month with her mother. Maggie isn't a churchy person, but even she can admit there's something special about St. Paul Lutheran. A plain white wrapper on the outside, a come-to-Jesus organ inside, with color, color everywhere, the most amazing of which is the stained glass and the brilliant Wendish-blue walls.

A woman whose hair blends right in with those walls zeroes in on Maggie. "You're here for your mother. God bless you."

"Of course I am." Maggie moves closer to Boyd.

A stylish-circa-1970 woman with a gray bob takes the next go at Maggie. "We pray for you all the time. The power of prayer triumphs again. Praise God."

"You didn't get me here by praying. I came because it's my mother's wedding and reception."

Blue Hair turns to Boyd. "Senator Herrington, what a blessing to have you joining our congregation to celebrate sister Charlotte's marriage."

Gray Bob adds, "We'll pray for you, too."

Maggie grins as Blue Hair takes one of Boyd's arms and Gray Bob grabs the other. He looks like he's facing his personal judgment day. She uses their interest in an even bigger sinner than her to slip away and sit with Rashidi and Michele.

The short ceremony is a beautiful blur. When it's over, Maggie's drunk has worn down to a weary buzz. She walks from the nave toward the school with her expanded family, everyone chattering but her. Suddenly, Charlotte stops and hugs a woman with a killer bod whose back is to Maggie. "Leslie, so good to see you."

"And you, Charlotte."

"Let me introduce you to my daughter. Or daughters, I guess, now that Edward and I are married."

The woman turns. It's Maggie's squatter, her face as overly made-up and immobile as ever. Maggie is starting to wonder if she's on the autism spectrum or has had a stroke. "I know Michele. Good evening."

Michele smiles. "Hi, Leslie."

"And this is Maggie," Charlotte says. "Have the two of you met face-to-face yet?"

"Maggie." Leslie makes a face like she's sucking a raw turnip.

Maggie returns a bared-fang smile. "Leslie. Are you packed up to go yet?"

Leslie stares into her eyes without a flicker of response.

Edward ends the awkward moment. "My dearest, we're the guests of honor."

Charlotte takes Edward's arm. "Of course."

The two continue to the school, the site of their reception.

Leslie turns away, shaking a cigarette out of a pack as she walks to the parking area.

Maggie whispers to Michele. "Crazy-ass bitch."

"You've had a contractual misunderstanding. This is why it's worth it to pay those online VRBO sites their cut. It's a little something we savvy folks call 'arms-length transactions.'"

"Bite me. I've got to get out of here."

"No way, new sis. We're going to celebrate the union of our families."

Rashidi steps between them. "Give me the honor of escorting the two most beautiful women in Lee County."

"I'll take my daughter. You take her sister," Boyd suggests.

"Perfect," Rashidi replies.

Maggie grumbles but takes Boyd's arm and allows herself to be pulled along. Inside the school, they stop for punch and a cookie. Sugar to mask her breath, and damnation to Boyd for pointing it out.

Chewing a snickerdoodle, she looks across the room. The pastor is holding court with Charlotte and Edward. The look on Edward's face as he gazes down at her mother stops her heart. Dead stop. No beats for three seconds, she'd swear it. Edward loves her mother. And her mom? She's lit up like a supernova, leaving a trail of sparkles in the wake of her every movement, her face ethereal.

"They're happy." Michele bumps a shoulder against Maggie's bicep. Punch sloshes out of Maggie's cup.

Maggie holds her punch higher, dodging the spill. She smiles at her best friend and new sister. "They are. Like you are."

And like I pray I'll be someday, dammit. If it's not sacrilegious to pray drunk. In a church. With profanity.

As if she can read Maggie's mind, Michele says, "You will be, too."

"May not be in the cards for me."

Michele gives her head a stubborn shake. "You're a treasure. As soon as you realize that, good things are coming your way. Believe it."

"From your mouth past Satan's ears."

"Stop it."

Maggie scans the room. "Hey, I don't see Lumpy." And she hadn't seen him at his house that morning when she picked up the goats and fixed his fence. He and her mother are friends. No way he wouldn't come to this if he's in town.

"I haven't talked to him in a couple of days either." Michele leans closer to Maggie to whisper. "I got your texts. We'll talk lawsuit later. You have plenty of time to think about it. Right now I'm more troubled about the source for the TMZ story."

"My new friends aren't so friendly."

"Could it be anyone else?"

"Zero chance."

"Have any of them fessed up?"

Maggie looks at her phone and scrolls through the new texts in the string.

Wallace: *OMG!*

Ethan: *So sorry, Maggie.*

Michele: *We'll talk.*

Emily: *Oh, Mags, that's terrible.*

Maggie almost laughs. Mags. The name of her favorite bad gal in her favorite TV show. *Justified.* She misses Timothy Olyphant, who looks more like Hank than any person she's ever seen. Only Hank, unfortunately for her, is even sexier and harder to wash from her mind. "Nope."

"What do you want to do about it?"

"Nothing, I guess. Except be more careful about who I open up to in the future. I'm not interested in facilitating someone's fifteen minutes of fame by association."

"I'm really sorry. I'll let you know if I hear who did it."

Maggie downs her punch and sets the cup on an empty table. "Ready to go congratulate the crazy kids?"

Michele nods. They get in the long line behind Boyd and Rashidi to hug and kiss each parent and new stepparent. Charlotte smushes Michele and Maggie together in a group hug with her.

She draws back. "Do I smell alcohol?"

Michele shakes her head. "Listerine. Sorry. I have a toothache and didn't want to have bad breath."

Maggie pats her mother's back. "You guys have fun. We're going to get out of the way of your admirers."

Charlotte releases them, and Edward beams at the women. Maggie blows her mother a kiss.

As Maggie walks away, she talks out of the side of her mouth to Michele. "Thanks for the save."

"Don't get used to it. I'm cutting you a break because you're going through tough times, but I'm about to be all over your ass if this keeps up."

Maggie stiffens. "I've got me under control."

"It would be a first."

Stopping, Maggie scowls at her friend. "I'll slow down. On my terms. Soon."

"I'm holding you to it." Michele rolls her eyes. "Loving you is hard work."

Maggie's short snit breaks apart. She smiles, until her phone rings with an incoming call from the Lee County Sheriff's Department.

NINETEEN

It's a miracle Maggie makes it to Flown the Coop alive after the call from Junior.

Her shop is on fire. Completely ablaze. Her barn is burning, too. The house is safe at this point, but that's small consolation. According to Junior, firefighters are on scene, trying to salvage something, anything, but there are no guarantees.

Her entire livelihood is burning to the ground. Her entire *identity*, since she gave up the music world.

She smells smoke and hears sirens and the roar of the fire beast before she clears the last corner to the house. Turning into her parking lot, she drives helter-skelter through a barricade, jerking Bess to a stop beside Junior. She jumps out, but forgets to take the truck out of gear. Bess lurches and jerks to a halt, then stalls bare inches short of a big red fire truck with an enormous hose snaking from it. Two firefighters in full battle gear wrestle the hose like an anaconda as it spits a thick spray of hissing water at the shop. Junior leaps into Bess and sets the brake.

"Ring of Fire" loops in Maggie's head as she runs toward her Coop. Her heart seizes. Her father—she doesn't remember him fondly most of the time, but does now. Overspray and ash rain down on her. Visions of the burning woman return to her. Her eyes comb the windows, afraid of what they'll find there.

Strong arms arrest her flight. "Ma'am. No."

She struggles to break free. "My store. My stuff. All of it."

"I understand."

She continues fighting. "You don't."

Junior arrives and helps restrain her. "Maggie. Listen to me. Stop it. You can't do anything but hurt yourself. Let them do their job."

Maggie's knees buckle. Only Junior's grip on her arms keeps her from puddling on the ground.

"I don't understand. I don't understand. I don't understand. Two times in three days. I don't understand."

Junior hauls her up and shakes her gently. "Come on. Let's go talk."

Somewhere in the back of her brain she knows she should resist. Michele would tell her this conversation should wait for her to get there. And she'll be here soon, Maggie knows. Michele ran fast as a NASCAR pit crew to get Rashidi after Maggie repeated Junior's horrible news. They can't be far behind her.

But Maggie follows Junior anyway. She's too defeated to resist. He leads her to his Tahoe, parked perpendicular to the yellow tape barrier she'd run over with Bess. They pass county employees restringing the tape from sawhorses.

"Sit inside." He opens the back door of the Tahoe.

She crosses her arms, cradling herself. "N-no. Outside. I need to see. I need to hear."

"I think you'll be happier inside."

She shivers. "I'm c-c-cold."

"Shit. Okay, yeah, shock. Let's get you to the EMTs."

At the ambulance, they take Maggie through the familiar drill. Shock blanket. Loosening her clothes. Getting her to lie down. Junior keeps stealing glances at an unmarked vehicle next to the fire truck. It's an SUV with a light on top. Maggie follows Junior's gaze to Karen, the fire marshal, and the tall Fayette County sheriff. They're leaning against the SUV, watching her.

"Oh no. No, no, no." She stands, dropping the blanket. "No way."

Junior puts a hand on her forearm. "Maggie, wait."

But she takes off toward the fire, not listening to Junior. Junior isn't her friend. He's a deputy. This isn't the same young man she's known since before he joined the Lee County Sheriff's Department, back when he was just a local boy trying to find a decent job in a small town. Who she has always treated kindly—for her, at least—because of his not-so-secret crush on her. Either he's in on it, or he's being used. Either way, Fayette County thought they'd catch her with her guard down with her store burning before her eyes. Get her to incriminate herself while she's vulnerable.

Like that would make a difference. She's the victim here. The *victim*.

When she reaches the reconstructed barrier, there's a cluster of official personnel ten feet past it. Beyond them, the Coop is still ablaze, but the barn is only smoldering. Flames are no longer leaping for the sky and lunging out the windows.

She calls out. "Excuse me. I'm the owner. Can I get a status update?"

A female Lee County deputy looks over her shoulder. She walks to the barrier and faces Maggie across it. "Long way to go."

"Did they catch it in time?"

"If you mean in time to save the building or the contents, I'm afraid not. Most of the roof fell in before the firefighters got here. Not sure if there will be anything salvageable inside."

Maggie sucks in a breath, long and whistly.

"I'm sorry, ma'am."

"What about out back? The barn."

"Give me a minute. I'll ask."

The deputy works her way over to a firefighter. Maggie watches the two converse, the firefighter removing his helmet and unzipping the neck of his jacket while they speak. The deputy returns to Maggie.

"They've got that one out. And the damage back there isn't as bad."

"Did my renter call the fire in?"

"Who?"

"I have a short-term renter in my house. It's the building off to the side, between the store and the barn. Her name is Leslie DeWitt."

She rubs her forehead, leaving a red mark. "It wasn't her. A rancher saw it when he drove by and called 911. I don't remember his name."

"Have you seen Leslie?"

"I haven't seen anyone that isn't from Giddings PD or Lee or Fayette County. Except for you." She gestures toward a line of vehicles on the county road in front of Maggie's house. "Although it looks like people are starting to gather."

"Can someone check on Leslie?"

"We knocked. No one answered." The deputy puts her hand on Maggie's arm. "Why don't you get off your feet. You look beat."

Maggie jerks away. She moves in a tight circle, then points to the little silver sedan in the parking area. "That's her car." As much as she dislikes the woman, she won't be able to live with herself if she bears any responsibility for her being injured. "She was at St. Paul Lutheran earlier, but she must be back. I saw her leaving." She rewinds their conversation outside St. Paul. Leslie heading toward the parking area. Possibly leaving.

The deputy pulls a radio from her lapel. With her back to Maggie, she speaks into it. Then she turns to Maggie and says, "You're giving us permission to enter your home?"

"Of course. It's a life-or-death situation."

"It is in the shop. Not in your house." She leans in. "I shouldn't tell you this. But do you understand that anything in plain sight is fair game and could lead to a search warrant for the entire property?"

Maggie shakes her head. "What is it with you people? I'm the victim here. And I haven't been in my own house for weeks. I told you. There's a renter in there. Leslie. Let me call her. If she answers, there's no need to go in. If she doesn't, then, yes, break down my goddamn door and make sure she's okay, because there's a fucking fire back there."

Maggie can't take any more death. Gary, killed in a fire. Chet, beaten to death. Patrick, dead, and Hank, injured, from gunshots. *No more death. Please, no more death.*

She pulls out her phone and finds a number for Leslie in the call log. She presses it, then chooses CALL.

A commotion at the front of the Coop draws her attention. The firefighters are agitated about something. The deputy moves in front of her like she's trying to block her line of sight and directional hearing, but Maggie moves stealthily along the barricade until she can hear the phone ringing in one ear and the firefighters in the other.

". . . body . . . charred past recognition . . . female . . . no identification or clothing survived the fire . . ."

Her hand drops to her side. She feels limp. She stares at the Coop. *A dead body in the Coop. More death.*

"Hello? Hello?" There's a voice coming from Maggie's hand.

Like a sleepwalker, she stares into the distance, but she lifts her phone as she does. "Hello." Her voice is dull.

"Is this Maggie Killian?"

"Yes."

"Why are you calling me?"

"Oh, Leslie. Fire at the Coop. Making sure you're okay."

"What?"

"My shop burned down. Your car is here. The deputies knocked at the house and you didn't answer. I'm making sure you're okay."

"I'm on the way home from your mother's church reception, where I've been, unlike you."

"I was—" Maggie shakes her head. Not relevant. "Whatever. There's a fire. You're all right. When you come back, expect a whole lot of law enforcement activity."

"Great."

Maggie hangs up on her.

The female deputy has her head together with Junior. They look up at her.

Maggie shouts, "She's fine."

The deputy returns to Maggie. "What?"

"I just talked to Leslie. She's on her way home from the church. She's fine."

"So, to be clear, do we have permission to enter your house?"

"No. You do not."

"You wanted us to a moment ago."

"As I said a moment ago, only if I didn't get confirmation she is okay, which I now have. It's rented to her. I can't give you permission to violate her privacy without a good reason." As much as she'd like to.

"We're going to need to talk to her."

"That's between you guys and her."

A small, warm hand grips Maggie's shoulder. "Oh God, Maggie. All your hard work. I'm so sorry."

Maggie lets Michele rotate her into an embrace. Maggie leans on her shoulder.

Michele whispers, "Not another word to anyone in law enforcement. We'll talk to them all together tomorrow at our scheduled interview. Nod if you understand."

Maggie nods.

"Good. I need to get you out of here. Rashidi and I will take you back to your truck."

Another warm hand lands on Maggie's back. She doesn't have to look to know that it's Rashidi. She allows herself to be trundled away from the scene, but her eyes keep cutting back to her shop. Her livelihood. Her identity. Her light after darkness. Who is she without it anymore?

"Hold up, Maggie." Weaselly Rickey Sayles is fast-walking toward her, dragging a woman along by the hand.

Maggie doesn't give the woman a second glance. "Come to gloat, Rickey?"

"Of course not. But I did want to make sure I withdrew my offer. In front of witnesses. I would, however, be happy to take any remaining inventory off your hands for an acceptable markdown off wholesale. Say, fifty percent."

"I wouldn't sell anything to you at any price. Not before, not now."

The woman steps between them. "Are you sure? You don't have your famous fuck buddy around to prop you up anymore."

Maggie stares at her. She shouldn't have discounted the woman in the beginning, because the curvy redhead is a woman scorned. Jenny.

"My new offer expires at noon tomorrow. The next one won't be so generous."

She jerks her attention back to Rickey. "Get lost, Rickey."

Rashidi is suddenly in front of Maggie. "Leave her alone and get out of here. Both of you."

Jenny pops a bubble in her gum.

Rickey laughs. "Call off your dog, Maggie. I know you can't be a stupid woman, no matter what I read about you."

Rashidi's fist strikes Rickey's jaw, spinning him sideways and to the ground. Jenny screams and huddles over him.

"Oh, Rashidi," Michele says. "Not good."

"No, it was bad. As in badass." Maggie steps over to Rickey and Jenny. "What he said."

Michele marches ahead of Rashidi and Maggie toward Rashidi's Jeep, which is parked on the side of the road facing away from the house, like it's ready to drive toward Michele's. "You'll be charged."

"Well worth it," Rashidi says.

"For you. Now I'll be defending both of you in court instead of working on my next book."

Just as they reach the Jeep, an SUV pulls to a stop in the middle of traffic. Leslie hauls herself out. For a moment, with the way the light falls on the woman's face, Maggie gets a strong sense of déjà vu. Has she known Leslie in some other part of her life? Before she can place the memory, it's gone, leaving only the wooden-faced woman she's come to loathe.

"Leslie," she calls.

The woman slams the door of her ride, and the SUV speeds away. "What?"

"The deputies over there." Maggie points. "They need to talk to you."

"Why me? I wasn't here."

"Don't shoot the messenger."

"I'm going to bed."

Rage explodes in a starburst in Maggie's head. This woman is keeping her from her own home, at a time when Maggie's lost the two most important men in her life and now her store and inventory. Tonight's fire stripped her of her creativity, her passion, and her hard work. And Leslie won't answer a few simple questions to help find the person who did it? She wants to throttle her, but she has a better idea.

She speed-dials Junior from her Recents.

He picks up on the second ring. "Maggie. Where'd you go?"

"My short-term vacation renter is standing in the road in front of the house with me and can talk to you now." Maggie describes Leslie, then adds, "Short, robotic, rude."

"Tell her we're on our way."

"Bitch," Leslie mutters as she walks toward the ruined compound.

"Come on, hon." Michele holds open the front passenger door of the Jeep.

Before Maggie takes a single step toward her new sister, her attention is ripped away again. This time by a strange glow in the trees on the other side of the road. She squints at it. Not a glow. A person. A woman. A tall, pale woman with a long gray braid.

"Hey," she shouts.

Without even realizing she's doing it, Maggie runs across the road. A horn honks. Looky-loos cruising the fire. She doesn't spare the time to apologize. She has to catch the woman she just saw. *The woman from Michele's backyard. She got away before. Is she following me? Maybe she started the fire. Or saw who did.*

Michele's voice seems to float to her from a million miles away. "No, Maggie. Stop. Come back. Be careful."

Maggie keeps running.

The pale woman is farther away from her than she'd realized. Way, way back in the trees and thick yaupon. Thorns rip at Maggie's clothes and branches scratch her face. As hard as Maggie runs, she doesn't seem to get any closer. There's a tunnel between her and the woman that's growing longer and narrower with every step, pulling the woman away from Maggie like she's on a high-speed motorized walkway. But that can't be. She's just faster than Maggie. It's the only logical explanation.

Panting, Maggie shouts again. "Wait. Please."

She thinks she hears Michele, but far away. Rashidi shouts, too, the sound like his voice is coming from the bottom of a well. But she ignores both of them. All she cares about is catching the mystery woman.

The woman stops. Her eyes lock with Maggie's.

Maggie slows and holds out a hand to her. "I just want to talk to you."

Maggie is lying, though. She doesn't just want to talk. She wants to get the woman back to Junior. She wants her to give him answers that will explain all of this.

Suddenly, Michele is there, in front of her, but Maggie doesn't break her gaze from the woman. She's so sad-looking. Is that guilt about the fire? Or does she feel empathy for what Maggie is going through? And why won't she say anything?

Rashidi joins Michele. He steps in front of Maggie, blocking her view of the braided woman.

"No!" Maggie shouts and swats to move him out of the way.

He holds his ground.

"Shh, Maggie. It's going to be all right." Michele reaches up and puts a hand on Maggie's face.

Maggie ducks around Rashidi and away from Michele. She doesn't see the woman anymore. She pushes Rashidi. Frantic, she yells, "Where is she?"

"Where is who?" Rashidi asks, his voice gentle. Concerned.

"There was a woman here. The same one I saw earlier in the backyard."

"In *my* backyard?" Michele asks.

"Yes. She ran off then, too. I have to talk to her."

Michele sounds stricken. "Maggie, you can't go running after a stranger. A witness. That's a job for the cops."

"But I have to get her to tell them what she saw."

"Them who?"

"The fire marshal. The deputies. Law enforcement."

"Give them her description tomorrow."

"She could be long gone by then."

"Well, you're not going to find her out in the woods in the dark. And how do you know she didn't start the fire? She could be dangerous."

Defeated, Maggie's shoulders slump. "There's no 'could be' to it. If she started the fire, she is dangerous. They found a dead body in the Coop."

TWENTY

The unreality of the previous night still hasn't sunk in. Maggie rotates a coffee mug back and forth in her fingers—her fourth cup of the day already —on the tile inlay top of Michele's dining room table. The tiny author-athlete-sister-attorney is a miracle worker. She's emptied her house and assembled all the hot-to-question-Maggie law enforcement personnel, on home turf. Or as close to home as Maggie can get with Leslie not out of Maggie's house yet.

Michele's not only gained home-court advantage, she's kept the law enforcement ranks thin. This despite their original demand of a crowd of nine. They're limited to Karen—the fire marshal—along with one representative each from the Lee and Fayette counties sheriff's departments. Junior is here representing Lee and the big sheriff himself has come from Fayette. The three uniforms circle the table like buzzards around a carcass. If Michele is the guardian of the remains whose job it is to keep the flesh eaters at bay, Maggie is the rotting hunk of meat.

Louise peers through the back window, barking her fool head off, adding to a deep pain above Maggie's brow. She appreciates Louise's loyalty, though. She shifts her eyes over the dog's head and into the back-yard. She'd seen the pale woman from last night here, and she wonders if she'll come back. Friend or foe? Maggie's gut says the woman has something important to tell her.

Louise tests the glass, pushing against it with her nose, then trying to dig through it with her claws. Gertrude paces beside her. When Gidget died, little Gertrude broke through a glass window and went for help, finding Michele. Maggie would bet Michele is remembering that right now, too. It brings the slightest of smiles to Maggie's lips. If Gertrude can break glass, Louise surely can. She imagines the two of them busting through, teeth sinking into ankles, officers screaming and running like small children from the yappy, runty dogs.

It's a happy thought.

"You have exactly forty-five minutes." Michele hits RECORD in the Voice Memo app on her iPhone. "I suggest you get started, because I'm not extending the time. Ms. Killian's had too much trauma in too short a time frame to be forced to endure anything longer."

Karen presses something on her own phone. "For the record, we object to your terms."

"That wasted thirty seconds." Michele smiles at her.

Maggie watches as they waste another few seconds staring at each other. *With their thumbs up their asses.* She nods at Michele.

"We'll start, then. Ms. Killian has something she wants to say." Michele doesn't look at her, but she squeezes her sister's knee. They'd talked this through for hours the night before.

"No, I believe I will," the sheriff says. He'd introduced himself earlier— in a voice that's barely spent a day outside Fayette County—but Maggie's already forgotten his name. He points at Maggie. "Did you or did you not confess to a Lee County deputy that you spilled gasoline on yourself while burning down Gary Fuller's house?"

Michele jumps to her feet. "If you want to talk to my client, that's the last we're going to hear of misrepresentations and accusations. Those you can make at the station, if you arrest her, but not in my home. And not when you haven't even classified this fire as intentional."

"You can't tell me what I can and can't ask."

"I can terminate this interview."

"We'll arrest her, then."

"You'd like that, wouldn't you? It doesn't escape me, Sheriff, that you're under a bit of pressure to close this case. Traffic outside Gary's gate now is a constant gridlock. He's like Selena, for Texas rednecks. A folk hero. And they're convinced their guy was murdered. Their narrative is to blame a woman. This woman." She nods at Maggie. "But their agenda shouldn't dictate yours, and it certainly doesn't dictate ours. Ms. Killian did nothing wrong, and you aren't going to get away with harassing her. Not on my watch."

The sheriff guffaws. "Junior, hold my beer."

Karen looks pained. "Enough. Ms. Killian, unless your attorney is going to terminate this interview, please answer the question."

"Fine," Michele says. "If she wants to."

Maggie shakes her head, but answers anyway. "No, I did *not* make any kind of admission. And Junior damn well knows it."

Michele holds a hand up. "Thank you. Moving forward, she won't answer anything I tell her not to. You can't bully us. Now, as I said, Ms. Killian will kick things off."

Maggie nods. "I've already told Junior everything I knew about the vandalism of my shop, including the only people I could think of who might have a grudge against me. With respect to last night, I have no idea how the fire started. I'd spent the day there cleaning up from the last break-in and getting merchandise and displays ready for the antique show. I went home, did yoga, took a walk, went to Los Patrones and then to St. Paul Lutheran Church, where I was when I got the call about the fire from Junior. But some weird things have been happening, and my attorney thinks I should tell you about them."

"With all due respect, counselor, Ms. Killian is eating into the time we were told we'd have to question her," the sheriff drawls, his tone mocking and disrespectful of the tiny lawyer.

Michele ignores him. "Go on, Maggie. Just tell them what you told me."

"I've had a few odd visitors to the Coop since I got back. The first and most concerning was Rickey Sayles. He's opened up a rival business not far from here. He showed up uninvited trying to buy the Coop. He didn't make a threat per se, but his attitude was threatening. He was at the fire last night, too. With Jenny, no less." Maggie speaks directly to Junior. "The one I told you hated me because she didn't like sharing Gary. Strange coincidence that they're together now." She returns her attention to the officers as a group. "Given that he's been going around town telling people he's going to kill off the Coop, I find the timing of his visits very suspect."

"When was that first visit?" Junior says. He's looking a little green around the gills, working side by side with such senior Fayette officials.

"Saturday afternoon."

"I'll look into it." Junior makes a note.

"Go on," Michele says.

"Tom Clarke came to see me on Saturday, too."

"Who's he?" Junior asks.

"Gary Fuller's manager."

Karen's eyes bore into Maggie. "What was that about?"

"I'm not really sure. He said he was in town to meet with Gary on Friday."

"What?" the Fayette sheriff barks.

Karen puts her hand over his arm. "Sheriff Boland. Please."

Sheriff Boland. Boland is the asshole's last name. Maggie doesn't remember the first, if she ever knew it. "With all that happened, I'd forgotten about it, but Gary told me he planned to meet with Tom Friday. When we talked Thursday night."

"Did Gary tell you why he wanted a meeting with Tom?" Karen asks.

"He said he was going to fire him."

Karen and Boland share a long look. Karen doesn't remove her restraining hand from his arm.

"But when I saw him on Saturday, Tom claimed he was late getting to Gary's and by the time he got there Friday, Gary was *long gone.*"

"What did he mean by that?" Karen asks.

"He didn't say. He was acting crazy. The whole conversation went down on the side of the road near the Coop, and it didn't last long. I told him he needed to go to the authorities, but he said he couldn't because people would think he killed Gary."

Boland smiles at her, but it's really more a leer. "That's awful convenient, seeing as he's not here to confirm your story."

Maggie balls her fists. "Well, it's *your* job to find him and talk to him, not mine."

Karen says, "Why would people think he killed Gary?"

"According to Gary, Tom is a thief and was putting other clients' interests ahead of his."

"Why would Tom do that?"

"You'd have to ask Tom. But if I had to guess, he's been hedging his bets for if and when Gary's star falls. Gary was no sellout. Tom's been on him to become more commercial for years, but he wouldn't compromise his artistic integrity." *If singing about Lone Star longnecks and Friday night lights is artistic.*

"Do you have any proof?"

"Why would I have proof? I'm not a cop and it's not my business." Maggie narrows her eyes at the sheriff. "But from what I'd seen and heard, that was my belief, and it had come to be Gary's. In my opinion, firing Tom was long overdue. It shouldn't be hard for you to confirm Tom's been in town, if you don't believe me." She takes a deep breath. "I also ran into another person on the outs with Gary. Yesterday. At Los Patrones."

Boland smirks. "Suddenly no one is Gary's friend, or so says Maggie Killian."

"Do you want her help or not?" Michele retorts.

Boland makes a rolling "go on" motion with his hand and shuts his mouth.

"Thorn Gibbons is a musician and television personality. He claimed to me that he came to town to surprise Gary, and that he hadn't known he was dead. He quizzed me about whether Gary had mentioned him to me, and whether anyone knew how Gary had died yet. That was all weird, because Gary and Thorn weren't friends and didn't have business together, but the weirdest part was I saw him Saturday morning, too. I asked him about it, and he denied being in town."

Boland grunts. "Case of mistaken identity?"

"There's no such thing with Thorn. He's very hard to miss."

"But does he have a beef with Gary?"

"Gary didn't mention anything, but Google their names. The internet thinks so."

"Why don't you tell us about it?" Boland says, his voice rising.

"Because your forty-five minutes is ticking, and I don't have a lick of firsthand knowledge. And I'm not done."

"Go on," Karen says, ignoring Boland's glare.

"Three things stick out at me from Friday night, as I think back on it, things I didn't remember in the heat of the moment."

"Convenient again," Boland says with a snort.

"Sheriff Boland, you're not helping," Karen says.

Maggie tries to block out Boland and focus on saying the things she and Michele planned. "The first was that Friday when I drove from Round Top out to Gary's, the road was pretty clear. I only saw one car the whole time. It was a silver sedan. I don't know the type. It wasn't overly old. It wasn't overly new. Unremarkable. But given the timing, I wanted you to know. I didn't notice the driver. The other thing was that as I was running to the back of the house, I tripped over a hose. I was in a hurry, and I didn't stop to get a close look, but it had a cut in it. A long one. That may not be significant, but, there you go."

"We found the hose." Karen nods at Michele.

Maggie hesitates. She's scared to tell the last thing. She and Michele had talked for a long time about how to spin it.

Michele pats her knee. "One last thing, right?"

Maggie swallows. "Last night at the fire, as I was leaving, there was a woman in the woods across the street from the Coop."

Junior interrupts. "Who?"

Michele raises a brow at him. "Let my client speak, please."

Maggie answers anyway. "I don't know, but I'd seen her at least once before. Here." Maggie points past the agitated dogs. "In the backyard, looking in the windows at me. That time, I got up to go out and see what she was doing, but she disappeared. When I saw her after the fire, I chased her. But she got away." She remembers the braided woman in her rocking chair, but she doesn't mention it. It's enough that they know about the other times, or so she tells herself, because it had to have been just a dream. She'll sound crazy if she tells them about a woman who broke and entered just to rock in a chair by her bed. Even Maggie doesn't believe the woman was really there that time. Booze. Dreams. Hallucinations. Whatever it was, it couldn't have been real. The scarf, yes, it was real, but it doesn't mean the woman was.

Deafening silence fills the room like a screaming banshee. She's surprised them, and she has their full attention now.

Maggie clears her throat. "I don't know who she is. I'd only seen her that one other time, as far as I know. But if she's following me, maybe she saw something I didn't. Or, I don't know, maybe she's involved somehow."

"Did anyone else see her?" Junior asks.

"I don't know."

Michele squeezes Maggie's knee again. "Rashidi John and I went after Ms. Killian in the woods and reached her after she'd lost sight of the woman. We didn't see her, but we can attest that she was running after someone and yelling for them to stop."

Boland grins. "So no other people saw her."

Michele's voice is a whip crack. "Ms. Killian answered that and said she doesn't know. It wasn't her job to go look for witnesses. That's for Lee County to do. Go on, Maggie."

Karen holds up her hand. "Wait. Can we at least get a description?"

"Gray hair. Long. She wore it in a single French braid the times I saw her. She's tall. I don't think she's old. Maybe fifty, sixty at most? Or prematurely gray. She was medium build. Not fat. Not skinny. Pale. Very, very pale."

Junior guides the questioning now. The woman is a potential witness to the incident in Lee County. "Eyes?"

"Too far away to see."

"How did she dress?"

"Jeans and a buttoned shirt, tucked in."

"Country."

"Seemed so."

"Anything else?"

"Not that I recall."

"Would you be willing to help with a picture?"

"I can try."

Junior sits back in his chair.

Maggie looks at Michele, who motions for her to continue. "The only other things I wanted to say are, first, Gary pissed people off. If this fire wasn't an accident, then you need to know the truth about him. I may have been the best friend he had, notwithstanding our breakup. He was arrogant. He stole girlfriends and wives. He cut people off in traffic. He was ruthlessly ambitious. Second, about the vandalism and fire at my place, please make sure you talk to my vacation renter. Leslie DeWitt. She's been in my house for the last two weeks, and I have not been in my home at all during that time. More than half of it I was working estate sales in Wyoming. If there was anything to see, she would have been the one in a position to see it."

"We talked to her last night," Junior says.

"Good." Michele smiles at Maggie. "Anything else?"

"That's all. Other than I'm devastated."

Karen looks down at a notepad in front of her. "Thank you, Ms. Killian. Deputy?"

Junior stammers a little, then finds his gear. "Um, yes. What can you tell us about the body we found in your shop?"

Maggie's neck twitches. "It's awful. Do you know who it is yet?"

"We were hoping you'd identify it for us."

Michele ducks her chin and looks over her nose at Junior. "Have you checked missing persons?"

He nods. "Of course."

"No luck?"

"Not yet. Maggie—Ms. Killian—do you know how she got in the shop?"

"It's a she?" Actually, Maggie had overheard that at the scene when someone in law enforcement mentioned the gender of the corpse. But there was no other way to answer the question.

Junior stares without responding.

"I have no idea. The windows were busted out when it was vandalized. Anyone could have knocked the plywood out and gotten in that way."

"And the fire?"

"What about it?"

"You have any idea how that started?"

"As I told you earlier and also last night, none."

He looks at his lap as he asks, "How much insurance are you carrying on the place?"

"I don't remember for sure. I know it was about half the replacement value of the building and I'd estimate half the rough value of the items I had on hand. I am—was—carrying tons more inventory now than I do any other time of the year. Because of the upcoming show. Anyway, I can call my insurance company and ask. The premiums were really high, that's all I know for sure."

"We'll need you to get that for us. And give us permission to speak to them."

"Whatever."

"Is that permission?"

"Sure."

Junior says, "Your witness, Fire Marshal."

Karen leans toward Maggie. "I think Junior here gave you a heads-up"— she shoots him a side-eye that isn't friendly—"that we're in possession of Gary Fuller's phone and the texts and emails between you."

Michele smiles like a crocodile. "You're in possession of his phone. You're not in possession of their actual texts and emails."

"We'll see about that. We're in the process of obtaining corroborating records from the phone company now. And here's a subpoena for Ms. Killian's computer records." She pulls a sheaf of papers from a briefcase at her feet and slides them to Michele under two fingers.

Michele ignores the papers. "And we're in the process of working with a computer specialist to figure out how falsified emails were sent using Ms. Killian's email address. Meanwhile, we will voluntarily provide screenshots for you of the call logs and full text exchange between Mr. Fuller and Ms. Killian on the day of and the week before the fire." Michele opens a manila folder and takes out the top two pieces of paper, closes the folder, and hands the pages across the table.

Junior accepts them when Karen and Boland stare Michele down without moving.

"The text string Junior told Maggie about is not correct as represented to her by him. There were confirming exchanges between the two of them that show Gary invited Maggie over and that he was very eager and welcoming. There was also a lengthy telephone call the previous night."

Junior looks up from his perusal of the papers. "Initiated by Maggie. I mean, Ms. Killian."

"Correct."

Karen leans on her elbows, hands clasped in front of her. "So, Ms. Killian, you're claiming you didn't send any of the emails to Gary we saw on his phone?"

Michele laughs. "C'mon, Karen—she hasn't even seen the emails."

Karen raises a brow. "Did you send email to Gary, Maggie?"

"Very rarely. I can't remember the last time, actually. We texted. Face-Timed. Talked on the phone. Or didn't talk at all, for long stretches."

"Tell us about your relationship."

"Well, I already have. But we first hooked up about ten years ago, and we were together off and on ever since. I broke things off completely last spring. Then, I had a bad time of it last week, and I called him on my way home from Wyoming. That's when he invited me over, and I said yes."

"You broke up with him."

"Yes."

"That's not what he said."

"Actually, it is. He complained about it to everyone who knew about us."

"What do you mean 'everyone who knew about you'?"

"We were very private about our relationship. Only a few people knew about it, until I told you guys Friday night at the fire. Now the whole world knows. Before, most people just thought we were longtime friends."

"So give me an example of people he told that you broke up with him."

Michele raises her hand like a schoolgirl. "Me. My boyfriend, Rashidi." She winks at Maggie. "I'm happy to provide you with affidavits."

Karen doesn't look at Michele. "So your only communication to Gary between the breakup and now was the call the night before the fire?"

"And the texts." Michele points at the paper.

Maggie shakes her head. "I've also answered some of his other texts. And I texted him the week after the vandalism at the Coop, because I felt bad he was getting sucked into it. I don't hate him. I care—cared—about him. I was just . . ."

"Just what?"

Maggie wipes away a tear.

Michele puts her hand out, palm up, and Maggie takes it. "In love with someone else."

TWENTY-ONE

"That was a shit show." Maggie ruffles Louise's ears. The dog won't leave her side after the tense morning.

"*Al contrario,* senorita. A huge success. You have witnesses for Gary's admissions that you dumped him, screenshots of your phone disproving the contents of his, and no one arrested you. You gave them additional suspects. And a potential witness."

"They're going forward with the subpoenas, they don't believe me about the lady with the braid, and in general they have a massive hard-on for me as a suspect. I've been down this road before."

"I know, and me, too, but you do have a great attorney and two tickets to her movie premiere."

"Two tickets—who'm I gonna take? Louise?"

Michele smiles. "Sell one if you want. Bring a bodyguard. Put your purse in the seat. I don't care. But you have two. Oh, and you have mail." She holds out a cardboard envelope.

Maggie snatches it. "T-Mobile? My SIM card."

"Are you changing your number?"

"Yep."

"Why?"

"Nunya."

"Seriously, why?"

"So Hank can't torture me anymore."

"Maggie, it's a breakup. He'll stop soon."

Maggie pops out her old SIM card, pockets it, and puts the new one in. "You want my new number or not?"

Michele gets out her phone. Maggie recites the number to her. Then she sends a quick group text to everyone whose number she can remember, announcing her new digits.

"Now, would my client allow me to take her to lunch?"

"Your client would love that. I need strength for this afternoon. And someone to give me a ride back from Brenham after I drop the truck off for air-conditioning repair."

"I'll ask Rashidi if he can do it. Are you going back to the Coop?"

"What's left of it. And afterward, to reclaim my house. Can I get the goats later?"

"They're no bother." Michele laughs. "Or very little."

"Seriously, thank you."

"*De nada.* Anytime."

"In that case, I don't have to leave. Really."

"Don't let the door hit you in the ass on the way out."

Maggie crosses her arms over her chest. "Uh-uh. No take-backs."

That earns her a smile, but it fades quickly to Michele's serious face. "Speaking of take-backs, I've been meaning to ask—did Leslie ever PayPal you for those extra two days?"

"Shit. I haven't followed up on that. I need to, so I can take it out of her in blood if she didn't actually pay."

"All right. Now, can you be ready in five? We have to meet Ava. She's shopping the stores that have opened early for the antique show. There's a gallery I'm dying to see. We'll grab lunch after."

Maggie's nonexistent brows rise an inch. "Um, no?"

Michele laughs. "You and Ava. What's with the two of you? You've both grown up. Moved on. Time to get over it."

"Her massive purchase yesterday at Flown the Coop helped thaw me toward her a little. But I'm still not up for the shopping. Call me when your lunch plans are set. Then, maybe."

Michele laughs. "I foresee a future where the two of you are best friends."

"You're all the best friend I need, *amiga.* Now go. So I can do the other thing I need to give me strength for this afternoon."

"Please tell me it's not Balcones."

"Nope, although that's a great idea. It's . . . a nap."

"Good. Because we're out of whiskey, and I'm not buying you any more." Michele winks as she grabs her zebra handbag and flounces out of the house.

TWENTY-TWO

Maggie plants herself on the couch after a quick shower. Before she can forget, she decides to log in to PayPal to check for Leslie's payment. As a small business owner, she's very familiar with all forms of taking payment. *Venmo, PayPal, Square, cash, or check, please.* She enters her email and password. The log-in fails. She hates logging in on a phone, but she surrendered her laptop to Michele's computer expert first thing that morning. She types the password in again, more carefully this time. It doesn't work.

"Dammit."

After a few more attempts, she gets a message that she's locked out for a few hours, with a link to reset her password. She never remembers new passwords, so she decides to wait and try again from her laptop, where the password is stored in memory. Since she's still awake, she checks her messages. There's no new texts or calls, so she decides to pop her old SIM card back in and check it, since her phone had been buzzing like mad earlier. Her heart quickens. Maybe she'll have something from Hank.

She has twenty-three text messages, fifty emails, and nine voicemails on her old number. None from Hank. She skips the email, which she can check anywhere. Perusing the texts, all she sees are expressions of shock and support about the Coop. Rather than listen to the voicemails, she just scrolls through the names. Franklin from the insurance company. Returning her call, no doubt. Her mom. Boyd. Her mom again. And Merritt Fuller,

Gary's mother. She sends another change-of-number text around to her close contacts. Then she hits PLAY on the message from Merritt, but something wacky happens to her screen and it disappears before her eyes.

"What the hell?"

Easy come, easy go. She puts the new SIM card in and reboots the phone, then closes her eyes while she waits for it to come back up. Moments later, she's sound asleep, Louise snoring on the floor beside her.

Sometime later, her ringing phone wakes her. The remnants of a dream follow her from sleep. Something about Lumpy. By the time she fumbles for the phone and answers, the dream is nothing but a vague impression. Caller ID announces Michele, but the phone stops ringing. She missed it. Michele had to be calling about lunch. Maggie is nauseous with hunger.

Before she can call Michele back, Lumpy's image pops into her mind again. Why is she dreaming about him? She tries to remember details, but nothing comes to her. She really wants to see him, to thank him for his help with the goats. It was odd that his truck was home yesterday but he wasn't, and that he didn't come to her mother's wedding thingy. Her throat closes. But it's especially odd that he didn't show up at the fire at the Coop. Lumpy listens to police scanners as a religion. He knows everything that happens in a five-county area *before* it happens.

Maybe that's the best confirmation that he's traveling. Only without telling Michele or her, when he's goat-sitting? No, it doesn't make sense. Besides, he hasn't answered her texts. Notwithstanding he usually does his answering in person, he never ignores her unless he's completely out of range.

The phone rings again.

She answers quickly. "Michele?"

Static crackles in Maggie's ear. In between spurts, Michele's voice is recognizable even if not decipherable.

"Where are you guys?"

Crackle—"pie"—crackle—"meet us"—crackle.

There are two nearby restaurants with Pie in the name. Royers Pie Haven in Round Top and the Pie Shack in Carmine. "Haven or Shack?"

"What?"

"Round Top or Carmine?"

"Can't"—crackle—"you."

"Text me."

"Me"—crackle—"Lee"—crackle—"Ava."

"Never mind." Maggie calculates the odds. Ava has the hots for the antique show, and that means Round Top. "I'll meet you there."

After the call, she hits her hair with a diffuser and smears in as much moisturizer as her skin can absorb, plus a smidge, but no makeup. She adds the oversized sunglasses that hide her singed brows and lashes. Her burns seem to be scabbing up, so she gives them a break from the bandages. She jumps into a second-skin denim minidress with bustier top and a lace vest, plus her favorite old boots. *Eat your heart out, Ava.*

As she trots toward the door, mulling whether she'll get pie or quiche— or both—at the Pie Haven, Louise chases after her. "You. Stay with Gertrude."

The dog's eyes accuse her of betrayal, but Maggie resists them. She shuts the dogs inside, then goes for Bess. The temperature is slightly less African today, so she's not sweating when she gets to the truck. She points it toward Round Top, putting the pedal down hard. The wind through the windows dries her hair the rest of the way. She parks in front of the Humble Donkey store in Henkel Square half an hour after her spotty call with Michele. She glances at her phone before she gets out. Texts from Michele.

Royers Pie Haven in Round Top. Bad news. We ran into Leslie here, and she's attached herself to me. I'm sorry. But can I get you coffee, quiche, and junkberry?

Michele knows her well. There's no way Maggie will meet them with Leslie there. Ava's already a big enough test.

A loud slap on the back end of the truck makes her jump in her seat.

"Maggie." Rashidi grins through the passenger window.

Collin's form appears behind him with his face just out of the frame.

Maggie slaps Rashidi a high five. "If it isn't the middleweight boxing champion of Lee County."

"Don't mess with my girls."

Collin peeks over his shoulder. "As a sworn peace officer, I'll pretend I don't hear the two of you discussing criminal battery."

Rashidi laughs. "You meeting Michele and Ava?"

Maggie says, "I was. But my psycho-renter Leslie's joined up with them. No offense, Collin, but Ava was all I could handle. Leslie puts it over the edge."

Collin leans in. "Don't tell her I said so, but Ava's all I can handle, too. Eat with us. Where are we going, Rashidi?"

"Teague's Tavern."

"Hell yeah." She isn't in the mood for pie anyway, or so she tells herself. Who's she kidding, though? She's always in the mood for pie.

Maggie texts Michele back: *No can do on Leslie. Love you, my older and kinder new big sis. Lunching with the guys instead, then on to Hades.*

She doesn't wait for the reply.

TWENTY-THREE

In the mood to spice things up, Maggie orders blackened shrimp and cheese grits when the waiter drops off a jalapeno deviled eggs appetizer for her and Collin, which Rashidi—a Rastafarian—is foregoing. She licks her fingers and looks around. She'd requested their table. Pub-height with stools, in the bar area. It gives her a good view of the door, easy access to the bathrooms, and a direct line of sight with the bartender, in case of emergency.

"The artwork in here is eclectic," Collin says, then pops an egg in his mouth. He points at the trophy mount of a longhorn bull with a twist. It's covered in vibrant upholstery fabric and fringe. On the opposite wall, a donkey stares back with a slightly Picasso attitude from an enormous canvas.

"The food's eclectic, too," Rashidi answers.

"How did you get off on a Monday, Rashidi?" Maggie says.

"I worked this morning. But I don't have any appointments this afternoon, so I'm giving Collin a break from shopping."

"My estrogen production went into overdrive," Collin says. "Balls shriveled up, and I think I'm wearing a C cup."

"Hey, I hear you need me to follow you in to drop your truck at the Ford place? Michele said you need the air conditioner fixed."

She had told Michele that. But she realizes she needs the truck for the hard work ahead of her at the Coop and in the barn. She'd smelled a hint of dog puke on the way to Round Top, though. Remnants of Louise's sickness driving home from Wyoming. She'd have to clean the interior herself, ASAP. "I've been rethinking that. I need Bess to make hauls to the dump this week now."

"Right. We'll come help you. In the evenings."

"You've got guests."

Collin says, "Fine. Talk about me like I'm not even here. I'll forgive you if you'll tell Ava I'm required to help you this afternoon."

"I'm not getting in the middle of anything with Ava. Self-preservation."

"Always smart with her. But let me tell you a secret. That video Emily sent Ava? It really knocked her for a loop. She doesn't like being showed up. But she does like making money, and honestly, your video was the best thing since sliced bread for that."

Maggie nods. "I would have felt the same." Then she rolls her eyes. "But I'll tell you a secret. I think Ava writes catchy tunes. And for some reason, Emily knew better than to send that video to me. I hate it." Like she hates that someone in that group of Amarillo friends talked to the media about her.

Rashidi puts a finger to his lips. "By the way, Collin lost a fiancée over Emily once. We try not to talk about her in front of Ava."

"Emily or the fiancée?"

Collin signals for the waiter. "Either one, if I want to keep my nads."

A squeaky-clean-looking twenty-something appears. Not the one who'd taken their order. "Yes, sir?"

"Shiner, please."

"Of course. For you, miss?"

Maggie wasn't going to order a drink, but how can she resist a young person who doesn't call her ma'am? "Balcones, on the rocks." She only feels guilty for a second. She hadn't promised Michele she wouldn't drink today. Only suggested it wasn't planned at the time.

"Let me check if we have that."

"You do. Unless you're out. In which case, I'll take Jack in its place."

"And you, sir?"

Rashidi shakes his head. "I'm good with my ginger ale."

When the waiter leaves, Maggie turns to Collin. "I'll bite. How did you lose a fiancée over Emily?"

Collin blows a raspberry. "I was a drunken idiot. I had a crush on Emily all during her first marriage. By the time she got a divorce, I was engaged. I declared myself to Emily anyway—or hit on her, or whatever—and my fiancée, Tamara, saw the whole thing. Emily turned me down flat, by the way. The rest is history."

"Man, you blew that one."

"No complaints. Every woman I've ever known fades in comparison to Ava. The real story is how I can like this joker so much when he used to live with my woman." Collin slugs Rashidi in the arm playfully.

Maggie laughs. "My God. It's like incest around here."

The waiter returns with their drinks. "Would you like a chilled glass, sir?"

Collin takes the bottle. "Nah, why ruin perfection?"

Maggie holds her nose in the mouth of the whiskey glass and swirls the rich mahogany Balcones. The strong fruity smell reminds her of bananas.

Rashidi says, "Michele said it went well this morning, Maggie."

She savors a sip of the whiskey in her mouth. Buttery, like toast and orange marmalade. As she swallows, the flavor turns to spicy caramel. "To say it like Michele would, *más o menos*."

"Much more than less," Collin says. "I'm a cop. You didn't get arrested, even though they like you for Gary's death. You had a good day."

"We'll see how good it ends up being after I spend the afternoon reclaiming my desecrated house and ruined store. I hope the insurance company continues being helpful. I wouldn't love me right now if I was them." She combs her fingers through her hair and is sorry she tried. The wind through Bess's windows had really done a number on it. "Proving my lost income opportunity from the fall antique show is going to be a daunting, depressing task."

An accent straight from the wrong side of the small-town Texas tracks whips Maggie's head around. "Well I'll be dipped in shit and rolled in bread crumbs. If it isn't Maggie Killian."

Rashidi's mouth drops. Collin grins ear to ear. Maggie closes her eyes for a split second and gathers herself. What are the odds she'd miss a call from Merritt and run into her in the same day?

She stands and holds out her arms. "Merritt Fuller. Sorry I missed your call earlier. Then my phone ate your voicemail."

"I don't have the foggiest idea what you're talking about." Gary's mother moves close enough to give Maggie a stiff hug while still making it obvious that she doesn't want to touch her. "Maggie. You remember my youngest daughter, Kelly?"

Maggie barely registers Merritt's nonsensical comment. She's too busy choking back surprise at seeing Kelly.

The bleach blonde in painted-on jeans and a tight Western-cut shirt, open to show young, firm cleavage, simpers at her. "Maggie."

"Kelly. Wow. You're all grown up."

"Have been for years now."

At seventeen, the girl is overstating her case a bit. "I heard you did backup with Gary this year. Congratulations."

"Yeah, well, that didn't last."

Maggie feels like she's stepped in a steaming pile of dog shit and can't get it off her shoe.

Merritt pats her daughter. "It's okay, sweet pea."

Kelly tosses her hair over her shoulder. "I'm going out on a tour of my own. And my single is higher than his on the charts. Or it was. Until he died."

Maggie pastes on a sorrowful expression to cover her distaste. "Merritt, I've been meaning to call. I'm so, so sorry about Gary."

"Why are you sorry? He got rid of you a long time ago, didn't he?"

Behind her, Rashidi sucks in a breath. Collin coughs into his hand. It comes out sounding a lot like *bitch*.

Maggie doesn't flinch. "Will there be a service?"

"Family and close friends only."

Maggie reaches for the back of her stool, digs her fingers into the wood. As hard as she's trying not to react to Merritt, she's not sure she can hold her tongue much longer. "Great. When and where?"

Kelly's smile is smug. "Let me spell it out for you, Maggie." She raises her voice and speaks slowly. "You're not invited."

Merritt holds up a hand. "Kelly, enough." To Maggie she says, "I got a call from the fire marshal who's investigating the fire."

"I tried to get in, to get to him. I was too late."

"That's not—"

"He loved you so much. And he was a great guy. Even if we weren't together anymore, I still thought the world of him."

"I didn't—"

"I would have called. I should have. Things here got crazy and someone burned down my shop and there was a body inside. But I've been thinking about you all. I'm so sorry for your loss."

"Maggie, I don't want to hear this."

A loud humming noise starts in Maggie's ears. "Just tell me where and when it will be."

"You're a suspect in my son's murder."

"But you know I would never harm Gary."

"Maybe. I hope so."

The lump that forms in Maggie's throat grows until it blocks off her breath. She can't swallow it down, can't speak. She's uninvited to Gary's funeral. She may not have loved him, but he's been a big part of her life. His death is a huge loss to her. She works her jaw until her throat relaxes and the lump moves out of the way. "Fine. I'll stay away."

Kelly pops a hip. "Good. Don't make me tell you again."

"Hey, Kelly." Maggie leans in and whispers into the blonde's ear. "How's it feel to be a no-talent slut who'll never amount to anything now that her big brother isn't around?"

"You bitch." Kelly hauls back to slap Maggie.

Maggie catches the younger woman's arm in midair and mimics the accent of the two women. "Let me save you from splitting your pants and showing us all your religion." She smiles at Merritt. "So nice seeing you two. Again, my condolences." When she feels Kelly's arm relax, she lets it drop.

Merritt and Kelly glare at her. A wide-eyed waiter walks up carrying a loaded tray above his shoulder.

"Y'all skedaddle now. I won't tell anyone about Kelly's hissy fit."

Kelly huffs, but Merritt gives her a push and the two women walk to a booth on the far side of the bar. Two men are waiting for them there. Maggie doesn't want to care, but when she realizes who they are, she can't help it.

Tom Clarke and Thorn Gibbons. Together. Meeting Mama and Daughter Fuller.

Still in a redneck voice, Maggie sinks into her chair and says, "Butter my butt and call me a biscuit."

Collin snorts. "What the hell was that about?"

Maggie slams her Balcones, no longer caring about its nose, taste, or finish. "Gary's family. See 'em in that booth? They're cozied up with Gary's former manager and someone who is most definitely not Gary's buddy."

"What's going on?" Rashidi asks.

Maggie picks up her spoon, the better to dig into her shrimp and grits as soon as it's in front of her. "I don't have the slightest, but it can't be good."

"Ms. Killian," a familiar voice says.

She looks up. It's the cub reporter she'd seen a few days ago at the Valero station. She points across the bar. "There's your story."

The waiter puts her bowl in front of her. Maggie pounces, her spoon in attack mode.

The reporter looks in the direction she pointed, looks harder. Then recognition sweeps across his face. He lifts his phone and points the camera lens at the foursome.

Maggie blows on a spoonful of the hot shrimp and grits. "You're welcome."

TWENTY-FOUR

Maggie returns to Michele's for Louise and her things.

As she unlocks the front door, she finds herself talking aloud. "If you're out there, Gary, you know I didn't hurt you. Would never hurt you. I will always miss you. We had some good times. And I'm not upset with your mother. She loves you. Kelly? Well, someone needs to kick that girl's ass, and I'm only sorry you're not here to do it."

The sun beats down on her. She thinks she feels Gary's presence in the warmth. Live, his voice was like sitting on a warm, tumbling dryer, rubbing worn flannel against your cheek. Recording flattened it, took out some of the texture and channels. It was still nice, and it served him well, but she loved the warmth of Gary's live voice. The door swings open and the dogs greet her. She pats them, but keeps walking and talking to Gary like he's in the house with her.

"I wish you could tell me who did this to you. Hell, to us, Gary."

Gary doesn't answer, of course. She hadn't really thought he would, but it would have been nice.

Inside the house, she piles straps on her arm. A duffel bag. Her hobo bag. A laptop case. Her Martin case. With the other arm she takes the handle of her suitcase and rolls it with her to the door.

Gertrude makes a pitiful sound when Maggie closes her in the house alone. Louise doesn't give her best friend a second glance. She leaps in circles, then chases her tail until she collapses by the truck.

"It's not nice to gloat in front of Gertrude."

Louise grins up at her like a drunk college kid on spring break. Maggie tosses the duffel, guitar case, and suitcase into the truck bed. She looks over the side as they land in goat poop.

Bad call.

But it's too late now. After loading the dog and smaller bags into the cab, Maggie drives toward what's left of the Coop. She doesn't even lower the windows to let the heat out. Suffering is life, life is suffering. What's the lack of an air conditioner on top of everything else?

She rubs one eye with a fist, then the other eye, exhausted from the month, the night before, and the hard morning. When she'd finally fallen into bed after the fire at the Coop, she'd alternated between thoughts of her ruined shop and ruined love life. Wondered where Hank is. If he's gone back to Sheila or is still MIA. Damn him. He can't even stay out of her head long enough for her to properly mourn the loss of a friend and the loss of the Coop.

The truck takes the bumps in the dirt road like a downhill sled on a field of boulders. The jolts keep Maggie awake, but she can't wait to sleep in her own bed. She'd stashed her favorite sheets away at the bottom of her cedar chest, where they'd be waiting for her when she returned. *Dear God, don't let Leslie have found them.* But thinking about her sheets does funny things to her heart. She hadn't put them there to keep them fresh for herself. Her top-secret plan was to bring Hank back to Texas with her. She'd sprayed the sheets with her perfume before putting them away. Imagined the two of them showering off after the long drive from Wyoming. Pulling the sweet-smelling sheets from the chest, the scent wafting in the air as she dressed the bed. Slipping into the sheets together, their bodies touching, his skin setting hers on fire, she not caring how tired she was from the drive, needing him right then. Right that second.

"Fuck it." She picks up her phone and punches Hank's number in by memory. It rings four times. Then it goes to voicemail. She hangs up on it, then steers onto the county road with one hand. She voice-records a text with Siri's help and sends it.

Hank, this is Maggie. I hear you're AWOL. I'm worried. Call me. I'll pick up this time.

She hangs up and blows wisps of hair off her forehead. Unsettling. Unsatisfactory. And unwise. She'd just contacted the one person on her new number that she'd changed it to avoid. *Idiotic, Maggie.*

But she couldn't help it. It's been a full day since Gene phoned her. If she doesn't hear back from Hank within an hour, maybe she'll text Gene. Let him know she tried. Ask if Hank's shown back up at the ranch.

Or at Sheila's.

Maggie may love him, but he's someone else's fiancé now. She can help find him. But she can't have him. She has to remember that.

A noxious odor fills the cab.

Maggie rolls down her window with the crank handle. She glares at Louise. "You suck."

Louise wags her tail so hard it's like someone's rapping on the passenger door.

"And just so you know, it also sucks to be in love. I don't recommend it." Louise cocks her head.

"It's true. I've been in love with Hank my entire adult life, and we've been together a grand total of less than one week of it." She leans out the window and pounds her hand against the outside of the door, screaming, "Fuck my life. It fucking sucks. Motherfucker."

Louise puts her head on her paws. Maggie doesn't feel any better.

Neither does driving up to the dismal remains of Flown the Coop. The complex is like a law enforcement car show at the moment. Vehicles from two counties in multiple branches of their respective emergency response. And news crews. Unfortunately, Leslie's sedan is still there, too. Maggie parks outside the crime scene tape. She grabs a ball cap and sunglasses from her bag and puts them on, then checks the time on her phone. It's nearly noon. Checkout time was eleven.

"I'm going to kill her."

Louise jumps to her feet, ready to rumble with her.

"I've got to do this alone." She shuts the dog in the truck, windows down.

Louise frames herself in the open window, standing tall with her head out.

Maggie keeps her eyes averted from the county personnel and the painful sight of the ruined gray heap of her former store. She marches to her home and knocks authoritatively.

Leslie opens the door with a bright smile that drops immediately to a death mask. "What now?"

"Nearly noon. Checkout time has passed. I need in. You need to be out."

"You're not very good at this rental thing, are you?"

"Takes one to know one."

"I've decided to extend my stay."

"Glad you like Giddings. Now, move aside and I'll help you with your bags on your way to your new digs."

"No, I've decided to stay here."

"This isn't a hotel. This is a private home. Mine. And it's not available. Not for another night, and not to purchase, so you can quit telling people you've bought it." Maggie catches the brief flicker of surprise that crosses Leslie's face. "Yes, I've heard all about it. And it's not for sale."

Leslie's mouth creeps into a smile. She slams the door in Maggie's face.

"Open this door. Right now." Maggie bangs with her knuckles, then pounds with her palm. "Open the damn door, Leslie."

Louise lets loose a cacophony of barks.

Inside, the house is deathly quiet.

"Son of a bitch." Maggie tries the knob. It's locked. She gets out her key and tries it in the lock, but it won't turn. "What the hell?" She flips the key over and tries again, but it still doesn't work. She repeats the process unsuccessfully with the deadbolt. She runs to the back door, Louise's racket following her. The key doesn't turn the lock in the back either.

"No. Fucking. Way."

"May I help you, ma'am?" A deputy has come around the house. Her hand is on a gun on her hip.

Maggie doesn't recognize her. "Oh, how I wish you could."

"You need to move along now. We're working an active crime scene here."

"It's my house. No one's told me anything other than my store burned down and a body was found in it. How does that make it a crime scene?"

"It's being treated as potential arson and murder."

"Great. Thanks, Lee County, for the heads-up. Unfortunately, I can't get my renter to leave. She's overstayed her lease and changed the locks on my house."

"I'm sorry to hear that, ma'am. If that's true, you're welcome to start eviction proceedings at our offices."

"Can you take a complaint from me now?"

"No, ma'am."

"But aren't you with Lee County?"

"Yes, but we have a process."

"My life is in shambles. I've lost my business. I can't get back into my home. And your only response is that you have a process?"

"I'm sorry, ma'am."

"So am I." Maggie stomps through the grass that needs mowing in her side yard back to her truck. "And stop calling me ma'am. I'm no older than you. I'm not your damn grandmother."

She slams the door and sprays gravel on a Lee County Sheriff's Department Tahoe as she leaves.

TWENTY-FIVE

Maggie blows in under a good head of steam when she gets back to Nowheresville. Michele, Rashidi, Ava, and Collin are drinking mimosas and eating bagels and lox. *Bagels and lox. In the middle of the afternoon in the middle of nowhere, Texas.*

"Look what we found at a vendor for the antique show," Michele says.

Maggie stomps to the table, grabs Michele's mimosa, and downs it. "That bitch changed the locks. She won't leave. Then I got chased away by a deputy with a peashooter, who was no help whatsoever."

"Whoa, who? What?" Michele is on her feet.

Ava puts a hand over her mouth.

"You think this is funny?" Maggie points at her. "Five people have died around me in the last week, counting the corpse in my store last night. My so-called friends are leaking information to People.com. They're calling me a black widow and libeling me to the entire universe." Maggie throws Michele a look. "And you know my money is on Wallace for that one."

Michele's face is pained. "We don't know that."

"*We* might not, but *I* do." Maggie directs her wrath back at Ava. "And you. You might be a publicity whore, but I'm not."

"Hey, now, watch how you're throwing that word around." Ava crosses her arms.

"I'm a very private person. My heart is broken, my livelihood is destroyed, the cops are after me, and I can't get back into my own home. This is the *opposite* of funny."

Ava raises both hands. "I wasn't laughing. I promise. What's happening to you makes me sick."

"Damn." Collin puts a hand on Ava's shoulder. "This sucks big-time, Maggie."

Rashidi hands Maggie his mimosa.

"Thank you." She downs his, too.

Michele takes Maggie's hand. "Come into my office. We'll get her charged with trespassing."

"I tried that, and the deputy at my house wouldn't help me." Maggie allows herself to be led. "Can they haul her off my place? And what about the locks?"

"Possibly. Probably. Maybe. All right, I don't know." Michele shuts the French doors behind them and pulls out her phone. "But the sooner we start, the better." She pushes something on the screen. "Sadly, I have the sheriff's department on speed dial."

It is sad, but familiar. "You and me both."

Michele holds up a finger. "Hello. I need to speak to Junior. Sure, I'll hold." She hits the screen and sets the phone down.

After a few seconds of silence, Maggie flops into the chair in front of her. Louise paws at the French doors.

"No," Maggie says, shaking her finger at the dog.

Louise flops to the floor with a long-suffering sigh.

"Hello?" Junior's voice fills the room.

"Junior. It's Michele Lopez Hanson."

"Ma'am. Long time no talk to."

"It's your lucky day. You've got Maggie on, too."

He doesn't reply, his silence a vacuum of sound.

"Listen, we've got a problem. Maggie went to reclaim her house from her vacation renter, and the woman has changed the locks and won't let her in."

"Shit."

"Yeah. We have a contract past its end date, multiple verbal confirmations of the terms, and today a very heated and clear instruction to vacate the premises at the agreed-upon time. We need her charged with trespassing, and arrested and removed from the property. And Maggie needs in her house."

"Goddammit."

"That's not a very professional response. How about 'No problem, Michele'?"

"This is really bad timing."

Maggie raises her voice to be sure the speaker catches it. "Tell me about it."

"Seriously, there's, um, stuff, um, going on."

"What kind of stuff?" Michele asks.

"Evidence stuff. Relating to Gary's case."

"Well, that case is in Fayette County and has nothing to do with this case in Lee County."

There's a long silence before Junior says, "Can you bring in the paperwork?"

"How about you meet us with it?"

"Goddammit." His voice is sounding more resigned.

"So you said. See you soon." Michele presses the screen to end the call and shakes her head at Maggie. "Methinks something is going on here."

Maggie doesn't disagree. "What is it?"

"I don't know yet. But I have a feeling neither one of us is going to like it."

TWENTY-SIX

While the minutes tick by without Junior's arrival—or return visit, if the morning meeting with Karen and Boland is to be counted—Maggie checks her phone. She's hoping to hear from Hank. There's nothing from him, but she does have a message from Boyd.

Got a call from a People.com reporter. They want to do a piece about us to coincide with Michele's movie premiere. Joint interview?

Her finger hovers. The interview would help Boyd's political campaign and Michele's book and movie ticket sales. But it would hurt Maggie's own potential libel suit. Besides, she wants her star lower in the sky, now more than ever.

She deletes the text. "Has Junior sent an update?"

"Not since last time you asked. I'm emailing things to him, so he comes with the right paperwork."

"He hasn't left yet?"

"Hush, or he never will. Go do something and quit bothering me."

Maggie trolls the liquor cabinet. Gives the dogs some water. Eyes the liquor cabinet again. Checks her phone to make sure the ringer is on.

She pokes her head back into Michele's office. "I'm going for a walk."

"It's ninety degrees out there. Or more."

"I can't sit here." Waiting for Junior, worrying about her home, her future, and Hank—it's killing her.

"Junior should be here within an hour."

Maggie calls for the dogs. She tucks a cold water bottle under her arm, then goes to the front door. Both dogs shrink back.

"What? Don't like it out there in the heat of the day? Prefer the air-conditioning, little princesses?"

Gertrude tiptoes to Michele's office. Louise wags her tail but won't budge.

"Wimps." Maggie leaves without them.

First she heads to the goat pen. The goats are lying down in the shade. They don't get up.

"You guys, too?"

Omaha flicks his tail. Nebraska closes his eyes. They've eaten everything green inside their fence. She refills their feed and changes out their water. Cold, fresh water tastes so much better in the heat, something her father had ingrained in her as a child with her 4-H animals.

"Treat them like you want to be treated, Maggie. They're God's creatures, too," he'd told her.

"I'd want to go in the house," she'd replied.

"So give them the next best thing."

She'd cracked ice trays into the stock tank for her lambs in the worst of the heat after their conversation. That had been so long ago. A lifetime. She was a different person then. One who'd left her 4-H past behind for Nashville. Until two orphaned goat kids fell into her lap. They'd taken her back two decades to memories of her father. Good ones. Not the angry man who couldn't relate to his rebellious teenage daughter. Or the devout Lutheran worried for Maggie's eternal soul. But the kind farmer who passed respect and love for animals down a generation. The firefighter who risked his life to help others.

Unexpected tears sting her eyes. She hasn't cried for that old bastard in as long as she can remember. She swipes them away. She's not going to start now. By her mid-teens, he was a different person. Judgmental. Authoritarian. Yes, she'd run away, but when she came home to visit, he hadn't welcomed her. Because of his hardened heart, she hadn't repaired her relationship with her mom until after he passed.

She'd hurt him by leaving, Maggie knows. But pain is a two-way street with potholes big enough to swallow the John Deere tractor he used to drive.

She calls goodbye to the unimpressed goats.

She walks into the trees, seeking shade since there's no breeze. Why is she thinking about her dad now? It takes a few minutes before the answer hits her. She's at a crossroads. Again. Her reinvented life has caved in on itself. He would be pushing her for decisions, to finally make something of herself more pleasing to God. And even beyond the grave, he's found a way to be here doing it again.

"I'm fine, Daddy."

He'd criticize her distance from the church. The absence of a husband and kids. The profession, the career, or even a job—or lack thereof—wouldn't bother him as much. He wanted her to live a life of piety, a biblical life.

"Never going to happen, old man."

The funny thing is, her tears well up again at the thought. The image that comes into her mind is Hank. His ranch in Wyoming. The Bighorn Mountains casting a long evening shadow over the cabin in the foothills and overlooking the barns, stables, pens, and livestock. Horses, all ages, in every color, serene in the tall buffalo grass. Some of them superstars of the bucking horse circuit, but there on the ranch, just part of the herd. Cattle, the massive bulls separated from the rest, destined for rodeo greatness. At dusk, white-tailed deer appearing out of gulches, gullies, and trees, grazing with the livestock. Antelope crouching and crawling under the fences. Lily, the horse she'd come to think of as hers in one short week, nickering to be fed. The hands, Gene, and the family at the long dinner table in the main house, Hank's mother chastising someone, everyone. Maggie actually smiles remembering the sharp tongue on the old woman in the tiny body. Alzheimer's didn't keep her from ruling that roost.

Maybe some of the things her father wanted for her, that her mother wants for her now, aren't so bad. But they aren't ever going to be hers. Hank and Sheila will have a baby within a year, and a yard full of rug rats in five. Sheila will ride Lily. And Maggie will move on, without Hank. Without love, she's sure, because she knows now Hank was it for her. She'll find something to occupy herself. To sustain herself. Or maybe she won't. Maybe she'll sell the Andy Warhol and vintage Jaguar and travel the world.

As she's walking the fence line of Michele's property closest to the road, a big red truck pulls to a stop across the strands of wire from her. She double-takes. It looks like the truck Gary used to drive. A small woman jumps out, leaving the motor running.

"Merritt, what are you doing out here?"

Gary's mother comes to the fence. "We need to talk."

Her tone isn't warm and friendly, but then, her son just died. Maggie gets it. Merritt needs someone to blame for her pain. Merritt had raised

Gary and his siblings in a trailer. His father cut and run after Kelly was born and didn't surface again until Gary hit the big time. Gary didn't give him the time of day. But he doted on his mother. Built her a nice house and set up a trust fund for her. Even if Merritt hadn't ever been crazy about Maggie, Gary would want Maggie to be nice to her now. Nicer than the woman has been to her.

"Okay. But you didn't seem to want to earlier. At Teague's."

"I couldn't. Not in front of Kelly and the others."

"You *did* call me this morning, didn't you?"

"I did. And I tried to again after lunch."

"Oh shit. I changed my phone number today. Sorry." The conversation feels awkward across a fence. Maggie separates the barbed-wire strands and ducks between them, lifting her legs carefully to avoid being scratched. "Go on, then."

Merritt hugs herself. "Gary named me as the executor in his will."

"Makes sense." Maggie uncaps her water bottle. It's not cold anymore.

"Something real strange happened this morning. I met with Gary's financial advisor and this banker fella. They told me that Gary is nearly broke. That ain't like him."

"No, it isn't."

"He's got some cash, but he'd signed away a bunch of his investment accounts."

"Do they know why?" Maggie takes a swig from her bottle.

"No. But they told me they'd get to the bottom of it."

"I'm so sorry."

"That's why I called you, right after. I figured if anybody knew about it, it would be you."

"I wish I did."

"Me and Kelly met Gary's manager for lunch. Him and Kelly's boyfriend, Thorn. Tom is manager for both of them now. He's been real good to Kelly."

Maggie's tongue itches to ask whether Merritt thinks it's wise to let Kelly date a much older man like Thorn. Maggie had been down that road in her career. It was an ugly and dangerous one. But she doesn't want to risk the well of Merritt's information drying up, so instead she just says, "I saw."

"I told them about me being executor and Gary being broke and all. Tom pulled out this paper. He said I needed to know about it."

"What was it?"

"An investment paper. From Gary. Tom said Gary put money in their company."

"Whose?"

"His and Thorn's. Clarkethorn Tour Promoters."

"How much?"

"Half a million dollars."

Maggie drops her water bottle. "That's hard to believe." She squats and retrieves it.

"It didn't sit right with me. Which is why I came straight to talk to you."

"I'm glad you did. Gary would never have brought Thorn in on his tours. And he was way past the point of needing to invest in his own tours."

Merritt closes her eyes. "It wasn't for Gary's tours. It was for the one for Thorn and Kelly."

Maggie shields her eyes from the afternoon sun. "Merritt, he wouldn't have backed Thorn."

"But Kelly?"

"Do you really believe Gary would have sent Kelly on a tour with Thorn at this stage in her career?"

Merritt's forehead creases. "He wanted to help her."

"By teaching her the ropes. Giving her a start. Introducing her to people. Mentoring her. Protecting her. Not by throwing her to the wolves before she's ready. She's only a kid."

"Kelly's got talent."

"Sure she does, or Gary wouldn't have brought her on."

"He told you all this?"

"Yes. When he asked what my advice was, since I was a seventeen-year-old girl in the business once upon a time, too."

Understanding dawns in Merritt's eyes. "Oh. I'd forgotten about that."

"Yeah. It was rough. He didn't want that for her. I just wish he hadn't fired her. He didn't ask my advice about that."

"Oh, he didn't fire her. She quit."

Maggie's breath catches. Merritt is full of surprises. "What?"

"She and Thorn hooked up. And then Tom got that song for her. And Thorn and Tom invited her on the tour." Merritt bites her lip. "You're right. Gary didn't want her doing none of it. So she quit. And it broke his heart."

"I'm sorry." Maggie sighs. "There's something else you need to know. Gary was about to fire Tom."

"Why do you think that?"

"Gary told me so the night before he died. And it's all making sense now. He called Tom a thief and said that after he fired him, Tom could spend all his time on his hotshot new clients."

Merritt may have grown up poor and country, but she's nobody's fool. "Oh, Maggie. The tour money. Tom and Thorn. Maybe they stole it. Maybe it wasn't an investment."

"That's what I'm thinking. And you know what else I think?"

"What?"

"That getting fired because you're caught stealing half a million dollars is a pretty good motive for murder." Maggie's heart hurts for Gary and his mother, but she feels optimism for the first time in days. This could be her break. It could get Fayette County looking in the right direction instead of at her.

Merritt presses a fist to her mouth. "I don't know what to do."

Maggie pulls Gary's mother to her and hugs her tight. "Whatever you do, you've got to be very, very careful about it. Tom and Thorn have half a million reasons to protect themselves. Reasons Fayette County needs to know about, and fast. You've got to take this to the sheriff."

"Tom and Thorn told me that you might say things about them that aren't true. They said I can't trust a junkie."

Maggie would laugh if it weren't so serious. *Junker, not junkie.* "I hope you know I'm not lying to you. I cared about Gary."

She has a chilling thought. Why would Tom and Thorn be warning Merritt off her? Do they see her as a threat? Damn that TMZ article and damn Wallace. Tom and Thorn and the whole world know she and Gary talked before his death. And the two men had been probing her about what Gary had told her. *Shit.* They think she knows about their embezzlement. Maybe it's not a coincidence that someone torched her store after burning down Gary's house. Sweat trickles down her chest, between her breasts and into her belly button.

Merritt pulls away. Her eyes are dazed. "Let me think on it." She starts walking back to Gary's truck. She stops halfway there. "When all this is over, let's you and me look at old pictures and listen to Gary's music together. Lift a glass in his honor."

Maggie hides her distress and smiles at Merritt. "More like drink a twelve-pack."

Gary's mother laughs, but it changes quickly to weeping. Wiping her eyes, she says, "I'm sorry, Maggie." Then she gets in the truck and drives away.

Maggie crawls back through the fence. The afternoon is still and quiet without the loud engine. The sun is fierce. She ducks back under the strip of trees between the fence and Michele's driveway. She's completely alone. Her skin crawls, and she looks for Tom and Thorn behind every tree. She has to go tell Michele about what Merritt told her so they can call the cops. She can't wait for Merritt to do it. Hell, she can't trust Merritt to do it at all. Because if she was in Merritt's shoes, she'd be protecting her daughter, and there's no way this is going down without taking some of Kelly's ass with it.

Her phone rings. "Come on, Junior." She answers, expecting Michele, excited to share what she learned from Merritt. "Tell me something good."

"Maggie?" The voice isn't Michele's. It's younger. The accent isn't Texan.

"You've got her."

"You'd better not have my fiancé."

Maggie's brain doesn't connect the dots for several seconds. Then the answer is there with a cymbal crash. *Hank's fiancée.* "Sheila?"

"You know damn well it is."

"Sorry. I didn't—never mind." Sheila won't believe her, and it doesn't matter. But Maggie isn't going to cow to her. "Come again? What's the matter?"

"Don't play dumb with me. Where's Hank?"

"I have no idea. I haven't seen him or talked to him."

Sheila is silent.

Maggie's mind tortures her with an image of the tall blonde woman coming out of Hank's hospital room in Wyoming. Her words had been a knife stab to Maggie's heart. "Hank and I are getting married! My Hanky Panky's going to be a daddy!" She imagines their future family dinners, the kids Sheila teaches, and her bright-eyed Sunday schoolers. Bile rises from Maggie's stomach.

She pushes Sheila's image away, but it's replaced by another. Hank's face. Weather beaten. Eyes twinkling. The dimples in his cheeks when he'd smiled at her from the back of his horse. A time jump jerks her back fifteen years. Hank in his chaps, jamming his hat on as he picks himself up out of the Cheyenne arena dirt and then hops onto the rails to avoid the horns of the angry bull he'd just ridden. The first meeting of their eyes, seconds later. Hank lifting his winner's buckle. Hank across a table in Wheatland, Wyoming. Hank kissing her in the seat of a borrowed truck. Hank cradling her face in the Buffalo Lodge in Chugwater, whispering her to sleep. Then time leaps forward again, to last week. Hank bleeding in the Wyoming dirt, shot with his own rifle. Her own crazed race to save him.

She pushes the images away, but it's too late. The pain is fresh, and she comes out of her reverie ready to fight. How dare Sheila treat her like this? Maggie hasn't done anything wrong. Isn't it bad enough Sheila stole the love of her life right out from under her by trapping the man?

Her voice is toxic. "If you're having trouble hanging on to your man, that's your problem, not mine."

"If you—"

Then Maggie realizes this call has come in on her new phone number. "How did you get this number, anyway?"

"It's not hard to look up the numbers he's texting and calling on his account. His stupid password is the same to everything."

Maggie knows that password. She used it for Wi-Fi at Piney Bottoms. Buffalo2002. The year they met, the name of the hotel where they spent their one night.

Sheila is still talking. "You called him today. And texted him."

"I'm not Hank's keeper. And I don't answer to you." Maggie ends the call. Her tank top is molded to her belly with sweat. Her chest is heaving. "Goddammit!" she screams.

A horn sounds from the direction of the house. Two taps. Honk-honk. Her phone rings with a call from Michele. She takes a deep breath. Rails against her rage and pain. Junior is here. It's time to go take her life back.

Past time.

TWENTY-SEVEN

"I've got something big to tell you about Gary," Maggie whispers to Michele as they file into the house behind Junior. "It's important."

"Shh. After he leaves," Michele replies, finger to lips. Then, louder, she says to Junior, "So tell us about the evidence issue at Gary's."

He keeps his eyes on his feet. "I'm here about the trespassing complaint. Nothing else."

Michele rolls her eyes at Maggie, but Junior doesn't say another word. The three of them congregate in Michele's office. An hour drags by as they fill out and, at Junior's insistence on "correcting errors," re-fill out documents, scanning and sending them back and forth to the sheriff's department and the county attorney.

Maggie finally snaps. "Daylight is wasting."

"Evictions are tricky," Junior explains.

"This is arresting a trespasser, actually, one who has done damage to the property." Michele pulls a thumb drive out of the printer, where she has scanned some documents. Again. "Private home vacation rentals are less tricky than long-term rentals."

"Maybe. But it's still pretty emotional. People get nasty. Nasty people are dangerous."

Maggie leans against the wall, arms crossed. "Admit it. Lee County doesn't want to help. You guys and Fayette County have a boner for me. After I've lived here as a model citizen and property-tax payer for ten years.

And grew up here as a member of St. Paul Lutheran. But suddenly you think I'm some crazed arsonist and killer."

A smile quirks the side of Michele's mouth. Both women watch Junior for his reaction.

His face goes red, like a beet cooking in a microwave, five seconds before it explodes all over the inside. "That has nothing to do with it."

"Doesn't it? Then why aren't we at my house already? This isn't complicated. I own that house, and you have the paperwork in front of you that proves she's trespassing."

Louise comes to stand by Maggie. Maggie reaches down automatically to pet her. The dog licks her hand.

"We need notice and an opportunity to vacate first."

"Which we can do, quite nice-like, when we get to my house, even though I did it two days ago, yesterday, and today already. But we can't do it from here." *Dumbass*, she wants to add, but doesn't.

Junior holds his hands up. "This is bigger than me, Maggie."

"You expect me to believe you, yet you refuse to tell me why."

Michele steps between them. "She has a valid point, Junior. It shouldn't be bigger than you. It should be a simple matter of enforcing the rights of county residents. No matter who they are. Maggie hasn't been proven guilty of anything. Whatever happened to presumed innocence? She has the full rights of any citizen in this county. No more, but certainly no less." She lifts her phone. "I'm sorry, but I'm going to have to escalate this."

Junior hitches up pants that have sagged low over his nonexistent butt, saved only by his bony hips. "What are you doing?"

"Calling Len," Michele says, referring to the county attorney. She's already pressed his number in her contacts and has the phone to her ear.

"No. Don't call him." Junior's lips continue moving as he paces over to look out the window.

Maggie is pretty sure he's praying.

Michele doesn't end the call. She holds up a finger. "This is Michele Lopez Hanson." Michele stops, listening. "No, I'm calling about something else. I have a Lee County deputy here with me, and I'd asked him to enforce a property owner's rights to get a trespasser off her property. We're having some trouble. May I speak to Len, please?" Again, she waits. "Len, Michele. I've got Junior here. I'm putting you on speaker."

She doesn't mention Maggie, but neither Maggie nor Junior interject the fact of her presence.

"Junior?" Len's voice is country smart. His undergrad degree is courtesy of a Texas Tech football scholarship, but his law degree from Tech came from an academic full ride.

"Hello, sir."

"What's the problem with the property?"

"It's not what, sir. It's who. Maggie Killian."

Papers shuffle, then there's a *clack-clack* like they've been straightened into a neat stack on the surface of a desk. "She owns the property in question?"

"Yes, sir. Her house. Where the fire was yesterday."

"And she has a trespasser?"

"A short-term vacation renter whose term is up. Maggie says she's given the renter verbal notice to vacate repeatedly and that the renter has stayed past the term of the rental agreement and is refusing to go."

"Michele, can't Maggie work this out without law enforcement?"

Michele's voice is huffy, with a trace of the Mexico she's never lived in. "What about that explanation makes you think she hasn't tried? The renter changed the locks today to keep Maggie out and told her she's unilaterally decided to extend her stay. Believe me, the last thing Maggie wants to do is contact any area law enforcement for help right now, not with how she's being treated by them. But we don't have any choice, unless you're suggesting she take the law into her own hands. Let me know if you're prepared to deputize Maggie and waive the consequences."

"Slow down. You have to understand, Michele. We're in the middle of a homicide investigation here. Two of them. And arson."

"Are you referring to the fire in Fayette County or the fire at Maggie's store?"

"Both."

"Last I checked, you don't work for Fayette County."

"You know what I mean."

"I'm sure I don't. When the fire marshal and Sheriff Boland were at my home this morning—and Junior—they didn't call either incident arson or murder. But we can solve all of that by focusing our conversation on Lee County. Better yet, let's keep it on trespassing."

Maggie can't hold it in any longer. "This is all such utter bullshit. I didn't do anything. I have information that—"

Len growls, "Is that Maggie?"

The smile on Michele's face makes it into her voice. "Surprise, Len."

"Nice of you guys to tell me she was there."

"You didn't ask." Michele winks at Maggie.

Junior lowers his face into his hands. "Well, um—"

Michele doesn't yield the floor. "Let me make this simple for you, Len. There's nothing in your playbook that says a citizen under investigation loses her property rights. Every minute you delay is a violation of her civil rights."

"Her what?"

"You heard me."

"I don't follow."

"Then I'll give you a road map. Point A is where we're at now. Point B is I file a lawsuit against the county first thing in the morning. Point C is publicity, and Point D is a messy jury trial before the destination of Point E, your reelection campaign." Michele shoots Maggie a thumbs-up.

"There's no need—"

Michele pantomimes an explosion with her hands and fingers as she mouths "Boom" to Maggie, then points at her.

Maggie nods. "Hang up, Michele. I've heard enough. File the lawsuit."

"Stop," Len shouts. "Fine. Junior, get the trespasser out. Maggie, if you cross that barricade or do anything to tamper with evidence, so help me, we'll—"

Maggie's voice sizzles. "I can't tamper with evidence that doesn't exist, and it sure isn't going to be at the house I haven't been able to enter in two weeks, which, by the way, is not barricaded."

Michele smiles, then draws a line across her throat at Maggie. "We have what we need here. Thanks for doing business, Len."

"Whatever." He hangs up.

"Go," Michele says to Junior.

Maggie points at him. "You going to make any more problems for me on this?"

"No. I'll give you a ride."

Maggie throws her words over her shoulder as she spins and stomps out, Louise scampering after her with hindquarters tucked. "No way in hell. I'll meet you there." She shakes her finger at Louise. "Not you. You're staying here."

TWENTY-EIGHT

Maggie and Junior wait on the front porch of her house. Maggie is fuming, and Junior's eyes are down and away, careful not to make contact with the death rays shooting from hers.

He rings the bell and knocks again. "She won't answer."

"We'll see."

After he tries for the third time without success, he shouts. "Lee County Sheriff's Department. I'm with the homeowner, Maggie Killian. If this door is not opened within one minute, I'm entering by force with her authorization."

Something makes rustling noises and soft thuds inside. Junior leans his ear toward the curtained window pane in the door. At forty-five seconds, the door opens a few inches, displaying a security chain that is as new as the deadbolt locks.

"Leslie?"

"No."

Maggie's laugh is a near-hysterical cackle. "Right."

Junior adjusts his gun belt. "I'm told your name is Leslie DeWitt."

The woman Maggie knows as Leslie says, "I don't care what you've been told. That's not my name."

Maggie harrumphs. "Oh really? Well that's the name you used for our contract."

The woman's barely visible blue eyes narrow. "It's not my name."

Junior sighs. "Ma'am, whatever your name is, you need to leave. Now. This house belongs to Ms. Killian. She's told you that your contract is up and given you notice that you need to vacate the house."

"I have a signed lease."

Junior holds up the documents Michele gave him. "And the term of that lease is over."

"That's not what she said." A long finger points at Maggie.

Maggie shakes her head. "She is the biggest liar. Ever."

"I asked to stay, and you said I could."

"I told you to leave. Repeatedly."

"You said you'd pick up my check later." A check slips out the crack in the door.

Junior reaches for it and Maggie slaps his hand down. "Don't touch it. We never talked about a check."

"Assault of an officer," he whispers at her.

She glares at him and gestures to the door with a jerk of her head that doesn't move the hair sweated to her face.

Junior speaks to the door. "I need you to remove the chain so we can have a conversation out here on the porch."

"I'll do no such thing. You have no right to enter, and I don't know if you're who you say you are. I do know I'm scared of her."

Junior's lips move again and his head shakes like he's arguing with himself. Maggie steps on his toe and digs her heel in.

He jerks his foot away.

"She made unauthorized changes to the home by changing the locks."

Junior holds his badge up to the crack between door and frame.

Maggie jangles the chain. "And adding this. And God knows what else."

"I told this woman how scared I was after that fire and the dead body they found in her store. She told me I could change the locks so I'd feel safer."

Maggie looks up at the sky and grabs the hair above either ear. "Argh. It's all total crap."

"A word, Maggie?" Junior points at an oak tree in the yard. He walks over to the shade.

Maggie stomps after him. "What?"

"This isn't as straightforward as you led me to believe."

"Of course it's not straightforward. She's lying like a dog on a rug. She's also been going around town telling people I'm selling the house to her."

"Is that true?"

"Of course not! She's catfishing me. Stealing my life."

"It doesn't help your case."

"Do you see a for-sale sign out front? Come on."

"Can't you see it makes it sound like you're okay with her being there and are thinking about leaving?"

"Junior, it's not true. You have the paperwork, and what I've told you, which refutes that."

"It's your word against hers about the locks and the extension. And the sale."

A 2000-era Oldsmobile floats to a stop in the driveway. Maggie and Junior turn to it as one. Two doors open. Two sets of sensible shoes hit the ground, and two ladies with beauty-parlor-fresh hair climb out. Two doors close. Two sets of feet walk toward the house.

Maggie's voice is choked. "Oh Jesus. The church ladies. My mother's friends."

"Yoo-hoo, Maggie, hello!" Gray Bob calls to them, waggling her fingers. "Deputy."

Maggie pastes on a smile. "Hello, ladies."

Junior lifts a hand. "Ma'am. Ma'am."

Blue Hair stops at the bottom step. "How are you dear? I swear, I was just praying about you an hour ago."

"That's great. What can I do for you?"

"We're just dropping in to talk to Leslie about joining the church."

Junior shoots Maggie a long look.

Maggie smiles grimly. Leslie has said she's not Leslie. So she says, "*Leslie's* not here."

"That's her car."

"Yes, but *Leslie* definitely isn't here."

The ladies hem and haw, finally leaving with farewells and more promises to pray for Maggie, for the sake of her dear mother and departed father.

When they're gone, Maggie closes her eyes. Their visit makes her turn to prayer herself. *Dear God, please make this hell stop. Amen.*

Junior interrupts her confab with the big man. "Listen, I know you're upset. I know you want back in your house. But it's almost dinnertime. Can I get with the county attorney tonight and we do this first thing in the morning?"

"Really? *Really?*"

"If you'll just give the renter real clear notice that her permission to stay here is revoked—"

"Which I've done until I'm blue in the face."

"Work with me, Maggie. Revoke it, and let me hear you say that you did not give her permission to change the locks. I'll tell her I'll be back to arrest her tomorrow morning. I promise."

Maggie holds up a finger. She speed-dials her sister and updates her. "What do you think?"

"Sounds reasonable. I hesitate to say smart, even. Let's do this ultra-legal."

"I'm drinking heavily tonight."

"I release you from your promise to cut back, for one night only."

Maggie hangs up. Her words are barely a mutter, but loud enough for Junior to hear the acid in them. "If she's not out of here by eleven, there's a lawsuit against the county by noon."

"Understood."

"Then let's get this over with."

Junior follows Maggie back to the house to listen to her go through her lines, and Maggie reminds herself that Junior's dead body on her front steps won't help her cause.

TWENTY-NINE

Maggie needs to make a liquor store run in a bad way. It only takes her fifteen minutes to park, shop, and queue up in the checkout line at Stoney's.

The cashier is a pregnant woman with meth peg teeth. She mutters to herself as she rings it up. "Balcones. Single Malt. Two bottles."

"Can you special order a few bottles from a distillery in Wyoming for me?" Maggie asks, pulling out her wallet.

"You need to talk to the manager," she states in the form of a question. "He's in on Wednesdays. Two to four."

"How about leaving him a message?"

She gives Maggie her total and takes her credit card. "I'm just filling in."

Behind Maggie, two women are talking. She pays them no mind until she hears her name. Not addressed to her, but in their conversation about her. She gives up on passing a message to the manager through the cashier and turns to the women. She's immediately sorry she did when she discovers Gary's little sister and his skanky ex-lover.

Maggie sighs. "Hello, Kelly."

Kelly Fuller bats her eyes. "Maggie Killian. I didn't see you standing there. Did you see her, Jenny?"

The curvy redhead examines her nails. "See who?"

"So great that you found someone for a playdate, Kelly. You girls have fun."

"Oh, we will. It's hard not to when you're young and not going to jail for murdering my brother."

The cashier says, "Here's your credit card."

"Thanks. The blonde behind me is underage, by the way." Maggie shoves the card in her wallet.

"Bitch," Kelly says.

"Tell your mother I said hey." Maggie hustles out before she gives the girl the beatdown she's got coming.

When Maggie puts Bess in gear, she finds herself driving somewhere besides home. Lumpy's. It's past time for her to check on him, and it will only take a few minutes. His place is barely even out of the way.

When she reaches his property, his truck is parked at the house. She feels optimistic until two solid minutes of knocking convinces her he's not coming to the door. Calling the sheriff's department is out of the question for the obvious reason that they don't believe anything she tells them. Her next step is to look for Lumpy inside, but to do that, she'll have to break and enter. Lumpy doesn't believe in hidden keys. She decides to try one more thing before busting her way in. She'll just borrow his four-wheeler and make a quick circuit of the place to see if he's out working on fence or clearing brush or something. It will only take five minutes.

The four-wheeler is in the shed he uses for vehicles and sports gear. As she backs the utility vehicle out, she passes all his hunting and fishing gear, which look untouched. She starts her circuit of the property by riding his fence line. When she finishes the loop without finding any sign of him, she turns onto a trail that bisects his property perpendicularly. Halfway across, she sees a ladder on the ground, along with several pieces of plywood and two-by-fours. She parks the four-wheeler and cuts the engine.

A thready voice calls out, "About damn time."

"Lumpy?" Maggie looks around in all directions but doesn't see the big man.

"Up here."

Maggie cranes her neck up, then up some more.

Lumpy waves limply from high in a live oak.

"What the hell?"

"Would you mind putting that ladder against the tree? I'd really like to get down."

Maggie hurries for the ladder, shoving it around until it's in position. She spots Lumpy as he climbs down, ready to break his fall. The ladder creaks and groans under his bulk. As he steps off the last rung, he falls to his hands and knees. His hat topples into the dirt. He's a big man, even crumpled on the ground.

"Are you okay?"

He stands, brushing off his hat. His slow country accent is music to her ears. "Dehydrated. Hungry enough to eat a skunk. Tired. Weak like a newborn kitten. But I'm going to live. Help me over to the ride."

"Whew, you're ripe."

"Pardon me, ma'am, but there're no showers up there."

"I'm so glad I found you." Maggie props him on her shoulder. He's heavy, but he carries most of his own weight.

"Not as glad as I am." He climbs on the four-wheeler, making it look harder than it usually is. He scoots to the back to make room for Maggie.

"Did your ladder fall?"

"It did. But not without help."

THIRTY

Inside his stuffy house, Lumpy has a hasty shower, water and coffee—a lot of both—and two ham and cheese sandwiches thrown together by Maggie. Afterwards, he takes Maggie out to his porch swing, where he tells his story.

"I've been working on a new deer blind." He stands and hooks his thumbs in his suspenders, holding them away from his generous beer gut.

"You were too high."

"Are you going to let me tell my story or tell it for me, little lady?"

"Sorry." Maggie pushes off with her toes and starts the motion of the swing. It stirs a light breeze that fans the sweat on her brow.

"I'd been staging the ladder and materials out there, and Saturday I finally got some time to work on it. I was setting up a pulley system in the tree when I heard a woman's voice."

"Who?"

"I don't know, but she shouted 'Yoo-hoo,' and I waved to her. She was trespassing, but she was a purty little thing. Curvy. Nice, um, bosom."

"Bosom. Okay. Go on."

"I was sitting up on that high branch where you saw me when she walked to the ladder and knocked it to the ground, pretty as you please."

"What in God's name would she do that for?"

"She didn't bother explaining, other than to say I should be more careful who I pal around with. Then she waved again and took off. But that's a tall tree, as you noticed, and I was so high I had a view back to the house. The little vixen took some wire cutters to the goat panels in the pasture where I was keeping Omaha and Nebraska."

"Which I fixed. The goats are at Michele's now. But I don't get it." Suddenly, though, she thinks she might. "What did you say she looks like?"

"Jessica Rabbit."

Maggie laughs. "You were hallucinating, then?"

"No, she's a curvy redhead. Pretty young one."

Bingo. Maggie's damn sure she knows a curvy redhead who would stoop to endangering animals and a nice former Texas Ranger to get back at Maggie. Now she wishes she'd figured out which car belonged to Jenny at Stoney's so she could have keyed it.

"If you're up for reporting this to the sheriff tomorrow, I know who did it, and I probably know why." She tells Lumpy her suspicions and fills him in on the fire at the Coop and the dead body inside, even about Gary, Merritt, Tom, Thorn, and Kelly.

"Sounds like I was safer up my tree than you were down it. Sure, we'll go report this. Together, when we clear your name."

"Thanks. So you were up there that whole time, without food or water?"

"I had one bottle of water in my pocket. I was getting pretty parched, I don't mind telling you."

"Why didn't you climb down?"

"I tried, believe me. But that's not a climbing tree. I'd decided that if no one found me by tonight, I was going to have to risk jumping."

She stops the swing with her feet and holds on to the handrest. "Oh, Lumpy. You could have broken every bone in your body."

"Could have. Should have. Would have. Thing is, I didn't, because you came back for me. Thank you, Maggie."

"What are friends for?"

THIRTY-ONE

Back at Nowheresville, Maggie finds her laptop and a note on the kitchen counter.

Out shopping. Overnight to Austin w/R&A&C. Back around 5 to grab bags and update you. And hear how it went and what you need to tell me.

Maggie pours her Balcones and retreats with her laptop and dog to what is fast becoming her bedroom. She piles pillows on the bed, then balances herself on them, leaning on the headboard. Louise jumps up, uninvited.

"Warning, dog. I'm not in my happy place."

She hears Michele and her friends in the kitchen, bustling about.

"Knock, knock." Michele walks in.

"Make yourself at home."

"It is my house, after all."

"That's what Leslie says about mine, too. Hey, Lumpy's back. I found him up a tree."

"What?"

Ava appears in the doorway. "You want something to eat?" She's carrying a tray with a bud vase that's holding a plastic daisy. A banana, jar of salsa, bag of tortilla chips, and plate with a fat sandwich slide to one edge of the tray. "Whoops."

A smile creases Maggie's face. "It'll slow down getting my drunk on." To Michele she adds, "Lumpy's fine, but some Jessica Rabbit type knocked his ladder down and left him for dead."

Ava sets the tray down and Louise goes for the sandwich.

Maggie catches the dog by the collar. "Get your own, Fucker."

"I don't get it. About Lumpy." Michele scoots the dog out of the room and shuts the door.

"I'll tell you all about it tomorrow." Maggie gestures at the food. "This is probably smart. You didn't poison it, did you?" she asks Ava.

"I thought about it. I decided stress would probably kill you anyway, so I don't have to."

A laugh escapes Maggie's lips. "You guys are headed to Austin?"

Michele sits in the spot the dog vacated. "Chuy's and some band Ava wants to see at a club I'm going to hate. On a Monday."

"And you didn't invite me?"

Ava says, "Please. Like you'd say yes with me going."

"Depends on who would be picking up the tab."

Michele punches her arm. "Will you be all right?"

"Of course."

"You say that, but I have news."

"More bad news."

"Not bad. Just not good."

"Spit it out."

Ava goes to the door. "Later, you two." She wrestles past the dogs and closes the door behind her.

Michele smooths the full skirt of a red flowered sundress. "The tech guy says the email address used to send those messages to Gary is really yours."

"I don't understand."

"He thinks someone got into your account and wrote real emails. And that there are real answers from Gary's account. Could someone have your password?"

"I don't see how, but anything's possible."

"It's not OmahaNebraska, is it?"

"What's wrong with that?"

Michele groans.

"I'm just kidding. It's not."

"Do you have it written down anywhere?"

"On my laptop. But I had that with me. And on a paper taped under my desk."

"Where anyone that goes into your house could get it."

"It's not Grand Central Station."

"You could take tickets at your bedroom door. And you keep a key under your mat, with no security system, and rent to strangers you meet on the internet."

Maggie smacks her hip. "Kiss my ass."

Michele sighs. "Well, someone either got your passwords or hacked into your account. My guy said that happens all the time."

"But who would do something like this?"

"Someone you've really, really pissed off."

"You know me. I piss everyone off a little, but no one off a lot."

"True."

"My real problem is Tom and Thorn, though."

"Who?"

"Hold on to your pants for this one. I talked to Gary's mom today." Maggie relays the story about Tom, Thorn, and Gary's money quickly.

By the time she finishes, Michele is up and pacing the room. "*Dios mío*, Maggie. Why haven't you told me this already?"

"I tried."

"I'll be on the phone with Fayette County as soon as we're on the road. This is big."

"Thanks. I feel a little hope."

"Me, too. Now, keep the doors locked and dogs inside while we're gone."

Maggie holds up her banana. "Thanks again for dinner."

Michele leans down and kisses Maggie's cheek.

After Michele leaves, Maggie eats the dessert banana first, then nibbles on the sandwich between sips of Balcones. Time to find out everything she can about her crazy-ass renter.

She pulls up the original series of emails between Leslie and herself. Leslie DeWitt. What does she know about her? Very little, truth be told. They'd exchanged a few emails. Maggie'd thought she sounded okay. She didn't have a lot to steal in her little house, so she didn't worry overmuch about security. No background check was needed, because Leslie paid in advance originally. Maggie realizes that with her laptop back she can check on the supposed PayPal payment, since she couldn't get her blankety-blank password to work on her phone.

Louise whines at the door.

She clicks to log in with her saved information. PayPal returns a message that her password is invalid.

"Impossible."

She tries again. It doesn't work. She enters it manually. It fails. She looks it up in her list of passwords, types it again, and gets rejected a fourth time.

Her password has changed. It's the only explanation. Anger starts building inside her. There could be a damn good reason she can't find the email between Leslie and herself. And that reason could be that someone has a motive to jack with her PayPal and also has one to delete vacation rental emails, the same someone conveniently with current access to the password list. Her renter.

Maggie seethes. Well, hopefully all Leslie wants to steal is Maggie's house and not her money, because PayPal is connected to Maggie's checking account with overdraft protection from savings. Maggie clicks to reset her password. She chooses a new one, changes it on her list, and saves it in her browser during the log-in process. She repeats the game for her email in a new tab and realizes she's going to have to change all her passwords. She looks at the long list of accounts and groans. It can wait until after she's done sleuthing Leslie.

A niggling thought begins to worry her. If Leslie got into her email to delete VRBO messages, could she have messed with her other messages, too? The obvious answer is yes, she could have. But why would she? She had no reason to fabricate email between Gary and her. Of course, she was beginning to realize Leslie didn't need rational reasons for anything she did.

"Now let's see you log in to my shit, bitch."

Louise barks from behind the hollow-core door.

Maggie accesses her most recent received payments in PayPal. The Coop has been closed for nearly two weeks. First, because of reduced hours when she left for Wyoming. Next, because it was vandalized. And finally, because it burned to the ground. Her transactions have tapered off to just a few website sales, plus two rental payments. The first is Leslie's original payment. It's a big one for a ten-day stay. The second is for two additional nights.

"She paid for the extra days." Maggie is disappointed. More ammunition against Leslie would have been nice.

She stares at the screen, feeling more than seeing a difference in the two payments. But when she studies them closer, she zeroes in on it. The payment account names used are different. The first payment is from Leslie C. DeWitt. It has an email associated with it. LesliecDeWitt39@gmail.com. The next payment is from Leslie DeWitt, no middle initial. And the email is different: simonesays, from a Yahoo account. Maggie isn't sure what to make of it, but she has more than one account herself. One personal, one business. Maybe that's all this is.

Louise loses it and scratches at the door like a rabid anteater.

A quick review of payments made reveals nothing unusual. She double-checks in her bank account to be sure there are no unexpected withdrawals. There's not. Leslie hadn't been after her money.

Louise whines, barks, and scratches more.

"I'm fine, Louise." Maggie tears off a big bite of sandwich with her teeth, struggles to chew it, then washes it down with Balcones. "Go find Gertrude. Mama has to get to work."

Her phone vibrates. She'd turned the ringer off earlier when she and Michele were meeting with Junior. Caller Id announces her mother. She picks up, reluctantly, and swigs more Balcones before saying hello.

"Hi, sweetie."

"Hi to you and Edward."

"I'm so sorry about your shop."

"Thank you. And I'm sorry I had to leave your reception early."

"I understand. Do you want to come stay with us?"

Charlotte's house is in LaGrange. Maggie assumes Edward has moved in there, but she hasn't asked. She feels like a terrible daughter because of it and so much more. "No, Michele's place is closer to my stuff. Besides, we're sisters now."

"You are. Isn't it wonderful?"

"It is." She decides not to fill her mother in on everything else that isn't. Her life is a shit show.

"Maybe it's for the best, honey. You staying there instead of here."

"Why?"

"Leslie called. She told me you've gotten a deputy to evict her. She's on her way over to say goodbye on her way out of town."

Yes! Leslie is leaving! "Probably so, then." She can't believe her mom is taken in by such a lunatic, but there's no use debating with her. Maggie always loses, even when she wins. "Hey, Mom, I was thinking about Dad today."

"Oh?"

"Yeah, he pops into my mind every time I have another big failure."

"Stop that. You haven't failed. Your store burned down. That's not your fault."

"My memories today were of the good times, years ago. They don't jive with my later memories, before he died."

"There were lots of good memories. Before."

"What was wrong with him?"

"What do you mean?"

"He changed. A lot."

The silence is charged. "Why do you ask now?"

"Because I'm a grown-up, and I wonder. Plus, I just spent time with a woman in Wyoming who has Alzheimer's. She used to be sweet, but now she's a pit viper. It reminded me of Dad."

"Oh."

Maggie takes a sip of Balcones, then blurts out her real question. "Mom, did Dad have Alzheimer's?"

After long, silent seconds, Maggie hears soft crying on the other end of the line.

When Charlotte speaks, her voice quavers. "He, uh, he didn't want anyone to know."

The news should help, but it doesn't. For so many years, Maggie had worried that the change in her dad was because he hated the person she was becoming. But that hadn't been it at all. It wasn't Maggie. It was a disease. *Yet he would rather I think he hated me than admit to me he was sick?* His feelings were more important to him than his only child's. Maggie tries to contain the anger that rolls through her like thunder. Deep down, she knows that once he had Alzheimer's, he was no longer rational. The decisions he made then weren't the decisions he would have made as the dad she wants to remember. That dad would have put her first, not make her wait ten years to find out the truth. Easy to say, hard to accept. Maggie stashes acceptance away as a project for the future.

"I should have told you sooner."

"I wish you had."

"There's more."

"More what?"

"To his story. He got sick—real sick, real fast—but it's not the Alzheimer's that killed him. Not directly."

Maggie steels herself. She'd always been told her dad died of a heart attack. Whatever's coming can't be good. "What was it?"

Charlotte takes a deep breath before she speaks. "He killed himself."

The words are like a barrage of barbed arrows digging into Maggie's flesh. Painful. Under her skin quickly, finding their way to the grudge she's held against her father and working their way in. "How?"

"Hanging. In the barn. I—I found him. The church helped me keep it quiet."

"Oh, Mom. I'm sorry. I had no idea."

"No, I'm sorry." Her mother sobs. "For him. Because of that, he can't be with God."

"Don't say that."

"The Bible is clear on it, Maggie."

"You and I will have to disagree there." She puts her drink down. "Thank you for telling me this. But let's not talk about sad things anymore. How about we plan happy things instead. Can I take you and Edward to dinner tomorrow night?"

Charlotte sniffs, and Maggie can picture her dabbing at her eyes with a tissue. "That would be lovely."

"Good. Let's do it."

"And when we're together, I can show you that awful article online."

"I've seen it."

"There's one that just came out tonight. Leslie. She's my friend. But she said some pretty un-Christian things about you. If they're not true, anyway."

"Like what?"

"Like that you show up drunk all the time, all hours of the day, and that she's scared of you and thinks you had something to do with the death of Gary and the person in your store."

"Oh my God. Most definitely not true."

"She didn't feel safe there. I wouldn't have either."

"Then she should have left."

"Not everyone has the means to just pick up and go, Maggie."

"I can't speak for her. All I know is she was supposed to be out this morning, and she's refusing to leave."

"Such a shame."

"I agree. She shouldn't blockade me from my home. You understand that, right?"

"What I know is that the Lord calls for us to help others in need. 'For I was hungry and you gave me something to eat, I was thirsty and you gave me something to drink, I was a stranger and you invited me in.' Matthew 25:35."

"She's not in need. She's stealing from me."

"Forgive us our trespasses as we forgive those who trespass against us."

"This isn't a forgiveness thing. I want my damn house back. The Bible calls for double restitution, though—thanks for reminding me to think biblically. Her price just went up."

"We should all worry about our own sins first."

"I'm flat out of unblemished rams covered in silver to sacrifice for mine."

"Now you're just being sacrilegious."

"Mom, she lied to you. She lied to me. She lied to everyone. I didn't illegally break her lease, show up drunk—" Maggie has to ponder that one for a moment, but she thinks she's right. "—or kill anyone. You understand she's slandering me, suggesting I killed people?"

"I'm sure that's not what she intends."

Maggie throws her hand in the air. It's not like her mom can see her, but it makes her feel better. "Whose side are you on, anyway? A relative stranger, or your only daughter?"

"I can't believe you'd even ask that."

Maggie stares out the window. The waning light shortens her sightline, and she feels like Princess Leia with Han Solo and Luke Skywalker in the trash compactor room in *Star Wars*. Imprisoned, with everything shrinking in on her. She's not going to win this argument. Her mom has an unearthly ability to see the good in everyone. It's helped Maggie tremendously at times, so she can't fault it when it's working against her. Not completely, anyway.

She softens her voice. "I love you, Mom. I'll call you tomorrow about dinner."

"Love you, too, Maggie. Goodnight."

Maggie lets her head thunk back against the wall. The conversation was exhausting. Relationships are exhausting. People. People are exhausting. And another damn online article? Why isn't she getting a chance to comment before they're being posted? It could be her changed phone number, although she just did that today. Or maybe it's because her shop is closed and her house is under siege. She doesn't want to give junk journalists too much credit, though. Or herself. Lord knows she usually hangs up or says, "No fucking comment" on the rare occasions that she gets the calls. Now the news cycle of her life has accelerated, like a hit and run over her back.

Outside her door, something emits an eerie howl. Maggie jumps up, ready to lock herself in the bathroom against an invasion of werewolves, until she realizes it's just Louise. She opens the door a few inches.

"Hush your face, Louise."

She hops back on the bed. She doesn't want to, but she needs to read the latest tripe. She wakes up her laptop and types her name into the Google search bar. In the two seconds it takes for the results to appear, she bites her lip and tastes blood. She'd walked away from the pursuit of fame after rehab. In the past decade, she hasn't read a single word about herself until the last week, other than the true crime novel Michele penned, and that was different. A favor to a friend. Maggie doesn't lie about who she is, but she doesn't offer it up. Her real self deserves protection.

Louise pokes her head in the door.

Maggie sucks the blood from her lip and reads.

"Superstar Gary Fuller and the Black Widow, Former Music Sensation Maggie Killian." "How the Mighty Maggie Killian Has Fallen." "Where Are They Now? Maggie Killian." And many more of their ilk.

The dog hops up on the bed beside her. Maggie gives her a quick pat.

"Parasites will say anything to sell ad space."

She scrolls down further, finding the one she's looking for but doesn't want to see. "Does Black Widow Maggie Killian Have a Black Heart toward Her Renter?"

"Nice."

Former recording artist Maggie Killian has been making news lately. It seems like every man close to her is getting murdered, and law enforcement in Wyoming and Texas have been looking hard at her for the deaths, reminding us of her old hit "I Hate Cowboys." Maybe she truly does.

She's still under investigation in Texas.

"She's like a black widow," an anonymous source says.

Maggie snorts. "Whatever."

But that's not all the mischief the washed-up alt-rocker has been up to lately.

Maggie clenches and unclenches her fists.

A renter of hers in Texas reports that a drunken and belligerent Ms. Killian has attempted to break her lease and even have her thrown out by the local sheriff.

"It's scary enough living here, with all the people that conveniently die when Maggie Killian wants them out of her life, without her targeting me for removal, too," the renter, a school teacher from Houston, says. "This isn't new behavior for her. I heard she broke her contract with her old band and kicked them all out in the middle of a tour once. And she's been doing stuff like that ever since, no matter whose career she destroys."

Maggie's split with her band isn't new news, and we've written about it on this site before. You can read more about the fate of Davo, Brent, Celinda, and Chris here in "Breaking Up with the Band: Maggie Killian."

We couldn't reach Ms. Killian for comment. Maybe the woman once famous for singing about being a "Buckle Bunny" is back for a much-needed stint in rehab. Or otherwise indisposed by law enforcement.

"That bitch," Maggie screams.

She clicks on the author's name. A hoodied millennial stares at the camera ironically, holding up a Monster Energy drink as if mocking her.

"Cocksucker. Lazy journalist."

Below the article is a picture of Maggie with her old touring band. She takes in the faces she tries not to remember. Yes, she feels guilty that she dumped them, but she didn't cause their deaths or ruin any careers. Maggie's gaze lingers on Celinda. She had felt sorry for her. Chris had used her and pushed her over for a real buckle bunny he picked up in Cheyenne.

"Not my fault, though. And she amounted to nothing because she had no talent."

Enough of that. She texts Michele the article link. *More fodder for the libel suit.* Now Leslie DeWitt needs her unwavering attention.

But before she goes back to cyberstalking Leslie, she goes for a pit stop. On the way back to the bed, she trips and nearly falls on nothing but wood floor. Too much whiskey, not enough food. She opens the chips and salsa and digs in hungrily. Salsa dribbles down her chin. She scoops it back up and into her mouth with a chip, then offers one to Louise.

Louise crunches it like it's a beef rib.

Maggie lays her phone on the bedside table. As she does, she notices a missed call banner. She leans closer to read who it was from, and she spits chips and salsa on the screen.

"Hank!"

Louise jumps up, wagging everything.

Hank called her. She looks at the number in her Recents. He'd called her that afternoon. She counts back hours. Probably when she was at Lumpy's. Why had her phone betrayed her and withheld this information? No ring. No notification of any kind. Until now.

She doesn't have an indicator for voicemail but she opens the screen anyway. Just in case.

But there's none.

Sometimes when she's out in the sticks her phone doesn't tell her about voicemail for days. She calls in to listen for new messages.

Nothing.

She presses CALL BACK, smearing salsa on her phone screen. It rings once, twice, three, four times.

"Come on, come on."

It rolls to voicemail.

"No." She redials. "No."

Hank's voice prompts her to leave a message. Just the sound of it brings a tingling rush between her legs, to a place that misses him like a freeze misses the warm.

"You've got Hank Sibley of Double S Bucking Stock, and I've got your mother buckers. Leave me a message."

She feels her cheeks smiling without her permission. "Hank, this is Maggie. I saw you called. If it was on purpose, call me back. If it was a butt dial, then listen to your butt. It's telling you something." She recites her new number, even though he already called it, and if he hadn't, he'd have it from the record of this call anyway. Better safe than sorry.

She puts the phone down on the bedside table. Then she picks it up to check the ringer. It's on. She sets it down again. But she hadn't turned up the volume. So she picks it up again. Checks the volume. It's on max. She lays the phone down. Pats it. Stares at it.

Louise walks to the edge of the bed to play the game, too.

"Watched pot. No boiling."

The dog deposits herself on one of the pillows and wriggles to find a spot good enough for her sensitive hide. The princess and the pea, canine version.

A mental kick in the pants is in order. Maggie smacks her cheek—tap-tap-tap—with her fingers, then does the same thing to the other side. She slackens her lips and gives her head a shake. Lifts her arms and wriggles her fingers. The distraction of waiting for Hank to call back is so intense she can't remember what it was she sat down to do.

Maybe the Balcones has something to do with it, too.

She scans the room. Pictures of Michele with her kids and her deceased husband, Adrian. A Hawaii Ironman triathlon poster. She's at Michele's because she can't be at her own place, thanks to that horrible bitch Leslie. And that's what she was doing. Researching the renter from hell. Something she should have done before handing over her keys in the first place. Giving her head one more shake, she repositions herself on the bed, knees bent, leaning against the pillows and wall.

"Ready or not, Leslie DeWitt, here I come."

She types the woman's name in a search box. She hits ENTER and starts reading down the results. Facebook. Facebook. Facebook. Instagram. Tsunami survivors. Google Plus. Twitter. Maggie bites the inside of her lip. Had she even spelled Leslie's last name right? DeWitt. Is that one *t* or two? With an *h* or without? She double-checks an email from Leslie before wasting too much time. Growls. Two *t*'s. She'd typed it with one. She fixes it, and the search results explode. Now she has sexual abuse trial verdicts, obituaries, and more.

She wants to drink herself numb. She wants Hank to call. She wants to research Leslie DeWitt like she wants to sign up for a month of Sundays at church with her mother. But she's out of other options. Nothing left to do but do it. She rolls her neck. It cracks, releasing stress, but not enough.

She browses, looking for clear profile pictures. There are nearly twenty Leslie DeWitts on Facebook alone, but none of the profile pictures look like the right Leslie. She pulls up the profiles without pictures. There's not enough information in any to rule them in or out.

She flips back to her Google results. Her Leslie isn't the woman convicted of sexually abusing a kid she'd coached. That Leslie is in her early twenties and lives in Seattle. And she doesn't know where her Leslie lives. Even if she did, that wouldn't guarantee a match. Lots of people use their hometowns or fake information online. She decides to limit her search to records inside the United States, but she can't narrow it any more than that.

But she thinks she saw Leslie's home address somewhere in their contracting process. Scanning the emails between herself and Leslie, she doesn't see an address, even in the message confirming the dates of her stay and working out the details of payment. PayPal. That will give her Leslie's address. She pulls it back up. Houston. It jogs her memory. She flips back to the newest People.com article.

"A school teacher from Houston," she reads aloud.

She adds the new information to her search. The results are better—narrower, fewer hits—but not good enough yet.

Her Balcones is calling. She sips it, dredging up everything she knows about Leslie. Age? About forty. Accent? The voice she hears in her mind is atonal, without accent. She wouldn't even call it Middle American. Which is weird, because it's rare she can't pinpoint a region.

She goes back to the twenty Facebook records, studies the pictures again. Looks can deceive. She eliminates the non–United States profiles and the women who are obviously too old or too young. She keeps five of them, even though they don't look like the woman in her house. One of them seems somewhat familiar, but even if her Leslie had long gray hair, this wouldn't be her. Too old. And the eyes are too dark.

Could it be Leslie was telling the truth, and that she isn't really Leslie at all? If that's the case, Maggie's back to square one. She's not ready to face that possibility, but she doesn't have to yet. Not when there's still more information to review. She sets the Facebook profiles aside for the moment and moves to other social media. Instagram and Twitter yield similar results. No matches to her Leslie. She doesn't understand Google Plus, so she skips it, along with the social media Michele's kids use. Snapback or Smackchat or something? Maggie isn't part of that younger generation, and Leslie isn't either.

Maggie racks her brain for more searches she can try. Why is this so hard? Her eyes are bleary from staring at the pictures. Maybe one of the women she's seen is Leslie. Or maybe not. Maybe Leslie goes by initials or something. She saw a middle initial for her on PayPal. Leslie C. Thus, L.C. She'll try that next. Or maybe Leslie isn't even on social media and this is a big waste of time.

She takes a slug of Balcones. An idea forms. She runs a few Google searches using the email addresses she'd found in PayPal for Leslie. She finds an image for the first email. Her pulse quickens and she leans in. The woman in the picture has gray hair, long and wavy, pale skin, and dark eyes. Nothing like her Leslie and the tight, expressionless face caked in makeup to cover her scars, with blue eyes so light they're like clouds.

Maggie snorts. Because it's *not* her Leslie in the picture. It can't be. Even with a haircut, a dye job, colored contacts, and plastic surgery, her Leslie is twenty years younger than the woman in the picture.

But why would Leslie use someone else's picture with the same email she uses on her PayPal account? Trying to figure it out hurts her head. She's exhausted, physically, mentally, and emotionally. Maggie lies down. Just for a minute, she'll ponder this from the horizontal. But before she can close her eyes, blue and red lights flash through the window and on the wall beside her.

THIRTY-TWO

"What the hell?" Maggie walks to the window and peeks through the blinds.

Three county vehicles are parked outside, lights strobing. Junior is leading the charge to Michele's door, with Boland and what seems like a legion of law enforcement personnel behind him. Maggie clutches the windowsill. The doorbell rings. Louise leaps from the bed like a flying squirrel and is sprinting before her paws hit the ground. Her barks join with Gertrude's, reverberating through the house.

Maggie runs to the bathroom. She squirts toothpaste on her finger and brushes her teeth as she walks to the front door. Her steps are slow, her heart pounding like she's climbing the steps to a hangman's noose. Her lungs shut like metal doors, refusing entry to the air she tries to breathe in. Why are all these officers here, after Michele was going to call Fayette and Lee County about Tom and Thorn?

This can't be good. Not good at all.

The door hardware is icy cold under her hand as she opens it. Louise and Gertrude dash past her to Junior's ankles. They sniff him thoroughly then move on to Boland, who shoves Louise away with his foot.

Maggie says, "Don't kick my dog. She won't hurt you."

Boland says, "Restrain her."

"Louise, come."

Louise comes, although not eagerly. Maggie grabs her by the collar.

Junior rubs his lips together. "Maggie Killian. We have a warrant to search the premises, as well as your vehicle."

Maggie's a search warrant neophyte. She'd feared arrest, not a search. Can they even search the house without the owner present? She has no idea what to do. "Michele isn't here."

Boland pushes his way around Junior. "Step aside, Ms. Killian, unless you want us to arrest you for obstruction of justice."

She doesn't budge from the center of the doorway. "I need to call Michele. I'm just a guest here."

"No one's stopping you. But meanwhile the law allows us to do what we've come to do. This is the last time I tell you to move out of the way. Next time, you're taking a ride to lockup."

Maggie turns to the side. Boland, Junior, and several deputies and other county personnel she doesn't recognize file past her into the house.

"I need to see a copy of the warrant," she says, trying to remember what she's seen when she'd been boozed up and watching old cop shows on late-night television, something Gary loved to do.

Junior hands it to her. Louise struggles against her as she reads. The words swim on the page before her eyes. It might as well be in hieroglyphics. Around her, things move at hyperspeed. Officers don gloves. Boland barks orders that don't register with Maggie, and his minions disperse. She tries again to read the warrant. This time she can make out words, but she doesn't comprehend much. It's a Fayette County warrant to be executed by ten p.m., dated that day, specifically for the home of Michele Lopez Hanson and the Ford pickup belonging to Maggie Killian, for the purpose of looking for fire accelerants, electrical communications and data relating to Gary Fuller and setting fires, and Rohypnol.

Rohypnol. The word jumps out at her. What is rohypnol? The officers are all inside now, so she lets Louise go. The dog tears off to join Gertrude and they run around with their sniff on. She snaps a picture of the warrant, texts it to Michele, and hits speed dial for her sister's phone number. Just as Michele is picking up, Maggie places the word. Rohypnol. Roofies. Date-rape drugs.

"Hi, Maggie. We're just walking into Chuy's. Are you okay?" Michele asks.

"No, I'm not. Lee and Fayette County deputies—and Boland himself—are here executing a search warrant."

"At *my* house?"

"Yes. And for my truck. I'm so sorry. I texted you a copy. What do I do?"

"Watch them like hawks. Take pictures. Video or audio if things seem hinky. But let me read the warrant first. Hold on."

Maggie sits at the dining room table with the phone on speaker. She bounces her leg, watching strangers pawing through Michele's drawers and cabinets. It's wrong. Just wrong. Louise and Gertrude shadow them as best they can, but they're far outnumbered. How can Maggie watch everyone at once any better than the dogs?

Boland emerges from the hallway to Maggie's room. "You'll get an inventory of the things we're taking, but for now, know that pretty much everything in that bedroom is coming with us."

"Wait. What do you mean? Not my guitar, laptop, my bag, my toiletries?"

"Everything."

"You're taking my IDs and credit cards?"

Michele's voice is hard and loud. "That's bullshit, Boland. You can subpoena her records, but you can't take her keys, cards, and cash. And that guitar is expensive and priceless."

"Who the fuck do you have on speakerphone?" Boland demands.

"Michele Lopez Hanson, my lawyer and the owner of this house. I believe you know each other from the quality time we spent together this morning."

Michele's voice takes no shit. "Leave her purse after you search it, Boland. And I'll consider it a personal affront if you take that guitar. One that I'll feel compelled to get noisy about."

"We'll try to eliminate the purse and guitar onsite. No promises."

"None from me either. When can you have a copy of her hard drive made and get her laptop back to her?"

"We're a small department. We'll do the best we can."

"It's a simple dump to an external hard drive. We'll bring you the hardware in the morning so you can have her computer back to her by noon."

Boland turns around, muttering, and heads back toward Maggie's room.

But Michele's not done. "Why didn't you return my calls, Boland? I've left you three messages in the last hour. We've got evidence for you."

Boland stops. "Call me tomorrow. I'm busy here."

"You'll look like a jackass by tomorrow if you don't hear what I have to say now, before the media gets hold of it."

Maggie jumps to her feet. "There are two men in town who the estate of Gary Fuller thinks stole half a million dollars from him. One is the manager Gary planned to fire last Friday. Tom Clarke. The other man, Thorn Gibbons, is having sex with Gary's seventeen-year-old sister. We'd already told you about them, before we even learned about the embezzlement today."

Boland rolls his eyes like a pubescent girl. "Thanks, Nancy Drew."

Maggie's eyes burn, not with tears, but with rage. The kind of powerless rage she can't do anything about without getting arrested.

Michele's voice goes super soft. "Don't say we didn't try to warn you, before you did this. And now you know."

Boland takes a toothpick out of his breast pocket and starts cleaning and sucking his teeth. "Duly noted."

"Have you found the witness to the fire at the Coop? The one Maggie told you about?"

"Not my concern. I'm here about Fayette County."

"Well, has Lee County found her?"

"Ask Lee County."

Michele growls. "Exactly what are the grounds for probable cause for this warrant?"

"Besides the emails between them, Ms. Killian has a history of substance abuse and proven ability to obtain drugs, in addition to motive, means, and opportunity for administering them and starting the fire."

"What does Maggie's history have to do with anything?"

"Someone—we suspect Ms. Killian—roofied Gary Fuller before the fire."

Maggie's mouth goes cottony and she feels suddenly, horribly sober. Gary was drugged. Drugged and left to burn to death. She clutches her stomach and rocks. A sob lodges in her throat, halfway up, stuck.

"Dios mío. A roofie now has nothing to do with Maggie and cocaine addiction ten years ago. That isn't probable cause. This is the cheesiest excuse for a warrant I've ever seen. I'll get it tossed with one hand behind my back. Everything you're collecting now, all fruit of the poisonous tree."

"Knock yourself out, counselor."

"What are you trying to do, other than harass my client?"

"Prove the person who died in the Coop was roofied, too, because then your client will be going down for both murders." Boland sticks the dirty toothpick in his pocket, winks at Maggie, and disappears down the hall.

THIRTY-THREE

Maggie jerks out of a deep sleep. By the time she realizes she's awake, she's bolt upright, her shoulders rigid. Sweat drips down her neck onto her heaving chest. A thunderous herd of Wyoming horses gallop in her ears. At the foot of the bed, Louise whines plaintively.

She can't remember what it is, but she knows something isn't right. Is the wrong thing in a dream? But she smells the overripe half-eaten banana and the astringent odor of the open Balcones on the bedside table. This isn't a dream. Boland and his crew were here. They tore the place apart. Took everything she had except her wallet and truck keys, and left with Boland looking pissed because, she assumes, they didn't find what they were looking for. The fact that they accused her of burning the evidence in the Coop makes her assumption seem pretty darn reasonable.

Maggie was so drained after the officers left that she toppled onto the bed in the wrecked room. She was out in seconds. Until moments ago, when she awoke. She didn't have to go to sleep to have a nightmare. Her life already is one.

Maybe she heard something outside. The curtains are open, the moon is full, and light is streaming through the window. Outside, the skinny oak trees are like dancing skeletons. She looks for movements along the ground but sees nothing. She holds her breath so she can hear, but there's nothing out of the ordinary. So what woke her?

"Michele? Rashidi?" she calls. They aren't due home until after midnight. Michele had offered to come home during their call earlier, but the search would have been over before she made it back. It was pointless. Maggie had thanked her and declined. She looks at the time on her phone. Ten thirty.

No answer. Her skin prickles. She's being paranoid, though. The dogs would be barking if someone is in the house. *Snap out of it, Maggie.*

She gets up. In the bathroom, she splashes cold water on her face. She isn't drunk anymore, although she wishes she was still under the influence of something to take the edge off. Anything to escape this feeling that she's trapped in a garbage barge, lost at sea. It's been years since she's craved coke, but if there were lines in front of her now, she'd snort them and damn the consequences. She stares into the mirror. The chance for a relationship with Hank is ruined. Gary is dead. Her store is burned to ashes. Law enforcement is harassing her for it. What does she have to stay clean for anymore?

She walks back to bed in the dark and huddles under the covers, replaying the last few minutes. All those things that are wrong—she's convinced they aren't what woke her up. She thinks harder. Before the search team came, she was researching Leslie. She hadn't found much. But it's Leslie, she realizes. Leslie is what woke her. She missed something. She has to go back over her search results. Her subconscious is screaming that there's an answer in there that she skipped over the first time.

She doesn't bother turning on the bedroom light, just flops on her tummy and gropes for her laptop. When she doesn't find the hard plastic rectangle amidst the bedding, she remembers Boland took it.

"Shit!"

She furrows her face, concentrating. What is it about Leslie that woke her up? She hadn't thought she'd found anything earlier. Now she's convinced she did, if only she could put her finger on it.

Louise barks at her.

"Keep your pants on."

Maggie opens the door and Louise follows her out, the dog circling Maggie's legs all the way to the living room. "Need to go out, girl?"

Gertrude pads up, dreadlocks swinging.

"Girls, plural. Sorry, Gertrude." She lets them out the back door, gets herself a glass of water and a handful of grapes, then returns to the door. She opens it to let the dogs back in, but they're not there. "Louise. Gertrude. Come."

She waits on them a moment, remembering the woman she'd seen in the backyard that weekend. Her mind plays a funny slideshow of images. The woman in the backyard. The woman across the road from Flown the Coop the night of the fire. The pale braided woman with the dark eyes she'd seen in the rocking chair.

"Son of a bitch."

The woman she's picturing in her mind is the spitting image of the pictures she'd found when she ran a search using Leslie's PayPal email account. Enough to be her sister. Goose bumps rise on her skin. It makes no sense. But one thing is clear. Maggie can't wait for morning to look for answers. She needs to know Leslie is out of her house, right now.

And if she's not, she has a whole lot of explaining to do, starting with the identity of the pale, braided woman.

THIRTY-FOUR

On her way out the door, Maggie grabs the shotgun Michele keeps there on two wooden pegs. It's for scaring off whatever needs scaring. Coyotes, bobcats, prowlers. The gun is only a 20-gauge, but it makes a powerful noise. If Leslie's still at Maggie's house, Maggie can blast a few shots outside the bedroom window. Maybe it will scare Leslie off like it does the varmints.

Shotgun under one arm and keys in the other hand, Maggie runs to the truck. She opens the truck door, and Louise jumps in first, without permission. She hadn't even known the dog followed her out the door. Putting her back in the house will take too long, so she lets it slide. She'll make her stay in the truck when she gets to her house. Maggie lays the long gun on the floorboard, business end pointing toward the passenger-side door. Louise settles on the seat above it.

Maggie peels out of the driveway and onto the road, taking the turns like Bess is on rails. The shotgun slides and bangs into the passenger door. To have lived in Texas all her life, nearly, and not have a gun rack behind her seat—it feels unpatriotic. And dangerous. She wishes she had one now.

She drives by an oil derrick lit up like a Christmas tree. A flare burns pressure off an oil well across the road. She hits a patch of old pavement on the mostly gone-back-to-dirt road as she takes another curve. The tires squeal. She slows down. All she needs now is a wreck and the delay and publicity of a DWI. But she's too jacked to drive the speed limit. There's no calming her down, even with the cooling night air blowing in the open windows, not after the night she's had. The day. The week. The month. The life.

Maggie reaches her house in record time, ten minutes door to door from Michele's. Leslie's car is still there, parked partially out of sight from the road behind a copse of trees, but in front of the house. Light spills out two of the windows.

"Leaving tonight, huh? Doesn't look like it."

Louise bobs her head, almost like she's nodding.

The Coop rubble is no longer lit up for crime scene technicians, but Maggie's headlights illuminate the yellow tape barricade as she pulls into the parking area. She skirts it and drives over the lawn, like Leslie must have. When she's close, she angles Bess toward the house, pointing the high beams through the front door and down the central hall.

"Take that, squatter."

Now that she knows Leslie hasn't left town yet, all thoughts of the pale, braided woman she's seen in real life, dreams, and online fly out the window. Maggie rolls the window down halfway, tucks the shotgun under her arm, and holds Louise at bay while she shuts the truck door. Marching toward the front of the house, she calls, "Stay," over her shoulder.

Louise howls in her best sad-coyote imitation, but Maggie ignores her.

She bangs on the front door of her house. She's not surprised when there's no answer, but Leslie has to be there. Not just because of her car, but because the chances of her still being at Charlotte's at eleven o'clock on a Monday night are nil.

Maggie isn't leaving without satisfaction.

She walks around the house. At the master bedroom window, she shouts, "I know you can hear me, Leslie. I've spent the evening getting to know you online."

Maggie pauses, listening. She hears a moan. A sex moan. Who would have sex with Leslie? She's attractive, but such a robot. And a bona fide head case.

Maggie yells again. "You hide online behind pictures of someone who isn't even you."

This time she hears a muffled yell, then an impact and a grunt. It gets her attention. If that's sex, it's not the good kind.

"Leslie? Are you okay in there?"

She presses her face to the window, her chin above the ledge. There's a little sliver not covered by the curtains, big enough to see into her bedroom.

It's a small room. All the rooms in her old farm cottage are little. Her queen-size four-poster bed takes up most of the space, leaving just enough room for a rustic bedside table, a tall antique dresser, and a matching dressing table with a gilded mirror. Her favorite Gidget painting, *Front Porch Pickin'*, hangs over the head of the bed. A large urn on the dresser usually holds fresh flowers. Now, dead sunflower heads loll over its side. She'd left them for Leslie before her drive to Wyoming. Her white duvet is in a heap on the floor. The overhead fixture is out, but a lamp she'd made from an old milk jug sheds light on two people on the bed. She almost pulls back, the thought of Leslie mid-coitus giving her a wave of nausea. But she can't force herself to look away.

Feeling like a voyeur, she realizes what she sees. Someone is tied to the four posts, spread-eagle, naked. Not Leslie. A man. Leslie crawls over to him and throws a leg astride his hips. She has a cigarette in her mouth, the end a glowing red.

What the hell?

Maggie shouts, "Fine. Don't answer. I'll see you tomorrow morning, Leslie, with the deputy here to arrest you. Goodnight, bitch."

She stomps her feet on the ground, hard, then softer, then softer still, but doesn't leave. She keeps her eyes on Leslie through the slit in the curtains. Let the woman think she's given up. She isn't going anywhere.

Leslie takes a drag on the cigarette then stubs it out on the man's chest. He barely reacts save for a light moan into a gag in his mouth. Leslie tosses the butt away, stands up, and pours the contents of a bottle of Balcones all over him. Maggie's skin crawls. Leslie sets the bottle upright on the bedside table. Then she walks out, leaving the man tied there, alone.

Bess's headlights are still pointing into the house. Maggie can't get away much longer with the charade that she's given up and left. She hoists herself onto the window sill, struggling to get a better look at the guy, wondering if she should call 911. Then she sees his face.

Horror washes over her.

It's Hank. Her Hank, and he's tied up in her bed, covered in Balcones, and this isn't sex, good or bad. It's some awful other thing that she doesn't have time to understand.

She bashes one of the window panes out with the butt of the shotgun. As fast as she can, she batters the wood frame to bits and the other panes with it. She lowers the gun inside the window, drops it to the floor, then pulls herself in after it. Her landing is rough, the glass digging sharply in her palms. She rolls onto her knees beside the shotgun and looks up. The first thing she sees is Leslie, back in the room on the other side of the bed from her, setting down a gas can and lighter.

The second thing she sees is Hank, and once she does, he is all she sees. Up close, his predicament is even worse than she'd thought from outside. His mouth is gagged with a blue-and-white scarf. Each wrist and ankle is held fast in a noose that holds him fully extended. The material doesn't look like rope. More like a plastic-encased steel cable. He's naked, like she thought. His hair is matted and dark with sweat.

As her inspection crosses his face, he opens his eyes. *I'll get you out of here. Hang on, Hank.* She imagines the two of them under a big Wyoming sky, riding side by side on a mountainside, and tries to send the image to him, but his eyes flutter closed again.

Leslie's voice brings her back. "This will be perfect. Murder-suicide. The finale to the drama. Your Wyoming lover dumped you, he shows up in Texas to tell you once and for all to stay out of his life, you drug him like you did Gary, tie him to your bed, and set the house on fire for revenge, then, overcome by grief, you shoot yourself as you're going up in flames with him."

Maggie looks up at Leslie and into the short, lethal barrel of a steel gray handgun. She feels a flash of recognition. Why does she always feel like she knows this crazy woman, not like knows her from the present, but from sometime before?

Her voice sounds less like C-3PO now. "Throw the gun out the window. NOW."

"What did you give him?"

"A roofie. I'm glad I had one left, since it was a lucky surprise he showed up here asking for you. I offered him a beer while he waited on my dear, sweet friend Maggie to get home. Easy as pie to crush a roofie up and watch him guzzle it down with Shiner Bock."

Maggie puts her hands on the shotgun.

"Good girl. Out the window."

Leslie's chilling voice rings in her ears, but Maggie doesn't move. She's been in this moment before. In Wyoming. Hank shot. Bleeding on the ground. No one else around. The moment when she realized she had to run for help.

"Don't do anything stupid, Maggie."

She'd abandoned the gun then, and she'd figured out how to save him. There's no alternative now, just like there hadn't been one then. She'll come up with something to get them out of this mess. She has to. Her refusal to take shit or ever give up are all she has.

She climbs to her feet, glass digging into her knees, fingers tight around the shotgun. She grimaces. Her left palm stings like a scorpion bite, a memory from a childhood playing in the woods in these parts.

"Easy," Leslie warns her.

Moving slow and calm, Maggie tosses the shotgun through the busted-out window. It thuds on dry grass and dirt below. Blood trickles down her wrists. She rotates toward Leslie, holding her hands shoulder high. "Okay?"

With her head level and still, Maggie shifts her weight through her hip and drags the other foot forward without lifting it.

"Keep your hands up."

Maggie doesn't drop them. "So, who are you, anyway?" She repeats the process with the other hip and foot, gaining a few precious inches toward Leslie.

"Fuck off."

Other hip. Other foot. "Who *are* you?"

"The woman who has Hank's life in her hands."

Hip. Foot. "You're not Leslie DeWitt."

"Yeah. And I guess you're not as much smarter than the rest of the world as you always thought you were, because I told you that earlier."

Maggie searches the room for a weapon. Something to stab with? A screwdriver. A knife. A pen. Something to use as a club—flashlight, wrench, glass bottle. All are normal items in her life, but tonight, she has none of them in her room. Then, like a gift from above, she realizes the sting in her palm is a piece of embedded glass. A long one. She folds her fingers over and tries to grasp it. The glass is too short to lodge between her fingers or to curl her fingers around.

"You don't look like your picture online." She brings her hands together, slowly. "Ouch," she says.

"I said keep your hands up."

"Glass. Give me a second." She digs the glass out and acts like she's discarding it, but keeps the shard between the fingers of her right hand. She raises her hands again. "You're younger. You have lighter eyes." Maggie sneaks a look at Hank. His eyes open, then roll back in his head again. She repeats her hip-foot sequence.

"Stop," Leslie barks. "No closer."

"I'm stopped."

Suddenly Leslie bends at the waist, clutching at her gut. Her back heaves. Maggie thinks she's having some kind of medical episode, until Leslie straightens. Tears are running down her cheeks. She's laughing.

"If you haven't figured out who I am, you deserve this even more than I thought."

"Figured what out?"

"You hurt everyone in your life, you know it? You never give a shit what happens to the little people. And we're all little people to you."

"I knew you? Before this week?"

"Duh."

"Your eyes are familiar."

Leslie grins. It's pure mockery. She pretends to play keyboard, then brings the barrel of the gun to her mouth like a microphone. She breaks into Martina McBride's "Independence Day" in perfect pitch. She stops suddenly. "We shared a room for two months on the road. You'd think you'd at least remember that."

The blood runs from Maggie's face, and it's like her life draining out of her. She remembers the night in Cheyenne like it was yesterday. Getting into an argument with her guitarist, Davo. Refusing to go back onstage. Standing outside the bar, talking to Hank. Hearing Davo introduce the next song, "Independence Day." And the woman who sang it. Maggie's backup singer. Why hadn't she seen it sooner? The scars, sure, the scars, the age and weight, different hair, but she *should* have recognized Celinda Simone, even if she last saw her fifteen years before in a van in Wheatland, Wyoming, before her band drove away to an accident that killed all of them, except one. "Celinda."

Celinda slow claps.

"You're so different. Not just how you look."

"I am different. I'm not a doormat anymore."

Maggie bites the inside of her lip. Celinda had been a doormat. She let Davo force her to the mic in Maggie's place, when Celinda wasn't ready to front the band. She slept with Chris, their drummer, who turned around and took up with Hank's ex right in front of her, and Celinda didn't do a thing about it.

But through all of that, Maggie had never once asked Celinda if she was okay. Maggie had just latched onto Hank and rode off into the sunset, however brief the ride was.

"I'm sorry."

"The old me died in the crash, along with my face. This?" She vogues like Madonna around her face. "This is a lot of plastic surgery later. You didn't make it to any of the funerals. Flowers and cards don't get you off the hook with me, not when you shot to the top by climbing on our backs."

"I, uh, I'm—"

"How many people like me are there, Maggie, hmm? In your life? How many people did you use up and throw out?"

Maggie stares at her. Names rush through her mind. Not just Celinda, Chris, Davo, and Brent. Her manager, Randy. Her mom, whose heart she'd broken. Rudy, a fan she'd blown off, who'd come back to haunt her in Wyoming because of how she'd treated him. Her dad. Yes, even her dad. Her mouth moves, but she doesn't say anything.

Hank's voice croaks, and both women whip their heads toward him. His scarf gag is chewed partly in half and hanging below his mouth on one side. His voice slurs, the words coming between long pauses. "It's my fault. I pushed her away from you guys. Then I dumped her. She was depressed."

Maggie can't make sense of what he's saying. That's not how she remembers it. She'd thought he had loved her. Then, very slowly, very deliberately, Hank closes one eye, the one closest to Maggie, and she realizes he's winking. She's not going to let him take the blame. Celinda is crazy, and Hank is defenseless.

"No. It's my fault." Her voice is firm.

"There's plenty of blame to go around. Maggie, you took my career. Hank, your slutty ex–buckle bunny took Chris away from me. I actually loved him—can you believe it? And then he died in the crash, before I could get him back." Celinda flicks her lighter. "How does it feel, Maggie, to lose stuff?"

"Bad."

"Not bad enough."

"I'm sorry. I'll do anything you want. Please tell me how to make it up to you."

"It's too late. Funny, because I thought I was over it. It helped that you messed up your life. Your rehab was my rehab. Then I read a stupid article online, one of those 'Where are they now?' bullshit pieces. And I realized, nope, you got away with it all, so I'll never be over it."

"Celinda, I—"

"Shut *up*. I came here, and that stupid bitch renter you had—Leslie— wasn't you. So I moved her out of the way and started taking your life like you took mine. Your friends. Your mother. Gary, until he chose you. Your shop. Your house. Your reputation. I was working on your sanity. And Hank —well, I don't think he's going to be on my side in this. But I'll still get to take him, one way or another." She points the handgun at the gas can and mouths "pow" and mimics a recoil.

"Gary?"

"Yeah, he was fine sleeping with me until you called. Got him back, though. Not just the fire. Before that, I got into his email on his phone, just like I got into yours. His phone wasn't password-protected. You let Leslie stay here with your password taped under your desk. Not smart, Maggie. Neither of you is very savvy about security."

Maggie's knees feel weak. Leslie. There really had been a renter named Leslie. If Celinda isn't Leslie, then Leslie is missing. Maggie's voice is a whisper. "Where is she? Where is Leslie?"

"Where you and Hank are going."

Shit. Maggie touches the sliver of glass. It's too small and won't do her any good. This woman is a murderer, and Maggie and Hank are next. She needs to call for help. Where is her damn phone? She tries to picture it. Is it in one of her pockets? No. She gets a visual. Louise. The seat in the truck. That's where it is. Beside Louise.

Hank jerks his eyes sideways, toward the window. He's telling her to leave. She'll do as he's asking, but not for the reason he intends. She has to get to that phone. Call 911. Pray that because Celinda hasn't killed Hank so far and knows Maggie is onto her, that she'll just make a run for it. That she'll leave Hank alone and look out for herself.

"Trust me," Maggie mouths at Hank.

Then she wheels, fast as she can, and takes two giant steps and dives headfirst out the window. Leslie reacts, but too slowly. Behind Maggie, bullets rip through the air and embed in the window frame. She catches herself with one arm, but it collapses and her shoulder hits, then her head. The ground is harder than she expected. It knocks the wind out of her. Her shoulder feels like it's broken. Her head rings from the impact. She drops her worthless piece of glass and tucks her shotgun under her arm. She wants to roll and groan and hug all the parts that hurt. She's in no shape for combat or rescues or escapes, but she's all Hank's got. She staggers to her knees, then her feet, and runs for the truck.

Behind her, she hears an evil whoosh and more glass breaking. A shock wave knocks her forward into the air-conditioner condenser. Somewhere in her mind is her father's voice: *Your mom will be here soon,* then Johnny Cash singing about the burning ring of fire. An excruciating pain in her ankle keeps her tethered to a world tilting back and forth. She presses down into the grill covering the fan blades, fighting to stay upright, fighting through the pain.

When her vision clears, she sees a figure running. The front yard. Celinda. A million miles away, but maybe not so far.

Celinda howls at Maggie. "You shouldn't have done that."

Maggie tries to run, but her ankle gives way. She half skips, half hops, using the shotgun as a sort of crutch. An eternity later, she makes it to Bess and her phone, leans against the comforting metal. Celinda is almost to her own car, fifteen-feet away. Maggie takes aim and shoots wide and high. She pumps and shoots again. The car's wheels blow out and glass shatters in a spray of shot.

"Bitch," Celinda screams.

Louise howls and squeezes herself through the partially rolled-down window, squirting onto the ground like a newborn calf. She's up in an instant, black-and-white fur aloft as she launches herself at Celinda. The woman falls, shrieking in a three-octave soprano, with the dog on her back.

Maggie dives into the truck's cab. When she has her phone, she dials 911 and holds it to her ear with her shoulder, grabs the shotgun again, and rushes back to the side of the house. Flames are shooting out the open master bedroom window.

"911, what's your emergency?"

She sprints around to the front door. "Fire. There's a man in the house. She's getting away." She shouts the address into the phone, then drops it on the front stoop.

Staring at the house, her heart hammers. She's always the one running from, not running to. From that long-ago fire of her childhood. From home to chase a music career. From Hank in Cheyenne. From Wyoming last week, and even though it wasn't her fault, from Gary's house as he burned to death. But not now. She can't now. Nothing can keep her from running into this fire, to this man. Nothing.

She tries the front door, but it's locked. She throws her body weight into it, beats it, kicks it, but it won't budge. Using the butt of the gun, she batters out the sidelight window beside the door. She can't crawl through the space, but she can reach the doorknob and deadbolt. Broken glass slices open the not-yet-healed burns on her forearms. The pain will come later. Now, with a truckload of adrenaline coursing through her, she's impervious. She turns the door lock. Celinda hadn't thrown the deadbolt, and when she twists the knob, the door flies open. Maggie stumbles through, still clutching the gun under her left arm. She pulls her right arm from the sidelight, cutting it even worse and not caring.

Smoke billows out through the door, but no flames. She runs into her kitchen and rips off her shirt. With water from the sink, she drenches it, then puts it over her mouth with one hand. The cool water on her face is instant relief from the smoke burning her eyes, and it blocks the stench of gasoline and char. As she's about to take off, she grabs the gun. It's been an important tool so far, and she may need it again.

She pounds through the living room, running past burning furniture and who knows what else, down the short hallway toward the master bedroom. With all the smoke, she can't really get a last look at the irreplaceable collection of art on the walls. Gidget's treasures. A memory, fleeting, consumes her. Playing an art gallery opening in Houston. The wildly eccentric but gorgeous owner, Gidget, who took an interest in her. She'd never met her mother again. She'd only later discovered the woman Gidget was through her magnificent paintings and the personalized collection of artistic gifts she'd amassed from all the notable artists of her time. She hadn't had enough time with her, with them, but there's nothing she can do to save them now.

Maggie may be losing Gidget tonight, but she's not going to lose Hank.

The bedroom door is locked. She leans over sideways using the shotgun as a fulcrum, kicking like a deranged mule, over and over. The door gives way and slams into the wall. There are things burning in the room—the area rug, the comforter, the trash can—but Celinda hadn't taken the time to douse everything in the room thoroughly with the gas before setting it on fire. So Maggie can still see through the flames to the bed. Before her eyes, though, the wadded top sheet at the foot of the bed ignites.

"Hank," she shouts through her shirt.

He coughs then says something, but the sound is too muffled for her to understand him.

She's on him in an instant, dropping the gun on the bedroom floor. "The restraints. It's steel cable."

He wheezes. "Attached by spring latches."

Maggie slides her hand up a cable. Sure enough, the chain is doubled around a bedpost and fastened on itself with a spring-tooth latch. She pulls back a lever and the spring releases. She unhooks the latch and loosens the noose around Hank's wrist. Hank rolls away on one shoulder from a flame that's crawling across the bed toward him. Maggie beats at it with her shirt. He groans and coughs, pulling the cloth gag from the corner of his mouth.

She makes quick work of his feet and other hand. "Can you hang on to me? Bury your face in my neck, and I'll drag you?"

"Yes."

She sits on the bed. He locks his arms around her shoulders, then pushes off the bed to help her stand. He's big, taller than her and far heavier, and the drugs make him weak and unsteady, but the increasing roar of the fire gives her a strength she's never had before. She holds her shirt over her face again. Leaning over as far as she can without faltering under his bulk, she walks under the worst of the fire, one arm out for balance. It's achingly slowgoing. A few times, Hank yells as the flames claw at them. She'd scream, too, but she's breathing too hard from the exertion of carrying him. The hallway—which has felt so short every time guests have loitered outside her bedroom—now feels miles long.

Twice she goes down. Once to her hands and knees. Another time, all the way to her chest. Hank's weight flattens her. For a moment she pants, dazed, aching, and sure they're both done for. Then she rallies. They aren't dying now, not like this. Straining, she pushes upward. Her muscles tremble. Hank puts some weight on his feet, relieving her burden enough that she's able to get to her knees, then push off her thighs with her hands, then stagger to her feet. Her hands burn. Even her boot soles are hot. She ignores it all and slow-marches on, only sure she's heading in the right direction because she keeps bumping into the wall to her left.

Ahead of them, she hears shrieking and growling. Inch by hellishly hot inch, Maggie gets closer to the sound. As she tumbles through smoke down the steps and out of the house, she feels fur under her hand.

"Louise."

A wagging tail hits her in the face.

"Get this fucking dog's fangs off of me."

Maggie ignores Celinda's voice, even though it's so close she knows she could touch the woman if she wanted. She hauls herself and Hank farther out into the yard, her thighs quivering. The heat on her back is still intense. She collapses. The grass under her cheek is a cool sip of mountain stream water. Hank touches her face, something blue clutched in his fist fluttering in front of her.

"Good dog, Fucker," she croaks, then passes out.

THIRTY-FIVE

"Louise deserves a medal," Junior says, leaning over Maggie, who's sitting on a stretcher while an EMT dresses her cuts and burns.

"She's a good dog."

"Can't believe you stole her from me." Hank's voice is a barely audible rasp. It still sounds woozy from being drugged. He's on a stretcher, too, but flat on his back, still holding his scrap of blue fabric.

Maggie pries it from his fist. "You foisted that mutt off on me. Now that she's the second coming of Lassie, you want to rewrite history."

"Sir, I need you to quit talking or we'll have to tape your mouth shut." The second EMT is teasing, but stern. "Seriously, I do need to put a mask over it now." He holds up an oxygen mask. "Your bronchial tubes are swelling. They're not letting in enough air. This will help." He lifts the back of Hank's head and slides the strap around it, placing the mask over his mouth and nose gently.

"Tape hers shut, too." Maggie jerks her head toward Celinda, who is nonstop complaining about her injuries from Louise's teeth. "She's lucky Louise didn't rip her throat out. It would have served her right."

Maggie opens her hand to look at the blackened piece of scarf Hank had carried out of the house. Blue with dirty white stars. It looks familiar. She stuffs it in her pocket, then takes several long sips of water. She's desperately thirsty, but the water still hurts going down. Her second fire in a week, before she'd recovered from the first one. She hopes it's her last. For sure there will be no mirrors allowed in her near future.

Junior pulls on his chin. "I have news."

"If it's good news, I'll take it."

Before Junior can answer, the EMTs push Hank's stretcher into the back of the ambulance. Maggie stands and attempts to climb in after him.

The EMT who had been helping Hank with his oxygen mask turns to her and says, "No, ma'am. We'll send another for you."

"I'm not letting him out of my sight."

Junior puts a hand on her shoulder. "I'll drive you. We can talk on the way."

She winces and jerks away, trying to remember how she hurt her shoulder. The dive out the window? Glass? Burning embers? Wrenching Hank along and to safety? All of the above? "I'm riding with Hank."

Karen appears, getting out of an unmarked SUV with a light on top.

"Shit," Maggie mutters. "Tell me she's not here to hassle me."

Junior follows her gaze to the fire marshal. "I don't think so."

The EMTs start to shut the doors to Hank's ambulance.

"No. Please." Maggie blocks them with her arm.

"Sorry, ma'am." The EMT removes her arm and closes the door.

Junior says, "Maggie, wait. We have an ID on the body from the Coop."

Maggie tries to pull her hair back, but her bandaged hand makes it impossible. She flits her glance to Junior, her eyes wild. "Who was it?"

"Leslie DeWitt. And she was roofied. Like Gary."

"And like Hank." Although Junior's words don't surprise her, they're a gut punch nonetheless. Leslie. The real Leslie. Her arm drops. Her hand finds the scarf in her pocket, and suddenly she knows why it looks familiar. She's seen it before. In the hair of a pale, braided woman, rocking in her room at Michele's, left in the chair. How had it gotten here? She pulls it out and squeezes it. *Oh, Leslie, I'm so sorry.* "It's my fault."

"Why?"

"Celinda. Her." Maggie points at her old bandmate. "She came looking for me and found Leslie. All of this. Gary, my shop, even befriending my friends and family, Hank, and now the house. All of it was for revenge."

"She's not just a sick puppy?"

"Oh, she's sick all right. But she claims I'm the reason she's sick."

The ambulance engine fires up.

"Let me drive you, Maggie."

She hesitates for a split second, then pounds on the ambulance door. She shouts, "Let me in." Then to Junior, "Make them let me in."

He doesn't move.

"Make them, Junior. After all you guys have put me through—that you've been a part of—you owe me."

He sighs, walks to the driver's door, holds up a hand. She peers after him, watches him speaking. The rear doors open, knocking into her, but she doesn't care. Out of her peripheral vision, she sees Karen join Junior.

The EMT inside the door says, "He needs care. Either get in, or stay out, but choose fast."

Maggie's inside and holding Hank's hand in a blink.

THIRTY-SIX

Two days later, under the midday sun, Maggie takes Louise to the charred ruins of her home. "All of this would have been yours, girl."

Louise whines and strains. The dog is on a leash, since the entirety of Maggie's compound is a crime scene.

The usual suspects are arrayed around the train wreck of her life, but Maggie ignores them. Media. Curious neighbors. Gary's groupies. Karen. Junior. Sheriff Boland. Other county personnel in uniform. Maggie's doctor had refused to let her be interviewed the day before, to give her voice a rest after the smoke strain. She'd given a statement first thing that morning, though, so the law enforcement types leave her alone now. She's no longer under suspicion, either. Not just because she and Hank could have died, but also because they were corroborating witnesses to Celinda's crazed confessions. Just for good measure, Maggie had told them about Lumpy and her goats, and about the redheaded woman who'd kicked his ladder over and left him treed for days. She wishes the authorities could pin that one on Celinda, too, but she feels certain Jenny did it. With Lumpy's ID, they should be able to nail her for it. The county is currently over its limit in crazy women who'd be better off locked up.

A very sane-looking woman, her face shaded by a straw cowboy hat with a pink band, is sitting on a folding lawn chair between the parking area and where the house used to be. Merritt Fuller stands. Maggie's lips are cracked and dry. She has even sparser eyelashes and eyebrows than after the fire at Gary's. No makeup, no moisturizer, not even a hat or scarf in her hair. She feels unprepared for a conversation, but she has no choice.

Maggie lifts a hand in greeting. "Merritt." She walks the rest of the way to the older woman, assisted by Louise pulling ahead of her.

"Maggie. I read what happened. I came here as fast as I could." She holds up a twelve-pack of Lone Star.

Tears prick Maggie's eyes, but she blinks them back. "Does this mean I can come to Gary's service?"

"Better you than those dickheads Tom and Thorn." She sets the beer in the chair. "You were right. They were stealing from Gary, for Thorn and Kelly's tour. Which went in the crapper when Gary got Thorn fired from *The Singer*. Served him right. I've already sicced the cops on them both. They were arrested this morning." Merritt's face droops. "But I don't think Gary ever got over Kelly quitting on him. He thought he was doing right by her."

"And Kelly?"

"She coughed up the whole story when I confronted her. Even signed affidavits against them."

"Did she know about the money?"

"Says she didn't." Merritt shrugs. "She's my baby girl. Corrupted by older men who should have known that if you mess with one Fuller, you mess with them all."

"I'm glad she did the right thing."

Louise winds her leash around Maggie's legs. Maggie twists in the same direction to avoid getting tangled up.

"She loved her brother. And she feels real bad about everything."

Now that her tour is on ice and her manager and boyfriend are being charged with embezzlement. If the world is a decent place, Thorn will get an adder for statutory rape, too. Maggie has a strong suspicion that Kelly should be in the clink with them, but maybe she's learned her lesson. "But you've kicked her ass, right?"

"She won't walk for a week."

"Good."

"How about I keep the beer on ice for us, and we'll toast Gary after we lay him to rest?" Merritt gives Maggie the details for the services in Boerne. "It would mean a lot to me for you to be there."

Maggie hugs Gary's mother with her nonleash arm, gingerly to avoid the injured places. "I wouldn't miss it."

Merritt walks back to the parking area with the chair and the beer.

Louise tries to follow her, but Maggie tugs her back. She's glad the conversation with Merritt is over, even if it was a good one. She's here for her house. Her shop. For closure.

Her phone rings. She glances at the screen. The call is from Emily. She walks into the shade of the lone surviving tree on the front of the property, a barren, singed oak. Louise scurries around her six-foot-diameter world, checking out the new scents.

"Hello?"

"Maggie! Wallace and I are calling to make sure you're okay. He was on my ass to call you. About your place. The fires. The person who died. I told him we should give you more time, but he's persistent."

In the background, Wallace's voice calls out, "Hi, Maggie!"

Maggie closes her eyes and lifts her face up to the sky. Her shoulder hurts. And her palms, her knees, and her bruised ribs on the side where she'd been thrown into the air conditioner by the fireball. The emotional pain of facing betrayal is more than she feels equipped to deal with right now. "Wallace needs to stay off the gossip rags and get a life."

Emily hesitates, then repeats Maggie's words to Wallace. There's a scuffling sound.

Wallace's voice comes on the line. "Seriously, are you okay?"

"Hi, Wallace. Yes, I'm fine."

"People dot com made it sound like you nearly died."

"I guess I did. Hank was closer to dying than me, though."

Louise darts between her legs. Maggie steps over the leash. Her patience with the dog's manners is growing thin.

"Is he as delectable as his picture?"

"Yeah."

Hank's smiling, dimpled face flashes through her mind. Saying his name makes her heart ache. Maggie had tried to talk to him repeatedly yesterday. He'd been in treatment or asleep every time. This morning her calls to his room went unanswered and the ones to his cellphone had gone to voicemail. Now that the danger of Celinda has passed, there are things she needs to know. Like why he came to Texas, whether he regrets it, and what his intentions are, toward her, Sheila, and Sheila's baby. But if he'd wanted to talk to her, he'd surely have called her back by now.

She draws in a sharp breath. She can't think about those things now. She has to deal with Wallace, and him leaking details of her life to TMZ. "Wallace, if we're going to be friends, it's not okay to talk to reporters about me."

The pitch of his voice rises. "What?"

"I know you're the one who told TMZ I was headed to see Gary last week. I understand. But it can't happen again."

"It wasn't me, I swear." His voice sounds sincere.

But Maggie has been fed plenty of earnest denials in her life. "I can be friends with someone who tells me the truth, even if they've messed up. But I can't be friends with a liar."

Wallace grows insistent. "Listen, I didn't tell People.com you were going to see Gary. I've never talked with anyone at TMZ. TMZ doesn't know I exist, damn them."

There's the sound of another struggle over possession of the phone.

Emily comes back on. "Oh God, Maggie, don't be mad at Wallace. It really wasn't him."

Maggie unwinds herself from the leash as Louise doubles back and tangles them both up again. "Kind of hard to believe. He's the one with the obsession with celebrity gossip."

"It's true. I know it's not him, because it was me."

"What?" Maggie stops fighting Louise.

"I'm so sorry. I only told Laura. And apparently those jerks writing for TMZ were in Sheridan trying to dig up dirt on you through Hank. They cornered Laura in the hospital. I know she didn't mean to hurt you. She was trying to get them off her brother. She feels terrible. I feel terrible."

"Oh my God."

Louise hits the end of the leash hard.

Maggie reaches down for an untangled section of the leash and jerks her back, then extricates herself. "Stop it, Fucker."

Emily's voice is aghast. "What?"

"Sorry. Not you. The dog. You were saying?"

"If I'd ever have dreamed it would turn into what it did, I never would have said anything to Laura."

This. This is why Maggie doesn't have female friends. Because they can't keep from running their mouths to each other. Except for Michele. She's different, thank God. "You told Hank's sister. Of all the people to tell, you told his *sister*."

"I know. In retrospect, it was a bad call. At the time, I had this misguided feeling that I was helping Hank get over you so he could move on to become a father and husband without reservations. But it was none of my business, and I shouldn't have done it."

Damn straight, you shouldn't have. Maggie sucks in a shuddering breath. "Okay."

"So don't be mad at Wallace. Be mad at me."

"And Laura."

"Well, yes, me and Laura. But I am sorry."

"Me, too. Very, very sorry."

A squirrel runs up the tree beside them. Louise goes after it, nearly jerking Maggie's arm out of socket. She's had it with reining the dog in. It's her own property, after all, so if the law enforcement types don't like it, tough shit. She unclips the leash. Louise bounds like a drunken reindeer toward the county personnel working the scene.

"I hope someday you can forgive me."

Maggie sighs. Emily cares about Hank. Lord knows Maggie does, too. "It will be okay. Can you let Wallace know I'm sorry I blamed him?"

"I will. And thank you."

"Just remember this when I do some dumbass thing that pisses you off."

Emily laughs. "I will. By the way, Jack says hello."

Maggie hadn't heard a sound from Jack, but she can't help a small grin. The wooden Indian thing he does is pretty funny, whether he means for it to be or not.

After they end the call, Maggie walks through the disaster area. She expects to feel anguish, but all she feels is numb. Junior waves to her from the far side of the scene. He's restraining Louise by the collar. Maggie waves back, but she doesn't go for her dog. She isn't eager to interact with Junior or any of the rest of them. Especially Boland. He'd tried to railroad her. At best, he harassed her needlessly. At worst, he nearly made her a victim of his lazy police work. And now, when she needs a moment with her place, to say goodbye before she figures out her next steps—Sell the land and buy another shop? Rebuild? Liquidate her inheritance and travel?—they're all here, keeping her from finding peace. Junior releases Louise and turns back to a conversation with his colleagues.

Maggie calls her dog. Louise sprints to her, the very portrait of joy.

"Come with me, girl."

Maggie and Louise walk past the former shop and burned-down house to the partially intact barn and workroom. The roof and walls are intact, and the place is no longer barricaded, so she follows Louise in. It's dark inside. She pushes her sunglasses onto her head, where they catch in her unruly hair. She'd rather not break her hair with her glasses, so she carefully removes them and hangs them on the neck of her crumpled, one-day worn T-shirt.

The first thing she sees is a big Dodge Ram truck with Wyoming plates. Hank's truck. Realization hits her. This is why she hadn't seen it out front the night of the fire. If she had, finding Hank in her house—and bed— wouldn't have been as big a surprise. Maggie's fists ball with a desire to find Celinda and snatch her baldheaded. The woman is clever, Maggie will give her that, but, whatever she has coming to her from the legal system isn't enough.

Louise sniffs, greedy for the barn scents, although all Maggie smells is smoke and chemicals. She moves past the truck and examines the remains of her professional life. How many hundreds of people and creatures have touched the salvaged treasures over their combined centuries of existence? Yet how meager they look postfire. She trails a few fingers over the tortured remains of a typewriter and a pencil sharpener on a blackened metal desk. Franklin is going to be sick when he comes out to process the insurance claim. Everything is ruined, whether from smoke, fire, chemicals, water, or a combination of them all. He should just call it a total loss and be done with it.

Her life in a nutshell. Ruined and a total loss.

Behind her, she hears voices and the sound of footsteps drawing near. People. More people intruding. She looks around for a place to hide. But no, that's childish. She reaches up to her cheeks. No tears. She fills her lungs with air, turns, and walks to the door, chin up.

"There you are." It's Michele's voice.

Maggie tents a hand to shield her eyes from the blinding sun overhead. Michele, Rashidi, Ava, Collin, Edward, and her mom. She'd texted Michele on her way over: *Don't worry about me. Just dropping by the house and shop. See you soon.* She should have kept her whereabouts to herself.

She lifts a hand in a tepid wave.

Charlotte wraps her in her arms. "My sweet girl. We didn't want you to face this alone."

Maggie pats her mother and steps out of the embrace. "I'm good."

"Let we take you for a bite," Rashidi says in full island accent. He scratches Louise between her ears.

Ava looks like a bird-of-paradise in a coal pit, standing by the burned buildings in a bright green top and pink leggings. "Collin and I leave after lunch. It's our treat. As a thank-you for putting up with us."

"Come on." Michele moves close enough that she can whisper in Maggie's ear. "You've lost weight. You have to eat."

"You're all very kind. But I have to do this. Alone. Now." Sounds of protest rise, and she lifts a hand to shush them. "I'll eat. I promise."

She allows herself to be hugged and bids Collin and Ava farewell.

"Thanks for not trying to steal my man," Ava says, smiling at her.

"Who says I didn't?"

Ava's mouth makes an O for a moment.

"Just screwing with you. This one's not a whore. Good job."

"Why do I feel like I've just been insulted?" Collin says, scratching his head.

Michele kisses her sister's cheek. "She has a special way with that. See you back at the house, Maggie."

When it's just the two of them again, Maggie sinks to the ground with the dog, her legs folding into a crisscross. Louise sits in front of her, dutifully stirring up dust from the dirt floor with her tail.

"Even with all of them gone, you make it impossible to be still with my thoughts."

"You don't do me any favors either."

The male voice behind Maggie jolts electricity to the tips of her fingers and toes. She doesn't turn her head, just continues to talk as if in a conversation with the dog. "My, what a deep voice you have, Louise."

"Woof, woof," Hank replies.

Long legs stop beside her. He dangles a brown paper grocery bag from one hand, the kind with handles. "How about you come up here instead of me down there. I've had more limber and pain-free days in my life."

Maggie stands facing Hank. Six inches separate them. Close enough to be in his pheromone zone. And what pheromones they are. *Oh, the smell of this man.* She breathes in, trying not to let him see she's huffing him. "How's this?"

"Perfect. I'm almost close enough now to see what little eyebrows and eyelashes you have left. It makes you look extra surprised to see me." He grins. "But you're still the most beautiful woman I've ever seen."

She almost melts right back to the floor. She clears her throat and says, "What are you doing out of the hospital?" in a strangled voice.

His dimples beg to be touched. "You know why I didn't do steer wrestling or calf roping?"

"Why's that?"

"Because I always broke the barrier too early."

She can't help smiling. "How'd you get here? I found your truck." Maggie points back at the barn.

"Hell, I Ubered. Paid the driver a big-ass tip to drive me around until I found you."

Warmth floods her body. Upward. Outward. Downward. "You didn't call me back."

"You weren't answering your damn phone."

Maggie checks her phone, flustered. It's dead. "Sorry. It must not be holding a charge."

"I knew where you'd be, although I can't say I was eager to come here again." Hank puts a finger under her chin and lifts it, aiming her gaze exactly where he wants it. Into his eyes. "Thanks for saving me—again."

"You're welcome. Again."

"I brought you something."

Maggie shakes her head. "You didn't have to get me anything. I got to see you naked, tied to the bedposts."

He raises his eyebrows.

"Sorry. Too soon?"

But he laughs. "No. And I did bring you something. It's why I came. You forgot it back in Wyoming. When you ran away. Again." His hand disappears into the grocery bag and pulls out his belt and Cheyenne Frontier Days buckle.

She takes a step back. "I didn't forget it."

He takes a step closer. His step is bigger than hers. Now they're three inches apart. He reaches around her waist with the belt, his arm brushing hers. She shivers. His other arm meets it mid-back, encircling her.

Her mouth goes dry. Her heart thrums madly. She's afraid to breathe. "What about Sheila?"

He presses the belt into her back. Then he slides his hands apart along its length. Gently, he pulls each end around the sides of her waist. When he joins the ends in front, he tugs with just enough pressure to scoot her toward him. Now only one inch of warm air separates their faces. "What about her?"

"She said you proposed. That you're going to be a daddy."

"She's not pregnant, if that's what you thought. She was talking about her daughter Phoebe. You know, the nine-year-old secret daughter she pretended to the world was her sister?"

"Oh my God. But I thought . . ."

"You thought wrong. I never proposed."

"Aren't you two getting married?"

"She suggested it while I was under surgical anesthesia. When I woke up later, I said no."

"Well, shit. That changes things."

He smiles with those killer dimples and closes the last inch between them, first with his lips, then with the rest of his body. "Good. So you're not running away this time?"

The barn spins around her as she sinks into his kiss. *Yes, this changes everything.* "Not a chance, cowboy."

DEAD PILE (MAGGIE KILLIAN NOVEL #3)

A WHAT DOESN'T KILL YOU TEXAS-TO-WYOMING ROMANTIC MYSTERY

ONE

Maggie tilts her chin, pushing up the back of the slate-colored ponytail beanie framing her black bun. All the better to lock eyes with the cowboy looking down at her. He's leaning against the door of a red barn, looking like an ad for Marlboro cigarettes. Or sex. A hand-lettered sign on a weathered board hangs overhead. PINEY BOTTOMS RANCH, SHERIDAN, WY. She likes the one even better that's just visible inside the barn above the window into the office. WYOMING: WYNOT?

"Nice belt buckle," he says, using it to pull her to him with a jerk.

She catches herself with her hands around his waist. Her chest bumps a little below his, through the bulky Carhartt jackets they're both wearing. Her legs are longer, but he's still got a few inches on her. "Got it off a dead-beat bull rider." In truth, the buckle was part of Hank's haul when he won the bull riding championship at the 2002 Cheyenne Frontier Days Rodeo.

He displays two killer dimples. "I hope you didn't catch anything."

"Just him." Her stomach flip-flops, its usual response to the damn hollows in his cheeks. "But you wouldn't believe how long it took to reel him in."

A single snowflake falls on the cowboy's nose, then another on her own. The snow tickles hers. Melts on his. She sneezes.

He lifts a faded navy-blue bandana to wipe his cheek. "Nice. I think you missed some of my face with that. But not much."

"So you don't want to kiss me?"

The cowboy—Hank Sibley—growls deep in his throat. "Like hell I don't."

His lips are cushiony and warm despite the cold air, like the bed they'd heated up that morning. Maggie melts into the kiss, merging their respective ChapStick flavors—cherry for her, spearmint for him—and drops a hand to his muscular buns.

"Get a room." A much shorter man with twinkling dark eyes and the dark skin and hair of his Mexican heritage doesn't break stride as he heads past them into the barn. Gene Soboleski, Polish last name courtesy of his adoptive parents.

Hank and Gene have been partners in their Double S Bucking Stock business for nearly two decades. Friends longer, from their early days riding bulls for beer and gas money through their later success that seeded the purchase of Sassafrass, the original broodmare for their bucking broncos. But Gene's only recently become Maggie's stepbrother, thanks to the union of her mother and his birth father, after her lifetime as an only child. Not only that, the marriage came with a stepsister, too: her best friend, Michele, back in Giddings, Texas, where Maggie's industrial and homestead salvage business, Flown the Coop, lies in tatters.

Hank talks against Maggie's lips. "Get a life. Or a woman of your own."

Maggie releases Hank after one more long, slow kiss. She isn't stopping on Gene's account. But she doesn't want to scandalize Andy, Double S's Amish hand, at least not this early in the morning. The top hand, Paco, she's not so worried about. Number one, because he's on vacation. Number two, because he'd probably yell "Let 'er buck" and slap Hank on the ass.

She murmurs into Hank's neck. "Take me for a quick ride before it snows."

"I thought I already did, music girl."

Maggie has mixed emotions about the nickname. Hank had called her that when he first met her, fifteen years before, in her old life. But it's outdated now. *Junker girl, more like.*

Gene walks back by carrying a bale of hay. "La la la. Don't hear you."

She sticks her tongue out at Hank. "Not that kind of ride. I want to ride my horse."

"That pregnant Percheron, big as an elephant, stubborn as a mule?"

Gene rounds the corner out of the barn. His voice is tinny in the cold. "First you'll have to catch her. Miss Houdini has done it again."

Maggie runs to join him. There are horses everywhere in the paddocks, the ones leaving later in the week for the Prairie Rim Circuit Finals Rodeo in Duncan, Oklahoma. But the big black mare is nowhere to be seen, her solo paddock empty. "Lily's out?"

"Yep. That damn mare's a pain in the ass."

Behind them, Hank says, "She's your horse, all right, Maggie. Every time I turn around, she's run off again."

Maggie shoots him a slit-eye look. "Funny."

To Gene, Hank says, "We'll find her."

"Better do it fast. This is supposed to be our first good storm of the season."

As if in response, a gust of wind from the north blows in. Maggie raises the collar on her jacket. Poor Lily. She's due in a month. Most horses gravitate toward a herd. But not her. The mare is a loner, which makes her harder to find and harder to catch. Maggie shivers. These are no conditions for Lily to be out alone in.

"It's only October. Is this weather unusual?" She heads back for the barn, following Hank, Gene following her.

Both men guffaw.

Hank swats her on the tush as she passes him to enter the dark, cavernous interior. "What would Pretty-shield say?"

Maggie had been reading and rereading the book about the Crow medicine woman, which Hank had bought her on a trip through the Montana reservation. She's gone her whole life not knowing she is one-eighth Crow on her father's side, until the previous month. As a Crow-come-lately, she's making up for lost time.

"It's not like a Ouija board. Or an almanac. It's a biography."

Gene says, "The October moon has a lot of different names with the Native Americans in the region, Maggie May. The Cheyenne call it the moon of the freeze on the stream's edge. The Shoshone link it to rutting season. The Lakota named it for the wind that shakes off leaves, the Arapaho for falling leaves, and the Sioux for changing seasons. Seems like those last three all had the same idea."

"I'm not hearing anything about snow, though." Maggie tosses her head and feels her bun flop.

"Ah, but we are nearly on the face of the Bighorn Mountains."

"So will it be safe for us to ride out in this?"

Hank dimples up. "This is nothing."

"It's still in the nineties in Giddings."

"That's hellfire hot to me. Oh, sorry. I didn't mean it that way."

For a moment, Maggie lets herself remember her darling house and cute shop, then shuts it down. It hurts to think about her murderous former bandmate going on a torching spree the month before. Besides her store and house—including all the priceless original artwork painted by Maggie's deceased birth mother—the fires killed Maggie's tenant and an old boyfriend, country star Gary Fuller, and nearly burned up Hank to boot. The fires lit off a conflagration of publicity that has been the last thing Maggie wants. She's glad to have Hank's family ranch, Piney Bottoms, as a refuge while she's waiting on the insurance payout she needs to rebuild her business. She's even more glad that she and Hank are *finally* together, after their years of crossed wires and missed opportunities. His recent almost-fiancée, Sheila, doesn't share Maggie's gratitude. "It's okay. I know what you meant."

"But now you look sad."

"I was just thinking of all Gidget's paintings I lost in the fire." Maggie hadn't known her birth mother while she was alive. An image flashes in her mind of her favorite, *Front Porch Pickin'*, which had depicted a guitarist both melancholy and joyful. "It was all I had of her. Sometimes it gets to me."

"I know. I hate that for you."

Maggie is lost in memories until a floppy-eared head bumps her knee. She bends to pet Louise, the short-legged union of a determined corgi and surely embarrassed border collie. But the dog's nudge is a hit and run. Louise trots past her and up the stairs to the hayloft to hunt rats.

Suddenly Maggie realizes Hank is leading two geldings to the hitching post inside the mouth of the barn, when she hadn't even realized he'd gone. She was more than lost in memories—she'd fallen into a mental black hole. She snaps herself out of her thoughts and moves to help him with them. The horses are lookers. A buckskin and a blue-roan with a graying muzzle. In the distance, she sees Andy in an animated conversation with another man, who she assumes is Amish because of his long beard and distinctive hat and dress.

Hank eyes her over the withers of the buckskin. "Thought I'd lost you there for a few minutes."

He's been worrying about her too much lately. Yes, she's had a tough time. Is having a tough time. But inside, she chafes at herself that she's showing weakness. Outside, she puts up a smoke screen. "Sorry. I should have had that second cup of coffee. Who's that talking to Andy over there?"

Hank's eyes flick to the bunkhouse then back to the buckskin. "That's his father. Reggie Yoder."

"They don't look like they're happy with each other."

"Reggie is hard on Andy."

Gene walks in with a brown-skinned young man whose long black hair is braided, jeans creased, and worn boots oiled. "Hank, this is Michael Short. He's looking for a job."

Hank strides toward Michael, arm out, and the two men shake.

"Nice to meet you, sir. I'd love to work on your fine ranch."

"I'm sure Gene told you we're not hiring full-timers right now, but that could change in the blink of an eye."

"Yes, sir, he did."

Gene nods. "You and Maggie better get going. I'm going to chat a little more with Michael while I give him a tour."

Hank puts a hand on the blue-roan's neck. "Nice to meet you, Michael."

Gene escorts Michael back out of the barn.

To Maggie, Hank says, "You'll take Don Juan. He was my mom's last horse." A shadow crosses his face. His mother's riding days are over. She's wheelchair-bound and has Alzheimer's. She still lives at the ranch, with Hank and a live-in helper, although Hank still provides a great deal of her care. It's a round-the-clock job bigger than any one person.

"So you're not using me as a crash-test dummy on some up-and-comer—that's good."

The up-and-comers will get a road test at the rodeo that weekend. It will be Maggie's first time seeing the Double S buckers in competition, and she's looking forward to it. Like really, really looking forward to it, even though she was never much into rodeo before Hank.

"Last thing I'd ever want is to harm a single hair on your pretty head." Hank hands her a brush and takes another to the buckskin's coat. "Lily likes Don Juan best of all the riding horses. She likes sweet feed even better, so you'll be carrying a feed bag full with you. I'll take Tatonka here." He bends to reach under the roan's stomach, then catches himself with his hands on his knees, grimacing.

Maggie pauses, brush poised over Don Juan's back. "What is it?"

"Another one of my damn headaches. They're coming on fast with no warning." He drops his brush and crouches on his boot heels, elbows on knees, head in hands.

Maggie tosses her brush into a bucket and hurries to him. Her fingers graze his shoulder. She knows he doesn't want anyone in his space when a headache hits. "Where's your prescription?"

Hank's eyes are squeezed shut. "Back pocket."

She pries the pill out of his tight jeans, retrieves a bottled water from a refrigerator that doubles as a holder of human drinks and of animal medications, and brings both back to him, first removing the pill from the wrapping he has trouble mastering when his head crashes. "Here."

He opens his mouth for the pill, accepting it on his tongue. She puts the bottle to his lips. He drinks, swallows, grunts.

"You want a cold rag?"

"No."

"Maybe I could help you into the office?"

He snaps at her. "Quit hovering."

"What did I do?"

"Just leave me the hell alone."

Normally Maggie has a smart comeback for any situation, but his volatile response short-circuits her system. She stands frozen for long seconds. Her eyes burn. Her breath comes out in little puffs of vapor cloud. His abrupt personality change stings. Feeling bad isn't an excuse to act like a jerk, but now's not the time to discuss it.

She picks up the brush he dropped and begins grooming Tatonka. When she's finished, she continues with Don Juan. She's unsure whether Hank will be able to ride, but she needs to do something. Slowly she curries their manes and tails, then picks their hooves. She scrapes botfly eggs off their legs. When the horses are both groomed to the nines and saddled, she gives them sweet-feed mash and hangs a bag of feed for Lily on Don Juan's saddle horn. Half an hour has passed. She puts bridles on the horses. Snow begins to accumulate on the ground in the stable yard. Hank hasn't moved. She's run out of ways to stall with the horses.

"Hank?" she whispers.

He startles. "Yeah?"

"Are you okay?"

"I musta dozed off." He rolls his head, stretching his neck. "I'm feeling a little better. I think we caught it in time."

"Amazing you can sleep in that position."

He holds a hand up to her, and she takes it. "Thanks for helping me."

"You didn't seem to appreciate it much earlier."

He puts a little weight into her hand as he lumbers to his feet. "What?"

"You weren't all that nice."

He looks confused, then he closes the blinds to his emotions with a snap, leaving only blankness. "I'm sorry. I was out of my head."

She doesn't know what worries her more, the fact that he's being evasive and doesn't seem to remember his behavior, or the pain and personality change. "Have you been to a doctor?"

"That's how I get the magic pills."

"I mean recently."

He checks the cinch on his horse. "Yep. Every three months."

"Wait, what? How long has this been going on?"

With his back to her and voice matter-of-fact, he says, "Nearly fifteen years."

Maggie feels as confused as Hank had looked moments before. "Why am I just now learning about it?"

"You've seen me have headaches before."

"You know what I mean."

"Whining like a child isn't the bull rider way."

"Would you stop fiddling with that horse and talk to me?"

He turns and meets her eyes. "Let's ride out. I'll tell you on the way."

TWO

They mount up. Maggie's not an expert rider, but Don Juan feels solid underneath her as she adjusts her reins. Louise runs down from the hayloft and follows them into the stable yard. Maggie's Texas goats, Omaha and Nebraska, are visiting Wyoming, too, and they bleat at her.

"Lawn mowers, do your thing," Hank had said after breakfast, and staked them in the yard on the barn-facing side of the main house, a white two-story wooden structure, where Maggie is staying with him.

Apparently they don't want to do their thing without Maggie anymore. Or maybe they're nervous with the change in weather. Fuss buckets. She makes a mental note to put them up when she and Hank get back with Lily.

Hank clucks and Tatonka takes off at a trot. Man and horse lead the way through several gates, heading south, until they—and Louise—are riding across a pasture so large there's no opposite fence in sight. Theirs is not a long-term partnership. Hank's go-to gelding, Wolf, had died a month before. But Tatonka moves like he's reading Hank's mind, which Maggie knows is partly training and partly Hank's clear body cues and leg pressure.

Hank gestures at the monochrome before them in shades of white varying from marshmallow on the ground to ash in the sky. "Lily has a few favorite spots. We'll check those first."

Don Juan is a slow-goer. Maggie fans her legs at his sides as he falls behind Tatonka. Big flakes swirl around Hank's body, and snow puffs explode from Tatonka's hooves. With ten yards separating them from Maggie, they look like a scene in a snow globe.

Hank swivels his head back toward her. "Smack your thighs with the reins. That usually does the trick."

She smacks, but Don Juan doesn't so much as flinch. She tries again. Once, twice, three times, with increasing velocity. Her thighs sting from the smacks, and the last time she does it, she catches the saddle's pommel. It makes a sharp sound. Don Juan snorts and speeds up to a reluctant trot.

In the distance, she sees the black silhouettes of cattle, all facing the same direction, huddled together. Their backs are dusted white. Louise cavorts like a puppy, snapping at falling snow. The wind is gusty, but not ferocious, and it's strangely less cold than she'd expected. If she wasn't worried about Hank and Lily, in fact, the ride would be lovely. She can even make out the Sibleys' tall, rustic cabin on the mountain and the road winding up to it. Austere. Beautiful. Mysterious. Hank has promised to take her up to see it soon.

"Okay, cowboy, we're riding. Time to talk," she says as Don Juan catches up to Tatonka.

Hank shifts his weight back in his saddle. Tatonka slows to match pace with Don Juan. "You remember me telling you I retired from bull riding because I got hurt?"

"Yes." She glances at him.

"I came here to recover."

"Right."

He nods.

She does a mini eye-roll. "Thanks. That clears it all up for me."

He twists in the saddle, stretching his lower back one direction and then the other. "Bull riders get hurt. Often. I was always too tall for it, really, and prone to whiplash."

"Okay. And?"

"I went down at NFR."

It takes her a second to remember that NFR is the abbreviation for the National Finals Rodeo. "After winning in Cheyenne?"

"Yes. A few months after that. I hurt my head pretty bad, along with some other parts. Another in a long line of head injuries, to tell the truth. It took a long time to heal. Never did completely. I've been on meds and seeing doctors pretty much ever since."

She reaches toward him, trying to touch him. "I'm sorry. I didn't know."

He lifts his hand and brushes hers, then their horses skitter too far apart for them to maintain contact. "It's called traumatic brain injury. Although we didn't have a name for it back when I was riding. Like football players, boxers, and soldiers get."

"And bull riders."

"Yep." His face is stony.

Maggie sees a long-legged mating pair of sandhill cranes alight from the snow. The big birds don't appear flight-worthy, but they surge skyward where their awkward size turns into effortless grace. They're headed south, it appears, but behind schedule. It makes her feel restless. For a brief moment, a flicker of worry about the wreck of her professional life distracts her. Then another flicker pushes it away. An image of Hank, riding at Frontier Days. Wearing a cowboy hat. "Wait, didn't you wear a helmet?"

"No. And don't ever mention that in front of my mother."

"Why?"

"It was always a point of contention. And arguing about it again doesn't fix anything now."

The horses lean into a climb. By the time they crest the rise, they're both breathing hard.

"But it's under control, right?"

"As much as it can be." He cuts into a stand of aspen trees.

"What's that mean?"

"It gets worse over time. Makes me more susceptible to things."

"What things?"

He looks straight ahead, his jaw tight. "Darkness. Mood swings. Confusion. Forgetfulness."

The gnawing in Maggie's stomach from earlier restarts with intensity. This sounds serious. And Hank has a history of neurological issues in his family anyway. Father dying of Lou Gehrig's disease. Mother with Alzheimer's. She wants to crawl into his saddle and hold him to her. If she's scared, how must he feel? But she knows the last thing he wants is to be coddled.

"Okay, then. Good thing you told me so I can help."

He shrugs. "I appreciate you wanting to, but I don't see how you can."

"Don't underestimate me."

Truth be told, she doesn't see how she can yet either, but she's always believed her refusal to give up when the odds are against her is one of her best traits. They break from the aspen grove. Before she can think of a response, Hank points.

"There she is."

Maggie doesn't see anything but white on white. "Where?"

"Take your sunglasses off. You'll see better."

"It's glary."

But Maggie tucks them down the front of her jacket. She blinks away the glare and the falling flakes. When her eyes adjust, she sees steam rising from an irregular shape in the snow. A black tail swishes and snow scatters. Lily.

"Why isn't she moving?"

"My guess is she's got a halter and lead tangled in something."

"Why would she have them on?" Maggie's voice holds a note of rising panic. She knows the Double S horses are left bare to prevent exactly this.

"Someone probably left her tied up after feeding her. It's good for her. Teaches her patience."

"Teaches her she can break lead lines, too, looks like."

"I imagine she pulled it loose, and we're running shorthanded with Paco on vacation, so no one had been by to put her up yet. We don't tie her off with hard knots. She's broken a hitching post or two before. Damn mare is strong as a freight train."

"And obviously clever."

Don Juan nickers at Lily. Lily is watching them, but she doesn't answer the gelding. Maggie jumps off her horse when they're twenty feet away.

"Wait, Maggie. I'll get her untangled."

"No. Let me, please."

Hank unsnaps a belt scabbard. "Take this. You'll probably need to cut the end of the line to get her loose."

"Thanks." Maggie hands Don Juan's reins to Hank. She attaches the scabbard to her own belt, then unties the feed bag and slings it over her shoulder.

"You always need to carry a knife out here. To deal with whatever comes your way, in case help doesn't."

"I don't have one."

"Keep that one for now." Hank tosses her an extra halter and lead rope he'd coiled on his saddle horn. "And if all else fails, just take off her halter and put this one on."

Maggie trudges toward Lily. The snow isn't deep, but it's wet. Don Juan tries to follow the feed bag, but Hank holds him back.

Lily's line is tangled in tall, thick brush. She strains toward the feed bag, tossing her head and ignoring Maggie altogether. "*Buh-buh-buh, buh-buh-buh, buh-buh.*"

Maggie laughs at her eager sounds. "Lily, you're a mess." She slips the feed bag over Lily's ears and pats her muscular neck.

A buck jumps out of the brush not fifteen feet from Maggie and Lily. Maggie jumps. Lily doesn't. Maggie checks the mare carefully for injuries, but doesn't find so much as a scratch. Lily's round belly looks warm and inviting, so Maggie presses her cheek against it. Inside, a hoof strikes out and thumps her.

Maggie laughs delightedly. "I felt the foal kick."

Hank grunts, but he smiles. "Cut her loose and let's shake a leg. We have to pony her back, and she's going to want to slow us down."

"Pony?"

"Lead her along while we're riding."

Maggie examines the line. "She's wrapped it up tight."

"Can you salvage some of it?"

Maggie loosens the upper coils of the rope, making her way to the bottom. "All but about two or three feet."

"That's worth saving, but we'll have to use the longer line to pony her."

Maggie pulls the knife from the scabbard. It's black, with the Double S brand. "Cool knife."

"We used to have a bunch like that. I think it's the only one left now."

She saws through the lead. It's harder than it looks, what with bad footing and prickly bushes. When the line and horse are freed, she exchanges the old line for the new line and leads Lily to Hank, then removes the feed bag, but not without a tussle.

Hank takes the rope and hands Don Juan's reins back to her. "Let's get out of here."

Maggie clips the old lead line to a ring on her saddle and puts the feed bag over the horn. As she mounts, she catches a glimpse of sun through breaking clouds. In the near distance, she sees big, dark birds circling. "Are those golden eagles?"

Hank glances up, then turns his attention back to Lily, who's trying to bite Tatonka. He twirls the end of her line between the two horses. She quits her attack, but she doesn't back away. "Nope. Buzzards."

Maggie points at a large snowy hump with a few trees to one side. "Is that another animal out there?"

"Probably."

"Should we go help it?"

"Take a closer look."

Maggie squints. "Oh. Is it dead?"

"It, and about ten others."

"What the hell?"

"It's our dead pile."

"Your what?"

"Where we put the livestock that die."

Maggie is drawn to the pile of carcasses like a fly to manure in August. She leads Don Juan toward it.

"Where are you going?"

"I just want a closer look."

"Be careful. There's a buffalo jump on the other side of it. Rock at the bottom."

Maggie knows what a buffalo jump is from reading about Pretty-shield and other Crow, who chased buffalo to low cliffs, where some of the fleeing beasts would fall over. Women would wait at the bottom, knives ready, to finish them off. "Okay."

"When our pile gets too big, we burn it. Then we push what's left over the jump with the tractor."

As Maggie draws nearer to the pile, Louise joins her and bounds up to it. "Oh no, bad idea."

The dog ignores her. She dives in, and soon her head completely disappears. Maggie looks away. Louise barks. Her wagging tail is about the only thing visible when Maggie turns back to her, reluctantly. "Come on out now."

Louise growls and tugs, growls and tugs. The top of the pile shifts on one side. The dog falls backward, a cowboy boot in her mouth. A bright red one with hand-tooling and high heels.

"Hank, Louise has found something, and it's not a cow."

"Could be a horse," Hank hollers. "Everything dies eventually."

"Horses don't wear cowboy boots."

"What?" Hank gives Tatonka a firm "Yah," and they canter to the pile, reaching it just as Maggie does.

The horses stop as one, unwilling to go any closer. Louise wags her tail beside them, the boot still in her mouth.

"Hank, what the hell is going on?"

But she doesn't have to ask. Thanks to their closer perspective and to Louise and her tunneling and tugging, they can both see another distinctive red high-heeled boot in the pile, as well as the back of a dead man's belt that's easily readable even upside down: PACO.

Hank pulls out a satellite phone.

"What are you doing? Shouldn't we help him?" she asks, even though the rational part of her knows Paco's past saving.

Hank is already speaking into the phone. "We've got a suspicious death out at Piney Bottoms Ranch. I think it's our top hand. Paco Lopez. And he's frozen in our dead pile."

THREE

Maggie shakes like thunder from the wet, the cold, and the shock of finding Paco's body. Back at the barn at Piney Bottoms, she and Hank update Gene and Andy. Hank had called Gene earlier with the bare bones of the news. There's not much to add. Just that they expect someone from the sheriff's department any minute. Then she and Hank turn out the horses in silence. They retreat to the main house, where Hank shuts Louise in the mudroom out back.

Maggie dashes upstairs. All she wants is hot coffee and dry clothes before law enforcement arrives. Luckily, Trudy, the ranch cook, has a large pot of coffee percolated by the time Maggie returns in fresh jeans and one of Hank's University of Wyoming sweatshirts. Maggie groans with pleasure when she recognizes the smell of the Panama dark roast from Pine Coffee Supply, the new house coffee.

In the dining room, Maggie heads for the sideboard, which holds the coffee and beverage service. Calling the space a dining room is really a misnomer, though. It's more a mess hall with a long plank table for ten at its center. The entire room is paneled in whitewashed shiplap. Rusted relics hang from the walls, a testament to the ranch's history. A PB branding iron. A wooden-handled scythe. Barbed wire. The dining area opens into an industrial-size kitchen with all modern appliances except for a big wood stove. White shiplap in the kitchen contrasts with dark green painted cabinets and thick plank countertops.

The cook is nowhere to be seen. As Maggie's stirring sugar and cream into her mug, a horn honks outside.

"Who is that rude person out front?" a querulous voice asks.

A wheelchair appears, in it the wizened body of white-haired Mrs. Sibley, and, pushing the wheelchair, Laura, Hank's dark pixie sister. Maggie imagines Mrs. Sibley as a younger woman. She must have looked a lot like her flinty, pretty daughter. Laura's wearing a T-shirt that shows off lithely muscled arms that Maggie envies. Laura's come by them honestly. A ranch kid turned jockey, she's retired now and running an equine therapy camp for troubled youth in New Mexico, on the family ranch managed by her husband.

Hank is right behind them. "It's okay, Mom. I've got it." He kisses his mom's cheek. His face has drawn in and his eyes have sunken, just in the last ten minutes.

Maggie's afraid his headache is back. She pours Hank a cup, black, then backs out of his mother's sightline. It's usually better if Maggie doesn't attract her ire. Evangeline "Vangie" Sibley isn't Maggie's biggest fan.

Laura is up to speed on Paco. She nods at Hank. "Let's go get some tea, Mom."

"I want coffee."

"The doctor says you need to stay away from it."

The older woman pouts. "I want to greet our company."

Laura laughs. "I'm your company, Mom. I just got here last night. Let's go have a visit."

Louise chooses that moment to set up coyote-worthy howling from the mudroom.

Mrs. Sibley's nose wrinkles and her mouth puckers. "Do something about that dog. You know I don't allow ranch animals in the house."

Laura's reply is inaudible as she pushes her mother toward the kitchen. Hank slams his entire cup of hot coffee and winces. He thunks it down on the sideboard, then heads toward the front door. Maggie follows him, still sipping from her mug.

"She didn't even look at me. Laura, I mean. She hates me, too."

"No one hates you." Hank pulls the door open and squints as sunlight blasts him in both eyes.

"Yeah, right." Maggie dons sunglasses from the pocket of the jacket she left hanging on a peg by the door, then puts the jacket on, too. Her head, still protected by her knit beanie, is starting to itch. She rubs the beanie against her scalp.

The cold is sharp now, and it freezes the hairs inside Maggie's nose. The sky is a brilliant baby blue, with the snow a blanket of rainbow crystals sparkling in the sun. She thinks she can make out the circling buzzards over the dead pile in the distance. In the opposite direction, a single set of tire tracks snake from a white sheriff's department Ram 1500 truck back toward the ranch gate. The rumbling engine silences. A grizzly-like deputy gets out. He's zipped into a jacket whose size must have multiple Xs before its L. He stomps his way through new snow over to Maggie and Hank.

The two men lean in for a one-shouldered guy-hug, clapping each other on the back and making small talk about family and football.

Hank turns to Maggie. "Travis and I have known each other since he was a little squirt hanging out watching the big boys ride bulls."

Of course. Hank and his family trace their Wyoming roots back to the late 1800s, when their ancestors homesteaded their land. Deep roots mean something here, and from what Maggie has seen, Hank knows and is respected by most of the people in northern Wyoming and southeastern Montana, even east into the Black Hills of South Dakota.

Travis grips Maggie's hand with his cold, dry one and shakes. "Ms. Killian. Good to see you again." They'd met the month before when there was a series of burglaries at the guest cabin Maggie was staying in, and later when Rudy Simon, a spurned fan of Maggie's, attacked Hank.

"Deputy Travis. I'm not sure about good. At least not for Paco."

"Yeah, Mr. Lopez. Bad business." Travis nods. "Sorry I had to come alone. We're shorthanded."

"You'll do, buddy." Hank steps onto the road back to the outbuildings. "Come on. We can talk on the way. We've got a Ranger gassed up and waiting."

Maggie takes a step and immediately feels her foot slide, so she slips her hand through Hank's arm for balance. Hank's changed his footwear from cowboy boots to tactical boots that look like they're waterproof.

Travis is wearing snow boots. "Tell me what you saw, then."

Maggie looks down at her feet and has a sharp and sudden case of boot envy.

"Maggie'd never seen our dead pile. When she got close, her dog brought out a boot. One of Paco's. He was buried in the pile. But the dog excavated enough that we saw his legs and the back of his belt."

"You didn't see his face?"

"No. We didn't want to disturb anything, so we backed away, and I called 911."

"Good. When was the last time you saw him? Alive, that is."

Hank cocks his head at Maggie. "Two, three days ago?"

Maggie counts it on her fingers. "Three. At breakfast on Friday. He was taking a long weekend."

Travis says, "So today is Monday. Wouldn't you have expected him back by now?"

"Sort of. Maybe." Hank shrugs. "If he hadn't come back by midweek, I would have worried. Otherwise, I would have just assumed it was Paco blowing off steam."

Travis's forehead crinkles. "Did he say where he was going?"

Hank stops at the gate to a paddock. He puts his foot on the bottom rail and leans a forearm on the top. "Actually, no. He said he was following the fun."

Maggie glances at the northern sky and sees a dark gray wall of clouds advancing like a steamroller. The mountains block the view of northern fronts until they're bearing down on the ranch.

Travis crosses his arms, surveying the ranch in a one-hundred-eighty-degree arc. "What did he mean by that?"

Hank smiles, but his eyes are sad. "Paco liked cards, women, and whiskey. When he came back from time off, he was usually dropped here by an angry woman squealing tires out of the place, and looking like he'd been mule-kicked all the way back from Lynchburg, Tennessee."

"You'd suspect a woman, then?"

"Maybe. But I've never seen one mad enough to kill him and leave him on our dead pile."

"Who would be?"

"Personally, I wouldn't know. Someone he beat at cards, stiffed when he lost, or ran out on when they caught him cheating? A boyfriend or husband who didn't like to share?"

"Any you know?"

"Like I said, none personally. Just his legend."

"What about family, friends, a steady girl?"

"His family's in South Texas. I guess we were his friends, although he also palled around with some of the hands on the area ranches. And I've never known him to tie himself down to one woman."

"Who benefits from his death?"

Hank rubs his chin. "I don't rightly know. He had a little bit of life insurance through Double S. Not enough to kill over, I wouldn't think, but maybe to someone. I don't know who gets it or if he had anything else worth much. He had a real nice roping saddle. That's about it." His face darkens. "And, well, he had this job. If someone wanted it, I guess that's something."

"Or if someone wanted him out of it."

Hank doesn't respond.

"Kind of hard for someone to get out to that dead pile without anyone here noticing."

"There's miles and miles of unmonitored fence line on this place."

"Inhospitable fence line."

"Unwelcoming. But not inhospitable."

Travis changes tacks. "You said Paco was your top hand. Will someone get bumped up with him gone?"

"We only have one other full-time hand. Andy. An Amish kid."

"He'll be promoted, then."

"Maybe. That isn't a sure thing. But the Amish are nonviolent, and Andy wouldn't hurt a fly." Hank resumes walking to the barn, Travis behind him and Maggie beside him.

"Did you have any relationship with Paco, Maggie?"

Maggie feels icy snowflakes pelting her face as the gray clouds close in on them. "He helped fix my truck once. But really, nothing other than small talk at meals. I've been teaching Andy to read music and play the guitar, but Paco wasn't interested."

Travis says. "Really? I read online that you'd given up music."

Maggie stops, and Travis bumps into her. She just loves all the media attention lately. *Not.* "I gave up performing music professionally a long time ago. I didn't forget how to make it."

Hank snorts. He wants her to play more. Since he reentered her life, the music is coming back to her, but it owned her once before, and she's not going through that again for anyone. This time, music is on her terms or not at all.

The wind picks up as they reach the stable yard, where Travis greets Gene and Andy. Travis barely glances at Andy's homemade blue pants and oilcloth coat, distinctive wide-brimmed hat, and blousy work shirt.

Travis takes Gene and Andy through the same type of questions he'd already gone over with Hank and Maggie, making occasional notes in a spiral pad. Gene confirms most of what Hank said, although he expresses more consternation about Paco extending his vacations. The only new information comes from Andy.

"He had a girl. Back in Texas. Her father was none too happy with Paco because the time had come for him to go back for her and marry. Paco was dragging his feet. He hasn't been faithful to her. He's something of a ladies' man."

Maggie isn't surprised about the ladies' man part, although the fiancée is a shock. Paco is—was—a charmer who loved to recite raunchy cowboy poetry. He had mischievous eyes, a compact, muscular build, thick, wavy dark hair, a black mustache, and a square jaw. He wasn't her type, but he was definitely attractive.

Travis's eyebrows rise. "Have you met her?"

"No. I've seen a picture. He keeps it under his mattress. One time he showed it to me when he'd been drinking."

"What's her name?"

"He called her Maribel."

"Last name?"

"He didn't say."

"Why was he dragging his feet?"

Andy looks around like he's the stray dog and Travis the dogcatcher. There's nowhere for him to run. "He liked his freedom."

Travis closes his notepad. "I'll need to search his quarters."

Gene says, "He has a room in the bunkhouse."

"I'll swing by after we go see the body. Could we get that room locked up in the meantime?"

Gene nods. "No problem."

Andy and Gene wave as Hank, Maggie, and Travis pile into a four-seat Ranger, with Hank at the wheel. They stop at the house for Travis's crime scene bag, then continue into the white pasture. The wind has picked up, and Maggie wishes she'd brought a scarf. She dons the gloves she keeps stuffed in her pockets. It's slowgoing. The two-tracks are rough and starting to drift. Twice the Ranger bogs down and they have to dig it out with a folding shovel from the storage compartment.

The second time, Hank taps the gas gauge. It doesn't move. "Andy gave us the one with the broken gas gauge, dammit. But it should be almost full."

When they reach the dead pile, they park and walk closer, up the hill. Maggie is glad when she hears the others breathing as hard as she is. Travis surveys the scene as he catches his breath. Maggie huddles into Hank's chest. The snow feels pelletized and the wind is lashing it against her face, where it then slides down her neck.

After walking a complete circuit around the dead pile, Travis retrieves crime scene tape and stakes from his bag in the Ranger. The wind whips the tape as he cordons off the area, then begins taking pictures. Several times he brushes snow aside to expose items for photographs, but Maggie is too far away to identify them. Occasionally Travis slips things into plastic baggies that he stuffs down the front of his bulky coat.

Just as suddenly as they began, the snow and wind stop and the gray clouds move south. Even with the sun coming out, though, it feels far colder now than it had when Maggie and Hank were out here earlier. Maggie is grateful for the temperature in one respect: the dead pile is frozen and odor-free. Travis works his way carefully up the pile to Paco's body, about ten feet off the ground. She wouldn't want to be in Travis's shoes, climbing and digging through dead bodies, however stiff they are. She watches as Travis excavates around Paco until his torso is visible. Hank turns away.

"What a waste," Hank says. He shakes his head.

"How could he even have ended up in there like that?" Maggie asks.

"We use the tractor to dump livestock there."

"You think someone used a Double S tractor?"

Hank is facing the pile again. His voice is like sandpaper. "It's possible. If not, it sure would have been difficult for someone to get a tractor on our land without us knowing about it. But hell, maybe he climbed up there himself. He could have been drunk and sleeping it off. Or hiding out."

She remembers his terse exchange with Travis earlier, when he'd insisted Piney Bottoms was easily accessible. He's contradicting himself a little now, but she gets it. If he admits his fears to Travis, he's pointing a finger at his own people. Protecting his own might mean failing to defend Paco. He's in a tough spot. Either way he leans goes against the type of man he is.

Suddenly, Paco breaks free from the space he's wedged into, between the remains of what looks like a steer and a young heifer. Travis scrambles out of the way as the body tumbles down the pile and lands face-first in front of Hank and Maggie, the body making snapping and cracking sounds on the way down.

Maggie gasps.

"Son of a bitch," Hank says.

There's a knife lodged in the base of Paco's skull, its white handle sticking out like an accusatory finger pointing at Hank.

Maggie says, "I'm guessing he didn't climb up there himself after all."

FOUR

Dinner that night is a somber affair. At the far end of the table, Gene and Andy are in deep conversation with the two day hands—they get three squares with their paychecks, although they don't live onsite—when Mrs. Sibley arrives, quarreling with Laura. Seated by Hank across the enormous table from mother and daughter, Maggie has a front-row seat.

The old woman sniffs. "All I'm saying is I left my batteries in the bathroom, and they're gone now."

"Mom, they were used batteries. They didn't work anymore."

"They were mine. Someone stole them."

"No one stole them. They were trash. I threw them away."

"I didn't raise you to steal."

Laura squeezes her eyes shut. Maggie notices dark circles underneath them, with skin that seems transparent. When they open, they're fixed on Hank. "I couldn't get her to nap. How do you and Tom do it?" she says, referring to Mrs. Sibley's caretaker, who's taking vacation while Laura visits.

"I feel ya, sis."

Trudy hollers from the kitchen. "Sorry, you guys. Just a few more minutes." Her red hair spills from its low bun. Her normally serene face is smudged with flour.

"It's okay," Hank tells her.

"Thanks, boss," she calls.

"Mickey's not going to let me come anymore. I'm worn to a frazzle when I get home, every time." Laura smiles to show she's joking. Her husband, Mickey, doesn't make it up to Wyoming much, Hank says. Maggie has never met him, but she's heard good things. She figures he's a saint if he's survived marriage to feisty Laura.

Hank pours himself and Maggie iced teas. Maggie thinks how much better her sweet tea would be with Koltiska liqueur in it. A sweet TKO, as it's known locally, since the liqueur goes by the KO family ranch brand.

Hank says, "You're earning your spot in heaven. How are things back at home?"

"Where's my dinner?" Mrs. Sibley demands.

"Soon, Mom." Laura puts a hand on her mother's. "Things are crazy right now. Farrah wants to quit the University of New Mexico and go to Amarillo College. To be closer to Greg, her boyfriend. He's working in a dance club, with the lofty aspiration of being an EDM DJ."

"Electronic dance music? Wow. So they're into rave culture," Maggie says.

"Maybe. I've gotten too old to get it."

Hank guffaws. "You were probably always too old to get it, sis."

"Bite me, Hank. But I am tired all the time. I'm just thankful the equine therapy camps are over until next summer. Ever since we let Farrah go to Bonnaroo with Greg and his friends last spring, she's been sliding off the deep end. Now she says Greg is a ghost producer for some famous DJ. All I know is he stays up all night and dropped out of school." She laughs, a harsh sound. "I suck as a mother. I've never been able to nurture anything, not even a plant. The only thing I've ever even kept alive was a succulent from Walmart, but after I congratulated myself for my green thumb, Mickey showed me the damn plant was fake. God knew what he was doing when he made me barren after all."

Hank shakes his head at her. "Don't say that. You're a great mother to Farrah."

Maggie remembers Hank telling her that Mickey and Laura had fostered Farrah and only adopted her as a teenager. She's been in Farrah's shoes herself—she was obsessed with music at her age—so she tries to reassure Laura. "I've been there. I'm sure she'll be fine."

"Really? And how did that go for you?"

Trudy whisks in with a colossal covered platter, which she sets beside the butter plate. A bag of Cheetos is on top of the platter. She tosses the bag to Gene and winks. He catches it. His cheeks redden.

Hank squeezes Maggie's knee.

She's seething. Laura has taken the gloves off, referring—Maggie is sure —to her famous rehab stints and the undeniable reality that she is no longer in the business. She musters a sweet smile and purrs musically. "A number one album, a Grammy, and international fame."

Trudy reappears with a covered pot and ladle. "Keeping it simple tonight, everyone. Cornbread and chili."

Gene smiles at her. "Thanks, Trudy. Are you joining us?"

"I'm busier than a one-armed paperhanger. Y'all dig in."

Gene seems lost in thought, watching her walk back into the kitchen.

Laura nods at Maggie. "How wonderful for you. I'm not into your kind of music, so you'll have to excuse me."

A backhanded compliment at best. Maggie's hackles rise and she tries to formulate a retort about the obscurity of quarter-horse jockeys compared to alt-country rockers.

Luckily, Mrs. Sibley interrupts before the two women put their backs into it. "Isn't it about time for grace, Henry?"

The table goes silent. It's a clear sign that Mrs. Sibley is having a bad day when she thinks Hank is her deceased husband, Henry.

"I'm Hank, Mom. Will everyone bow their heads, please?" Hank clears his throat. "Dear Lord, thank you for your many blessings, the nourishment of the food on this table, and the hands that prepared it. We ask for your grace and peace as we mourn the loss of your son Paco. Please welcome him into your kingdom and help us find justice on earth for whoever did this horrible thing to him. In Jesus's name we pray, amen."

A chorus of amens echoes his.

Everyone remains quiet as they pass around platters of cornbread, then bowls for the chili that Hank ladles. Trudy pops her head in to check that everyone has what they need. She wipes her hands on a ruffled pink-and-green gingham apron that's far more old-fashioned than she is, then brings another pitcher of iced tea. Sweat beads on the pale skin at her hairline.

"Thank you, Trudy," Gene says.

She curtsies, holding out one side of her apron over her Wranglers and the snap-front Western shirt with a feminine cut that shows off her curves.

After she disappears back into the kitchen, Gene and Hank share a glance. Hank nods.

Gene says, "Thank you all for cooperating with law enforcement today." Crime scene techs, an additional detective, and the county coroner had joined Travis soon after he examined the dead pile, and the group had only packed up and left half an hour before dinner. "We're real broken-up about Paco. I know you are, too."

"Who's Paco?" Mrs. Sibley says, her voice reverberating.

Laura distracts her with a discussion about honey for her cornbread.

"We've been in touch with his family. They've agreed we can have a memorial service for him here. We were thinking Prairie Dog Community Church. Unfortunately, though, I'm going to be in Oklahoma with some buckers, but Hank will have that covered."

The service conflicts with the Duncan rodeo? Maggie's disappointment is deep. Does this mean she and Hank won't be going? But it's not the time to ask.

"Will they be coming to collect him?" Andy asks.

Gene nods. "Soon. But we'll have time for the memorial first. Unfortunately, this is a busy time for us. We're defending our NFR Stock Contractor of the Year title, with NFR only a few weeks away." Gene doesn't mention that they'd only reclaimed their NFR contract a few weeks before, after the murder of their neighbor and competitor, Patrick Rhodes. Everyone has been in a mad scramble to get ready since then. "We're going to have to bring on another full-time hand, immediately."

Andy studies the wooden slats in the tabletop.

"We have a good candidate. I've called him to come in tomorrow morning, to have him try us on for size and vice versa."

Pink creeps over Andy's ears.

"Andy, we'd be much obliged if you'd accept a promotion to top hand for us."

Andy's head lifts. His beard covers most of the blush on his face. "Th-th-thank you. I'm honored."

"Congratulations, Andy," Hank says, lifting his iced tea glass to salute him. "I'm sorry it's under these circumstances, but you've earned it."

The day hands, Maggie, Laura, and Trudy join in the congratulations.

Gene smiles at him. "I'm leaving on a scouting trip tomorrow. Hank and I will be counting on you to bring the new hand on right."

"Yes, sir. Absolutely, sir."

Maggie's phone vibrates in her pocket. She sneaks it out and glances at the screen just as it notifies her that the caller—Charlotte, her mother—left a voicemail. She suppresses a groan. There's only one reason Charlotte is calling, and that is to pressure her to come back to Texas. She already feels enough of that pressure from inside herself. She doesn't need it from her mother, too.

When Maggie left the music industry, she was in a death spiral. She'd lost her contract, been through rehab twice, and alienated everyone she'd ever worked with. Then her record company went belly-up, and she'd accepted her little antique shop and house in lieu of payment for her albums and songs. It had been a slow climb back from dead busted to self-sufficient. A few years ago, she discovered she was adopted and had a secretly rich birth mother—Gidget—and a politician birth father—Boyd. She inherited everything when Gidget died. But she's only rich on paper. She can't bear the thought of selling off treasures like the Andy Warhol or the vintage Jaguar, much less Gidget's farm, especially after she lost everything else in the fires. So she's rudderless, between careers, and cashless. The only place it seems she can solve these problems is back in Texas, but the thought of leaving Hank in Wyoming is like a death sentence.

As if she's reading her mind, Mrs. Sibley says, "What does that woman do to support herself? Lord knows she isn't doing a lick of work here, and she's eating up our food and sleeping under our roof."

Maggie chokes on the cornbread that is suddenly dry in her throat. She can't argue with the accuracy of Mrs. Sibley's complaint. She only hopes Hank's mother doesn't realize exactly where under their roof she's sleeping.

Hank slaps Maggie's back until she recovers. "Mom, that's uncalled for. Maggie is my guest."

Laura smirks. "It *would* be nice to hear Maggie's plans."

Maggie feels like there's a knife sticking out of her back, and she gets an uncomfortable rush of imagery. Paco in the dead pile, stiff, the knife in his neck. It makes her think of the knife Hank lent her. She'd left it on the nightstand earlier when she changed into dry clothes.

Hank glowers. "Laura, please."

"What? You told me she doesn't have a home or business back in Texas. I'm interested."

His voice grows even louder. "Laura. Stop it. Now."

Maggie clears her throat. "It's okay, Hank. Laura, I'm trying to figure that out right now. I'll have to go back to Texas soon one way or the other, once I get some figures back from my insurance company and some quotes from contractors. The adjuster was headed out to my place today."

Mrs. Sibley sniffs. "Take the goats with you when you go. This isn't a goat ranch."

"Ignore her. And don't be in a rush." Hank squeezes her knee. "You just got here."

She looks at him, and she's shocked to see his eyes are damp and emotional.

"Yeah," Andy says, his voice cracking. "We've just started my guitar lessons."

Maggie scoops chili into her mouth so she doesn't have to answer anyone, especially not Hank, not in front of the group. She hasn't told him that what she really wants is for him to move Double S to Texas and come south with her. Piney Bottoms belongs to his mother. Gene is from Texas, where there are more rodeos anyway. Running Double S from Giddings makes good sense to her. There's a long-term tenant at Gidget's old place now, but when the lease is up, there'd be plenty of room for the bucking stock. Especially if they leased the neighbor's place, too, and that old coot Lumpy would love the income. It wouldn't hurt to contact a realtor and see what's available in the area, either. That way when she brings it up with Hank, she'll have complete information on the possibilities to wow him with. She's just worried it won't strike the same chord with Hank.

Into the strained silence, Gene says, "Have you told your family you're learning the guitar, Andy?"

"No. Some of them feel that playing instruments is a show of vanity. Not all of them."

"But you're on Rumspringa, aren't you?" Gene asks. He's referring to the time before baptism into the church when Amish youth are allowed to go out into the English—non-Amish—world, before they decide whether to make a commitment to formally join their church and community.

"Yes."

Maggie says, "Do you still live by Amish rules while you're on Rumspringa?"

"To the extent you want to. I do, mostly. It's important to my father."

"Except for your beard." Gene smiles. "And Andy's father, Reggie, has been known to show up here without warning to check on him."

Maggie remembers seeing Andy talking to Reggie earlier. "I thought your family was in Montana?" Maggie says.

"They are. He rides into Sheridan with a former Amish several times a week to work."

Gene helps himself to a second bowl of chili. "What will Reggie and the rest of your family think about your promotion?" He grins at Maggie. "Andy has nine younger siblings."

"They'll be proud of me."

Maggie pushes her bowl back. The spicy chili was good, but she's not very hungry. "Are you going back when Rumspringa is over?"

Andy mumbles something.

"What?"

"I'm not sure."

Mrs. Sibley interjects again. "At least that young man works, like what *she* should be doing instead of freeloading off my husband while she tries to take him from me."

Hank puts a hand on her arm. "I'm Hank, Mom. Your son. And Maggie isn't trying to take anyone."

She glares at him, her eyes deep, dark, and round, like she's been possessed by a demon.

Laura stands. "That's our cue." She wheels her mother away from the table. "Good night, everyone."

Mrs. Sibley drags her heels on the plank floor. "She's trying to steal everything from me."

"Come on, Mom."

"No, you can't make me. No, goddammit, no."

Laura prevails, and the two disappear, although Mrs. Sibley's strident voice echoes into the dining room. Maggie has never heard the old woman use the Lord's name in vain before.

"I'm sorry," Hank whispers to Maggie.

She stares into his sad eyes. Her own father had Alzheimer's. Her memories of him in his last years aren't pretty. She covers Hank's hand with hers. "No. I am."

FIVE

The dinner group breaks up slowly after apple cobbler and ice cream and gathers in the great room at the front of the house. Mrs. Sibley's wing downstairs and Hank's suite upstairs are family-only, but the common areas are set up for everyone at the ranch to enjoy, with computers, a television, games, a beer refrigerator, and books. Maggie pulls Hank away to his rooms, stopping first to take a bouncy, happy Louise from the mudroom to a sabbatical outside.

"Are you ready for bed?" Hank asks when they reach the top of the stairs.

"Maybe." Maggie picks up a vintage wooden mortar and pestle from the sofa table behind a leather couch in Hank's private living area. "I love this."

"You and old things. That's a family heirloom. Come to bed with me, and I'll show you another."

"Oh?" She sets them back down. "More old junk?"

"Bite your tongue. The family jewels."

She rolls her eyes. "Like I said."

"Just meet me in there."

"You going somewhere else first?"

"Trust me."

Maggie slips into his bedroom suite and strips down to her bra and panties. The emotions of the day rush over her—Hank's revelation about his brain health issues, Paco's death, the exhausting reality of Mrs.

Sibley's condition, Laura's disapproval of Maggie—and mix with her lingering sadness over her lost home and business. She retrieves her Martin acoustic guitar from its battered case. As she stands in a stream of moonlight from the window, something melancholy forms in her mind, and her fingers translate it into a melody on the strings. Words emerge from deep inside her. Maggie sings softly as she picks to an appreciative audience of one black-and-white dog curled up on a pillow under the window.

"Lost. What once was here now is gone. Lost. Will it ever be found? It's lost. Lost."

"What's that?"

Her fingers still. She turns toward Hank, setting the Martin back in its case. "Nothing. Randomness."

"Don't stop, music girl."

Her eyes take him in, head to toe, lingering on the triangle of his strong neck and shoulders. Muscles honed through hard work, not on machines in a gym. She strolls to him, her music-warmed fingers outstretched. She traces his collarbone and manages a shirt button before the rest of her reaches him. Rocking and humming to the slow melody that plays on in her brain, she finishes the buttons and stops with her fingers on his belt. "You want me to play for you some more now?"

His eyes glint in the same moonlight she'd bathed in while playing her guitar. "Don't stop."

She laughs. "Fickle man."

"I'm not, actually."

She drops her forehead to his chest and kisses the contours there. "I know."

"I can't believe we had to wait fifteen years for this."

"Did you? Wait?" She leaves her lips on his chest, breathing him in, waiting for his answer.

"I've been with other women since. As have you. Men, I mean."

Maggie laughs. "That wasn't what I meant."

Hank whistles and his hand slides down her back to her ass. "Liar."

Maggie draws in a deep breath. She's been holding something back that Gene told her, waiting for the right time to talk about it. Now. Now is that time. "When were you going to tell me you came after me?"

The room is quiet except for the sounds of their breathing.

Finally, Hank says, "So you knew?"

"Not back then. Gene told me a few weeks ago. That you came to one of my shows in Denver and got turned away. And that you showed up for me at rehab."

Hank's hand slides around her waist. "I also tried calling. Your publicist and manager were real assholes."

"I'm sorry. They never told me."

"That's a relief. At the time, I thought they were following your orders."

Maggie tilts her head back so she can see his eyes in the dimly lit room. "Not on your life. There's a million reasons I couldn't take that life. Everyone thinking they could control me for their own reasons was a big one. I wish they'd told me."

"Water under the bridge."

"I don't think I completely trusted you until Gene said you'd tried to reach me." She kisses his chest again, this time in the center, high.

"At least one of us reached out."

"Believe me, I followed you as best I could. I wrote a whole album trying to draw you out." She moves down an inch, drops another kiss.

He laughs.

"Then you kind of fell off the face of the earth, while I got sucked further and further into that crazy world." Another inch, another kiss.

"I heard you on the radio once. A big national show. Aaron Cryor." He pulls her up, kisses her lips hard, then nips them. "You really kicked his ass."

Maggie remembers and groans. "What a jerk. Pretending he was all sanctimonious, then the things he did to me in that studio. The things he expected me to do to him. Total asswipe."

"You got him fired, didn't you?"

"And that got me national attention, which was the beginning of the insanity that shot me like a rocket to the bad ending." She rubs her cheek against his.

"I think it all turned out okay. But maybe that's just because you're in my arms now."

"I kind of like being here. And I believe there's rising evidence that you like it, too." She unbuckles his belt, then pulls it off and drops it to the floor.

"We could test the theory."

Backing away toward the bed, she pulls him by the belt loops to follow her.

"Wait. I have a question for you." He resists. "Why are you in such a hurry to go? When you just got here."

"You mean to the bed?" She unfastens his jeans, then tugs them and his briefs down at the same time. "We can do this wherever you want."

He kicks them off. "No." His jaw bunches. His Adam's apple bulges. "From Wyoming. From me. Back to Texas. When we've just found each other after all this time."

Maggie puts her hands around his waist and pulls, bumping him into her, and together they tumble onto the four-poster bed. Another heirloom. She gathers her courage for the words she's been scared to say to him. "Why don't you come with me?"

His body stiffens on top of her, and not in the good way that leads to fun and games. "I've got the ranch here. Your home, your business in Texas, they're gone."

"But I have family, friends, and a brand. Horses and bulls can live anywhere."

"I'm here, Maggie. I'm tied to here."

She cuts him off with a kiss. Now isn't the time to debate this. She'll make another run at the topic later, when she can be rational and persuasive. When emotions aren't so charged. "So am I. We're together. Nothing is going to change that."

"Together. Or *together?*"

"*Together.* Through the good and the bad and the worse. Together. Let me show you how very much together, cowboy."

A surge of wanting him consumes her, and she flips him onto his back. She grabs him, taking charge, rough and urgent. He responds in kind. They're wild, reckless, and lost. In the midst of their passion, there's a loud crack under the bed. It falls to the floor, mattress, box spring, and all. Louise yelps and scrambles to the door.

"Shit." She's so close, so close to something bigger and better than she's ever felt before. She thrusts against him.

He pulls back.

She presses her forehead into his. "Don't be a quitter, Hank."

Hank yells. "Argh."

"Yes, baby." Maggie sinks her teeth into his chest. "Yes."

"No." He pushes her off of him. "No."

She lands on her back beside him. He rolls into a fetal position, clutching himself.

"Hank? Are you okay?"

He groans. "I think we broke it."

"The bed? I know. I'm sorry."

"No. It. My, um . . ."

She finally gets it. Sees what he's holding on to. Understands why he stopped. "OH. The family jewels?"

"Yes."

"Let me see."

He covers himself with both hands. "Give me a minute."

A sharp knock at the door jerks them both upright. Hank still holds his hand like an athletic cup over his personal parts.

Maggie scrambles for a sheet and whispers, "Did you lock it?"

Laura's voice is so distinct it feels like she's in bed between them. "Hank? Are you in there? I need help with Mom."

"Son of a bitch," he mutters. Then, louder, "Be right down."

"Your . . . jewels." Maggie reaches for him. "What can I do?"

He finally manages a grin. "Don't give up on me. I've had worse injuries in my rodeo days, and I recover fast." He crawls to the edge of the bed, wincing, then walks gingerly to his pile of clothing. He looks down. "Damn, I think it's changing colors."

"Seriously, do I need to take you to the emergency room?"

"Nah. I'll get ibuprofen and an ice pack on my way back up." He zips and buttons his jeans and pulls on a T-shirt from a chest of drawers. He stops at the door. "I love you, Maggie."

He's out before she can tell him that she loves him, too, in a crazy way that scares her. But who's she kidding? He's told her he loves her over and over now, and she always finds a way not to utter the three little words.

SIX

Maggie slides down the broken bed like it's a ski slope and hops over the frame to the floor. On her hands and knees, she peers under. Even in the dark, she can see that one of the support slats is broken. The mattress and box spring are tipped inside the frame. Naked from her romp with Hank, she uses her legs and back to take the weight off the remaining slats while she redistributes them inside the frame, then jerks the mattress and box spring back into position. It's a temporary fix, at best.

She's broken a lot of things in her life, but never a bed. Or a penis. Poor Hank.

She crawls out as her phone chimes with a new voicemail notification. The room feels colder. Where is her phone? She finds it in the pocket of her jeans. She scurries back to bed and burrows under the covers. She reads the screen. The notification is new, but the two messages from her mother are from earlier. Her T-Mobile coverage here and throughout Wyoming is hit-or-miss at best.

The first message: "You didn't return my call yesterday. Some reporter contacted me about you. A new one. Amos something-or-other. I told him no comment. Call me."

The second: "Are you mad at me for getting married without telling you? Because I can't think of any other reason you'd move to Wyoming and cut me out of your life. Call me."

Oh, Mother, Mother. She's not ducking her. Life has just been hectic.

And this thing, this beautiful thing she has with Hank, has been all-consuming. Surely her newlywed mom can understand that, a woman so in love she eloped without telling her only child. Listening to the squeaky chirp of a night bird, she decides to call Charlotte back in the morning. An owl screeches, raising hackles on her skin. *It will be going after the little bird*, she thinks.

She wraps herself in the comforter and pads over to the window. Louise whines, and Maggie reaches down to pet her head. She doesn't find an owl, but in the beam of the outdoor lights, she sees a man running toward the bunkhouse. *Odd.* She leans all the way to the cold glass. He's short, with dark hair and dark skin. And bright red knee-high boots.

Like Paco.

But that can't be—Paco's dead. She shuts her eyes to clear her vision and tries again. It has to be someone else. It could be Gene. Gene is short and dark. He shouldn't be running to the hired hands' cabin, though. He lives in the opposite direction. And he doesn't have red boots. At least she doesn't think he does. Maybe she's just wrong about the boots. Can she even see red in the low light?

But there's no way to know for sure, because when she opens her eyes again, the man is gone. The landscape is night-bare and lonely. A gust of wind rattles the window and pushes snow through the ranch grounds like a schoolyard bully.

The door to the bedroom opens, and she turns away from the window. It's Hank, and the hall behind him is pitch dark. He moves into the relative light of the room. His shoulders are slumped—more of an inverted U than a V now—and he walks like a man thirty years older than he is.

"Is your mom okay?"

He collapses onto the bed and lets out a short bark.

"What?" Maggie stands in front of him.

"Ice pack. Frozen peas and carrots to the junk."

"It's like you're making a stew. Sausage and veggies."

"God, I hope not." He laughs, then shakes his head. "And about my mom—she's not really okay tonight."

"What's the matter?"

"She's sundowning."

Maggie sits beside him and runs her fingers through his hair. Even though Maggie's father had Alzheimer's, her parents had kept his diagnosis from her as a teenager. She'd never heard the term *sundowning*. "What's that?"

"She has trouble functioning at bedtime, then can't fall asleep and gets up over and over during the night, each time more irrational than the last."

"Does it happen often?"

"More than it used to. Laura hasn't dealt with it before. She's going to have a tough night, I think, but she says she can handle it."

"God, Hank. I'm sorry."

He throws the bag of vegetables toward the bathroom. They hit the tile floor and skid out of sight. "To hell with icing. What I need is your arms around me."

Maggie puts her head on his shoulder, careful to keep her weight off his injured spots. "How's this?"

He doesn't answer, but his breathing speeds up and his chest heaves.

She touches his cheek, and her fingers come away wet. Tears. "Hank?"

"Damn, Paco. I never knew he had a fiancée. I thought of him like a little brother. Or the son I'd never have." A sob breaks free, but he reels it back in quickly. "How could someone do that to him? And why put him in our dead pile like an animal?"

Maggie strokes the tears dry on his cheek.

"And my mother, suffering. So young. Both my parents. They're good people. They didn't deserve this."

"Of course not."

"Thank you for being here, Maggie. I never get a chance . . ." He stops, holding his breath.

"To have feelings?" she says, and kisses the place where she'd dried his tears.

Again his chest shakes, and when he doesn't answer, she stays quiet, listening as his breathing settles into a rhythm and soft snores escape his lips. Then she drops her own lids and lets herself fall asleep in his arms, with her cheek pressed against his big, aching heart.

SEVEN

Mrs. Sibley is absent from breakfast, but Laura shows up to fill two plates.

"Did you get any sleep?" Hank stands, holding out the skillet of his mother's favorite cowboy biscuits.

Laura takes two, scoops strawberry jam, and slices a large pat of butter. "I'm okay."

"It usually takes her a day or two to recover from a bad episode. Hopefully she'll start a resting cycle today." Hank puts two slices of bacon on each plate.

"Want me to pour you coffee?" Maggie is already up, grabbing cups off the sideboard.

"Thanks." Laura adds a generous helping of scrambled eggs to one plate, none to the other.

"Black?"

"That's fine."

Maggie pours, then walks the cups to Laura. "I can carry them for you."

Laura and Hank exchange a look. Laura exhales extra breath, a sort of sigh. "Probably not the best time for an encounter. But thank you. Let's just make room for them on the plates."

Hank crouches at the sideboard and comes up with a tray. "Here."

He arranges the plates and cups on the tray. When she's set, Laura leaves without another word. What was already a quiet breakfast with the absence of Paco turns maudlin. Andy mumbles something about prepping the horses for transport and leaves with a bacon biscuit in each big paw and the day hands trailing him. Maggie picks at her food, head down.

Gene breaks the silence. "I've got to get on the road. Sorry to leave you with all this and dealing with transport."

The haulers are coming for the rodeo livestock today. The animals have a long drive and need plenty of rest before performance time, which starts for them on Thursday.

Hank puts his napkin on his plate. "It's fine."

"Michael should be here any time. I haven't had time to finish his background check, but we'll make this probationary, and I'll have it done by the end of the week. You're okay putting the service for Paco together for Thursday?"

"Trudy is helping me. Doing most of it, actually."

"Well, if there's one thing I know, it's that we can count on Trudy." Gene stands. "See you later, new sis."

Hank's chair clatters back. "All right."

Maggie jumps up, too. "Have a safe trip."

As Gene leaves, Hank heads for the door as well.

Maggie touches his elbow. "You okay?"

Hank's eyes are flat, his cheeks without his smile dimples. "I'll be fine." He steps away from her. "Sorry about last night."

"Why?"

"Dumping all that on you."

"Dump all you need to. Do you, um, need any ice or ibuprofen, for your injury?"

The trace of a smile flickers, teasing, then fades. "I think it will survive."

"Phew. And your head?"

"Maggie, I'm fine. Don't fuss."

Andy pokes his head back in the dining room. "The new hand is here."

Hank turns to Maggie. "See you later." He follows Andy out.

Maggie lifts her fingers and waves at his retreating back. "Mm-hmm."

Alone, Maggie contemplates her options. Today she'll call her mother, maybe run some online searches for potential property for Hank near Giddings, and she'll connect with Franklin, her insurance adjuster. It's past time for some answers. She's mired down in indecision without information. Not that she's complaining. Wyoming is a lovely place, and being with Hank is a dream come true.

But first she heads outside, where she's met with a surprise: except for patches in the shade, the snow has melted. It's colder in the house than it is outdoors. She shucks her jacket immediately and hangs it on a peg inside the door. As soon as the door swings closed behind her, Louise is at her side.

"Hey, girl." Maggie leans down to fondle the dog's ears and sees something sticking to her muzzle. She puts her hand under Louise's chin, tilting it up to get a better look. It's something white, and—when she touches one—soft. She rubs it between fingers, then groans. It's down. As in feathers-from-a-baby-bird down.

Louise wags her tail, which rocks her head and sets her long, patchy black-and-white-freckled ears swaying. Maggie straightens, looking for the source of the down. Louise, reading her mood change, ducks and turns. Maggie's eyes follow the dog. Ten feet from the entry steps, she sees it.

"Oh, Fucker, no." Maggie uses the nickname the dog earned almost immediately after she'd adopted Maggie as her person.

Maggie walks briskly to the little mound of feathers, looking around to be sure no one is watching. Louise slinks a few steps away. Blood-spotted white-and-brown feathers are camouflaged into the dead grass and snow in the shade thrown by the house. Using the toe of her boot, Maggie tilts the creature up and over. Its head flops, neck broken. Staring at her from round, sightless eyes is a dead baby owl. On either side of its head, tufts of feathers stick up in horns. Like a tiny devil, only cuter.

She uses her firmest voice, but quietly, knowing that killing animals can get Louise in a lot of trouble on a ranch. "Bad, bad dog."

Louise lowers her head.

Maggie's phone rings. She looks around. No one is watching her. The owl is her secret. She glances at her screen. It's her insurance adjuster—she has to take this call. "Bad," she says again to Louise for good measure. She answers. "Hello?"

"Maggie Killian, please."

"Speaking." Maggie moves back into the sun and sits on the stoop. The sun is delicious.

"Hi, Maggie. This is Franklin Best."

"Do you have good news for me, Franklin?"

Louise noses Maggie's hand. Maggie glares at her and moves her hand away. It's too soon. She can't pet the head that just murdered a baby owl.

"I wish I did."

"What's the matter?"

"I was at your place yesterday, but I couldn't get into the barn. It was padlocked. Looked like one of those kinds of locks law enforcement uses when they're done with a scene."

"Shit."

"I can't finish without getting in there to inventory the condition of what you have left."

"Can't you just cut the lock?"

"No, ma'am. It's against policy."

Maggie shoves her thick hair back. She needs a hat or a headband. "Fine. I'll have someone go out and do it."

"I'd recommend you call the sheriff's department first."

"Oh, you can count on that."

"Well, let me know when I can get in. Sorry."

They hang up.

Maggie fetches a hat, pondering. On the way back downstairs, she speed-dials a number she wishes wasn't in her Recents.

"Lee County Sheriff's Department," a female voice says.

"Junior, please."

"The deputy isn't available right now. Can someone else help you?"

"Tell him Maggie Killian called. I'm having the padlock on my barn cut. And I'm pretty pissed he didn't tell me it was there."

"Is there a number where he can reach you?"

"Oh, he has it."

When she ends that call, she's standing in the common room. Maggie doesn't hesitate. She hits a number in her Favorites.

"Michele Lopez Hanson."

"I hope you're having a better day than me."

"Maggie! How are you? How's Wyoming?"

"It's fine." Michele is a worrier. There's no reason to burden her with the whole truth. "I need a favor, though."

"Anything. Well, almost."

She says that, but she's already done too much lately. The scale between them is way out of balance. "Junior padlocked my barn shut, and the adjuster couldn't get in to finish my claim. Can you or Rashidi cut it for me?"

Michele's voice changes as she speaks away from the phone. "Rashidi— do we have anything that will cut a padlock?"

"A big one," Maggie adds, walking into the kitchen for a cup of tea.

She hears Michele's boyfriend's lilting island accent. "Yah mon."

Trudy is coming in the back door, an empty garbage can in hand. Maggie smiles at her and lifts a hand in greeting. She returns both. Suddenly, Maggie forgets about the tea. She knows how to dispose of her owl problem. She grabs two trash bags from the pantry and waves to Trudy again as she exits.

Michele continues talking to Rashidi. "Can you drop by Maggie's and cut one off her barn?"

"Soon," Maggie says. She winces, hating to push when she's imposing already. She opens the front door and squints in the bright sun.

Rashidi says, "I leaving now for College Station. I do it on the way."

Michele puts her mouth back to the phone. "Consider it done."

"Thank you both. Very much. I promise I'll be back soon and won't be asking any favors again for a very long time. Anything up with you?"

Michele hesitates. Maggie hears rattling keys and something that sounds like a kiss, then seconds later, a door closing.

"Oh, just a few little things. Rashidi's got a new contract with an organic grocer. Belle is in love again, although I haven't met him. Sam and Charlie are good, and his girlfriend Rachel is around a lot more again. I've finished *Baby's Breath* and my agent is on me to start a new book."

"Isn't it enough that you've got a *New York Times* bestseller and block-buster movie out at the same time?"

"Alas, no. But I wasn't done with my update. There's a new shrine up to Gary in Round Top. Garish. It's like a mecca for the trailer-park crowd. You'll hate it. He'd love it."

"Great."

"Your mom and my dad are grossing out everyone in town with their PDA. She wants you to call."

"Tell me something I don't know."

"And . . ."

"And what?"

"Ava wants your number. Can I give it to her?"

Maggie walks over to the owl and crouches, giving herself time to think about how to answer the question. Ava. Her onetime nemesis. Michele's friend. Currently the indie darling of the pop charts. She puts her hand in one of the trash bags, then pulls it inside out to cover her hand. She uses the bag like a glove to pick up the owl, gently, then turns the bag right side out again and releases the bird inside. She ties the bag shut.

"What does she want? I don't need any bullshit."

Michele laughs. "No bullshit. I think she has a proposition for you."

"What kind?"

"Work stuff."

"I'm a junker. Does she want to stake me in my new store?"

504 PAMELA FAGAN HUTCHINS

"Don't play dumb. *Music* work stuff."

"I'm a retired Texana singer. She's a pop superstar. And she's wasting her breath."

"A Grammy winner, which is more than she can say. And it's her breath to waste."

Louise approaches Maggie and sniffs the bag.

"Bad."

"What did I do?"

"Not you. The dog. Long story."

"So I'm giving her your number."

"You already did, didn't you?"

Maggie hears a smile in Michele's voice. "Nice talking to you. Tell Hank and Gene I said hey."

EIGHT

Carrying her grim package and trailing one hangdog mutt, Maggie walks to Lily's paddock. The black horse spares her a glance, then pretends to ignore her. Using the rope halter hanging on the gate, Maggie catches her and leads her to the barn. She fastens her to the hitching post, then sets the bag of baby bird against the side of the barn.

A tall blond man she's seen at the ranch a time or two before is with Andy and the two day hands, examining horses lined up in a loading chute. At the other end of the chute is the trailer already half-full.

Maggie fetches her gear from the tack room. On her way back out to the mare, Hank and the new hand, Michael, appear.

"Hi. I'm Maggie. We met yesterday, Michael. Welcome to Double S."

Glittering black eyes fasten on her. "Thank you. I'm glad to be here."

"We didn't expect it to be so soon, but we're lucky you came along." Hank claps him on the back.

"Who's that?" Maggie points at the man working with the hands.

"Doc Billy. The vet. Doing wellness checks on the stock for Duncan."

"Gotcha."

To Maggie he says, "You riding out?"

"Yeah. Pretty weather."

"You got your phone?"

"Yes. And your knife." She pats the scabbard on her hip. Her load is getting heavy, so she hoists the saddle, blanket, and bridle higher.

"I'd feel better if you weren't alone."

She grins over her shoulder at him. "I won't be. I have nearly a ton of horse and my superhero dog." Louise had caught the arsonist last month in Texas. She couldn't ask for a better protector.

Hank grunts. "At least tell me where you're headed."

"Um." Maggie knows safety should be her first priority, but if she tells him, he'll raise a stink. "Out toward Rudy's old house. I'll stick to the fence lines and be back before lunch. Have a good first day, Michael."

Maggie grooms and saddles Lily, then ties the trash bag and its contents behind the cantle of the saddle. The men depart in a Ranger. Just as she's about to mount, Andy rides over on Tatonka. He ties up at the space Lily and Maggie vacate.

"Hey, Andy. Want to work on your guitar later?"

"If I can break free. I have a lot to do with Paco gone. And that new guy here."

Something about his voice stops her from putting her foot in the stirrup. "You don't like Michael?"

Andy blushes. He turns to Tatonka and starts unsaddling him. "It's not that I don't like him. I just grew up on the edge of the Cheyenne reservation. My father hates them all. Some of them are okay. But a lot of them expect something for nothing, like life is all a big government handout. And they drink a lot of alcohol. Take a lot of drugs. Michael's not from a good family."

Maggie has never heard Andy say a negative word about anyone before, so his words are a shock. "I'm sure it will be fine."

"Yes. Hank and Gene are counting on me. I won't let them down."

"I know you won't." Maggie mounts Lily and whistles for Louise, who, from the sound of the squeak, is chasing something small and furry in the barn.

Maggie makes good time, despite gates and Lily begging to graze the brown grass every few yards. Maggie urges the heavy mare into a low trot. She doesn't want Lily to overdo it, but it's the only way she knows to keep the mama-to-be's nose out of the grass. Louise runs circles around them, literally. Huge circles as she hunts and digs.

The phone rings in Maggie's pocket. Lily is calm, so she checks the caller ID. It's a 615 area code phone number. Her stomach flips. It's been years since she's taken calls from Nashville, so she picks up.

"Maggie Killian."

"Maggie, this is Jeff Franke with Goliad Records. How are you today?" The voice is young and energetic.

Goliad Records. She's not familiar with the name. "I'm fine. What's this about?"

"Um, right down to business—okay. We bought your albums—*Throwback*, *Texana*, and *Buckle Bunny*—when your prior record company went out of business. I believe you'd already sold the royalty rights in the music to them, and we have those as well."

Louise flushes a jackrabbit, who bounds across the field between patches of white and brown.

"Good for you."

The man laughs with an ironic edge. "Recently you've been getting a lot of publicity, which has been great for our revenue from your music. We —Goliad—is wondering if you'd like to cut another record. With us."

"You're offering me a record deal?"

"With contingencies, of course."

"Contingencies?"

"For, er, behavior. Morality clauses, if you will."

"Moral behavior."

Lily clomps onward, but Maggie feels the horse tense. She's not oblivious to the drama unfolding from her back.

"Yes."

"Like the Ten Commandments type of behavior?"

"More like drugs. No substance abuse. Or addictions."

"Addictions. So if I'm addicted to, say, sex, then you're saying no fucking."

"No, I mean, I don't know, I—Shit. People warned me that talking to you is like cuddling a hedgehog. Well, they were right."

Riding the fence line against a dirt road off property, Maggie sees a beat-up truck pass. Something about the driver makes her double-take. She could swear he was wearing an Amish beard and hat. But hadn't Andy said the Amish don't drive? She has to have been mistaken.

"What was your name again?"

"Jeff Franke."

"Jeff, you realize I am a recovered drug addict. I can't erase the addict part. So by the very nature of your morality clause, I can't enter a valid contract with you. Or if I get desperate enough to do so, you'd have grounds to screw me anytime you want to. I may have a checkered past, but I'm not brain-damaged. Still got all my marbles."

"I wasn't suggesting that—"

"What's in it for me, then?"

"Money, of course, and redemption. Another shot."

She thinks of the new songs she's been working on. Goliad isn't getting them, that's for sure. "I suspect you don't know a thing about me, Jeff, or you'd know that I don't give a shit about redemption or another shot, and if I did, I could finance those without your help."

Lily snorts. The big horse lowers her head and shakes it.

"Label backing would legitimize—"

"I'm a Grammy winner. I don't need a two-bit label fleecing me back to legitimacy. Fuck off, Jeff. And tell your buddies at Goliad to fuck off, too."

Maggie hangs up the phone. "Patronizing asshole. User. Millennial."

It's a small leap from her irritation about the record company to her irritation with the insurance company. She needs to let the adjuster know the lock has been cut. She texts Michele: *Confirm Rashidi cut padlock? Adjuster waiting to hear.* Then she takes a chance, texting Franklin: *Padlock cut. When can you go back out?*

The phone rings in her hand. Lily snorts and dances. She tosses her nose, pulling the reins looser. She half trots, half walks in an arc back toward the ranch headquarters. Maggie pulls up the slack in the reins and uses firm legs to set the horse back on course. "Whoa." Lily huffs. There's no doubt how she feels about Maggie's level of attention.

Maggie squeezes the phone tight, not wanting to talk to Jeff again. But the call is from Charlotte. All her good intentions to call her mom back disintegrate. She presses DECLINE and thrusts the phone into her pocket. She's had enough aggravation for now. Who did that little weasel think he was, calling up and acting like he was doing her a favor? Like cutting an album with an unknown would give her legitimacy. She'd be the one giving them legitimacy, at the cost of her pride, privacy, and peace. And leading with morality clauses. They'd never worked with her before. All they were doing was piggybacking on the conclusions drawn in lazy journalism.

After traversing a gulch where Louise spooks a whitetail doe with a fawn minus most of its spots, Maggie is still fighting mad, but she spies vultures. Her destination is close. Five minutes later, she crests a rise and sees the pile of dead livestock, complete with yellow crime scene tape. She'd forgotten about the tape. She dismounts outside the perimeter and drops Lily's lead rope to the ground.

"Don't you run off."

Lily mows grass and swishes her tail.

Maggie unties her cargo. The place feels spooky and unsettled. If she stands at the edge of the tape closest to the pile, she thinks she can heave the bird onto its final resting place. It's not the dignified ending she'd envisioned, but she can do it without violating the crime scene. Well, without violating it with anything other than the baby owl.

"Sorry, baby owl. My dog is an asshole." She grasps the limp bird and turns the bag inside out. The animal looks worse for the transport, and it makes her sad. She throws it like a football toward the pile. It lands with a soft thud.

Louise sprints after it, like it's the ball in a game of fetch.

"No, Fucker."

Louise turns to her, wagging her tail.

"I wonder if I've just broken any Game and Fish laws?"

Lily nickers, low and rumbly. Maggie turns to see Deputy Travis, this time on a gray horse half Lily's size with big dapples on his rear end. She doesn't recognize the animal or the brand, which looks like a T intersection.

"What do you think you're doing, Ms. Killian?"

Maggie lifts her hands and flexes her palms up and out with a shrug. "Shit. I'm sorry. My dog killed an owl. I didn't want her to get in trouble, so I brought it out here where no one would know she'd done it."

Travis's squinty eyes and wrinkled brow tell her he's not buying it. "Out of thousands of acres, the only hiding place you can find for it is in the middle of my crime scene?"

"When you put it that way, it does seem crazy, but I promise it made perfect sense to me."

Travis stares at the owl. "So this has nothing to do with Paco?"

"Nothing. How could it?"

He turns his horse so that he's facing her. "Have you seen anyone out this direction in the last few days?"

Maggie frowns. "I haven't been out here. I see Hank, Gene, and the hands headed out from the ranch buildings all the time."

"Did any of their movements seem out of the ordinary?"

"Um, no, I don't think so. The only odd movement I've seen around here was today."

"Odd in what way?"

"Just that I saw an Amish man driving a truck on the road, as I was riding out here."

"So not odd in relation to Paco or this pile?"

"No."

"What about at night?"

For an instant, she remembers seeing someone running to the bunkhouse the night before. Someone in red boots. But her gut tells her not to mention it, so she doesn't. "I can only speak for Hank. And he spends the nights with me."

Travis's horse spins in a circle, but Travis quiets and reorients him. "Last time we met, he was with Sheila." His tone suggests he's Team Sheila. He's local, so chances are he knows her or is related to her, but that doesn't numb the sting.

She drills him with laser eyes. "What's your point?"

"None. Sorry."

"If there's nothing else, then?"

"We're waiting on the conclusions about manner and time of death. When we get that, I may be back."

"Fine. Do I have to remove the owl?"

"Hand me your bag."

Maggie gives the bag to him. Travis dismounts, gives her his reins, and walks carefully to the pile. He rebags the owl and ties the bag closed. He hands it back to her.

"Thanks." Her voice mocks the word.

He grunts. "Have a good day, then, Ms. Killian."

She wheels Lily, whistles for Louise, and sets off at a trot for home. Halfway back to the ranch, she stops in a patch of grass that doesn't seem too rocky. Using her borrowed knife, she digs a hole just deep enough for the little owl and buries it, bag and all.

NINE

Back at the ranch headquarters, Maggie unsaddles Lily. As she's walking into the barn to put up the saddle and tack, a man is hurrying out, and runs into her.

"Oh, sorry." He grabs her by both arms to keep from knocking her down. "The sun was in my eyes."

"That's okay." She remembers the blond man. "Hey, are you the vet who was checking out the horses this morning?"

"Yes. Folks call me Doc Billy. Or just Doc." He releases her arms and clasps her hand instead. They're standing too close to shake.

"I'm Maggie Killian. I'm a friend of Hank's. Do you have a moment to look at my mare?"

"Um—" His eyes dart to his truck, parked on the other side of the driveway to the barn.

"She's just tied to the hitching post right there. The black Percheron. She got caught out in the storm yesterday, out by the dead pile, and she's really pregnant. Just a once-over."

He sighs and looks at the hitching post. "Oh, Lily. A Double S mare." Then he smiles. "A quick look. All the way out by the dead pile, huh?"

"Yes." Maggie leads him to her. "Normally, I'd have just asked Paco to doctor her up. He was my go-to for that kind of thing. Did you know him?"

Doc Billy stiffens, then shakes it off and runs a hand along Lily's neck, back, and rump. "Yes."

"What do you think?"

"I think he had a way of intruding on other people's territory." His voice is icy cold, but he doesn't look at Maggie, just continues examining Lily, looking at her gums, her eyes, pinching her skin, prodding at her udder, and lifting her tail.

She's taken aback. "He was just trying to help the ranch."

"I wasn't talking about—oh, never mind. Yes, he was good with the horses." Doc Billy stands and pats Lily. "She isn't scratched up, and she doesn't seem stressed or dehydrated. But I do think she's going to have this foal early. I was around for her first few, and she hasn't gone to term once. Her udder and teats are filling, her pelvic area is relaxing, and she's starting to wax a little. Keep a close eye on her. Call me if she looks like she's having any trouble."

"Can I still ride her?"

"Pleasure riding, sure. Exercise is good for her."

"Thank you, Doc."

"I'm late for lunch with my wife. Nice to meet you."

"You, too."

Maggie returns Lily to her paddock with some sweet feed, then hustles into the main house just in time to catch the end of lunch.

Hank's eyebrows lift when he sees her. "You ever think about checking your cellphone?"

Maggie checks. There's no missed calls. Her phone also claims she has no service. "T-Mobile, remember? I don't always get them. Sorry I'm late."

"Well, Laura and I are leaving now to take Mom to a doctor's appointment. If you eat fast, you can meet us at the truck after we get her loaded up."

Laura shakes her head. "No, Hank."

"What?"

"I said no."

Mrs. Sibley, who is clutching her sandwich like it will run away if she relaxes her grip, sets it down. Her expression is reptilian. "I don't want that woman with me at the doctor." Then she attacks her sandwich again, chewing as if her life depends on it.

Maggie ignores the bite of the words. She wishes she'd known Hank's mother before Alzheimer's. She concentrates on building her sloppy joe. She adds salad and chips to her plate. "I can sit in the waiting room while she's in with the doctor."

Laura gives Maggie the side-eye. "I'm sorry, but I get practically zero time with my brother, and we have things we need to talk about."

Hank's voice is deadly. "You're being a b—"

"No problem. I have things to do anyway." Maggie cuts him off before he can escalate the awkwardness in front of the hands, who already look like they wish they'd eaten at the dead pile or manure dump. Anywhere but here.

Laura nods. "Thank you. Hank, I'll meet you and Mom at the truck." She pushes her jet hair behind one ear as she leaves.

Hank says, "I'm sorry about that. Laura hasn't had any sleep."

Mrs. Sibley speaks through a mouthful of food. "Don't talk about your sister behind her back."

Hank sighs. "And neither has my mother. Andy, the place is yours. I'll be back before dinner. Maggie . . ."

"I already told you. I have things to do. Including a guitar lesson for Andy, if he's done in time." She lifts her sandwich. Filling falls to her plate. She takes a bite and more gushes out.

Andy wipes his mouth. "I'm taking Michael to check the herds, ride fence, and trade out some pastures. Probably best after dinner."

Maggie smiles at him, finishes chewing, and swallows. "That's best for me, too."

Maggie knows Hank stood up for her to Laura, as much as she let him, anyway. But Laura's words still hurt her. It's not rational, but even though she's not choosing Andy over him, she wants Hank to feel her pain, too.

A hurt look flickers in Hank's eyes. "All right. Well then, we're off. Mom, let's go."

Mrs. Sibley jerks her sandwich toward her shoulder, like Hank is trying to pry it from her hands. "I'm not finished. The portions that new cook serves are far too big. Wasteful."

"Can you wrap it up for her?" he asks Trudy, then mouths, "Sorry."

She winks at him. "Let me save this for you, Mrs. S."

Mrs. Sibley relinquishes her sandwich and her plate to Trudy, who disappears into the kitchen.

"Laura served your plate, and Trudy isn't new here, Mom. It wasn't nice to talk like that in front of her."

"Are you saying I'm not nice? I was just being truthful."

He pulls her wheelchair back from the table. "I'm not saying anything."

They're still arguing over whether or not she was nice as they exit. When the door slams shut behind them, the room grows even more tense.

The hands are evenly divided on each side of the table, with Andy and Michael stark contrasts across from each other. Andy is blond and self-contained, with a full beard and homemade clothes. Michael is clean-shaven, dark, and bristling with energy.

Trudy brings in a platter and lifts a dish towel from it. "Too bad the Sibleys had to miss dessert."

Maggie tries to lighten things up. "Yum, apple strudel. Thanks, Trudy." She helps herself to a slice and passes it to Andy.

He takes one and slides it to the middle of the table. The day hands grab pieces. So does Michael.

There's a knock at the front door.

"I'll get it," Trudy says, and cuts through the dining room.

Maggie and the hands eat apple strudel in silence heavy as a down comforter.

Trudy comes back in, shivering, and points at Andy. "Deputy Travis is here. He wants to talk to you, Andy. But take a coat. I can't believe this weather. There's another storm blowing up."

Andy says, "M-m-me?"

"Yes."

"I don't understand."

Maggie knows what it's like to have the cops up in your grill for no reason. "Want me to come with you?"

"If you don't mind."

"Lunch was great, Trudy." Maggie walks ahead of Andy into the common room.

"Thanks." She watches them with concern in her eyes.

In the great room, Deputy Travis is staring out the window. He speaks without looking at them. "Yesterday was a dusting of powder. Today's storm is supposed to get wicked. Winter is coming early."

In the last half hour, frost has crept from the edges of the windows, working its way to the centers, but thick gray clouds are still visible through the center of the panes. The house groans and creaks as the wind batters it. The trees struggle to stay upright. Maggie can't believe she was out riding comfortably an hour before.

Travis turns to Andy. "What's your full name again?"

Andy catches the back of a couch and grips it. "Andrew Reginald Yoder, sir."

"What's this about?" Maggie asks. She walks all the way up to Travis and crosses her arms.

Travis ignores her. "So your initials are A-R-Y?"

"Yes, sir."

"Do you own a folding knife with a bone handle?"

"Yes, sir. I bought it for myself after I took this job."

"Are your initials, A-R-Y, etched into the blade?"

"Yes, sir."

"Can you get it for me and show it to me?"

Andy clears his throat. He starts to speak but only a croak comes out. On his second attempt, he says, "No, sir."

"Why is that?"

"Because I haven't seen it in a week."

"That's convenient."

"I'm not trying to smear your eyes. I left it in the barn, and I haven't been able to find it."

Travis rubs his chin. His five-o'clock shadow looks closer to two days old. "I'm sorry, but I'm going to need you to come in with me for some more questions."

Maggie bristles. "Whoa. You've been watching too much *Amish Mafia*. Why can't you just ask him what you need to here?"

Andy's eyes are terrified, but now his voice is steady. "No. It's okay. I don't have anything to be afraid of, because I ain't done nothing wrong."

"Is he under arrest?" Maggie demands.

Travis inspects his nails. "If he was, I'd be reading him his rights."

She gets between Travis and Andy, facing her friend. With all the protection Michele has showered on her recently every time the cops have harassed Maggie, it's time to pay it forward. "I'm driving you, then."

Travis talks to her back. "I'd prefer he ride with me."

She doesn't turn to face him. "I'm sure you would. Andy, you're with me."

TEN

The blizzard hits full force from the north while Andy and Maggie are on the road to Sheridan. Visibility is shit, and Maggie creeps along the interstate in Bess, her vintage magenta Ford pickup. Not the best vehicle for the conditions, and without chains. Hank had encouraged her to get snow tires a few days before, but she'd put it off, not understanding why it was important when she was just visiting. Now she gets it.

"Should we go back?" Andy asks.

"We're over halfway. Maybe we'll drive through the storm and out the north edge. If we turn for home, we'll be in the thick of it. I think we should keep going. We made a commitment to get you in for an interview, anyway." What she doesn't say, since it's pessimistic, is that she wants to be as close to Sheridan as she can get in case they end up on the side of the road. She glances at her phone. Especially since there's no cell service where they are.

"Okay. I hope Michael got the animals taken care of."

Before they left, Andy had overcome his issues with Michael enough to have an urgent conversation with him about bringing in the expectant mares. Most had foaled in the spring. It's not ideal for them to give birth in the winter, and usually doesn't happen unless by accident. Lily the escape artist had managed to get herself knocked up at the wrong time of year when she let herself into a pasture with a stallion while she was in heat. So she's on the short list of mares that need to be stabled, which is why she's being kept in a paddock near the barn. The cows are all pregnant but not due until spring.

"He seemed to have it under control. And the day hands will be doing their part."

"It's his first day."

"Gene and Hank wouldn't have hired him if they didn't believe he's capable." Although Gene hadn't gotten around to Michael's background check yet.

"Then it's on them, because I wouldn't have picked him."

"He'll get it done."

"If he doesn't knock off at the dinner bell." His eyes are blazing. "A cowboy works until he gets it done. The animals come first."

Andy seems more upset about Michael and the animals than he is about being under suspicion and questioning for a friend's murder. Something about it gives Maggie pause.

"Is all this distrust about Michael just because he's Cheyenne?"

Andy's face clouds. "It's funny timing. Him showing up asking for work on the day Paco is found dead."

"Did they know each other?"

"I don't know."

Doc Billy's reaction to the mention of Paco flashes through her mind. "I'll tell you who didn't seem to like Paco, and that's the vet. What's that all about?"

An eighteen-wheeler suddenly bears down on them, driving far too fast for road conditions. It honks, then whips around them, fishtailing as it passes them. Maggie gasps as her own truck veers to the right. She fights to keep it under control and lets off the gas. The deeper snow on the shoulder grabs the tires and moves the steering wheel of its own accord. She taps the brakes three times, and the truck straightens. She steers it gently back into the right lane.

"Idiot," she says, her voice squeaky. She shakes a fist after the truck.

Andy's face is pale and his eyes wide. "Good job."

When her heart slows, she quickly checks her cell again for service. There's none. Not only does she wonder what would happen to them if they went off the road here, it kills her that she can't call Hank, Gene, Michele—who is an attorney in addition to being a successful author—or John Fortney, the only lawyer she knows in Wyoming, to get help for Andy.

And Maggie is very sure Andy needs help.

She'd left a message with Trudy to tell Hank where she and Andy have gone, but by the time he gets it, it will be too late. She slows the truck more as they encounter more traffic. Only a few miles to go to the first exit into Sheridan now. She keeps one eye on the rearview mirror for more tractor-trailers, and the other on the road, where she can barely tell where the pavement edge is under the swirling snow—it's hard to even tell up from down. Thank God for the hazard bumps on the side of the road that alert her when she loses her way.

Her tension eases a little when they reach the Fifth Street exit. Bess takes the ramp like a champ, and they do well on the city street, too, thanks to the snowplows already at work.

As they near their destination, she says, "If they had more evidence, you'd be under arrest."

"What do you mean by *evidence?*"

A snowplow flings snow and road debris onto her windshield.

She slows down to a crawl. "Fingerprints. DNA. A witness."

"They won't find any evidence."

"Have you been fingerprinted before?" She takes a right on Main. There's road construction ahead, but she can't see the hazards through the snow. Her stomach tightens. She remembers a section of this road where she'd seen a three-foot drop the week before.

"No."

"They're going to ask to do that today, then."

"Fine."

"Not fine. I don't think you have to unless you're charged."

"But I didn't kill Paco."

"It doesn't matter. They need a suspect. If they focus on you, they'll lose any interest in finding another one. No fingerprints unless charged."

"What about justice?"

She sighs. How sheltered his life in the Amish community has been from the "English" ways of justice. "Oh, Andy. I wish we could trust in justice. Even more, I wish I could have reached an attorney to meet us there."

"Hiring a lawyer's mighty spendy, ain't it?" He pounds his fist in his hand, his first outward sign of intense emotion over his situation. "I really had the bull by the tail, moving along. And now this."

"Let me worry about how much it costs."

"I don't take handouts."

"I know you'll work it off in trade if you have to, and that's fine with me."

Maggie parks Bess, sure that she'll never make it out of the already drifted lot when they're done. She's also sure that she needs a pair of winter boots. Andy catches her by the arm and prevents her from going down on the slick sidewalk. Just as they're entering a tan brick building that looks like any other government structure built in the 1970s, her phone chimes. She has cell service.

"You go on in. I've got signal. I need to call to get you some help."

"Out here?"

"I don't want people in there hearing your business."

"Can you call and leave a message at my father's country store phone? I want him to know what's going on."

"I don't see how he could get here in this weather."

"Father often works here in Sheridan."

Maggie takes the number from him and makes the call. After she leaves the message, she says, "Good luck. I'll be waiting for you when you're done. If I'm able to get an attorney, I'll send them in. And Andy, say as little as possible. Don't explain. Just yes, no, or I don't know, if you can."

The look he gives her is defiant, and she knows his ethics dictate cooperation and create an expectation in him that others will operate by a strict code, too. Maybe he's morally right, but in her experience, the code in the actual justice system is so different from his.

He disappears into the lobby. A blonde woman exits through the interior vestibule door he holds open for her. She's bundled up in a puffy jacket, scarf, and furry boots. Her ponytail cascades through a hole in her wool cap like Maggie's from the day before. She looks Wyoming-winter fashion-forward, if there is such a thing.

Her blue eyes meet Maggie's when she gets to the front steps, and she stops in her tracks. "You."

Maggie's finger is poised to speed-dial Hank when she realizes who the woman with the unlined face is. Sheila. His sort-of fiancée, until Hank ditched her to come after Maggie in Texas. But only sort of, since Sheila did the asking while Hank was medically incapable of operating heavy machinery or making matrimonial decisions.

Maggie's voice would curdle milk. "Sheila."

"What are you doing here?"

"You mean in Wyoming, or here at the Sheriff's Department in particular?"

"Never mind." Sheila starts to push past her.

"What are *you* doing here? A little trouble with the law?"

Sheila stops, eyes blazing. "As if. I'm renewing my concealed carry permit."

That doesn't give Maggie a peaceful, easy feeling. She frowns.

Sheila smirks. "Don't like guns? I'm an instructor. Why don't you take a class from me? We rarely have fatal accidents. I could make an exception for you, though."

"Pass."

Sheila starts to walk on, then flounces to a stop. "Have you ever heard the expression 'Live by the sword, die by the sword?'"

"Excuse me?"

"In this case it means if you have to steal a man to get him, expect to lose him the same way."

"I didn't *steal* Hank. He was mine long before he was yours. And I didn't have to trick him into an engagement while he was sedated, either."

"You're engaged?"

Maggie hadn't anticipated that interpretation. "What *we* are is together. What *you* are is not." Maggie shoos her with her fingers. "Now move along. Hank's waiting on my call."

"Is he, now? I just saw him in the bar at the Rib and Chop. With some woman that wasn't you."

"Don't you have young minds to brainwash?"

"They let out before lunch because of the storm. And don't you even want to know who he was drinking with?"

"No, because I already know."

Sheila smirks. "You're looking at her."

Maggie controls her reaction, unwilling to give Sheila satisfaction.

"Yeah. So you have a nice day thinking about him having a drink with me without telling you." She waggles her fingers in a goodbye gesture that mocks Maggie's earlier shooing motion.

Maggie turns her back on Sheila and presses Hank's number. The message Maggie leaves for Hank is less lovey-dovey than it would have been before running into his ex.

"I'm at the Sheridan County Sheriff's Department with Andy, who was strong-armed into coming in for questioning. I'm also worried about how we're going to get home in this blizzard. If you're still in town, can you come here? I hope your time with Laura was good and that your mother is okay. Oh, and how was that drink with Sheila?"

She tries Michele. No answer. Gene. No answer, but not surprising since he's on the road in a state not known for excellent rural cell signal. She calls John Fortney, the attorney in Buffalo. An outgoing message announces his offices are closed for the day due to the blizzard. And she'd heard how Wyomingites are so weather-tough. What is this, the storm of the century?

She texts Michele: *Need legal advice. Hank's top hand being questioned in a murder. Big storm. I can't find anyone to help me. Call if you can.*

The snow has worked its way into her coat. In Texas, what she has on would be considered severe-weather wear, good for anything except rain. Her heavy brocade coat is lined with fleece and flares over her hips. But it's yet another thing for her list of items that need a Wyoming upgrade. She hurries into the lobby and takes a seat, grateful for the double doors of the vestibule that are keeping most of the cold out where it belongs.

Minutes tick slowly away. She asks the receptionist for an update and gets nothing. She checks her phone and ringer obsessively, to no avail. To pass the time, she surfs property for sale near hers in Giddings, focusing on acreage. A three-hundred-acre ranch seems promising, so she emails the realtor for more information. After about half an hour, the inside door opens to let in an Amish man with brilliant blue eyes and a long beard. He looks familiar. Her mind offers up an image of the Amish man she'd seen earlier talking to Andy at the ranch. Could this be the same man? Whether he is or not, he can only be here because of Andy. Before Maggie can intercept him, he approaches the receptionist.

The man's voice booms. "I'm here for Andrew Yoder."

"And you are who, sir?"

"His father. Reggie Yoder."

ELEVEN

The receptionist confers with a colleague, then returns to the glowering man. He slowly turns a round-brimmed hat between his fingers.

"Sir, he's in an interview. You're welcome to take a seat."

"How long will he be?"

"There's no way to know at this point."

"But he will be free to leave with me when the deputies are through with him?"

"That's my understanding, sir. Subject to change if they find a reason to hold him over."

"Such as?"

"Well, if they arrest him."

Anger hangs over Reggie like a dark cloud. He wheels and stalks stiff-legged to a chair several feet away from where Maggie sits.

"Sir?" Maggie says.

At first he doesn't register she's addressing him.

"Mr. Yoder?"

His head jerks in her direction. "You speaking to me?"

Reggie has a medicinal odor to him. She wonders if it's cough syrup, but he's not coughing. "Yes, sir. My name is Maggie Killian. I understand you're Andy's father?"

"That conversation was not for your ears."

Maggie grinds her teeth. "Andy asked me to be on the lookout for you."

"Who are you to my son?"

How to explain this? "My boyfriend, Hank, is one of the owners of Double S, where Andy works. I gave Andy a ride to town today."

"This is a family matter. Your services are no longer needed. He'll be coming with me."

Heat consumes her ears. She'd expected politeness, if not gratitude. "I'm not sure I understand."

Maggie hears the door from the interior of the station open. She looks up to see a visibly distressed Andy. He notices his father immediately, and she sees a mask of self-control slip over his features.

"Ms. Killian. Father."

Reggie snatches his hat from his knees and stands. "Old Mr. Gregory is waiting with the truck. I'll meet you out there."

"For what?"

"Our ride back to the community."

"Father, I can't go with you. I have a job. They need me at Double S."

"This is not a discussion."

As they're leaving, the receptionist calls out, "Need a shovel?"

Maggie stops. "What?"

Andy says, "No, we've got one."

To Andy, Maggie says, "What was that about?"

"Digging out."

The three of them move outside. In the parking lot, Maggie sees why the receptionist offered them the shovel. The snow has piled up even higher while they've been inside. Plows are out clearing the roads, but not the parking lot.

Andy stands taller, his wool scarf flapping, his back like a flagpole. "Thank you for coming, Father. I sure am sorry to shame you like this, although I ain't done nothing wrong. But I've got livestock to tend to, and this weather puts them at risk. You always taught me about responsibility and hard work. Those animals and that ranch are my responsibility as top hand, and I can't just leave them."

Reggie stomps away, seeming not to even notice Andy's mention of his promotion, however subtle. Maggie's eyes follow him and she watches the profile of his beard and hat in a beat-up Chevy truck parked just a few feet away. The truck backs up. The wheels spin, then grip. It reverses course, fishtails for a moment, then disappears within seconds.

Andy's voice is strangled. "Let's go."

He pulls a snow shovel out of the truck bed.

Maggie asks, "Where did that come from?"

"I threw it in before we left. Due to the weather. There's an ice scraper in the glove box." He shovels, clearing a path.

"Oh."

She feels worthless—and worse, naïve—as she scrapes snow from the windshields. It hadn't occurred to her to check for snow tools before driving to town. Being stuck in a parking lot is one thing—a minor irritant. But if they go off a road, there could be no help for hours. Or days. She ticks off things it would be a good idea to have in the future. Not just a shovel and ice scraper, but a satellite phone. Blankets. A bag of kitty litter or sand for traction. Chains. Water. Nutrition bars. Flares. Taking things for granted here could be deadly.

She and Andy get in the truck. He doesn't look at her.

She exits the parking lot. "Are you okay?"

"It's humiliating to accept help from a woman in front of my father."

Maggie tries to stifle the offense that rises in her. Now is not the time to fight a gender battle. "Don't be ridiculous. We all need help sometimes. No shame in taking it."

They ride in silence through town. Maggie hopes he'll open up, but he doesn't.

Finally, she can't hold back any longer. "How did it go in there?"

"Fine."

"Did you learn anything new?"

"My knife killed Paco."

"Andy, I'm so sorry."

"They'll be contacting everyone at the ranch about the knife and my alibi."

"They have a time of death?"

"Not exactly. But I gave them my whereabouts ever since Paco left."

"Did they fingerprint you?"

"Yes. And I gave them hair for a DNA sample, too."

Maggie bites her tongue. She wants so badly to chastise him for giving law enforcement things they have no right to yet, but it won't change anything now. And she understands Andy's reasons, even if they're different from her own.

The worst of the storm has passed, so the visibility is far better than on the way into town. Maggie lets the ride pass in silence. When they reach the ranch, she drops Andy at the barn—per his request to go make sure Michael took care of things right—then parks at the ranch house. The snow is soft and powdery under her feet as she walks to the front door. Just as she touches the knob, her phone starts issuing notifications rapid-fire. Messages, voicemails, emails. Just inside the door, she stops to check them. Apparently her signal hadn't been good enough to receive anything while she was driving back from Sheridan. Everyone she'd contacted had reached back out to her, although a fat lot of good it did Andy now. She even had a return call from Franklin.

Before she has time to read or listen to a word of them, she sees headlights creeping toward the ranch house. The battered truck she'd seen earlier stops by the front door, and Reggie Yoder covers the ground in a few long strides, a large satchel in his hand. His knock is forceful and continues until she opens the door.

"You again," he says.

"Mr. Yoder." She nods.

"I want to speak to Andy's employer."

Maggie steps back, once again getting a whiff of something astringent. She ushers him into the common room.

Hank calls to her from upstairs, his voice a raised whisper. "Bring Mr. Yoder to my sitting room up here, please. I'd like to keep it quiet downstairs so Mom and Laura can get some rest."

"After you, sir." Maggie beckons Reggie ahead of her on the stairs. In the second-floor sitting room, Hank is nowhere to be seen. "Please, have a seat. I'm sure Mr. Sibley will be with you any moment."

Reggie sets his satchel down and stands at attention.

Maggie goes back downstairs to shuck her boots and outerwear at the rack and pegs by the door. When she returns, Reggie is holding the Sibley mortar and pestle.

"Family heirloom," Maggie tells him.

He doesn't reply or make eye contact, so she continues on to the room she shares with Hank. Louise meets her at the door.

Maggie goes inside and closes the door with a soft click. "You let the dog in. Thanks."

Hank's buttoning a flannel shirt. "I was just getting in the shower. How come you never called me back?" His voice is stiff, and he doesn't make a move toward her.

She approaches him and kisses the cheek he doesn't offer. What's he doing mad at her when he was the one having a drink with Sheila when he was supposedly at the doctor with his mother? She backs away, her temper starting to flare, but she holds it in, for now. There's a visitor on the other side of the wall. "My phone wasn't working for incoming calls. I just got a ton of voicemails and stuff when I came inside the house. I haven't had a chance to listen to them yet."

His eyes flick to hers. "Is Andy okay?"

"As much as he can be. They didn't arrest him, anyway."

"What's up with Reggie?"

"Andy left word for him about what was going on, and Reggie showed up at the sheriff's department. He demanded Andy go back to Montana with him, and Andy refused. Told him he had work to do here. Reggie followed us home. That's about it."

"Anything else I need to know before I talk to him?"

Before she consciously thinks it, Maggie says, "That he smells like rotgut."

"Booze?"

"To my nose."

"The Amish don't drink."

"Maybe it's bad cough syrup. Or something."

"Has to be."

Hank leaves the room. Maggie's slow burn turns into a boil. It's been a shitty day, and Hank doesn't have to make it worse. For a moment she wonders if he's having a head episode. Or if maybe things went badly with Laura and his mother. But that just makes her angrier. Tough times are for working out with her, not with his ex over drinks. Otherwise, there's no future for Hank and her. And if there's no future for the two of them, then that just makes it even more important that she figure out what to do about her ruined home and business. She balls her fists and closes her eyes. To think she'd been searching for a ranch for him in Texas earlier. Louise sidles up to her and nuzzles her hand. Maggie strokes the dog's long, furry ears.

Raised voices from the sitting room draw her closer to the door. She can't make out what they're saying. Hank had shut the door on his way out, but Maggie turns the knob silently and creates a crack of several inches. Immediately she's able to hear their words.

"—English corruption. It's the wrong place for my son. If he was home, none of this would be happening."

Hank sounds placating. "This is a safe place. We've done nothing to corrupt him."

"I disagree. He's a suspect in a murder because of you."

"Andy's innocent. He was only in for questioning."

"You're exposing him to murder and immoral relationships."

Maggie puts her hand over her mouth.

Hank's voice hardens. "We didn't cause Paco's death. And what do you mean about immoral relationships?"

Louise whines.

"You, and that . . . woman . . . that drove him to town."

He's talking about her. She's the immoral relationship. Her blood boils.

"You're out of line, Mr. Yoder."

"And you're a heathen. I want my son released immediately."

Hank's laugh is a snort. "He's not our prisoner."

"Then send him home with me."

"If he wants to go, he'll go. I won't be assisting you in kidnapping a grown man."

Downstairs, the front door opens and closes.

Andy's voice calls out so softly that Maggie barely hears it. "Hank?"

"Up here, Andy. With your father."

Booted feet ascend the stairs with a soft clomp-clomp-clomping. The sounds grow more distinct, then stop. "Father."

"Pack your things, Andrew. We're leaving tonight."

"I already told you, I'm staying here."

"You're risking your eternal soul."

"Father—"

"And shunning by our community."

"I ain't broken no church rules. I'm not even baptized, Father."

"Come and confess your sins, and all will be forgiven."

Andy's voice is firm. "You're embarrassing me. I work here. You need to leave."

Maggie feels her lips turn up with a smile she hadn't expected. Andy's standing up for himself.

Hank chimes in, and she hears the smile in his voice, too. "You heard the man, Mr. Yoder. Time for you to go."

The boots on the stairs recede. These clomps are far louder. At the bottom, they stop, but the door doesn't open. Maggie steps out into the hall, curious, and Louise bolts ahead of her to sniff Hank, giving him a thorough going-over. Andy and Hank are both inspecting their feet. After a few more long seconds, the door slams, and moments later, she hears a truck drive away.

TWELVE

Maggie trips over a dead mole on the front steps as she's leaving the house the next morning. "Gross, Louise!"

Hearing her name, the dog bounds toward Maggie. Maggie kicks the mole off the porch with her hard-toed cowboy boots, as far as she can. It lands ten feet away, partially hidden in the snow.

"This one is going over the fence. I'm pretty sure you won't get in trouble for killing a pasture nuisance."

And Maggie sure doesn't want any more trouble. Mrs. Sibley is on the warpath this morning, irrational and angry. After two nights without sleep, Laura didn't show up for breakfast, which was probably for the best. Mrs. Sibley is convinced Hank is her husband. Nothing he says or does persuades her otherwise. That makes Maggie her rival, out to steal her husband from her, so she threw a biscuit that missed Maggie's head by inches. Trudy covertly made Maggie a to-go plate, and Maggie snuck out the back door with it, then around front to eat alone in the great room.

Trouble isn't limited to Mrs. Sibley, either. Maggie and Hank went to bed without talking. Not about the handful of ibuprofen he dry-swallowed for his broken man parts, the migraine meds she saw him take, Paco, Andy, or Maggie's lack of progress in Texas. And especially not about his drink with Sheila. Hank tossed and turned in his sleep, muttering and occasionally flailing and crying out, which means Maggie is exhausted and on the ragged edge this morning.

Now she's got a bloody varmint to deal with, too.

Sighing, she opens the door to go back for a garbage bag to cart it off in. The door gives too easily, and she falls forward into Gene on the other side.

"Whoa there." He catches her and boosts her back upright.

"Hey, Gene. I thought you were on the road?"

"I was. But I was headed south, where it's even worse than here, on my way to Oklahoma. So instead, I'm on my way north, to fly out of Billings." He grins. "And decided to drop in here for a few things. What has you exploding into the house?"

"You don't want to know."

"I heard I missed some excitement."

"Yeah, poor Andy. I don't know which is worse—his father or the deputies. Andy really doesn't like Michael, by the way."

Gene shakes his head. "They need to get over it. The Cheyenne don't like the Amish, the Amish don't like the Indians. They're Double S employees now."

"Did you get a chance to look into Michael's background? Andy is convinced he's from a family of drug-abusing drunkards on the federal dole."

"No, but I'll call around from the road."

Hank clomps down the stairs. "Ready, Gene?"

For the first time, Maggie notices the overnight bag at Gene's feet.

He throws it over his shoulder. "Off to Billings."

Maggie's brow creases as she looks at Hank. "Both of you?"

Gene grins. "He's my chauffeur."

Hank doesn't smile at her. "I'll be back tonight."

Maggie chafes at his lack of communication. She hates the coldness between them. "Is that extra tank of gas really cheaper than parking?"

Hank shrugs. "Gives me a chance to pick up a few things, meet with a few people."

Under her breath, Maggie's voice is seething. "And you were going to tell me about this when?"

He looks past her and doesn't stop. "All in a day's work. Here for breakfast, here before bed. What does it matter where in between?"

Gene raises his eyebrows at her. "What's up your ass, Sibley?"

Hank hops in the truck. "Ask her." He slams the door.

Maggie growls. "Ask him why I had to hear it from Sheila that he had a drink with her yesterday."

"Oh shit." Gene puts his hand on the truck door. "I think I'll leave this to the two of you. Other than to warn you that trust is a big deal to Hank."

"Then he should be trustworthy."

Gene steps back to get closer to her and drops his voice. "No. *Being* trusted. He considers himself an honorable guy."

"He shouldn't have gone out with her."

"Who's to say he did?"

"What?" Maggie is confused for a moment, then it hits her. She doesn't know who asked who or if there was any asking at all. She's so accustomed to the man-whoring ways of her old boyfriend Gary, she'd just assumed. Still, hearing it from Sheila instead of Hank? Although, her phone wasn't working yesterday. And she still hasn't listened to all her messages.

Gene nudges her with a shoulder. "Listen, I'll talk to him, but consider *asking* him when he gets back."

Her face prickles, a sure sign she's blushing. "Thanks."

Maggie salutes him and waves to Hank, who lifts his hand. A dead fish has more life than him. Gene has a point, but Hank needs to quit acting like an oversensitive drama queen and just talk to her. The truck pulls away, and immediately she feels a ferocious tug on her heart. She runs after them, wanting another chance to get goodbye right. But she's too late, and the truck bounces down the snowy dirt road toward the gate.

"Shit. That didn't go well."

Louise licks her fingers. Maggie jerks them away, not wanting dead-mole tongue on her skin. Louise wags her tail.

"Come on, Fucker. Let's get rid of the evidence of your latest crime."

THIRTEEN

After throwing the mole over the fence and then taking an apple to Lily, Maggie returns to the warmth of the house to check her messages. Before she can even access her voicemail, though, her phone rings. It's Boyd Herrington, her birth father.

"Hey, Boyd."

"Maggie! How's the great white north treating my daughter? Have you managed to get up to the Crow reservation to learn about our ancestors?"

"White and cold. And yes, I have. You need to come see it sometime. Maybe next summer for the Crow Fair. It's a big powwow."

"That would be great. Are you serious about white and cold?"

"Big blizzard yesterday."

"Wow. It's eighty-five degrees in Round Top right now. I believe I'll make my visit in the summer."

"I'm not sure which weather is worse."

"Listen, I have some exciting news."

"What's up?"

"My campaign is a go."

Boyd had withdrawn from a run at the presidency during the last election cycle when news broke that his sister Julie murdered Maggie's birth mother, and a few other people along the way. That was bad, but what made it worse was that she was Boyd's campaign manager, and that she'd committed the crimes to cover up Maggie's parentage. The truth had come out anyway, and when Maggie learned his identity, she was horrified to remember that he'd hit on her the year before. Her new father was a notorious horndog. What could be worse than learning you'd slept with your own daddy? Ugh. Thank God she'd turned him down. But to Boyd's great credit, he celebrated the news that he had a daughter from the moment he learned who Maggie really was to him.

"That's great. I wish you success." She wonders for a moment what office he's campaigning for, but she assumes he'll just be trying to regain his senate seat.

"Michele's book and movie have really neutralized any attempt to paint me in a bad light about you and Julie." *The Love Child and Murder That Toppled the Herrington Dynasty* was a bestseller and blockbuster hit. "And they've been great for name recognition. Better than a reality show."

Knowing Boyd as Maggie now does, she realizes he's probably trying to get one. Maggie shudders. *Please, God, no.* "Yeah, I'll bet."

"But my publicist wants us to push the ball a little further down the field. That's where you come in."

"Oh?" Maggie slips off her boots and flops onto the bed with her hand over her eyes. She braces. The other shoe is about to drop.

"Joint interviews. What do you think?"

"You and who?"

"Me and *you*, of course."

Maggie would rather crawl through snow naked carrying dead baby owls in her bare teeth than submit to interviews. She's had bloggers on her tail for the last few months, ever since her latest rise in notoriety in a "How the Mighty Maggie Killian Has Fallen" piece. It had the horrible timing of raising interest in her just as she was accused of murder. That led to her former bandmate Celinda finding her and exacting revenge for their disastrous past through arson, murder, and identity theft, which only added fuel to the flame of Maggie's notoriety. Her music plays on the radio regularly now. Reporters stalk her friends and family. So why would she offer herself up for more public humiliation?

Boyd fills the silence. "We could set any ground rules you want."

She knows that never works. "It's a bad idea, Boyd."

"Just one? It would really help me."

It's not that she owes him anything. He'd never been there for her, but then again, he'd never been given the chance. Maybe blood is thicker than water, because she hears herself saying, "One and done."

"Thank you. I'll owe you."

"Big-time."

"When are you coming home? We can do it in person, together."

"I don't know. I'm working on it."

"I miss you. We just found each other, and now you're gone. Maybe I should just come visit you in Wyoming after all, and we can do the interview there."

"Don't bring reporters here."

"I didn't—"

"I'm serious, Boyd."

"Okay, okay. I'll call you when the plans start to firm up. Email me if you want to set some topics off-limits. Or if you have any broadcast journalists you prefer to work with. Or not."

She agrees and they end the call.

Lying on the bed, she listens to her voicemail.

Hank: "I just got home. Call me as soon as you know anything about Andy. And give me a break about Sheila. Laura and I had lunch there with Mom after her appointment. They sat us at a table in the bar. Sheila came in and invited herself to sit down. She had a drink, then we left. I can't believe you don't trust me."

Maggie feels sick to her stomach. She wishes she'd listened to her messages the day before. Sunlight streams through the window and across her face. She's not used to being in a grown-up relationship with a good man. Or being the good woman in a grown-up relationship herself.

She texts Hank: *Finally had time to listen to your voicemail. I'm sorry. Sheila manipulated me. I shouldn't have let her. I trust you. I miss you. Let me make it up to you later? xxox*

Michele had texted back general advice that agreed with Maggie's inclinations. Andy had defied most of it, but Maggie felt relieved she'd been right in giving it. To Michele she sent a *Thanks, love you* text.

And finally she listened to the voicemail from Franklin, the adjuster. "I went by your place this afternoon and have what I need. I think you'll be pleased with the amount. I'll call you when it's final—probably tomorrow."

Maggie's heart flutters. She has to figure out a course of action that will protect her finances without having to sell off Gidget's two remaining treasures or the little farm. It's bad enough that all Gidget's paintings burned up. Maggie loved the paintings, her house, and her store. She has goodwill and a brand remaining from the Coop, not just a piece of land.

Surely if she rebuilds the shop, the land will be more valuable. She'll have time to acquire new stock while the contractors are at work. Then, whether she returns to run it or sells it, she'll be in good shape to make a decision. Maybe Hank will develop a hankering to raise bucking stock in Texas. It could happen.

Or maybe the house would be the more important thing to rebuild. More people are in the market for a house than an antique shop. But would they prefer to build their own, if they were buying new construction? Ugh. Why are the decisions so complicated?

What she needs is some estimates so she can compare her options. And a number from Franklin, so she'll know her parameters. She decides to reach out to some of the contractors she's been in touch with already, back when the project was nothing more than repairs from vandalism. When she opens her email, she has one from the realtor she emailed yesterday about the ranch. She reads it after she sends messages to the contractors about getting quotes.

> *Ms. Killian:*
>
> *I hope you don't mind me saying, but I know who you are and about your nice property outside Giddings. I am very sorry to hear you lost your house and shop in fires. If you're interested in selling—or even just talking about the possibility—I'd be happy to get together. I drove by the place, and it looks like your barn is still standing. County property records show you own twelve acres. I could list it for you. Maybe $95,000 or $100,000? As for the ranch, let me give you a tour. It's a turnkey cattle ranch, with a three-bedroom farmhouse."*

Only ninety-five thousand for her place? Maggie's heart drops. She has a small savings account and an even smaller checking account. Franklin's claim estimate better come back big bucks, or Maggie's in a bigger pickle financially than she'd thought.

FOURTEEN

Maggie wakes with a start. Someone is calling her name. A woman. The voice is coming closer.

She stretches and wipes drool from her face. "I'm in here."

Laura appears in her doorway. "We missed you at lunch. I just wanted to be sure you're all right."

Maggie sits up and shuts her laptop. "I was working. I must have dozed off."

Laura turns to go. "Trudy said she was putting a plate aside for you."

"Thank you. For checking on me." Maggie smiles. "I would have thought you'd be relieved if I went missing."

Laura puts her hand on the door frame and looks back at her. "I don't *dislike* you, you know."

Maggie laughs. "You do a great imitation of it."

"You broke my brother's heart. He's never lived a normal life, because of you. Just when he has it together, you show up again and break up his first mature relationship. I hate where this is going for him."

"Wait, what? He broke *my* heart."

"Whatever. I lived through it with him. Dad's illness. Hank's injury and depression. His loneliness. Between Mom and my own problems, I don't have the bandwidth right now to go through that again with him."

"Laura, I care about Hank. I want the best for him."

"That may be true. But you're not exactly the poster child for stability. Or sobriety. Hell, I used to be a fan."

"I thought you said you weren't into my kind of music."

"I said I used to be a fan. I actually saw you perform in Waco, at a dinner theater. You were wasted. When did you quit smoking, by the way?"

"What?"

"I saw you talking to the cops, smoking like a chimney."

"Rehab. I quit at rehab."

Laura nods. "Anyway, you were a real letdown. I don't think I ever listened to you again after that. And this was before Hank had even told us about you. He didn't confess until years later. I guess he was afraid of disappointing me."

Maggie bristles. "That wasn't a good time in my life." She's remained calm, but Laura's getting personal, whether she's right or not. "But I've been a business owner and pillar of my community for ten years. You're out of line and unfair."

"Once an addict, always an addict."

Maggie advances on her. "For the sake of your relationship with your brother, I think this conversation should be over."

Laura stares at Maggie, deep into her eyes. "I'll be in his life long after you're gone." Then, before Maggie can answer, she leaves.

Fuming, Maggie jerks on her boots, then goes to the bathroom and wipes the sleep from her eyes. She stomps down the stairs to the kitchen. Trudy is gone, but on the counter are two plates of food covered with plastic wrap.

"I hear Trudy left me a plate."

She turns to see Michael. "You missed lunch, too, huh?" She points at the covered meals.

"Yeah. I got an ATV stuck in a drift." He smiles, showing perfect white teeth, except for one that's missing. An eyetooth. "I'm taking a horse out this afternoon. They're a little more reliable in these conditions."

"How's the weather?"

"Cold, but clear and sunny. The sky looks like the Caribbean Sea. Not that I've ever seen it, except on TV."

Maggie eats her beef stroganoff and rice with a spoon, standing at the counter. Michael follows her lead.

"It would have been nice to ride out in twos, but we're kind of slammed with Hank and Gene gone, and Andy, um, missing part of yesterday. And then tomorrow people will be gone for Paco's service."

"I'll bet."

"Although I'm not sure Andy would ride with me anyway, even if he could."

Maggie rinses her plate and avoids eye contact. "Oh?"

"I think he has a thing against the Cheyenne."

"Why do you say that?"

"The Amish are our neighbors, but we're not neighborly."

It sounds like an admission, so Maggie follows up on it. "So do you have a thing against the Amish?"

"No more than anyone else I know back home. I don't like how they treat their animals, but maybe Andy will be different."

"What do you mean?"

"The Amish I know ride their horses into the ground and starve them. I was pushing cows with some Amish this summer, and I had to take my saddle off my horse and walk him back—he was that beat. The Amish just whipped theirs up and ran them home. Their feet were awful, cracked, turned up. Most of them were half-lame." He snorts. "Not their teams, though. They treat their teams real good. But then again, if they're your transportation and your tractor, you better keep 'em running."

"Andy's been nothing but good to the animals here."

"He moved away. That says something. And the best farrier I ever saw was Amish. Or ex-Amish. I do some blacksmithing myself, and he won every competition I ever saw."

"Are you from the reservation?"

"Yeah. But I left a few years ago. I'm trying to stay out of the res scene. There's nothing for me there. But it's hard. I'm pretty broke."

Maggie remembers leaving home younger than him, a lifetime ago. Broke, too. Everything had been so much simpler, until it wasn't. If what Andy says is true, things aren't simple at all for Michael back on the res. "Well, I hope the two of you will get along. Since he'll be your supervisor."

"I'll be fine."

She looks out the kitchen window. Not a cloud in the sky. She has decisions to make, and there's nothing like wide-open Wyoming to clear her head. "I make a pretty good second. Or at least I can dial 911 in an emergency. If there's signal."

He laughs. "You beat out all the competition, but it won't get me in trouble with Hank, will it?"

She scoffs and checks for a text back from Hank. There's none. "Of course not."

FIFTEEN

Lily is sassy after twenty-four hours in a stall, where the hands had put her when the weather went to crap the day before. She dips her head and shakes it as she canters along behind Michael and his horse.

"Who are you and what have you done with my lazy pregnant mare?" But Maggie understands. She likes her freedom, too.

Ahead of them, Michael is doing a post-storm welfare check. He counts heads of cows and calves. It's easier said than done, because they don't stand still for it. When he's done, he turns back and frowns. "I'm short two head. Can you see what count you get?"

"Whoa, Lily." Maggie counts, keeping track by fives on one hand. Lily fidgets in a circle. Maggie uses leg pressure to push her back. "I got thirty-two."

"Shit. That's what I got. And after I've been lucky all day."

"Do you know which tags are missing?" All Double S bovines wear numbered, colored ear tags.

"Nope. If we have to, I can ride back and get them. But I need to check the fence and break up some ice, too, so let's start by riding it."

"Break ice?"

They take off, riding single-file along the fence. The cold makes her breathing stuffy. She rubs some Mentholatum under her nose and coughs, then returns the little tube to her pocket.

"In the tubs."

"Aren't they automatic?" Maggie thinks about all the ranchers she knows in south central Texas. Their tanks have floats for refilling. Even in the coldest weather, the water usually replenishes.

"No. We don't use floats this far north. Ice breaks floats, and broken floats kill. Animals die fast here without water. Plus a broken float can waste the water itself, spill it all out on the ground, where it doesn't do them any good."

"What about the creeks and ponds?"

"They don't freeze as fast, so we can break the ice by hand. But when it gets too cold, we'll have to bring the livestock where we can keep them fed and hydrated, I imagine. That's what most everyone up here does."

Maggie imagines the overcrowded barn conditions. "There's not room for them all in the ranch buildings."

"Oh, they're fine outside. Especially the horses. They adapt pretty well to cold forage. Better than cattle. The cows are known to hunker in ravines that fill up with ice and snow, then starve their damn selves to death. Horses move to higher ground where the wind blows the snow off the grass leftover from the growth months. Horses can even get their hydration from eating snow. Cattle don't."

"But it gets so cold here. And so windy. Won't they freeze to death?" Maggie's plenty cold now, even with the sun out. She leans back as Lily picks her way down a steep incline. The horse slides a few feet. Maggie clutches the saddle horn, but Lily seems nonplussed.

"You'd be surprised. I've heard an unclipped horse's ideal weather is twenty degrees. I don't know about that, because I haven't ever been able to get one to tell me, but I've seen our horses on the res refuse to take shelter even when we offer it, in double digits below zero."

"How do they survive?"

"They just huddle together with their butts against the wind."

"But two cows aren't enough for a huddle. I hope they didn't get loose."

"Most likely they're just over a ridge, enjoying the sun. But we'll make sure."

Lily snorts and jerks her head up. A red fox darts in front of them in a crazy zigzag pattern, then across the snow to the fence line. Maggie remembers the brown jackrabbit hopping over the grass only a day or two ago. This landscape is nothing if not constantly changing. The sky is crazy clear and the snow sparkles like diamonds. On the face of the mountain, the rustic family cabin looks like a Swiss chalet. A bald eagle swoops up and down the ridge, letting out a series of high-pitched whistles.

Maggie tents her hand to peer after the raptor. "It sure doesn't make a very powerful sound."

"Doesn't have to. The eagle knows he is mighty. We are blessed by his presence. He comes to us from heaven."

Maggie smiles. "A visitor from heaven. Really?"

"That's what my grandfather says. Maybe this one is sent by your friend Paco."

"Maybe." Maggie doesn't bother to sound convinced.

Michael's head moves slowly left to right and back as he scans the landscape, looking for signs of the missing cattle. "I only met him once. Did you know him well?"

"A little. He was full of life. A charmer. And good with mechanics. Like, things with engines. He helped me when my truck broke down."

Michael stops and stares at something for a moment, then he urges his mount forward again. "My Cheyenne name is Talks to Eagles. When I was a boy, an eagle flew through my bedroom window. He was not happy. He went crazy, flapping his wings, breaking things. I talked to him until he calmed down. I told him I was his little brother and I would help him. He finally let me pick him up. I carried him outside and released him to kiss the sky."

How different her childhood and whole life would have been if she had known about her own Native American ancestry and lived closer to that side of her family. Suddenly she really wants to find out who they are. Not just that they are part of the Crow nation, but who the people are. To meet them. She needs to ask Boyd for their names.

"Was the eagle hurt?"

"Only his pride, I think."

Maggie smiles, enjoying the thought of eagles kissing the sky as she watches the eagle continue its journey along the ridge.

"Eagles are sacred to my people. They represent truth, courage, wisdom, and freedom. So my eagle's visit was like a visit from the divine. Because of this, I was treated with the deep respect that people reserve for him."

His words are moving to Maggie, but she doesn't know how to express it. So she stays quiet and thinks about this young man and his family. He certainly isn't telling a story that sounds like it is filled with drunks and druggies.

"His visit has been the source of my strength in many hard times. I've had many visitors since then, because of him. Spirits, sometimes in the form of other animals. Even the dead."

"How do you know? I mean, when you get the visitors, how do you know?" Maggie has had visits from the dead herself. Several, in fact, from her renter, Leslie, after she was murdered, but she doesn't mention this to Michael.

"I just know. My eagle taught me to trust in my power."

Maggie warms inside. Maybe she needs to trust more in her own power. Her own wisdom. She'd doubted her visitor was a dead woman, but it had turned out she was. She looks back up at the eagle. She can barely see it now as it flies off into the distance up the mountainside, past the Sibleys' cabin. Her eyes drop, and as they do, she catches a glimpse of a man. Stooped. Hat pulled low. Not dressed for the weather. Red boots glaring out from the snow. He's headed down a ravine, and she knows it's Paco. Even though it can't be, she knows.

She draws in a sharp breath. "Paco."

Michael raises his hand for her to stop. "Hello there." His voice echoes in the stillness.

The man doesn't react.

"You see him, too?" Maggie asks, her voice thready.

"Our visitor? Yes. He could be walking the in-between world, looking for peace."

"So I'm not crazy."

"I can't say that. But this doesn't make you crazy. Just perceptive. If I didn't know better, I'd say you were Indian."

"I am. Partly. Crow." She remembers the red-booted man she'd seen the night she found Paco's body. The one running to the bunkhouse. Could that have been Paco, too?

"See that?" Michael points down a ravine at two black furry bodies. One of them moos. "That's where Paco was headed. He's still doing his job."

Maggie looks back for Paco, but he's disappeared. She shivers and pulls the collar of her coat closed tighter. "The little bastards. They can't hide from us."

"Help me push them back to the herd?"

"Do we need to do anything about Paco?"

Michael looks at her like she's crazy now. "He's not in this world anymore. There's nothing we can do for him. But we can take care of these cows."

"What do I do?"

"We'll fan out behind them, maybe five yards back."

Michael and his horse drive the cows out of the gully and past Maggie. She urges Lily after them and positions the horse to the left of their retreating backs, nose-even with Michael and his horse's rump. She barely has to guide Lily, who seems to know exactly what to do.

"You're a natural."

Maggie smiles. She's not sure about that, but she's taken to ranch life far more than she'd ever thought she would.

SIXTEEN

Maggie showers and dresses, checking her phone every five minutes. She still hasn't heard back from Hank, and she's getting worried. The weather is clear, but that doesn't mean bad things can't happen on the road between the ranch and Billings. Semitrucks with overly aggressive drivers. Ice. Deer. Sleepiness. Trouble with his head.

She texts: *Let me know you're okay. I can't wait for you to get home.*

This time she gets a reply. *Hey, sorry. Signal spotty. Driving. All good. Home by 10.*

Maggie's relief makes her giddy. She responds with a heart emoticon, feeling like a silly adolescent. She stops just short of begging him not to be mad at her. When things aren't right between them, things aren't right with her. Hell, she may not be able to say the L-word, but she knows she's a goner for this cowboy.

Dinner is quiet. Laura has taken Mrs. Sibley into Story to the Wagon Box for chicken fried steak, a tradition the older woman keeps with her caregiver. Gene is probably in Oklahoma already, and Hank won't be home for hours. It's just Trudy, Maggie, and the four hands.

Michael breaks the silence, teasing Maggie about her new cowgirl skills.

"I told you I was the right person for the job." Maggie twirls spaghetti noodles on her fork. The thick meat sauce slides off, so she scoops it back onto the fork.

Andy has a funny look on his face. "Hank is pretty protective of her. I'd be careful if I were you."

Trudy plops down at the table. She serves herself spaghetti. "He's fine, Andy."

Maggie wipes her mouth and swallows. "Hank doesn't get jealous. Besides, I'm a grown woman. If I want to push cows, I'm going to push cows."

"Michael works here. You don't. And I think you've got Hank running around a stump."

"What?"

"The man doesn't know up from down with you around. Why do you think he took off today?"

"Gene needed a ride."

Andy harrumphs. "Maybe so. But Hank is trying to worry something out. And you're the only thing he worries about. Remember, we're with him here when you're not."

Trudy stabs the air with garlic bread. "Andy, I think you need to shut it down."

"I don't want in the middle of that," Michael says, shaking his head.

Maggie squeezes the cloth napkin in her lap. "You're not in the middle of anything. It's okay. Hank doesn't mind me teaching Andy guitar." She takes a deep breath and lets it out quickly, twirls up more spaghetti and lets it hover in the air. "Speaking of which, are we on tonight, Andy? It would be a good distraction for you, I think."

"I've been thinking on that. The roads are clear. Would you be willing to take me to the Occidental tonight for the bluegrass jam instead?" Andy puts his elbows on the table and takes another bite.

Maggie wonders if his worries are more about Michael than Hank. "You go on. A saloon? On a work night?"

He blushes and ducks his head.

"I think it would be fun. And good for your own playing to watch musicians jam."

"You don't think it's disrespectful, this soon after Paco's, um, after he's gone?"

"What would Paco say?"

A grin lifts one side of Andy's beard. "He'd be the one asking me to go with him."

"Music is always appropriate in my book."

"If you don't think it will look bad to the sheriff. Like I don't care about Paco."

Or like he's guilty. But he's not. "The deputies will figure out the real killer. Listening to music isn't evidence. I'd be more worried about what your father will think."

"I'm on Rumspringa. It doesn't matter." He pushes his bowl away and scoops whipped cream onto an enormous apple dumpling, then pulls that bowl toward himself.

"I've been meaning to ask you about him."

"What?"

"I saw an Amish man that looked like him, driving a truck. Outside the ranch."

"My father doesn't drive."

"Okay. I did think it was odd."

"Are you sure he was Amish?"

"Not a hundred percent."

"All right, then."

Michael glances between the two of them. "My sister loves the jam. She's a musician."

Maggie can tell he's waiting for an invite. He and Andy need to work things out and move on to something normal. But she's not going to force it on Andy when he's already got so much to deal with. And Andy doesn't respond.

Well, so be it. Maggie considers an apple dumpling. She never thought she could get sick of apples, but she is. She stands. She'll skip dessert. "Let me change. I'll meet you out front in twenty minutes?"

Andy nods, his mouth overfull of apple dumpling and a look of bliss on his face. Michael scowls and attacks his dessert.

Upstairs, Maggie puts on heavier boots and swaps out her sweatshirt for a cable-knit sweater over a button-down. After she swipes on lipstick, she texts Hank again.

I'm taking Andy to the Ox in lieu of music lesson. Home by 9.

Andy's words replay in her head. "Hank is trying to worry something out. You're the only thing he worries about." She knows she jumped to conclusions about Sheila. She shouldn't have blamed him. Hopefully that's all he's worrying about, but she knows he's concerned about her plans. Her place in Texas. Their future. She is, too, but only because she hasn't figured out how to get him to Texas yet. Tomorrow she'll call that realtor about the ranch for sale. She needs to know about cross-fencing and facilities and set up a time to see it. A time when she can get Hank down there with her.

Forty-five minutes later, she and Andy find two seats next to each other in the Ox at a table for four with a smiling couple in matching plaid shirts who are noshing on burgers and french fries. Maggie loves the greasy-spoon smell, the jovial atmosphere, and the authentic décor. Especially the décor, from the bullet holes in the ceiling to the heavily lacquered hand-hewn tables to the wildlife mounts of every animal known to Wyoming, plus a few. A waitress with a blonde braid weaves over and takes their order. If Maggie had a dime for every blonde braid she's seen in Wyoming, she'd be a rich woman. Maggie opts for one TKO and one coffee. She's not eager to learn how good her winter driving skills are after a few drinks. She'll pace herself, very slowly.

Andy orders a ginger beer. "Will you play tonight?"

"Oh no. Not on your life."

"I really wish I could see you." He gestures at the players, who are warming up by running through snippets of songs. There are six of them. An old guy in dusty, baggy jeans with a red bandana around his neck, a pimply teenage boy, a soprano-voiced banjo player with long dark hair, a foreign-accented woman on the fiddle, and two more old guys who look like twins. "They're good, but I've listened to you play. Live, at the ranch, and on your albums."

"My albums? How?"

"Cassette tapes. Hank lent me his stash. There's a boom box in the bunkhouse."

Hank has a stash of her albums, on cassette. That means he got them back in the years they were apart. And kept them. Every piece of evidence that he really loves her is a sunburst in her chest. "Wow. I didn't know."

His brown eyes plead. "Please play."

Andy's had such a terrible week. War wages inside Maggie. How can she deny him this? It's only her ego standing in the way. She flinches. Yes, her ego. She doesn't want people to see her perform less than perfectly. Even retired, she's a professional musician. But an out-of-practice one, out of her element and playing with strangers. There's no way she's going to be perfect if she gets up there. Maybe no one but Andy will figure out who she is, though.

She sighs. "Fine. What do I do?"

SEVENTEEN

Andy beams and claps his hands once, loud and sharp, one hand going up, the other away. "Just go tell them who you are."

"Oh no. I'll play the jam, but only if it's anonymously," Maggie says.

"Well, say hello, anyway. They'll invite you in. It's how they've done it here at the Ox the times I've seen them before. When Paco brought me here."

She shakes a fist at him. "If this goes bad, I'm coming after you, Andy."

"You'll be the best they've ever heard."

"I doubt that." She turns sideways and sidles between chairs. "Excuse me. Pardon me."

People move out of her way with no grumbling. At the front of the room, the jamming musicians are between songs.

She approaches the old guy with the bandana at the vocal mic. "Hey. I hear you let musicians work in?"

"Sure do. What do you play?"

Maggie surveys the instruments. Piano. Standing bass. Banjo. Fiddles. Acoustic guitars. Tambourine. Washboard. "Everything you've got."

"Did you bring an instrument?"

"Nah. I had no idea this was an option." She takes a step back. "It's okay if I can't."

"Nope. Just checking. How about you start on the piano? We rotate up to the vocals through the instruments we each know. When you get the vocal mic, you announce your song and key and set the tempo."

"Sounds good."

"Name?"

"Maggie."

He turns to the group. "This here's Maggie. She's working in, starting on the piano."

Friendly, curious faces greet her and offer names. Penny. Brad. Donna. Hal and Cal. The old guy says his last. "And I'm Wally."

"Nice to meet you, Wally."

"Song is 'Rocky Top.' Key is G."

He's picked something she knows, which is a good start. She seats herself on the piano bench. Wally announces the song to the bar and introduces her. She waves. A few hands in the crowded bar lift. Andy's is high and vigorous. Wally counts off, and the musicians launch into a joyful noise. Maggie's chords are complementary and rhythmic. The players are all quite good and have obviously played together many times. The banjo-playing girl with the long black hair is a standout. *Penny. That's what her name is,* Maggie thinks.

It's an easy way to work in, being in the background. She can't help smiling and bobbing her head. By the end of the song, she's exhilarated and embellishing. Okay, she misses this. Not solo performance, but this. Being inside a song, even an amateurly delivered jam song. It lifts her soul and fills her with a light she hadn't realized was burned out. When they finish the song, the crowd applauds with vigor. Andy stands up and whistles with two fingers.

Wally scoots onto the piano bench. "You play this thing like you've been pounding keys all your life."

"Something like that." She moves on to the standing bass.

Piano is the least of her skills. Give her anything her fingers can pick and strum, and she's in her element. As she cycles through the bass, the banjo, the fiddle, and the tambourine, they play old standards. "Cherokee Shuffle." "Will the Circle Be Unbroken." "Old Joe Clark." "Whiskey Before Breakfast." Then it's her turn at the vocal mic, with the guitar. She ponders song choices. She needs something bluegrass that she knows all the words to, when what she really wants to play is "Kickapoo Redemption," something she heard recently from Shea Abshier and the Nighthowlers. Her choices are limited by her experience and her memory. She'd do better with a list to choose from. The other musicians huddle behind her. Just when she's about to ask them to offer up a tune, Wally nudges her.

"We voted. We want you to play 'I Hate Cowboys.' We'll bluegrass it up a little for you."

Maggie bites her lip. "Um, I . . ."

"You didn't think we wouldn't figure out who you are, did you? That face of yours is way too famous, and word's out about you and that Sibley boy. But we had a hint, too."

Maggie scans their faces. What hint? She glances at Andy, but he looks innocent and oblivious.

Wally laughs. "Ole Hal here knows all your songs by heart. He's even had us play 'em a time or two."

Hal tips his hat. Cal tips his, too.

She bows to them, then blows a kiss. "I usually hate playing my own stuff. It blows my cover."

Wally claps her on the shoulder. "You're amongst new friends. And I'm not sure you have much cover to blow. Now, give us a treat."

She makes eye contact with Andy and nods at him. Into the mic, she says, "'I Hate Cowboys,' key of E. This one is for my friend Andy."

Just as she launches into the music as familiar to her as her own breath, she sees Andy isn't looking at her. He's looking past her. She glances back and catches Penny's gaze locked on Andy. A chuckle escapes her, but she ends it in time to sing the lyrics Hank inspired so many years ago. She strums and sings along to the accompaniment of the bluegrass musicians. The music feels different on a strange guitar, and she misses her Martin back at the ranch. She becomes aware a buzz is growing in the room. How long has it been since she sang this song in front of humans? Ten years? Twelve? When she reaches the ending, she sings the chorus one last time.

I hate cowboys—especially bull riders—
I hate cowboys.
Their buckles look funny,
And they call their girls bunnies.
I hate cowboys. I hate bull-riding cowboys.

She shakes the guitar gently, drawing out the sound of the last note. The saloon patrons are on their feet, cheering. Calling her name. Her secret is definitely out. Andy basks in the glow and nods at her. Wally claps her on the back so hard she falls forward from the stool.

He catches her. "Sorry! Just a little excited. That was real special for us."

The rest of the musicians surround her. She accepts hugs and handshakes. Penny holds out a Sharpie and asks her to sign the back of her banjo.

"Oh no. Anything but your beautiful instrument. How about the case instead?"

The girl agrees and returns with a beat-up case covered in bumper stickers. Maggie signs and tries to hand the marker back.

"You're going to need it." Penny points.

A line has formed.

Wally takes the mic. "We're going to take a break to let you folks thank Ms. Killian for gracing us with her talent. Back in a few."

Maggie signs autographs and chats while keeping one eye on Andy. He beelines toward Penny. She barely meets his eyes, but she nods. The girl is shy, that's for sure. After they exchange a few words, she joins him at the bar. A few minutes later, Maggie sees fresh ginger beers in their hands. Maggie finally begs off from the patrons wanting to talk about her music to join them.

"Hey, you two. Penny, you have a great sound. What did you think, Andy?"

"I think she is wonderful."

The two stare at each other like there's no one else in the room.

Maggie laughs. "I meant about the music, Andy. You're here as my student."

Penny breaks eye contact and swivels to Maggie. "You teach? I'd love to take lessons from you."

"Well, Andy's my first student. Ever."

"I can be your second."

"She could take lessons *with* me," Andy suggests. His voice quivers a little, like he's not used to being this forward with girls. A non-Amish girl, at that.

Maggie shrugs. "We could do that." She recites her number, and Penny types it into her phone.

Andy says, "There's the woman Paco was sparking."

He doesn't point, but he nods at a curvy brunette in her late twenties or early thirties standing near the pool table in the back room. She's sipping her drink through a straw, then stirring the ice cubes. There's a cluster of women around her. One looks familiar to Maggie. Had she seen her out on a date with Gene a few months before?

"Maggie. Didn't you just bring down the house?" A female voice drips sarcasm to Maggie's left, even as it slurs.

Maggie looks over. Sheila. She's way, way drunk, and probably carrying concealed under her puffy lavender vest. "Time to scat, Andy."

"But . . ."

"What, Maggie, are you running away from me?" Sheila says.

Maggie turns away from Sheila, imagining a bullet through the back. She ignores Sheila and answers Andy. "You can meet me outside, then."

"No! I mean, I can't let you go out there alone." He shoots a glance at the glowering, staggering Sheila, then turns his attention back to Penny. His brow furrows. "I, um, I don't have a phone, Penny." Maggie knows this is an Amish thing, and she aches for him for a moment. Dating outside his community in Montana is a challenging thing. "But I'd like to see you again."

"We're going to take music lessons together."

"How about I get the two of you together Monday night?" Maggie suggests.

Sheila stares daggers through her. "Hello?"

Penny looks down. "Sounds good."

"I'll see you then." Andy's face relaxes.

Penny smiles sweetly. "Thanks for the drink. Nice to meet you, Maggie."

Sheila's voice elevates to a screech. "I'm talking to you, Maggie Killian. You can't ignore me just because you think you're some big hotshot."

The curvy brunette and the familiar-looking friend appear beside Sheila, and now Maggie is sure it's the same girl she saw out with Gene.

She narrows her eyes at Maggie. "You."

Andy takes Maggie's elbow. He's never touched her before. "Let's go."

"Definitely."

Andy hustles her ahead of him toward the door. Maggie is really glad she's sober, or she'd be ending this night in a public catfight.

Sheila's voice isn't far behind them. "Run like a little bitch."

"What did Hank ever see in that beast?" Maggie mutters.

The cold slaps her in the face when they hit the sidewalk, but it's not nearly as shocking as what she sees. Hank is standing there, arms crossed and legs slightly apart, looking like a Remington bronze.

"Hank!" She throws her arms around him, but stops short of climbing him and biting his neck like she wants to. "You're here." Their noses bump, and his is icy cold.

"I decided to come straight here instead of stopping at home."

She nuzzles into his neck. "I'm so glad. I missed you. I'm sorry I was jealous yesterday." She cranes her head back and catches a sight of the dimples. Something inside her chest flutters.

He presses his lips to her ear. "I missed you, too. Let's get your boy home and crawl into bed."

She shivers. "I'll race you."

EIGHTEEN

Before Maggie, Hank, and Andy can leave, the door to the Ox flies open. Sheila barrels out with her two sidekicks.

"There she is," Sheila says. Then, "Oh. With you."

Maggie and Hank lock eyes.

"Unprovoked, I promise," Maggie says.

"She tried to cause a problem yesterday. Why should today be any different?" He kisses her, his warm lips all the reassurance she needs. "Let me see if I can stop this."

They break apart. Sheila is still bristly, but starting to deflate.

"Enough, Sheila. I told you yesterday. You're a great woman. But I'm not the guy for you."

Her eyes glisten. "You were. You could be again."

"Come on, Sheila." The brunette tugs on Sheila's arm. Then to Hank, she says, "Sorry."

"Thanks, Mary." To Maggie he says, "This is Mary Marton. You already know June, I think?"

Sheila jerks her arm away from her friend. "Get her away from me, June."

Maggie says, "Nice to meet you, Mary. Hello, June."

Mary says, "Nice to meet you."

June scowls and moves between Mary and Sheila.

Two men a few years older than Andy walk out. One says, "Hey, thanks for playing, Maggie!"

She waves. "You're welcome."

Hank shoots Maggie a questioning look, but then turns back to Sheila. His voice is rock solid. "No, I never will be again. My heart belongs to Maggie."

"You said she's moving back to Texas."

Maggie's mouth flies open.

Hank holds out an arm, stopping Maggie before she can advance on Sheila. Or him. "You asked me about her place in Texas. I told you she's going back to take care of things. And that's all I said. You need to stop this. Get on with your life." He turns to her friends. "We're leaving. Get her back inside. Better yet, get her home to sober up. She's got to teach in the morning."

The women nod. Sheila crosses her arms and plants her feet.

Hank takes Maggie's arm and starts walking her away. "I want you and Andy to drive ahead of me. Andy, you're on duty."

Andy falls in step with them and pats his ribs. "Don't worry, Hank. I'm carrying."

Maggie smiles. "That's not very Amish of you."

"Hank left me in charge of you."

"Is that why you were upset that I rode out with Michael?"

"Not exactly."

"What?" Hank asks.

She looks over her shoulder. Sheila and her friends are still arguing. The temperature is falling, and the cold is seeping into Maggie. She wraps her arms around her midsection. "I'll tell you at home, babe. I've got to get Bess's heater on."

They walk a little farther and reach Maggie's magenta truck behind the courthouse.

"I'm back on the street out front. Come around and wait for me so I can follow you."

Five minutes later, Andy and Maggie chug off with Hank behind them. Bess finally heats up five minutes before they reach the ranch.

Andy says, "I'll walk from the main house."

"Are you sure?"

"Yeah. It's not far."

"Okay. Thanks, Andy."

They get out. Hank parks beside Bess. All the lights are off, inside and outside the house. Andy waves and slips away into the darkness.

A hard body crashes into Maggie. Her squeal is cut off by warm lips, her fall arrested by strong arms around her. They lean into the cold metal of her truck. She hooks a leg around Hank's hip, pulls herself up, then wraps the other around him and locks her ankles, all without breaking their intense kiss. But then she pulls her lips away and sinks her teeth gently into the base of his neck.

Hank groans. "Don't let go of me."

She doesn't.

Somehow they make it in the door, up the stairs, and to the bedroom without Hank crashing or Maggie falling. He kicks the door shut behind them, then staggers to the bed, where they topple.

Maggie laughs as it crashes to the floor. "Whoops. I think we need a permanent fix."

"I'm on it. Just not right now." He grabs her face and holds it between his hands, his pressure possessive and just the right side of rough. "I fucking love you. It's driving me crazy. I thought it was bad before. When we were younger. But I feel like a kid again."

"Oh God. Me, too."

His lips rove across her face to her ear, then down her neck. He stops suddenly. "It's not always a good thing, but it's always amazing."

Maggie knows exactly what he means. "Less telling. More showing. If you can. With your broken unit and all."

"My unit is fully functional." He laughs. "Did I mention I fucking love you?" Then he rips off his shirt, and all telling stops.

NINETEEN

"I can't decide what I like best about sex with you. Wanting you, having you, or the afterglow." Maggie traces her finger across and around his sculpted chest.

"Stop. You're going to kill me."

"Is it hurting you?"

"Is what hurting me?"

"Well, you're, um, looking ready to go again. And you did injure yourself, after all."

He smiles. "The bruising is bad, and it's crooked. I look like I got the worst of it with a bull hoof to the crotch."

"But it's treatable, right?"

"Bull injuries?"

"No. Sex injuries."

"What the hell kind of nonsense is that?"

"If it hurts, then you should get it looked at."

"It will only hurt if you laugh at it."

"I won't. But if it does."

"Maggie, I didn't see a doctor for a broken back. I'm sure not going to see him for a crooked penis."

"Let me see."

"No."

"Seriously, just stand up."

He sighs, but stands naked in the moonlight.

Maggie tilts her head. "It's black and blue. Mostly black."

"I told you so."

"And you look like you're signaling a right turn." She scoots to the right on the bed. "You want me to keep going? I feel like I should run a lap around the room. To the right, to the right."

"Didn't we just discuss you not laughing at it?"

She makes a zipping motion over her lips. "Not laughing. But I don't think you should run around naked in public anytime soon."

He takes the left side of the bed and pulls the covers up over them. "No public nakedness. Unless I tie my horse to sagebrush."

"You lost me, cowboy."

"Have I never told you that story?"

"Um, obviously, no."

Hank puts his arms around her and pulls her against him, a little spoon to his bigger fork. "I was working for an outfitter to make extra cash during hunting season."

"Before you met me?"

"Yep, but not long before. I was moving our camp while he took the clients out. It was Indian summer, perfect weather, and after I finished setting up the new camp, I took my favorite horse from the string—Dollar—down to the creek"—which he pronounces *crick* in the Wyoming fashion—"where there was a hot spring. The only thing near the water was sagebrush, but Dollar was a good old horse, so I looped his reins around it. I took off everything but my hat, and I got in the hot spring and relaxed the dust off. All of a sudden, I saw a big gray horse running by me back to the old camp, dragging the sagebrush. I jumped out and into my boots and started after him, walking slow so as not to spook him."

"In nothing but your hat and boots?"

"Nothing but."

"Did you catch him?"

"I sure did. But not until after I scared the bejeezus out of two women hikers, who couldn't quite look me in the eye. One of them pointed behind her and said, 'Your horse went thataway.' So I tipped my hat and said, 'Yes, ma'am. Thank you. You ladies have a nice day,' and skedaddled after him."

Maggie starts to chortle. Her laugh builds to a hee-haw. "Oh, Hank. I'm going to pee."

"Not on me." He tickles her, and she rolls away, screaming and clutching her sides, with tears running down her face. "Someone is ticklish."

Tickling turns to kissing, and kissing into round two. When they're back to the afterglow stage, she pokes him.

"You're a mess. I can just picture you in the boots and hat. You know, you could have taken the hat off and covered yourself."

"There was a lot going on. It didn't occur to me until too late." He smiles at her. "I've matured. And now I have stable income, so I don't need to go running off naked after horses into the mountains."

His words jiggle loose a thought. She should update him. About her day. Her altercation with Laura. The ride with Michael. The email from the realtor. She stalls. "How was Billings?"

"Makes me as glad as ever that I live here and not there. I spent a lot of money. Met with a few ranchers and a rodeo organizer. Made it without hitting a deer in both directions. About as good as it gets. How was your day?"

"Laura and I had . . . words."

"Oh no."

"She doesn't like me."

"I like you."

"Thank God for that. I also napped. Michael got an ATV stuck, so after lunch I rode Lily out with him to count cows and got to cowgirl up and help him herd in two strays."

"Michael doesn't need your help for that," Hank says in a grumbly voice.

"It was fun."

"You could get hurt."

"Stop. There's more. We saw an eagle."

"Not uncommon around here, but nice."

"Yes. Oh, and I got a call from a record label. The ones that bought my music when my label went under."

"You're a rock star. What did they want?"

She snorts. "They wanted me to record a new album. To capitalize on my current notoriety. But they insisted on a morality clause since I'm such a live wire."

"You're shitting me."

"Nope. So I told them to fuck off."

"Good for you. Although I do wish you'd play again, music girl. But you don't need it like that."

She summons up her courage for the tougher topic. "I also contacted a real estate agent."

He squeezes her. "You're putting your place on the market?"

She hears the smile in his words and feels guilty because she knows she's going to burst his bubble. "Well, not exactly."

"What, then, exactly?"

"I might. Eventually. Honestly, I've been waffling back and forth about what to do. Selling my place is a consideration. Even fixing it up and selling it. But also fixing it up and working it." She turns to face him and puts her hands on his cheeks. "Just listen for a second, okay?"

"I'm not liking this."

"Shh." She touches a finger to his lips. "I've got Gidget's farm. It's a hundred acres. There's a place next to it, about the same size, that we could lease. And I made an inquiry on a few hundred more acres nearby. Just to see what it would cost to set up down there."

"Set up what?"

"Double S." She gnaws the inside of her lip.

"I already told you, I can't do that."

Can't or won't? His words are stinging nettle, but she covers up her hurt. "Okay. Well, I still need to figure out how to compare apples to apples on my options. I've contacted some contractors for estimates. What would I make rebuilding and running it versus selling it as is versus fixing it up and selling it." She withholds one option: selling off her inheritance of Gidget's farm, the Warhol, and the antique Jaguar. She doesn't want to let them go. Plus, it just seems dilettante. Not like her. She wants to support herself, and the inheritance is a last resort.

Hank is so quiet he seems to be soaking in sound like a black hole in space.

It eats at her until she blurts out, "I'd think you could trust me and be happy for me. I'm trying to follow my heart."

"Follow your *heart*? I thought you followed your *heart* to Wyoming. To me."

"You know what I mean."

"Honestly, Maggie, I'm not a hundred percent sure I do. Last time we ended with you running off to work in Nashville. Now it sounds like you're gearing up to run back to work in Texas. I can tell you one thing. I've spent fifteen years apart from you, wanting you. I'm not spending another fifteen that way." He turns his back on her and hauls the covers up in one swift move.

"Hank."

"Good night, Maggie."

"Don't be this way."

He flips over, his mouth inches from hers as he speaks. "Funny, that's exactly what I was trying to say to you." Then he rolls back over, leaving her alone and shivering on her side of the bed in the dark.

TWENTY

Hank is gone before Maggie wakes the next morning. She sits up. He must have left early, because he didn't let Louise out. The dog is whining like she does when bacon's frying on the stove and she isn't getting any. *Spoiled mutt.* Maggie only let her in after Hank fell asleep the night before, so it's not like she's been trapped inside for long.

Maggie feels like whining, too. She can't figure out whether their rift is her fault for bringing up Texas or Hank's for being stubborn and sensitive, but she knows she doesn't want to fight. Her heart hurts. *Damn, love is hard.* Love, or whatever this is called. There may be a reason she's never succeeded in a real relationship before.

She checks the time on her phone. It's after seven. So much for breakfast. She throws on sweatpants and one of Hank's extra-large Wyoming Cowboys sweatshirts with some Uggs. As she's dressing, she sees Hank's suitcase by the door. For a moment, she panics. Why is he leaving? Then she remembers they're leaving today for Oklahoma and the rodeo. She puts her hand on the suitcase, then walks to his chest of drawers. She's not sure why, but she opens his top drawer. Snooping isn't her thing, usually, but this up and down with Hank has her outside herself. She doesn't even know what she's looking for, but she looks anyway. Feeling around, she shoves her hands under his stack of folded underwear. Folded? She doesn't even fold hers, and she's a woman. She finds a flat box and pulls it out. Opens it. Holds her breath.

Inside is a piece of folded paper, like the kind torn from a hotel memo pad. Unfolding it, she sees the logo for the Buffalo Lodge and the address in Chugwater, Wyoming. Her heart hitches in her chest. She reads her own words in her scribbled writing:

> *Best night of my life, cowboy. I hate missing breakfast, but Nashville called and I have to go. The truck will be at the airport. Come get your belt buckle.*

It's signed with a big heart, an *xxox*, her name, and her old phone number back in Nashville, so many years ago.

Hank had kept her note. The one she'd left him fifteen years ago. Tears well in her eyes. She wipes them, chagrined at her emotionality. What does it matter if he keeps romantic notes if they can't get along for more than a few days at a time?

She stomps to the front door and lets Louise out. Louise scampers toward the barn for breakfast with the ranch dogs, nose to the ground and tail up the whole way. Maggie shuffles into the kitchen in search of scraps. She'll pack after she eats. Trudy is there, the eye of a tornado. Around her in the kitchen are baked goods and casseroles of every description. The whole place smells like powdered sugar and angel kisses. The obligatory apple pie—*God, let that be the last of the apples for the season*, Maggie prays—and a basket of icebox rolls. A glazed pound cake. Potato salad. A steaming pot of baked beans.

"You're killing it in here. What's the occasion?"

Trudy squints at her. "Paco's memorial."

"Oh shit. I forgot. Can I help?"

"Don't you need to eat breakfast and get ready? We have to leave here in half an hour." Under her voluminous white chef's apron, Trudy is in ironed jeans, a purple snap-front shirt, and black boots. Her hair—normally scraped into something that's half falling apart from hard work—is in a neat French twist with strawberry-blonde tendrils framing her perfectly oval face. Gold earrings in the shape of feathers dangle nearly to her shoulders.

"Good idea. Have you seen Hank?"

"He grabbed coffee while I was making breakfast. He was doing his grizzly bear impression." Trudy glances at Maggie, like she's checking for a reaction, but Maggie doesn't give away her emotional state. Closing the oven with her hip, Trudy holds another apple pie aloft. "There are apple cinnamon muffins in the bread box. Coffee on the stove." She keeps a percolator hot and full all day.

Maggie rolls up the lid and snatches a muffin, even though she would have sold her soul for blueberry. Banana nut. Carrot. Anything but more apple. "Thanks. I'll be back down to help as fast as I can."

"No bother. I have Andy and Michael loading the truck for me. We're in good shape."

Maggie stuffs half the muffin into her mouth on the way up the stairs and regrets not pouring herself coffee. Or a glass of water. She struggles to swallow, but follows up with the other half before she turns on the shower in the bathroom. Dry shampoo will have to work for her hair, since she's out of time before she's even getting started today. She's in and out in five minutes. Taking her cue from Trudy, she opts for country Sunday attire. She's sliding a black sweater over her head to go with her jeans when Hank comes in.

Without a word, he turns the shower back on.

"Hank."

He shuts the bathroom door.

She opens it and then closes it again, leaning against the inside for support. "Don't do this."

He shucks his clothes. Dammit, she can't help admiring the view, even when things are like this between them. She loves every scar and indentation on his beautiful body.

"My head hurts. I can't talk right now."

She flows across the floor and takes his hand. "Let me help you."

He looks at her. His eyes are glazed with pain or medication or both. "Let me be okay, like I am."

"I can do that." She turns on cold water and holds her hands under it, then places one on his forehead. "Feel good?"

He moans. "Do that again."

She puts the other hand in its place, then kisses his temple. "You take your meds?"

"No."

"What am I going to do with you?" She tears open a packet and hands it to him.

He closes his eyes and dry-swallows. "Love me forever."

"Oh, Hank." The image of the note he keeps in his top drawer flashes in her mind. She wraps herself gently around his naked body and puts her head on his chest. "I have. I will. I just wish it was easier. Were we always this up and down?"

His voice is a rumbly vibration against her cheek. "We were together less than twenty-four hours."

One snort-laugh escapes her. "It was a lifetime ago. We were so young. I remember it as so much longer. So much more."

He rocks her. "It was. It was everything."

A loud knocking on the bathroom door makes them both jump. Laura hollers at them. "Are you guys riding with Mom and me? Because we're leaving."

Hank winces. "Meet you there?"

"So I don't get your help because you have to sneak a shower quickie when we have things to do? It's not enough that I'm taking care of Mom while you play with your horses and girlfriend the rest of the time?"

"Whoa there, sis. Who do you think gets up with her nights and covers Tom's days off when you're in New Mexico?"

Maggie's rage is instantaneous. She throws open the door, revealing Hank's nude body.

"If you don't mind, your brother is having a horrible headache. You're not helping. I'm trying to. I don't think he'll be able to drive. You can either wait for us, or I can bring him to the church. Your choice. We'll be downstairs in ten."

She enjoys a glimpse of Laura's round eyes and mouth before she slams the door in her face. Then she points at the shower and raises her eyebrows at Hank.

"There's the girl I love. You're so damn cute when you're fierce."

She winks. "I'll pick you out some clothes while I pack a bag for our trip. Want the lights out?" It sometimes helps him.

"Sure."

She flicks the switch.

Hank's head peeks out from the curtained shower. "And Maggie?"

"Yes?"

"I'm sorry."

"I'm sorry, too."

TWENTY-ONE

The one-room white clapboard church is packed tight, humid with humanity as the pastor finishes a short service for Paco and announces the hymn. Frost on the windows partially obscures the white landscape surrounding the building. The tables in the back are groaning under the offerings of food. The front of the nave looks like an ad for a florist. Maggie wishes Paco's blood family could have been here to see his church family show up en masse to wish him farewell. Fifty voices offer up "Amazing Grace" slightly off-key while the Danish musician Maggie met at the Ox plays the fiddle and Wally the keyboard.

Deputy Travis is in the row behind her, not singing. Maggie is sandwiched between Hank, who is holding her hand, and Andy, who's shifting uneasily. Beside Andy, Trudy warbles in a pure soprano. Next to her, Laura has her arm around Mrs. Sibley and is whispering in her ear. The older woman is growing increasingly agitated, turning her whole body in her chair to look back at the door.

The song ends. The pastor opens the mic to the congregation, and people offer brief eulogies. Hank goes last. He gets choked up at the podium, but manages to bid Paco Godspeed and give Gene's regrets for not being able to be there. Maggie knows Paco would have understood and agreed with Gene's decision to get on the road to meet the bucking stock in Duncan. Livestock comes first on a ranch, that much she has already learned.

The pastor releases everyone to eat and visit. Folding chairs scrape the floor as people move from them and form a line for the food.

"I've got to get Mom home," Laura announces, wheeling Mrs. Sibley in front of Hank.

Mrs. Sibley lets loose a string of curse words that impress Maggie with their crudeness and creativity. Where had Mrs. Sibley picked up "dick smack" and "asswipe?"

Hank pulls at his bolo tie. It's black with a bronze bull rider on a silver oval. "I'll help you load up, but I can't go yet." Since Laura had waited for Maggie and Hank to ride over together from Piney Bottoms, they only have one vehicle now. "Want to drive around and come back for us, or should we cram in with Trudy and Andy and the dishes?"

Laura pushes her short hair back. She looks haggard. Maggie almost feels sorry for her, but after earlier, not quite. "I'll drive into town and get her a hamburger, then come back for you. Maybe she'll fall asleep on the way."

Hank turns to Maggie. "I'll be back in a minute."

"Of course."

People part to make way as Hank and Laura walk out together with their mother.

Andy appears beside Maggie and whispers to her. "Is the deputy here to keep an eye on me?"

"I think it's pretty standard for law enforcement to come to the funerals of murder victims."

"Why?"

"What I've heard is that often the murderer will be there."

"Like me. Great."

"Come on. He's not here for you."

"Then why do I feel like he's spying on me?"

"I'm feeling a little spied on myself." Maggie glances pointedly at Sheila and her girlfriend on the other side of the room. They're staring at her and whispering.

"Why don't we get some food? It might make us both feel better."

"Lead the way."

At the buffet line, she and Andy converse across the tables with Wally and the fiddler, who she is relieved to hear Wally call by name. Donna. Maggie steers the conversation to their instrumental backgrounds and away from herself. Suddenly, Penny is in line with them, too, her long black hair shining and hanging in a curtain down her back.

"Hey, everyone." Her eyes are red like she's been crying.

"Penny. Good to see you." Maggie grabs a paper plate and rolled napkin full of plastic cutlery.

Andy turns red to the roots of his sandy hair. "P-p-penny."

"Hi, Andy."

"I didn't know you knew Paco." Maggie skips the apple pie and takes a big slice of pound cake instead.

"We hung out a few times."

Andy looks away.

Penny was another of Paco's admirers? "I'm sorry for your loss."

Penny inclines her head. "Well, I just wanted to say hi. My ride is here. I'll call you about the lesson Monday, Maggie." She glances at Andy. "Bye, Andy."

"Goodbye." He watches her go.

Maggie adds a slice of ham and a link of Basque sausage to her already heaping plate. "Did you know she was friends with Paco?"

Andy concentrates on ladling potato salad. "Uh-huh."

Nothing is making much sense to Maggie. "So you knew her before last night?"

A tap on her shoulder saves Andy. Maggie nearly dumps her plate against the stomach of Deputy Travis's bomber jacket. Andy backs away and disappears into the crowd.

TWENTY-TWO

Travis jumps back, one eye on Maggie's load of food. "Can I have a word, Ms. Killian?"

Maggie tilts her head at her plate. "Kinda occupied here."

"There are two empty chairs over there." He nods. "You eat. I talk."

Maggie's sigh is long and dramatic. "Really. At a funeral."

Travis takes her free elbow. She jerks it away but walks to the two chairs near the window. It isn't until she takes a seat that she notices Sheila and her friends standing next to the chairs. Today Sheila's puffy vest is black and matches boots with fur lining peeking out, which Maggie guesses is in deference to Paco. Her hair is down in a blonde cloud. She snorts and pokes Mary, the brunette from the Ox. Mary doesn't react. Her eyes look as red as Penny's. More. She's staring out the window.

Maggie scooches her chair until its back is to them. She ignores Travis, too, by digging into the sausage, even though her mouth is dry and the meat tastes like dirt.

"I have some follow-up questions for you."

With her mouth full, Maggie tries to say, "I thought you said I'd eat and you'd talk." It comes out as, "I taught you said I eat and you tock."

Travis seems to understand her anyway. "You can drag this out if you want. I've got all day."

Suddenly, Sheila is in front of them. She bends over nearly into Travis's lap. "Trav, how are you? I missed you at homecoming."

A flash of irritation crosses his face. He pulls back from Sheila as far as he can in his chair. "Work. You know."

"Oh, hi, Maggie." She shows all her teeth in a fake smile.

Maggie hadn't realized Sheila looked so much like a beaver. It makes her happy.

Sheila uses a conspiratorial tone with Travis. "I ran into Maggie and Andy last night at the Ox. And the day before when, um, they were at your *office.*"

Travis lifts an arm and uses it to guide Sheila away from his personal space. "All right, Sheila, we were in the middle of something. I'll be seeing you."

She pouts prettily. "Travvers. All right. Don't be a stranger." She drops the pretense and gives Maggie a death mask, but keeps her voice sugary sweet. "Maggie."

Maggie tests the baked beans without responding, and Sheila rejoins her friends. Funny how talking to Sheila makes Travis slightly more palatable.

Travis lowers his voice. "I've heard a few new details about Paco that disturb me."

Maggie dips a carrot in ranch dip and nibbles.

"One of Paco's buddies, a guy named Emile, said Paco was concerned before his disappearance."

"About what?"

"About Hank."

Maggie puts her carrot down. "Hank? Why?"

"Hank warned him off you, apparently."

"That's crazy."

"Is it?" Travis looks at Hank, who's standing in the doorway, red-cheeked and staring at the two of them. "He's a volatile guy with a reputation for solving his problems physically."

Maggie swallows a big lump. This isn't the first time the Sheridan County Sheriff's Department has targeted Hank because of fighting. She'd had a front-row seat to the fight with Patrick Rhodes that made Hank a suspect in the man's murder, until Maggie handed Travis the real killer. Plus Hank's told her stories. Confessed to using his fists, when he maybe should have walked away. And then there's his head injury and headaches. Volatile? With her, at least lately. She won't win a debate on this issue with Travis, so she won't go there.

"And you think I'm his problem?"

"Or Paco was. What was your relationship with him?"

Maggie's eyes lock on Hank's. He starts walking toward her. "Nothing special. He worked for Hank and Gene. We ate meals as a group. He'd saddle my horse sometimes. He worked on my truck. He was a nice guy, but he was younger, and he was always going on about some woman or other. I was nothing to him but his boss's woman." She stands and puts her plate in the chair. What she doesn't say is that Hank had warned her that Paco thought she was "hot." But that was before she got back together with Hank. When he was dating Sheila. There was nothing wrong with Paco noticing her, or even Hank telling her. Hank just didn't want her to make a mistake and get hurt. *Right?*

"So Emile is lying?"

"Or he misunderstood. Or Paco distorted the truth."

"Can you account for Hank's whereabouts in the two days before you found Paco—every single hour?"

Of course she can't. Hank works on a very big ranch, and she doesn't follow him around like a dopey kid with a crush. Before she can think of a way to answer Travis, Hank puts his hand on her shoulder and squeezes. She reaches up and catches his hand, squeezes back, and holds on.

"Harassing my girl, deputy?"

Travis reaches for Hank's other hand and shakes it at the same time that he rises from his chair. "Just finished. You two have a good day."

Hank holds Travis's hand a second longer than necessary. "You, too."

Travis grimaces, and Maggie knows Hank just crushed the bones in his hand. *Bad timing, Hank.*

Travis shakes his fingers. "Nice grip, Sibley."

Hank guides Maggie away. She looks up at his profile. He's smiling, but there's not a dimple in sight.

TWENTY-THREE

Maggie and Hank drop Laura and Mrs. Sibley back at Piney Bottoms, hitch a trailer to Hank's truck, load Louise, and hit the road for Duncan, Oklahoma. The roads are clear and the sun is out. The temperature is a balmy fifty. The seasons here are so short. The window is open again on summer, but it will slam shut for the rest of the winter soon enough.

The winds, however, are hurricane strength—a year-round phenomenon—and they buffet them all over the interstate. Louise whines from the back seat of the extended cab.

Hank winks at Maggie. "Relax. I'm used to this. I've never flipped a trailer."

She's gripping the armrest so hard she leaves nail imprints. "There's always a first time. Why are we bringing the big windsail anyway? We aren't towing any animals."

"You never know what we'll want to bring back. Plus, we need a place to sleep."

"What's wrong with a hotel?" The truck veers from a gust, and Maggie pushes both feet into the floorboard.

He shoots her a disbelieving look. "I'd lose all credibility if I paid good money for a hotel when I could sleep in my rig on the grounds. Plus, I might miss something. It's a big networking thing, hanging out in lawn chairs, drinking, and telling stories."

Maggie surfs the radio until she finds a country station out of Laramie. "I hate missing day one of this thing."

"If we don't make good time, we'll miss another day. It's a sixteen-hour-or-more drive."

Suddenly, Maggie hears her name on the radio. It used to be a common occurrence, but in the last few years, less so. And lately it makes her blood run cold, because no one ever has anything good to say about her. Hank hears it, too, because he lets go of the steering wheel with one hand and turns it up. The truck swerves, and he double-grips the wheel again.

"According to Amos Hardy, a reporter out of Denver, the Black Widow has spun her web south of Sheridan and caught Wyoming's own Hank Sibley in it. You remember Hank, folks. The 2002 bull riding champ at Frontier Days. He had a helluva career before he was sidelined permanently with a wicked back and head injury. Nowadays he and a partner run Double S Bucking Stock. Pretty successfully, too. A former NFR Stock Contractor of the Year, even. Death seems to follow Maggie everywhere these days, with the most recent man down being the top hand from Double S, right on the heels of her ex, country star Gary Fuller, rival stock contractor Patrick Rhodes, one of her renters in Texas, and a Wyoming electrician. We're not ones to gossip, but these two have a history, with Maggie ending up in rehab twice in the wake of their previous breakup. Will they make their eight seconds this time, or will one of the popular duo get thrown? Only time will tell. And, yes, she wrote this song about him."

"I Hate Cowboys" starts to play. Maggie releases a breath she hadn't known she'd been holding.

Hank turns off the radio. "So, what did you and Travis talk about back at the church?"

The abrupt change of subject would have been welcome if it were to any other topic. Maggie had hoped Hank would forget about Travis's interrogation. She needs to mull it over more before talking to Hank about it. He's feeling so much better—she doesn't want to be the reason for a setback.

"He wanted to go over the timeline of my whereabouts since the last time I'd seen Paco." It isn't a lie. It isn't the complete truth either. She hopes it's enough.

"At the funeral. Come on, man."

"I know, right?"

"Anything else about Andy?"

Now she relaxes. On this point she can tell the whole truth and nothing but. "Not a word." She glances at him. In profile, he is stalwart, strong, and achingly gorgeous. She swallows. "I need to tell you something."

He grunts, and she takes it as "Go ahead."

"I found the note you kept. The one I left for you in Chugwater."

"Found it. In my drawer. In a box." He dimples up.

"I, um . . ."

His dimples are deep and sweet. "I don't care, Maggie. I don't have anything to hide from you. If you need to look around to satisfy yourself on that, be my guest."

She hesitates. Does he expect her to return the offer? She doesn't own anything to hide. Not after the fires. But she's not sure how she'd feel about him snooping if the tables were turned. Not that she's hiding anything, just the general concept. "You kept it."

"Of course I did."

Maggie picks up her hobo bag from the floorboard. From a secret compartment in her wallet, she retrieves the note he'd left her. She reads it aloud to him. "Best night of my life, music girl. Between you and Big Sky, I'm walking off the stiff and sore. Back in an hour with coffee and breakfast. Don't get dressed, gorgeous. Hank."

He reaches for her hand. "So you kept yours, too."

"I've had it with me ever since."

"Big Sky was one lucky draw."

"So that's your reaction to me sharing that with you?" She punches him.

"If I hadn't drawn him, I might not have won, and we might not have ended up together."

"I'll let you in on some late-breaking news: I was yours whether you won or not."

He chuckles, and she leans over the console and puts her head on his shoulder. She wakes up with a sore ribcage and crick in her neck on the south side of Casper. Hank smiles at her. "Wake up, sleepyhead." He gets out of the truck.

She sits up and stretches. By the time she has her bearings and looks outside, Hank is working his credit card at the gas pump.

Maggie comes around to stand beside him. "Time to trade off drivers after I'm back from the loo?"

Louise barks.

"And take Louise to pee?"

Hank sets the automatic pumping switch on the nozzle. "Sure. But I'll take her."

Maggie peers into the back window. Plastic sandwich bags and newspaper are shredded all over the seat. "Oh my God."

"What is it?"

"Louise got into the bag of treats Trudy sent with us."

Hank shakes his head. "Bad dog. Buy me some venison jerky, then?"

"Got it." Maggie heads inside.

After the stop is over, Hank falls asleep before Maggie wrestles the truck and trailer back onto the interstate. "Right in Time" by Lucinda Williams plays on the radio, drawing a smile from Maggie as she looks over at Hank. Louise snuffles daintily in the back seat. The miles fly by, with more stops, more trading off driving duties, and more naps. The scenery is monotonous this time of year. Tan, brown, and beige, broken up every half hour by small towns. But Maggie has eyes only for Hank beside her, and no complaints.

They make it safely to Duncan in the wee hours, with Maggie finishing her book, *Plenty-coups*, about the great Crow chief during one of her riding shifts. Hank is driving when they get there, so he parks their rig and they settle in for a few hours' sleep in the living quarters of the trailer. Maggie wakes, disoriented, when it's barely light outside, troubled but unsure why.

"Hank." She rolls over and puts her head on his chest.

He groans. "Too early." Then he goes rigid. "What's that smell?"

That's it, Maggie realizes. A noxious odor is what woke her. Then she hears the thump-thump-thumping of a tail. "Oh, Fucker."

"She didn't."

"I'm pretty sure she did. Five feet away from us. Rock, paper, scissors for who cleans it up?"

"I got it." Hank levers himself up on an elbow. "But tomorrow night, she sleeps back in the stalls."

Maggie gags and doesn't argue.

TWENTY-FOUR

Hank leaves with Gene to check on their hooved athletes not many hours later, with a promise to text and catch up with her soon. Maggie sleepily trolls the grounds, after walking Louise and leaving her to nap in the trailer. On the outside of the covered arena, colorful banners tout the Prairie Rim Circuit Finals Rodeo. Prairie Rim isn't a nationally known rodeo, but it's a Professional Rodeo Cowboy Association event that draws contestants from Kansas, Nebraska, and Oklahoma, so it's plenty big. Food trucks line a crowded parking lot, and the aroma of funnel cake is making Maggie salivate. Vendors are hawking wares ranging from Western wear and rodeo gear to jewelry, farm equipment, and—Maggie's favorite—home décor, not unlike the things she salvages and repurposes at her store in Texas. Or did, anyway.

As she weighs out whether to give in to funnel cake for lunch, her phone sounds its tone for voicemail. She pulls it from her jeans pocket. She has three voicemails from yesterday that only just appeared on her phone. The coverage had been spotty on the drive, which she is used to in Wyoming, but she'd expected better of eastern Colorado and the Texas Panhandle. One is from Charlotte, another from Franklin, and a third from a Colorado number. The Colorado call is the most recent, so she plays that message first.

"My name is Amos. I'm a freelance reporter, and I've written a few pieces on you. I saw you online in a video from the Occidental Saloon in

Buffalo, Wyoming. Wait, did I get that right?" There's a pause. "Yeah, The Occidental. Anyway, I'm swinging up that way and hope I can interview you. Please give me a call so we can arrange a time to get together."

Amos. The name is familiar, but she doesn't think she knows one. Was he the reporter being quoted on the air yesterday, talking about her? He sounded so smug it makes her itch to punch him. She hates reporters automatically, but she's sure she'll hate him specifically, too. And video? She should have known someone would post it from the Ox and mention her. She considers deleting his message without calling him back, but experience tells her if she does, he'll show up anyway, pester her, and interview everyone she's ever pissed off in Buffalo and Sheridan. Starting with Sheila.

She calls him back.

"Amos speaking. Hit me."

His voice sounds too old to be a hipster wannabe–cool cat. She shudders. "Absolutely not."

There's a silence. Is he there? "Sorry, I had to look at the incoming number. Is this Maggie Killian?"

"Unfortunately it is. I'm sorry, but I can't meet with you. I'm just passing through the Buffalo area."

"That's not what I heard."

Now she feels certain he's the reporter quoted on the air yesterday. "I can't control what you hear. Or the rumors you spread. Buh-bye."

She hangs up. Hopefully the call will be enough to keep Amos south.

She listens to Franklin's message next. It's a hang-up. She growls and calls him back, but the call fails to connect. She tries twice more. Same result both times. She moves on to Charlotte. Before she can play her mother's message, a text comes in.

Where's my woman?

She grins, stops, and types. *Looking for her man.*

Ready for the nickel tour of the Double S setup, then some grub?

A big, warm paw lands on her shoulder.

She startles, then smiles, matching the dimples winking down at her. "Hey, cowboy."

"Someone told me, once upon a time, that you hate cowboys. Especially bull riders."

"I'm experiencing a change of heart."

"You're having a flashback. You pretend not to like them, but I think rodeos turn you on."

Maggie laughs. "Or something."

"Behind the chutes we go, then."

"Aren't the chutes inside and your animals outside?"

"Details."

Together they stroll through the pens outside the arena. Hank can't walk five steps without someone hailing him up, slapping his back, and asking about how the Double S buckers look for the event. Nearly everyone talks about his storied past as a bull rider. Many mention what a blessing and miracle it is to see him hale and hearty, referencing his spectacular career-ending injury. Maggie is in the presence of rodeo royalty, and she revels in the respect shown Hank, and her own anonymity. He introduces her by her first name only, which she appreciates. People are nice. But Hank is the star. She feels a flash of irritation as she remembers Travis's insinuations at Paco's funeral. Hank isn't a jealous killer. Not the Hank she knows, that all these people revere, not even in the throes of the worst of one of his brain trauma episodes. It's preposterous.

Hank stops her at a pen of muscular horses in a rainbow of colors. She recognizes some of them from the ranch. They're a little jacked, milling about, lifting their heads over the metal rails and bumping into them with loud clangs.

"Every one of these beauties traces back to Sassafrass, our original broodmare."

"The one you bought with your Frontier Days winnings?"

"Yep."

"And losings."

He shrugs. "It's true. I'm not proud of that. But it's part of the history." Hank had taken money to stay out of the winner's list each day, until he met Maggie and she'd convinced him she only dated winners. He'd incurred the wrath of his Argentinean "employer" then by winning it all. Mafia thugs had chased Maggie and him over half of Wyoming, but here they were as a result.

"The man, the myth, the legend." Maggie bumps him with her hip. "Do you ever see Christiano Valdez?" He was the bull rider the mafia family had backed.

Hank bumps her back. "You're not going to believe this. Paco worked for him a few years ago. Small world."

"What did he do for Christiano?"

"Shovel shit, mostly. But I haven't seen Christiano in many years. Last I heard he was back in Brazil, fat and rich."

"Good." For many reasons, Maggie thinks. Her thoughts return to the buckers. "Don't you risk genetic issues with so much of one bloodline in your horses?"

"Lots of other bloodlines in the mix, too. We've been careful to keep it diverse. There are incredible champions in all their parentage."

"You sound like a proud papa."

"I am. We are. It's very rewarding. And exciting." He waves at the pen. "This here is a crop of youngsters. You remember we hold inside events at the ranch for up-and-coming cowboys, to evaluate our three-year-olds?"

"Yes, and I can't wait to see one."

"They're a party." Hank nods. "These horses passed that test and are working their way up to bigger venues."

"Will any of these be bucking at the National Finals Rodeo next month?"

"Nah. They'll have to earn that later. Only the best of our best, the seasoned warriors, buck at NFR."

Maggie remembers Hank explaining before that they cross draft horses into the herd to keep them hearty, and colder-blooded horses for their athletic ability and fight. "Are any of these horses related to Lily?"

He rubs his chin, then points. "That big mare, the blue-roan. This is her first season on the road. She's draftier than we usually see in our successful buckers. But nobody told her that. She's like nitroglycerin in a brick house."

"She's my favorite."

Hank smiles. "Of course. Want to go see the bulls? Gene's over there."

Maggie climbs on the rail, looking for bulls. The humped backs give them away. She spots Gene outside a pen. While her attention is off the horses, the blue-roan mare charges at her, snorting, then ducks away.

Maggie jumps down, startled. "She's feisty."

"Her blood is up. She knows it's almost showtime. If you approached her in the pasture back home, she'd ignore you."

They amble to the bulls through a repeat of the glad-handing and introductions.

One old-timer breaks away from a group. "Mr. Sibley, the first time I met you, you was wandering through the parking lot of the fairgrounds in Mandan, South Dakota. It was the middle of the night, and you wasn't wearing nothing but a long-john top. Not a stitch." The storyteller pulls at the handlebar mustache hiding his smile.

Maggie socks Hank's arm. "Wait, you were naked?"

"I was changing clothes beside my truck after a few shots of whiskey. I accidentally locked myself out. So I was looking for a pay phone. Only I didn't have a quarter."

The geezer winks at Maggie. "I hope for your sake it was only the cold that made him so—"

"Okay, that's enough." Hank claps him on the back.

He cackles and wanders back to his friends.

Maggie raises her eyebrows. "You certainly have a colorful past."

"Mostly lies and exaggerations."

"What part of streaking around bare-assed was a lie, and what part was an exaggeration?"

"Well, that was mostly true."

She loops her arm through his, and they resume walking toward Gene. The smell of bull manure grows stronger with every step.

Maggie holds the back of her hand under her nose. "Why does bull shit smell so much worse than horse shit?"

"An age-old question. And why do bovines taste so much better than equines? There's another for you."

"You've eaten horse meat?"

"I'm speaking theoretically."

Gene spots them and doffs his hat at Maggie. "What do you think of it all?" He opens a bag of Cheetos and offers it to her.

She's hungry, but the thought of food so near the bull manure turns her stomach. She holds up a hand to decline. "That you guys have come a long way from the broke-ass bull riders I met in Cheyenne. I can't believe you even scraped up enough money to buy your fancy broodmare."

"Sassafrass?"

"Yeah. Hank spent his stake of the money for her on a getaway truck for us in Wheatland."

Gene cocks a brow. "You're right, Maggie May. And I nearly killed him for it. But everyone loves a Frontier Days winner, lucky bastard, and we had just enough that they gave us a short extension."

Hank thumps his chest. "I came up with the money."

Maggie says, "You're a better man than me not to have killed him, Gene."

He grins. "Thanks. I think. Anyway, Hank's point man on the horses, but the bulls are my babies."

"Babies? Hardly. These are monsters." Maggie leaves a five-foot buffer between herself and the bull enclosure.

"Nasty, ugly muscleheads. Just how we like 'em."

"Which make more money, the horses or the bulls?"

"Used to be the horses, hands down. With the advent of bull-only events like the Professional Bull Riding shows, we've got a growing market for the uglies. But every rodeo has two bronc riding competitions—saddle and bareback—and only one bull-riding event. So it's a toss-up."

Hank slaps his thigh with his hat, back and forth, knocking off the sod the blue-roan splattered him with earlier. "The horses are a little fussier. More prone to hurting themselves."

"At events?"

"No, at life. Horses are experts at doing stupid stuff. One time we had a hand who parked a truck across an open gate. One of the horses decided to jump out, over the hood and windshield of the truck. He almost made it too, except for a back hoof. New windshield. Lotta stitches. Three-month bucking hiatus while he recovered from his injuries."

Gene nods. "A bull would have just rammed the truck and walked away."

"But both require a lot of special care traveling to and from events. We had a harder trip here than these animals. Twelve to fourteen hours of rest for every ten spent on the road. Standing in a half foot or more of sawdust to cushion their hooves and legs. A veterinarian on call at every event. At the slightest sign of strain, we pull 'em, rehab 'em, and call in an expert if needed. Anything to keep them in tip-top shape during rodeo season. It's not cheap to run the operation."

"But it must be worth it."

The two men grin at each other and answer at the same time. "Oh yeah."

Hank slings an arm around her. "We make more money than we did rodeoing, and nothing beats this life."

Maggie loves the feel of his taut frame and strong arm. She leans in. "It's making me remember how much fun the events were back when I was touring and performing. But I'd forgotten about all the vendors. It's a pretty diverse enterprise of businesses."

"A lot of the vendors just follow the rodeos all season. Like us. And some of the rodeos dwarf Prairie Rim. Money to be made, for sure. Now, let's go to our box. Time to watch our brand in action."

The seed of an idea germinates in Maggie's mind. But hunger calls first. "And feed your woman."

Hank squeezes her to him. "And that, of course."

TWENTY-FIVE

An announcer's voice reverberates through the arena. "Next up we have the saddle bronc riding competition."

He keeps talking, but it's just yammering to Maggie. She turns to Hank, accidentally kicking what's left of the nachos she got at the concession into the seat-back in front of her. She braces for an explosion, but the woman who's now wearing chips and nacho cheese on her sweatshirt is oblivious. It's not *that* bad, so Maggie isn't going to be the one to clue her in.

"What's her name?" she asks Hank.

"Who?"

"Lily's blue-roan bucking baby."

"Crazy Woman."

Like an echo, the announcer says, "First up will be Josh Cassidy on a fine young mare from Double S Bucking Stock, Crazy Woman. Josh is coming off a big win in New Braunfels, Texas at the Comal County Fair. Let's see how he handles a bona fide descendant of Sassafrass, two-time winner of the PRCA Saddle Bronc of the Year."

Maggie screams with delight. "Go, go, go, Crazy Woman!" That earns her a few looks, but she doesn't care.

The blue-roan mare explodes out of the gate. Even though Hank rode bulls in his day, saddle bronc riding has always been Maggie's favorite event. And something about Lily's high-spirited daughter has lit her fire. The young mare does not disappoint. Within two jumps, she's bucking like a catapult. The cowboy on her back is clinging with his legs to the saddle, his rein hand high and other arm flailing. Maggie sees air between his butt and the seat. That's the end of the line for him, she knows.

"Go," she shouts again. "Come on, Crazy Woman!"

Beside her, Hank joins in. "Get him, girl. Get him."

And the powerhouse mare does. Her hooves rocket upward with her head down and body fully and beautifully extended. The crowd exclaims en masse. Has a horse ever bucked this high or looked this good doing it? Maggie doesn't think so. At the height of her buck, Crazy Woman twists. Her front feet are still two feet off the ground as her back half torques sideways. Everything seems to move in slow motion to Maggie now. Like a demon-possessed toy top, the horse spins before she lands. The cowboy tumbles through the air and into the dirt. Then Maggie's slo-mo ends, and the horse bucks riderless in real time.

The buzzer sounds. The cowboy is already on his feet and picking up his hat. Meanwhile, Crazy Woman attacks likes she's trying to take down the sky. Two pick-up riders make their way to her, but when they get near her, she morphs into a heaving race horse. The three horses streak down one side of the arena. Crazy Woman pulls ahead in the curve, then the pick-up horses gain on her in the straightaway again as she continues to kick and buck. At the end of the second lap, the chasers finally get close enough to remove the sheepskin flank strap. They peel away, and she slows to a lope, tail and head high, black mane flapping, sweaty sides heaving. She's a sight to behold. The crowd stands and cheers.

The announcer says, "That round goes to Crazy Woman. I can't decide if she's named right or if they should have called her Blue Lightning. Better luck next time, Josh."

After they sit, Maggie leans to Hank. "How often do horses get standing ovations?"

One corner of his lip quirks. "It's rare."

"So she really is special?"

"It appears she may be."

"I love her."

He laughs. "I know you do."

The rest of the rodeo flies by in a blur for Maggie. She cheers for the Double S stock, drinks a few beers, and eats a cool hot dog with too-sweet relish. When it's over, she's jazzed like Crazy Woman. She holds Hank's hand as they wait in line to exit.

"What now?" she asks.

"We circulate."

"Where?"

"In the parking lot. From trailer to trailer. It's a progressive party out there."

"Sounds good. Where's Gene?"

"One of the bulls was pulled because he's got a cut or something. He's going to find out what happened."

They swing hands and joke around until Maggie's phone rings.

Hank drops her hand. "It's okay if you want to get it."

"Thanks." She pulls it from her pocket and checks the screen. It's a Giddings number. "Hello?"

"Maggie Killian, please."

She doesn't recognize the woman's voice. "Who's calling?"

"This is Trish Jasper. I'm a real estate agent in Lee County, Texas. If this is Maggie, you contacted me about one of my listings."

Maggie shoots a glance at Hank. He's waving like a pageant queen. She lowers her voice. "Now's not a good time."

"Okay, can we talk quickly about you listing your place, then? I think I have a buyer who'd pay cash and promise a quick close."

Irritation burns through Maggie. *How presumptuous.* She whispers, "How can you have a buyer when I don't have it for sale?"

"Based on comparables, I have a fair idea of the value. Assuming you'd accept an offer in that ballpark, this buyer is ready."

"Ballpark as in the numbers you emailed me?"

"Yes."

"Not interested."

"Okay, then. What number would you be interested in?"

Hank stops, striking up a conversation with some really dusty cowboys. Maggie realizes they are competitors from the night's rodeo.

She holds up one finger at Hank and mouths, "Just a minute."

He nods and keeps talking.

"I'm not," Maggie says.

"I have an idea. How about we list your place at a number above what you're interested in, and just see what you get? You don't have to accept an offer. Your property is safe and remains yours if you'd like, but you get an idea of its worth on the current market."

"How about not."

"Okay, well, if you change your mind, please let me know. And if you'd like, we can talk about the ranch listing tomorrow."

"I'll call you." Maggie hangs up.

Hank is leaning against the wheel cover of a black trailer. He salutes her with a can of Bomber Mountain. "This is my girl, Maggie. Maggie, meet some of the poor saps that got their asses kicked out in the arena today."

The cowboys clustered around him are mostly a head shorter than Hank. Zero percent body fat or thereabouts with sinewy muscles and more tobacco bulging in their cheeks than butts in the rear of their jeans. One of them spits brown juice in the dirt.

"Hi, guys," she answers, to a chorus of hellos.

The dustiest of the cowboys says, "I hear your horse threw me."

"My horse?"

"Crazy Woman," Hank says. His eyes are smiling and don't leave her face.

"Does that mean you're giving her to me?"

He pops the top on another can of Bomber Mountain. "What's mine is yours, sugar."

The cowboy thrown by Crazy Woman lifts a bottle of tequila. "A toast, to Crazy Woman." He tips the bottle back. His Adam's apple bobs four times before he passes the bottle to Maggie. "She's your horse, so drink up, Miss Maggie."

"Miss Maggie? That sounds like something a chauffeur would call his elderly passenger."

"Hell no. Miss Maggie, like the smokin' hot Maggie."

"Excuse me?" Hank says.

"I'm just saying, your girlfriend is very nice-looking, Mr. Sibley."

He grumbles something that isn't a thank-you.

"Are you going to drink to your horse or not, Maggie?" the cowboy asks.

He's cute, Maggie realizes. And, while lean, he exudes strength and a cocky, self-assured manner. Like Hank. It almost makes her laugh. "Tequila makes me sad, mean, and headachy. I've outgrown self-sabotage."

Hank slides an arm around her waist and pulls her backward into him. "Have you, now?"

"Mostly. Enough that I prefer anything *but* tequila."

The cute cowboy says, "What would you like? We've got a full bar in the trailer."

"If I had my way, a sweet tea spiked with Koltiska."

He salutes. "One sweet TKO coming up." Then he disappears inside the trailer.

Hank nibbles her ear. "Just like old times. All the cowboys want my woman."

"And you won my heart, fair and square." She snuggles against him. "Now I'm just Sibley's old, worn-down nag."

"Far from it." He snorts. "Are you sure you want that drink? If not, I can think of other things to do."

"You win the prize." Maggie takes his hand and two steps toward their own trailer. "Again."

He hoots, she laughs, and they run to the trailer together.

TWENTY-SIX

Saturday afternoon, Hank and Maggie shop the vendor booths outside the arena. Maggie is intrigued by the home décor and kitsch, but they linger in a booth with a frightening display of knives.

"Do you like these?" Hank holds up a wicked-looking knife in one hand. A leather belt scabbard with beading depicting a sunset and a pigging string knotted through a leather thong hangs from his other.

"Gorgeous." Maggie runs her fingers over the beads of the scabbard.

"And useful." He stabs over his shoulder. "In case of a mountain lion attack."

She laughs.

"I'm not kidding. We're just guests in their world up at the ranch. They stalk and attack from behind. By the time they're on you, the only thing that works is a knife. If you're lucky and fast."

"Comforting. Makes me wonder why anyone ever settled in Wyoming in the first place."

"The grizzlies and Indians were far more dangerous. And the weather."

"Case in point."

Hank hands the items to the attendant, who rings them up. "For you, my dear."

"But you already gave me a knife."

"I gave you my knife, and I want it back." He presses the bag into her hand. "Practice with it. A lot. And keep your mutt with you."

She salutes. "I will. Thank you. But you should be scared I'll use it on you when you snore."

He raises an eyebrow. "Snore? That would be you, princess."

"What? I don't snore."

"You did last night. Like a chainsaw."

"The hell you say."

"Which is exactly how I slept. Like hell." He swats her on the behind, and they walk on.

She stops to admire more home décor.

Hank holds up a barbed-wire cross. "This looks like something you'd make."

There's a good market for all things religious in Texas, and, it appears, at rodeos in general. Person after person is checking out with different sizes and types of the barbed-wire crosses. Crosses mounted on tin siding. Crosses festooned with bows and boots. Crosses accenting painted homilies on weathered barn wood.

Before she can respond to Hank, a slight guy with a hat bigger than his torso corners him. Hank listens and nods, then steps over to her.

"Maggie, give us a moment? Gotta solve an issue with a horse."

"Not Crazy Woman?"

"Yeah, but it'll be fine. She's just got more buck than we bargained for. She may be better than this rodeo. That's a good problem."

Maggie feels a warmth in her chest. Pride? "Go on. I'll be fine."

She's admiring some horseshoe art, thinking about the plentiful supply of that particular raw material at Double S, when her phone rings. Charlotte. She never called her mother back yesterday. Hank's still occupied, so she picks up.

"Surprise!" It's Boyd's voice on her mother's line.

"It's both of us," her mother adds in a trill.

Speakerphone. Both of her living parents, birth and adoptive. "Wow." Don't you two barely know each other?

Boyd's voice holds a smile. "We joined forces over lunch, since we share a common interest."

"You," Charlotte explains.

"Yes, I got that, Mom."

Boyd continues. "We need to know when you're coming back."

Charlotte's voice is giddy. "Because I'm making a big Thanksgiving dinner. For everyone!"

"Define everyone."

"All the family. Edward. Boyd and his wife. Michele, Rashidi, Belle, Sam, and Charlie. Gene, if he can make it down. And you."

Her mom hadn't included Hank in the list. Intentional or not? "I'll be there. Hopefully with Hank. My boyfriend."

"That's great. How's it going on your house and the Coop?" Boyd asks.

"Baby steps."

Hank saunters back, looking satisfied.

"Listen, I'm at a rodeo in Oklahoma. I've gotta run."

Boyd and her mother pledge their love, and Maggie returns it before she hangs up. Maggie and Hank walk into a livestock supply booth.

"What was that about?" he asks.

"Thanksgiving. At my mom's. Wanna come?"

"Sure. We can drive up through New Mexico on the way back to Wyoming. Stop and see Mickey and Laura."

Maggie bites her tongue. She expects to be back in Texas long before Thanksgiving, hopefully with Hank, and neither of them returning to Wyoming after. And she can't think of anything worse than going to visit Laura.

Hank picks up a silver bag. "This is what we need for Crazy Woman."

Maggie reads the label. "What does Mare Magic do?"

"Makes a mare less like a hysterical woman."

"I'll give you two point five seconds to retract that explanation in favor of something that will keep you warm in bed tonight."

"It takes the hormonal edge off a difficult mare. Sometimes."

Maggie ponders. "Would it make Lily stop running off?"

"Maybe. But so would latching her gate better."

Maggie buys a bag.

"You're wasting your money."

"Mine to waste."

"There's also anecdotal evidence that an ounce per day in the last trimester is helpful for the uterus and hormones. So I guess it can't hurt."

"Good. Now buy me a funnel cake."

As they exit the booth, the cute cowboy from yesterday—the one too young to flirt with her—appears.

"Hey, you left without your drink, Miss Maggie." He whistles. "Damn, you're even more beautiful today, and twice as hot as the actress who plays you in *Love Child.*"

She tenses. He figured out who she is. *Please be smart*, she thinks. But apparently he's landed on his noggin a few too many times.

"You know if you get tired of this has-been, I'm your man."

Hank moves, quick as a big cat. Suddenly, the young cowboy is dangling two inches off the ground against the side of a box trailer.

"Don't come near her ever again. Got it?" Hank's voice is lethal.

"Hey, man, I was kidding. I didn't mean nothing."

"Hank"—Maggie puts her hand on his arm—"put him down."

"He's disrespecting you, Maggie."

"I don't think it's my honor you're concerned about. Put him down, *now*."

Hank drops him.

The cowboy shakes his head. "I've always heard you were a crazy son of a bitch." He walks off, still muttering.

"I'm sorry," Maggie calls after him.

Hank growls. "Don't go apologizing to him for what he did."

"I'm not. I'm apologizing for you."

Volatile. Physical. She tries to unremember her conversation with Travis, but she can't. Neither can she hold it in any longer. "You want to know what Deputy Travis said to me at Paco's funeral?"

"I thought he was checking your alibi."

"No. He was checking yours. Because he's started hearing rumors about your jealousy, and he's been putting it together with your volatility and violence."

"Jealousy? I'm not jealous. I'm protective. Of you."

"And some guy told Travis you warned Paco to stay away from me."

"I wasn't jealous of Paco. You and I weren't even together then. I was just trying to keep him from hurting you. He's a complete womanizer."

"Well, now Travis is wondering about you. To me. Like wondering if you could have killed Paco."

"But you can't think that of me." All of a sudden, his eyes look hollow and dark, his skin pallid.

"Even though you have killed someone." She feels bad bringing it up. Sure, it was in defense of his mother, but dead is dead.

"You know what I mean."

"Honestly, I don't know what I think." She stalks away, toward their trailer. Too late, she realizes it sounded like she doesn't know whether or not he killed Paco. That's not what she meant. Or not really, anyway. She's good and pissed at him, and worrying about it a little might be good for him.

Hank doesn't follow her.

TWENTY-SEVEN

Two hours later, Maggie heads to the arena for the finals of the rodeo. Hank hasn't shown up, called, or texted. She's not going to miss seeing what she came for—the Double S stock in all their glory. But with Hank's latest explosion, Travis's words are haunting her.

Gene shouts over a line of people at the gate. "Maggie, wait up."

She waves and does.

"Have you seen Hank?" he asks.

"Not since he almost beat a guy's ass for flirting with me."

"Shit. Then he's probably half a bottle of whiskey down at a trailer somewhere out there, with an old-timer who doesn't realize he needs to send him on his way."

Maggie pulls Gene out of line, away from all the ears. "What's with him, Gene? Is he always like this? He's scaring me."

Gene sighs. "Which question do you want me to answer first?"

"Just tell me what's going on."

"Let's walk." They head inside the arena, where the sounds of the "Star-Spangled Banner" begin and swell as the crowd sings along. He raises his voice in her ear to be heard over the music. "Okay, first, he's not always like this."

Maggie exhales, loudly. "Thank God."

"He is occasionally."

"I liked your first answer better."

"You know about his brain injury? God—I hope you do, or I'll catch hell for spilling it."

"I do." Maggie shows her contractor badge to the attendant at the entrance, as does Gene.

"Good. From time to time, he needs adjustments. The headaches start again. Mood swings. Loss of control."

They head up a ramp toward the box with their reserved seats.

"But the adjustments work?"

"They always have before."

Maggie balls her fists. "So he needs to see his doctor."

"That's the challenge."

"Why?"

"By the time he needs it, he's less rational."

"Tell me about it."

The two of them swim upstream against traffic in the corridor, weaving around clusters of people like salmon in a river full of boulders. Their box is on the exact opposite side of the arena from the entrance, so it's a long swim.

"More emotional."

"Um, yeah."

"And less open to suggestion."

"Completely."

"But the jealousy—that's a new thing."

"Protectiveness."

"What?"

"Hank is just trying to protect me."

"Okay, protectiveness. That's since you. Other women just haven't mattered that much before."

"That's a backhanded compliment if I've ever heard one."

"But the point is, I think you can get him there. To the doctor. *Because you matter to him.*"

"I hope so."

"Me, too." Gene's phone rings. "It's Laura."

Fear grips Maggie, along with a little guilt. Hank doesn't need any more blows right now. Should she have gone easier on him, since she knows he's having trouble? "Take it."

Gene listens, frowns, paces, and finally says, "I'll get on it."

"Well?"

"Mrs. Sibley is threatening to slaughter your goats."

Maggie barks out a laugh.

"They got out—"

"Again."

"Again. And they left pellets all over the front steps and jumped on the hood of her car and dented it. She said to tell you, and I quote, 'They're meat, not pets.'"

Maggie enters the box. "Hopefully we can get back before she proves it."

After she's settled, Gene returns to the pens, and Maggie watches the rodeo alone, sipping a beer and dining on peanuts she buys from the beer guy roaming the stands. She tosses her shells to the floor like everyone else around her. Her mind races, and only the bucking events capture her attention. The Double S broncs and bulls are magnificent, if she does say so herself. Or if the rhinestone-bedazzled couple next to her does. They're quite taken with the bucking talent, and she's bursting to pass along their compliments to Hank, if only he'd respond. But he doesn't. Not to her five texts or two calls.

With only a few contestants to go in the last event, she bags it. She and Hank have been planning to drive through the night and be home by sundown the next day. As she sidles out, her phone buzzes with a group text with Hank from Gene. She waits to read it until she's outside, standing near the exit. The wind has picked up, pushing warm air. An ill wind. *It's a little late to blow now,* she thinks.

Gene: *If I don't see you guys before you take off, drive safe. I've got things from here. See you in Casper.*

Hank's response is immediate. *Thanks, buddy.*

Maggie wants to send a blistering text to Hank along the lines of *You sorry SOB, I know you've been getting my texts and calls.* But Gene's words still ring in her ears. She needs to get Hank in to his doctor. ASAP. So she just texts back: *Casper?*

Gene: *My return flight takes me there. You guys are picking me up tomorrow afternoon on your way home.*

Somehow she'd missed that in the planning, but it makes sense. If he returns through Billings, someone will have to drive two and a half hours each way north to get him.

She hustles to their rig through the parking lot, moving from darkness to pools of light, over and over, from light pole to light pole. The big Double S trailer is under one, and Hank is spotlit, sitting on a wheel cover, talking on his phone. His face is somber, and he has the dark circles under his eyes that tell her his story. He puts the phone down.

When he speaks to her, he blows out a bottle's worth of Jack fumes. "Before you say a word, I'm sorry." His words slur, but not as bad as she expects. "Please believe in me, Maggie. I need you to."

She grabs a finger and kisses it, then puts his hand to her chest. "I know. I do. And we can talk about it more later. For now, I'll pack while you're on your call, then we can leave."

"I think I'll be able to drive by then." His expression is serious.

She makes a sound that's a cross between a laugh and a snort. "Not on your life, cowboy." And her heart lifts like it's on wings. Something about this strong but vulnerable man does it for her like nothing and no one ever has. Or will again.

TWENTY-EIGHT

Hank and Maggie make Douglas, Wyoming by eleven on Sunday, trading driving and napping shifts again, although Maggie's first shift was a triple while Hank slept off the previous night's excesses. Since then, Maggie has snuck in reading a few more chapters in her latest book on the Crow, *From the Heart of the Crow Country*. She must have drifted off again, though, because Hank's voice pulls her from sleep.

"Wake up, beautiful," Hank says.

Maggie yawns. Her ass hurts on the side she landed on when Lily bucked her off weeks ago. She turns her seat heater on. "How long was I out?"

"Since Cheyenne."

More than two hours. Yeah, she did more than drift off. "Are we stopping?"

Even as she's asking the question, they pass the last exit. Town gives way to farm and ranch land again. Mountains on the left. Treeless prairie on the right and in front of them northward as far as the eye can see.

"We can make Kaycee on our gas—that would be ideal, so we only have to gas up once before we get home—if you don't need a stop. And if my Excedrin holds out." He grins. "I feel like shit."

"So why'd you wake me? I could have slept another—what?—hour?" She wrinkles her nose. The truck cab is starting to smell stale, bordering on rank, after ten hours with two unshowered humans, the remains of their snacking, and one farty dog.

He offers his hand and she takes it. "I was lonely. And a little sleepy. Keep me company until we pick up Gene?"

She stretches, arching her back and rotating her neck until both pop. "Sure." She opens the lid on her mango Bai and adds, "It'll cost you, though."

"I'm good for it."

They smile at each other. Hank is clear-eyed. His phone rings from the passenger floorboard.

"Want me to get that?" she asks.

"Who is it?"

Maggie dives for the phone and reads the caller ID. "Looks like the main line from Piney Bottoms."

"Yeah, if you don't mind."

Maggie answers it. "Hank Sibley's phone."

"Uh, yes, this is Andy."

Andy doesn't have a cellphone, Maggie remembers. "Hey, Andy. It's Maggie."

"Oh, good. I was wanting to talk to you. I didn't know your number."

"What's up?"

"Deputy Travis was here."

Maggie's mouth goes dry. "What did he want?"

"He interviewed Penny."

Her mind churns his words. Why would Travis question Penny? And why would he come talk to Andy about it? "Have you talked to her?"

"I ain't got her number. She gave it to you."

Maggie's phone is plugged into the charger. She picks it up and looks up Penny in her contacts. "You ready?"

"For what?"

"Her number."

"Oh, I can't call her."

"Why not?"

"I was hoping you would."

Andy is shy and lives by a different operating manual than most people. She gets it. And she does want to know what Travis talked to Penny about. For Andy's sake, for Hank's, and for her own. "All right. But what did he want with you?"

"To go over my alibi again."

"Does he have a problem with it?"

"Only that I ain't got one for the nights Paco was gone. I was in the bunkhouse alone."

Hank looks at her and mouths, "Is everything okay?"

She shakes her head at him and mouths, "No." To Andy, she says, "Any idea why he mentioned Penny to you?"

"He thinks I'm sweet on her."

Maggie smiles. "Aren't you?"

"He thinks I was jealous of Paco. Because he dated her. And that I wanted his job."

Motive. "Oh. I'm sorry."

His voice is stricken. "Will you call her? Make sure she's all right?"

"I will. We'll be home in about five hours. Do you want me to call you back or talk to you then?"

"Then. I have to work. With Hank and Gene gone, we're mighty busy."

"Of course you are. Try not to worry about it, and I'll talk to you soon."

"Thank you."

Maggie ends the call. She briefs Hank on Andy's side of the conversation.

"That's bullshit. The last thing Andy would do is kill someone. The second to last thing he would do is try to take something from someone else. A job. A girl. Anything. The kid is moral to the core."

"He sure seems that way to me."

Maggie presses Penny's number. "Maybe Penny will have some answers." The phone rings four times and goes to voicemail. "Penny, this is Maggie Killian. We met at the Occidental and Paco's service. I hope we're still on for our music lesson tomorrow night." She is about to tell her the reason for the call, then doesn't. Something tells her the girl won't call back if she knows it's about Paco's murder. "Could you give me a call back, please? As soon as you can. Thanks." She hangs up.

They pass an exit with a Kum & Go gas station. Maggie stifles an inappropriate urge to laugh. *Whoever came up with that name had to have known how vulgar it sounds.* Hank exits the interstate. The rest of the drive to the airport is traffic lights and industrial, with a few bars sprinkled in doing brisk midday Sunday business. If Maggie was up for karaoke, they could make a detour into the Alibi Lounge. But she's not. She wants to do something, though, she realizes. She wants to feel useful.

"Hank, put me to work."

"What?" The look he gives her is one part confused, one part amused.

"On the ranch. You have plenty of work to go around. Let me do some of it."

"Where did this come from?"

"From me feeling like a freeloader." *Something not going unnoticed by your mother and sister,* she thinks.

"All right."

"Starting tomorrow."

He laughs. "All right."

"I mean it."

"So do I."

"Good. Thank you. And I want to be paid."

"Of course."

"But not in cash."

He waggles his eyebrows. "I feel so objectified."

"I already get *that*, Hank. I need something else."

"Your wish is my command."

"I want you to see your doctor. ASAP."

The temperature in the truck cab falls ten degrees.

"Hank?"

"Huh?"

"Did you hear me?"

"I heard you."

"And?"

"And tomorrow I'll call my doctor."

"With me present."

"You're killing me."

"No, and I don't want anything else to either."

He sighs. "With you present."

She leans across the console and kisses his cheek. "Thank you." She feels like a lead weight has fallen off her chest. Now all she has to do is make him follow through.

He turns into the Casper/Natrona County International Airport. Two minutes later, they see Gene. He wads up and throws away a Cheetos bag, then sticks out his thumb, hitchhiker style. It's slightly orange. Hank pulls to the curb, and Maggie throws open her door, bracing it against the wind. The last time she saw Gene, she was angsting about Hank's volatility, with Hank a rodeo-no-show. She wonders if he's thinking about it, too.

Gene is already throwing his bag into the bed. "You lovebirds want me to drive so you can canoodle in the back seat?"

There's no way Maggie is getting back there. Between the stench of Louise and the truck blowing all over the road, she'll be carsick in minutes. "My turn to drive. You get in the back and stretch out."

Maggie and Hank exchange places. He grins, in sync with her.

"If you're sure." Gene gets in the back seat. "Oh, hello, Louise."

Hank hits the locks. "I think you just got suckered, bud."

"Jesus, when was the last time you gave this dog a bath?"

Maggie passes pronghorn antelope grazing by the parking lot, then pulls out of the airport. "A month ago, maybe? When she barfed all over herself and the inside of my truck."

"That's thirty or more dead-animal rolls ago. *And* she gets carsick?"

"Not if you sing 'You Are My Sunshine' to her while rubbing her belly," Hank says.

Gene laughs. "Screw you." Then he stops abruptly. "Hey, guys, I got some news."

"About Andy's alibi?" Maggie asks.

Gene leans over the console between Maggie and Hank. "What? No. About Michael. You have news about Andy?"

Hank turns sideways in his seat. "You go first."

"The background check on Michael came back. It's not good."

TWENTY-NINE

Maggie chews the inside of her lip. She likes Michael. Has she been wrong about him? "Bad news in what way?"

"He just got out of jail, for one thing," Gene says.

Hank cocks his head. "For what?"

"Burglary."

Maggie merges onto the interstate, heading north.

"Shit."

"Yeah. So I had a friend up in Lame Deer ask around. Apparently Michael's family is bad news. Drug dealers, big into opioids. The assumption is that they steal them to sell them."

"Was that what Michael was stealing?"

"I'm not sure. My friend said Michael's conviction came after a string of arrests that didn't stick. But he also said that burglary doesn't mean the same thing on the reservation as it does to us off of it."

Now he has Maggie's attention. "In what way?"

"It goes back centuries. Successful raids against other Indians was a respected activity. A way to prove manhood. Stay battle-ready between battles. Show superiority over an enemy. My friend says the Cheyenne considered it a sign of skill and intellect. Some still do."

Hank nods. "I've always heard that."

Maggie compares what she's learned about the Crows to what Gene is telling her about the Cheyenne. It makes sense. They crest a hilltop with large rock outcroppings and stunted evergreens, then head downhill into the sea of brown prairie again.

She asks, "What does that mean for Michael and Double S?"

Gene turns to Louise. "Get off me, mutt." In the rearview mirror, Maggie sees him push the dog to her side of the back seat. "It makes me real nervous, having a convicted thief living on the place. But we need the help. What do you think, Hank?"

"Too big a risk. I think we should cut him loose as soon as we can replace him."

"Hank!" Maggie says. "At least give him a chance. He seems like a good kid."

"A chance to steal from us? He's a grown man, Maggie."

"He's poor, Hank. Maybe now that he's away from bad influences and has a steady income and a different cultural environment, things will be better."

"Maybe. Or maybe he's a con artist who has you hornswoggled already." Hank winks. "Hand me a bag of potato chips and a water, will you?" he says to Gene.

Gene finds them in a convenience store bag and tosses them to Hank. "How about we talk to him about it and see how he responds? If he knows we know, maybe it will keep him on the straight and narrow."

Hank opens the bag, and chips erupt out the top from the release of pressure. Maggie snatches one that lands on the console. She crunches it and puts her hand out for more.

Hank deposits a handful in her palm. "I guess we could do that."

Maggie's phone rings.

Hank picks it up. "It's a 307 number."

"Put it on speaker."

He presses something on the screen, and the phone connects to the call.

"Hello?" Maggie says.

A girl's voice enters the truck with them. It's clear and bell-like. "You called me."

She smiles at Hank. "Hi, Penny. I'm driving. I have you on hands-free, okay?"

"Okay."

"Andy said the police came by to question you."

"How does he know that?"

Maggie leaves the lee of hill cover to cross a bridge. The wind roars through the creek bottoms, knocking the truck and trailer to the shoulder, near the railing. Sweat beads on her brow. She muscles the wheel left, slow and steady. Just as quickly as it rocked them, the wind disappears behind another hill as they climb back up to the prairie.

Maggie swallows hard. How many seconds have passed without her answering? "Sorry. It's really windy. Um, Deputy Travis came out to the ranch. He told Andy about it. We were all worried about you."

"I'm fine. He just wanted to know about me and Paco."

"What do you mean?"

"Like did he break up with me. Was I upset with him. When I saw him last. But I told him I was the one who broke things off. Paco dated a lot of women. I didn't want to catch a disease or something, you know?"

Oh God, how Maggie knows. She used to ask her on-and-off boyfriend Gary Fuller to bring a clean bill of health and a bottle of penicillin for her when he'd come off the road from touring. "So you hadn't seen him in a while?"

"I saw him last week. At the Ox. But we barely talked."

"And that's what you told Deputy Travis?"

"Yeah. Oh, and he wanted to know when Andy and I got together. That made me laugh. I was like, um, 'Never.' I'm used to guys who only want one thing. Not Andy. He's too shy to have a girlfriend."

"But he likes you."

"Do you think so?"

"I do. Do you like him?"

"He's cute. But kind of religious. Mary's husband is religious like that— he's Mormon, though—and he was all, 'I'm going to kill that Paco' and going on and on to Mary about how she's going to hell for committing adultery and breaking the Ten Commandments."

Hank's eyebrows shoot up, mashing his forehead like a hand organ.

Behind her, Gene whispers, "WTF?"

"Wait a second, what about Mary's husband?"

"He thought she was going to hell."

"No, he said he was going to kill Paco?"

"I think so. That's what Paco told me."

"What did Deputy Travis think about that?"

"He didn't ask me about Mary."

Another wind gust hits the trailer. If Maggie were piloting a sailboat, she'd be a contender for the America's Cup with this kind of velocity. Each creek valley is the same, but less terrifying as she becomes accustomed to cheating her steering left against the wind.

"Sounds like something he'd want to know."

"Paco didn't necessarily believe her. He said Mary had a higher-than-average need for drama."

"But the deputy could figure it out."

"Yeah."

A long, tense silence fills the truck cab. Hank rolls his hand at Maggie, like *Get on with it*. Ahead of them to the west, the silhouette of the sloping shoulder of the Bighorn Mountains appears. The rolling landscape becomes even more dramatic, with crazy tilts and drop-offs punched out of the grassland like the footprints of giants. Overhead, black and gray clouds roil. *No,* Maggie thinks. *No weather while I'm driving.*

When Penny doesn't offer anything more, Maggie looks a question at both men. Gene shakes his head. Hank shrugs.

"All right, then, Penny. I'll let Andy know you're good."

"Okay."

"Bye, then."

Maggie hears dead air through the phone. Her first reaction is happiness. Another suspect for the deputy: Mary's husband. Or even Mary herself. The more suspects there are, the less need they have to go after Andy. Or worse, Hank.

Gene says, "Well, I'll be a monkey's uncle. Paco and a Mormon wife girlfriend."

THIRTY

Maggie wakes from the sleep of the dead before dawn Monday morning, still hungover from the drive and some nightmares she can't remember. Hank is stretching beside her, looking rested and happy.

"No, it's too early for today," she moans.

"Says someone who didn't grow up on a ranch. I let you sleep in."

"Stop being logical."

"I thought you'd be up with the sun this morning. It's a big day. You're my new hand. I've agreed to let you be there while I call my doctor. Light a fire under it, girlie."

Maggie huddles under the warm covers. "Who you calling girlie, boy?"

Hank spoons her and kisses her neck. Before she can snuggle into him, he's up. Cold air rushes her body as he rips the covers from the bed.

"Hank!"

"Better not be late on your first day. I hear the Double S boss is a real hard-ass."

She mumbles something about jackass, then races into the bathroom ahead of him and locks the door.

He laughs as he pounds on it. "Let me in. You're going to miss the middle of your back without me."

"You wish. You're just afraid I'm going to use all the hot water up. Which I am." She turns on the shower. "But I'll let you in if you tell me the magic word."

"What's the magic word?"

She shucks her nightgown. "If you don't know, you're not getting in."

"Please?"

"Unimaginative. Strike one."

"You need some of that Mare Magic you bought for Lily."

"Strike two."

"You're the most beautiful woman in the world."

She opens the door. "Was that so hard?"

"No, but this is."

She looks at his midsection, only a little lower. "It's so much easier to get clean that way. Come on."

He follows her in, and just as she predicted, they both end up with a cold shower, but neither one of them complains. When they're dressed and ready, Maggie straps on her new scabbard and knife.

"You can have your knife back now," she tells him.

"Hey, that looks nice." He picks up the black Double S knife. "I'll put this back in the barn."

"I can take it for you."

He hands it to her. She straps it on, too, then notices for the first time that Louise isn't in the room with them.

"Where's my dog?"

"She was whining to go out in the middle of the night."

"You let her?"

He dimples. "She didn't jump out the window."

Maggie bites her lip. She's been keeping the dog in so she won't leave dead animals on the front porch. Cute, dead baby animals. *Oh, Louise, please have been good.* "Buy me breakfast."

"Done." Hank sneezes, then looks traumatized. "I'm getting sick."

She pats him. "Take some vitamin C."

Together they walk downstairs, with Hank sniffling and clearing his throat.

Maggie says, "I'll meet you in there. I just want to check on Louise first."

She pokes her head out the door. At first she thinks she's in the clear, then she sees an adorable little lump on the landing. On closer examination, the lump is a baby porcupine. Dead, of course.

"Dammit, Louise!"

The wiggly dog comes running, pleased at Maggie's reaction to the tribute. Maggie's not sure if anyone will care about the death of the little porcupine—Louise still hasn't gone after any ranch animals—but it's painful to see it. Coatless, she wraps her arms around herself and pushes the animal off the steps with a toe. Then keeps pushing it, until it reaches the side of the house and is out of sight.

Shaking her head, Maggie walks into the dining room. "Good morning, all."

"Your cheeks are red. Been out for a morning jog?" Laura asks, straight-faced. She's pushing her mother away from the table. "Or in a knife fight?" She points at the two knives on Maggie's hips.

Maggie doesn't dignify her jibes with an answer.

Mrs. Sibley sniffs. "Decent folk have finished eating. Gene and that new hand have already left."

Maggie notices that Mrs. Sibley is mentally sharp, if as unpleasant as usual.

Hank pours Maggie a cup of coffee. "Mom, have a good day. And be nice."

"I'm always nice."

Laura mouths, "Oh my God," and she and her mother make their exit.

Maggie takes the coffee. "Thanks, Hank." She makes herself a plate and eats quickly while Hank talks her through morning chores.

"Sounds like I should have gotten started before breakfast."

"Tomorrow."

She laughs. "What have I signed up for?"

Trudy puts out a second basket of apple muffins. "Muffin? I'm trying a new recipe."

Maggie and Hank stand.

Maggie pats her tummy. *No more apples.* "You're bulking me up. Gotta say no. Thanks. That egg soufflé was delicious."

Trudy buses Maggie's plate. "I've got to master soufflés." She looks down at the toes of her boots. "Since I've been accepted to the CIA."

"The CIA?" Maggie halts at the door.

"Culinary Institute of America."

Beside her, Hank covers an anemic cough. "You're going to do great. But we're going to starve to death."

Trudy laughs. "Hardly. I'm working on finding you someone to replace me." She disappears into the kitchen.

"You knew?" Maggie asks as she and Hank walk to the front door.

"She told Gene and me last week. Wanted to keep it quiet, what with Paco and all. Gene's pretty torn up about it."

"Why?"

"You haven't noticed? He's sweet on her."

Maggie grins. "Maybe now that she won't work here he'll do something about it."

"Nah. He thinks she's too young." Hank sneezes.

"Age is just a number. Or so they say. Are you going to get a doctor's appointment today?"

"I emailed them about it last night. I have an appointment at noon."

"I'll meet you at eleven fifteen to ride together." She dons her jacket from the hook by the door.

He gives her a miserable look. "Can we leave early to stop at Walgreens? I need cold medicine."

She wonders how he went so fast from a few sneezes to this level of pitifulness. "If you don't die from the flu before then." She ducks out before he can formulate a comeback.

The snow has melted, leaving electric golden aspen and bright red and orange buckbrush behind. The wind is calm today. She's struck by the stunning beauty of the mountains. How did she get lucky enough to end up in this amazing place, with her amazing man? She's elated—relieved—to be needed, to be helping today. As she walks toward the barn, she checks her phone. There's a slew of voicemails. Several contractors wanting to talk estimates. And somehow she has another missed call from Franklin.

This voicemail has content, though. "I have your claim finished. Call me so we can talk through it."

She calls him immediately and trades voicemail. "Keep trying. I need numbers so I can get contractors started."

Disappointed, she resumes her walk to the barn. First, she unstraps her extra knife—Hank's—and hangs the scabbard from his saddle horn in the tack room. Then she starts filling dog food bowls, then water tubs.

Lily nickers, low and deep.

Maggie can't see her, but she knows her voice. "I'm coming, I'm coming."

She hustles into the barn to fill feed buckets, feeling like a badass for slicing open a bag of feed with her knife. She stacks the buckets in a box on the back of a four-wheeler. She'll do hay later.

She feeds Lily first. The mare eats like she's starving and doesn't say thank you. Maggie places her hand on the enormous belly, hoping for a kick from the foal. She gets one, and it's powerful.

"Whoa, Crazy Woman better watch out. This one is a little buckaroo."

She distributes the feed to the rest of the penned horses, then goes back for bags of cubes, which she slides across the open tailgate of a ranch truck, into the bed. One bag for each pasture, different types for bovines and equines. And a special bag of alfalfa pellets for a pasture of retired champions, the revered senior citizens of the ranch.

She pats the phone in her pocket. Should she call the contractors back about the estimates while she still has some cell signal? It should make her agitated that she has all this Double S duty today when she's getting all the calls about her life in Texas. But it doesn't. Instead, she feels a strange but very welcome inner peace. She decides to hold off on the calls.

THIRTY-ONE

She's smiling as she gets into the driver's seat and shuts the door. She's going to relish this. The beautiful day. The gorgeous scenery. The wonderful last twenty-four hours with Hank. Feeding the amazing ranch animals, so full of life. She fires up the engine.

A knock on the truck window startles her. Michael is staring in at her. Her stomach knots. Just when everything was looking rosy. All the information Gene dumped on them yesterday about Michael—she can't help but be impacted by it. She pastes on a smile to cover it up.

She rolls the window down. "Hey, Michael, what's up?"

"You're going to want some help with the gates."

"Why?"

"Because the livestock will meet you at each one and try to push through to you."

"Oh."

"They like their chow."

"I hadn't thought of that."

"I'll come with you. I have an hour before the transport is due to arrive from Duncan."

Again, unease twists inside. Is he just using them, and her? But she wants to give him a chance. Needs to, after she advocated for it to Hank and Gene. "Thanks. Hop in."

When he's seated, Maggie guns the truck to the first gate. Michael was right. She's met by a herd of horses. He opens the gate and waves them off long enough for her to drive through and him to close up. Then he walks behind her, doing visual checks on animals while she drives slowly to the feeding area. They reach it nearly simultaneously.

"I got it," he says. "This will go really fast together." He vaults into the truck bed and opens a bag of the horse cubes, then pours them in a U on the ground around the truck bed.

Horses jostle into position. There's some kicking, biting, and squealing, but enough space for everyone once Maggie moves the truck forward, emptying the center of the U. A herd of deer vault the fence and move cautiously closer, although Maggie isn't sure whether it's the truck, the people, or the horses they're afraid of.

"Keep going. I'll meet you at the gate," Michael calls.

They repeat the process in the next few enclosures, moving in a large circle around the property. At a pasture of bulls, a big fellow with hide like a patchwork quilt refuses to budge for the truck. He paws and faces down a waving, yah-ing Michael.

"What do you want me to do?" Maggie asks through her open window.

Michael shrugs. "Push him. Just remember he's worth more than he looks. I don't want to get fired."

"Great," Maggie mutters.

She puts the truck in gear and eases off the brake. The truck moves faster than she wants, so she pushes it partway again and rides it. The truck nudges the bull. He bellows and throws his head, his horn clanging against the front hood. The nudge turns into a heave-ho and he gives way. His tail twitches angrily as he trots off to join his brethren, looking no worse for the encounter with a two-ton dualie. Maggie exhales.

Michael joins Maggie in the cab for a longer stretch of driving. The truck bounces so hard on a rock hidden in a mud puddle that Michael catches himself with a hand on the ceiling. They both laugh.

Michael points behind them. "Your dog followed us."

"Shit. That damn dog."

"What's wrong with her?"

Maggie sighs and stops the truck. "She's a stone-cold killer."

Michael opens his door, blocking muddy Louise from getting in the cab. He hoists her into the bed. Maggie resumes driving.

"What does she kill?" he asks.

"Moles. Mice. Rabbits. Today, a baby porcupine."

"Dogs will be dogs."

"Yeah. But that baby owl was so cute."

"Baby owl? What kind?"

"The adorable, innocent kind. I don't know the type. I gave it a decent burial."

"Burial? Where?"

"Out near the dead pile."

"We have to dig it up."

"Why?"

"You don't bury an owl. That's mixing the above world with the underworld, and it's bad medicine. You leave it out, so that the spirit can return to the sky."

"Bad how?"

"Bad like bad things will happen. Maybe to you. Maybe to someone you care about. I just hope it isn't too late."

"Shit, Michael. You're scaring me."

"I'm sorry. But it's important. As soon as we finish with the animals, we'll go get it."

Her mind offers up an unexpected use for her new knife. Digging up a dead baby owl from hard, cold ground. "Then what do we do with it?"

"We find a nice rock. Or build a stack of sticks. Something respectful, but open to the sky."

"Okay."

He purses his lips, staring out the window. When he turns to her, he's deadly serious. "Maybe your dog has special powers and saved you from a shapeshifter."

Somehow Maggie has not only missed owl burial but shapeshifting in her research on her heritage. God, she's a shitty Crow. "I'm not following you. Again."

"Witches and bad medicine men sometimes transform into owls. If it was a screech owl or great horned owl, that's what I would think."

"Maybe."

"When did this happen?"

"A few nights ago. I found it in the morning."

"Has your dog ever done anything like that before?"

"Well, she's killed those other animals."

"No, I mean saving people."

"As a matter of fact, yes. She tried to pull a man out of a burning house. And she chased down an arsonist and pinned her to the ground so she couldn't get to Hank and me."

"Hmm. I'd take care of her if I were you."

Buried owls, bad medicine men and witches, and threats to her and her loved ones? A chill rips through Maggie. Somehow the thought of Louise with special powers to protect her is meager comfort.

She says, "How about we go ahead and move the owl now?"

THIRTY-TWO

God spare me the man-cold. Maggie is in Hank's passenger seat, and he's behind the wheel outside Walgreens, downing cold medicine. They'd driven to town separately, her with Andy, him alone. She left Bess in the Home Depot parking lot, where Hank will drop her when they're done with his doctor. Andy has a ranch shopping list for Home Depot and will wait for her there.

Maggie's still feeling a little anxious after what Michael said about the owl, but at least they'd moved it, so she won't worry about Hank's illness being her fault. Now she just has to worry about every other threat in the world to everyone she cares about.

She hands Hank lozenges and tissues. "Are we good?"

He moans. "Is it feed a fever, starve a cold? I'm really hungry."

"It's feed a *cold*, starve a fever. Lucky for you, we don't have time to stop for food."

"So I have a fever?"

She stares at him.

"Feel my forehead."

She obliges. He's cool and normal. "Nope."

"Are you sure?"

"Hank, I have bad news for you."

"What's that?" He reverses the truck.

"You're going to live."

"Maybe not."

"And I have a question for you."

"I might be too weak to answer."

She rolls her eyes. "Why haven't you guys brought in any female hands at Double S?"

"Well, we have you."

"I'm a volunteer. And this is my first day."

"Seriously, no women have ever applied for the job."

"Why?"

"Would you want to work in thirty-below weather if you had other options?"

"Good point. Now, where's your doctor's office?"

"New York."

Her head whips around to him. "Come again?"

"I Skype with him."

"So what are we doing in Sheridan?"

"Using the free Wi-Fi outside the library."

"We had Wi-Fi back at the ranch."

"Yeah, but you have to be back from Walmart in time for Trudy to cook dinner, and you wouldn't have made it if you'd waited to leave until after my call with Dr. Clark."

His logic is convoluted, but it works. "All right, then. I haven't been to the library."

After they park, he leads her to a wooden bench outside a picture window. "We'll get good signal here."

He unpacks his laptop and boots up. Maggie looks around outside while she waits. The library is a dark fortress of a brick building, but the grounds are spacious and well kept. Right across the street is a park with a sign that reads WHITNEY COMMONS, so the library green space—or tan space, this time of year—seems immense.

Hank says, "I'm making the connection, if you want to come sit with me."

Maggie scooches onto the bench beside him. "I don't plan on saying anything."

"You can if you want to."

"I just want to know what's going on. As long as you're completely open with him, you won't hear a peep from me."

He side-eyes her. "Right."

A surfer-dude-looking man in a white doctor's coat answers. "Dr. Clark."

Dr. Clark's voice is clipped and Bostonian, about as unlike a surfer dude as Maggie can imagine.

"Hi, Dr. Clark. Hank Sibley here for my checkup."

Dr. Clark doesn't waste a second on idle chitchat, but launches into a detailed quiz into Hank's condition and symptoms since they'd last talked. Maggie only has to jab Hank once when he squirms out of full disclosure about the problems with his headaches, mood, and mental functioning. He clears his throat and supplements his answer, then looks to her for valida-tion. She smiles and bumps his knee with hers.

"Is there someone there with you?" Dr. Clark asks.

"My girlfriend, Maggie. She's been, um, concerned. She's here to keep me honest."

"Good. Maggie, did he leave anything out?"

Hank shifts the laptop so the camera lens picks her up.

"Hello, Dr. Clark. I think he downplayed everything a bit, but essen-tially that's it. And you're the brain doctor only, right? Not someone to talk to about an injury to his, um, man parts?"

"Man parts? You mean penis or testicles?"

Hank groans. "Maggie . . ."

"Penis. From sex. It's crooked."

"Any pain, Hank?"

Hank partially covers his face with his hand. "Right after it happened, but it's better now."

"Go see a urologist if it doesn't straighten out completely. They can fix it, usually. Better than I can fix your head."

Hank whispers to Maggie, "I'm going to kill you."

She gives him a smile worthy of a halo.

Dr. Clark shifts into a review of Hank's most recent lab work. When he's done, he doesn't take a breath before moving into regime changes for Hank. "You're not responding to the pills anymore. We need a better method of delivery. You're going to have to learn to give yourself shots a few times a week. If you don't see significant improvement within three weeks of starting that, set up another appointment."

"Got it."

"Stick with the rest of your regimen—food, sleep, exercise, low stress, and your other supplements and meds. It won't be overnight, but you're going to feel better, Hank."

Hank and the doctor discuss the details of the injections. Practice, timing, procedure. Maggie takes notes. They hang up.

"Well?" Hank says.

"He seems good. And he took your issues seriously and made changes."

"Yes. I like him. He costs me an arm and a leg, but he saved me, back when conventional medicine failed."

She's encouraged, but Dr. Clark's last words linger. "It won't be overnight." A lot can happen in a few weeks. A lot has happened. And there's a lot that might have happened that she prays didn't. *Thanks, Deputy Travis, for putting that in my head, however unlikely it is.* Hank's no killer, at least not when he's himself. But when he's not himself, how can she really know for sure?

THIRTY-THREE

"I'll meet you back at the truck, all right?" Maggie lifts the last bag into her cart from the checkout carousel. After Hank dropped her at Home Depot, she and Andy headed to Walmart.

Andy puts new work boots and several pairs of socks on the belt. "All righty."

Maggie's cart is full to the brim. She's shopping for the ranch table, mostly, and for herself and Hank, a little. She pushes the cart out to the parking lot and alongside Bess. As she hefts a fifty-pound bag of dog food into the bed, Andy appears with a bag on one arm.

"I could have helped you."

"It's a beautiful day, and I need the exercise."

And it is beautiful. The sky is a summery blue with only a few wispy clouds floating by. It's in the high fifties, and Maggie's in a short-sleeved T-shirt, jeans, boots, and the Frontier Days belt buckle. She's even wearing her long, white-streaked black hair down, since there's no wind to tease it into a fright wig.

She's getting out her keys to open Bess's old-school locks when she becomes aware of a big white pickup pulling into the empty space beside Andy. A bulky figure appears beside him.

"Ms. Killian." Travis tips a ball cap.

"Deputy Travis."

"I was on my way out to Piney Bottoms when I saw your truck."

"Well, she's hard to miss."

"True. I think this will save me a trip." He puts a hand on Andy's shoulder. "Andrew Yoder, you're under arrest for the murder of Paco Lopez." He holds up a pair of handcuffs. "Do I need to use these here? I can wait to put them on in the truck if you'll come peaceably."

Maggie runs around the truck. God forgive her, but her first reaction is gratitude that it isn't Hank. Her next is to wonder what the hell they have on Andy that Travis has arrested him. The boy's no murderer. It's crazy. And why is Travis doing this in a public parking lot? She wants to take him down with a knee to the balls, but she doesn't want to get arrested.

"What the hell?" Her voice is shrill.

Travis raises a hand to stop her. "No closer, Ms. Killian."

Andy stares at the deputy without a word, but Travis seems content to let him remain uncuffed for the moment.

"Mr. Yoder, you have the right to remain silent. You have the right to refuse to answer questions. Anything you say can and will be used against you in a court of law." Travis recites the rest of the Miranda warning to Andy. "Do you understand these rights as I've explained them to you?"

Andy's eyes are round and pale as a blue moon. Unlike most of his generation, he didn't grow up hearing the Miranda warning umpteen times a week on TV cop shows. The unfamiliar words must be confusing and intimidating. Despite the lack of cuffs, people are stopping to stare, too, adding further pressure to the situation. A young mother in yoga pants gapes, while her toddler son darts between parked cars. A woman closer to middle age, based on her less taut skin and muscles, grabs hold of him and puts her body between Andy and the child. Three teenage boys in high-tops, shorts, and tanks stop to watch, jostling and pushing each other.

"That'll be you, man," one says.

Another says, "Nah, cuz I ain't got no religion."

The third cackles appreciatively at their wit.

Travis ignores them all and says to Andy, "You'll need to answer verbally, son. Yes, you understand you have these rights, or no, you don't."

"I don't know, sir. I guess I do all right."

"Is that a yes or a no?"

"Yes. I understand."

"Good. Let's get you loaded up, then, and I'll take you in."

Maggie can't stand it any longer. "You're making a mistake."

Travis huffs at her. He opens the back door of his truck, then puts a hand on Andy's head to protect it as the young man climbs into the seat. "Why? You think I should arrest Hank with him?"

"Of course not. But there are other suspects. What about Mary's husband?"

"Who?"

"Mary. Paco's girlfriend."

"You're grasping at straws."

Maggie remembers what Andy had told her the day before, that he didn't have an alibi for the nights after Paco was last seen. "But you can't take Andy in just because he sleeps alone in a bunkhouse and can't prove where he was. It doesn't mean he killed Paco."

"No. But his fingerprints on the knife handle are pretty solid evidence. His knife." Travis gets in the driver's seat and shoots her one last look before shutting the door.

She knocks on the window.

Travis glares at her, but he lowers it. "What?"

"Can I come with him?"

"It won't do any good."

"What can I do, then?"

"He'll meet with a public defender later today, unless he gets his own lawyer. And I imagine he'll have a bond hearing tomorrow. You can help with those. That's all you can do." He raises the window and backs out of his space.

With Travis and Andy gone, the crowd loses interest and disperses quickly, but Maggie gazes after the truck as it leaves, feeling like she's failed Andy in some fundamental way. After a few moments, she gets her wits together enough to text Gene and Hank. *Andy arrested for Paco's death. In jail. Bond hearing tomorrow.*

Gene: *Shit. I hate that I'm not there.*

Hank: *Calling an attorney for him now.*

Maggie slumps into Bess and rests her head against the seat back. Then she bolts upright. Travis is wrong. The attorney, the bond hearing? That's not all she can do. If the sheriff's department won't look for the real killer, she can do it for them. For Andy.

THIRTY-FOUR

The next morning, Hank, Maggie, and Gene are at the county building for Andy's bond hearing. From its architecture, it's hard to tell if the courthouse wants to be a pagoda or the Wyoming homage to Frank Lloyd Wright. It doesn't put a best foot forward. The public entrance is almost like a loading dock. Half the walkway is cordoned with safety tape, cones, and warning signs so that visitors aren't killed by ice avalanches from the roof.

Outside the third-floor courtroom is a sign for the Fourth Judicial District Court of Wyoming and the Honorable Judge John P. Johnson. The inside has an Old West feel with vertical dark wood paneling and a beamed ceiling, green patterned carpeting and upholstery, and even a brass and velvet rope to mark reserved rows in the gallery. Because it's the new West, there are laptop-friendly counsel tables and a projector and big screen.

Andy is there, wearing his normal work clothes, dirty and wrinkled. At least he didn't have to wear prison garb. The attorneys, the judge, the bailiff, and the court reporter are all present, too. Paco's death isn't big news in the community. It's a murder, of course. That got people's attention. But Paco was a Mexican ranch hand from Texas, not someone from a local family, and that makes a big difference. There are a few people in the gallery, though. Reggie, glowering. Trudy, which warms Maggie's heart. And—surprise—Penny, which confuses her. She'd told her about the hearing in a text canceling the music lesson the day before, but she didn't think the girl was that into Andy. She doesn't get a chance to talk to her before the bailiff calls court to order, though.

The attorneys make their appearances, but the proceeding is anticlimactic. John Fortney does a good enough job for Andy, but he doesn't have a challenge. Hank and Gene have already pledged adequate bond, with the bondsman present to hand over the check to the court. One hundred fifty thousand is steep to them—they'll never see fifteen thousand of it again, the fee to the bondsman—and low to the county for murder, at least according to the heated objections of the county attorney. The judge seems to buy Fortney's argument that a twenty-year-old Amish man who doesn't drive, fly, ride trains or boats, or own a passport is not much of a flight risk.

Andy spares a brief smile for his supporters as he turns to walk up the aisle without cuffs, although he's rubbing his wrists like he still feels them there. He sees Penny, and his face lights up like the girl is the present he never dreamed Santa would leave under the Christmas tree.

Reggie steps in front of Andy, blocking his view of Penny. His face is cold, his tone harsh. "Come with me."

Andy ducks around him to keep Penny in his sight.

"Did you hear me, Andrew?"

Andy returns his gaze to his father. His jaw flexes as his head inclines. Maggie is sure he's about to say "Yes, sir" when Penny steps up beside Reggie.

"I'm happy they released you, Andy."

Andy's suddenly two inches taller, his shoulders rising up and back. That brief smile returns, directed straight at the brunette. "Thank you."

"I mean, I'm sad Paco died. But I'm sure you didn't do it and they'll find who did."

Maggie is torn between agreeing with Penny and the fear that the someone they'll find will be Hank. But she won't let that happen. He's standing ramrod straight beside her, no dimples, no smile, but his eyes are kind.

"Andrew, now," Reggie says, in a deep hiss.

Andy shakes his head. "No." He clears his throat. "No, sir." He turns and extends his hand to Hank. Then to Gene. "Thank you both. More than I can say."

Both of his bosses shake his hand.

"I'll pay you back."

Gene crosses his arms. "You're a good man, Andy. And we know you're a good investment."

Penny steps closer. "Could you use a coffee, Andy?"

Andy laughs, starting to seem more his age. "Yes, I believe I could."

Hank and Maggie share a look. *Maybe Penny has gotten over her religious objections*, Maggie thinks.

Hank says, "If you don't mind, we have some errands to run. But we could pick you up and give you a ride back to the ranch from there."

"Oh, and before I forget, let's reschedule that music lesson for the two of you. How about tonight?" Maggie asks.

"That will work for me," Andy says.

Penny nods. "And Java Moon is just down the street. The weather is so pretty. Would you like to walk, Andy?"

"Enough of this. You're defying the faith before my eyes." Reggie's face is so red it's almost purple.

Andy speaks softly, but firmly. "No, I'm not. Goodbye, Father."

Reggie storms out of the courtroom, looking like the poster child for a movie on Old Testament vengeance.

Gene whistles. "That's not a happy man."

"You staying in town?" Hank asks.

"Nah, I'll get on back to the ranch. See you there."

Fortney joins them as Gene departs. The attorney talks about Andy's next steps in the criminal justice system and promises to call the ranch to set up an appointment for trial prep. After the attorney takes his leave, Andy walks out with Penny.

Hank offers his arm to Maggie. "I thought we'd walk to the compounding pharmacy to pick up my prescription."

"That's sexy talk, cowboy. I'm so excited for you to start the new treatment."

They walk along busy Coffeen Avenue chatting and holding hands.

Maggie says, "I was thinking about Andy's defense."

"Fortney will do a good job."

"I know. But there's no substitute for someone who really cares about and knows Andy. Should we hire a private investigator?"

"Maybe. The state still has to prove he did it, though, and I don't see how they can."

"It would help if we could show them who did."

"But we don't know who did."

"I'd like to try to figure it out."

"So hire the private investigator."

"Okay. I'll just do a little digging first, so I can start a PI in the right direction."

"That sounds like a good way to get yourself killed."

They enter the pharmacy. Hank's prescription is ready. While he pays, Maggie Googles for private investigators in the area. She doesn't come up with anyone promising. Plus, she starts wondering about the impartiality of a small-town investigator when all the suspects are likely to be local, too. Everybody knows everybody here.

Hank shakes a white paper bag at her. "Got it."

"I'm proud of you."

On the way back to downtown, they talk about Hank's injection schedule.

"Are you scared to give yourself a shot?"

"I'm not looking forward to it, but I've given injections to animals nearly all my life. I'll be fine."

"Don't you get the vet to do the injections?"

"You wouldn't ask that if you knew what Doc Billy charges. We take very good care of our livestock. They're our income. But what we can do ourselves, we do."

"What about labor and delivery?"

"Now you're thinking about Lily?"

"Yes."

"She's done it by herself several times now. We'll be there to help her if she needs it. But unless there's a problem, we won't call Doc Billy."

Halfway down Main toward Java Moon, Maggie stops and stares into a window. "I love their displays."

"Twisted Hearts. Girly stuff."

"And what's wrong with that?"

"You might not have noticed, but I don't wear many dresses."

"On account of your bowlegs?"

"Very funny."

The door to the shop opens. Three women emerge with navy paper shopping bags.

Maggie groans. "Don't look now, but it's the Witches of Eastwick."

Hank says, "Shit. Well, Mary's nice, but June and Sheila aren't my biggest fans right now."

"Or mine."

Turn the other way, turn the other way, Maggie wills them. "Let's go." Maggie takes Hank's elbow and pulls.

But it's too late. "Hank Sibley, are you going to pretend you don't even see your ex-fiancée?" June asks.

The three women are upon them in an instant.

Sheila pulls a pair of pants from her bag. She drapes them across her. "I hope when I'm nearly forty I can still fit in these."

Maggie pulls her embroidered top up with her free hand, looking down at her tight tank. "I'm sure glad I don't have to stuff socks in my bra to look like a grown woman."

Hank clamps his hand over Maggie's on his elbow and propels her forward with two big steps. "Come on, before Penny and Andy run off and elope."

A mewling sound whips Maggie's head around. It's coming from Mary. "Penny? I don't think so." She looks close to tears.

Maggie's strange feeling from earlier returns. What is it about Penny? She stops, which wrenches her hand out from under Hank's. "Why?"

"Don't listen to her," June says. "She's crazy when it comes to all things Paco Lopez."

"I am not. And Penny is the one obsessed with him. Paco'd been trying to foist her on Andy for weeks."

Sheila reloads her merchandise bag and leans to whisper in Mary's ear, but just loud enough that Maggie overhears it. "Mary, honey, why do you think he was using that religious freak as a beard? Because he could make it look like something it wasn't. Andy was a safe place to park his other woman. So quit lying to yourself. Up until the day he died, Paco was still giving it to Penny every bit as often as he was giving it to you."

THIRTY-FIVE

On the drive back to the ranch, Andy is more like a lovesick puppy than a man charged with murder.

Maggie's still reeling from her interaction with the three witches. What's Penny's angle? Is she using Andy for something? Lying to the police and everyone else about her relationship with Paco? "You seem upbeat."

"It will all work out. I didn't do this. The lawyer feels I won't be convicted."

Hank turns right on Main, taking the back way out of Sheridan to US Highway 87 and on through Story. "But I don't think that's the reason you look so happy. I think it's the girl."

"A Cheyenne girl at that. I thought you didn't like Indians?" Maggie says.

"Depends on the Indian."

"Are you allowed to date non-Amish?" Maggie can still picture the glowering face of Reggie when Andy agreed to coffee with Penny. Maybe religion will save Andy from Penny. If he needs saving.

"During Rumspringa, yes. But outside marriages are against Ordnung—community rules. So if I go back and get baptized, I have to marry Amish."

The religion and the community fascinate Maggie. From growing up Wendish, she can relate to the isolation and the extreme views. "Can people convert to Amish?"

"It's very difficult. Rare."

"But not impossible."

He smiles. "No, not impossible."

The news isn't as good as she'd hoped.

THIRTY-SIX

That evening, Hank and Maggie exit the dining room with Andy, Michael, and Gene, to find Penny in the great room waiting for the music lesson.

"Hello, Penny." Hank kisses Maggie's cheek. "I'm going to take a shower."

"See you in a few." To Penny she says, "You ready?"

Andy's face turns the color of a beet. "Penny."

"Hi, Andy."

Michael's eyes narrow, and he looks confused. "What are you doing here? You could have called me if you needed something."

She hugs her purse to her side. "Sorry. I'm not here to see you."

Maggie's hackles rise. How widespread are Penny's affections?

"Oh?" Michael says. "Who are you here to see?"

"I'm taking a music lesson from Ms. Killian."

"Like Andy." His brows draw together.

"Yes."

"Is this lesson with him, too?"

"Yes."

Michael studies her face, then Andy's. The air is thick with something that Maggie wants away from.

She points at the stairs. "Let's go make some beautiful music together." She immediately regrets her word choice.

Michael stares after them as they go.

THIRTY-SEVEN

Half an hour after the music lesson ends, Maggie and Hank lay intertwined.

Maggie is limp and sweaty. "The bed didn't crash. That's good."

"I Maggie-proofed it."

Maggie laughs. In the background, Alison Krauss is crooning "Stay."

"Definitely the afterglow. My favorite part, I mean."

Hank kisses her clavicle. "You think? I'm all about the pursuit."

"So if I'd stayed with you in Wyoming originally, we would have been over before we began? Because to you it's all about the pursuit?"

He runs his finger down the centerline of her body, from the hollow of her throat to just below her belly button. "In case you haven't noticed, you require a lot of pursuing."

"Don't try to talk your way out of this, cowboy."

He chuckles, and she touches the indentations in his cheek. "I believe I just pursued you to Texas. And up the stairs. And around the bedroom."

Maggie is mollified. She worries about leaving him to go back to Texas, if she can't get him to come with her. It's not that she'd require chasing, but she would want him to come after her. The thought of being apart makes her jangly and anxious. That reminds her she has two estimates sitting in her email inbox, a result of having no time to call the contractors back the day before. She hasn't even opened the emails.

"Hey, where'd you go?" he jostles her toes with his.

"Sorry. Thinking about Andy." She crosses her eyes instead of her fingers as she tells the white lie. "He and Penny were all googly-eyed on the porch after the music lesson. He's moony over her."

"You don't sound like you approve."

"I don't *dis*approve, but something isn't right with that girl."

"She seems nice enough."

"Harrumph."

He laughs. "You sound like Andy's mom."

Not what she wants to sound like when she's naked in bed with Hank. "Enough of that. Did you do your shot?"

"I did."

"Good."

Louise scratches at the door.

Hank growls. "Damn dog."

"She keeps getting shut out whenever we . . . you know."

"I don't need her watching my performance."

"You think she's going to critique you. Like, 'Hey, Mister, aren't those things usually straight?'"

"Too soon."

Maggie laughs. "About Louise. I have a confession on her behalf."

In the hall, the dog sighs and lies down on the floor with a loud, dejected thump.

"Uh-oh. As long as this isn't a story about Louise and one of your previous boyfriends, I'll be good."

"I got Louise here. In September. How fast do you think I work?"

"We were apart for a few weeks."

She nips at his nipple, eliciting a groan. "Louise has been keeping the ranch safe from small creatures. Rodents. Rabbits. Porcupines. Even an owl. I told Michael about it, and he thinks the owl was a witch, and that Louise saved me. That Louise is my protector."

"That's one bloodthirsty animal."

"Were you even listening to the punch line?"

He rolls her onto him and tips up her chin. In the moonlight, his face is shadowed, but his breath is warm and sweet on her lips.

"If Louise is protecting you, she's my favorite animal in the world."

Maggie nestles her face in the center of his chest. Hank holds her tight against him. Soon, his breathing is rhythmic and snuffly. Louise snores from the hall. Maggie is drifting off herself when she hears a screech and sees a shadow against the window. *Is it another owl?* But sleep pulls her under before she can decide.

Sometime later, Maggie wakes with a start. She's on her back, arms flung out.

"Waddafock," Hank mutters.

Her heart is kicking like the hooves of Lily's foal against the inside of her chest. She puts her hand on her throat. It's slick with sweat. There's an odor in the room. She sniffs. Something rank. Rotten. Dead?

Louise scratches on the door and whines. She sounds like she's digging for moles in the hall.

Maggie pushes herself to a seated position against the headboard. An image is fading from her memory. A dream? It's Paco's face, Paco's red boots running from the dead pile. He's pointing at something, or someone behind her. Hank is there. Gene. Michael. Andy. Penny. Her. She runs, gasps. Paco's image fades. What was he pointing at? Was he trying to show her something? His killer? She clutches at the covers pooled in her lap. Her hand closes over something warm, soft yet hard, and wet. She screams and rockets out from under it, landing on the floor with a thud on her side.

Hank is on his feet, fists swinging. "What? What? What?"

Maggie's voice is strangled. "Something was in my lap. I don't know what it is."

Louise scratches more frantically. Maggie doesn't tell her to stop, even though she'll have a sanding and staining job to repair the damage later. Hank switches on the bedside light. He hurries to her, leaning over to get a closer look.

"I'm fine. It's up there. On the bed."

He stands and searches the covers. She knows the second he finds it—whatever it is—because his expression of revulsion is unmistakable.

He crouches beside her, puts the back of his palm against her forehead. "Are you sick?"

"What? No. I was having a . . . a . . . nightmare, and I woke up."

"It's vomit."

She feels her chin, her neck, her chest, her mouth. "It's not from me."

"Or me. And Louise is in the hall."

The dog redoubles her efforts at the sound of her name.

"Having a cow."

Hank uses his alpha voice. "Louise, stop it."

Silence in the hall.

Maggie holds up her hands. "It's on me."

Hank grabs her wrists and gives them a gentle shake. "Go wash up. I'll try to figure out what's going on."

She nods and accepts his help standing up. Together they stare at the drippy bundle stuck to the covers.

"Are those *bones*?" she asks.

"Yes."

"And fur?"

"Yes."

"It's like something from a voodoo curse, or a witch doctor."

"Funny you say that."

"Why?"

"Last night you told me Michael thinks you had a visit from a witch."

"So?"

"This is from an owl."

"Owl vomit?"

"Yes."

"An owl couldn't get in our room."

Maggie runs to the door and lets her frantic dog in. Louise scrambles around the room, hackles up, growling. Hank and Maggie stare at each other.

"Hank, what the hell is going on?"

THIRTY-EIGHT

After the discovery of owl vomit on her in bed, Maggie and Hank can't get back to sleep. They decide to get a jumpstart on the morning chores and do the feedings together early.

After breakfast, Hank stops to hug her at the front door. He and Gene are on their way to meet Paco's family in Sheridan. "Don't let the dog out of your sight."

"I won't." She Eskimo-kisses him. "I hate that I'm not going with you."

"I'll be fine. Besides, I appreciate your help here."

"But the morgue."

"Not the first time I've been to one. Seriously, I'm good."

Gene walks up behind them. "You coming, Sibley?"

Hank picks up a travel mug of coffee he'd set on the sofa table on the way through the great room. The two men leave. Hank turns back for a moment, flashing her some dimples, and she waves to him from the open front door. Louise gives herself a side rub up against her leg. As the men back out and drive away, Maggie is alone, except for the dog. Her unease amps up.

Footsteps from the other direction draw her attention away from the ranch exit. She sees Andy walking up to the main house from the bunkhouse, his head down. His presence is comforting.

"You missed breakfast," she calls.

"Morning chores ran long." He doesn't look up.

As he skirts her to enter the door, she sees something dark around his eye. Purplish green, dark blue, and red. Like a blackened eye.

"Andy, wait."

He stops, not facing her.

"What's wrong with your face?"

"Nothing."

"Let me see."

He starts to walk away, but then he turns to her, revealing the mother of all shiners.

"Did you get kicked?"

He sighs, shaking his head. "Michael found out I like Penny."

"He punched you? But aren't you his boss?"

"Yeah." He clomps toward the kitchen. Then he turns back. "But I'm still going to marry her."

"What?"

"I asked her to marry me. She said yes."

"Whoa, what?" This doesn't feel like good news for Andy. "That was fast."

He trudges away.

"Wait," she calls after him. *And what the heck is Penny to Michael,* she wonders, but Andy doesn't hang around for her to ask more questions. She starts to chase after him, but decides she needs more information first. If she disapproves of their engagement, she'll drive Andy away. But if she figures out for herself who Penny is and what she's up to, well, then she'll have a better idea of what to do.

Maggie heads to the bedroom. Remembering her missed calls and emails, she quickly reviews the building estimate emails that came in two days before. The numbers are a little higher than she'd hoped, but one of them is close to workable. She sends a reply to that contractor, letting him know he's in the ballpark but needs to come down further.

She yawns. A quick makeup nap is in order after the rough night. There will be plenty of time after it to tackle the rest of her chores and her list of follow-ups, both in relation to Texas and to keeping Andy out of a bad marriage and prison. She's asleep almost before her head hits the pillow.

Loud knocking at the front door wakes her. No one answers the door, and the knocking just keeps going and going. She hears barking, growling, then yelling. *Shit.* Louise is outside. So much for Hank's request that she not let the dog out of her sight.

Maggie scrambles out of bed and downstairs, pushing wild hair out of her eyes and checking her breath on the run. She throws the door open. "Where's the fire?"

A puffy man dressed all in black is pinned on top of a Prius. Louise is lunging and snapping the air around it. She shoots Maggie a look as if asking what took her so long, then runs to her master and dances around her, tail wagging.

Maggie isn't about to scold the dog for protecting her. No one local drives one of these tin-can cars. It's a recipe for getting stuck on the side of the road in a pothole or snowdrift, or being killed when hitting one of the many deer who insist on suicide by vehicle. "Who's your friend, girl?"

Louise runs back to the muddy little car and resumes haranguing the visitor.

"Call off your beast, dammit." The man is holding his nose, giving his voice a nasally quality. Still, it sounds familiar.

Maggie crosses her arms. "Not a good idea to show up unannounced around here, mister. Who the hell are you, anyway?"

"Amos. We talked on the phone."

"Sic 'em, Louise."

His scream is high-pitched like a young girl. His arms flail the air, and he releases his nose, ducking his head and face. "No, no, no."

Louise doesn't know any commands. Even "come" and "sit" are still beyond her, no matter how many treats Maggie has offered her to learn them. But Amos doesn't need to know that.

"I told you not to come." Maggie's nose wrinkles up. "God, what's that horrible smell?" She's been so focused on the unwanted visitor, she just now realizes she's standing beside something dead and seriously rank. Not rank like owl vomit. Rank like . . . she searches the ground around her. Yep. Rank like a baby skunk. "Louise, bad girl."

"She smells like a skunk."

"You think?"

"It's making me nauseous."

The dog slinks to her, but she looks proud, not chastened. Her tail wags harder and harder. She smells as bad as the dead animal. Maggie is about to banish her to the barn until she can bathe her, but decides against it. She can take it, and it appears the sensitive flower from Colorado can't.

"If you don't like it, the interstate runs north and south, just a few miles that way." Maggie points.

His voice is icy. "Are you always this nice to people who drive hundreds of miles to see you?"

"No. Sometimes I call the cops." She opens the door to the house and starts to go back in. "Stay out here, Louise," she tells the eager dog.

"Wait! We got off on the wrong foot. Talk to me. Please."

She shuts the door. From the sound of the dog's growl, Maggie can tell she's rushing the Prius again. Amos screams. Maggie smiles and sits on the couch to check her phone.

Andy runs up, hollering at Louise. *Dammit.* After a short conversation, Andy pokes his head in the door. "Maggie?" he hollers.

"Right here."

"Oh. Sorry. There's a reporter here to talk to you."

"I know."

"What should I tell him?"

"That I'm not available. But I already did."

"Louise is terrorizing him. And she got a skunk. But I'll bet you already knew that, too."

"Sure did."

"I'm going to take her out to the barn and put her in one of the stalls."

"A shame. She was being such a helpful girl."

"Maggie."

She grins. "I'm kidding."

"He, um, he asked if he could interview me, since I know you."

"Suit yourself."

"You don't mind?"

"I don't recommend it. Reporters are vultures."

"I've never been interviewed for a magazine."

"E-zine. Blog. Or worse."

"What?"

"Do it, then. It's fine. Get it out of your system. Have fun."

"Can I bring him in here?"

Maggie nods. "I'll take care of Louise. I have work to do outside anyway."

Andy's eyes light up. "Thank you."

"I wouldn't thank me." Maggie follows Andy out, stepping over the skunk, and grabs Louise.

"You've decided to talk to me?" Amos asks from his dented rooftop.

He's finally looking at her without his hand clamped over his nose, and a bad feeling starts in her stomach, like the kind she gets from too much sugar. She knows this person. His salt-and-pepper hair is longer than she remembers it. He's wearing a beard on his formerly clean-shaven face. But she'll never forget the face of the man who used to be one of the top disc jockeys on the radio, until he harassed Maggie in an interview. Aaron cum Amos's fascination with her and his smears thinly veiled as news make sense now. He's got a hard-on for revenge.

"Not a chance. Especially not now that I see who you really are, Aaron Cryor."

"I don't use that name anymore."

"Freelancer now. My how the mighty have fallen."

"If that isn't the pot calling the kettle black, I don't know what is."

"No argument here. Come on, Louise."

Louise lifts a leg on the Prius like a boy, then follows Maggie to the barn. Maggie doesn't look back at the former shock jock. At the barn, she gives Louise a hose bath with skunk shampoo she finds with the dog supplies in the feed room. After Maggie rinses her, Louise shakes immediately, dousing Maggie.

"Stop." But Maggie laughs. She's going to smell like a skunk, too, but the temperature is a gorgeous fifty-five outside, and a little stinky water won't kill her. She goes for buckets and fills one with all-stock feed for the goats and another with sweet feed for Lily. They've already been fed, but she feels like spoiling them. She goes to the goats first. They're tethered behind the guest cabin she'd stayed at in August, before she and Hank were back together.

"I need to make you guys a pen before Mrs. Sibley has you butchered."

They don't seem overly concerned. She lets them loose. They follow her—and the feed buckets—to Lily's paddock.

"You're looking like an elephant today, my pretty one," she says to the horse.

Eyes on the feed, Lily jukes and jives as light-footed as if she weighed three hundred pounds less. She starts her funny *buh-buh-buh*, like a motor having trouble starting on a cold day. Maggie sets the goat bucket outside Lily's gate, then pours the horse's feed into her trough. The goats and horse eat quickly. When they're all done, she pushes the goats in with Lily. Louise squeezes in after them. The creepiness of last night and irritant of Amos's visit slip away in the presence of her favorite animals, just as she'd hoped they would.

She tips her head back, eyes closed, and soaks in the Indian summer sun. A flapping noise makes her open her eyes. A flock of Canada geese wing in front of blue sky and fluffy white clouds, then turn. She rotates with them and admires their silhouettes in front of the yellow orb of sun, like they're fleeing from a world on fire.

A blue-roan in the next paddock turns sleepy eyes on Maggie. The docile animal looks familiar.

With a start she realizes it's Crazy Woman. "Hey, superstar." She walks to her pen and holds out a hand. The horse rubs her nose on her foreleg, then goes back to dozing. "No love for your fans, huh?"

She's going to miss this in Texas.

Her phone rings in her pocket. Franklin. Finally they're going to connect. "This is Maggie. Give me some good news, Franklin."

"Oh, um, hi. I expected to get voicemail again."

"You need to learn what to do with it."

"What do you mean?"

"I've been waiting on this claim information, and you're holding it captive."

He clears his throat. "It's our policy not to leave it in a message."

"Then spit it out already."

The line goes dead.

She stares at the phone. "Dammit, T-Mobile. Dammit, Wyoming."

It rings again.

"Yes?"

"I lost you."

"Talk fast."

He gives her a number for reimbursement on rebuilding. It's less than half the amount of the lower of the two estimates she'd read earlier. And those were already for no-frills buildouts. Not nearly as nice as the originals.

"Come again?"

He repeats it.

Maggie is silent. She walks into the pen with Lily, the goats, and Louise. Omaha and Nebraska bleat at her and butt her legs. She reaches down and trades off between them, scratching behind their horns.

"Are you there?"

"I'm here. This is me being speechless."

"Are you okay?"

"How could I be okay? That amount won't pay for me to rebuild a shed, much less a house, a shop, and a barn."

Franklin hems and haws. Maggie doesn't listen.

"So what do I get if I don't rebuild?" she asks.

He names a far lower number. That, plus selling the land at the price the realtor suggested a few days before wouldn't give her enough money to buy a new place. She can't rebuild, and she can't afford to replace what she had. Not to mention she can't afford to give up the rental income on Gidget's place, and she sure can't afford to lease Lumpy's place, nor can she qualify for a loan to buy ranchland for Double S. She'd been living in a dream world.

"What the hell was I paying for with my premiums all these years? You guys are screwing me."

"This isn't personal."

"Getting screwed is always personal. Expect a call from my attorney next."

He tries again to explain, but she ends the call in the middle of his sentence. Lily stares at her and swishes her tail.

Maggie kicks the gate. It hurts. "Son of a bitch."

THIRTY-NINE

After finishing the rest of her ranch chores in a blue funk, Maggie takes her laptop into Hank's sitting room and plops onto the brown leather couch. It's worn but still feels plush under her. She puts her feet on the coffee table. Typing ninety-to-nothing on her phone, she shoots off an email to Michele about the insurance payout. Then she texts her: *SOS. Sent you an email. Getting effed over on insurance.*

As always with Michele, the reply comes fast: *See know more. Dammit. Trying out voice recognition. Quitting voice recognition. Seriously, I'm on it. Don't worry another minute.*

Maggie smiles for the first time since she talked to Franklin. *Thanks.*

"Maggie, is that you?" It's Trudy's voice from downstairs.

"Hi, Trudy. Yep, it's me."

"I have a surprise for you. Can I come up?"

"Of course." Maggie boots up her laptop while Trudy climbs the stairs.

The woman appears bearing a small plate in one hand and a steaming tin mug in the other. Maggie smells coffee.

"You seem to be sick of apples."

"I, um . . ."

Trudy sets the mug down by Maggie's feet, then hands the plate to her. On it is a sugar-sprinkled scone with some kind of reddish berries. "It's cranberry."

"I freakin' love cranberry scones."

"Good." Trudy brushes her hands on her jeans. "It's my own recipe."

Maggie bites into it. She moans. "It's still warm."

Trudy smiles. "Do you have a sec?"

Maggie pats the couch and takes another bite.

"Did Andy tell you he's engaged?"

Maggie nods and rolls her eyes, still chewing.

"Yeah. Me, too. Do you know anything about her?"

Maggie sets the scone on the plate and the plate on the coffee table. "She's a wonderful banjo player. She used to date Paco. Michael beat Andy up over her. And two days ago she thought Andy was too religious for her. That's all I've got."

"That's more than I had. What's her name?"

"Penny."

"Penny what?"

Maggie stares back at Trudy. "You know, I don't have a clue. I told myself I was going to do some hunting around for information on her this afternoon, but I'm not going to get very far without a name."

"She's Crow?"

"Well, Native American at least."

"No, I remember. Cheyenne. Andy told me."

That thickened the plot with Michael, for sure, since he was from the Cheyenne reservation. "Should narrow it down some."

"I have to admit I'm surprised. Andy hates Cheyenne."

"There's that."

"I'm worried this is just some kind of rebellion he'll regret."

"He's smitten with her, but I agree. Even if it's true love on his part, this relationship has regret written all over it."

"If you find anything out, let me know, okay? I can't stand the thought of him getting hurt."

"I will. You, too."

Trudy's face is pensive as she walks away.

Maggie's laptop is booted up. She eats the last bite of scone and sips her coffee. Time to do some good for Andy. She decides to research Mary, since she has a last name to go on. Martin. She types *Mary Martin, Sheridan, Wyoming* into Google. The search engine asks her if she meant Mary *Marton* Sheridan, Wyoming. She thinks about it, replays the sound of Hank introducing the woman to her in her memory. Mar-TAHN. Yes. *Marton.* She clicks to accept the change, and more search results appear on the screen.

Mary Sanders Marton. The Facebook profile picture is definitely the curvy brunette. Born in Sheridan, Wyoming. Graduated Sheridan High School. Married to William Marton. His name is not highlighted, so it doesn't appear he's on Facebook. Mary graduated from Eastern Wyoming College. Works at Sheridan Vet Clinic. Occupation: Vet Tech.

Maggie scrolls down Mary's timeline. She finds pictures of her with June. With Sheila. With Sheila and June. One is at the Ox. She pulls it up and enlarges it to see the other people in the background of the shot. There's a flash of red on the feet of a cowboy sitting with his back to the camera. He has his arm around a woman in profile. A woman with a sheet of long black hair. Penny. The photo is creepy, since it brings life to a dead man, but it doesn't tell her anything new. She keeps scrolling. Mary likes to post selfies with her four-legged patients, as well as rescue animals from the local shelter. Maggie sees pictures of Mary on horseback at brandings, in the mountains on a four-wheeler, and fly-fishing in waders. What she doesn't see is any pictures of Mary with a man—Paco or her husband, or even friends or family.

She Googles Sheridan Vet Clinic. The website is factual and functional, with no pictures of the staff. Maggie reruns her search on Mary and sifts through the results. Mary has volunteered with rescue events, and she's competed in some 5K runs.

The sound of the front door opening and closing tears her attention away from Mary. Heavy boots clomp through the great room.

"Who's there?" she says, loud enough to be heard downstairs, but not shouting.

"Michael."

She pushes the laptop onto the couch and jumps to her feet. "Wait up." She runs down the stairs in her stocking feet.

He's waiting, and looking puzzled. "What's up?"

"Are you getting coffee?"

"Yep."

"I thought I'd join you."

"Free country, except on the res." There's an edge to his voice, and he doesn't meet her gaze.

She follows him into the dining room. It's empty and so is the kitchen. Michael grabs a mug from the stack by the percolator and pours coffee into one. He sets it aside and pours another, nodding at the first one. She doesn't need more coffee, but it seems like the right thing to do.

"Thanks." Maggie gets pumpkin spice creamer from the refrigerator. "I saw Andy earlier. He looks like shit." Michael had filled the mug nearly to the rim, so she's not able to get in as much as she likes.

"Yeah? Well, he had it coming." Michael walks to the door.

She stirs in her creamer. "It's a good way to get fired, and to hear you tell it, you really need the money."

He stops at the door. "Some things are more important than money or jobs."

She wishes she knew whether Gene or Hank talked to Michael about his time in prison. Bringing it up first herself wouldn't be right. "Like punching your boss?"

"Like Penny." He spits out the words like pellets from a gun, then turns on his heel to go.

"But why?"

He disappears without answering her.

FORTY

Maggie takes a late-afternoon shower to wash the day and dust off before dinner. When she gets out, she dries off, then uses the towel to turban her hair. She pads dripping into the bedroom. Hank is on the bed with his hat over his face. She removes the hat and kisses his cheek.

He opens his eyes, and his dimples are like the Grand Canyon. "Hello, beautiful." He reaches for her.

She wags a finger at him. "Time for me to dress for dinner. How was Paco's family?"

He sits, his long legs swinging over the side of the bed and his boots hitting the floor. "Sad. Nice. We took them to eat. Then they got on the road."

"Such a sad journey for them." Her dream image flashes back through her mind. She hopes his spirit went with them, if that's what it was.

"You sure you're in a hurry?"

She shimmies into panties. "I'm sure. I skipped lunch. But I'll take a rain check tonight." She doesn't tell him that she's still too depressed about the contractor estimates and insurance claim news to get her sexy on now. Somehow she doesn't think her bad news will be as bad to him as it is to her.

"Probably for the best. My head is killing me. I'm going to take some stuff."

"Did you do your shot?"

He mouths a pill in the doorway, talking around it, glass in hand. "Yeth-terday." He swallows the pill. "Don't be pushy, woman." But he smiles.

Her phone rings.

He swallows his gulp of water. "Aren't you going to get it?"

She picks up her phone and groans. "It's Amos, that reporter from Denver. He showed up here today uninvited. But get this: Amos is a pseu-donym. It's *Aaron Cryor*."

"That asshole DJ you got fired?"

"None other."

"Give me that." He takes the phone from her and answers. "This is Hank Sibley. Listen, asswipe, leave my girl alone."

"That won't make it better." Maggie holds her hand out for her phone.

"And don't come on my property again without an invitation. That's a shooting offense up here."

"Give me the phone, Hank."

He slaps it into her palm. "I feel better."

She shoots him a look. "Aaron, don't bother me anymore."

"Amos. I texted you the link to today's article."

"Super." He must have written it in real time as he did the interview.

"Take a look. I'll hold."

"That's okay."

"Please. Your hand said he doesn't have technology. He wants you to show it to him."

"Fine." She puts him on speaker and switches to her texts, where she clicks the link he sent.

The first thing she notices—"Black Widow Steals Other Woman's Fiancé"—is a box quote from Sheila. *Maggie stole Hank from me. We were engaged to be married.* And then a picture of Maggie with Lily, Louise, and the goats, captioned *Country star to country girl.* Sneaky bastard taking pictures like some paparazzo with a telephoto lens.

Hank reads over her shoulder, squeezes her, and kisses her neck. "Want me to talk to him again?"

"I hear you, you Neanderthal," Amos says.

From downstairs, a woman's scream rings out.

Hank says, "Shit, that's Mom. You okay?"

Maggie points at the door. "I'm fine. Go."

Hank runs out.

"Maggie?"

"You're a jackal."

"The interest in you is huge after these murders you were involved in."

"I wasn't *involved* in any murders. Murderers were involved."

"Add all the rest to it, and you're great reading. You're dating a real cowboy, your superstar ex died, your old bandmate burned down your house, your father's running for president, and your new bestie is Ava Butler."

President? Oh, Boyd. That won't keep the scavenging press away. "I wouldn't call us besties."

"What would you call it?"

"We're . . . friends of friends."

"Well, people are interested. You can let me write about you, or someone else will."

"You have a grudge against me. No thanks."

"My articles are creating renewed interest in your music."

"Good—the record label that owns my tracks thanks you for helping line their pockets."

"Seriously, you should do something with it."

She doesn't tell him that Goliad Records had the same idea. "I don't want to do anything with it. I just want to be left alone."

"I'll be here a few more days if you change your mind."

"Digging up more dirt like you did with Sheila?"

"Satisfying public interest."

"That you create. Potato, potahto, shock jock."

"Have it your way."

After the call, she finishes dressing. While she's blow-drying her hair, another call comes in. It's not totally unexpected. Michele had warned her. Aaron had too, in his own way.

Maggie turns off the blow-dryer. "Hello, Ava."

Ava's island patois lilts over the line. "Maggie, you still up there freezing your backside off in Wyoming?"

"It's lovely here. And, yes, I'm in Wyoming."

"Girl, you need to do something with your music."

"It's not mine anymore."

Ava drops her accent. "I saw a video clip of you playing with some rednecks. You still got it—comes through even on a shitty cellphone video."

"Great."

"And that article. Some reporter asshole sent it to me. Amos. He said you referred him to me."

"I most certainly did not."

"He had my personal number."

"Not from me, he didn't. Please don't speak to him."

"I didn't. But listen, you're too talented and hot right now to let this go. And I have an idea."

"Why do I think I'm going to hate this?"

The accent returns. "Because you always been a sourpuss."

"Just tell me what it is."

A baby cries in the background. "I gotta make this quick. Collin is hungry. Collin Junior, that is. Well, probably his dad, too, but not that kind of hungry."

"Spare me."

"Let's do a mash-up."

"What?"

"Let me remix one of your old songs."

"I don't own the recordings anymore."

"But you own the songs. Like if someone records them, you get paid, right?"

"No. But I have lifetime rights to re-record them myself without paying royalties."

"That will work."

"Work for what?"

"We're going to record together. My producer is a genius. You'll make a mint, and I'll get tons of crossover fans from whatever it is you call what you do."

"I do antiques."

"Musically. Western shit."

"Texana. Or alt-country. Americana. Folk. Alt-rock. Any of those. But not Western."

"Yeah, well, that's what I want us to do together. Your shtick and mine. Your songs."

Ava is running her own show. Maggie wonders how much different her dead musical career would have been without an agent or manager calling all the shots and a label making demands. She has new respect for Ava. Not enough to cave, though. "Sounds fun. No."

"What do I have to do to get a yes?" She names a number. It's higher—three times higher—than the insurance payout. "Plus ongoing royalties, of course."

Maggie's breath hitches. It's more tempting than she'll admit. "Ava, I'm not part of that world anymore. I'm in Wyoming. Hell, you don't even like me."

"You've grown on me. But sleep with my man, and I'll cut you."

Maggie can't help it. She laughs. "Back at ya, sister."

The baby's cries escalate to earsplitting screeches. "Think on it. I'll be in touch again soon."

The call ends, and Maggie stares out the window, calculating whether Ava's offer would be enough to cover the delta between the chickenshit insurance payout and the cost of her Texas rebuild.

FORTY-ONE

Maggie sips a cup of light and sweet coffee on the back porch after morning feeding and breakfast. She's in a red long-john top with her boots, jeans, and Hank's Frontier Days belt buckle. The clouds tumble like petals from a dandelion in the sky, and the breeze in her hair is mild and pleasant. On the mountain, the old summer cabin looks mysterious but inviting and close enough to touch. Louise is rolling in the grass—in something dead, from the smell of it—but even that can't spoil the glory of a perfect day. Last night she'd told Hank about Andy, Penny, and Michael and updated him on the status of her nightmare in Texas. It had felt good to share the burden, and Hank had been steady and helpful.

Things may not be perfect, but they're damn good.

The wooden floor creaks under Hank's boot treads. "What are you doing out here?"

"Admiring the view."

"Are those elk coming down the mountain?"

"What?" She squints. "Maybe. But I was admiring the summer cabin."

He drops a kiss on her neck. "I need to run up there to check on the old girl. Want a tour?"

Maggie adores old things, and she's dying to see the cabin. "I'd love it!"

"Grab a jacket. It's windier up there."

Half an hour later, the two are driving up a narrow, single-lane road in Hank's truck with Louise in the back seat. Maggie grips the armrest. It's one dead-man's curve after another, and she's on the uphill side, so all she sees is blue sky on the driver's side. The big cabin looms over them, straight up the road.

"It's crazy steep." She looks up at the cabin to take her mind away from the drop-off.

Hank grins at her. "It is. It took Dad and Grandpa two years to build this place. And half of that time was spent just hauling materials up this road."

"Does anyone come up here in the winter?" This road would be a ski jump with ice and snow.

"Sure. We used to a lot, but mostly on snowmobiles. There's a snow-plow in the barn, and an old Snow Cat." Hank spins the truck around a nearly one-hundred-eighty-degree switchback for the final approach to the house.

"Wow." Maggie can't find any other words that won't get stuck in her throat.

Somehow, the cabin site is just flat enough to accommodate a small parking area and the footprint of the cabin. It's as tall as it looks from down below, too—four stories built into the face of the mountain. The walls are hand-hewn logs encircled by a deck balancing over the drop-off below it. The green metal roof blends into the tops of towering ponderosa pines.

"Pretty cool, huh?"

"Amazing." Maggie jumps out and slams her door, then lets Louise out. The dog sniffs the ground like it's crack for an addict. After huffing for a few seconds, she takes off after a chipmunk that disappears into a woodpile. The air is thinner, crisper than at the ranch. "This is what Pine-Sol wishes it smelled like."

Hank laughs.

"And the view. Oh my God. This view." She points toward a ridge that juts eastward from the mountain range.

"It's special. Usually in this part of the state you're either looking at the mountains or you're in the mountains and see nothing but trees and rocks. Here you get both because of that ridge, plus the view of the buttes to the east, the foothills below, and the valley along Piney and Little Piney creeks."

"I didn't even know that gulch was there." She points at a fold lined with gray-and-red rock cliffs. "It looks like heaven for mountain lions."

"Oh, it is." Hank walks back and forth, staring at the dirt driveway, his lips pursed.

"What is it?"

"Someone's been up here."

"Is that bad?"

"Well, usually I'm the only one who comes all the way up to the cabin, at least unsupervised. I come up every week or two for maintenance. It's totally off the grid, so I make sure everything is working, keep the rodent population down, and arrange workers and deliveries." He points at several big propane tanks.

"Even in the winter?"

"Even more so in the winter. Can't afford to let it freeze or the pipes will burst."

"I didn't know you were up here so much."

"I have a strong sentimental attachment. And she requires a lot of care." He pats the edge of a log. "Come on in. I'll show you around."

They enter into a cozy kitchen with an old-fashioned wood-burning stove. The interior walls are simply the other side of the external logs. The effect is rustic and everything a mountain cabin should be.

"It's beautiful. Perfect."

Hank steps into a three-story great room with a black iron stove and tall chimney. "You should see it lit up with a giant Christmas tree and fires in all the stoves."

Maggie peers upward. The top floors overlook the lower ones with log railings instead of interior walls. She has a flash of inspiration. The Wyoming pieces she bought last summer, the ones that survived the fire, anyway, would look wonderful here. Music plays in her head, music she can picture making in this space. "The acoustics must be amazing. Why don't you live here? This place is magical."

"It's too big for a bachelor pad. And not convenient with Mom's condition. All these stairs and levels. Plus at the ranch house we're half an hour closer to help and have onsite cooking to share with the hands." He squats and examines the carpet.

"It's huge. How many bedrooms?"

"Six."

She's getting tingly, and she's not sure why. "And bathrooms?"

"Um, six and a half."

"It's big enough to be a bed-and-breakfast. A lodge. A guest ranch."

Hank frowns at the floor. "This boot print wasn't here last time I was."

"Maybe Laura came up?"

He traces the print with his finger. "Too big. And these are work boots, not cowboy boots like we wear around the ranch." He stands. "Damn, I wish I'd put up a game camera."

"Or you could use some of those Wi-Fi cameras you can check on the internet."

He nods slowly. "Maybe so." His phone rings.

"You have cell service up here?"

"Line-of-sight internet and 4G signal. It's better than down at the ranch." He looks at the screen. "I'd better take it. Laura and Mom were headed into town."

Maggie wanders off to explore on her own. She'll come up here and install the cameras herself, she decides. She is a ranch hand, after all, and it would give her another excuse to visit. In the dining room, wooden-framed windows show off the view. Deer wander down the slope, grazing. A mature buck, two does, a yearling spike, and some summer fawns that have lost their spots. Tears prick the corners of her eyes. How can physical beauty have this emotional impact on her? It's like this is the place she's been waiting to find her whole life.

Hank's voice booms with authority in the other room. "I'm leaving now. Hang on."

Maggie hurries back to the mezzanine and stands beside an old piano. "What is it?"

Hank's face is pale. "They're at the hospital. Mom collapsed. Laura thinks she's had a stroke."

FORTY-TWO

Louise hunkers down outside the cabin and refuses to load in the truck. The dog's no fool. She's found heaven.

"We don't have time for this." Hank revs the engine.

Maggie grabs Louise around her torso. "She's heavier than she looks." She hefts the dog into the back seat. Once in her own seat, she buckles up. "Ready."

The trip down the mountain is far faster than the one up, and Maggie presses her feet into the floorboard like it will help with the brakes. She closes her eyes on the scariest parts. Once they reach the relatively flatter road back to the ranch proper, Hank speeds up. The truck goes airborne between potholes. He stops so hard at the main house that Maggie's seat belt arrests her.

He puts it in park and turns to her. "I'm in a hurry."

"Then go."

"Aren't you getting out?"

"Not unless you want me to."

He throws it back in gear. "Thank you." His words are clipped, his face is stony, his eyes dark and sunken.

She reaches across the seat and touches his knee. "Of course."

He drives left-handed and holds her hand in a crushing grip the entire drive to Sheridan. Maggie texts Laura for him when they're five minutes out. When they park, Louise whines. Maggie had forgotten she was there. Hank doesn't seem to notice, so Maggie cracks her window.

"I'll come check on you in a little while with some water."

Louise wags her tail. Life is always an adventure to her.

Inside the hospital, Laura meets Maggie and Hank in the front lobby.

"No one is telling me anything." Laura collapses into Hank.

He bends down, and her head slides up to his shoulder. Maggie feels out of place. Until she acquired her two stepsiblings, she'd never had a brother or sister. She can't relate to Hank and Laura's reliance on each other. But she does understand they love each other, and that they love their mother. That they share the pain of the loss far too young of a father they adored. That once upon a time, their grouchy, confused, wheelchair-bound mother was a vital, loving spouse and parent.

Like her own father had been. A sob burbles up in Maggie's throat. She chokes it back. She rarely thinks about him. Feels sad about him even less often. But being here, remembering the change in her father and his death, knowing he had Alzheimer's like Mrs. Sibley, it all crashes down on her.

Hank hears her. His eyes find hers over Laura's head. His face is slick with tears, his eyes red-rimmed, and his lips tight and trembling. If Laura didn't have her arms around him, Maggie would scoop him up. His pain is her pain, and she aches to touch him. He reaches out to her, but they're interrupted.

"Are you the family of Evangeline Sibley?" A woman with white pin curls and a smock over her gabardine pants and polka-dotted blouse walks up on squeaky shoes.

Laura releases Hank and mops her face with her hands. "We are."

"The doctor would like to speak to you."

Maggie moves beside Hank. She slips her hand into his.

Laura holds up her hand. "Family."

Hank's face darkens.

"Please, Hank."

Maggie puts a hand on his elbow. "I'll be waiting for you here in the lobby."

His tight lips open, but Maggie interrupts before he says anything that makes the moment even harder.

"I'm good, Hank. I promise."

"Are you coming, Hank?" Laura says, avoiding Maggie's eyes.

Hank moves toward Laura, leaving a gap between him and Maggie.

Every step he takes widens it. It's painful and surprising. Maggie wants to run after him. Instead, she settles into an uncomfortable seat in the lobby.

After a few minutes, Maggie's thoughts wander to her financial predicament. She doesn't have the money to rebuild her shop and her house. It's one or the other, unless she liquidates her inheritance: the Andy Warhol and the Jaguar have immediate value. She can put Gidget's little ranch on the market, but who knows how long it would take for it to sell? Or, she could take either Goliad Records or Ava up on their offers. Capitalize on her current resurgence of fame. In other words, sell out. She hates the idea of Goliad, but Ava . . . well, she's not completely opposed.

It might be fun.

But she hates Ava.

Or maybe she doesn't.

She's no closer to a decision when Hank pulls her to her feet.

Maggie moves to him, keeping their conversation private from Laura and her censure. "How is she?"

Hank looks like he's losing weight before her eyes, drawing in, winnowing out. "It's a massive stroke. They don't think she'll recover, even if she lives."

"I'm so sorry." She throws herself into his arms and squeezes him tight.

His lips move in her hair and his words are muffled. "Thank you."

"What can I do?"

"Love me forever."

She digs her fingers into his back. She already does. A flash in her mind foretells her future. Alone, in a hospital waiting room, losing Hank. A cry of pain escapes her lips.

"What is it?" Hank holds her away from him.

Everyone dies. One of them—her or Hank—will go first. Suddenly she hopes it's him. She doesn't want him to endure the pain she just felt at the thought of living without him. She doesn't admit to her terrors. "I hate this for you."

"Me, too." He draws in a long, deep breath. When he speaks, he turns to include Laura. "Let's go get some food, ladies. We have a lot to talk about."

Laura grimaces. "*We* have a lot to talk about, but not all of us. Did you bring your own car, Maggie?"

Hank wheels on her. "I'm sick of your shit, Laura. No more of it. Maggie is with me. If you don't like it, go eat by yourself."

"I know you're with her, and that's fine, but we need to discuss important *family business*, Hank."

"And we will. With or without you."

He propels Maggie with his body, arm around her shoulder. "Do you mind the cafeteria? I want to stay close in case they have news about Mom."

"Of course." As nasty as Laura has been, she feels sorry for her, but she doesn't know what to do about it. The younger woman's pain is palpable. It has been for the last week. Before this incident with Mrs. Sibley, and above and beyond any ill will she feels toward Maggie. Call it women's intuition or whatever. She may not have known her as long as Hank has, but she senses there is something else wrong.

Hank releases her at the cafeteria line. They fill their trays in silence. When they reach checkout, Maggie sees Laura in line behind them.

"I've got theirs," Laura calls out to the cashier, waving at the two trays in front of the register.

Maggie bites her lip.

Hank's voice is casual. "Thanks. I'll get us a table."

At a round table big enough for six, they huddle on one side. Hank pats Maggie's knee, and they eat in silence for several minutes.

Laura stares at a gravy lake in her mashed potatoes. "We've waited too long to talk about dividing property. Even if Mom lives, we have to figure this out."

"Say what's on your mind, sis." Hank takes a bite of meat loaf.

Maggie got it, too. It's a little dry, but surprisingly good.

Laura puts a thimbleful of potato on her fork. "I don't want the land."

"Land is all they have."

"Land can be sold."

Maggie holds her breath. Laura wants Hank to sell the ranch where he runs Double S?

Hank pushes his plate back. "The value of the place is far greater than the price it would bring. To me."

"I understand that. But I need money. Mickey and I need money. Very badly."

"What are you saying?"

"I need us to put it on the market."

"You understand my entire livelihood is built around that property? Couldn't I just buy you out of your half of it?"

"How would you propose to do that?"

"In monthly installments."

She shakes her head and pushes back her tray. "I need the cash now. Could you get a mortgage?"

"Maybe. But I don't have W-2 type income. Banks don't like to lend money to guys like me. I don't own anything to put up as collateral."

"I'm sorry for your situation. But when it sells, you can use the money to get another place."

The sound Hank makes can't be described with mere words. The closest Maggie can come is a strangled cat in a dryer. "Did you have a time frame in mind?"

"As soon as humanly possible."

"Gosh, then, sis. You'd better hope Mom doesn't make it." He's on his feet like a jack-in-the-box. His hip jars the table and knocks over condiments and drinks. Ice and tea race across the table toward Laura.

Laura grabs napkins and sops liquids off her lap and legs. "Aren't you going to help me clean up your mess?"

"Not feeling helpful," Hank says from his clamped jaw. "And thanks for humiliating me and showing your true colors in front of Maggie."

Laura's voice escalates. "I warned you this was a family discussion."

Hank pushes down on his hat like he's walking into a stiff wind. "If only that felt like family." To Maggie he says, "Let's get out of here."

"I'll meet you up front."

He nods and strides off.

Maggie turns to Laura. "What's the matter?"

Laura finishes wiping down the table. "Other than my brother is a selfish asshole?"

"Why do you need the money?"

"That's none of your business." Laura lifts her tray with a jerk.

"Laura, I know you don't believe it yet, but I'm not the enemy. If there's something I can do to help, I want to."

"How can you help?"

Maggie follows Laura to a conveyor belt, carrying her own tray and Hank's. "I don't know. Talk to Hank, at least."

"I can talk to my brother myself, thank you very much." She slams her tray down on the belt.

"If you change your mind . . ."

"I know you'll be lurking around."

Maggie bites back what she wants to say, but she thinks it. *You don't have to be such a bitch about it.*

FORTY-THREE

Gene joins Hank and Maggie at the Mint Bar after Maggie sends him a distress signal text. Hank's been drinking for an hour. Maggie's taken Louise for a constitutional and drink of water. She's catalogued every animal head trophy and photo in the place. An email came in from the contractor in Texas, offering to work with her on a design that meets her budget. She made an appointment with him for the end of the next week. Now she's just trying to keep Hank upright.

Maggie side-talks at Gene. "I'm so glad you're here."

Gene holds up three fingers in a question to her. She holds up five. His eyes widen.

He nudges Hank with his shoulder. "Buddy, I'm so sorry about your mom."

"I lost all the rest of my fam'ly today."

"No, buddy, your Mom's still with us. And you've got me. Maggie. And Laura."

"Not Laura. Fam'ly doesn't try to sell your life out from under ya."

Gene looks to Maggie for interpretation.

"Laura wants the ranch to go on the market, ASAP." She takes a sip of her Koltiska original, straight.

Gene's eyes fly open like someone has cattle prodded him. "Put it on the market?"

"She's dead to me." Hank downs the whiskey in front of him. He holds up a finger.

Maggie curls it down. "You're getting too far ahead of me, cowboy." Like four ahead, but she doesn't tell him that.

He slant-eyes her. "You don't drink as much as you used to."

She realizes he's right. Not that she doesn't drink, but that she was drinking way too much for a while. She smiles. "You're the only drug I need. How about you?"

Hank locks eyes with her and shakes his head back and forth. "Doesn't appear so."

Ouch. She hopes he took his shot, because he needs all the help he can get. Grief and anger are doing a number on him. She rolls her eyes at Gene.

He's chewing his bottom lip. "We can make Laura an offer."

"We don't have the money to buy her out."

"Maybe she'll take a promissory note."

"She wants cashhhhh." Hank throws a twenty on the bar.

Maggie adds another.

"We gotta get back to the hoshpital."

"I'll drive." Maggie snatches the keys from his hand.

Gene says, "I'll be there in an hour. You got him until then?"

"Yep. He's safe with me."

A few minutes after Gene leaves, Maggie props Hank on her shoulder. "Time to go."

"Do you need a hand?" It's Penny's voice at her elbow.

"Hi, Penny." Maggie almost says no, then changes her mind. This is a good chance to talk to the girl. At least find out her last name. "Sure."

"I need to go to the bat'room," Hank announces. "Bleed the lizard. Drain the main vein."

"We can get you there, but after that you're on your own," Maggie tells him.

One on each side, she and Penny support Hank as he stumbles to the men's room.

"You gonna be okay?" Maggie asks him.

He salutes her as he falls through the door.

"Not good." Maggie leans against the pool table. She likes the small room in the back of the bar with historic ranch brands burned into the paneling, hand-carved wooden booths thick with varnish, and her favorite photographs in the place, all black-and-whites. A plane dating to the early days of flight with the mountains in the background. Snow-covered cattle and cowboys. Sheep at a mountain lake.

Penny nods. She gazes into the jukebox. "He's pretty hammered. His mom had a stroke, right?"

"Yes."

"Michael told me."

That's one of the subjects Maggie wanted to talk to her about. "Michael."

"Yes."

"You talk a lot?"

"Kind of. Not as much as we used to."

"You were close?" Maggie walks over to the jukebox, too.

"We still are. But we used to have an apartment in Sheridan."

"You lived together."

"Yeah." Penny dips her head. Her hair falls forward.

Maggie can only see part of the girl's profile. "Before you dated Paco?"

"Yeah."

"I heard you were still close with Paco when he died."

Penny closes her eyes. "We broke up."

"But you were still close?"

"Yeah."

Maggie breaks a long silence. "And now you and Andy are engaged. Congratulations."

She shakes her head. "I broke it off with him. It's probably for the best. But I thought he would be a good dad."

"Why did you do that?"

"Michael. But I didn't tell Andy that. I don't want to cause trouble between them."

"You mean trouble like Michael blackens Andy's other eye?"

"That was from Michael?"

"You didn't know?"

"No." Her hand covers her mouth, and she backs up to the jukebox.

"How did Andy take the breakup?"

She shakes her head. "He's okay, I think. I just told him. I guess this means I won't be coming to music lessons with him anymore."

Maggie is more confused than ever, but at least Andy is free from Penny. She thinks that's probably a very good thing. "I guess not."

Hank staggers out from the bathroom.

"I've got it from here," Maggie tells Penny.

The Cheyenne woman stares at her with inscrutable eyes. "Whatever you say."

How can she know less about this woman every time their paths cross? Penny walks away, and belatedly Maggie wonders what Penny was doing at the Mint.

"Give me your arm, cowboy." Hank throws it over her shoulders.

Maggie and Hank make their way to the door like the last-place team in a three-legged race. Once they're outside, Maggie turns right down the alley. They're parked in back. Not ten feet down it, they meet a man coming the other direction. A man dressed in the Amish style.

He looks up. The angry face is familiar. Reggie Yoder.

When Maggie is three feet from him, she gets a blast of the medicinal odor from his breath. If she didn't know he was Amish, she'd think it was moonshine. "Good day, Mr. Yoder."

"It ain't looking like a good one for my son's employer. What kind of man is drunk in public? Midday, no less."

Hank looks up, bleary-eyed. "I hear congraduelashions are in order, Reggie."

Maggie can't help but raise an eyebrow at his slurred pronunciation.

"What do you mean? My son is charged with murder and subject to any number of bad influences working for you."

Maggie tries to interrupt. "Hank, no—"

Hank bumbles on, pointing in the air. "Your son Andy is engaged."

Reggie hesitates for only a moment, then sprays spittle. "That's impossible. I would know."

Maggie tries again. "Hank—"

"You would know if she wash Amish, and if you wern an asshole."

"What do you mean?"

"Surely thish isn't the first time someone has told you you're a jerk?"

"Not that."

"Penny. You met her in court. Pretty Indian girl. Cheyenne, right, Maggie?"

"I think so. But—"

Reggie's face turns crimson and he punches the air. "This will not stand."

Hank grins drunkenly. "You jus keep thinking that. Have a good day, Yoder."

Maggie considers correcting the situation, but Reggie Yoder is so completely unlikeable, she decides he deserves to stew in it. Andy can set him straight later.

FORTY-FOUR

After a quick stop at Walmart, Maggie and Hank return to the hospital. Something long-legged, blonde, and smelling like strawberry Lip Smacker rushes Hank at the door.

"Oh, Hank. You poor thing. Your mom. I'm so sorry." Sheila attaches herself to Hank like a baby koala to its mother, only a little less platonic.

Hank staggers back a step, but Sheila doesn't let go. Only the fact that Maggie is behind him saves them from toppling out the door and back onto the sidewalk.

"Uh, thanks." Hank pats his former almost-fiancée.

Maggie peels one of Sheila's arms off Hank and slings it back at her. Sheila glares from behind Hank's midsection. Maggie doesn't give a shit, so she slings off the other. Then she comes around Hank and gives Sheila a little push in the small of her back, to get her moving in the right direction. She nearly jams a finger on something hard. *Sheila's concealed gun, holstered high and tight.*

"Hello, Sheila." Maggie slides her arm through Hank's. "So nice of you to come."

"Well, when I heard, I just rushed right over. I've been comforting your sister, Hank."

Hank grumbles, "She's no sister to me."

Sheila looks confused.

Maggie mimes walking with her fingers.

"Where is she?" Hank's voice nears bellow level. "Laura?"

Sheila's voice catches. "She's up with your mother."

Maggie whispers, "It's about to get ugly."

Sheila's eyes flit to Maggie, to Hank, then back. She says, "I'll be praying for you, Hank," and leaves.

Suddenly, there's a loud, feminine wail from the far side of the lobby. "Hank."

Hank bows up, ready for battle, but when his tiny sister comes toward him, she's racked with sobs and walking with one hand on a couch back for support.

He runs to her. "What is it, sis?"

"Mom. Gone. Dead. Oh God, Hank. We've lost them both."

They fall together, their cries primal. When they release each other, Hank staggers to sit on the couch. He sinks down, his hat in one hand, his head in the other. Maggie sits beside him and slides herself under one of his shoulders. She wraps him in her arms and rocks him.

Long moments pass, and she becomes aware that Laura is sitting on the other side of Hank. Maggie looks across Hank's chest. The tips of Laura's hair are plastered against wet cheeks. Her face and neck are splotchy. She encircles her brother with her arms and grabs Maggie's elbow. The skin on Laura's hand is calloused and a little sandpapery, the palm small, and the fingers like the talons on a raptor. Her eyes meet Maggie's. She's given Maggie plenty of reason to hate her. But Laura is Hank's baby sister, and their mother and father are dead. Maggie puts her hand on Laura's elbow, so they're locked forearm to forearm.

"I'm sorry. I'm so sorry." Maggie gives the words a lullaby quality, repeating them over and over until both Sibleys start to breathe normally. "I'm so, so sorry."

"I know it's for the best." Laura's fingers dig even harder into Maggie's elbow. "She wouldn't have wanted what was coming for her. With the Alzheimer's."

Maggie feels a kinship with Laura in that moment. "My father had Alzheimer's. It was horrible. So bad that he killed himself."

Laura sits upright, her jaw slack and eyes round. "I didn't know. I'm sorry."

Face against Hank's chest, Maggie nods.

Laura stares out the window into the parking lot traffic. "Mickey's dad has cancer. And no insurance. That's why we need the money. For his treatment."

Hank lifts his ravaged face. "God, sis, why dincha just tell me?"

"He's embarrassed to be a hardship to his family. And Mickey feels like a failure because we don't have the money to help him."

"Thank you for telling us," Maggie says.

Laura gets to her feet, scrubbing at her eyes with her fist. "I told the nurse I'd be right back. There's paperwork."

"I'll come, too." Hank doesn't move.

"No. It's fine. I'll be back as fast as I can."

"I wanna say goodbye."

"They promised they'd let us know when it's time for that."

Hank nods. She leaves, looking back once at Maggie on her way out. Maggie wipes tears from Hank's face.

He focuses on her eyes. His words come out in a low croak. "Don't let me end up like my mom."

She grabs his face with both hands. "Oh, Hank. We all go somehow. Sometime."

"Promise me."

Maggie can't do that. "It will be okay, Hank. It won't be like this."

"I never gave her a gran'child."

"She had Farrah."

Hank shakes his head. "Who'm I kidding? I'll never have a child."

Maggie feels like a cold wind is blowing through her. They haven't talked about kids together. She hadn't thought about it much, but she realizes she assumed that they would have them, some way, somehow. "Why is that?"

"Because you're going back to Texas. Arnchoo?"

"I don't want to be anywhere without you," she says carefully, and reaches for his face again. Of course she has to go back and salvage her professional and financial situation. Is now really the time to discuss the complexity of her options, though?

He shucks her off, and stomps away unsteadily. Each step feels like it's landing in the middle of Maggie's chest.

FORTY-FIVE

A man's voice breaks through her consciousness. "Maggie. Wake up, Maggie."

Her eyes fly open in the dark. She throws an arm out, feeling for Hank. His side of the bed is cold and empty.

"Come to the window, Maggie."

"Hank?" She tries to crawl out from under the covers, but she's stuck, her pj's like Velcro against the flannel sheets. "Dammit." She kicks and makes it worse.

"Hurry, Maggie."

She stops, clutching the sheet. *It's not Hank's voice.* Her eyes drill into the dark, searching for movement or a shape, but she sees nothing. "Who's there?"

Downstairs, she hears a cracking sound. Her eyes jerk from the window to the door. She holds her breath. Two long, high-pitched scrapes. Then a thud.

Louise, she thinks. She calls for the dog. "Are you in here, girl?" There's no response. *Yes, it must have been the dog.*

The voice is a hiss now. "You've got to hurry."

Something about it is familiar. Compulsion overcomes fear and she finally wrestles out of the bedsheets and runs to the window. No one is there. She's hearing things. She presses fingertips to glass and gets her face as close to it as she can without fogging it over. The glass is cold.

"What is it?" she asks, then she snorts. Like she expects an answer from someone who isn't even here.

"Too slow, Maggie."

She gasps. Someone *is* in the room. But where? She scans the nooks and crannies, but movement snaps her attention outside. There's a shadowy figure moving along the road, toward the barn. Her eyes lose it in the dark. It must be Hank, which would account for his absence from bed. Or Gene. Or one of the hands. People move around the ranch at all hours, depending on weather or the needs of the animals.

An image mirrors in the window glass, a man behind her. Compact. Muscular. Dark. Handsome. Mustached. Paco?

She wheels. "Paco!"

But there's no one there.

A coldness seeps down Maggie's face that isn't from the window glass or the fall chill. What had Michael told her about knowing when she sees the spirits of dead people?

She knows.

She hugs herself. *There's nothing to be scared of, Maggie. Paco won't hurt you. If it's even him.*

But where is Hank?

She burrows back under the covers, knees to her chest, shoulders against the headboard, eyes popped wide and brain spinning over all she saw and heard, until the sun finally makes its dramatic morning appearance across the eastern sky.

Finally, she sleeps.

FORTY-SIX

Michael attaches a wireless camera to a mount on a tree facing the front door of the summer cabin. Maggie is logged into the cabin's passwordless Wi-Fi, setting up the system through her laptop. The cameras' base station she put in a cabinet by the front door. Maggie bought a two-camera package at Walmart the day before, when she was taking a drunk Hank back to the hospital. Hank. The Hank she hasn't seen since dinner at the ranch the night before. At breakfast, Gene told her not to worry, but it's hard.

She examines the feed on her laptop. "Looks good. Now let's sync the other camera and mount it facing the back door."

They quickly sync it and install it. Michael says as little as possible during the whole process. He seems to be waiting for the boom. For her questions about Penny and Andy. But she's too exhausted to quiz him.

It's more than that, though. After the weird events in the middle of the night, she's unsettled. In the barn at the feeding earlier, she kept looking over her shoulder. Here, now, she has a strange sensation that someone is watching her. She doesn't know if she's looking for the mysterious shadowy figure or Paco, but she knows her sonar is pinging like mad.

Maggie closes her laptop. "I think we can take off now. Thank you." She heads for Bess.

Michael follows her. It's his first time at the cabin, and while he has played it cool, she's seen his big, amazed eyes. She knows just how he feels. It's an impressive place.

He stops, head cocked. "Is someone living here?"

"Why do you ask?"

"The tire tracks on the road when we were driving up. And I thought I saw someone in the window upstairs just now."

Shadows and light, she thinks. *Don't let this rattle you, too.* But Hank had said the same thing the day before. "Hank and I were up here yesterday. But I don't see a vehicle. How could someone be up here without one?"

Michael shrugs. "They could park in the barn."

Her eyes cut to it then back to the cabin. He's right. It could be an unwelcome visitor. Or maybe this is where Hank hides out when he's not fit for human companionship. Could he have stayed here last night? For a second, she considers knocking on the door, but then gets in the truck instead. If Hank's in there, she doesn't want to talk to him in front of Michael. She can come back later, if Hank doesn't show up by lunch. *Or not,* she thinks, remembering the footprint Hank saw yesterday.

An hour later Maggie and Michael are back at the ranch building a goat pen. Michael warms slowly as it becomes clear that Maggie won't be badgering him. She clamps a goat panel to a green metal post. Michael hammers in another post with the T-post driver. She hears a grinding sound she can't identify and looks around for the source. Nothing seems to match it.

Michael's voice ends her search. "Last one." He wipes sweat from his brow with the inside of his shirt neck.

He's driven four more posts while she's been standing there in a daze. She's a mess. Maybe he won't notice.

"Thanks." She puts another clamp in place and grips it with pliers. Her hands shake.

"You okay?"

She twists the thick metal ends of the clamp. "I'm just thinking about Mrs. Sibley. I wish I'd built this pen for the goats before she died. They drove her crazy."

"I don't think the pen would have helped with that."

She half smiles. "You're probably right. I just feel guilty."

A shadow falls across the panel she's working on. "I've got it from here, Michael."

Michael snaps to attention. "Yes, sir, Mr. Sibley." He disappears with the driver and an extra post before Maggie can disentangle herself from the panel.

"I saw you coming back to the ranch in the truck with him."

But from where, Hank? She holds in the game of twenty questions she wants to throw him into, right before she whups his ass. It will go better if she lets him tell her of his own volition. "So?"

"He's a felon, Maggie. Trouble. You need to stay away from him."

"He *works* for you, Hank."

"For now."

His eyes are black and hollow. Maggie knows what that means. It steals her breath away. "Gotcha."

She brushes dirt from the seat of her pants. Hank takes the pliers from her and leans over at the waist to get a clamp, then kicks a leg out for balance. With his tool and clamp, he squats and fastens the panels to the posts far faster than Maggie. He works without speaking. When the last panel is secured, he leaves one side loose as a temporary gate. Maggie hands him a chain latch. He loops it through and clips it back on itself, testing it.

"You can keep Louise in here, too."

"Why? Is she causing problems?"

"She left a dead squirrel on the porch this morning."

"That. Okay."

The awkwardness between them gets worse as they walk to fetch the animals. She halters the goats. Hank takes Omaha, and she leads Nebraska. She whistles for Louise. The goats bleat and fight the leads the whole walk over. Louise meets them at the pen. Maggie closes the gate when all three are inside.

"Crap. I forgot to put their food and water in."

Hank walks to the barn without further comment.

Maggie stands at the pen, fuming. So he's done and just walks away, without even explaining where he was last night? Why can't he just tell her he runs to the summer cabin? Give her that little bit of comfort? Anger propels her forward. She marches into the barn with a head of steam. A farrier's truck is pulling away when she gets there. Grinding. Horseshoes, she realizes.

"Where the hell were—?" She runs into Hank, and a full bucket of water sloshes on her.

Hank lifts the bucket shoulder high. "Watch out."

Maggie slings water off her arms and brushes it from the front of her jacket and her jeans. Her indignation fades. "Thanks. I'll get their feed."

She catches up with Hank at the pen. Louise is sitting in front of the gate, sweeping dirt with her tail and looking hopefully into Hank's eyes.

"I think you're all set." His face is inscrutable. He turns to go.

"Wait."

He stops and faces her.

"Thank you."

"Of course." He takes a step back, pivots, and starts striding toward the barn again.

She raises her voice. "I was up last night. You were gone."

He freezes but doesn't turn back.

"I was worried. Where were you?"

"Couldn't sleep."

"Like I asked. Where were you?"

The pause is heavy.

"I needed to be alone."

His boots start crunching again, but she doesn't watch him go. She's too busy staring at the dirt. The old Maggie would tell him she didn't deserve his bullshit. But his mother just died. His brain injury is an issue. So the Maggie who's trying to make the relationship work won't rip him a new one yet. But she's not sure how much longer she can hold out.

FORTY-SEVEN

Laura and Hank leave for the funeral home before lunch. Maggie only knows this because she runs into them on their way out when she's coming to the house to wash up. Laura nods at her in a more friendly way than she has in the past. Hank isn't unfriendly. He just isn't anything, other than factual.

Maggie walks them to Hank's truck.

"Back before dinner," he says, and gets in the driver's seat.

She watches them drive away. They turn north at the ranch gate toward skies dark gray with the promise of a storm. Well, she's not just going to sit around here and mope all day. Andy is still facing trial for murder, and she needs to figure out whether Mary or her husband are viable suspects. And she has an idea about how to finagle a conversation with Mary.

Louise. The dog needs vaccinations, heartworm medicine, and an exam. She can't get signal, so she returns to the house and makes a call to the clinic.

"Sheridan Vet." The voice is raspy and bleak.

"Is Mary Marton working today?" Maggie asks.

"You a friend of hers?"

"Uh, yes, sort of."

"Yeah, she's here."

"I've taken in a stray. This will be her initial visit. Do you have any time to see her today?"

"Doc's going into surgery at one. How fast can you get here?"

"Forty-five minutes."

"Yeah, we can squeeze you in."

Maggie makes it to the clinic on the southeast side of Sheridan in forty-six minutes from the time she ended the call. Louise strains against the leash on the sidewalk, pulling Maggie along for frantic examinations of garden gnomes, dog statuary, and a sign that says DOG RELIEF AREA. Once inside the tiny lobby, Louise goes bananas. The bags of dog treats. The Chihuahua in her owner's lap. The cat carrier, filled with a hissing cat, sitting on a chair. Maggie hauls her to the front desk, away from the cowering Chihuahua owner with the judgmental eyes.

The woman behind the desk looks like she's wintered outside for forty years, with wind-tanned skin, furrows instead of wrinkles, and hair like a Brillo pad.

Maggie says to her, "I called about bringing in my new stray."

The woman nods. "Can you control it?"

"The dog?"

The woman looks down her nose at Maggie. "I'm not talking about your bladder, lady."

Maggie senses a soul sister. "Not so much."

"I'll put you in an exam room to wait, then."

"Thanks."

"Yes, thanks," the Chihuahua owner says, her voice snotty.

Maggie considers letting Louise go and imagines the satisfying havoc. But instead she and Louise walk behind the receptionist to a boxy room with a stainless steel examination table and a bench on one wall.

"Mary will be along shortly. Doc, too."

"Sounds good."

Not a minute later, the staff door opens. Mary's curves are mostly covered by blue scrubs.

Her face is puzzled. "Have we met before?"

Maggie sticks out her hand. Mary takes it and shakes before Maggie answers.

"Yes. I'm Maggie. Hank Sibley's girlfriend. We met at the Ox last week. And a few other times."

Mary's eyes widen. "Oh. Yes." She smiles. "Sorry about Sheila. She's not taking the breakup well."

Maggie doesn't want to talk about Sheila. "This is Louise. She's a stray from Piney Bottoms ranch. I'm pretty sure she's never had vet care before."

"They do their own preventative care out there."

"She's my personal pet."

"Gotcha." Mary runs through a list of questions about Louise, most of which Maggie can't answer. "We need to test her for heartworm before we can put her on a preventative. But I'll go get the rest of the vaccinations ready." She rattles off their names. "Do you want all of them?"

"Yes."

"Doc will be in to examine her in a minute."

Before she can leave, Maggie says, "So you dated Paco."

Mary's face blanches. "Can you keep it down?"

"Sorry." Maggie lowers her voice to a conspiratorial tone. "Penny said Paco told her your husband wasn't very happy about it."

"We're trying to make things work." Mary puts her hands on her hips. "Paco had a big mouth. Penny still does."

The staff door opens again. Doc Billy enters.

Maggie says, "Hello, Doc Billy. We've met, out at Piney Bottoms. I'm the one who rides Lily."

He nods distractedly. "I remember. Sorry to be in a rush. We've got a dog about to go under sedation." He starts examining Louise, poking and prodding her, and says over his shoulder, "Honey, tell me about the dog."

Mary shoots a look at Maggie. "Sure, Billy." She repeats what she knows about Louise to him.

Maggie stares between the two of them. She remembers Mary's Facebook page. Husband: William Marton. William. *Billy*. Doc Billy. Of course. Gears start to mesh in her mind. How nice that with Paco dead the two of them can try again. Then Maggie's mouth goes as dry as the Wyoming badlands. Whoever killed Paco had to have access to the ranch. Doc Billy is out at the ranch a lot. Sure, so are a lot of people. Even the farrier today. But Doc Billy had motive. And he knows about the dead pile.

"Maggie, are you okay?" Mary says.

"Fine. Yes. You were saying?"

"I asked you whether or not you'd like Louise on a flea, tick, and tapeworm preventative?"

"Um, sure."

"She looks healthy as a horse," Doc Billy says. He takes off his exam gloves. "Nice to see you again, Maggie."

He puts his hand on Mary's shoulder, and they walk out together.

"Holy shit," Maggie says to Louise. "Holy frickin' shit."

On her phone, she looks up the website of John Fortney's law firm for his contact information. Email, that's what she wants. She writes one to the attorney as fast as she can thumb-type and hits SEND. Her next call is to Travis. She leaves him a message about what she's learned. She hasn't completely lost faith in Sheridan County yet.

FORTY-EIGHT

Back at the ranch, Maggie is still riding high from her discovery at the clinic. She puts Louise back in with the goats. The weather is continuing to worsen, and it looks like the rest of the day will be best spent inside. She goes in and washes her hair. While she's drying it she checks her phone. She has an email from Fortney.

"The other-guy-did-it defense. Works for me. Thanks!"

She feels a sense of progress. When her hair is dry, she decides to bring Louise up to the house. She puts on a sweatshirt and a fleece jacket. As she's walking out to the pen, she hears a commotion at the barn over the sound of the wind.

Andy's voice. He's yelling. "Get back in there. No. All of you. No. Bad dog."

A barreling gust of wind hits. The temperature feels like it's dropping a degree a second. She zips her jacket collar to her chin. A fully enclosed Ranger approaches her. Andy and Michael are in it, dressed for a norther. She hustles to meet them. At least Andy doesn't know Michael is the reason Penny broke off their very short-lived engagement. Still, they both look tense.

On the passenger side, Andy cracks his door open.

"Louise let the goats out." Andy points in the distance. "And Lily."

"How'd she do that?" Maggie shouts to be heard over the idling engine. "No idea."

"I'm sorry."

"No, I am. There's a storm coming, and we've got to tend to the rest of the livestock. That dog is trouble, but she's crazy smart. They'll probably come in them own selves. But if they don't, best you wait for Hank, okay?"

She looks north. The dark gray sky feels like it's closing in on them. Already her fleece jacket isn't enough to ward off the cold. "Do you need my help out there?"

"No, but thanks. It's a two-man job."

"Be careful."

Andy salutes and Michael accelerates toward the ominous wall of clouds. The wind rumbles like a runaway freight train. Dirt swirls in the driveway. Even the eaves whistle. She scans the pastureland and ridgelines within sight. No big black mare. No little red goats. No fast, low-slung dog with flapping ears. Andy told her to stay put, but she can't do nothing. She'll just look around the central ranch grounds, stay close to the compound. But first she needs better clothes for the conditions.

While she's upstairs changing, she hears the front door slam against the wall.

"Hello?"

No one answers her. The sound of the wind increases, and it beats the door rhythmically against the wall downstairs. Whap. Whap. Whap. She hears scratching and bumping on the stairs, then a knock against her door.

Her heart does a flip-flop. "Who's there?"

The familiar sound of Louise trying to dig her way through the door breaks her tension. She opens the door, and fifty pounds of cold fur barrels into her legs.

"You're a bad girl." Maggie rubs the dog's ears to warm them.

Louise flops on the floor and wriggles. Maggie goes to the window to look for the other animals. Icy snowflakes pelt the glass, but she can still see down to the barnyard. Omaha and Nebraska are standing in the entrance to the barn, no fools they. But Lily is nowhere to be seen. Not at the barn, the paddocks, not grazing in the yard to the house. Somehow the thought of her with two noisy goats and a superhero dog wasn't as terrifying as the thought of her alone. Big and quiet, with a horse's predilection for injury, and a baby on board—Maggie doesn't like it.

Maggie runs down and shuts the front door, then finishes gearing up. She grabs her knife and scabbard along with the ATV driving goggles she uses against dust and sun. They should help with the blowing snow.

She opens the door, letting the storm in the great room with a whoosh of wind. "Come on, Louise."

The dog cowers behind the couch.

"Oh no. This is your fault. I need your help."

Reluctantly, the dog comes after her, hunkering low and moving fast. At the barn, Maggie puts the goats up in a stall. She grabs the keys to an extra Ranger and fires it up. Louise jumps into the seat beside her. Maggie drives out of the barn. Even with the plexiglass windshield and plastic doors, the wind comes right through. Louise hops down onto the floorboard, where she's more protected.

For fifteen minutes, Maggie drives in circles around the house. She grows more confident about driving and more concerned about Lily as time passes. By now, Maggie is wise to Lily's favorite flight paths. She's exhausted all her close-in spots. Maggie will have to go farther out.

For a moment, she second-guesses herself. Lily is a big, strong animal, and she's smart. But she's alone. And if anything happens to her, especially after fucking Louise let her out, Maggie will never forgive herself. If only she'd kept Louise inside. It's her fault.

Despair wells up in her. She's failing at this ranch-hand thing. Failing like she fails at everything. Faking it like she's faking everything these days. Faking at being a Crow. At being a Wyomingite. At being a girlfriend. Things are so much easier for her in Texas. She knows how to be a junker, a washed-up singer, and a free-and-easy single woman. Suddenly, it's hard to breathe. All her life she's been the risk-taker, ready to jump. Running off to Nashville at seventeen. Touring the country playing for tips at eighteen. Even trading the rights to her recordings for her shop and house in Giddings in her early twenties had been a huge risk.

But those risks had been about her music and her livelihood. Now that it's her heart at stake, it's not nearly so easy to be brave and real. To tell Hank she loves him. To commit to a future with him. To confront him about not shutting her out.

Going after Lily isn't nearly as hard as those things. She points the Ranger into the wind and guns the engine. Whether Maggie is faking it or not, Lily is out there, and Maggie's the only one who can help her.

FORTY-NINE

An hour has passed, and there's been no sign of Lily. The snow is falling horizontally, and it's almost a whiteout. Maggie follows fence lines to keep herself from getting lost. Twice she's come upon hulking black objects, but both times she finds cows huddled in small groups. Sweat drips down her face. How can she be so cold and so hot at the same time? She wiggles her fingers. There's barely any feeling in them or her toes. She's not sure how much longer she can stay out here. The gas gauge on the Ranger doesn't work, and running out of gas in this storm would be bad news for a flat-lander like her.

It's time to head back in. She hates it, but she knows it is.

She decides to make a circuit of the fence in one last pasture, even though it's not one of Lily's haunts. The land out here is wild, she knows, prone to unseen gulches, rock formations, steep hills, mini-cliffs, and irriga-tion ditches. There's no two-track inside this fence as there has been in the others. The Ranger putts along slow and steady, up, down, and over terrain and obstacles unfamiliar to her.

Suddenly the steering wheel is wrenched from her hands, and the whole unit tips. With no seatbelt to hold her in place, Maggie braces herself against the steering wheel and floorboard. The Ranger lands on its side, ripping its door apart. Louise falls on top of Maggie's side, but Maggie manages to hold them both suspended over the snowy, rocky ground. The roof is on the downhill side, and the ATV begins to slide. Snow and mud cover Maggie head to toe in seconds. There's a painful scraping sound and the Ranger comes to a jarring stop.

"Oomph." Maggie shakes her arms and legs and rotates her neck. She's all right.

But the Ranger isn't. She opens the other door. Dog and woman crawl out. Maggie takes a few steps around the Ranger to inspect it. There's no way she can right the thing. She feels as much as hears a crunch and finds her driving goggles under her boot.

"Come on, Louise." Maggie scrambles on her hands and knees to the top of the ravine. She holds her hands out and walks slowly until she finds the fence, which just skirts the top of it, leaving no room for an ATV to pass, which would explain why she ended up at the bottom of the little gulch.

Just as she's about to retrace their path and start the long, cold walk home, she hears a whinny.

"Lily!"

A horse whinnies again. In the wind and weather, Maggie can't get a fix on the direction the sound is coming from. She doesn't even know for sure if it is Lily. But she can't go back in without checking, when the horse is so close.

She follows the fence out in the direction they'd been headed, calling every few seconds. Without the goggles, Maggie is nearly blind, even with her scarf wrapped around her forehead as a shield. She and Louise trudge on.

Then Louise barks once, a shrill yip. Maggie takes another step, then another, calling for Lily, and runs into something large and unyielding.

FIFTY

Maggie screams and jumps back, but not before she realizes the something is also warm, and it snorts. She moves back to it and brushes snow from a big animal's back and uncovers black fur. She works her way to the head and gets a big puff of Lily's breath in her face.

She smashes her face into Lily's long, hard one, holding the horse's head with both hands. "You big, dumb horse. What are you doing out here? Why do you always have to be so damn independent? Look what it gets you. In trouble. Alone." She lifts her head, kisses Lily's velvety muzzle. "Let's go home."

Maggie is wearing a halter and lead over her torso, bandolier style. Lily submits easily to them. But when Maggie gives the lead a tug, the horse doesn't move an inch. Steadily increasing pressure does nothing either. Lily huffs.

"What's the matter, girl?" Maggie strokes her nose. She gets out her phone and uses the flashlight to inspect the animal.

Barbed wire is wrapped around three of Lily's legs. Panic rises like a tsunami in Maggie's chest. "Oh no, Lily. Don't move."

She pulls her knife from the scabbard. But Lily isn't in rope and bramble like last time she'd rescued her. This is wire. And what good is a knife against wire?

Think, Maggie, think. She's going to have to unwind the wire to get Lily free. Thank God the horse is standing still instead of giving in to the instinct to fight against pressure. Squatting, Maggie searches hand over hand for an end to the wire. She can't unwrap Lily only to send her into more. She traces the piece to a post, where she finds four individual strands attached, all of which lead back to Lily. A whole fence's worth.

There are no ends. The fence is down. Lily walked into it.

Okay. That's all right. You can do this. One strand at a time.

She crouches by the least tangled strand. Louise presses against her, and Maggie appreciates the dog's warmth and loyalty. "It's okay, Lily. Good girl." She takes a deep breath and starts pulling the wires apart, inch by inch. Her gloves are shredded in seconds. She takes them off and works bare-handed. Now the wire nips at her skin. Blood drips into the snow, and she's not sure if it is coming from her or the horse. The cold makes her fingers stiff. She can barely feel the wires. Lily snorts and shifts her weight, but she doesn't move her feet, even when Maggie removes barbs embedded in her hide.

"Such a good girl, Lily." She strokes the horse's belly, then gets back to work.

It takes about ten minutes for Maggie to liberate the first strand. She moves it as far as she can out of the way, then repeats the process with the other three pieces. It's hard to stick with it. Her feet feel like pincushions from the cold. The wind is burning her face and making her eyes water so badly that she can barely see what she's doing. But she can't give up, and she's desperately glad she came. Lily was—is—in trouble and needs her.

When she finally has all the barbed wire far to one side of the mare, she runs her numb hands up and down Lily's legs. Her fingers come away bloody. She sweeps her forearms under Lily's enormous belly. The foal kicks out. Her arms come away bloody.

Maggie tries not to panic. It's a long way back to the ranch house, and Lily is injured. It's too dark to see how badly. She can only assume it's better to walk her in than to leave her out here, but what does she know? Moving her could make it worse. There's no one here to make the decision for her, though. She puts her tattered gloves back on and makes the call—they're going home.

"Come on, big girl."

This time, Lily offers no resistance to being led. They walk the fence in the blowing snow, the only sounds their breathing and the wind. Occasionally, Maggie has to high-step through drifts above her knees. Louise lunges and leaps to get through them and disappears under snow with each landing. The exercise keeps Maggie's core warm, although now she's sweating so hard her clothes are wet from the inside out. The only thing really cold anymore is her face, feet, and hands, and the ripped gloves aren't helping matters much. At times she can't feel the rope in her hands. Or, when she does, the line is so slack she doesn't think Lily is back there. But she is. The horse knows where they are going, and she's on board.

Time slows to a crawl. Maggie isn't sure how long it takes them to reach the two-track at the corner of the pasture. It could have been fifteen minutes or it could have been an hour. She's tired. Very tired. And sleepy. In her flashes of alertness, she has a new worry. What if she passes out?

In the distance, she sees lights blinking. At first, she's worried she's taken a wrong turn. Those can't be the ranch lights. But then she sees them moving. It's some kind of vehicle. But who, and how far away?

"Hey!" she yells. "Over here." *Idiot. They can't hear you. They can't even see you.*

She urges the horse and dog faster, worried about Lily hurting herself worse, but even more worried they'll freeze to death in their own dead pile. The snow is packed somewhat from her Ranger tracks, so the going is easier. Trotting, they make the next fence line, intersecting the path of the approaching lights. Maggie waves frantically, which makes Lily back a step. Maggie loses her balance and falls after the horse onto her butt. She hears the puny honk of an ATV, and Maggie waves from the ground in relief.

FIFTY-ONE

Michael doctors Lily as the storm rages against the barn walls.

"Is she going to be okay?" Maggie asks.

"Yeah." He pats the mare's haunch. "Horses heal fast. Faster than people. You'll hurt worse than she does."

Maggie's hands had looked like bloody pincushions, purple and swollen from cold, but they're washed, dabbed with ointment, and wrapped now. "Do we need to call in the vet?" Doc Billy isn't someone she trusts or wants to see. But she'll suck it up, if Lily needs him.

"Nah. She's good. Can I walk you back to the house? We'll be fired if we lose you twice in one day."

Andy walks into the barn, dusting snow off his jacket. He doesn't look at Michael, and Maggie feels the ongoing tension between them.

"How'd you know I was gone the first time?"

Andy answers. "I was closing up the barn, and the Ranger was missing. Didn't take much to figure after that, since you and that mutt were gone, too. You didn't even take one of the walkie-talkies." He puts one back on the charging station. "So I took one and waited here, and Michael went with the other in the ATV."

"I'm so sorry. I feel like an idiot. I'll take the offer of the escort, Michael, but let me feed Lily first."

Maggie mixes an ounce of Mare Magic in sweet feed. She hopes it's helping strengthen Lily's uterus, because it hasn't stopped her running off.

Maggie opens a stall door and pours feed into a trough. Then she leads the horse in.

"What will I do about you when I'm back in Texas?" Lily doesn't appear to listen, all her attention on the oats, corn, and molasses. "I sure can't go until after your foal comes." She thinks about the appointment she made to meet with the contractor. Maybe she can push it back some.

"What happened here?" Hank is standing in the doorway to the barn.

Andy has disappeared. Michael is cleaning up veterinary supplies. His hands and clothes are stained with blood.

Michael looks nervous. "Lily got out, then caught herself in some barbed wire."

Hank's eyes lift. He looks in Lily's stall and sees Maggie, with her two bandaged hands. "Maggie." He hurries to her and grabs her by the wrists, holding her hands in the air. "What happened to you?"

"Lily's barbed wire."

"You went out with them to get her?"

"Not really."

Hank frowns. "What does that mean?" Then he turns to Michael. "Give us the barn, please."

Michael doesn't need to be asked twice. "I have to meet someone in town anyway. Chores are all done. Good night."

"Good night, Michael." Maggie lifts her chin at Hank. "I went alone."

"How?"

"A Ranger. And I remembered to take this." She holds up her knife in its scabbard, hoping to lighten the mood.

He glowers, his eyes taking inventory around the barn. Maggie sees the second he starts counting machinery and comes up short.

"Where's the Ranger?" he demands.

"About that. I'll pay for the damage."

"You wrecked it?"

"I'm really sorry."

"You could have gotten yourself killed out there."

"But I didn't. And Louise and Lily are fine, too."

"You're too damned independent for your own good. But I guess that shouldn't surprise me. You've been running off since the day I met you."

"I didn't run off. I went to find Lily. That fucker Louise had let her out. Michael and Andy told me not to go, but I wasn't going to be able to live with myself if she got hurt or died."

"Great. You could have gotten the hands killed, too."

"But I didn't."

"And every time I turn around, you're holed up with Michael."

"That's ridiculous."

"Maggie, I'm having a rough week, in case you haven't noticed. I need something I can count on. You're not it."

Her first thought is that his brain injury is making him irrational. "Bullshit. You can count on me and you know it."

"Really?" He points at her. "I read your phone last night."

"You what?"

"You have meetings set up with contractors in Texas. Next week."

A meeting. Singular. Her second thought was that the pot was sure the hell calling the damn kettle black, but she's too busy defending herself to point it out. "I was going to tell you. There hasn't been a chance."

"But you didn't." Hank stomps out of the barn.

"I was going to reschedule," she calls after him. Then, softer, "I'm sorry."

He disappears into the snow. Then she realizes what she should have said instead, those words she can't get out. That she loves him. Because she does. She's in love with Hank, and she wants to help him through his injury and the loss of his mother. She's in love, and it feels fucking . . . terrifying. Can she do this love thing? Because right now it feels like she's messing it up big-time.

Maggie shuts Lily in her stall, then walks alone through the storm back to the house. She enters, then sinks back against the door and sits on her heels with her head in her hands.

FIFTY-TWO

Maggie wakes to the sound of loud snoring. She smiles. Hank. She rolls over, and Louise licks her face.

"Not you, Fucker."

Thump-thump-thump goes a tail.

Hank had been here when she fell asleep—sullen, uncommunicative—but he's clearly not here now. She wishes she'd found the courage to tell him how she feels. She kept waiting last night, waiting for a perfect time that didn't come. But in the light of day, she knows the perfect time is a fallacy. *Now* is the perfect time, and *now* passes by all too quickly. Case in point, Mrs. Sibley's funeral is set for Tuesday. Time marches on. People lose each other. She needs to make the most of every moment with Hank.

"Hank?" she calls.

No answer from the bathroom or hallway. He's probably already out working, because of the storm. Animal welfare comes first. Maggie's nose is cold and her breath makes an icy cloud in front of her face. Sunlight is streaming through the window. Her phone sounds a notification from the bedside table. She picks it up. It's a motion alarm from the cameras at the summer cabin. In the small picture on her phone and with her bleary eyes, she sees the figure of a man, thick like he's bundled against the weather. Then her phone rings. *Hank.* She can't read the caller ID. She picks up anyway.

"Hello?"

"Hello, honey. It's Mom."

"Mom. Good morning. What time is it?"

"Seven thirty."

"Which makes it six thirty here."

"Oh no, did I wake you?"

Ya think? "It's fine. What's up?"

"I led women's Bible study at my house last night, and I just wanted you to know that it came over my heart that we should pray for you. We set up a prayer chain, and I've been calling the entire congregation this morning."

"Why? What did I do this time?" She checks the irritation in her voice. She shouldn't complain. She can use all the help she can get. "Never mind. I know why."

"Is it so bad to want you where you belong?"

"And where is that?"

"Back here, happily married, within your own faith?"

"Mom, I think we've been doubling back on this tired old gene pool long enough. Besides, don't you think that's ironic coming from a woman who just married outside the faith?"

"He's a Christian."

Maggie thinks of the Amish Christians, the Wendish Christians, Edward's Catholic faith, and Hank's cowboy Christian. There's Christian, and then there's Christian. "So is Hank."

"Everyone needs their own people, Maggie."

"I've got what I need."

"Do you? You're just like your mother."

"You're my mother."

"No, your birth mother. Running off from everyone and everything good in her life."

"Who says I'm running?" Her mother's words ring in her ears, an echo of Hank's. "Mom, this conversation is going nowhere. Thank you for praying for me. I love you. Now, I have to go. It's time for breakfast here. I'll talk to you soon."

"Maggie—"

Maggie ends the call and presses her fist to her mouth. Her mother thinks she's running from Texas. Hank's accusing her of running from Wyoming, and him. They can't both be right. But they could both be wrong. She's not running. She isn't.

And she's nothing like her birth mother.

The phone rings again. Sighing, she answers. She shouldn't have hung up on her mom.

"I'm sorry."

"Good, so meet me for breakfast at the Busy Bee." Not her mother.

"Who is this?"

"Amos. Is your caller ID not working?"

"I'm hanging up now."

"No. Not until I tell you I'm sorry."

"This I have to hear. Sorry for what?"

"For before. When you were on my radio show. I was a different person back then. I was angry at you for a long time. I blamed you that I was fired after that. But I don't anymore. I caused my own problems. And if I hurt you, I'm sorry."

"That's a lot of sorry to absorb."

"I think that's why I started writing about you. I've been following you a long time. For no good reason. I don't want revenge. I just needed to say that."

"What if I don't forgive you?"

"That's okay. And I still want to finish my story on you. Can you meet me?"

Louise noses her hand—sore, but unbandaged—and Maggie massages the dog's floppy ears. She wriggles until her upper body is splayed over Maggie's. Maggie chews her lip. She hasn't made up her mind about recording with Ava, but if she does, publicity sells records. The redemption of Aaron Cryor and Maggie Killian, two for the price of one. And isn't it far better if it's on her own terms? He's going to write about her anyway. This could be a trial balloon. If it were to go well, maybe she'd give Amos an interview with her and Boyd.

"Fine."

"One of these days, you're going to—Wait. Did you say 'fine'?"

"Yes."

"You won't regret it. What time?"

"How are the roads?"

"Bad, I think. But this is Wyoming. The plows have probably been out all night."

"Give me an hour. If I'm not there, order me scrambled eggs, hash browns, and bacon. And coffee. A lot of coffee."

FIFTY-THREE

Trudy is changing channels on the big-screen TV in the community room when Maggie gallops down the stairs in heavy winter boots. She fastens her scabbard to the belt loop of her jeans, then pulls her long, loose sweater over it. She straightens the Frontier Days belt that makes the sweater like a tunic. Today she's not driving off anything less than fully prepared for whatever Wyoming has to dish out.

"Wait. You missed breakfast. Let me bring you a biscuit and some coffee."

"I'm having breakfast in town. But thanks. Hey, have you seen Hank?"

Trudy returns her attention to the TV. "He took off after breakfast in the truck."

So he was at the ranch for breakfast. Maggie doesn't like that he didn't say good morning or goodbye. In fact, she's pissed about it. He could have texted. Left a note. Called. She's sick of him acting like the world is ending and she's not his partner. His mother died. It's very, very sad. But not her fault.

Maggie's voice is bright as she adds a scarf, wool cap, and mittens to her gear. "Okay, thanks. If you see him, tell him I'm in Buffalo."

"Will do. Be careful. The roads are bad."

Fingers flying, Maggie texts Hank. *WTF, cowboy? Maybe I should start taking off without telling you, too?* Her thumb hovers. She can tell him herself that she's going to Buffalo in this text. Or not. She hits SEND.

Maggie waves goodbye to Trudy, who heads back into the kitchen. Maggie opens the door. A frigid wind knocks her back. She tucks the scarf into the neck of her puffy jacket and wraps the end over her face. Louise bounds out, dipping her nose in the snow and tossing some in the air with her mouth. Maggie stomps to her truck. It isn't deep—maybe three or four inches—and it's powdery soft. She turns on her truck to let it heat up while she gets after her windshields with an ice scraper. This isn't going to be a warm or fun ride to town. A quick double check confirms she has a shovel, towrope, and chains in the bed and a blanket, bag of kitty litter, waters, flares, a first aid kit, and food bars of some sort under the front seat. Absent a satellite phone, she's remote-Wyoming-ready.

Forty-five slow and careful minutes later, she pulls into Buffalo. Amos was right. The plows were out, and the interstate is snow- and ice-free. But when she nears the Busy Bee, she discovers a police blockade in front of the courthouse.

She rolls to a stop and an officer comes to her window. It's Detective Lacey, a cop she became much too familiar with back in August when he zeroed in on Maggie as a murder suspect. His white-blond hair almost blends with the snow. His light blue eyes crinkle at the corners when he recognizes her. She'd pretty much solved his case for him, and she's not sure how he feels about that. Spoiler alert: the murderer wasn't her.

"Ms. Killian. Good to see you back. We've got a detour. If you can just turn right here, and skirt the downtown area, please."

"What happened?"

He checks the road behind her. It's clear of approaching vehicles. "Don't quote me on this, but there was a double murder back there." He points at the parking lot behind the courthouse.

Maggie's familiar with it. She'd parked there just last week when she and Andy went to the Thursday Night Jam at the Ox. "Oh my God. Who was it?"

"I don't know anything other than they're early twenties, an Indian girl and boy. And if I did know, I couldn't tell you until we notify next of kin. But keep it to yourself, okay?" He motions her on as another car pulls up behind her.

Maggie coasts along, thinking about the boy and girl found dead. Her stomach clenches. It's not like there aren't lots of Native Americans in the area, plenty of them in their early twenties, but the fact that she knows two has her heart in a vice grip. She cuts her wheels hard to the left, sliding across two lanes of oncoming traffic. Her tires lose traction and she slams into the curb hard enough that a newer truck would have deployed airbags. Her forehead bangs against the steering wheel.

"Shit."

She takes a moment to straighten the truck, then pushes in the clutch and turns off the ignition. She run-skates as fast as she can across the lawn of the Sheridan College annex, to the courthouse parking. When she's almost there, she slips on an icy patch and goes down hard on her tush.

"Son of a bitch."

She stares at the sky, her neck jarred and her butt smarting, a painful reminder of being thrown by Lily. When she's back on her feet, she moves more slowly, all the way to the police tape. An ambulance is parked fifteen feet away. She sees booted feet, pointed toes-up. Another set with the toes of the boots splayed. Nothing definitive for identification, until her eyes fall on the beat-up banjo case covered in bumper stickers. Even from where she's standing, she can see her own signature scrawled on it.

Penny.

With all the death in her life in the last few months, Maggie should be used to the blow to her solar plexus. But she's not. She clutches her midsection. Penny was an enigma. Maggie hadn't been in favor of Andy marrying her. But she was a living, breathing person, a beautiful girl, and a talented musician. She didn't deserve to be killed. Few people do.

One of the crime scene techs stands up, holding something in her gloved hand. Her movement leaves a sightline to the two people on the ground. The boy has a strong, recognizable profile.

It's Michael, Maggie is sure of it. She stifles a cry with her mittened fist. She can't tear her eyes away. She'd grown to care about him. Talks to Eagles had been kind to her. He'd be telling her right now that his spirit is heading skyward for another conversation with his friend.

The crime scene tech turns. A black object in her hand catches Maggie's attention. It looks like a knife. Maggie leans as far as she can across the barrier, then nearly collapses when she gets a crystal-clear view of a Double S logo. Hank's knife.

FIFTY-FOUR

Maggie can't get back on the road to Piney Bottoms fast enough. She drives without conscious thought, the miles flying by without her worrying anymore about the conditions. Just as she's slowing to take the exit from the interstate, an owl flies in front of the truck. A witch, Michael would have said. *And Louise not here to protect me.*

Maggie jerks her foot off the gas and fights the urge to swerve, but her automatic reaction is faster. The truck rumbles off the highway. If she over-corrects now, she'll flip back onto the blacktop. If she doesn't correct, she'll go over the embankment and down a good thirty feet before she hits the bottom. Holding her breath, she steers gently back toward the off-ramp and braces her leg under the steering wheel. The wheels grab pavement, and she navigates into the lane. The exit is steep and curved, so she isn't able to stop until she's made it safely through her turn and is on flatter road.

She pulls over, panting.

Her life is so out of control. She could have died back there. She could have died yesterday in the ravine under a Ranger. Or frozen to death on top of the ridge tangled in barbed wire and stomped by a giant, pregnant horse. And all the deaths around her. She's never been around so much death as these last three months. Just within the last week, Paco was murdered, Mrs. Sibley has died, and now Penny and Michael are gone, too—Hank's knife beside their bodies.

She shudders. Hank's knife may have killed them. A knife that anyone who enters the ranch house could have taken, but that was in Hank's bedroom. Hank, who had disappeared in the night. Who's volatile and physical, and under emotional and physical pressure right now. Who's protective of her when it comes to Michael.

No. Other people have stronger motives. Mary was jealous of Penny. Andy had reason to hate Michael, and to resent Penny for breaking their engagement. It can't be Hank.

She realizes she's clutching the steering wheel with both hands, and that her arms and shoulders are rigid. She lets go, flexes her fingers. Her breathing slows down. Her heart eases in her chest, although it feels like it's left her bruised from its wild pounding. She picks up her phone, not to call anyone, but because it makes her feel connected to the rest of the world. Convinces her she's not dead in a snowdrift on the side of the interstate.

But of course she sees messages.

Amos: *Are you coming?*

Hank: *Where are you?*

Charlotte: *Why did you hang up on me?*

She gets a strong image of Lily in the barbed wire, except in her mind she's the one trapped.

To Amos: *Almost home. Must reschedule. Sorry.*

To Hank she thinks about telling him about the murders over text, but decides against it: *On my way back from Buffalo. I have to talk to you. Are you at the ranch?*

Her mother she skips. She'll deal with her later. Right now, she has to get back to the ranch and break the news to Andy before he hears Penny is dead from someone else.

Maggie runs into the house. Hank's truck isn't out front, but she calls for him. "Hank?"

Trudy appears, wiping her hands on a flour-dusted apron. "He's not back."

Maggie is out of breath. "Andy?"

"Nope. What's wrong?"

Maggie sprints to the barn without answering Trudy. "Andy, are you in here?" She hears a vehicle engine outside, then it shuts off. Footsteps, soft thuds in the snow, approach.

Andy appears from the hayloft. "Yes?" His head cocks, his eyes study her. "What's wrong?"

Maggie doesn't have time to explain before a Buffalo police officer walks in. Lacey.

"Ms. Killian."

"You're off traffic duty."

He nods and looks up at Andy. "Andrew Yoder?"

"Yes."

"I'm Detective Lacey, Buffalo Police Department. I'd like to ask you to come with me."

"Is he under arrest?" Maggie steps between the detective and Andy. Her need to protect him is strong, even as a horrible place inside her tells her that if they focus on Andy, they won't suspect Hank.

"No, just some questions for him."

"About what? What's going on?" Andy's confusion is giving way to panic, and his voice rises in pitch.

"Do you know a Penny Short and a Michael Short?"

Short. Both were named Short. Maggie doesn't understand. Were they *married?* Separated? Divorcing? That might explain Michael's reaction to Andy.

"Yes. Why?" Then he groans. "Oh God, no. Please, God, no. Don't let something have happened to Penny." Andy lurches and falls a few steps into the wall, where he holds himself up.

"Where were you last night, sir?" the officer asks.

"I, um, here?"

"Do you have any witnesses to corroborate your whereabouts between ten p.m. and four a.m.?"

Andy's eyes are wide and wild. "N-n-no, sir."

"They were murdered. We'd like to talk to you about it."

Andy nods. Tears gather in his eyes.

"Can't you talk to him here?" she says.

"We'd prefer not to."

She knows what Andy will say before he says it.

"It's fine."

Maggie takes his arm. "You know the drill, Andy. You're riding with me." She'll just have to tell Hank and Gene later. Andy is the first priority now.

FIFTY-FIVE

In the police department reception area, Maggie waits for Andy. She kills time rearranging her schedule for the next week and soul-searching her options in Texas—Hank's absence makes it impossible to reach a decision. She'd thought Hank would respond after she group-texted him and Gene about Michael and Penny. Gene had. He was upset and also understandably worried about the ranch and finding a replacement for Michael, even more so after she told him the police had Andy in for questioning. She hadn't heard back from Hank.

"Ms. Killian?" the receptionist says.

Maggie gets up and walks over to her. "Yes?"

"Detective Lacey asked me to tell you he expects a long interview. Would you like me to text you when they're done?"

"Yes. Thank you." She recites her phone number.

Freed, Maggie walks down Main Street, with no enthusiasm for the cute stores. Luckily, she runs into Amos. She lets him interview her over a cup of coffee at the Busy Bee. It goes well enough. He'd heard about the murders and their link to Double S, but he doesn't spin it as related to her. At least not to her face. When they're done, she gets up to go.

"I really am sorry about before," he says.

"Thank you."

"I'll send you a link when I post an article."

"I hope I didn't make a mistake talking to you."

"You didn't. And text me if you have any news. Please."

"I'm not newsworthy."

"Let me be the judge of that."

Back outside, she stands at the railing of the bridge over Clear Creek and calls Travis, even though he'd never called back after her message about Mary and Doc Billy.

He picks up. "Ms. Killian."

"Deputy. Thanks for taking my call."

"I got a call from Lacey in Buffalo."

"So you already know about the deaths there."

"Long since."

She takes a quarter from her pocket and feeds it into a machine that dispenses fish food. Doling the pellets out one by one, she watches the trout dart from the shadows for the treats. "You're the one that pointed them toward Andy, aren't you?"

"I mentioned his name."

She throws another pellet. "I'm in Buffalo now, waiting on the police here to be done with him."

"And you're calling me why?"

"Andy and Penny were engaged." *With an emphasis on were*, she thinks, but doesn't elaborate. With Michael and Penny dead, who will there be to contradict the old information?

"So?"

"He adored her. He wouldn't hurt a hair on her head." A fish jumps out of the water to beat a competitor to a pellet.

"The greater the love, the greater the crazy. That's what we've been discussing with respect to your relationship."

She tosses the rest of the food, creating a frenzy in the water below. The fish thrash, their bodies like writhing serpents. Then the food is gone, and the turmoil ends. "I've never discussed my relationship with you."

"Fine. We've talked about Hank, then."

This is a subject she wants to avoid at all costs. "Did you follow up on the information I gave you about Mary Marton and Doc Billy yet? There's got to be something there. Mary was very jealous of Penny."

"Maggie, you're like a horse with blinders on. I'm doing my job. Now, if there's nothing else?"

Horse with blinders? Takes one to know one. "No. Nothing. You have a nice day, Detective."

She hangs up, fuming, and checks her texts. *Travis is*

so . . . so . . . so . . . smug. And close-minded. Nothing from the police department receptionist. The gurgle of the creek is less now that the water level is
fall-low, but it's still soothing. Taking deep breaths, she lets it do its magic
on her until she's breathing calmly and freely again. She can only think of
one more way to pass time, so she takes Bess to the gas station, parks at a
pump, and starts filling her up.

"Maggie." A female voice makes her name a statement instead of a
question or greeting.

Sheila. *What the hell is she doing in Buffalo?* Maggie looks at the display
on the pump. She has a long way to go before the tank is full. "Sheila. You
get around."

"I'm interviewing for an assistant principal's job here, not that it's any of
your business."

Young, pretty, and ambitious. God, how Maggie hates this woman. "Do
they need a character reference? I'd be happy to talk to them."

Sheila flips her hair, with her middle finger raised. "Where's Hank?"

Maggie gives her a dirty look.

"You don't know where he is, do you?" Sheila's smile is wide.

Maggie doesn't answer.

"I'll bet you were wondering if he was with me."

"As a matter of fact, no."

"Go ahead, ask me."

"Eff off, Sheila."

Sheila's boot heels grind salt as she walks into the c-store. Maggie
swears she can hear her laughing. The nozzle clicks off. She returns it to the
gas pump and puts the cap back on the tank, seething at Hank for going
AWOL, at Sheila for general bitchiness, and at herself for letting Sheila
manipulate her. Suddenly Maggie remembers that when Hank was sort of
engaged to Sheila, he'd disappeared and ended up tied up in Maggie's bed.
Never mind that Maggie wasn't the one who tied him up and that he nearly
died, the fact remained that Hank had gotten cold feet and come after
an ex.

No. That was different. He hasn't been with Sheila. Maggie and Hank
are meant to be together. They both know it. It's why she's in Wyoming and
sticking by a man with traumatic brain injury and unexplainable behavior.
Shit. It doesn't sound good when she thinks about it that way. Is she being a
fool? Even if Hank hasn't done anything worse than act erratically, is she
crazy to hitch her wagon to him? She doesn't have to sign on for a life of
helping him through the ups and downs from his old injury.

Does she?

A text notification comes in from the receptionist at the police station. Andy is ready for her. She pushes her worries about Hank to the back of her mind for now.

Less than five minutes later, Andy is in the truck, wringing his hands. "Thank you. For everything."

"Of course. I'm so sorry about Penny. And Michael, although I know the two of you didn't get along that well."

His eyes are vacant. "She was in a family way."

Maggie doesn't understand. "What?"

"Penny. She was going to have a baby."

"Oh my God." Whose baby? She can't ask Andy.

"She was going to let me be the father, too. Until Michael messed it up."

Panic laps at Maggie. Did Andy kill Penny and Michael? "What are you saying?"

"I have to go home."

Even if he killed them, he's not a danger to her. This is Andy, after all. What was done in the heat of passion is not the core of who he is. "I'll get you back to Piney Bottoms as fast as I can."

"No, I mean I need to go to *my* home. In Montana."

She knows he's devastated. He's also even more exhausted than she is. But she doesn't get it. If anything, the Andy she knows would feel an even greater sense of responsibility to the ranch with Michael gone. "What's going on, Andy? Why home now?"

He wipes tears from his eyes, a furtive gesture. "I have to talk to my mother. I've brought shame on my family. She has to know from me I ain't done this, before she hears it from anyone else. I should have done it before, after Paco died, but it didn't seem real. Now it does. And I have to get to her."

Maybe he didn't kill anyone. God, she hopes not. "Okay. Do you want me to make a call for you to find a ride?"

He stares at his hands. "Could you maybe take me?"

"Um, no problem." She gets her phone out. "I need a minute, then we can be on our way."

His voice is strangled. "Thank you."

She texts Hank. WHERE ARE YOU? *I'm taking Andy home to Montana. I need your help.* She stares at the phone. *I need YOU.* She sends it, willing Hank's text bubble to appear. Willing a response to come in from him.

She gets nothing.

She gallops her fingernails on the steering wheel. Who is she kidding? Trusting Hank was a huge mistake. She needs to kick the rest of her life into gear. What was the name of that real estate agent who offered to list her place? She scans through her emails until she finds what she's looking for: an email from Trish Jasper. The woman's number is in it. Her finger hovers over it. She has to move forward. She can't stand still. She pushes it.

"This is Trish Jasper. May I help you find your dream home today?"

"Maybe. This is Maggie Killian."

"Maggie! Are you calling to list your property? That ranch you had your eye on is still for sale, too."

"I want to list my place. Ten acres and a damaged barn—the house and shop are a total loss and I'm bulldozing what's left of them. Then I need you to find me a new place, less land, with a house and barn already in place. Not the ranch. I'll be using the sale proceeds to pay for the new place, and not a cent more." She doesn't mention the insurance payout. She'll need that to finish out a new store and restock inventory.

"How exciting. Are we in agreement on a listing price for your place?"

She names the number from their last conversation.

They're not, but what choice does she have? "That's fine."

"Great! I'll get the listing up within the hour and have someone out to take pictures later today. But honestly, I think one of my clients will have an offer in to you by tomorrow. And watch for an email from me tonight with some properties for you to preview."

The answer should make her feel good, but it does the opposite. "Thanks."

Maggie hangs up and puts the truck in gear. Her skin prickles with the sensation of Andy's eyes on her face. "What?"

"If I had someone who loved me I'd choose that over any place. Much less some new place that means nothing to you."

She thinks about Hank. How much does he really love her if he keeps hiding from her? *Not enough. Not nearly enough.* A sob threatens, but she swallows it down and presses Bess's accelerator.

FIFTY-SIX

A little more than two hours later as the sun is setting, Bess bounces onto the rutted road into the Amish community. It's surprising to Maggie. As hardworking and conscientious as Andy is, she'd expected it to be clean and orderly. Instead, it's broken-down farm implements, cobbled-together fencing, and a hodgepodge of buildings that don't look sturdy enough for Montana winters. The muddy snow doesn't improve the picture, even though the community is set before a beautiful mountain ridge overlooking the Tongue River.

There are horses everywhere, pulling carts, carrying kids of all ages, milling in corrals. She sees a few women, all in drab dresses down to their ankles and with white scarves on their heads. They're standing in front of houses with babies in their arms. Men converge on the houses, looking like they're coming home from work.

"That's my house." Andy has been perking up ever since they left the Cheyenne reservation fifteen minutes before. He points at a large, boxy structure that boasts a roof, covered windows, and a door, but doesn't have much else to recommend it as a place to live.

"We've made it."

He smiles, eyes soft, and waves at some children who are hanging off a wooden fence.

Maggie pulls to a stop in front of the Yoder home. "I'm glad you're going to get some time with your family. Will you need a ride back to Piney Bottoms?"

"I'll hitch with someone tomorrow afternoon."

Stern-faced Reggie approaches the vehicle.

Andy gets out to greet him, leaving the door open, so Maggie can hear their exchange. "Father."

"Why are you here?"

"A weekend visit. There was a tragedy today. My friend—" His voice breaks and he tries again. "Penny is dead. So is Michael. He worked with me."

Reggie grunts. "Well, there's plenty of work to go around," he says, as if he didn't hear the last of Andy's words.

"Yes, sir."

A short, round woman with friendly eyes joins Reggie. She whispers in Andy's ear. The two have a brief conversation.

He turns to Maggie. "Can you stay for dinner before you drive back?"

"I can't impose."

Again, the woman whispers.

"It's no imposition."

"Thank you, then. That's very kind." Maggie follows them into the house, conscious of curious eyes on her back.

The conditions of the house are worse inside than outside. The walls are partially Sheetrocked. The floor is bare plywood. Black tar paper is tacked up over the insides of the windows. There are children everywhere, but they grow silent when they see her. Gene had mentioned before that Andy has nine siblings. Ten kids. Two parents. Twelve people in this house, plus her makes thirteen. It hardly seems big or strong enough to contain them all.

A large table is already set, and a teenage girl ushers her to a seat. The trapped feeling from earlier returns, the one she had when she was driving home from Buffalo. It was a mistake to accept the dinner invitation. She feels suddenly desperate to get out of the house. To get out of the state of Montana, then Wyoming, and all the way back to the safety of Texas. But Maggie sits and steels herself with a deep breath. She doesn't have that choice right now.

After the rest of the family has filed in and sits down, Reggie begins the meal with a lengthy prayer. Maggie sneaks a glance around the dining and cooking area while he's still at it. She sees a mortar and pestle on the kitchen counter. At first, she thinks it looks a lot like the Sibley's family heirloom.

Then she grows suspicious. Is it the same one? Did Andy take it and give it to his family? She can't believe she's having doubts about him. His moral code doesn't allow for stealing, so it can't be the same one. Mortar and pestle sets can't be all that different anyway.

After grace, they eat quietly. The food is simple but good. She takes homemade bread and butter, then serves herself stew with carrots, potatoes, onions, and some kind of meat she can't identify. Andy's mother and oldest sisters clear the table when they finish and bring out dessert, a rhubarb crisp. Maggie takes a no-thank-you bite and starts the countdown until she can leave. She'll be out of here in ten minutes. Fifteen tops.

Andy unfolds some printed pages from his wallet. "I was in this article. It's about Ms. Killian. She's a music star."

His family passes it around, rubbing their hands over it and his picture in it.

When it reaches the head of the table, Reggie wads it up and throws it to the floor. "Pride, Andrew. You're indulging in pride. That's a sin. I hope now that the Indian whore is out of your life, you will sin no more."

Everyone looks down. Andy's neck flushes. The silence is sharp as razors.

Maggie bites back a comment. This is not the environment for it. Instead, she puts down her spoon. "Thank you for the delicious dinner. I hate to be rude, but I have a long drive back on dark roads."

"And the snow." It's the first time Mrs. Yoder has spoken to her directly.

Maggie smiles at the woman. "Exactly. You have a lovely family. Andy, I'll see you later."

He stands, fists clenched. "She wasn't a whore, Father. And Michael may not have been a good brother to her, but he was a good person who tried to protect her. It's terrible that they died."

Brother. Michael was Penny's brother. Things begin to make more sense to Maggie. The baby had to have been Paco's.

Mrs. Yoder speaks with her eyes down, cutting off Maggie's line of thought. "Of course it is, son. Please sit back down."

He does. Maggie doesn't. She feels twenty-four eyes watching as she hurries out.

FIFTY-SEVEN

Maggie opens the door to her truck. This has been one of the weirdest days of her life. Time to get the hell out of here and back to the ranch.

She smells cheap booze, then a male voice close behind her says, "Drive me back to Sheridan with you."

She jumps, startled. In the dark, she can't make out a face, but she knows it's Reggie, and that he's a secret drinker. "Mr. Yoder?"

"I need to pick up Andy's things. He won't be coming back."

"I can't let you do that without hearing it from him."

"I am the head of this household, and my word is final."

"But you're not head of household at Piney Bottoms, Mr. Yoder."

"Fine. I have to work in Sheridan tomorrow. I can stay out at the ranch in his cabin."

Internally Maggie resists, but manners win out. "Not my call. You can certainly ask." She knows he's still going to try to take Andy's belongings, but Gene and Hank can deal with that when the time comes.

The two of them pile into her cold truck. She checks her phone. No signal, so of course no new messages, from Hank or anyone. Despite her earlier dip about him, he's the one she wants to talk to now. She types him a text. *Heading home from Montana with Reggie Yoder. He wants to stay in Andy's cabin. Yes or no? He's giving me the creeps. So much to tell you.* She'll send it when she's in range.

As she drives out of the gate, she says, "Thank you for dinner with your family, Mr. Yoder."

He doesn't respond.

Maggie fiddles with the heat, trying to get more of it flowing. "Do you have a ride into work tomorrow?"

He nods.

Her mind returns to the Yoder's home, her disquietude there. "The mortar and pestle in your kitchen. Where did you get them?"

"Them's women's things."

"So you don't know if they came from Double S?"

He grunts noncommittally.

So this is how it's going to go, then. Maggie finds a staticky station on the radio and fills the silence with country music for the rest of the two-and-a-half-hour drive, with the occasional grumble about heathen music from Reggie. It's dark as pitch when they arrive at the ranch gate.

"You've been to Andy's cabin, before, right?" she asks. Her voice cracks from lack of recent use.

He nods.

Maggie realizes she forgot to call and ask permission for Reggie to stay, but she's too tired to take him back to Sheridan anyway. It will just have to be okay. In front of the bunkhouse, she takes her foot off the gas. Something hard jabs her in the side.

"Ouch." She turns toward the pain and Reggie.

"Keep driving."

"But we're here. What is that?"

"A gun. I don't prefer to use it."

"I—"

He pummels her with his words. "Drive. Now. Or I shoot."

Maggie's brain feels like it's stuck in quicksand. This doesn't make sense. Reggie is unstable. He's upset. He has a gun. She needs to do what he says and calm him down, even if she doesn't understand why yet. "Fine. Fine. Where am I going?"

"Where I say. Turn here. And throw your phone out the window."

She hesitates, hand on the window crank. They're heading into the south pastures. Her phone is the only way she can summon help, but she won't have signal much further anyway. She glances at the screen. Her message to Hank is still in a text box, unsent. She hits SEND.

His voice is edgy, cracking to let a higher pitch through. He jabs her again. "Do it now."

"Okay, okay." She opens the window and tosses it out. They reach the first gate and she stops. "Are you going to get the gates?"

"No. You are."

"I'm not strong enough for some of them."

"I suggest you will be."

"What's going on, Mr. Yoder?"

He doesn't answer.

"What do you want from me?"

He doesn't even look at her.

Maggie's adrenaline spikes, making her light-headed. She's still close enough to make a run for the house. She gets out of the truck. Instead of walking to the gate, she bends low and takes off at top speed, which isn't very fast over the rough, slippery ground, in cowboy boots. The ground wins. She goes down.

Reggie's door opens. "I'm a good shot. If you make me shoot you, I'll still have a mostly full magazine left. Who do you think I'll go for next? Your boyfriend? His partner? Your dog?"

The snow on her sore hands is wet and cold. She pushes to her feet. Now she's really scared, but she does her best not to show it. Without looking at Reggie, she goes to the gate and opens it, returns to the truck and pulls it through, then closes the gate and returns once more.

The road through the next pasture is rough. Maggie barely notices. All of her energy is going toward a plan to get away from Reggie. Her brain cycles through one useless idea after another. Jump on him and wrestle the gun away? Wreck the truck? But into what? And what would she do then, without wheels, alone with him and his gun?

She sees a horde of eyes shining in the headlights. Expensive, mean rodeo-bull eyes. She slows down.

"What are you doing?"

"Trying not to hit a bull."

"They will get out of your way. Keep driving."

"You'd think that." But she speeds up, and, luckily, the eyes in front of her shift to the side and soon are behind them. Her mind churns again, and she decides her only option is to figure out what's wrong with Reggie and try to talk sense into him. "I know you're upset. I'm sorry about everything that has happened. If you want to pick up Andy's things, I'd be happy to help you."

"Open the gate and turn."

It's too far back to the compound to make a run for it, plus he still has his gun, so Maggie does as he asks. As she struggles with the wire loop, she hears a bovine snort and a heavy hoof pawing the snow. "Whatever you're thinking, no. He's got a gun, you big dummy."

He doesn't back away. What if this is one of the star bulls? And he charges, and Reggie kills him?

She waves her arms in a crisscross over her head. "Shoo. Go away." She gets the gate open, then drives the truck through. The bull barrels through the gate and past them. *Great.* This one is going to have a sexcation with the cows, because that's what's in the pasture.

She shuts the gate. When she returns to Bess, Reggie is in the driver's seat. He points her to the passenger side. She gets in and Reggie drives on. As they cross the next pasture, Maggie's fear turns to terror. She sees the mound in the distance and knows exactly where Reggie is taking her.

FIFTY-EIGHT

It only takes five minutes to reach the dead pile, and they're the shortest minutes of Maggie's life. Reggie parks so close to the edge of the cliff—the old buffalo jump, where the dead pile gets pushed over with a tractor—that she's scared the ground will crumble and drop them the hundred feet to the rocks below. Her hands start shaking violently in her lap. She clutches them together.

"I'm putting the truck in neutral. We're going to get out. But don't try anything stupid. I have the gun pointed at you."

She exits the truck, looking for a place to run and hide. There's nothing. Nowhere and nothing.

Reggie is out and around the truck before she can come up with a plan. "Now you're going to push." He jams the gun between her shoulder blades, forcing her to the tailgate.

She stares at her truck and shakes her head.

He digs the barrel in harder. "Push."

A silent wail reverberates inside Maggie. She puts both hands on the truck she's loved since first sight. "Too heavy."

"Push!" Reggie shouts. "Now!"

She bends at the knees and waist and pushes. The truck doesn't budge. She crouches further and uses all her strength and weight. The truck starts to roll, and her feet slide out from under her. The truck stops. On the way down, her chin smashes into the trailer hitch. The pain is blinding.

"Ow." She cradles the gash with her palm. To buy herself time, she asks, "Why are you making me push my truck?"

"Everything about you is evil. I have to destroy it all."

"Bess hasn't done anything wrong. I haven't either."

"Get up. Be quiet."

"I—"

"Shut up or I shoot."

Maggie crawls to her knees, leaving a bloody handprint in the snow that she can just barely see in the dark. Her head spins as she stands.

"Push again."

"I've tried. I'm not strong enough."

"Like with the gates, tonight you will be."

Maggie swivels and digs her heel in the snow until she reaches the grass below, then does the same with her toe. She repeats the digging with her other foot. Once she has traction, she pushes again, every muscle in her body straining. Her chin pulses with pain. She cries out, and it turns into a long scream of effort, fear, and rage.

The truck moves forward again.

"Don't stop."

She takes a breath and lets out another scream. Bess rolls another few inches, gathering momentum on the slight decline. Bess. Her beloved truck. He is making her push a piece of herself over the cliff to its death. She can't. She just can't. Maggie hates this man. She desperately wants to turn the tables on him. But try as she might, she can't think of a way to do it. Best to play along a little while longer.

She empties her lungs on a final war whoop of a scream, and the truck topples over the edge. When she hears it hit something hard down below, Maggie crumples to the ground. "Bess."

"Walk."

She hesitates just too long, and he smashes her ribs with the gun.

Again, she cries out, but at the same time, she fights to get to her feet. "I'm g-g-g-g-oing, asshole."

He marches her to the dead pile. "I hereby judge you as the corruptor of my boy, forcing your immorality on him. Playing the guitar is nothing but prideful vanity. I won't let you continue to ruin him. Just like that Paco who took him to bars. And that whore who was tempting him with her loose ways."

His words are horrifying. This isn't a one-time break brought on by the stress of Andy being a suspect in the murders. This is madness. Reggie Yoder is a multiple murderer.

She has to keep him talking. "What about Michael?"

"The Indian boy?"

"Yes."

"May God forgive me for him. But he showed up as his sister's protector, and I had no choice. Just as I have no choice with you if I want to save my son."

"I haven't been corrupting him. I promise."

"Hush!" He holds up his gun and points it at her. "This time, no one will pin it on my Andrew."

She'll never be able to talk him out of this. Her mind whirls. She has to fight back, now. She searches around her for something to use as a weapon. Her size and strength are no match for his, much less for his gun. But in all the snow, she can't see anything heavy, even though she knows there are rocks and debris near the pile.

She makes one last try to keep him talking. "Doesn't the Bible tell us to let God judge?"

"You have no understanding of God's words or commandments."

"Help me understand. Please." Suddenly, she remembers the knife and scabbard concealed under her sweater. The one Hank made her promise to carry. The one Reggie will thrust in the back of her skull if he sees it before she can use it. How had she forgotten it? Her sweater is already partially hiked up over one hip. Slowly, she pushes the bottom edge up further until she can rest her hand on the hilt of her knife.

"Impossible." Reggie strikes her across the temple with his gun. "You'll never understand."

She falls toward the snow, time slowing, a metronome in her head counting out the ticks of seconds passing. Her face hits first. It's cold, cold, cold, especially in the cut on her chin. Thank God for the cold, because it keeps her awake. She closes her eyes and wraps her fingers tightly around the handle of her knife, using her thumb to open the snap on the strap that holds it in place.

Suddenly everything is clear to her. She wants nothing more in the world than to stay alive, here with Hank, on this ranch, in Wyoming. The emotion is so strong that it paralyzes her for a beat. Why has she been too proud to tell Hank she loves him? To fight for him and help him through his treatment change and the death of his mother? She's been distant. Short-changing him with her emotions. She wants to give him everything she has and is. She needs to tell him she loves him. And that's not all. She sees that Charlotte is right, but also that she's wrong. Maggie does need her people, but what her mother doesn't realize is that Maggie's people are *here*. Maybe she had to run to find them, to find Hank. Like Gidget did. And maybe being like her birth mother isn't the insult people have always intended it to be.

Reggie grunts. "I thought you'd have more fight in you."

He steps closer, snapping her out of her haze of thoughts. He pushes her with his foot, but she plays possum. After a few moments, he holsters his gun. She hears his breath as he leans over her. Through slitted eyes, she sees him reach for her wrist. His legs are by her torso. She rips the knife from the sheath and stabs backward into his calf.

His shriek is inhuman, the cry of a screech owl, and scarier than anything he has said to her all night. She pulls the knife out of his leg with a twist. She rolls away, pushing herself, and her knife jams in the ground and rips from her hand. Reggie leaps on top of her. He lands a punch on her cut chin. Stars flash in her vision. Then he's pressing down on her chest and something above her glints.

He has the knife, and he's a witch.

She braces for the blade, her eyes closed. Then she hears a noise like the rhythmic beating of a bass drum. Her eyes fly open. Reggie looks startled, and he hesitates. Seconds later, snow sprays in Maggie's face. Reggie grunts and falls to the side, all of his weight off of her except a leg. She crab-walks out from under him as fast as she can.

When she's free of him, she glances back. She barely processes what she's seeing. It's like a Tasmanian devil is attacking Reggie. Their bodies are writhing and turning, so intertwined it's as if they're one. Reggie is stabbing at the thing with his knife hand. The little devil is black. A bear? A wolf? No, it's too small. Wolverine? No, there are none in Wyoming. Tasmanian devils either, for that matter. The black fur is long, with white markings. Too big to be a skunk. The sound it's making is like a growl. Or a whine. Or a . . . bark.

"Louise!" she shouts. She has to help her dog before Reggie stabs her wonderful, loyal, hero of a dog to death.

But it's not just Louise. Lily is stomping, pacing, and pawing behind them. There's no time to wonder how they got there. As she scrambles to her feet, her hand touches something icy cold, smooth, and hard. Really hard.

Reggie's gun. It must have dislodged from his holster in the struggle with Louise.

She's no gun expert, but it's big and black and looks deadly. She fumbles with it. If there's a safety, she can't find it. She holds it up and aims it at man and dog. They're a churning mass, slamming over and over into a small tree. There's no way she can shoot Reggie without risking Louise. She gets as close to their fray as she can without being swept into it, then she smashes the gun down with all her strength. Louise yelps, but she doesn't loosen the jaws she has clamped over Reggie's arm.

"I'm sorry, Louise."

Without hesitation, she hammers the gun down again. She hears a sickening crack and Reggie cries out, then releases Louise. He rocks on the ground in the fetal position. Conscious? That's not good enough for Maggie. She has better aim now that he's not wrestling the dog. Grunting, she hits him again with the gun, harder, this time on the back of his head.

"Umph." Reggie's body goes limp and silent.

Louise barrels into Maggie, licking her and trying to push her away from their attacker at the same time.

Maggie hugs her tight. "You are such a good, good girl. Such a good girl." She looks up at Lily. "I rescue you, you rescue me. Good girl." She checks Louise for injuries. Sticky blood mats her fur, whether hers or Reggie's, Maggie doesn't know. But Louise doesn't seem to be in pain or distress.

Maggie paws through the snow around Reggie looking for her knife. She's not taking a chance he'll wake up and jump her with it. The blade finds her first, drawing blood. She sucks her hand, then jams the knife into its sheath. As she starts to snap it in place, she stops. Thinks. Decides. She drags Reggie to the tree and props him against the trunk. Then she pulls the pigging string out of the scabbard, pulls Reggie's wrists behind the tree, and wraps the pigging string over and over around them before tying it off. *This wasn't on the list of things Hank told me I could do with a knife and a string.*

When she's done, Maggie's hands are like ice. She walks over to Lily. "Help me out, girl?" She warms her hands between her body and the mare's belly. Lily turns her neck and puts her muzzle on Maggie's hair. Louise leans into her leg.

Maggie's adrenaline has worn off, and her energy is sapping out of her quickly. "Let's go home, guys."

Louise leads the way in the dark. After ten minutes of high-stepping through snow and going through one gate, Maggie begins to wonder if she'll make it back. Her clothing and boots aren't made for winter hiking. Wetness has crept into her boots, and her feet are now as cold as her hands. After another ten minutes, she's fairly sure she won't make it.

Louise seems to sense the quit in Maggie. She whines and bumps against her. Losing her footing, Maggie falls. She reaches up and her hand lands on the dog's collar.

Time stops. Her face hurts. She can't remember where she is. It's snowy and quiet, though. Louise barks and head-butts her.

"Stop it."

She's holding something. Louise's collar. The dog strains and Maggie allows herself to be pulled until she's standing up. With one step, though, she slips again and lurches forward, headfirst into something big, warm, and unyielding. She touches it with her hand. A horse. Lily. The mare bumps her muzzle into Maggie's face. Reaching up, up, up, Maggie clutches a handful of coarse mane and buries her face into warm fuzzy horse hair.

The warmth rejuvenates her, and her brain tries to make sense of everything again. She realizes she's in the ranch pasturage. Because? Reggie. She's out here because Reggie brought her. She groans. He made her push Bess off the buffalo jump. And he tried to kill her and put her on the dead pile. He's still out there. Tied up, but he could escape. She has to get home. Get help.

"You gonna help me, girls?"

With Louise pressing into her lower legs from one side and Lily's wide barrel against her head and shoulder from the other, Maggie keeps a tight grip on Lily's mane and stumbles along between them. Little, big, and bigger, abreast, they keep moving for what seems like forever. Maggie's feet, hands, and face are like ice, and she still slips, but Lily keeps her upright, and the warmth from the animals is a big improvement. They don't do much for her brain, though, and she has trouble keeping the story she's fought so hard to remember straight in her mind.

Headlights appear in the distance.

"Over here," she says, her voice barely above a whisper. She feels a strange sense of déjà vu. "Over here."

She's babbling incoherently when a truck pulls up beside her.

Hank jumps out. "Maggie, oh my God. We've got to get you warm." He lifts her in his arms.

"Lily and Louise saved me."

He pushes her into the truck and turns his heater on full blast. "Are you okay?"

Louise jumps into the front seat with Maggie. Hank ties Lily to a metal loop in the side of the truck bed, then he gets in and closes the door.

Maggie shivers. Her hands and feet feel like they're being stabbed with needles. Her face burns, except her chin, which throbs. "I tried to text you."

He starts rubbing her hands briskly between his. "I got your message about dropping Andy in Montana."

"Montana. Yes."

"I'm sorry, Maggie. I'm ashamed of how I've been treating you. I can't lose you. I had to get away where I could protect you from what I was becoming, until the treatment started to work. So I went to Denver to get something for you. While I was there, I started to feel better, more human again. I think it's working, the program and the shots."

Maggie groans. She's only partially processing his words, but the sound of his voice is soothing. The rubbing isn't.

"I came home as fast as I could. You should have been back already, but your truck wasn't there, and I couldn't find you. You weren't answering your phone. When I saw Louise and Lily were missing, too, and there were fresh tire tracks out toward the south pasturage—not ranch truck tracks, but skinny like the ones from your funky old truck—I was so scared."

"Bess," Maggie whispers.

"What?"

She shakes her head. He puts his warm face against hers.

It hurts so good. She sighs.

"Wait, where is your truck?" Then he holds up her arm. "Is this blood?"

Maggie smiles at him. It hurts her cheeks. "You didn't do it."

"What?"

"Neither did Andy."

"I'm not following you."

Maggie shakes her head. Her brain starts to come back to her. She points in the direction of the dead pile. "You'll understand when you see the surprise waiting for you and two counties worth of deputies at the dead pile."

FIFTY-NINE

An unfamiliar truck pulls up the lane toward the ranch house two mornings later—looking like it shares a birth decade with Bess, but hasn't aged as well —with Travis in his Sheridan County truck on its bumper. Maggie is walking back from the barn, where she's been feeding Louise and Lily a special thank-you breakfast. She would have done it the day before if she hadn't spent all of it either being questioned by doctors or law enforcement personnel. It's not only the animals that have had to wait. She and Hank have barely had a moment to themselves either.

A toothless man at the wheel of the ancient truck leans out the window and spits a stream of tobacco juice. Part of it splatters behind him on the rear door. He parks in front of the house. A light snow begins to fall as Andy gets out of the passenger side and walks toward the entrance. Travis pulls in beside him but leaves the motor running.

Hank meets Andy at the door, and Maggie begins to trot, her long hair falling from the stretchy headband she'd pushed it up and back in. The headband falls down to her neck like a scarf, sticking to her ChapStick for a second on the way. She catches Hank and Andy mid-conversation.

"You're welcome back here, any time." Hank has a hand clamped on Andy's shoulder.

"Thank you, sir. I know that. But I'll be staying in the community. My mother needs me now, to help with the family."

Maggie is only a little out of breath. "Is that what you want?" Returning to the community means baptism and is a point of almost no return.

"My father ain't my religion. I can keep the pieces separate. This is what is right."

The lump in Maggie's throat nearly chokes off her air. "You're a good person, Andy Yoder."

"So was my father. Before. I wish you could have known him then."

Hank holds his hand out to Maggie and she takes it, gripping it tight.

"Before what?" Hank says. "You've lost me, son."

"Before the rotgut ate his brain."

"Alcohol." Maggie isn't surprised. It confirms what she has smelled and suspected. And she knows substance abuse can destroy a human one brain cell at a time. She wonders if they'll find bottles up at the summer cabin—she'd reviewed the new security camera shots in the hospital the day before. The mysterious figure she'd seen in the alerts? Reggie Yoder. "You knew?"

"Others did. The truth is out now."

"Maybe he can get treatment in prison?"

"That ain't the Amish way. We don't always understand God's will, but I know my father never would have done those things before."

Maggie isn't sure how it could be God's will that Reggie kill off the people Andy cared about, but now is not the time to wrestle her theological demons. Whatever God's will, Reggie's quest is fulfilled: Andy is returning to the community. But if she remembers one thing from all her religious upbringing and education, it is not to confuse God's will with man's. Reggie made the choice to start drinking, not God, and that was the choice that led to all his other ones. Or that's the way she sees it as a two-time survivor of rehab, and success story of sorts, anyway. Her head hurts from even that little bit of religious contemplation, so she forces her attention back to the conversation.

Hank is saying, "If it's about money, Andy, we can help."

"That's a very kind offer. Especially after all my father did. I'll be sure my mother knows about your generous nature. Maybe someday she'll support me coming back."

"I'd like that." Hank pulls him into an embrace.

Maggie takes her turn hugging Andy. She expects him to hold back from her touch, but he surprises her with a warm bear hug. "We could continue your guitar lessons."

Hank shoots her an odd look.

"I'd like that. Well, I'll just pick up my things, then, and be off. I'm visiting my father and his court-appointed attorney before I go home."

They wish him good luck, and he returns to the passenger seat of the decrepit truck. It isn't even in gear before Travis gets out and walks over to Maggie and Hank.

He shakes hands with both of them. "If you're going to make a habit of solving our cases for us, we'll need to put you on the payroll, Ms. Killian."

"If nearly getting killed by the murderer is what you call solving a case, then I don't want the job."

"You knew who didn't do it, and you never quit trying to prove it."

Hank clasps her around the shoulders. "Don't let her good looks fool you. She's stubborn as hell. And no one gets to tell her the sky is blue. It's whatever color she damn well says it is."

"Well then, I guess you two are a good match."

Maggie watches the old pickup pull up to the bunkhouse then says, "I hope you're not here to tell us someone else is dead."

Travis smooths his shirt and adjusts his belt. "Nah. I just dropped by to tell you I'm sorry. It was nothing personal."

"You mean about Andy?" Hank says.

Something on the horizon becomes mighty interesting to Travis. Then he sighs. "Hank, you're one volatile and physical son of a bitch. I don't take that back. But I was wrong about Andy, and I was wrong to suspect you. Don't get me wrong. It's my job to question everything. I just want you to know that everyone out here at Piney Bottoms is A-OK, as far as I'm concerned."

Hank looks at Maggie. "You had my woman questioning me, too."

Maggie holds up her thumb and forefinger. "Only a little bit."

Hank makes a wider space between his hands. She shrugs. Travis chuckles.

"Looks like you've got her snowed again, then." Travis backs a few steps. "I've gotta hit the road. Stay out of trouble."

"No promises," Hank says.

Maggie waves.

As soon as Travis closes the door of his truck, Hank flips Maggie around so her shoulders rest against the front door of the house.

"What was that about? The thing you said to Andy."

"What?" She gives him an innocent smile.

"Teaching him guitar lessons if he ever comes back someday. I thought you were on your way back to Texas."

"Well, how can I be, with no truck?"

He grins at her. "About that."

"About Bess?"

"Yes. I took a look at her. She got lucky on her landing. I think we can fix her back up. It'll take a while, but if you're not going anywhere soon, maybe we'd have time."

Tears threaten the corners of Maggie's eyes.

From the barn, Gene's voice interrupts them, shouting. "If y'all hurry, you'll get here in time to see Lily's latest. She's about to drop it."

Gene and Hank have been working since four a.m. with the day hands and some neighbors who insist on pitching in until Double S can find help, now that Paco, Michael, and Andy are gone. The two men have to be exhausted, but they don't show it.

Hank grins and takes Maggie's hand. A laugh escapes her throat as they trot to the barn. The snow falls faster—big, pretty flakes. When they reach the entrance, Maggie pulls him to a stop as she catches her breath and a whiff of sweet-smelling hay.

"I'll always be on my way somewhere, Hank. That's who I am. And it so happens I have things—people, too—in Texas. From time to time, I'll have to take care of them."

"What do you mean?"

"I'll leave sometimes. But I'll always come back where I belong."

Hank takes her other hand. "Jesus, Maggie. Are you leaving me or not?"

"Not. I'm staying. I've figured out how to support myself here." She lets go of one of his hands and holds up a finger. "I can teach music lessons." Then another. "I can be your first permanent, part-time female hand." She lifts a third. "I can sell my salvage pieces on consignment or at rodeos with you." When her pinky finger rises, so do the corners of her mouth. "And maybe I can use some of them to decorate the summer cabin."

He pulls her to him and kisses her long and hard. "That is the best thing I've ever heard. All of it." Then his face falls. "If we can keep the place, which Gene and I are going to try like hell to find a way to do."

"About that. I have an offer for you and Gene."

Gene appears. "Hank and *me*? I'm not into that kind of thing, thank you very much, Maggie May." Then he laughs. "You two look like snowmen. Come on."

He leads the way to the birthing stall. Maggie and Hank drop snow as they follow him.

Maggie turns to Hank in the corridor. "I have insurance money coming, and I'm going to sell my place." And according to an email from Michele, she should expect double the number the insurance company offered. "I was thinking you might let me buy in. Not in Double S. But in the property. Piney Bottoms. I could run a music camp in the summer cabin a few times a year. And, um, Ava has offered me a deal to record together." Maggie had called Ava just that morning, and the two of them had reached a deal. If Ava keeps being so reasonable, Maggie is even going to have to admit she likes her. And after Maggie's meeting with Amos, he'd sent a link to a semi-positive piece on her, with a promise he'd be all over any collaboration with Ava. "She'll front us the rest of the money to buy Laura out, an advance on royalties. So that Laura and Mickey can cover the cost of Mickey's dad's treatment ASAP."

Hank's fingers grip her arms so tightly it hurts, but she's not about to ask him to let go. "Are you serious?"

"Holy shit," Gene says.

"It's taken me a while to work through the options, but I think this is the best one. So, yes, I'm serious. What do you think?"

Hank's eyes shine. "We can live there together. At the summer cabin. With lots of room for your friends and family to visit."

"No, thanks, I've got a place," Gene deadpans.

Maggie makes a raspberry at Gene and says to Hank, "Your friends and family, too. Except Laura, because she hates me."

"She doesn't hate you. She's had a tough time. But thanks to you and Ava, things will be much better for her soon." He kisses her forehead and lowers his voice so that only she can hear. "But what about my condition? My brain—that's forever."

She moves her mouth by his ear and speaks softly. "You said yourself the treatment is helping. And I've got a few issues myself. If you haven't figured them out already, I'll let them be a surprise."

He presses his forehead against hers. "Then you can't run off again when things get tough."

She leans back to give him the evil eye. "Look who's talking, Mr. Denver."

"Oh shit. I forgot. I have a present for you. The thing I went to Denver to pick up."

"It had better be damn good."

He grins. "Only if you like signed prints of *Front Porch Pickin'*, a Gidget Becker original. And a pair of snow boots, which I think I'm delivering a few days late."

"Oh my God, Hank. It's the best gift ever. Thank you. Thank you. Thank you." A signed print of the prized original she'd lost in the fire, plus boots? This man gets her. She locks her lips on his, crushing their faces together. Steam rises around their bodies as snow melts from the heat of their kiss.

When they come up for air, Hank says, "I'm serious. You'll crush me like a grape if you ever leave."

"I'm not just your lover, Hank. I'm your partner. We'll do the hard stuff together. Like your mother's funeral tomorrow. Like telling my mother I'm staying here."

"Yeah, you can do that last one by yourself if you want."

She socks him in the chest, and he catches her fist, laughing.

Gene's voice comes from inside the birthing stall. "If you lovebirds don't mind the interruption, Lily has something to show you."

Hank and Maggie tear their eyes from each other and lean over to look in the stall. Lily is licking a bundle of wet black fur that's mostly long legs that seem to stick out in every direction.

"Way to go, Mama. Is it a boy or a girl?" Hank says.

Gene approaches mother and baby. "Hey, girl. Let me take a look at what you got there."

Lily nudges at her foal, and not gently. It begins scrambling and rocking. She keeps pushing it insistently until it stands, only to wobble and tumble immediately. Maggie clutches her throat, but Gene and Hank laugh.

Gene says, "I got a glimpse down under. Looks like a girl to me."

Maggie claps. "Go, Lily. Bucking girl power."

Hank turns to Maggie. "Are you sure you're ready for that kind of partnership? The forever kind."

"I am."

"Promise on the life of that little one in there?"

"I promise on the life of the Black Widow."

"The Black Widow?"

"Those spidery legs. She needs a killer name for a killer bucking career, so she can follow in her sister Crazy Woman's footsteps." Maggie spits on her hand and sticks it out with a grin. "And oh, by the way, I love you."

Instead of shaking it, he pulls her into his arms, but not before she sees the dimples that curl her toes. "Now that didn't hurt so much to admit, did it, music girl?"

SURPRISE! You've got two more goodies to read in this box set!!

1. R-rated and a little sexier than my other books, next up is *Bombshell*, featuring Maggie's nemesis, Ava Butler, in *Bombshell*, set in the Caribbean and New York City. Just keep scrolling to read the whole book.

2. PG-rated *WDKY*-spinoff *Switchback*, a Amazon Top-25 novel and a Wyoming mystery set in the 1970s, featuring the adventurous young doctor Patrick Flint and his family: feisty wife Susanne, troublesome teen daughter Trish, and undersized tween son Perry (based on my real-life family and late 70s Wyoming adventures).

Don't like sexy books? Flip past *Bombshell* and go straight to an excerpt from *Switchback*.

To Eric. Thanks for helping me find my inner romantic and deal with my old junk.

OTHER BOOKS BY THE AUTHOR

Fiction from SkipJack Publishing

The *What Doesn't Kill You* Series

Act One (Prequel, Ensemble Novella)

Saving Grace (Katie #1)

Leaving Annalise (Katie #2)

Finding Harmony (Katie #3)

Heaven to Betsy (Emily #1)

Earth to Emily (Emily #2)

Hell to Pay (Emily #3)

Going for Kona (Michele #1)

Fighting for Anna (Michele #2)

Searching for Dime Box (Michele #3)

Buckle Bunny (Maggie Prequel Novella)

Shock Jock (Maggie Prequel Short Story)

Live Wire (Maggie #1)

Sick Puppy (Maggie #2)

Dead Pile (Maggie #3)

The Essential Guide to the What Doesn't Kill You Series

The *Ava Butler Trilogy*: A Sexy Spin-off From *What Doesn't Kill You*

Bombshell (Ava #1)

Stunner (Ava #2)

Knockout (Ava #3)

The *Patrick Flint Trilogy*: A Spin-off From *What Doesn't Kill You*

Switchback (Patrick Flint #1)

Snake Oil (Patrick Flint #2)

Sawbones (Patrick Flint #3)

Scapegoat (Patrick Flint #4)

Snaggle Tooth (Patrick Flint #5)

Stag Party (Patrick Flint #6): 2021

The What Doesn't Kill You Box Sets Series (50% off individual title retail)

The Complete Katie Connell Trilogy

The Complete Emily Bernal Trilogy

The Complete Michele Lopez Hanson Trilogy

The Complete Maggie Killian Trilogy

The Complete Ava Butler Trilogy

The Complete Patrick Flint Trilogy #1 (coming in late 2020)

Nonfiction from SkipJack Publishing

The Clark Kent Chronicles

Hot Flashes and Half Ironmans

How to Screw Up Your Kids

How to Screw Up Your Marriage

Puppalicious and Beyond

What Kind of Loser Indie Publishes,

and How Can I Be One, Too?

Audio, e-book, and paperback versions of most titles available.

ACKNOWLEDGMENTS

The Maggie books are set one foot in Texas and the other in Wyoming, while Maggie's life is a little bit junker and a little bit rock and roll. My own love affair with Wyoming started at an early age when my family moved to Buffalo. Then my parents "ruined my life forever" by moving us back to Texas a few years later. I didn't return to Wyoming until 2014, and then only because I took Eric for his first visit in July, as opposed to January. My mama didn't raise no fool.

Two cabins later, my Virgin Islands–native husband drives a snowplow and owns more coats than his famous sandals. I wrote all the Maggie stories from our Snowheresville, Wyoming, in a big, beautiful, remote, off-the-grid, and, above all, *rustic* cabin on the eastern face of the Bighorn Mountains. It's not easy shuttling between two homes in Texas and one in Wyoming, but Eric does it with a smile on his face and adventure in his heart. I am beginning to think he loves me.

The animals in this book are based on Pippin, one of our granddogs, and Katniss, my Percheron cross mare. The truck, Bess, and store, Flown the Coop, are rooted in the lives of Tiffany and Jeff, who live near our Nowheresville, Texas. I am grateful to a colorful cast of Wyoming characters (Jeff, Christina, Brenton, Colter, Mandy, Travis, Ron, Eric, and many others) for endless anecdotes. Thanks for the inspiration, all of you!

Thanks to my husband, Eric, for brainstorming the *Maggie* stories with me despite his busy work, travel, and workout schedule. He puts up with me recycling bits and pieces of our lives in the stories as well. I'd say he does it without reservation, but that would be a lie. I guess that makes it even more remarkable that he smiles about it in the end.

Thanks to our five offspring. I love you guys more than anything, and each time I write a parent/child (birth, adopted, foster, or step), I channel you.

To each and every blessed reader, I appreciate you more than I can say. It is the readers who move mountains for me, and for other authors, and I humbly ask for the honor of your honest reviews and recommendations.

Thanks mucho to Bobbye and Rhonda for putting up with my eccentric and ever-changing needs.

Maggie editing credits go to Rhonda Erb and Whitney Cox. The beta and advance readers and critique partners who enthusiastically devote their time—gratis—to help us rid my books of flaws blow me away. The special love this time goes to Angie, Caren, Pat, Tara, Karen, Ken, Kelly, Vidya, Ginger, Mandy, Susan, Jim, Ridgely, Melissa and Linda.

Thank you Alayah Frazier, for working with Bobbye to create amazing vector art for the covers, as we took Maggie into (for *What Doesn't Kill You*) uncharted visual territory.

SkipJack Publishing now includes fantastic books by a cherry-picked bushel basket of mystery/thriller/suspense writers. If you write in this genre, visit http://SkipJackPublishing.com for submission guidelines. To check out our other authors and snag a bargain at the same time, download *Murder, They Wrote: Four SkipJack Mysteries*.

ABOUT THE AUTHOR

Pamela Fagan Hutchins is a *USA Today* best seller. She writes award-winning romantic mysteries from deep in the heart of Nowheresville, Texas and way up in the frozen north of Snowheresville, Wyoming. She is passionate about long hikes with her hunky husband and pack of rescue dogs and riding her gigantic horses.

If you'd like Pamela to speak to your book club, women's club, class, or writers group, by Skype or in person, shoot her an email. She's very likely to say yes.

You can connect with Pamela via her website
(http://pamelafaganhutchins.com)
or email (pamela@pamelafaganhutchins.com).

PRAISE FOR PAMELA FAGAN HUTCHINS

2018 USA Today Best Seller
2017 Silver Falchion Award, Best Mystery
2016 USA Best Book Award, Cross-Genre Fiction
2015 USA Best Book Award, Cross-Genre Fiction
2014 Amazon Breakthrough Novel Award Quarter-finalist, Romance

What Doesn't Kill You: Katie Romantic Mysteries

"An exciting tale . . . twisting investigative and legal subplots . . . a character seeking redemption . . . an exhilarating mystery with a touch of voodoo."
— *Midwest Book Review Bookwatch*
"A lively romantic mystery." — *Kirkus Reviews*
"A riveting drama . . . exciting read, highly recommended." — *Small Press Bookwatch*
"Katie is the first character I have absolutely fallen in love with since Stephanie Plum!" — *Stephanie Swindell, Bookstore Owner*
"Engaging storyline . . . taut suspense." — *MBR Bookwatch*

What Doesn't Kill You: Emily Romantic Mysteries

"Fair warning: clear your calendar before you pick it up because you won't be able to put it down." — *Ken Oder, author of* Old Wounds to the Heart
"Full of heart, humor, vivid characters, and suspense. Hutchins has done it again!" — *Gay Yellen, author of* The Body Business
"Hutchins is a master of tension." — *R.L. Nolen, author of* Deadly Thyme
"Intriguing mystery . . . captivating romance." — *Patricia Flaherty Pagan, author of* Trail Ways Pilgrims
"Everything about it shines: the plot, the characters and the writing. Readers are in for a real treat with this story." — *Marcy McKay, author of* Pennies from Burger Heaven

What Doesn't Kill You: Michele Romantic Mysteries

"Immediately hooked." — *Terry Sykes-Bradshaw, author of* Sibling Revelry

"Spellbinding." — *Jo Bryan, Dry Creek Book Club*
"Fast-paced mystery." — *Deb Krenzer, Book Reviewer*
"Can't put it down." — *Cathy Bader, Reader*

What Doesn't Kill You: Ava Romantic Mysteries

"Just when I think I couldn't love another Pamela Fagan Hutchins novel more, along comes Ava." — *Marcy McKay, author of* Stars Among the Dead
"Ava personifies bombshell in every sense of word. — *Tara Scheyer, Grammy-nominated musician, Long-Distance Sisters Book Club*
"Entertaining, complex, and thought-provoking." — *Ginger Copeland, power reader*

What Doesn't Kill You: Maggie Romantic Mysteries

"Murder has never been so much fun!" — *Christie Craig, New York Times Best Seller*
"Maggie's gonna break your heart–one way or another." — *Tara Scheyer, Grammy-nominated musician, Long-Distance Sisters Book Club*
"Pamela Fagan Hutchins nails that Wyoming scenery and captures the atmosphere of the people there." — *Ken Oder, author of* Old Wounds to the Heart
"You're guaranteed to love the ride!" — *Kay Kendall, Silver Falchion Best Mystery Winner*

OTHER BOOKS FROM SKIPJACK PUBLISHING

Made in the USA
Columbia, SC
27 November 2020